THE
ASSASSINI

THE
ASSASSINI

THOMAS GIFFORD

BANTAM BOOKS
NEW YORK • TORONTO • LONDON • SYDNEY • AUCKLAND

THE ASSASSINI
A Bantam Book / September 1990

Grateful acknowledgment is made for permission to reprint excerpts from the following: "The Love Song of J. Alfred Prufrock" in Collected Poems 1909–1962 *by T. S. Eliot, copyright 1936 by Harcourt Brace Jovanovich, Inc., copyright © 1964, 1963 by T. S. Eliot, reprinted by permission of the publisher. "Have Yourself a Merry Little Christmas" by Hugh Martin & Ralph Blane, copyright 1943 (renewed 1971) by Metro-Goldwyn-Mayer, Inc., copyright 1944 (renewed 1972) by Leo Feist, Inc. All rights assigned to EMI Catalogue Partnership. All rights controlled and administered by EMI Feist Catalog, Inc. International copyright secured. Made in U.S.A. All rights reserved. Used by permission.*

Library of Congress Cataloging-in-Publication Data

Gifford, Thomas.
    The assassini / Thomas Gifford.
      p. cm.
    ISBN 0-553-05728-6
    I. Title.
    PS3557.I284A87   1990
    813'.54—dc20
                                    90-30533
                                         CIP

Published simultaneously in the United States and Canada

Bantam Books are published by Bantam Books, a division of Bantam Doubleday Dell Publishing Group, Inc. Its trademark, consisting of the words "Bantam Books" and the portrayal of a rooster, is Registered in U.S. Patent and Trademark Office and in other countries. Marca Registrada. Bantam Books, 666 Fifth Avenue, New York, New York 10103.

PRINTED IN THE UNITED STATES OF AMERICA

RRH   0 9 8 7 6 5 4 3 2 1

FOR
Elizabeth

AUTHOR'S NOTE

S pending nine years researching and writing a book is a remarkably daunting task. Countless people, both from within and from outside the Church, helped and hindered the work. Each doubtless had sufficient reasons for what he or she did, whether selfless or despicable. But for each one who tried to stop my completing this book there were many more who gave of their time and energy and insight to help me. They know who they are, heroes and villains alike. But three people were utterly indispensable.

Charles Hartman inspired every aspect of the undertaking. Without him there would have been no book. He was a source of constant encouragement; he was tireless when I was at the end of my tether; at the darkest times, when the obstacles seemed too great to overcome, he never failed me.

Kathy Robbins negotiated her way through the impossibly dense thicket of emotions, conflicting aims and egos, and the vast accumulation of legal documents with the skill and good humor and wit of a great diplomat. For nearly nine years she slew the dragons, even when the dragons seemed to be winning.

Beverly Lewis joined the effort when it had reached its greatest crisis and with the clear intelligence and the determination of a Jesuit made it all come right. Her skill as an editor is exceeded only by the one quality that sets the great editors apart from the rest— her utter respect for and understanding of the author's intention.

Whatever may be wrong with the piece of work you are holding is my doing; whatever is right I gladly share with these three.

Thomas Gifford
London
November 1989

PROLOGUE

October 1982
New York City

He looked like a bird of prey, all black and swooping against the silver sheen of ice. He was an elderly gentleman. He was very good on the blades.

He was enjoying himself, hearing the hiss of his skates carving neat, precise patterns in the ice, feeling the crisp autumn breeze on his face. His senses were unusually acute, as they always were on such important days. The task at hand brought him to life in a unique way: on such days he was one with his destiny, one with his God. The point of his existence was clear to him on such days.

The world was clearer, too. Everything around him lost its mystery. On such days he understood. The mist of the morning had blown away and sunshine was streaming past the high white clouds. The towers of Rockefeller Center rose above him and the music from the loudspeakers set his pace and he was able to lose himself in the grace and power of his skating, almost able to ride them back through time.

As a boy he had learned his skating on the frozen canals of The Hague. The somber houses, the snowy parks, the leaden sky with heavy clouds lowering over the ancient city and the dikes and the windmills: they all stuck in his mind with the peculiar tenacity of childhood impressions, things you never forget. It didn't matter that there weren't many windmills anymore. They were still there, slowly turning, forever in his mind. The thought of the slow-moving arms of the windmills and the sibilant swishing of the blades on ice always worked to relax him. On such days as this, when he had work to do, he always prepared by relaxing. A younger generation might call it meditating, but it all came down to the same thing. You wanted to reach a level of pure, perfect concentration, so perfect that you no longer noticed that you were trying. He was almost there. The skating was taking him there. Soon time would cease to exist. He would become a single, all-seeing eye, aware of everything, missing nothing, capable of being one with his task, one with God's purpose. Soon. Very soon.

He wore the black suit with the clerical collar and a black raincoat which furled out behind him like a cape as he moved gracefully among the other skaters, who seemed mostly to be teenagers. It had never occurred to him that the blowing coat might give him a threatening, ominous appearance. His mind didn't work like that. He was a priest. He was the Church. He had a remarkably reassuring, kindly smile. He was goodness, not someone to fear. Nevertheless, the other skaters tended to make a path for him, watched him almost furtively, as if he might be judging them morally. They couldn't have been more mistaken.

He was tall with wavy white hair combed straight back from a high, noble brow. His face was narrow with a long nose, a wide, thin-lipped mouth. It was a tolerant face, like a good country doctor who understood life and had no fear of death. His face wore an almost translucent priestly pallor, born of a lifetime spent in dim chapels, badly lit cells, confessionals. A pallor born of long hours of prayer. He wore steel-rimmed spectacles. The skating, the concentration, brought the faintest of smiles to the wide mouth. He was lean and very fit. He was seventy years old.

As he skated he held his hands before him, palms out, as if he were dancing with an invisible partner. He wore black leather gloves that fit like skin. From the loudspeakers came a scratchy recording of a girl singing something from a movie he'd seen on the Alitalia 747 that had brought him to New York. She sang that she was going to live forever, that she was going to go out and fly . . .

He weaved among the skating children, slid gracefully among the pretty girls with the tight Guess jeans and long swinging hair and strong, hard-muscled rumps about to burst the seams. Girls of a certain age had always reminded him of frisky colts. He had never seen a naked woman. He'd hardly ever thought about such a thing.

He gently kicked one leg before him, skating on a single blade, deftly switching back and forth, arms slowly pumping the air before him, eyes narrowed as if seeing into the core of time while his body skated onward, powered by the engines of memory. He moved like a great black bird, circling the rink, eyes fixed ahead of him, ice-blue and clear, as if they had no bottom, like a lake high in the mountains. There was no hint of emotion in his eyes. They just weren't participating.

Some of the girls whispered, giggled as they watched the old priest glide past, austere, formal, yet there was an air of respect in their glances, respect for his skating, the strength and the style with which he moved.

But he was busy thinking about the rest of the day and he barely noticed them. The girls doubtless thought they were going to live forever, and were going to go out and fly, which was fine, but the elderly priest knew better.

Now, ahead of him on the ice, he saw a very pretty girl of fourteen or so fall down abruptly, sit with legs splayed out before her. Her friends were laughing, she was shaking her head, the ponytail bobbing.

He swept down on her from behind, caught her under the arms and lifted her upright in a single, fluid motion. He saw the look of surprise on her face as he flickered past like a mighty raven. Then she broke into a wide grin and called a thank-you. He nodded solemnly over his shoulder.

Soon afterward he looked at his watch. He skated off the ice, returned the rented skates, reclaimed the briefcase from the check-room. He was breathing deeply. He felt supremely at ease and in control with a nice edge of adrenaline running.

He climbed the stairs out of the rink. He bought a hot pretzel from a vendor, smeared a bit of mustard on the salt-studded surface, stood eating it methodically, then discarded the napkin in a trash can. He walked the length of the arcade of shops to Fifth Avenue. He crossed the street, stood looking up at St. Patrick's Cathedral. He was not a sentimental man, but the sight of great church buildings—even so recent an example—inevitably moved something in his breast. He had hoped to say a prayer, but the skating had gone on too long, and he could pray inside his head anyway.

He'd come a long way to keep this appointment.

It was time to go.

Rome

The man in the bed wasn't watching the soccer match on the large television screen. One of his secretaries had put the cassette into the VCR and thoughtfully turned it on before withdrawing, but the man in the bed had begun, of late, to lose interest in soccer. If it crossed his mind at all, it was in the form of memory, boyhood matches he'd enjoyed in Turin many, many years before. As for the stuff on the cassette, recently arrived by courier from São Paulo, well, he just didn't give a damn. The World Cup wasn't a part of his plans anymore.

The man in the bed was thinking about his own impending death with the sense of detachment that had always served him well. As a young man he'd mastered the trick of thinking of himself in the third person, as Salvatore di Mona. With part of himself standing off to one side, wearing a bemused smile, he'd observed Salvatore di Mona's diligent, systematic climb through the ranks, had nodded appreciatively as Salvatore di Mona forged alliances with powerful and worldly men, had witnessed Salvatore di Mona reaching the final lofty peak of his profession. At which time Salvatore di Mona had, in a manner of speaking, ceased to exist: at which time he had taken the name Callistus, had become the Vicar of Christ, the Holy Father—Pope Callistus IV.

Eight years as Chairman of the Board: he was neither a modest man, nor a particularly deep one, but he had been both very lucky and extraordinarily practical. He was not much given to the elaborate hocus-pocus that went with his job and he'd always looked upon his career as only marginally unlike that of any CEO of a major multinational corporation.

It was quite true, of course, that only the Emperor of Japan occupied an older office on Planet Earth, but still it had never occurred to him that, for instance, God literally expressed His will through the man who had been Sal di Mona, the bright-eyed eldest son of the prosperous Fiat dealer in Turin. No, mysticism was not his cup of tea, as Monsignor Knox had once said in his charming English manner.

No, Callistus IV was a practical man. He didn't much care for drama and intrigue, particularly in the years since he'd managed to get himself elected by the consistory of cardinals, a maneuver that had required a certain simple, heavy-handed intriguing of the sort that left no doubt of the outcome. Money systematically parceled out to relevant cardinals with the aid of the powerful American layman, Curtis Lockhardt, had gotten the job done. Cardinal di Mona had built on a solid core of support, headed by Cardinal D'Ambrizzi. The money—bribes, to give the parcels a name—was a tradition that had put more than one sweating *papabili* over the top. Since becoming pope, he'd tried to keep all the curial plotting and whispering and tinkering and slandering to a minimum. But he had to admit that in a hothouse society like the Vatican, he was fighting a losing battle. You couldn't really alter human nature, certainly not in a place where there were at least a thousand rooms. He'd never been able to get an accurate count, but the obvious reality was simply that if you had a thousand rooms, somebody was always and inevitably up to no good in some of them. All in all, keeping a semblance of control over the curial machinations had pretty much worn him out. Still, it had been amusing as often as not. Now it just wasn't amusing anymore.

The bed upon which he lay, once the resting place of the Borgia pope Alexander VI, was an impressive affair that possessed a history he enjoyed imagining. Alexander VI had doubtless put it to better use than he had himself, but from the look of things he was at least going to die in it. The rest of the bedroom's furnishings could be described only as Apostolic Palace Eclectic—some pieces of Swedish modern dating from Paul VI, a television and a videocassette recorder, huge Gothic bookcases with glass doors once filled with the immense collection of reference works Pius XII liked to keep close at hand, chairs and tables and a desk and a prie-dieu which he'd turned up in a storage room under dust a century or two thick. It was a motley collection, but for the past eight years he'd called it home. Regarding it with a dour glance, he was relieved that he didn't have to take it where he was going.

Slowly he eased his legs over the edge of the bed and slid his bare feet into Gucci loafers. He stood up, swaying slightly, steadying himself with a gold-knobbed stick an African cardinal had with touching foresight presented him a year previously. He was never entirely sure which of his two afflictions caused which symptoms, but the dizziness he attributed to the brain tumor. Inoperable, of course. So far as he could tell from the doddering curia-approved sawbones who attended him, it was going to be a photo finish as to what actually would carry him off: the heart or the brain. It didn't make a great deal of difference to him.

Still, there were things to be done in the time remaining.

Who would succeed him?

And what exactly could he do to choose his successor?

Malibu

Sister Valentine couldn't seem to stop crying, and it was pissing her off. She'd done some reckless things in her life, she'd sought danger and certainly found plenty of it, and she'd known fear. But that had been the spontaneous kind of fear that everyone all around her was feeling: the fear of the rifle shot cracking along the lonely road, the fear of one of the truth squads or one of the death squads, the fear of the government troops or the hungry guerrillas coming out of the hills looking for trouble or blood. In some parts of the world that was just your average everyday or garden-variety kind of fear, and it was the kind of fear you knew about going in, the kind of fear you consciously chose.

The fear she felt now was something very different. It was attacking her will and her nervous system like a ravenous cancer. It had come from a long time ago, but it was still alive and it had found her, singled her out, and now she was going home because she could no longer face it alone. Ben would know what to do. Somehow he'd always known.

But first she had to stop crying and shaking and acting like a fool.

She stood at the edge of the patio, her toes dipping off into the damp grass, watching the silver, pitted boulder of moon in the blue-black sky. Tattered clouds drifted past, looking like a corny cover of a Moonlight Sonata album from her childhood. The sound of the surf crashing on the Malibu beach far below blew up the face of the cliffs, rode on the ocean breeze that brushed her bare legs. She wiped her eyes on the sleeve of her robe, pulled it tighter, and walked across the grass toward the white railing at the top of the cliffs. She watched the surf foam, fan out, and recede, then begin again. A few pairs of lonely headlamps poked along the Pacific Coast Highway. In the distance, through the haze, the Malibu Colony glowed faintly like a spaceship settling down at water's edge. Fog rode offshore as if it were holding the enemy's navy at bay.

She moved along the fence until she felt the dying heat from the coals where they'd grilled sea bass for a late supper. Just the two of them, a bottle of Roederer Cristal and sea bass and hot crusty sourdough bread. A meal he was addicted to, accompanied by the same conversation they'd had in Rome, Paris, New York, and Los Angeles, all during the past year and a half. Conversation, debate, argument, call it what you will, it was always the same. She felt herself giving in to him, like a breakwater unable to resist the tide, but she fought not to crumble, wasn't quite ready to crumble. For God's sake, she *wanted* to crumble, collapse, fall into his arms, but she couldn't now. Not yet. Not quite yet. Damn. She was crying again.

She turned and walked back toward the low, sprawling hacienda, past the swimming pool and the tennis court, crossed the flagstone patio, and stood looking through the glass wall with its sliding door. An hour before she'd made love in that bed.

He was a large, solid man with a face like a good-looking bulldog. Determined. His gray hair was cut short and carefully brushed and it never seemed to get mussed. He wore dark blue pajamas with white piping, a monogrammed *CL* on the breast pocket. His right arm lay across the side of the bed where she'd lain earlier, as if he'd gone to sleep to the rhythm of her breathing, her heartbeat. He lay still now. She knew he smelled of their sweat and Hermès's Equipage. She knew so much about him, more than she had any business knowing. But then, she'd never been a conventional nun. The fact was, as a nun she'd been a royal pain in the ass. To the Church, to the Order. She'd always known what was right: that was the way she'd been born and nothing much had ever happened to change it. She knew what was right and she knew what was wrong and very often her ideas and the Church's had been at odds. She'd gone her own way and defied *them* to do anything about it. She'd gone public, she'd written two best sellers, she'd become a heroine of her time in the eyes of a great many people, and the publicity had ensured her safety. She had dared the Church to admit it was too small, too petty, too mean, to include her—and the Church had backed down. She had made herself an indispensable centerpiece in the great facade of the modern Church of Rome, and the only way they could ever get rid of her was—in her view at the time—feetfirst.

But all that had happened before she'd embarked on the researches of the past twelve months. Now, she reflected wryly, wiping her eyes one more time and sniffling, all the causes and speeches and publicity had only been a warm-up. Nothing, however, could have adequately prepared her for the past year, for the growing fear. She thought she'd seen it all. She thought she'd seen evil in all of its disguises and forms, and love in a good many. But she'd been wrong. She hadn't known diddly about evil or love, but, by God, she'd been finding out.

Eighteen months earlier Curtis Lockhardt had told her that he loved her. They were in Rome, where she was at the jumping-off point for her new book, which would deal with the Church's role in World War II. He had been called to the Vatican to take a hand in covering over the ever-growing scandal at the Vatican Bank, which encompassed everything from fraud, extortion, and embezzlement to simple murder. Lockhardt was one of the few laymen that the Church—in this case Callistus IV—would turn to in a time of extreme crisis. Most laymen couldn't imagine the toughness of mind, the utter ruthlessness that controlling an octopus like the Church required. Lockhardt could: he'd made a career out of precisely those qualities while remaining the most sympathetic and charming and devout of men. As Callistus was fond of saying, Lockhardt sat very near the center of the center of the Church within the Church.

She had known Curtis Lockhardt all her life. When she had been Val Driskill thirty years earlier, dancing on her parents' lawn in the sweeping arcs of the sprinklers, in her ruffled bathing suit, looking like a fancily wrapped piece of candy, ten years old, Lockhardt had been a youthful lawyer and banker bearing the imprimaturs of both the Rockefellers and the Chase. He had frequently visited the house in Princeton to talk money business and Church business with her father. As she pranced, showing off, glistening wet and tanned in the sunshine, she'd heard the ice clinking in their glasses, seen them from the corner of her eye sitting in white wicker chairs on the shady porch.

"You were an enchanting sprite at ten," he told her in Rome that night. "And at fifteen you were a sexy tomboy. Damn near beat me at tennis."

"You kept watching me, not the ball." She was grinning at him, remembering how she'd known he was finding her desirable as she dashed about the court, the breeze blowing her tennis skirt and drying the sweat on her face until she could feel the saltiness crack. She'd liked him, admired him. She'd been fascinated by his power, the layman who could make the priests sit up and listen. He was thirty-five at the time and she had wondered why he'd never married.

"By the time you were twenty I was flat out scared to death of you. Afraid of the effect that I knew you were having on me every time I saw you. And I felt like such a fool. And then . . . do you remember the day I took you to lunch at The Plaza, the Oak Room with the murals of fairyland castles in mountain kingdoms, and you told me what you intended to do with the rest of your life— remember? The day you told me you were going inside, joining the Order? My heart did a half gainer into the tomato bisque. I felt like a spurned lover . . . and the fact was, had I been entirely sane, I'd have been looking on you as a girl, as Hugh Driskill's daughter . . . a child.

"But the point was, of course, that I wasn't sane. I was in love. And I've stayed in love, Val. I've watched you, followed your career, and when you came to Los Angeles I knew I'd have to start seeing you again. . . ." He shrugged boyishly, and the years fell away. "The bad news was that I was still in love with a nun, but the good news was that I knew the wait had been worth it."

Their love affair had begun that night in Rome in his apartment high above the Via Veneto. And he had also begun the campaign to persuade her to leave the Order and marry him. Betraying those vows—coming to his bed—had been the easy part. Those vows had always been the coercive part of her job, the necessary evil, the price she'd paid for the opportunity to serve the Church, to serve humanity through the powerful instrument of the Church. But leaving the Order, leaving the framework within which she'd built her life—that had proved to be beyond her thus far.

Now, only an hour earlier, out of their mutual frustration they had quarreled coldly, regretfully, neither accepting the other's inability to understand, but still loving, always loving. Finally they had found consolation in passion, and then he had slept and she had slid from the bed, gone outside to think. To be alone with the things she couldn't dare tell him.

Before her, out of the night and wispy fog, wings flapped, a gull swooped down, a blur going past her, and landed on the patio. It strutted for a moment, peered at itself in the glass, took wing as if frightened by its reflection. She knew just how it felt.

Suddenly she thought of her best friend, Sister Elizabeth, in Rome, in whom she had seen certain mirror images of herself. Elizabeth was also an American, several years younger, but so bright, so incisive, so understanding. Another modern nun, doing the work she wanted, but not the troublemaker Val was. They had known each other at Georgetown when Sister Val had been in the doctoral program, Elizabeth a precocious, liberal M.A. candidate. They had forged a friendship that had lasted through nearly a decade of extreme tensions within the Church. And in Rome it was to Sister Elizabeth that Val had confided Lockhardt's marriage proposal. Sister Elizabeth had listened to the whole story and waited before speaking.

"Play it by ear," she said at last, "and if that's casuistry, blame it on my basically Jesuitical nature. Situation ethics. Remember your vows but think it through—you're not a captive, you know. Nobody's locked you in a cell and thrown away the key, left you to rot."

Good advice, and if Elizabeth were in Malibu now, she'd have more good advice: what would it be? But then, Val knew what it would be because Sister Elizabeth always went back to it.

"If you're going to keep sleeping with him, Val," she'd said, "then you've got to get out of the Order. There's just no sense in going on the way you are. You may think it's a technicality but, face it, buster, it's no technicality. You took vows. Anybody can slip. But to go on slipping, make a way of life out of slipping—no way.

That's just stupid and dishonest. You know it, I know it, and the Supreme Being—she knows it, too."

Remembering the certainty of Sister Elizabeth's words, she felt only drained and afraid. The fear was blotting out any other emotions.

It had begun with the research for the book. The damn book! What she'd give never to have thought of the book! But it was too late for that now and it was the fear that had brought her back to the United States, that would take her home to Princeton. It was the fear that made her so hesitant about everything—about Curtis and love and staying in or getting out. . . . You couldn't think straight when you were consumed with fear. She had ventured too far in her researches, had kept digging when she should have had the sense to stop short and get out, go home. She should have forgotten what she'd found, attended to her own life, to Curtis. But it wasn't just for herself that she was afraid. Overshadowing every- thing else was the greatest fear. Her fear for the Church.

So she'd come back to America, intending to lay it all out for Curtis. But something had warned her, told her to stop, something she hated identifying. What she had discovered was a kind of infernal device, a bomb that had been ticking for a long, long time. Curtis Lockhardt either knew about it, or—God help him—was part of it, or he knew nothing at all of it. No, she couldn't tell him. He was too close to the Church, too much a part of it. That much, at least, seemed to make sense.

But the bomb was there and she had stumbled across it. It reminded her of the time at the house in Princeton when her brother Ben, rooting around in the basement looking for the old hickory-shafted golf clubs from their father's youth, had come across the seven cans of black powder left over from some long-ago Fourth of July. She had followed him down the steps, past all the accumulated mountains of the family's history, wary of spiders real or imagined that might drop into her hair, and had suddenly become aware of his voice, dropped to a whisper, telling her for Christ's sake to go back, and she had said she was going to tell on him for swearing.

Well, that was when he'd told her the house could blow up at any moment because that black powder had been in those cans since before they were born and was damned unstable. The water heater in the same room had a short in it, was shooting sparks. She didn't know anything about black powder, but she knew her brother Ben, and Ben wasn't kidding.

He'd made her go into the stone-walled stable while he had carefully, dripping with sweat, carried one can after another up from the basement and out across the back lawn past the family chapel all the way to the edge of the lake at the back of their property, back beyond the apple orchard. When he called the police in Princeton they'd sent some firemen, and the chief of police himself had come in the black DeSoto and they had wetted it all down and Ben was a real hero after that. The policemen gave him some kind of honorary badge, and a week or so later Ben had given it to her, a present, because she'd been a brave soldier, too, and followed orders. She'd been surprised, had cried and worn it every day all summer long, slept with it under her pillow. She was seven and Ben was fourteen and for the rest of her life she'd always gone to Ben when she needed somebody who would be a hero for her.

Now she had this bomb of her own, unstable and capable of blowing the coming papal election to smithereens, and she was going home to see Ben. Not Curtis, not her father—at least not yet. But she knew she would go back to Ben. She always smiled to herself when she thought about Ben, brother Ben, the lapsed— "collapsed is more like it," he used to say—Catholic. She could lay it all out for him, tell him what had come to light in the Torricelli papers and in the Secret Archives. He would laugh at her predicament and then he'd get serious and he'd know what to do. And he'd know what they should tell their father, how they should approach him with the whole story. . . .

New York

The Rolls-Royce was waiting at Kennedy when Lockhardt's private jet arrived, and took them directly through light traffic into the heart of midtown, arriving a half hour ahead of schedule. Lockhardt told his driver to drop him in the short block called Rockefeller Plaza which ran between the RCA Building and the Rockefeller Center ice rink. In the commodious backseat he looked into Val's eyes, took her hand. "You're sure there's nothing you want to tell me now?"

There was so much more behind the question than was showing. He hadn't told her about the call he'd received a week before,
when she was still in Egypt, from a friend at the Vatican. There was
concern in high places about what she was doing, the research trail
she'd come upon, her determination in pursuing it. Lockhardt's
friend in the Vatican was asking him to find out just what she'd
learned, to convince her to lay off.

Lockhardt had too much respect for Val's motives and work to
bring the Vatican's curiosity into the open. In any case, the Vatican
did not impress Sister Val. But he also had a strong sense of self-
preservation which he could easily enlarge to include her. For that
reason he was disturbed by the inquiry. It never did you any good
to have someone in the Vatican all over your case. And the call
wouldn't have been made on a whim. Something was seriously
bothering someone, and the word had been passed on. But he
couldn't press Val. She'd tell him what she'd been up to but he had
to give her time.

She smiled nervously, shook her head. "No, really. You've got
plenty on your mind right now. Callistus is dying. And you, my
darling man, have got to decide who is going to be the next pope
. . . the vultures are gathering."

"Do I strike you as a vulture?"

"Not at all. You're beating the vultures to it, as usual."

"When it comes to naming popes, I don't have a vote."

"Don't be disingenuous. Didn't *Time* call you the cardinal
without the red hat?" She grinned at his scowl. "You have a great
deal more than a vote. You named the last pope—"

"With your father's help, Sister." He laughed. "And we could
have done worse—"

"Barely," she said.

"My God, I love you, Sister."

"And you're in a position to name the next pope. Let's be
realistic. And I love you, too. You're not all that bad for an older
man."

"You're not supposed to have much basis for comparison," he
said.

"Believe me, I don't."

He took her hand. "Val, I wish you'd trust me, too. This terrible
secret of yours—it's driving you crazy. You're completely worn out.

Whatever it is, it's taking a hell of a toll on you. You're thin, you're tired, you look run-down—"

"You sweet-talking, silver-tongued devil—"

"You know what I mean. Take it easy, relax, talk to Ben. . . . You've got to get this off your chest."

"Curtis, cut me a break on this one, okay? I don't want to look foolish if my imagination has run away with me. This can all wait until tomorrow. Then maybe I'll lay it all out for you." She squeezed his hand. "Now you go see Andy." She leaned forward and kissed him softly, felt his hand in her hair, cupping her head. His mouth brushed her ear.

He got out and stood on the sidewalk, watched her wave as the car pulled away, and then the blackened window rose and she was gone. Next stop Princeton.

He'd lived so much of his life in the corridors of power that for a very long time he'd mistaken satisfaction and discreet camaraderie for happiness. Then Sister Valentine had revealed the mysteries of utter happiness, solved the great puzzle. Now he was sure they'd be together for good.

It was in this frame of mind that he stood gazing down at the skaters gliding rhythmically around the rink. It was true that he was worried about Val. She'd been in Rome, Paris, and had gone as far afield as Alexandria, Egypt, all in the name of research. He had tried to put the pieces together. He knew she'd also been working in the Secret Archives. And then he'd gotten that damned call from Rome.

From his vantage point at the railing above the ice he smiled at the sight of an elderly priest, full of grace and dignity, skating among the kids. He watched with admiration as the priest with his black raincoat blowing out behind him swept down and plucked a pretty girl from the ice where she'd fallen. He doubted if he had ever seen a more solemn and serene face.

He glanced at the Patek Philippe, a golden wafer on his wrist. Monsignor Heffernan, only forty-five now, destined for the red hat within the next five or ten years, was waiting. As Archbishop Cardinal Klammer's right-hand man, he had already accumulated considerable power in one of the wealthiest sees of the Church. He was not known for his dignity, certainly not for his solemnity. He was known for getting things done. And for such a hail-fellow-well-met, he was a punctual bastard who expected punctuality in others.

It was time to go.

The Church's involvement with the square block directly to the east of St. Patrick's Cathedral dated back to the late nineteenth century when it had built a rather pedestrian church, St. John's, on the site which later—after the Church sold the land—saw the construction of the famous Villard houses, which reminded some observers of the austere Florentine dwellings of Medici princes. Too expensive to remain in private hands following World War II, the glorious houses were abandoned and sat waiting, elegant and empty memories of another age.

In 1948 Francis Cardinal Spellman, Archbishop of New York, who was accustomed to looking at them across the traffic of Madison Avenue from his residence at St. Patrick's, decided to reacquire them. In no time the Church with its countless official selves spread through the magnificent buildings. The Gold Room at 451 Madison became the conference chamber for the Diocesan Consultors. A reception room overlooking Madison became a conference room for the Metropolitan Tribunal of the Archdiocese. The dining room was transformed into the tribunal's courtroom and the library became the Chancery office. Pushing down corridors and up marble staircases, the protean entity of the Church spread . . .

Times change, however. By the 1970s, the real estate boom of the 1960s had collapsed and the Church found itself unable to unload the Villard houses, which once again sat empty, representing an annual tax burden of $700,000. The economic problem was acute.

They were rescued by Harry Helmsley, who offered to lease the Villard houses and the adjacent Church-owned properties to construct a hotel. The Archdiocese assisted Helmsley with the red-tape problems, and, in the end, the houses were saved intact, the Church still owned the site, and Helmsley had a long-term lease. He built his hotel around the houses.

Like a Renaissance prince, he called it The Helmsley Palace.

It was this palace that Curtis Lockhardt entered beneath the nineteenth-century bronze and glass marquee on Fiftieth. He went directly through the hushed reception area with its mirrors and the rich French walnut paneling, turned abruptly right, and went into the small enclosure that contained a concierge's desk and the out-of-the-way elevators servicing the topmost floors, the penthouses.

It was typical of Andy Heffernan to have reserved the Church's triplex penthouse for the meeting. In the highly political world he inhabited, Curtis Lockhardt was one of Monsignor Heffernan's trump cards, and he wanted to maintain as much secrecy as he could. Lockhardt was talking about a sum of money so large that not a shred of rumor could be permitted to leak out. The choice of the next pope was on the table, nestling up close to the money. Had they met across the street at St. Patrick's, the rumors would have beaten them to the street. Power, luxury, worldliness, and secrecy: that was Monsignor Heffernan.

Lockhardt knew that the Dunhill Monte Cruz 200 cigars and the Rémy Martin cognac Andy favored would be ready. Monsignor Heffernan often remarked off the record that you took all the perks you could get and the more you took the more there were to take.

Lockhardt got out of the elevator at the fifty-fourth floor and padded through the deep carpeting to the end of a long hallway running parallel to Madison Avenue. There was nothing to indicate anything out of the ordinary behind any of the doors. He pressed the buzzer and waited. A voice from a small speaker said: "Come in, Curtis me lad." It sounded as if the good monsignor might have enjoyed a two-martini lunch.

Although he was accustomed to luxury, Lockhardt was always impressed by the sight of what lay before him. He stood at the top of a curving staircase with an elaborately carved banister. The huge room below was two stories in height, completely glassed in, with Manhattan spreading out beyond like an isometric map.

The Empire State Building, the suave art deco spire of the Chrysler Building, the pristine modernity of the World Trade Center towers, beyond them in the bay the Statue of Liberty, Staten Island, the Jersey shoreline . . .

Radio City, Rockefeller Center, the luminous patch of the ice rink . . . and almost straight down was St. Patrick's, its twin steeples rising majestically above Fifth Avenue.

He felt as if he were standing on a cloud. He held the carved railing as he slowly descended the thickly carpeted stairs. He couldn't look away from the view. It made him feel like a child confronted by toys beyond his wildest dreams.

"I'm having a quick pee." Heffernan's voice floated out from behind some hidden door. "Be with you in two shakes."

Lockhardt turned back to the view, almost mesmerized by the clarity and detail of the city. He was standing with his nose nearly pressed to the glass, staring down at a view of St. Patrick's that its builders must never quite have imagined. God's view. It was like looking at a blueprint that had come to life, developed a third dimension rising up at you.

"God bless our little home." Monsignor Heffernan, a large man with thinning red hair and a nose that seemed to have been pilfered from a clown, lumbered toward him. He was red with sunburn that was peeling. He was wearing a black shirt and a priest's dog collar, black trousers, and black tasseled loafers. His watery blue eyes blinked behind a scrim of cigar smoke. He had battled his way up from Irish poverty, South Boston variety. He was already a very important man in his world and by cementing his alliance with the great American kingmaker he was becoming even more so. Conveniently, they were able to use each other, which the monsignor thought was as good a definition of friendship as you were likely to come across. Andy Heffernan was a happy man.

"You're looking very fit and virtuous for a rich man, Curtis. Have a cigar." He pointed to a wooden box on the corner of a cluttered trestle table topped by a slab of glass two inches thick.

"You've twisted my arm," Lockhardt said. He lit the Monte Cruz with a Dunhill cigar match and savored the flavor. "Where did you pick up the look of a lobster?"

"Florida. Just back yesterday from a week of charity golf. Great week." He went to the chair behind the table and sat down. There were several folders, a legal pad, a telephone, the cigars, a heavy ashtray. Lockhardt sat down facing him across the field of glass. "Great guys, Jackie Gleason, Johnny and Tom and Jack, all of them. Lots of great guys down in Florida. Do anything for the Church. Hell of a benefit for the Our Lady of Peace children's wing. Lotsa golf. You're not going to believe this, but I missed a hole in one by no less than three inches! Damned if I didn't! Shoulda been on the TV—six iron pin high, three crummy inches to the left. I got one in Scotland once, at Muirfield . . . ah, happy days, a hell of a long way from South Boston. What more can a man want, Curtis? Enjoy, enjoy, we're a long time dead—"

"Whatever happened to the life eternal, the choir invisible, big sets of wings—"

"You and your nuns' theology! Gimme a break." Heffernan laughed in his characteristic all-out way that was supposed to make you think he was as wide open as a whorehouse on Saturday night.

"You want a break *and* ten million bucks?" Lockhardt smiled back at him and blew a smoke ring. The figure was so large that on the few occasions it had come up specifically in their conversations it had been very rewarding to watch Heffernan's reaction.

"Ten million bucks . . ." Heffernan's laughter died quickly. That much money was very serious business, even to the right-hand man of Archbishop Cardinal Klammer. Lockhardt always wondered what was going on in the man's mind when he was talking about holes in one with Johnny Miller and laughing that way. He never seemed to be on his guard. Yet he never seemed to make a mistake.

"The ten million," Heffernan said softly, liking the sound of it. He touched his fingertips before him, tapped all ten against one another. "You believe ten million will swing this whole deal?"

"More or less. I can always come up with more. There's always a deep pockets reserve."

"Like Hugh Driskill, maybe?"

Lockhardt shrugged. "Andy, you can make any assumption you like. But do you really need to know? Do you really *want* to know? I rather doubt that."

"Whatever you say. You come up with the money, I'll help you see it into the right hands." Heffernan sighed like a man who knew he was well off, a smiling Irishman. "Klammer just kills me, Curtis. All this hands-off bullshit, all his deniability rap—"

"American cardinals are different. They tend to think their votes are sacred things rather than trading chips. I suppose he doesn't want to touch any of this himself, he doesn't know it ever happened. Bribes scare them—"

"Gifts, gifts!" Heffernan made a face. "The B word must never pass our lips. Ten million. What are we actually getting for the money, you and I? Is it, in a word, good for the Jews?"

"A rock-solid American core of support. You put that together with Fangio, the cardinals Callistus named who owe us . . . bottom line, Andy, is we name the next pope. The Church stays on track. We see to it." For a moment his mind stuck, hearing Sister

Valentine, hearing her tell him that what she'd turned up could affect the choice of the next pope. . . .

"No defections in the ranks?"

"Why should anyone defect? Saint Jack is seventy-six years old. He won't last forever and then . . . well, by then you'll be wearing the red hat and the Church will have had a great man as pope for a time. And this old Church will have been moved on into the twenty-first century, going the only direction it can go if it's going to survive. It's a new world coming, Andy, and the Church has got to hit the ground running. It's as simple as that."

"I gotta hand it to you, you make it simple. The money is certain?"

"I never deal in mere probabilities, Andy."

"Well, this calls for a libation." Monsignor Heffernan reached for the Rémy Martin on a tray beside two handsome pieces of Baccarat crystal. He poured and handed one glass to Curtis Lockhardt. "To money well spent."

The two men stood at the vast expanse of glass, drank a toast against the awesome backdrop of Manhattan. It was as if they stood on a man-made mountaintop, a peak they'd achieved together, Lockhardt leading the way with his faithful monsignor.

"To jolly old Saint Jack," Lockhardt said quietly.

"To the future," the monsignor echoed.

It was Heffernan who saw him first. He smacked his lips, looked up, and saw an old priest. Somehow he'd come in unheard, descended the steps while they'd been enjoying the view, and congratulating themselves. Monsignor Heffernan cocked his head quizzically, his red face smiling sunnily. "Yes, Father, what can I do for you?"

Lockhardt turned, saw the priest. It was the skater. Lockhardt smiled, remembering the scene at the ice rink. Then he noticed the gloved hand coming up, and there was something about it . . .

While Lockhardt watched, strength draining from his body and being replaced with biological, chemical, uncontrollable shock, he tried in the fractional instant to grasp what was happening. This priest was all wrong. He didn't come from Curtis Lockhardt's corridors of power. There was a gun in his hand.

It made a strange muffled sound, like an arrow hitting a wet target.

Andy Heffernan was slammed backward against the vastness of

glass, silhouetted against the light, arms outstretched as if waiting for the nails to be driven home. The sound came again and the sunburned face came apart—irrevocably apart, ended in every way: the thoughts tumbled through Lockhardt's brain as he stood, unable to move, to run, to throw himself at this gunman—the face he'd known so many years came apart in an explosion of blood and bone. A web of cracks appeared in the blood-spattered glass wall, radiating away from a hole the size of a man's fist.

Lockhardt stared down at what was left of his friend, stared at the slippery crimson trail he'd left on the window. Lockhardt felt his way along the edge of the desktop, moving slowly as if in a dream, moving backward toward the body of Monsignor Heffernan. He was only barely functioning. Everything seemed so far away, dim, as if things were happening at the end of a tunnel.

Slowly the priest swung the gun around to face him.

"God's will," he said, and Lockhardt struggled to comprehend, struggled to decipher the code. "God's will," the old priest whispered again.

Lockhardt stared into the gun barrel, looked into the old priest's eyes, but he was seeing something else, a little girl in a frilly bathing suit dancing and laughing and showing off in the rainbow of a sprinkler's arc, dancing in the sunshine, on the wet, newly mown grass that clung to her toes as she danced.

Lockhardt heard his own voice, couldn't quite make out what he was saying. Maybe he was calling to the little girl, calling her name, trying to reach her before it was too late, trying to get there, scrambling back into the safety of the past, the safety of the net of time. . . .

The priest waited, his face kindly, as if he were giving Curtis Lockhardt time to reach safe ground. . . .

Then the old priest pulled the trigger.

Curtis Lockhardt lay with his head against the glass, where it met the carpet. He was drowning in his own blood, his lungs filling. There was a dimming of his vision, as if night were falling fast now, and he couldn't quite see the prancing child anymore. In her place he could make out the shape of St. Patrick's Cathedral blurring far below him. The spires seemed to be reaching toward him, like fingers pointing.

He saw a black trouser leg beside his face. He felt something blunt pressing against the back of his head.

Curtis Lockhardt blinked hard, trying to make out the sprightly dancing figure, but instead he took one last look at St. Patrick's.

PART ONE

PART ONE

1

DRISKILL

I remember that first day quite clearly.

I was summoned to lunch at his club by Drew Summerhays, the imperishable gray eminence of our well-upholstered world downtown at Bascomb, Lufkin, and Summerhays. He possessed the clearest, most adaptable mind I'd ever encountered, and most of our luncheon discussions were both illuminating and amusing. And they always had a point. Summerhays was eighty-two that year, the age of the century, but he still ventured down to Wall Street most days. He was our living legend, a friend and adviser to every president since Franklin Roosevelt's first campaign, a backstage hero of World War II, a spy master, and always a confidant of the popes. Through his close relationship with my father I'd known him all my life.

On occasion, even before I'd joined the firm and subsequently become a partner, I'd had his ear because he'd watched me grow up. Once, when I was about to become a Jesuit novice, he'd come to me with advice and I'd had the lack of foresight to ignore it. Oddly enough, in such contrast to his austere, flinty appearance, he was a lifelong football fan and, particularly, a fan of mine. He had advised me to play a few years of professional football once I'd graduated from Notre Dame. The Jesuits, he argued, would still be there when I retired but now was my only chance to test my ability at the next level. He had hoped that fate might deliver me to the New York Giants. It might have happened, I suppose. But I was young and I knew it all.

I'd spent my Notre Dame years as a linebacker, caked in mud and crap and blood, all scabby and hauling around more than my share of free-floating anxiety and rage. Two hundred and fifty pounds of mayhem stuffed into a two-hundred-pound body. Sportswriter hyperbole, sure, but Red Smith had so described me. The fact was, in those days I was a dangerous man.

Nowadays I am quite a civilized specimen in my way, kept in one psychological piece by that fragile membrane that separates us from the triumph of unreason and evil. Kept intact and relatively harmless by the practice of law, by the family, by the family's name and tradition.

Summerhays hadn't understood the simple truth that I'd lost whatever enthusiasm I'd ever had for playing football. And my father wanted me to become a priest. Summerhays always thought that my father was a bit more of a Catholic than was, strictly speaking, good for him. Summerhays was a realistic Papist. My father, he told me, was something else, a true believer.

In the end I hadn't played pro football and I had gone off to become a Jesuit. It was the last bit of advice I'd ever taken from my father and, as I recall, the last time I ignored a suggestion from Drew Summerhays. The price for my lack of judgment was high. As it developed, the Society of Jesus seemed to be a hammer, the Church an anvil, and the smiling linebacker got caught between. Bang, bang, bang.

It wasn't just that I didn't become the Jesuit my father had hoped for—young Father Ben Driskill, mighty Hugh's boy, chucking old ladies under their chins at rummage sales, shooting baskets with the neighborhood toughs and turning them into altar boys, giving smelly old wino Mr. Leary the last rites, arranging for the teens' hayride with Sister Rosalie from the Visitation Convent School, leading the caroling at Christmas . . . none of that for me.

No, I said good-bye to all of it, turned in my rosary, hung up the reliable old scourge, packed away the hair shirt, kissed them all farewell.

I haven't been inside a Catholic church in twenty years, except to honor my sister Valentine, who picked up the standard that I'd thrown down and become a nun of the Order. Sister Val: one of those new nuns you kept hearing about, running around raising hell, driving the Church nuts. Val had made the covers of *Time* and *Newsweek* and *People*. Old Hugh—to his considerable dismay, at times—had sired a hellion.

Val and I used to joke about it because she knew where I stood. She knew I'd gone inside the Church and glimpsed the machinery glowing red-hot. She knew I'd heard the sizzle. And she knew I'd been burned. She understood me and I understood her. I knew she was more determined than I, had more guts.

The only thing I didn't enjoy chatting with Drew Summerhays about was football. Unfortunately, as I'd feared, football was on his mind that day. It was the season, late October, and there was no stopping him as we set out on foot for one of his many clubs. He wore his impeccable chesterfield with its perfectly brushed velvet collar, a pearl-gray homburg, his tightly rolled Brigg umbrella tapping the narrow sidewalk where the jumble of financial district workers seemed miraculously to part and make way for him. It had become a raw, blustery day down at our end of Manhattan, heavy smudged clouds like thumbprints moving in after a sunny, perfect morning. There was a taste of winter working its way up the island, starting with us. Grim gray clouds were pressing down on Brooklyn, trying to drown it in the East River.

As we sat down and commenced lunch, Summerhays's dry, precise voice was going on about a long-ago game I'd played in Iowa City against the Hawkeyes. I made seven unassisted tackles and had two sacks that day, but the play that was lodged in the old man's mind was the last of the game with Iowa on the Notre Dame four-yard line. The tight end had run a brutal little post pattern, I'd had to fight off two blocks, and when I looked up, the ball was floating toward the tight end in the back of the end zone. We were six points ahead, there was no time left on the clock. The end zone was flooded with receivers alert to the possibility of a tipped ball. So I'd made a frantic leap out of the mud sucking at me and intercepted the pass. Anybody standing there could have done it. It happened to be me. My nose had been broken to start the fourth quarter and a gash over my eyes had blinded me with blood, but I got lucky and caught the damn thing. The interception became a Notre Dame legend that lasted the rest of the season, and Drew Summerhays, of all people, was remembering it and wanted to hear the whole boring story again.

So while he was bringing down all that old thunder from the skies I remembered how it had felt when it had struck me during a summer scrimmage that I quite suddenly *understood* the game. I could see it all, as if it were a single piece of fabric: the quarterback across the humped tails and helmets of the down linemen, his eyes moving, the cadence of his raw, hoarse voice, yes, I could somehow *see* his voice; I saw running backs tense; as if I could chart the movement of molecules, I saw the receivers shift their weight, strain at the leash. I saw the linemen thinking out their blocking assignments. I saw inside the quarterback's head, I knew what he was thinking, how the play would develop, how I should react.

And from that day on I understood the bloody game, saw each play developing as if it were in slo-mo. I understood the absolute essence of what was going on and I became one hell of a football player. Made the *Look* All-American team and got to shake hands with Bob Hope on TV. Football.

You tell yourself later on that you learned a lot about life from playing football and maybe you did. You learned about pain, about the wild-eyed crazy bastard down in the silt at the bottom of your psyche; you learned about locker-room jock humor and gung-ho for the Fighting Irish and old grads who turned on you if you lost the fucking game; you learned that just because you were a football player it didn't mean you were going to get anywhere with the blondes with big tits on the *Bob Hope Show*. If that was life, well, I guess you learned something about life from football.

But nothing I've ever known since quite equaled that moment of summer scrimmage when I saw it all so clearly. Drew Summerhays never understood football like that. And what he understood I simply never grasped. Summerhays understood the Church.

I watched him complete the neat, surgical slicing and spearing of the last morsel of Dover sole which he ate without any accompaniment whatsoever: no salad, no vegetables, no rolls and butter. A single glass of Evian water. No coffee, no dessert. The man was going to live forever, and what I really wanted from him was the name of the person who did his shirts. I had never seen such starch work. Never a ripple, just shirts like perfect fields of snow. I felt like a peasant sopping up the sauce in which the last of my osso buco lay. His face was expressionless, unless patience with my appetite constituted an expression. He urged a choice Fladgate port on me and the wine steward scurried away to the club cellars. Summerhays slipped a gold hunter from his vest pocket, checked the hour, and got to the point of our luncheon, which had nothing to do with Notre Dame and old gridiron exploits.

"Curtis Lockhardt is coming to town today, Ben. Have you ever spent much time with him?"

"I hardly know him. I've met him a few times. That's since I've been a grown-up. He used to hang around the house when Val and I were kids."

"That's one way of putting it. I'd have described him as your father's protégé. Almost a member of the family. That's how I'd have put it, anyway." He ran a knuckle along his upper lip, then shifted away from the possible implications I might recognize about Lockhardt's relationship with my sister. Whatever *that* might be. It was none of my business, what your new nuns got up to these days.

"He'll be seeing me, of course," Summerhays went on. "And your father, too . . . ah, thank you, Simmons. Precisely what I had in mind for Mr. Driskill." Simmons placed the bottle on the table, allowing me the privilege of pouring my own. I slid it around the glass. The port had legs, I had to give it that. Simmons reappeared with a Davidoff cigar and a clipper. In no time at all I decided that reminiscing about the Iowa game had been a small price to pay.

"And," Summerhays said softly, "I'd like you to spend some time with him. It occurs to me that given some of the firm's interests—" He may have shrugged. It was so subtle I may have imagined it.

"Which interests would those be, Drew?" I felt a draw play coming my way. I was being suckered into committing myself too early. If I didn't watch out, Drew Summerhays would have a first and goal inside the ten.

"I wouldn't try to mislead you," he said. "We're talking about the Church here. But, Ben, the Church is business, and business is business is business."

"Let me see if I've got this straight, Drew. You're saying business is business?"

"You have grasped the essence of my thought."

"I was afraid of that."

"Two lawyers," he said, "being cute." A smile flitted across his thin lips. "You may have heard that the Holy Father is unwell?"

It was my turn to shrug.

"That's why Lockhardt is coming to town. He's firming up plans for choosing a successor to Callistus. He may want our counsel—"

"Not mine," I said. "Most unlikely."

"And I want you firmly in the picture. It is valuable to the firm that we have sufficient lead time when this sort of decision is being made. Or seriously contemplated."

I rolled about ten dollars worth of port on my tongue. I puffed a bit on the cigar while he waited with vast serenity. "I thought the College of Cardinals still elected the pope. Did they change the rules and not send me the letter?"

"They haven't changed anything. They pick the popes exactly as they always have. You know, Ben, you've got to keep a firm rein on your anticlericalism. Just a word of advice."

"It's served me pretty well so far."

"Things change. Almost everything changes. But not, as it happens, the Church, not at its heart. You mustn't think I would ever ask you to compromise your principles."

"Thank God for that, Drew."

The irony was lost on him for the moment. "But the firm works closely with the Church," he said. "There are things you should familiarize yourself with . . . things that are somewhat out of the ordinary run. Why not start with our friend Lockhardt?"

"Because the Church is my enemy. I can't make it any clearer than that."

"You're losing your sense of humor, Ben. Your sense of proportion. I'm not suggesting that you aid the Church in any way. I merely want you to listen, to become more informed about our dealings. Forget your personal problems with the Church. Remember, business—"

"Is business."

"That's it in a nutshell, Ben."

*   *   *

It certainly was turning out to be my day for the Catholics.

When I got back to the office Father Vinnie Halloran was waiting for me. I felt a groan welling up inside me. He was a Jesuit, about my age, and I'd known him a long time. The Society had put him in charge of handling the last will and testament of the late Lydia Harbaugh of Oyster Bay, Palm Beach, and Bar Harbor. It was a marginally nutty document that left the bulk of her vast estate to the Society of Jesus. There was a good deal of Jesuitical concern about its ability to withstand the challenge from three understandably truculent, short-changed heirs presumptive.

"Look, Ben, the dowager empress of Oyster Bay gave two sons to the Jesuits. Is it any wonder that she wanted the Society to benefit in a large way? As her will clearly indicates, let me hasten to add. Hell, it isn't as if the other three offspring—have you seen them, Ben? God at His cruelest—they aren't getting shut out. Coupla million apiece for them. Greedy little bastards." I hadn't seen Vinnie in his clerical collar more than five times in my life. Today he wore a Harris tweed jacket, a striped shirt, a bow tie. He looked at me in hopes of encouragement.

"They're going to offer a lot of evidence that she was a batty old dipsomaniac for the last twenty years of her life. Very persuasive case, in my view. And under the influence she made a patently absurd will. Jesuits camped at her bedside. And so on."

"Is that any way for *our* mouthpiece to talk?" Vinnie came from money so, contrary to popular belief, money meant a great deal to him. Halloran money from Pittsburgh was nothing like Driskill money from Princeton and New York, but it was enough to get you into certain habits.

"Is this really what the Church had in mind for you, Vincent? Hovering over the doubtful wills of rich old ladies?"

"Don't get moralistic on me, Ben," he said blandly. "It's a doggie-dog world out there."

"Dog eat dog," I corrected him. We'd been doing that bit for years.

"The Church is no different from any other big organization. You know that. The Church, and the Society, we have to look out for ourselves because sure as hell nobody else will. I do my part by rounding up odd bits of loose change here and there. The Church has got to own itself—"

"Vinnie, Vinnie, this is me, Ben. The Church hasn't owned itself since the days of Constantine. It's always out whoring for someone. The pimps change but the Church is always back on the street the next day."

"By Jove, laddie, you may be this Antichrist we've all heard so much about. What a red-letter day for me . . . still, you might make the perfect Jesuit yet. Except you fight for your piddling little idea of the great truths too zealously. You never learned to speak your piece and shut up. The truth is you never understood what the Church was about. You were never able to force the cuddly little lamb of idealism to lie down with the fierce lion of realism and make nice-nice. Which is what the Church is *all* about."

"What a happily pragmatic fellow you are!"

"Have to be. I'm a priest." He leaned back and grinned at me. "I've gotta live with this mess. And it is a mess; the Church is not a tidy place. Because man is never tidy. We all just run around doing the best we can and if we're right fifty-one percent of the time, well, hell, that's about all you can ask for. Believe me, the Dowager Harbaugh wanted the Society to have this moola. And if the old bat didn't, she should have."

What mattered to Vinnie and all the other Vinnies was that they *believed*. Halloran's faith was intact. He'd always told me that I'd had a faithectomy somewhere along the line. His belief and faith were not only in God—maybe not even mainly in God—but in the Church itself, which was where we really parted company. I'd observed them at work and I'd learned you could find God a convenient myth or you could believe He lived in your dishwasher and spoke to you during the hot-dry cycle, none of that mattered. But, by heaven, you'd better believe in the Church.

After lunch I stood in the corner office I'd occupied for most of a decade and looked out at Battery Park and the towers of the World Trade Center and the Statue of Liberty, which was only barely visible through the fog and mist that was thickening by midafternoon. It was the kind of office Hugh Driskill's son was expected to have, and expectations were very much a part of our lives at Bascomb, Lufkin, and Summerhays. There was an English partners desk from Dickens's day, a Louis XV refectory table, a Brancusi on top of it, an Epstein bust on a pedestal, and a Klee on the wall. It could give you the shakes if you weren't feeling pretty confident. Gifts from my father and my former wife, Antonia, and all very eclectic and smashing. *New York* magazine had once done a piece on power offices, and mine had been among them and it had taken me a long time to live it down. I'd picked the carpet and both Hugh and Antonia thought it looked like the bottom of the canary cage which was, if memory serves, just about the only thing they ever agreed on. In the end all that Antonia and I had shared was a deep distrust of the Roman Catholic Church, but it hadn't been enough to save our marriage. I always felt that she had inherited her attitude at birth while I'd acquired mine the old-fashioned way. I'd earned it.

The fog was rolling in from the direction of Staten Island, blurring familiar landmarks, like clouds of memory overtaking the everyday trivialities. When you reached the middle of your life, one of the revelations concerned memories, or so it seemed to me. They seemed so important and they would not be pushed aside. They exercised their claim on you and you began to wonder if they held all the keys to all the locked doors in your psyche. It was a little scary.

There had always been lots of priests hanging around the house while Val and I were growing up. By the time Father came home from the war in 1945 I was ten, and it was summer. In those years when Father was out of the country and we couldn't see him except on leaves, there was an elderly priest with a great deal of white hair billowing from ears and nostrils who made an impression on me. He was Father Polanski, who came to say mass in our chapel. He sometimes puttered about in the gardens with Mother and me and once gave me a trowel of my own but we didn't really know him any more than we knew the man who kept the skating pond neat and smooth or the fellows who came to do the lawn, mow it and rake it and prune the trees in the orchard.

It wasn't until our father came home from the war that we really noticed a priest as a human being, and that was a matter of comparative necessity. He brought one with him, an actual Italian who spoke English with a heavy accent. Val and I somehow got it into our heads that Father—or was he Monsignor?—Giacomo D'Ambrizzi, in his long cassock and high-topped, bulbous-toed, thick-soled black shoes, was a trophy of the war that Father had bagged in some peculiar way—akin to the dusty, moth-eaten stuffed bear standing in one corner of the tack room and the lion and rhino heads in the lodge in the Adirondacks. In some childlike

way little Val, who was nearly four, and I figured that Father
D'Ambrizzi belonged to us. He seemed to enjoy the relationship,
too. There's no way to count all the piggyback rides, the games of
checkers and animal lotto and croquet he played with us that
summer, how many hours he spent with us in the first autumn of
peace, taking hayrides and learning to bob for apples along with
us, carving jack-o'-lanterns and trying to get the hang of ice skating
out on the pond beyond the orchard. He seemed as innocent as Val
and I certainly were. If the other priests I came to know had shared
his virtues, I suppose I'd be a priest now, but that kind of
supposition is pretty much of a dead end these days.

Father D'Ambrizzi liked doing things with his hands and I used
to sit by the hour, entranced, watching him. He built a swing out
in the orchard, hanging the ropes from the stout limb of a large
apple tree. I'd never seen anything quite so wonderful—but then
he surpassed himself with a tree house reached by a rope ladder.
And even more impressive than that was watching him lay bricks,
the way he slapped the mortar around and leveled them with such
certainty. He did some work on the chapel that had taken to
crumbling in a couple of places. I was spellbound. I took to dogging
his footsteps wherever he went other than when he closed the study
door to do his "work." I could tell that his work was terribly
important. No one ever bothered him when he was at his work in
the study.

But when he emerged, there I'd be waiting for him. He would
pick me up in his long, hairy, simian arms as if I were a doll. His
hair was thick and black and curly, cropped close to his boulder of
a skull like a cap. His nose was like a banana, his mouth curled
like a prince in a Renaissance painting. He was a good six inches
shorter than my father. He was built like Edward G. Robinson,
according to my mother. I asked her what that meant and she
thought for a moment and said, "Well, you know, Benjy. Like a
gangster, darling."

Father didn't have D'Ambrizzi's easy grace with children. He
must have felt moments of jealousy at the crushes Val and I had
developed on this exotic specimen. We never thought to wonder
why he'd come to stay with us: we were just content to worship
him. And then, one day, he was gone, had gone in the night as if
we'd made him up, as if he'd been a dream. But he left us each a
cross of bone, Val's filigreed like lace, mine solid and masculine.

Val still wears hers. Mine is long gone, I suppose.

Father talked to us about D'Ambrizzi a little later in what for him was a pretty subtle tactic. He didn't mention D'Ambrizzi's name, but Val and I exchanged a glance because we knew. Father was explaining to us why we shouldn't confuse priests—"men of God"—with God Himself. While the one had feet of clay, the other had no known feet at all, not so far as anyone knew. That's what it boiled down to, though it was quite a long time in the telling. Afterward I can recall sneaking looks at the feet of the priests drinking scotch in the library with Father or marching off to say mass in the chapel for Mother. Never saw any of the clay, and that confused me. Val in her quiet, little-girl way went to work with her jars of modeling compound and produced quite a remarkable rendering. Mother came into the playroom, stopped, did a double take, and asked what those things were. Val piped up, clear and sweet, "Feet of clay!" Mother found that extravagantly amusing and had Father come take a look. Later on she brought a friend from the Church to see them, but Val said she'd scrunched them all up to make something else. I knew it wasn't true. She'd hidden the feet of clay inside her big bass drum with the clown painted on the side panel. She had pried one of the panels up and used the space inside as her most secret place. It was years before she discovered that I knew about it. I never found a great place like that, but then, I never had any great secrets. Val was the curious one, the one who had stuff to squirrel away.

I was remembering Val as a little girl, learning to skate on the pond with a kind of natural ease while I floundered around like a fool, cold and wet and bruised and generally irritable. Winter sports always struck me as unhappy pursuits, punishment for unnamed offenses, but Val thought I was a goof.

And I suppose I was.

I was thinking about Val when Miss Esterbrook, my secretary, came in and cleared her throat behind me. I turned back from the fog and memory.

"Your sister's calling, Mr. Driskill."

She left and I sat at the desk for a moment before picking up the phone. I do not trust coincidences. "Hello, Val? Where are you? What's going on?"

My sister sounded funny and I told her so. She laughed and

called me a goof but her heart wasn't in it. There was something wrong but she said only that she wanted me to get out to Princeton, to meet her at the house that evening. She had something she wanted to talk over with me. I told her I'd thought she was in Paris or someplace.

"I've been all over. It's a long story. I just got home this afternoon. Flew in with Curtis. Will you come tonight, Ben? It's important."

"Are you sick?"

"I'm a little scared. Not sick. Ben, let this wait until tonight, okay?"

"Sure, sure. Is Dad there?"

"No. He's got a board meeting in Manhattan—"

"Good."

"What's that supposed to mean?"

"Just the usual. I like plenty of advance warning if he's waiting in the shadows to bushwhack me."

"Eight-thirty, Ben. And, Ben? I love you, even if you are a big goof."

"Earlier today Vinnie Halloran told me I was the Antichrist."

"Vinnie always erred on the side of overstatement."

"I love you, too, sis. Even if you are a nun."

I heard her sigh and then she hung up. I sat for a while trying to remember if I'd ever known her to be afraid before, with the fear seeping into her voice. I decided I never had.

I left the office a little early for me since my customary day had a tendency to wind down between eight and nine. I wanted time for a shower and a change of clothes before I ransomed my Mercedes for the drive to Princeton.

The cab dropped me at Seventy-third and Madison. The light had faded behind the fog and the streetlamps were on, glowing their moist penumbrae. I walked toward the park, still trying to figure out what was going on with my sister. The streets were slick and shiny. The World Series had ended just over a week before and suddenly it was cold as winter and the mist was turning to biting little pellets.

Sister Val . . . I knew she'd gone to Rome to get started on a new book, had then sent me a postcard from Paris. I hadn't expected to see her in Princeton until Christmas. She stuck fiercely to her research and writing schedule, yet here she was, taking a break. What had scared her enough to bring her home?

Well, it looked like I'd be finding out that night. You could never be sure what kind of hell my sister Val was raising. All I knew was that she'd been researching the Church's role in World War II. Had that brought her home? It was hard to imagine how. But you never knew about Val. She wasn't the kind of nun we knew at St. Columbkille's Grammar School. That thought always put a smile on my face and I was grinning like a fool when I got to my brownstone. There wasn't going to be anything Val and I couldn't handle. There never had been.

I crossed the Hudson by way of the George Washington Bridge, headed toward Princeton, and felt the cold and the damp and the tension of my foot on the gas pedal setting off the old ache in my leg, a souvenir of my Jesuit days. The Jesuits had left their mark, all right. The traffic finally thinned out and I was alone with the sweep of the windshield wipers and the Elgar cello concerto coming from the tape player. It had become a foul, slippery night, the rain turning to a slushy half-ice, the car always on the verge of aquaplaning me into the next world.

I was thinking of another night rather like it, twenty-odd years before, only then it was the utter dead of winter and white not dirty gray, but there had been the same feeling of things out of kilter. I'd been heading back to Princeton then, too, dreading the talk I was facing with my father. I didn't want to tell him what had happened and he certainly didn't want to hear it. He wasn't much for sob stories and failures, which in his view were always nothing but goddamn cowardice. The closer I got to Princeton the more I wanted no part of it. There I was, in the middle of what Bulwer-Lytton might have called a dark and stormy night, ice and snow sealing me off, running like a thief in the night from the gloomy, crenellated battlements where I'd tried to be a Jesuit. Tried to be the man my father had always wanted me to be.

Hugh Driskill liked the idea of my being among the Jesuits, liked knowing I was entwined in the rigorous discipline, the demanding intellectual life. He liked knowing I was taking my place in a world that he understood. It was also a world that my father felt he could control to some extent. He liked to believe in his own egocentric way that he, because of his wealth and devotion

to the Church and the accomplishing of good works and the
wielding of influence—he liked to believe that in the end he was
one of those who defined the Establishment, the Church within the
Church. I always felt that my father rated himself rather too highly
but, hell, what did I know?

More recently it has occurred to me that he may have had a
pretty accurate view of himself after all. Drew Summerhays had
confided a few things to me over the years that tended to legitimize
my father's belief in his own importance. Summerhays had long
been a mentor and friend to my father in much the same way my
father was to the ubiquitous Curtis Lockhardt. And now Summerhays was telling me that my father and Lockhardt were laying plans
for the choosing of the next pope.

Of course I remembered things from my own life that lent
weight to my father's view of himself. When I was a kid, Cardinal
Spellman—he must have been bishop or archbishop then, who
remembers?—was always coming over from New York to Princeton
for dinner, which must have meant we were something special. He
came to both the Princeton house and the very grand Park Avenue
duplex which we gave up after Mother's accident. Sometimes I
heard my parents calling him "Frank," and once I marveled when
he told me he was wearing alligator shoes. Perhaps I'd been
inspecting him for feet of clay.

It must have been the call from Val that had gotten me worrying
and thinking about the old days, and now I was remembering
Spellman and my father and alligator shoes and the Jesuits and that
long-ago night when the road was slippery and the snow was
blowing and I was driving home alone with a load of bad news,
wondering what my father would say, wondering how he'd confront
the newest disappointment I'd devised for him.

Twenty years ago, more.

In the early morning, when the snow had almost stopped and
dark of night had eased up a bit, the highway patrol had gone
looking for victims of the storm. They found my Chevy racked up
against a tree, totaled, the car and the tree and damn near me, and
there was no evidence I'd tried to stop the car on the icy, crusty,
snowy road. So they knew I must have fallen asleep. It happened
sometimes. Well, that was all bullshit. I had a broken leg and I was
half frozen, but the important thing was that I'd realized in the

middle of the night that dying was preferable to telling my father about the Jesuits and me.

Epiphany. It was the only true moment of epiphany I'd ever had. Naturally, as it developed, my father knew the truth of what I'd tried to do that night. It was there in his eyes, the burning fires of unquenched despair, like beacon fires on a dark and treacherous shore beckoning me home, home. He knew. He knew I'd had my go at suicide, the final Catholic sin, and it was one more thing he could never forgive.

Thank God there's Val. He actually said it to me in the hospital afterward. Not to insult me, nor to humiliate me, but just muttering to himself under his breath. And by then, having consciously tried to end my own life, having once chosen the void, having excluded my father from the decision-making process, I no longer gave a goddamn what he thought. That was what I told myself. That was my triumph.

I skirted the edges of Princeton, turned off onto the two-lane blacktop where I'd learned to drive my father's Lincoln, and before I knew it the headlights were poking through the whipping curtain of rain and sleet, reaching into the darkness toward the house. The long driveway passing beneath and between rows of poplars was soft with slush sucking at the tires. The gravel turnaround was yellow and muddy, the rosebushes forlorn, as if no one had been home this century. The low gable-roofed stone garage sat glum and dark on one side of the forecourt. No one had turned on the welcoming coach lanterns to light my arrival. The house itself stretched out to the left, the fieldstones glistening in the headlights like pebbles at the bottom of a streambed. The house was dark and the night was black, impenetrable, soaked. In the distance the glow of Princeton wavered pink in the rain over the treetops.

Entering the darkened front hall sent a chill rattling along my backbone. But when I flipped the switch the lights came on and everything was as it always was, the polished oak floor, pegged not nailed, and the cream molding and staircase, the olive-green walls, the gilt-framed mirrors. I went directly to the Long Room, the two steps up from the foyer, where we seemed to do most of our gathering when we returned home.

The Long Room. It had once been the main public room of the original eighteenth-century inn around which the rest of the house

had been built, as was still evident from the blackened beams
overhead, the scarred and scorched fireplace six feet high and ten
wide, the pot hooks. But it had picked up bits and pieces over the
years: the flowered slipcovers, the walls of bookcases, the enormous
hooked rugs of mustard and scarlet, the coal scuttle, the mustard
leather wing chairs drawn up around the stone fireplace, the yellow-
shaded brass lamps, the bowls and copper pots of flowers, and at
the far end of the room looking out toward the orchard and the
creek, the easel where my father did some of his painting. The
current canvas was large and covered with a dropcloth.

It was cold in the room, the damp chill seeping in from outside.
The ashes in the grate were dead and damp and smelled like
autumn with rain dripping down the chimney turning them to
mud. In the old days William and Mary lived in their own quarters
and would have been bustling around, stoking the fires, greeting
me with a toddy, bringing the place to life. But now William was
dead, Mary had gone into retirement in Scottsdale, and the couple
who served my father lived in Princeton, not in the rooms over the
east wing.

I knew she wasn't there. I called her name anyway, just for the
company of the sound, and it died away in the silence. I went to
the foot of one of the several staircases scattered about the place
and called her name again. I heard the old scampering sound from
above, like dry newspapers blowing along a gutter. The cold and
rain had driven the field mice inside from under the eaves and now
they were running around trying to remember where they were,
which was where countless generations of their ancestors had been
before them.

When we were kids Val and I had decided that the noises we
heard in the walls were made by the ghost whose story we seemed
to have heard at birth. He was a boy, the tale went, who had killed
an English officer behind their lines and made his escape with a
couple of redcoats in hot pursuit. An earlier Ben Driskill had
hidden him in one of the attics, but after a week the British search
party came to the Driskill holdings and searched the house. They
found the boy cowering in the darkness, half dead from pneumonia,
and declared him guilty on the spot. They told this long-ago Ben
Driskill they were going to hang him with the boy, an object lesson
for the countryside, which prompted Ben's wife, Hannah, to appear
in the doorway with a blunderbuss and the promise to put a couple

of ounces of sudden death into that redcoat's breadbasket if he
didn't satisfy himself with the one prisoner and beat it. The Brit
bowed, suggested that henceforth Ben should think twice before
giving aid and comfort to an enemy of Good King George, and
stalked off with the killer in tow. They took the lad to the orchard
and hanged him with a length of Driskill rope from a stout Driskill
apple tree, from which Ben cut him down shortly thereafter and
buried him beneath the tree. His grave was still marked and we
used to play out there. And we listened with wide-eyed fascination
to the story of this brave rebel's death and ghost.

I climbed the stairs now and waited but nobody—not a ghost,
not a squirrel, not my sister—was going to answer me. I thought of
my mother in one of her flowing nightgowns and lacy robes
standing in the hallway, her hand out as if she were trying to reach
me from far away. How long ago had that happened? Her lips
forming words which I must have heard then but could no longer
recall . . . Why couldn't I remember what she'd said while I could
recall exactly the scent of her cologne and powder? And why was
her face lost in the shadows of the hall? Was she young? Or was
she gray? How old had I been when she'd come forward, hand out,
saying something, trying to make me understand something?

I went back downstairs, took an umbrella, went outside. The
rain was blowing sideways in the ghostly glow of the coach lights. I
pulled the trench-coat collar up and went to the little underpass
between two wings of the house and ducked underneath. The rain
rattled on the mullioned windows above and in the lead gutters,
spewed out furiously, slowly turning to ice that would build up and
eventually block the drainpipe. Some things just never changed.

I set off across the lawn where we used to play croquet and
badminton. The lights from the windows of the Long Room cast
yellow fingers pointing the way toward the chapel.

We had our own chapel, of course. My father's father had built
it in the twenties to satisfy one of my grandmother's whims of iron.
It was "of the period," as they say in guidebooks, brick and stone
and black and white trim with what my grandmother used to call
"a very nice steeple, not too proud of itself," which was always in
need of repair. We weren't English Catholics like Evelyn Waugh's
and we didn't keep a tame priest of our own on the family payroll,
but we pretty much supported those who served at St. Mary's in
the nearby village of New Prudence. Growing up, I thought that

having your own church was insane but I learned to shut up about it. When I went to the St. Augustine School, having your own chapel didn't seem quite so preposterous. Some other kids were in the same boat.

Now the chapel was dripping in the rain like something you'd find in an old English churchyard, in a poem. It was dark and dreary and full of mice. The grass needed cutting. It was lacquered over with a thin coating of ice. I grabbed the handrail and climbed the steps to the iron-bound oaken door. The ring handle squeaked slightly when I gave it a tug. A single candle guttered in the rush of air from the doorway. One little candle. The chapel was utterly black beyond the halo of light, almost as if it were just emptiness. Still, Val must have been there to light the candle. And then she'd gone off somewhere.

I went back to the house, turned off the lights. I couldn't bear the idea of making myself at home in that cold house without Val. It wasn't like her to leave me hanging. But it was a rotten night and she may have had errands and gotten slowed down somewhere. She'd show up later.

I was hungry and needed a drink. I got into the car and took one look back at the lonely old house in the pelting rain, and drove in to Princeton.

There was a pleasant buzz of conversation in the downstairs taproom of the Nassau Inn. The bar was crowded. There was a haze of smoke, the faint air of clubbiness that clings to the name if not to the actual place itself. There were the framed photographs of Hobe Baker and other heroes of another age, the deep carvings of generations of Tigers in the tops of the tables. The smoky haze might have been the mists of time.

I sank into a booth and ordered a double dry Rob Roy and realized how tense I was. It was Val and the fear in her voice, and now where was she? She'd been so insistent, and now nothing. Had she put a match to that single candle?

My cheeseburger had just arrived when I heard someone call my name. "Ben! Ben boy, a blast from the past!"

I looked up into the boyish, blue-eyed face of Terence O'Neale—Father Terence O'Neale, who was between Val and me in age but would always look like a freshman somewhere. Everybody used to call him Peaches because he had one of those perfect peaches-and-cream complexions, eternally youthful, ever innocent. We'd known Peaches forever. We'd played tennis and golf and he'd always contended that I'd gotten him drunk the first time, out back in our orchard. He was smiling down at me, blue eyes glinting, dangling over the chasm of the past.

"Take a load off, Peach," I said, and he was sliding into the booth across from me with a beer of his own. He hadn't started out to become a priest: that was pretty much Val's doing. Golf and motorcycles and the world beer-chugging record, that's what Terence O'Neale had seen when he looked into his future. That and a wife and a bunch of kids and maybe a job on Wall Street. Val was supposed to be Mrs. O'Neale. It had sounded fine to me. Now I hadn't seen him in four or five years but he hadn't changed. He wore a white buttondown and a tweed jacket. Vinnie would have approved.

"So what brings you back to the scene of our crimes?"

"I'm a workingman, Ben. Got a job over in New Pru. I'm the padre at St. Mary's. It's a little spooky—I keep looking out during the homily and I keep thinking I'll see us, you and me and Val." He grinned at the Lord's mysterious ways.

"Since when? Why didn't you call me?"

"Just since summer. I've seen your father. You should have seen him do a double take. I figured I'd catch you at Christmas. Val said she might get a skating party together out back of the orchard. She said I shouldn't expect you at mass."

"She got that right. I've been going straight for twenty years, as you damn well know."

He plucked a french fry from my plate. "So what are you doing here? Your dad says you don't get home much."

"How true. Of course he's still wondering if I'm really his son. Maybe there was a mix-up in the maternity ward. It's the only hope he has left."

"You're awfully hard on the old boy, aren't you?"

"Nope. Anyway, I didn't come out here to see him. I got a call this afternoon from Val, all mysterious and determined to get me out here tonight. So I came through all this crud and she's not home to meet me." I shrugged. "When did you see her? What's this skating party thing? I hate skating—"

"When she was passing through last summer on her way to Rome, we had dinner. Old time's sake." He took another fry. "I think you're right about that mysterious sound—there's something going on, she's been doing some pretty heavy research . . . she wrote me from Rome, then Paris." His face clouded for a moment. "She's writing this monster of a book, Ben. World War Two and the Church." He made a face. "Not a time the Church likes to brag about—"

"With good reason," I said.

"Don't look at me. I didn't have anything to do with it. Pius was Pius and I was just a little kid in Princeton, New Jersey."

He finished off my fries, grinning at me. I felt a surge of warmth. Val had been pretty serious about Peaches, had told me she might just marry him. They became lovers when she was seventeen.

Val had felt a good bit of Catholic-schoolgirl guilt when she lost her virginity to him one summer night out in the orchard. Later on, when she got to thinking seriously about the Church, Peaches thought it was a phase. Then he thought she was caving in to pressure from Dad. Then he figured she'd just gone crazy. But Val wanted her life to mean something special—to herself, to the world she lived in, to the Church. Kennedy had been assassinated and Peaches said, hell, you want to save the world, go join the Peace Corps. She wouldn't fight with him about it. It wasn't that she needed the Church, she said, but rather that the poor old Church needed her. Val never had any trouble with her ego.

John XXIII was her idea of a new start after the reign of Pius, whom she counted an embarrassment. But Paul VI seemed willing to lose what had been gained, seemed content to have the Church sink back into the past again. She saw the world changing and the Church needed to keep moving, growing into a new and humanistic role. She saw Kennedy and Martin Luther King and Pope John and she wanted to join them in making a better world. And Peaches, well, if he couldn't have Val, he didn't want anybody else. In time he became a priest and it all went to show you that you never knew how things were going to turn out.

He was walking me down the length of the bar when he noticed the guy he'd been waiting for in the doorway and pulled me over. "Ben, I want you to meet a friend of mine."

The man in the doorway was wearing a yellowing old mac and a dark olive snapbrim with a narrow leather band. Bushy gray eyebrows arched outward over pale gray eyes set deep in a pink-cheeked face. A flash of white dog collar peeked from behind his dark green scarf. He was five seven, maybe in his early sixties. The laugh lines at the corners of his mouth and eyes made him look like Barry Fitzgerald, who often played priests in forties movies. Fitzgerald had also played a pixilated Irishman in *Bringing Up Baby* and a crafty old avenger in *And Then There Were None:* I could see both possibilities in the face before me. There was something distant and cool in the flat gray eyes. They didn't seem to go with the rest of his crinkly, smiling face. I recognized him from his publicity photos.

"Ben Driskill, this is the Church's poet laureate, Father Artie Dunn."

"Faith and begorra," Dunn said. "Forgive young O'Neale, Mr. Driskill. You aren't by any chance Hugh Driskill's boy?"

"You know my father?"

"By reputation, of course. I'm told he is not one of my readers." Dunn's face cracked into a quick grin. He took his hat off, revealing a bald pink scalp with a fringe of gray hair curling over the tops of his ears and scarf.

"At his age he can only take so much sex, violence, and confession." I shook his hand. "Maybe I'll present him with your collected works at Christmas."

I had seen Father Dunn on television once, being interviewed about one of his novels, and he somehow worked the subject around to one of his passions, baseball. Phil Donahue had asked him if, like so many ballplayers, he had any superstitions. "Just the Catholic Church," he'd said, and the audience was in his pocket.

"Don't settle for paperbacks," he said. "My hardcover jackets are every bit as shameful."

Peaches chuckled. "The priest who looks like Tom Selleck is being ravished by a Joan Collins clone in half a dress."

Dunn said: "Why don't you join us, Mr. Driskill?"

"How about a raincheck? I've got to meet my sister—"

"Ah, a *respectable* writer. A true scholar and an activist. A unique combination."

"I'll tell her you said so."

I left them and walked back to the car. It was fully in character for Peaches, a bit of a free spirit, to know Father Dunn, the iconoclastic priest/novelist whose books were always best sellers that drove the Church hierarchy quietly nuts. He had devised a manner of somehow producing moral object lessons within the context of stories devoted almost exclusively to sex, power, and money. My father doubtless felt that Dunn had made himself a rich man desecrating the Church. Desecration aside, since Dunn was a diocesan priest free to keep any money he earned, he certainly was well-heeled. Like my sister, he was so well-known that the Church had to exercise considerable restraint in dealing with him. In practice they found it advisable to look the other way.

It was still spitting sleet and the sidewalks were treacherous. From the shop windows all of the paraphernalia of Halloween stared into the night. Witches rode on broomsticks and bowls overflowed with black and orange candy. Jack-o'-lanterns grinned, gap-toothed. I headed home, eager to sit down in front of the fire in the Long Room with my sister Val and help her get things straightened out.

The house was still dark and empty, the rain still blowing in sheets and turning to snow in the headlights, dusting the rutted and freezing mud in the driveway. I pointed the car at the garage and walked ahead in the lights, looked through the windows. There was a car inside. I pulled the doors open. The car was wet. But it had been raining for hours and the engine was cold. I went back to my car, pulled it up by the house, and got back out. It was ten-thirty and I was beginning to worry about her.

I'm not altogether sure why I walked back out toward the orchard. Maybe I went for a walk because the rain had turned to snow, the first of the year, and the quiet seemed surreal after the chatter of the Nassau Inn. I stopped, called her name just in case she'd had the same impulse, but all I succeeded in doing was start a dog to barking in the black distance.

I was standing in the orchard before I'd given it any thought, and when I looked around I saw I was under the tree where the priest we never talked about had hanged himself a long time ago. It seemed like my entire life had been spent living with the stories attached to the house and the orchard—priests from the rubble of World War II and priests working in the garden and saying mass for Mother and priests drinking scotch with Father and the one poor devil who'd hanged himself, all of them stories with the power of myth, stories reflecting this family of mine, its history and concerns and, inevitably, its religion.

The orchard was always cropping up in family stories, but I'd never been particularly fond of the place. The only reason I'd ever spent any time out there was because Val had liked it. When she was four I taught her to play poker on the grass out of sight of the house. But I'd once eaten an apple and found half a worm inside and the orchard and I had parted company about then.

We used to have Fritz the gardener show us the exact tree from which the priest had hanged himself. We'd stare at it while Fritz showed us the precise limb and made a face with his tongue sticking out and his eyes rolled back, and then he would laugh and suggest that just possibly the orchard was haunted like the attic. I never even saw a newspaper article or photograph about the tragedy and the poor damned dead priest. I asked my mother about it and she'd brushed the question away, saying, "It was all a million years ago, it was just too terribly sad, Benjy," and my father had said that it was just bad luck. "He could have picked anybody's orchard, anybody's tree. Bad luck he picked ours."

By then I'd begun to feel foolish standing out there in the falling snow remembering a suicidal priest of damn near fifty years earlier and wondering where the devil my sister was. She hadn't been in the house; she hadn't been in the chapel.

I walked back and stood looking at the chapel, frosted with snow like something in a fairy tale. The wind had come up from out back, whistling across the creek, through the orchard.

I climbed the slippery steps and swung the door open again, stared into the damp, cold stillness. The little candle had gone out. I left the door open for the pathetic bit of light it provided and felt along the wall for the light switches. I flipped the first one. The entry was enveloped in a dim grayness, antediluvian. I felt like a diver in the depths of a flooded ruin. I flipped the second switch and another set of dim lights came on in the chapel proper. I heard the leathery flutter of a bat or two overhead in the darkness.

There were only ten pews divided by a center aisle. I took a few tentative steps, called her name. Never had a room been so empty. The single syllable, *Val,* ricocheted off the walls and the stained glass windows. I heard the steady drip of a couple of leaks, the roof and steeple needing repair yet again.

Then in the gloom, between the first and second rows, I saw a flash of red. A red wool and blue leather sleeve, a bit of antique warmup jacket. I recognized it. It was my old letter jacket from St.

Augustine. It would have the intertwined *SA* on the left breast. It didn't belong on the floor of the chapel.

In the catacomb of St. Callistus deep below the Appian Way there is the tomb from which Pope Paschal, in the ninth century, removed the body of St. Cecelia. He laid her to final rest in a sarcophagus of white marble under the altar of the Church of St. Cecelia in the Trastevere quarter of Rome. Years ago I visited the catacomb of Callistus and emerged from the darkened gallery into the pool of light where the body of a girl lay in what seemed to be a peaceful sleep. For an instant I felt as if I had intruded on her privacy. Then, of course, I recognized her as the work of the sculptor Maderna, the body of Cecelia as she had appeared to Cardinal Sfondrati in a dream. It was an extraordinarily realistic rendering, and as I looked down at the body of the woman in our chapel I felt as if I, too, like the cardinal of centuries before, were lost in a dream, as if I were confusing this woman with the martyred Cecelia.

She lay crumpled sideways, fallen where she'd been kneeling in prayer. She lay still, like Maderna's sculpture, peaceful, her head turned toward the floor, the one eye I could see closed. I touched her hand, the rosary clutched in the cold fingers. She'd worn my old warmup jacket to make the walk from the house to the chapel. The wool was damp. I held her hand. The fingers were stiff.

My sister Val, always the brave little soldier, full of the courage I lacked, was dead.

I don't know how long I knelt there. Then I reached out to touch her face, so empty of her spirit, and I was seeing her as a little girl, hearing the happy lilt of her laughter, and when I touched her hair I felt the crusty blood, felt the singed hair breaking at the touch, saw the smeared wound where the bullet had entered. She'd knelt in prayer and someone had held the gun within an inch of her head and put her out, like quenching a candle. I was sure she hadn't felt a thing. Maybe, for some inexplicable reason, she'd trusted her killer.

My hand was sticky with her blood and hair. Val was dead and I was having trouble catching my breath. I rolled her head back the way it had been. My sister, my dearest friend, the person I loved most in the world, was dead at my feet.

I sat back in the pew, held her hand trying to make it warm

and failing horribly. My face was frozen in grief and I didn't want to cope. I didn't want to stand up and do something.

A wisp of cold, a draft, fluttered something caught in a sliver at the corner of the wooden bench. I plucked it from its niche. A triangular piece of fabric, black, waterproofed like a raincoat. I was barely registering it at all, just holding it, something for my hand to do.

I heard the chapel door creaking, then footsteps on the stone floor.

The footsteps came down the aisle while I tried to stop trembling. I hoped Val's killer had returned to have a go at me. I'd kill him with my bare hands. I wanted to die killing him. I looked up.

Peaches was peering down at me. He'd taken one look and everything was registering on his face. All the color had drained away, no more peaches and cream. His mouth had slackened open but he wasn't saying anything.

Beside him Father Dunn was staring down at her. She looked so lonely. "Oh shit," he whispered in a tone of infinite sadness.

I thought he was commenting on my sister, but I was wrong. He reached down and took the bit of black fabric from my hand.

It didn't take long for the machinery of death to start clanking away. Sam Turner, the police chief, arrived with a couple of his cops and shortly thereafter an ambulance and a doctor with his black gladstone bag. Sam Turner had been a friend of the family's all my life. He'd obviously been awakened and brought back out into the hellish night: his gray hair was doing a Dagwood Bumstead, and his face wore a gray fuzz outlining his drooping dewlaps. He wore a plaid shirt and windbreaker and corduroys and green Wellies. He shook my hand and I knew he was hurting, too. He'd known Val from when she was a little girl and now he was heading through the rain and snow to the chapel to see how it had ended.

Peaches, tight-lipped and pale, made coffee and brought it into the Long Room on a tray with mugs and fixings. He and Dunn had come on impulse to see if Val had shown up all right: Peaches had been worried about the chance of a car accident. Seeing the light in the chapel, they'd come in to find me holding my dead sister's hand. While Peaches and I drank coffee, Dunn went back to the chapel with Sam Turner. He was probably researching a scene for a novel.

Turner was wet and cold when they came back. He took a mug of steaming black coffee and slurped it noisily. Through the window I saw them putting Val's body, wrapped in an oilcloth bag on a stretcher, into the ambulance. The rain and snow drifted slowly through the lights in the forecourt.

"Jesus, there's not much to say, Ben. I'm sealing off the chapel and we'll get some scene-of-the-crime boys up from Trenton. You don't have any idea what happened, do you?"

"Only the obvious," I said. I thought about Val's state of mind when she called me, but I couldn't imagine how to start in on that with Turner. "She just got in today. Called me in New York, asked me to come out and meet her tonight." I shook my head. "I just assumed she was late, doing some errands. Went into town for a burger, came back, looked around again, found her. That's it."

He sneezed into a red bandanna and rubbed his nose. "Comin' down with a bug," he muttered. "It's funny. I got a call from her this afternoon myself. She mention that to you?"

"No. What did she want?"

"Well, that's what's so crazy. You'd never guess. She asked what I knew about that priest who hanged himself out in your orchard, back in 'thirty-six, 'thirty-seven, whenever it was. It was the first year I was on the force here, lowest man on the totem pole. About the time you were born. Just one of those nutty things, a priest killing himself in the Driskill orchard. Poor bastard. She didn't say why she was asking, just said she wondered if we had a file on it." He shook his head, massaged the gray stubble on his chin.

"Well? Do you have a file?"

"Hell's bells, Ben. I don't know. I told her I'd be a monkey's uncle if I'd seen one, but I said I'd dig around in the old boxes down in the basement at the station house. I mean we *could* have a file, I suppose. But it's been a long time, could've been thrown out years ago." He pinched off another sneeze. "I got to thinking about it after we got off the phone and old Rupert Norwich came to mind. He was deputy chief back then, sorta broke me in, then he was chief for twenty-five years—hell, you remember old Rupe, Ben."

"Gave me my first speeding ticket," I said.

"Well, Rupe's in his eighties now, lives down by the shore, down Seabright way. Still pretty spry. I figured I might give Rupe a call on this one . . . 'course, now there doesn't seem to be a helluva lot of reason. We don't know what Sister Val wanted the file for." He sighed, remembering why there was no reason.

"Why don't you look around for the file anyway?" I said. "You know Val, she's always got her reasons."

"Guess it couldn't hurt." He looked me over, staring. "You all right, Ben? Quite a shock—"

"I'm all right. Look, Sam, the way I look at it—ever since she spent that year in El Salvador she's been on borrowed time—she led a charmed life in some ways. Her luck ran out tonight."

"She liked it right out there on the edge, damn tootin', you're right about that." He went to the window. "Oh, it's a shame, Ben. A cryin' shame." He paused. "Oh boy, looks like your father's home. Jesus, I hate stuff like this." His eyes were bloodshot and his hair was plastered down with rain now. He took off his glasses and wiped them with the soiled bandanna. "You want me to break this to him, Ben?"

"No, Sam," I said. "This is a job for Superman."

My father.

You'd go broke mighty quick betting you could shock my father. Or scare him or fluster him or break him. He simply wasn't prey to the same pressures that regularly cracked the rest of us. His life had been extravagantly colorful for one so obsessively secretive. He was seventy-four years old and knew full well he didn't look much past sixty. "Unless you get too damn close," he'd say. Get close to my father and you deserved a prize. Which was more or less what I'd heard my poor dutiful mother say a time or two.

He had been a lawyer and a banker and a diplomat and the overseer of the family's investments. In the fifties there had even been a presidential boomlet, which he'd squelched because he was a Catholic and everyone knew what had happened to Al Smith. Averell Harriman had held talks with him about the feasibility of announcing that Hugh Driskill would be his running mate if Harriman got the Democratic nomination but, in the end, my father said no, life behind the scenes suited him better. The truth was, my father didn't have a great deal of faith in the electorate. He used to say he wouldn't let them vote on what tie he was going to wear, so why did they have to be consulted on who'd occupy the White House.

As a bright young lawyer he had worked in Rome before the

war, in the late thirties, spending most of his time on the matters of Church investments in American companies, banks, and real estate. Some of the investments weren't awfully pretty and it was best if the Vatican's involvement were kept hidden. He helped to see to that, and as a result he developed a lot of friendships on the inside, and maybe an enemy or two. "That whole period," he once told me, "was for the experience. I was smart enough to know that the religion was one thing and the worldly form it took was something else, something that had to fight for survival. I wanted to see how the machinery of the Church worked. It was a much simpler world then, back in the days when Mussolini used the Vatican as a cover for his espionage operations. Talk about a learning experience! It was like getting a doctorate in Advanced Reality. Save your idealism for the religion. The Church is all practice, all mechanics."

All his life my father had been tremendously rich and bright and discreet. And very, very brave, my old man. He spent a lot of time in Washington when everybody knew we were bound for the war. His knowledge of how the Italian Fascists worked their spies under Vatican auspices came in handy, got him known in certain rather mysterious circles. He ran across a fellow Irishman, many years his senior, who turned out to be Wild Bill Donovan. When Donovan got around to setting up the Office of Strategic Services, the OSS, one of the first bright-eyed lads he brought on board was Hugh Driskill. Donovan was a Catholic and in those exhilarating early days when the issue of the world's fate was hanging in the balance he had surrounded himself with a bunch of good Catholic boys he could trust and understand. His inner circle even became rather famous, known by its nickname, the Knights Templar, precisely because they were all Catholics. My father was one of Wild Bill's Knights Templar.

As the war was ending in Europe, right about the time Dad showed up in Princeton with Monsignor D'Ambrizzi in tow, Jack Warner, who was running Warner Brothers, got together with Milton Sperling, the producer, and Fritz Lang, the director, and Ring Lardner, Jr., the writer, and probably around somebody's pool with the palms and the starlets swaying in unison they began kicking around the idea of an OSS movie. The idea was to commemorate the unsung, secret work of our intelligence services. They were going to create a composite hero, put him in a high-risk, behind-the-enemy-lines, all-purpose story, and run with it in that inimitable Warner Brothers way. It would bear a fictional disclaimer, but on the other hand they wanted a certain authenticity. The movie was the reason Bill Donovan came to the house in Princeton to talk to my father.

As it turned out, the composite figure was going to be a thinly disguised version of Hugh Driskill. One of his adventures in occupied France would form the basis of the plot, something about smuggling a guy out to freedom.

It got exciting for me when Gary Cooper showed up in Princeton one weekend. He was going to star and I was just about overcome with excitement. I can remember sitting on the porch steps with a big glass of lemonade, listening to Cooper, Donovan, and my father shoot the breeze about movies and the war and after a while Cooper took me out to the tennis courts and worked on my serve with me. My God, Sergeant York and Lou Gehrig were helping me with my serve and Cooper told me that Bill Tilden had told him it was ninety percent in the toss. That night the actor took out a sketch pad and did me and little Val, then one of Father and Donovan and D'Ambrizzi. He told me he'd always figured he'd be a cartoonist until he fell into the acting thing, sort of by chance. Before he left he told me to call him Frank because that was his real name, what his oldest friends called him, like the ones he'd made at Grinnell College in Iowa, he said.

I never saw him again except in the movies. And there he was on the screen the next year, 1946, in *Cloak and Dagger*. The funny thing was, the character he played really was a lot like Father. Hollywood added a standard love interest in the form of a young actress who was making her debut, Lilli Palmer, and it was made clear to me at home that all the mushy stuff was made up, pure fiction.

My father had doubts the more he heard of the Hollywood touches that were being added to the script. I remember Donovan sitting on the porch one summer afternoon with Father and Curtis Lockhardt, his protégé, and Donovan was kidding my dad. He was sitting in an Adirondack chair and I was perched on the steps as usual, swilling Kool-Aid, and I heard him laugh and say, "Well, Hugh, let's just hope they don't make you look like too big an asshole!" Father grunted doubtfully and said: "They'll never let Cooper look like an asshole." Donovan said: "Tell him, young

Lockhardt, tell him he's got to have some faith about these things."
Lockhardt nodded. "That's right, Hugh. Faith." I was listening to
them and watching my little sister prancing around in her new red
bathing suit, running back and forth through the sprinklers, showing off, hoping everybody was watching her. Even as a child she
had an eye on Lockhardt.

Behind me my father said, "My faith has never been in question,
gentlemen. It is Mr. Warner and his minions I distrust. From the
look of them, I doubt very much that they are papists."

Donovan roared with laughter and the conversation turned to
the chances of Mr. Cooper having sexual relations with Miss Palmer,
who was apparently quite a looker, at which time I was shooed
toward the gardens to help Mother, who was crouching among the
flowers, wearing a floppy sun hat and smoking a Chesterfield and
drinking a martini, weeding.

It was true that my father had been through a great many
crucibles of fire in his life and had been hardened and tempered
accordingly but that night, with the news of Val's murder coming
down on him, I saw more than the strength and toughness born of
experience. All that helped keep the surface under control, but it
was his faith, which had never been in question, that kept him
from falling apart. I had to hand it to the old bastard. He took it
like a man, never flinched.

He came in the front door looking huge and curious and ready
for damn near anything. He stood six four, weighed about two
forty, had thick gray hair combed back like iron from a widow's
peak. He saw me and Sam Turner behind me and said, "Why, hi,
Ben. This is a surprise. Sam . . . So what's the problem here?"

I told him and he watched me, his clear blue eyes fixed on
mine. When I was done he said, "Give me your hand, son. You
look a little peaked. It's time to hang together, Ben." I felt his
strength as if it were palpable, a charge flowing into me. "She lived
the life she wanted and she knew we loved her. She served God and
you can't have a better life than that. She wasn't sick and she never
knew the infirmities of old age. She's gone to a better place, Ben,
never forget that. And one day we'll all be together again and
forever. God truly loved your sister." His voice never faltered and
he put his arm around my shoulders. I'm six two myself and he
shook me in his grip. Everything he said was bullshit, sure, but it

pulled me together and I knew I was going to be okay. I could handle it.

"Sam," he said, "who killed my daughter?" He didn't wait for an answer but just led the way into the Long Room, surveyed the group, said, "I need a bracer." And he broke out a fresh bottle of Laphroaig.

Poor Sam Turner didn't know who killed my sister. He talked quietly with my father for a while. Peaches had a big fire going in the huge blackened fireplace. Father Dunn had become a part of the background once Peaches had introduced him to my father.

Peaches said he'd be glad to stay the night, just to sit up and talk if I wanted him to, but I said I was okay. I don't think he really wanted to go back to the parish house in New Pru to spend the night with his memories. But in the end Sam Turner left and then Peaches and Father Dunn finished up their drinks and left together, as they'd come. I stood at the window watching them depart. Father Dunn, the millionaire novelist, drove a new Jaguar XJS. Peaches had an old Dodge station wagon with a ding in one fender and mudflaps: it had come with the job.

When I turned back, my father was drizzling more scotch over fresh ice in our glasses. He was a little flushed from the heat of the fire. He handed me my glass. "It's going to be a long night. This might do some good. What are you doing out here, anyway?"

I told him the story of my day, feeling the single malt coursing through my veins, taking the nerves with it. I sank down in one of the mustard-colored leather chairs and stretched my legs out toward the fire.

He looked down at me, swirling the amber liquid across the ice, shaking his head. "Damn. What did that girl have on her mind?"

"Something to do with her research. Something she'd discovered or stumbled across—maybe in Paris or . . . well, I just don't know—"

"You can't tell me that digging her way through a bunch of musty junk dating back to the war could make her so upset now!" He was exasperated. "World War Two! What's any of that got to do with being murdered here in Princeton?" He was choosing anger over sorrow.

"Calm down," I said.

"It's ridiculous on the face of it. No, looks to me like we're reading way too much into this. We're forgetting we live in an age where everyday people die for no reason at all. She went to the chapel to pray and disturbed some madman trying to get out of the storm. Meaningless death!"

I let him go on trying to convince himself that Val had died randomly, that there was no point to it. He hadn't heard the fear in her voice. She was too afraid to have died a random death.

"Well," he was saying, "she called me yesterday from California, told me she and Lockhardt were coming to New York today. Said she'd be home this afternoon and he'd be out tomorrow probably. I had a meeting in New York today, I wasn't even sure I'd get home tonight. She didn't say a word about anything bothering her." He slipped out of his suitcoat and draped it over the back of one of the ancient wooden chairs. He loosened his tie and rolled his sleeves up. "You know what I've been worried about, Ben? I've had this nagging feeling she might be coming home to tell me she was going to leave the Order and marry Curtis—am I crazy? Is that shot on the table?"

"I don't know. I'd have thought Curtis was your idea of the perfect son-in-law."

"It's nothing to do with Curtis." My father made a face. "Use your head, Ben. It's Val. She's a nun and she was meant to stay one—"

"Like I was meant to be a priest?"

"God only knows what you were meant to be. But Val, she was meant for it, cut out for the Church—"

"Who says so? Not the Church, unless I've been reading all the wrong papers. Sounds to me like they'd take up a collection to buy her a one-way ticket. And anyway, isn't it up to Val? What she does with her life—she's got a vote, right?" I only barely realized it was all wrong. I was using the wrong tense. There wasn't any more of Val's life.

"I'd expect you to take that position. There's no point in arguing about it. Val and I are Catholics—"

"Funny, how I'm the one with all the scars—"

"If I were you, Benjamin, I wouldn't presume to know what scars others may try to keep hidden. And perhaps we could, just for tonight, be spared your poor battered psyche."

I had to laugh. Val would have laughed, too. It was an old battle by now and we both, Dad and I, knew there was no winner. We'd fight on and on until one of us was dead and then, if it had ever mattered before, it surely wouldn't matter anymore.

"Am I close," he said, "on this Val and Curtis thing?"

"She never talked about it with me."

"Just as well, assuming the advice you'd have given her." Suddenly he put a meaty hand up to his eyes and I realized how close he was to tears. It wasn't easy, not even for an old warrior. He stood up, halfheartedly poked at the fire. Sparks showered onto the hearthstones.

The clock on the mantelpiece struck a tinny two o'clock, a thin, reedy sound like an antique harpsichord. I got up, took a cigar from his humidor, lit it, and went to the far end of the room, stood near his covered easel, stood looking out the window into the rotten night. I was unexpectedly thinking about a dog we used to have, a Lab called Jake, who used to go crazy trying to take a bite out of a basketball. When he died Val insisted on burying a deflated basketball with him so he could get a grip on the damn thing all through dog eternity. Well, my father and I couldn't seem to get hold of things, what had happened to Val, what had happened to our world.

He yawned and said something about Lockhardt and I turned back questioningly. "Callistus is dying. I don't know the time projection, but it can't be long now. Curtis is getting ready in that busy way of his to back another winner. *Pick* another winner. He wants to talk to me. You can bet he's raising money."

"Who's his man?" I asked.

"Someone to lead the Church toward the twenty-first century. Whatever that means."

"Well, good luck to him."

"You never know about Curtis. I suppose it might come down to D'Ambrizzi and Indelicato. Fangio, maybe, as a compromise." He looked at that moment as if he didn't care: it wasn't true. He was just worn down.

"Who's your man?"

He shrugged. He'd played a lot of poker in his time. He had a candidate, a hole card, for playing at the last moment.

"I've never asked you this," I said, "but I've always wondered—why did you bring D'Ambrizzi back here after the war? I mean, it was great for Val and me, he was the perfect playmate, but what was your reason? Did you know him during the war?"

"It's a long story, Ben. He needed a friend. Let's just leave it at that."

"One of your OSS stories? The ones you never tell—"

"Let's just drop it, son."

"Suits me." D'Ambrizzi, Indelicato, Fangio. They were just names to me. Except for my memory of D'Ambrizzi.

My father's mysterious OSS days tended to give me a bit of a pain. So long ago and he still treated them as state secrets. Once he and my mother had taken us to Paris for a summer holiday, suites at the George V and *bateaux mouches* on the Seine and the Winged Victory at the Louvre and mass at Notre Dame and my first copy of a P. G. Wodehouse from Shakespeare & Co., close by the Seine. In some ways the high point of the trip—no pun intended—was a visit to the Eiffel Tower presided over by one of father's old friends from OSS days, Bishop Torricelli, who was by then quite an elderly man. He had the longest, most thoroughly hooked nose I'd ever seen, and I'd heard his nickname was Shylock. He carried a pocketful of little anisette candies. Val went for them in a big way. He told us the joke about Jacques and Pierre who had been lunching at the same small out-of-the-way restaurant three or four days a week for twenty years. Finally one day Jacques asked Pierre why they'd been going to the same place for twenty years and Pierre said, "Because, *mon ami,* it's the only restaurant in Paris from which you cannot see the damned Eiffel Tower!" We didn't really get it, but Val laughed like a madwoman because she was really hooked on that candy.

I heard my father and Torricelli make a few passing references to Paris under the Nazi occupation and Torricelli joked about my father emerging from a coal cellar after two weeks of hiding from the Gestapo, how he'd opened his mouth to speak and borne quite a resemblance to Al Jolson singing "Swannee," all coated in coal dust. It must have been quite a time, dangerous and exciting. But after all, he was my father, just my father, and it was difficult to see him as a spy, dashing through the night to blow up power stations and ammo dumps.

"You know, Ben," he said, speaking slowly, his brain half submerged in a small lake of Laphroaig, "I hate the idea of having to tell Curtis about this. He hasn't had to deal much with things that haven't gone his way. He's led a happy life, all things considered."

"Well, he's in for a rough patch now." I didn't give a damn about Curtis Lockhardt. He was one of *them*. And I wasn't wasting a whole lot of sympathy on my father, who was about as vulnerable as one of the gargoyles hanging on the walls of Notre Dame. I was sorry for my little sister, Val.

"I'll tell him tomorrow—"

"Oh, I wouldn't worry about that. It'll be on the tube and in the papers tomorrow. Val's a celebrity. No, he'll hear about it before we have to tell him. We'll have to mop up after his grief. I'm not looking forward to that."

He fixed me with one of his X-ray stares across the top of his glass. "You can be a reprehensible shit at times, Ben."

"Like father, like son? It's all in the genes."

"Probably," he said after a while, "quite probably so." He cleared his throat and finished his drink. "Well, I'm for bed."

"To face the demons of the dark."

"Something like that." He turned in the doorway, gave me a little wave.

"By the way, Dad . . ."

"Yes? What is it?" The shadows of the foyer were about to swallow him.

"Sam Turner told me Val called him today, asked him questions about the hanged priest—"

"What are you talking about?"

"The hanged priest out in the orchard. We have only the one, am I right or am I right? What do you make of that? Did she say anything to you about that?"

"Sam Turner's an old gossip." My father snapped out the words, impatient with fools. "How should I know anything about that? No, she said nothing to me about that old story—"

"What do you mean—*story*? It did happen . . . the dangling, frozen priest in the orchard—"

"That's ancient history. Forget it. We'll never know what she wanted and that's just fine. Now I'm going to bed." He turned away.

"Dad?"

"Yes?"

"If you have any trouble sleeping, I'll be awake, in my room,

staring at the ceiling, indulging in emotional weakness. So if you
want company . . ." I shrugged.

"Thanks for the offer," he said. "I think I might say a prayer.
May I suggest you try it? If you recall the process, of course."

"Very kind of you to care," I said.

"Well, I say it's never too late." There was a hint of a smile in
his voice though I couldn't see his face clearly. "Not even for a lost
soul like yours, Ben."

Then he was gone and I took a long time straightening the
coffee things and the drinks table and smoking my cigar and slowly
turning off the lamps.

The lights were still on in the chapel.

My bad leg was punishing me for my sins and the scotch hadn't
helped. I limped up the stairs, down the dark and drafty hallway to
my old bedroom. The framed photograph of Joe DiMaggio auto-
graphed to my father and me hung over the bed. I saw the faint
familiar brown stain on the ceiling where one night the rain had
poured through a hole gnawed by a squirrel secreting nuts.

I turned on the bedside lamp. The sleet was beating against the
windows. Gary Cooper's sketch of Val and me still sat in its silver
frame on the chest of drawers. Odd. I was now the only one of us
left alive.

I pumped down a handful of aspirin for my leg pain and tried
to escape the banshees of memory gathering on the lawn beneath
my window. I kept twisting and turning and trying to make my leg
comfortable, then dozing among troubled reflections and dreams
and ghastly, unhappy fantasies. And then somehow I found myself
among the Jesuits again, like an out-of-body experience. . . .

The black-uniformed army among whom I'd once made my life
swarmed out of the night toward me, as if they were fuzzy-wuzzies
hell-bent on overrunning my positions, reclaiming me for themselves. Which was not necessarily the way it had been, at least not
most days. The fact was I had enjoyed much of life as a novice.
From the first day I'd found a place among the smart-ass contingent
which always seemed to form the core of the Society of Jesus.
Professional smart-asses, valued more for their rebellious intelligence than for their piety. Those first weeks of basic training
quickly took on the quality of a challenge—a challenge to our
sharp-edged smart-ass individuality which we were supposed to

submerge in humility, prayer, the tedium of routine, the constant busyness, the sounds and smells of a religious dorm.

Then came the day Brother Fulton, only a couple of years further into the process than we were, called us in for a chat.

"You will have been wondering about some of the more exotic aspects of our happy little order," he began. Brother Fulton was a classic Jesuit smart-ass: lank blond hair, pointy, foxlike features, pale brown eyes that seemed to deny the possibility of treating anything *too* seriously. "We think of them as penitential practices, nothing to fear, because we are all brave fellows and the Society has our best interests at heart. We are primarily concerned with the strength of the spirit, the vitality and determination and growth of the inner man. However . . ."

He smiled at the group of intent young men waiting for the other shoe to drop. "However, we must not altogether ignore our physical selves. It is our experience here at Castle Skull—just a little Jesuit humor, men—that a whiff of mortification of the flesh never really hurt anyone. It may even occasionally do some good. Pain, I assure you, tends to concentrate the mind most wonderfully. But the pain is merely to remind us of our real purpose—you guys all on the right page here?—good, good. Suffice it to say that you will feel pain and your minds—if this thing works like it's supposed to—will turn to such fit subjects for meditation as your love of God. Are you with me?"

His lively brown eyes danced from one dutifully nodding face to another. "Gentlemen, take a look at these little doodads." From the drawer in his desk he took out two items and placed them casually on the blotter. "Go ahead, pick them up. Get the feel. Get to know them."

I took the braided white rope, watched it dangling like a valuable necklace from my fingers. Touching the chain was oddly exciting, almost shameful. I held it gingerly, as if it might come to life and lash out at me, while Brother Fulton went on.

"These little devices, a whip and a leg chain, will aid you. They will make it easier for you to reflect on your devotion to God. And your obedience. The rope or whip is largely symbolic. On Monday and Wednesday evenings you will strip to the waist and kneel beside your beds. The lights will be out. You will hear the tolling of the bell. You will then begin flogging your backs with an over-the-

shoulder flicking motion. You keep at it for the length of one Our
Father. No big deal."

"And how about this?" I swung the chain.

"Aha," Brother Fulton said. "You will notice the little signs on
the bulletin boards when you return to your rooms. 'Whips tonight,
chains tomorrow morning.' An old Jesuit maxim. Benjamin, do you
notice anything unusual about the chain?"

"The links," I said. "One side is filed down so it's very sharp.
The other side is just blunt, rounded off."

Brother Fulton nodded again. "Which side would you say, just
off the top of your head, is supposed to be pressed against the
flesh? Blunt or sharp?"

"You bring out the Iron Maiden next," Vinnie Halloran said,
"and I'm going through that door—"

"We save that for the seventh year," Brother Fulton observed.
"You'll be long gone by then." He smiled beatifically. "You keep
these things—the flagellum and the chain—under your pillows.
The chain is for hurting, I promise you. You will be fastening the
chain around your upper thigh, beneath your trousers, on Tuesday
and Thursday mornings." He stood up, a gesture of dismissal. "You
see the clasp, you figure it out. One thing, though. Tight. Clasp it
tight. Nothing worse than feeling your chain sliding loosely down
your leg until it rattles on the floor." He paused in the doorway
before leaving. "That happens and you're going to feel like a real
asshole. Mark my words."

I threw myself into the business of fleshly mortification with
customary determination. The chain was no joke. You put it around
your thigh, cinched the links tight while it pulled the hair on your
leg and pinched the flesh, and fastened it. You stood still while you
put it on and adjusted the tension. That wasn't so bad. But then
you started to walk. The muscles flexed. The sharp edges bit into
the meat, the welts rose and stung.

Novice MacDonald thought the whole thing was insane, shaved
the hair from his thigh, and held the loose chain in place with
adhesive tape. No one else would even discuss the chains. It was a
private battle and you fought it alone, the best way you could.

It hurt worst of all when you had to sit down. At mass. At
breakfast. In class. And the sharpened links raised the welts, then
dug the trenches in the flesh. All in a good cause. My father would
be proud of me. *Ad Majorem Dei Gloriam*. God. The Society of

Jesus. Saint Ignatius Loyola. *Sanctus Pater Noster.* The better to obey, to serve. I would rise above it. I'd be damned if I didn't rise above it.

We were swimming when Vinnie Halloran spoke up. "Hey, Ben, look at your leg, man. Just look at it." I refused to look. I'd been seeing it for a couple weeks. "You better take care of that, man. Really, that's not right. That's pus and green crud. Look at my leg, little red dots. MacDonald, you know he paints his little red marks on? No shit! But you, you got green stuff running . . ." Vinnie shivered, shrank within himself.

But I wouldn't give in. Not to a crummy Jesuit chain. Not Ben Driskill. That was just the way it was.

It was infected and gangrene had developed. In the end Brother Fulton found me passed out in the john, lying in a puddle of my own vomit. The doctors at St. Ignatius Hospital saved the leg and I was very glad they had. Explaining a missing leg to my father would have been murder. And I was willing to live with the residual pain that flared up from time to time. But what made me feel best was the other thing. I hadn't given in. Sometimes I lost, anybody could lose. But I never, ever gave in. Not even to the Jesuits. Not even to my father.

When I woke up there was a dim grayness at the window and I could see my breath in the cold of my bedroom. Dry snow blew along the windowsill, drifted through the open inch to wet my face. The telephone was ringing in the distance. I counted four rings and then it stopped. My watch said it was six forty-five. I next came out of the fog at eight past seven, leaving behind a dream of someone screaming.

The problem was I didn't leave it behind. The scream was part of reality, not left over from a dream. And it wasn't a scream, it was more of a strangled cry and it probably lasted no more than a second, maybe two, and then there was a hell of a crash, like a blind man trying to get out of a burning building.

My father lay at the bottom of the stairway. His robe was all twisted around him, his arms bent sideways, his face down, resting on the foyer floor. The moment seemed to drag on forever, and then I was kneeling beside him. He looked like someone else, an old man with one eye shut, the other staring up at me. Then the eye blinked.

"Dad? Can you hear me?" I cushioned his head on my arm.

One side of his mouth twitched, a smile. The other side did nothing at all. "Telephone," he said, fairly distinctly. "Archbishop . . ." He sucked some air through the side of his mouth. "Cardinal . . . Klammer . . ." Leave it to my father to get all the titles right. A tear trickled out of the closed eye, seeping away as if jealously guarded.

"He called? What did he want?"

"Lockhardt . . . Heff-Heffernan . . ." It was so difficult for him to speak. Hugh Driskill had come to this, drooling out of the corner of his mouth at the bottom of the stairs.

"Lockhardt and Heffernan," I prompted. Who the hell was Heffernan?

"Dead . . ." It was a whisper now, as if he were running down, batteries going.

"Christ . . . they're dead? Lockhardt's dead?"

"Murdered . . . yes-yesterday . . ." He blinked again. Fingers fluttered at my side. Then he drifted off.

I called the hospital. Then I went back and sat down beside my father, took his hand in both of mine, willed some of my energy into him, returning the favor.

I willed my father to live.

She jogged back to the modern tower on the Via Veneto and stopped to catch her breath in the marble and chrome lobby while she waited for the elevator. Sweat dripped from the tip of her upturned nose. Her tawny brown shoulder-length hair was held in place by a green band. She pulled the earphones out and an old Pink Floyd tape came to an abrupt end. She wiped her forehead on the sleeve of her gray sweatshirt.

She'd run three miles and was headed to the pool on the roof. She stopped at the eighteenth-floor apartment, shucked off the sweats, got into her bathing suit, wrapped herself in a thick terry-cloth robe, and ran up the three flights to the roof. She had the pool to herself and swam in a serious, disciplined way, pacing herself, thirty laps. The sun was purple, struggling up over the horizon, almost frightening seen through the dust and pollution of Rome.

By the time she was in her kitchen making coffee, it was six-thirty and she'd been up since five. She'd prayed and jogged and taken a swim and it was time to stop horsing around. It was time to get a handle on the day.

Sister Elizabeth enjoyed her life. She had not become a nun with unrealistic stars in her eyes: she'd thought it through in her organized way and things had gone well. The Order was proud of her. The apartment on the Via Veneto was owned by Curtis Lockhardt. He had personally spoken with Sister Celestine, who handled such matters for the Order from her office at the top of the Spanish Steps. There had been quick approval for her to move in. The Order tended to treat its members as adults who could be trusted and respected.

It was Sister Valentine who had introduced her to Lockhardt and made the suggestion about the apartment. Lockhardt had subsequently become Elizabeth's friend, too, and a valuable source of information useful in her work. It was a perfect example of the synchronicity which in a closed, stifling society like the Church made life so much more pleasant. The trick was always to make the machinery work for you, not against you. Elizabeth was gifted when it came, as it often did, to that arcane art. She was true to herself and true to the Order, and that was the foundation for making the machinery hum. Sister Val called it pushing the right buttons. They both knew how to do it though they weren't pushing the same sets of buttons.

She drank coffee and ate toast and took out her Filofax to check the day's schedule. At nine o'clock there was a delegation of French feminists, Catholic laywomen from Lyons, who were continuing a long-running guerrilla action against the Vatican and wanted coverage in the magazine. God help us all. . . .

She had been editor-in-chief of *New World*, the twice-monthly magazine funded by the Order, for three years. Its original audience had been Catholic women back during the height of the social and religious upheaval of the sixties. It hadn't taken long for a decidedly liberal attitude to suffuse the magazine; then came the charges of Marxist influences hurled from all sides by enraged conservatives; the result was to turn the liberalism to radicalism, which in turn acted as a magnet not only to all the legitimate voices of the left but to most of the wild-eyed nut cases in Christendom. The outcry had eventually roused Callistus from his pontifical slumber and he'd declared in camera to the powers at the top of the Order that the time had come to put a sock in it. For their own sakes.

Shortly thereafter Sister Elizabeth was named editor, the first American to hold the job. For the past three years she'd tiptoed along the line, addressing the major issues facing the Church in an even-handed way but dodging nothing: birth control, a married clergy, women priests, abortion, the leftist clergy in underdeveloped and third world countries, the role of the Church in international politics, the scandals at the Vatican Bank—in short, the works.

New World had quadrupled its readership, had become a kind of debating society for the Church's heavy hitters. She'd managed to stay just shy of bringing Callistus blinking back into the daylight. And now it looked as if she would outlast him.

All through the summer and autumn she, like every other journalist in Rome, knew that Pope Callistus was living on borrowed time. Death was lurking in the Vatican anterooms, clichés abounded in sleek bars, and at fancy parties attended by clergy, and in heavily draped villa drawing rooms overlooking the city. The atmosphere of pure expectation, a kind of unfettered, luxurious foreplay, reminded her of more innocent times, reminded her of her grandfather back in Illinois, in a little town called Oregon which she visited each summer from the family home in Lake Forest. It reminded her of the excitement and anticipation when he took her to the circus.

A circus was the perfect metaphor. The Pope would die and the circus would actually begin with the tawdry tinkle of the hurdy-gurdy and monkeys on chains, the trumpet fanfare of a Fellini movie and the clowns and all the freaks and aerialists joining hands, dancing, capering across the screen. Always with a few priests thrown in, a bow to local color. Rome was presently in the pre-circus phase, and she remembered her grandmother getting her up early, her grandfather gassing up the station wagon and driving out to the fairgrounds in the cool dawn, cloudless and blue, promising another scorcher. He wanted her to see what went on before the ringmaster cracked his whip and opened the show, wanted her to see that some of the best parts of the circus happened when no one was around to watch. The tigers and the elephants, prowling around or making the earth shake, how they stood on their columnar back legs and reared into the air, showing off . . . The circus before the show began.

That was the state Rome was in now. The *papabili,* the men with eyes peeled and fixed on the main chance, power, a line in the history books—they were gathering like the great elephants and tigers they were, shaking the ground with their weight, prowling with sabre teeth bare in ghastly smiles . . . the cardinals. The men who did what had to be done to ascend to the Throne of Peter. And their handlers, the power brokers, the deal makers, the fixers. Elephants, tigers, no end of jackals and hyenas, and not a lamb in sight.

My God, how she loved it!

She loved the politicking, the intriguing, the nerves of the contestants showing through, rubbed raw in the infighting, the backward glances, the fear of a symbolic knife in the back, in the dark of the confessional, a false step, a word in the wrong ear, a career shot to hell. Who could best manipulate the gathering of cardinals? Who could flatter and cajole and threaten? Would the Americans try to throw their weight and money around? Who would be the most pliant when offered a promise or two? Who knew the best headwaiters in the best restaurants, who would be invited to the best parties, and who would swoop down and pitch camp at the Hassler? Who might have waited too long to strike? Whom might rumor destroy?

That morning Sister Elizabeth wore the navy blue suit with the scarlet rosette in the lapel, the symbol of the Order. She was tall and rangy and had good legs and a very modern figure and Cardinal D'Ambrizzi thought she looked very sexy in the uniform and wasn't shy about saying so.

She went to mass in a good mood, counting her blessings. She was looking forward to accompanying D'Ambrizzi and a visiting American banker on one of the cardinal's famed tours of Rome. It was a good time to be watching D'Ambrizzi closely: she was working on a long piece about the *papabili* which would be published as soon as Callistus died, outlining an insider's view of the likely favorites, among whom no name loomed larger than D'Ambrizzi's. She was trying to handicap the field: she figured the leaders at about two to one, eight to five if you took them as an entry. And D'Ambrizzi was one of them. Saint Jack, as Sister Val called him.

In the small church she habitually visited for morning mass, she lit a candle, said a prayer for Sister Valentine. She was eager to hear from her because, when she gave way to it, Sister Elizabeth was worried sick about her. Val was about as tormented these days as you could be, and it wasn't just the Curtis Lockhardt thing. Elizabeth figured it roughly eight to five she'd leave the Order and marry the guy. And more power to her. No, it wasn't the Lockhardt thing.

It was all the other stuff Val had hinted at.

Once the Frenchwomen had departed she had a couple of hours to herself. She spent them at her desk, the blinds closed to deflect the bright sunshine, her managing editor, Sister Bernadine, taking all the calls in the outer office. Before her on her desk she arranged the files on the *papabili*. Slowly she read through her notes on the two leading candidates. Then she turned back to her Apple II and divided the glowing screen down the middle, typed in the names of the two men, and proceeded to begin a thumbnail sketch of each.

GIACOMO CARDINAL D'AMBRIZZI

Vatican moneyman, director of investments, power at Vatican Bank but not an officer, untouched by the scandal; worldly, well-known diplomatic presence; pragmatist, cultured, but looks like a squat, muscular old peasant *à la* John XXIII & plays his earthiness for all it's worth; chummy, friendly man with a crocodile's smile and hooded eyes; will of iron—says don't get mad, get even and then some; big eater, drinker, lover of good life.
A pragmatic progressive—on birth control, gay rights, women priests—he's open to suggestion, not a doctrinaire Vatican creature; there's a strong rumor that he's gotten religion and may want to divest

MANFREDI CARDINAL INDELICATO

If the Vatican had a CIA/KGB he'd be its chief (works as papal adviser under Sec of State); tall, thin, ascetic, somber, slick black hair (dyed?), very simple black suits— no pomp, lots of circumstance; remote from all but his personal clique; little known to outside world; a true disciple of Pius during the war; ties to Mussolini in thirties. Noble, ancient family, past full of clerics; brother a big-time industrialist murdered by the Red Brigade; sister married to movie-star legend Octavio Russo; his personal art collection in his private villa is priceless (Nazi loot?); hobby is chess, he endlessly replays the great games. A conservative, traditionalist, even the

Church of some of its morally questionable investments; big supporter
of human rights in totalitarian
countries; fear in certain circles that
he's gone soft/liberal in his old age.
Old friend of American Catholic
powerhouse, H. Driskill. What was
he doing at Driskill home in Princeton after war? *A mystery.* What was
wartime relationship with Driskill?
War years in Paris w. Torricelli.

curia is scared of him; advocates a
rich, powerful Church deeply involved in world of *realpolitik;* he and
D'Ambrizzi once close in prewar
years when both were getting careers started. D'Ambrizzi has become more of a humanist while
Indelicato has hardened in his original views. A disciple of Pius on
whom he has rather styled himself:
arrogant. Spent war in Rome with
Pius, said to have worked on "saving" Rome with Pius.

Wondering what lay behind such skeletal hints at the reality of
the two men, she was called back to her schedule by Sister
Bernadine. Monsignor Sandanato was waiting downstairs with the
limousine.

They rode in a Vatican Mercedes, the four of them—Kevin
Higgins, a well-connected banker from Chicago, Cardinal D'Ambrizzi, and Sister Elizabeth in the back with windows open, Monsignor Sandanato behind the wheel. Higgins was an old friend of
Sister Elizabeth's father and greeted her warmly, full of memory-
laden small talk. He had not visited Rome in many years and he
couldn't have been more delighted than to return in the company
of the cardinal and his friend's daughter. He must have felt, she
reflected, as she herself did whenever the cardinal was holding
forth, as if she were seeing the Eternal City for the first time.

D'Ambrizzi had greeted her with an avuncular hug and insis-
tence that she hang on for the distance. He needed a quiet moment
with her once Higgins had been sent on his way. Sandanato had
been formal, proper, undemonstrative, such a contrast to the
vibrant cardinal who had been standing beside the black limo, face
to the sunshine, already giving Higgins an earful, when the monsignor had brought her out to the street.

The drive through the hot, dusty, traffic-clogged city had been
punctuated by stops for walks through various sites. Cardinal
D'Ambrizzi had inevitably linked his arm through hers, as if he
were substituting her for the absent Val, who so often accompanied

him, and meandered slowly with Higgins trailing behind in Sandanato's care, the monsignor a dark shadow, ready to open a door or brush off a bench or light one of the cardinal's black Egyptian cigarettes.

The cardinal's commentary never flagged. At one point Sandanato reminded him to take some medication which he washed down with a *granita* from a street-corner vendor. And now they were driving along the Tiber, the cardinal finally quiet, smiling at her and the Boston banker, letting the newcomer soak up the sights and reflect on where they had been and what they had seen.

"It isn't simply that I love this city," D'Ambrizzi had said as they set off, his English excellent though colored by a rich accent. "I *am* this city. Sometimes I think I was here when Romulus and Remus were suckled by the wolf and have been here ever since—not a very Catholic notion but it is true, I feel it in my soul. I was here with Caligula and with Constantine, I was here with Peter and the Medicis and Michelangelo, I feel them, I knew them." He had looked out from the folds of his hooded eyes: there was something timeless and unknowable in the visage, then he smiled suddenly as if enjoying a secret joke or a magician's trick he couldn't explain to the children. Elizabeth saw in him at such moments all the things Val had described, how he'd played with Val and her brother during those months in Princeton after the war. "Like Montaigne," he was saying, "I can say I know the pagan temples of old Rome better than I know the palaces of today's Church. I can see them, I can hear the voices of the consuls and senators on the Capitoline Hill when all was grandeur and grace . . . and I can see the same hill more than a thousand years later when the monuments were done to dust and the great men replaced by goats nibbling at the scrub brush. Ah, here we are—let's get out and go for a walk." He was larger than life, stumping along in his plain black cassock. He was George C. Scott playing Patton.

They had traversed the Capitoline, or Campidoglio as it is known now, the center of Roman municipality, and everywhere they had seen the immortal cipher which far predated Christianity, S.P.Q.R., *Senatus Populusque Romanus.* Like the cardinal's own view of himself, the solemn inscription, now visible on everything from buses to manhole covers, linked the pagan and Christian eras across the centuries. It was the central fascination Val had always felt with the city, both as a historian and as a nun: that this one remarkable point on the planet had been the center of the pagan world, that all roads of the world before Christ had led to Rome, and that subsequently it had become the fountainhead of the Christian world.

Life was pulsing everywhere, all around them, in the noise and the color and the sense of time coursing backward and forward, past and present all one, pagan and Christian so inextricably bound together that what divided them was irrelevant. Sister Elizabeth felt a certain light-headedness, bred of wonderment at the sensuality and humanity of the city coexisting so easily with the Church's orders and denials, and when she turned she saw the cardinal watching her, suddenly solemn.

The roar from the Piazza Venezia faded away in the quiet of the Capitoline. They passed through the gentle little garden separating the Via San Marco from the Piazza d'Aracoeli. With a sweep of his arm D'Ambrizzi encompassed the palaces and the piazza and the cordonata of the Capitoline, spoke one word: "Michelangelo." He shrugged happily, drew her on toward the Piazza del Campidoglio.

There, burnished in the bright sunshine, was the elegant statue of Marcus Aurelius surging forward on his horse, hand outstretched, with the brightly glowing gold Palazzo del Senatore behind him. When Michelangelo first saw this survivor of the ancient world, he had been so moved by its sense of life that he had ordered it to walk. They paused now, looking at it, and D'Ambrizzi said, "It's a mistake, you know, that we can see it at all. In the Middle Ages, at a time of religious zealotry which produced a good deal of vandalism, it was thought to be a statue of the first Christian emperor, Constantine, and as such it escaped the melting pot. Had they known it was Marcus Aurelius, it would have been gone, along with all the others."

He waited while Monsignor Sandanato lit another cigarette for him. "Like your Chicago, Kevin, Rome is built on a foundation of legend. This one has it that when this statue appears once again covered with gold, the end of the world will be at hand and from the horse's forelock will come the voice of the Last Judgment." He took a deep, rasping breath, moved on. "The statue had many curious uses. It was once used for a banquet with wine flowing from one nostril, water from the other. Much like one of your bankers' conventions, Kevin. . . . One angry pope hanged a city prefect from the statue by his hair." He laughed deep in his chest.

"You tell me that you are interested in the violent side of Roman history." The moneyman shrugged self-consciously. "This was once a place of medieval executions. They executed people everywhere, wherever the mood took them."

She smelled the cypresses and the oleander blossoms baking in the sun, releasing their scent. She turned, saw Sandanato's large, dark eyes staring at her. She smiled but he merely turned his gaze back to the glorious garden.

D'Ambrizzi seemed most interested in showing Higgins traces of the world that predated Christianity, perhaps assuming that his awareness of Church-related history was more complete. They were entering the Passagio del Muro Romano when he pointed at some massive, weathered gray stone blocks which seemed hardly worthy of comment.

"All that remains of the Temple of Jupiter, you see before you. The sixth century before Christ. In those days the soldiers of Rome were nothing more than shepherds, and there was no concept in their minds of gods like people. And certainly no temples in their honor. The Romans worshipped in the open, at altars made of turf. But the immortal Livy tells us that the soldiers brought their plunder to this place and put it under an oak tree. Where the kings of Rome chose to begin building the Temple of Jupiter." He looked leisurely around, as if he saw or heard something familiar. "It was here that the great triumphs were held, the celebrations of the endless victories. The triumphant general's body was painted bloodred and they dressed him in a purple-flowered tunic, a purple toga embroidered with gold. He wore a laurel wreath and carried an ivory scepter and a laurel branch." The hooded eyes were wide now, as if he could see the spectacle before him: Elizabeth felt his enthusiasm sparking within her, the effect of a magus.

"There he stood, clad as a god, offering a sacrifice to Jupiter— and his enemies, held in the Mamertine prison down there, below us, were put to the sword . . . my dear Sister Elizabeth," he whispered hoarsely, "these triumphant pagan rituals exceed my powers of description. Surrounded by gold and marble and statuary we now consider a standard of grace and beauty, wearing their purple robes, they presided over the sacrifices of pigs and goats and bulls, the smell of blood was everywhere, people fainted from it, their togas were stiff with it, the squeals of the dying animals filled the air that was thick with the smoke of the roasting flesh, the piazza was slippery with blood . . . our ancestors . . . where we stand, they stood, they believed in their gods as we believe in ours, we are one with them . . . we are the same." His voice had fallen almost to nothing and the images gripped her. Higgins leaned forward, straining to hear. She was almost embarrassed by the fervor of the description.

Later they stood in the cool shade of a small garden from which they could see the stark ruins of the Forum through the haze of heat and dust. Higgins was speaking softly to D'Ambrizzi and she caught a fragment. "It's always been something that fascinated me, the paradox . . . the evil, the good, coexisting. Not unlike your own interest in the pagan forerunners of Christianity."

Sandanato was ahead of them, smelling flowers in the bright sunshine. "Paradoxes," D'Ambrizzi repeated. "They are, of course, what lie at the heart of the Church. Two sides, two conflicting approaches to life, always interacting in order to survive . . . I have tried to bring the diverse elements into harmony. After all, we are not an organization of ascetics, are we? Oh, we have those fellows off in monasteries praying, we have the good sisters who remain in the cloister—they do enough praying for us all, don't you agree? I've never spent more time praying than was required of me." Smoke curled away from the cigarette clamped between stubby, nicotine-stained fingers. "Sister Elizabeth, you are not given to great prodigies of prayer, are you?"

"No, I'm afraid not. Not prodigies." She smiled.

"I knew it," he said, satisfied. "You and I, wine from the same hillside, Sister. Take Monsignor Sandanato there, he's a great expert on the monasteries, loves them, monasteries in ruins, monasteries deserted and burned to the ground by infidels or following infestations of plague. He doesn't always approve of the emphasis I put on the secular world, the money and power games." He smiled, beaming from one face to another.

They had left the comfort of the shade and the sunshine flowed across them, blinding them momentarily. Sandanato was waiting patiently, a lean figure in black, a kind of Roman Calvinist.

"Games someone has to play," she said, inhaling the sweetness of the garden, "or the world devours us. Evil might triumph and wear the red paint and the purple toga—"

He nodded vigorously. "There are those who might say the world has devoured us already. In any case, it is a battle fought on the world's terms, not ours. So I play my games and let others, like my faithful Pietro, attend to the spirituality. The Church is big enough for us all." His eyes flickered behind the folds of flesh.

Later still she was out of breath in the steepness of another ancient Roman street, the Clivus Argentarius, on past the Basilica Argentaria which had once been the center of the Roman world's commerce. The sun was dipping low enough so that they were much of the time in shadows. As they entered the Via del Tulliano she wondered if the cardinal's tour had simply been an elaborate jest, a teasing effort to send a shiver along the banker's spine, and hers as well, or did he intend it as some kind of object lesson about the connections that forever tie the pagan and Christian worlds together? Perhaps it was, as he had said, simply a reflection of his own identification with the timeless, ambiguous city. Whatever his intention, her mind was reeling with the images and insights he had produced as if from a top hat, in a spotlight.

"There," he said, stopping to catch his breath, "on the corner, the Church of San Giuseppe dei Falegnami. Nothing out of the ordinary, but beneath the church is a fascinating chamber, the chapel of San Pietro in Carcere . . . consecrated as the prison where Nero had St. Peter himself held. Come, let me show you this place." He crossed the street flanked by Higgins, who was beginning to look a trifle bedraggled, and Elizabeth, with Sandanato trailing behind. "Tell them the history, Pietro." The cardinal was tired. The huge nose drooped over the full mouth which seemed always drawn back in a grin, exposing the yellowed teeth. The black cigarette with the gold banding was stuck on the heavy ridge of his lower lip, the eyes almost hidden as he squinted through the wavering pillar of smoke.

"His Eminence has a peculiar affection for some of Rome's grislier sights," Monsignor Sandanato said, "but never give up hope, we draw near the end. The Tullianum was nothing more ominous than a water cistern, probably constructed shortly after the Gauls sacked Rome. However, it was later converted to use as a prison, serving as the lower vault of the Mamertine which, you will recall from your Roman history, was the final home of such defeated enemies as Simon Bar Giora and Jugurtha and Vercingetorix, who were often as not starved to death, and such enemies of the state as the Catiline conspirators who were perhaps strangled. Dead is dead, in any case, and a great deal of dying went on here."

They descended the modern double stairway to the entrance of the chapel, then entered the upper chamber. She suddenly felt a fluttering in her chest, felt her breathing shorten, and perspiration break out across her forehead and on her upper lip. A moving screen of black dots appeared before her. She was on the verge of falling, stopped to lean on a railing. She was hot, then icy cold, and her stomach churned rebelliously. The warm day and the onset of her period, the long walk, the talk, the intensity of the cardinal's vision of Rome, the horrors and oddities he had described—they all seemed to be overtaking her at once. All she wanted was a moment to rest and somehow not disgrace herself. The three men swam before her, she felt herself nodding in a mockery of attention, faking it, grasping for handholds as inconspicuously as possible. It was dim in the chapel. She prayed, hating her own weakness, get me through this and I'll never be bad again. . . .

Sister Elizabeth closed her eyes, tried to force herself to be calm, wondering with a distant corner of her mind if she was about to pass out.

"There was only one exit from the Tullianum, which is where we are at this moment, and that was a drain leading to the Cloaca Maxima. It was sometimes said to be clogged with rotting corpses. Now, of course, we see above the altar a relief depicting St. Peter baptising his jailer . . ."

It seemed hours before they'd gotten back to the Mercedes. Now, with the breeze off the Tiber cooling her face, and the cardinal staring moodily out the window, and the banker disgorged at his hotel, the tour was over. She was worn out and they were headed back toward the Via Veneto, and she felt the semblance of equilibrium returning.

She smiled at the thought of telling Sister Val about the afternoon, getting her interpretation of the cardinal's tour. Saint Jack. Maybe the next pope . . .

And then Saint Jack took her hand in his great meaty paws, held her gently to keep her from breaking, and told her that Sister Valentine had been murdered.

3

DRISKILL

I sat in the hospital coffee shop and tried to figure out what was going on.

There was a television set in the corner and the story of the murders of Curtis Lockhardt and Monsignor Andrew Heffernan was getting a big play but the newscaster from the *Today* show had precious little to tell. I knew enough about the way the archdiocese worked to see the lid being slammed down, hammered into place. The NYPD had issued a statement four sentences in length. So the meat of the story was a quickly cobbled together obituary of Lockhardt and a brief recap of Heffernan's career.

The news of Sister Valentine's murder hadn't yet surfaced. It would soon enough, and I could imagine the television commentators putting two and two together. Getting four wasn't going to take a rocket scientist.

I stared out the coffee shop window at the Halloween world, looking past the decorations done by children who were patients, all the orange and black witches on broomsticks and grinning pumpkins. The more I thought about it, I seemed to see something grim and implacably evil, like an army of Vandals or Goths gathering on the horizon. Yet there was only a stand of stark-limbed trees, windshorn, a desperately inadequate windbreak out past the parking lot. But in my mind the ghostly, nameless enemy was gathering beyond those sorry trees. My sister had been caught in the Church's dirty work. The Church had just started screwing around with my life. Again.

A pair of doctors who had known my father forever finally came to the coffee shop stroking their chins like actors trying out for *Magnificent Obsession*. My father had suffered the standard massive heart attack you're always reading about. It didn't look good. But then, it could have looked worse. Mainly it was a waiting game. And for the moment they were worried about controlling press coverage, deflecting the possibility that the hospital might become a circus of reporters waiting to see if Hugh Driskill was packing it in. The hospital staff didn't know my sister had been killed and I wasn't going to get into that. They could hear about it like everyone else. About noon I left the doctor place, as Val had called the hospital when she was little, and drove through the hardening slush until I was home.

The couple working for my father, the Garritys, was on hand full of awkward comfort. I'd called them from the hospital, told them the sad story, and they'd come to do some cooking and straightening in case any guests slept over. They did a ham and turkey and God knew what else and then they were gone and I was alone. I made some other necessary calls, to my office and to my father's. When I got off the phone I was more alone than I'd ever been.

Late afternoon and the gray light was fading fast. I sat in the Long Room without the inclination to turn on the lamps or light the carefully laid logs in the dark fireplace. I was sifting through the jumbled events of the past twenty-four hours like a prospector peering for the glint of gold winking at him from all the false hopes. Then something struck me.

I went upstairs, stood looking down the dim hallway toward Val's bedroom, where the door stood open. I'd called Sam Turner from the hospital to tell him about my father. Sam said he had the crime-scene guys coming out to the house in the morning. The Garritys told me that they had indeed clumped around out in the chapel and gone through the house, but I saw no evidence of their efforts. The door to Val's room stood open. Had they gone through everything she'd brought home with her?

I was trying to fix on something. The golden wink, the hidden jewel in the slag which might draw one on.

The hallway, long and dark and profoundly quiet, seemed like the deserted gallery of a museum devoted to unidentifiable, half-remembered, repressed images and experiences, memories of my mother, unanswerable questions: why she'd died as she had, what it was she'd been trying to say when she'd reached out to me, the rings weighing so heavily on her trembling fingers . . . It was a museum of disappointment, whispered questions without answers, as if only bits and pieces of the paintings were visible within the frames and you were supposed to guess what the finished picture might actually represent. Our home had always been a puzzle museum, a palace of indirection where nothing was quite what you'd thought. I'd lived in the house and had never really known what was going on and now Val was dead, my father was dying, I was alone, and I didn't understand it any better than I had so long ago.

An hour later I stood in Val's bedroom with the contents of two suitcases spread out on the bed. A couple of skirts, sweaters, blouses, a wool dress, underwear, toiletries, cosmetics, stockings, knee socks, a pair of loafers, a pair of heels, jeans, wool slacks, two paperback copies of Eric Ambler novels, a small leather jewelry box . . .

I had searched every drawer, gone through the closet, looked under the mattress. I stood in the middle of the room, starting to sweat. There was something impossibly wrong.

There was no briefcase. No notebooks. Not a pad of paper, not a pen. Not a single sheet of notes. No diary, no weekly planner. No address book. But most of all—no briefcase. Years before I had given her a heavy Vuitton briefcase with a brass lock. It had become a permanent part of her daily life. She'd said it was one of those perfect things, like a Rolex or a perfectly balanced Waterman pen or an IBM Selectric. Her indestructible Vuitton briefcase. It was usually packed to bulging and it was always with her. I simply didn't believe she'd neglected to bring it home. She was writing a book. She'd never have gone anywhere, let alone home, without that briefcase. She might have left cartons of research material in an office in Rome . . . but the briefcase would have been with her, just this side of manacled to her wrist.

And it was gone. Someone had taken it. . . .

It was past six o'clock, dark as a lost soul, when I put down the telephone in the Long Room and lit the fire. My father's condition was unchanged. He hadn't regained consciousness. The doctor was blandly noncommittal and said he was awfully sorry about my sister. Word was getting about.

The flames took hold, licked at the dry bark, curled around the kindling and the thick logs. I sank back in the deep chair my father had used the night before: I felt his presence all around me. I smelled his cigars mingling with the woodsy smoke smell from the fireplace. In the shadows at the end of the room stood his easel, the draped painting he'd been working on. The sound of a car in the forecourt roused me from my reflections. The glare of headlights poked through the window.

I opened the front door and Father Dunn came in, followed by a sudden gasp of chill wind. He looked rumpled and calm, a comfortable man who fit in because he was never much aware of himself. The familiarity of his face was something intrinsic, not just manufactured from the dust jackets of his books.

He shucked off his trench coat. He was wearing his black clericals, the collar. "How's your father?"

"No change," I said. "But how do you know?" I stopped abruptly on the way into the Long Room and he passed me, dropped his coat over one of the wooden chairs at the table.

"Cardinal Klammer. You called him, right?"

"He'd just spoken with my father, telling him about Lockhardt and Heffernan, then it happened."

"Well, I've spent several hours with Klammer, trying to keep him from running naked onto Fifth Avenue screaming he had no part in any of it. His Eminence and Lockhardt were not pals, you see. So he sees himself as a suspect in that cute, paranoid way he has. Klammer, of course, lives in the sixteenth century, when men were men. You wouldn't have a wee drop of that Laphroaig?" I poured it over ice and he drained off half of it. "So, Klammer's not leading the mourners, but murder practically in his parlor does call for a quick change of underwear." Dunn smiled for a moment. I poured myself a drink. "I told him about Sister Valentine. I really had to—I daresay she'd have gotten a kick out of his reaction. Our archbishop cardinal put on his game face, gritted his teeth . . . as the immortal Wodehouse might have said, Klammer's face was that of a sheep with a secret sorrow. He actually said, 'Why me, O Lord, why me?' A bellyaching Teutonic nitwit through and through. I have a bit of news, Ben. I've had a busy day."

"What is it you actually *do*?" I said. "For the Church?"

"Today I did a whole lot of listening. And I'm a good listener. After Klammer I went to see the cop in charge of the murder investigation in New York—Randolph Jackson, I've known him for twenty years. He had some things to say . . ." He gave me one of his sharp looks, all gimlet eye and eyebrow like a privet hedge gone to rack and ruin. "May I trouble you for a cigar?" I nodded impatiently while he clipped and lit it, blew out a jet of smoke. "A thing like this, it looks impossible, two bodies at the Palace—what can you do? Well, Jackson started talking to people at the scene. And it leads back to your sister, Ben—you got your seat belt buckled?"

"Leads back to my sister," I said. The Vandals and the Goths were moving closer, faster.

"A secretary working for Heffernan saw the killer." He watched me while that sunk in. "She was down the hall programming a computer for him and she had some questions; she started down the hall to the penthouse suite. She saw this guy come out of Heffernan's door and go to the elevator. She couldn't get an answer to her buzz, she called on the phone—finally she just went in and got the surprise of her life."

"So? The killer?"

"She says he was a priest." He broke into a dour grin, like a man delivering the worst punch line in the world.

"A priest. Or a man dressed like a priest—"

"She says she can always tell a priest—she's worked for the diocese for thirty-five years. She's a nun."

"Aren't there any Protestants left in the world?"

"Not in this story, I'm afraid."

The wind came up hard against the windows and a flurry of drafts filled the room, shoving the curtains. The fire flared.

"She's absolutely sure," Dunn said. "But she says she can't identify him. Or describe him, really. She says all priests look alike to her. Except for his hair. This was an elderly man with silver hair."

"How to find him in New York?" I shook my head. Hopeless.

"Well, he's not in New York. He was here yesterday. I think he killed your sister, Ben."

My face was clammy. "I thought about it today. Three Catholics. The hat trick. It had to be the same operation."

"There was something in the chapel last night . . . you had it in your hand, you didn't even know it. Piece of fabric, torn on the back of a pew. I knew what it was. Today proved it."

He took something out of his pocket, dangled it before me. A small piece of black fabric. I said, "I don't get it."

"It's a piece torn from a raincoat. A black raincoat. I've seen a million of 'em. A priest's raincoat. I'm like that old nun. I'd know one anywhere."

Peaches called, insisting we come over to the St. Mary's parish house in New Prudence for dinner. He wouldn't take no for an answer.

I rode with Dunn in his Jaguar. When we reached New Pru, countless pint-sized goblins and ghosts and skeletons were out trick-or-treating. Parents waited on the sidewalks as their kids traipsed back and forth, house to house, clutching Mars bars and popcorn balls and little sacks of cookies. It was windy, misting faintly, the night full of shouts and screams.

Edna Hanrahan, Peaches's housekeeper, let us in the front door of the old Victorian house with its long windows and wrought iron fence and gabled roof. Peaches had just returned from a hayride with the parish kids. What ensued in the church basement was a kind of pandemonium I hadn't seen since I was a kid. Peaches was riding herd on the eight- to twelve-year-old kids, raucous, pink-cheeked, hysterical at their in jokes. Peaches had straw in his hair and was sneezing from the dust and looked like a commercial for the priesthood. He draped his arm around my shoulder. "Have a rotten day?"

"No, thanks," I said, "just had one."

We'd been making the same joke all our lives and he grinned sadly. His eyes were full of sympathy and history. "How's your dad?" Everybody seemed to know.

"It's a waiting game. He's not dead, anyway."

Peaches went off to get through the party. Pretty young mothers helped out, getting the apple bobbing going, opening casseroles and putting the franks into the buns and the potato chips into bowls. Dunn and I met at the hot dogs and loaded up, stood munching, watching the kids raising hell. Peaches had a touch with them, like a good teacher or coach. Finally Father Dunn couldn't resist the insistent requests by a ten-year-old blonde with pigtails: she led him over to the pin-the-tail-on-the-donkey, blindfolded him, and giggled merrily as he set off in search of the donkey.

Peaches came over and said, "Let's go outside, Ben. I need a break." We went onto the back lawn of St. Mary's which led away down toward a tumbling creek. The moon ducked in and out behind dark, gray-rimmed clouds and the mist was cold on my face. Peaches kicked at the crusty leaves poking out of the brittle, shallow snow.

"I'm not up for this party," he said. "Occupational hazard. The priest at St. Mary's has always done it, so this one will, too. You saw how much the kids enjoy it."

"You've got a way with them," I said.

"I do, I really do." The windows of the church basement shone brightly and I could hear the kids laughing, shouting. "Val and I would have had great kids, Ben."

I nodded. Nothing to say.

"Goddammit, why couldn't she just have gone straight? She'd be alive now. I'm a real half-assed priest, Ben. Gone as far as I can go, not like Artie Dunn in there, no big-deal pals in Rome, no inside dope. This is it for me . . . but I'd have been a good husband. A great father. Dammit. We'd have had a lot of laughs and been happy and we'd have grown old together. But instead she's dead and I'm running a Halloween party for other people's kids." He wiped a corner of an eye. "Sorry, Ben. I had to say all this to somebody."

We walked slowly along the creek bank, then turned slowly back toward the church. I told him what Dunn had said about the killer being a priest.

Peaches shook his head. "I know a couple of priests who are killers at heart but, well, this sounds a little crazy. One priest kills Lockhardt, Heffernan, and Val. Who knows what kind of hell Val was stirring up—but why Lockhardt and Heffernan? Members of the inner councils—it's crazy."

"Dunn seems to take it pretty seriously."

"Priests," Peaches said. "Reminds me. Mrs. Hanrahan's got something I want you to hear. Hang around while I wrap this party."

Edna Hanrahan had made a fresh pot of coffee. She pushed a plate of Pepperidge Farm Mint Milanos toward the middle of the table. Her hair was gray, her face ridged with laugh lines, her eyes perky behind thick lenses. You could see the girl she'd been. She had old-fashioned nuns' hands with a history of hot water and carbolic soap. She wasn't a nun, but she'd been taking care of the priests at St. Mary's for thirty-five years. As a girl at parochial school in the late thirties, she'd been a pupil of a teacher I'd never heard of, Father Vincent Governeau. What could she have to tell me?

"Tell them about Father Governeau, Edna," Peaches said. "What you told me this afternoon."

"Well, you know how silly girls can be, and he was so handsome, like a movie star. Like Victor Mature, I'd say." She stroked a Mint Milano as if it were the bone of a saint. "Dark, swarthy. And ever so nice to talk to. Very *sensitive*. Paintings, religious paintings, that's what he lectured to us about. He loved the paintings, like he knew the men who painted them. He showed us paintings of popes and he talked like he knew *them*. He was so familiar. We were all thrilled." She cleared her throat. "Cookie?"

I took one, and she sighed gratefully.

"What else did you girls talk about? You silly girls?" Peaches was grinning gently, a masterful interrogator.

"Well, we thought he was quite a dish. And he seemed to like us all right, so we'd flirt with him, outrageous we was—all in good fun, mind you. But we'd never seen a priest like this one." She sipped her coffee, savoring the memory from so long ago. "And there was a nun, Sister Mary Teresa, she was so pretty. Well, we saw the two of them talking, walking under the trees, they looked so sweet. And we used to think what a shame it was they could never marry. And some of the boys used to say that Father Governeau was having a, you know, *relationship* . . . and we wondered if it was with our Sister Mary Teresa, and we wondered how, for heaven's sake—" She gave us a plaintive look, as if she hoped we weren't holding all this against her. "Well, I'm sure we should have kept our noses out of other people's business. Then we graduated and left our happy schooldays behind us. I moved to Trenton and, you know, life went on."

"And then?" Peaches prompted her.

"I never saw Father Governeau again." Edna took another cookie, turning it slowly in her roughened fingers, staring at it. "Until I saw his picture in *The Trentonian*. He was dead . . . I just couldn't believe it."

"Priests do die," I said.

"But not like that! By his own hand! I'd never have believed it, not in a million years." She looked up at me. "But I thought you'd know all about Father Governeau, Mr. Driskill."

"Why's that, Edna? I've never heard of him before."

"Well, it was your orchard and all, what he hanged himself in . . . I just thought you'd know, that's all. 'Course you was so little . . ."

"We never talked about it," I said.

We were driving back toward Princeton with the defroster and wipers working on the frozen mist dimpling the windshield. I said, "Why was Val asking questions about the hanged priest? He hangs himself in our orchard and Val, never having shown the slightest interest in him before, turns up all these years later wanting to see Sam Turner's files."

Dunn stared at the slippery road. "Speaking as a writer of books, the hanged priest may be a red herring—"

"But she did ask to see the file. That's a fact. And I've got another fact for you—the person, *your* homicidal priest if you insist, who killed my sister also stole her briefcase, whatever notes she may have been carrying with her. Notes for her book or anything else. It's gone."

"How do you know?"

I told him and he nodded. "One book of mine, you wouldn't believe the reams of notes. The immortal Wodehouse said that the notes for one of his novels filled many more volumes than the manuscript itself. It took me eight years to plot that book of mine and I wrote it four times." He hummed tunelessly for a moment. "Hanged priest. Forty-plus years later she asks about the hanged priest and another priest kills her and steals her briefcase. We're already out there in the gap, my friend. When you're alone in the fog in no-man's-land, when you can't see where you're going or where you've been, when you're out there in the gap . . . the trick is not to step on a land mine. You've got to move carefully. Or the priest will come at you out of the night and kill you, too."

When we pulled into the drive leading up to the house the wind hit the car sideways, shook it.

"You were good at pinning the tail on the donkey," I said. "I saw you do it three times in a row. How'd you do that?"

"The only possible way. I cheated. Kids are very easy to fool. They love it. They expect it from a priest and I wouldn't want to let them down. It's all part of the great seduction. . . . It's the way we've always done it, you know that. Take a young mind in its formative years"—he smiled at me, holding the wheel in the frozen ruts, the snow graying in the headlights—"and seduce it. It's yours forever."

"Thank you, Miss Jean Brodie."

There was a police car parked in the forecourt. A cop was waving a red flashlight at us. "What's going on?" I asked.

"Oh, it's you, Mr. Driskill. Chief Turner figured we'd best keep an eye on the place for a few days. We're gonna switch off every four hours or so." He looked cold and his nose was red.

"Why don't you come inside, then?"

"That's okay, sir. It's warm in the car. Chief says we stay in the car. I got me a thermos of coffee, I'm fine."

"As you wish. I appreciate it."

Dunn watched the cop go back to his car. "We've gotten a bloody nose since last night, Ben. You know what my dad used to say to me? I'd come home from school, all banged up from a schoolyard scrap, he'd say, 'Artie, nobody ever died of a bloody nose yet.' So, get some sleep. Take a look at things tomorrow."

I went inside. The house was quiet in the way that a sailboat on Long Island Sound is quiet in the night. It creaked, it moaned, almost seemed to give underfoot. The fire was reduced to a clump of faintly glowing coals. I placed a couple of logs among them and pulled one of the leather chairs closer and watched the fire come back to life.

Father Dunn's remarks about cheating the kids, how easy it was, how the Church set out to seduce the minds of the young, came back to me and made me smile. He was a rascal. And he never had told me what his job was. But he had access to Archbishop Cardinal Klammer. And to cops who told him inside stuff. And what had Peaches said? Dunn had big-deal pals in Rome. . . .

I was feeling the pull of the Church, the insidious beckoning finger stretching toward me, the seduction. The march of my thoughts was disorderly and ragtag, darting from the Vuitton briefcase to the priest dangling from the limb in our orchard to some other priest calmly pressing the gun to the back of my sister's head to yet another priest unerringly pinning the tail on the donkey every time, and I was too worn out to impose my will on the mental chaos. There was no fighting back.

It had been so long since I'd thought of myself as a Catholic. A long time since I'd *been* a Catholic. Damn. Being a Catholic . . . it had been love and hate, right from the beginning.

It was less a dream than a memory bobbing to the surface. Between waking and sleeping, I saw the bird and smelled the wet wool and the years slipped away, and I found myself back in the darkening March afternoon so long ago.

A wet, cold day: spring had not yet declared itself. From the schoolroom window I saw the piles of dirt-encrusted snow melting away into the mud, the wet gravel driveway curving from the tree-lined street. The clouds lay low and gray over the town. The schoolroom was overheated, but I sensed the wind and the smell of the rain.

I was eight years old and scared half to death. I had loused up my catechism earlier in the day and Sister Mary Angelina had swept down on me, marched the length of the aisle between the desks, mouth clenched, eyeballs peeled back, holding the triangular metal ruler in her white, bony hand. I couldn't take my eyes from the thin, bloodless lips, the pale and unlined face, the habit rustling softly as she approached. The radiators hissed. My classmates turned solemnly, eyes wide, glad it was me and not themselves.

I heard her voice but was too frightened to fully comprehend her remarks. I stuttered, botched my response, forgot what I had memorized so carefully the night before. Tears sprang. The metal ruler flashed and the skin split across my knuckles. I saw a thin red line traced across my hand. I felt the hot flush blotching my face. I was crying. I swallowed against the need to cry out, heard the resulting shameful whimper.

I moped quietly through the rest of the day, kept my eyes

downcast, managed to avoid Sister Mary Angelina's gaze. But the
fear, and what I was beginning to recognize as hatred, was building
to an eight-year-old's crescendo, leaving me shaking in the boys'
toilet, running cold water across my knuckles. After lunch I
returned to class, my plan in place. Benjy Driskill had had enough.
I thought it over, tracing the arcs of possible consequences, and
couldn't see how anything could be worse than an endless train of
confrontations with Sister Mary Angelina.

At afternoon recess I worked my way to the back of the school
which loomed against the grayness, all porches and turrets and
recessed windows. Deep red building stones, black trim with dim
yellow lights glowing from within. A fortress. I was about to escape.

I waited in the shrubbery near an old unused coach house. The
afternoon dragged on, no one came looking for me. The schoolday
ended, the other kids burst out, ran for home or to waiting cars.
My plan had extended only so far as not having to return to class.
Once the grounds were empty of children and nuns I felt wonderfully daring, alone. Ground fog clung to the wet grass, formed itself
around the evergreens.

As I stood shivering, however, another hour passed and darkness began overpowering the afternoon, and I discovered that
having escaped Sister Mary Angelina was not altogether enough.
The excitement at the moment's triumph faded. It was time to go
home and face that music. I was edging along the high black iron
fence when I saw the bird.

It was impaled on one of the arrow-shaped points at the top of
the fence. It was dead and decomposing, little more than a straggly
handful of feathers stuck with blood to the spindly skeletal remains.
It hung there, an open glittering eye, unblinking, shiny, staring
malevolently at me.

In my eyes, terrified at not knowing my catechism for Sister
Mary Angelina, paralyzed at the sight of the painting of the gaunt,
agonized Christ crucified and dripping with gore just outside the
door of the third-grade room, the bird was incomprehensibly evil,
the climax toward which the long, unhappy day had been building.

I couldn't face Sister Mary Angelina anymore, the black eyes
burning behind the flat, round discs, the pale white face like a kind
of clown's that turned again and again to stare me down in my
dreams. . . .

I bolted, slipping and falling, running across the wet, half-icy grass. I reached the gravel path and tore down toward the towering black gate and the freedom beyond, away from the nuns and the dead bird.

Panting, dripping with sweat, I looked up as I approached the gate. My mother was coming up the walk. She didn't look happy.

Turning, I ran blindly back up the gravel path toward school.

And suddenly I was overwhelmed in a cloud of heavy, damp black wool. The scent overwhelmed me, like a gas, like the ground fog. I swung my arms, beating at the cape, struggling to free myself, but strong arms enfolded me, held me tight. I was crying, frightened, and ashamed and sick.

It was Sister Mary Angelina.

When I saw her face through the tears, all I could make out were the piercing eyes behind the glasses . . . the bird skewered on the point, the bleeding Christ, the darkness of the school halls . . . I saw the hatred and the fear, all the powdery white women in long black robes, the ravens swooping down on me. . . .

"Benjy, Benjy, it's all right, dear, really, it's all right, don't cry. . . ."

Sister Mary Angelina's voice was soft and she was kneeling beside me on the muddy gravel. The arm around my shoulders, her arm, softened its grip, and through the fists I'd flung before my eyes I saw that she was smiling gently, eyes shining and warm. I tried to speak but could only cough and hiccup and she was sheltering me with her arms, patting my back, cooing softly in my ear. "Don't cry, Benjy, there's nothing to cry about, nothing at all. . . ."

Everything in my small universe was spinning, nothing made sense, but I couldn't deny her touch, the loving voice.

She seemed young, not an old lady. She seemed someone else, a different Sister Mary Angelina. She was motioning my mother to wait. Whispering to me. Her woolen cape was dragging on the gravel, getting dirty, and she didn't seem to care.

I leaned against her shoulders, burying my face in the dampness. Inexplicably, everything was all right.

Sister was a person. And with that realization my first rebellion against the Church had ended.

Somehow nothing had been what it seemed.

The hatred had been put down by kindness. And Sister Mary

Angelina had been transformed, metamorphosed. She had become someone to turn to.

No one ever explained to me how it had happened. But I wanted to be close to her, I wanted to cling to her and feel her arms around me and the strength of her body.

It took me a long time to understand that the great seduction had just begun.

I was half awake when I heard the pounding at the front door. I shook loose from the past, yawned, and tottered across the Long Room into the foyer. The cop was calling my name while he had a go at the door.

When I opened it he wasn't alone. I felt my heart leap in my chest.

In the shadows behind him, outlined by the lights from the taxi swinging around on the gravel, was a woman. I couldn't see her face, but the sense of her was so familiar, someone I'd seen before.

"She says she's come from Rome, Mr. Driskill." The cop's voice was going on, but I wasn't hearing him.

I was staring past him.

It was Val. Something was wrong and I blinked like a fool, trying to come wide-awake. The height, the shape of the hair, the silhouette there and then gone as the headlights swept past her. Val.

She stepped forward into the hall light.

"Ben," she said. "It's me, Sister Elizabeth."

4

DRISKILL

Sister Elizabeth.

We stood in the Long Room. The shadows from the fire flickered across her face, in the hollows, shone in her green eyes. She took my hand, said things about Val, shook her head, her thick hair swaying: there was something about her physical presence that filled the room, crowded everything else into the shadows. She was tall and broad-shouldered, wore a heavy sweater falling low on her hips, a dark skirt, high, dark boots. Her eyes fixed me, alive with candor and energy.

She told me how Cardinal D'Ambrizzi had given her the bad news, how she'd put the magazine in the hands of her managing editor, packed a bag, and grabbed the first flight to New York. She'd had a limousine waiting to take her to Princeton. "I'm starving," she said finally. "Do you have horse? I could eat a horse and chase the rider."

Ten minutes later we were sitting at the kitchen table surrounded by what looked like an explosion in the Empire Diner. She wasn't a woman to hang back when it came to food. She looked up from the task. "It's tomorrow morning for me." She seemed to be building a four-story sandwich. "I always need explanations when I start to eat. Growing girl, that worked for years and years, but once I passed thirty I had to come up with some new material. You wouldn't have a Diet Coke on you by any chance?" She went to work with the mustard pot.

"No Diet Coke, I'm afraid."

"No, too much to hope for. Impossible to get in Rome. Any chance for a beer?"

I got her a beer and made a sandwich for myself. When I finished she said, "Maybe I'll have just one more sandwich . . . well, how about a half, okay?"

"You've got a beer mustache, Sister."

"Always happens. I can stand it if you can. Pete's Tavern. Irving Place. I remember."

"I'm surprised."

"Why? Look, I'm a nun but I'm also an earthling. I've been known to not only have a good time but remember it, too. Ben . . ." She uncapped another Rolling Rock and poured it.

I remembered it, too.

My sister had come to New York a couple of winters ago to receive one of those humanitarian-of-the-year awards from a national women's group. She gave a speech at the Waldorf in a gilded pillared hall where I'd once attended a dinner welcoming the Yankees back from spring training. A thousand people were eating creamed chicken and peas and she worked the room like a Las Vegas pro, towing me along in her wake as she filtered through the shoals of heavy hitters.

But after the dinner and the speech she'd arranged to meet another nun, a friend from Georgetown and later Rome. She took me by the hand. "You've got to meet her, you're going to hate each other!" And her mischievous laughter floated back at me from childhood.

The friend turned out to be Sister Elizabeth, and the first thing I noticed was how much alike they looked as they stood together in the dark blue lobby of the Waldorf with the great ornate clock saying it was ten o'clock. Thick wavy hair, shiny eyes, both well-tanned, live-forever healthy, Val's face more oval and her friend's rather heart-shaped. Sister Elizabeth and I shook hands, and when she smiled at me she had a slightly smart-ass, Jesuitical look, tilted her head a few degrees to one side as if she were challenging me to keep up with her. Val was watching us expectantly, two people who meant a lot to her. Sister Elizabeth surveyed me with a flat gaze. "So, at last I meet the fallen Jesuit."

I glanced at Val. "Blabbermouth here has apparently spilled the family's beans."

When Elizabeth laughed the irony was colored with warmth. "We are not going to hate each other, are we?"

"Well, in any case, we can't say we haven't been warned."

We wound up at a cocktail party being given by a friend of some Jesuits who were particular fans of my sister's. The apartment looked down on Gramercy Park. Lots of smoke and wine and arch conversation, full of jokes about the pope. Poor Val was the center of everything.

I gravitated to the cooling drafts of a partially opened window. It was just past Thanksgiving but a snowstorm had closed in on the city. Everything was turning white, giving Gramercy Park the look of a Christmas display window. Sister Elizabeth came to stand beside me, asked me if I thought anyone would be offended if we were to duck out for a walk in the snow. I didn't think so. Father John Sheehan, S.J., whom I'd known for years, gave her an appraising look as we passed into the hallway, made a circle of thumb and forefinger to me, nodded appreciatively. He had no idea she was a nun.

The snow was deep and she frolicked like a little girl allowed up late, kicking it with her leather boots, making big soft snowballs to throw at the trees past the iron fence. Gramercy Park had been turned into a snowy cloister, shadows like monks moving quietly to the chapter house. We walked past the dim lights glowing in the downstairs bar at the Players Club, then went off down Irving Place, where parked cars were turning into low ridges of snow.

We stopped at Pete's and had a beer at the scarred, ancient bar with the photo of Sinatra looking down on us like an icon, or the abbot of his own special order. She told me about her job at the magazine in Rome and I told her how peculiar it felt to be surrounded by Catholics, the first time in years. She asked me how my wife, Antonia, was and I told her that she wasn't my wife anymore. She just nodded and took a drink of beer that left foam on her upper lip.

When we left Pete's we ran into Val and Sheehan and the four of us walked all the way back up Lexington to midtown, laughing and horsing around like kids. We weren't thinking of Val as a candidate for a Nobel Peace Prize. We were for a moment rediscovering childhood and pretending that everything would turn out all right in the end. But it hadn't, and now my sister was dead.

"Ben, we've got to get down to cases. I loved your sister. But I haven't cried for her yet. I don't know what's the matter." Sister Elizabeth wiped the foam from her upper lip, squeezed the napkin into a tight little ball.

"Neither have I. Perhaps she wouldn't have wanted us to—"

"People always say that. Maybe it's true. Anyway, I'm too angry to cry."

"Exactly, Sister."

She wanted to know everything, and I told her. Lockhardt, Heffernan, Val, my father. Father Dunn and the theory of the priest killer. All of it.

"Well," she said, "you're right about the briefcase. It was her version of my Filofax. She took it everywhere. She had it the last time I saw her. Stuffed with papers, notebooks, Xeroxes, pens, Magic Markers, historical atlases, scissors—she kept her whole work world in that briefcase."

I said, "They killed her, stole the briefcase. What was she working on that was so important?"

"And important to whom? What made Lockhardt and Heffernan as well as Val such threats to them?"

"What would Lockhardt and Heffernan have on their minds?"

She gave me a shocked look. "You really are out of touch with the Church! Believe me, those two guys were talking about electing the next pope. That's the only thing anyone in Rome is talking about, and Lockhardt and Heffernan take Rome wherever they go. Who were they backing? Lockhardt always had an angle; I've heard people say he could tilt the scale. No kidding."

"But where would that leave Val? Wouldn't her support be the kiss of death for any candidate?"

She shrugged. "Depends . . . of course, she was so tight with D'Ambrizzi, the connection from childhood, your father and Saint Jack, all that history—"

"I don't see her playing papal politics—"

"But it *was* Lockhardt's field of play."

"But it was *Val's* briefcase."

"True," she admitted. "Too true."

"Maybe Heffernan was just a bystander. Maybe Val and Lockhardt were the intended victims."

"If that's the case, if Lockhardt was the object, why not kill him someplace easier? Now, think about this, Ben—how did the killer even know of the appointment at the Palace? Don't you see? We've got an internal proof here." She was talking fast, making all sorts of leaps, and I was trying to keep up. "The secretary who's so sure he was a priest? Well, she's probably right. Who but a priest, somebody inside the Church, could possibly know about a meeting between hotshots like Lockhardt and Heffernan? Val said Lockhardt was the most secretive man in the world with the possible exception of her father. Lockhardt *had* to be secretive with all the stuff he was into." She took a deep breath, rushed onward. "So you know he didn't tell anyone about the meeting. And Heffernan, he was an old poker player, close to the vestments. No, this is an in-house job." She stopped as if taken aback by the conclusion, an ambush of her own making. "At least murder is an old Church tradition. But somehow you think of that sort of thing as history, not something that could happen now."

"She was scared when she called me. She wanted to talk something over with me. Peaches said she was into some pretty heavy research that worried her. You were as close to her as anyone. What was she afraid of? Did she ever give a hint?"

"The last time I saw her was in Rome. About three weeks ago. She'd been working like a madwoman. In Paris, in Rome. In the Vatican Library, the Secret Archives. Not an easy thing to arrange. She didn't tell me what she was working on but it was old, I mean really *old,* fourteenth and fifteenth centuries, that's all she said about it—"

"But how the hell could *that* get her killed? What was she doing in Paris? I thought this book was about World War Two—"

"She'd been working there all summer. She had a flat. She did come to Rome every so often, she'd dive into the Secret Archives, then go back to Paris. When I saw her last she was heading for Egypt. Alexandria. I called her the Desert Fox after Rommel, all the stuff from the war she was digging into."

"The fourteenth century, World War Two, the hanged priest in our orchard—did she ever mention that one to you?"

"Never."

"But she comes home with all this other stuff on her mind and the first thing she does is ask Sam Turner about that old suicide." I felt my impatience growing and I couldn't stop it.

"Right before she left for Egypt I was really bugging her to tell me what she was after and finally she'd had enough of my pestering her. She told me to lay off. She said I was better off not knowing. 'Safer, Elizabeth,' she said to me, 'you're safer not knowing.' She was protecting me—but from what? Well, from getting killed, it turns out. It's something about the Church." She bit her knuckle, eyes narrowed. "Something *inside* . . . something so *wrong*—and she's found out about it—"

"In the fourteenth century?" I asked. "Someone reaches out from the fourteenth century and kills her? Or at the other end, some nut who wants to be pope blows her away? Come on, Sister!"

"When it's the Church, Ben, you just never know. It's like an octopus. If one tentacle doesn't get you, another one will. That was the title of the new book, by the way. *Octopus.*"

I heaved a sigh that shook the rafters. "If we only had a solid idea of what she'd uncovered, we'd have a motive. She didn't tell you because she thought it would put you in danger. She was going to tell me but didn't have time before they got her. But she must have told Lockhardt—"

"Or they thought she did. Same thing."

"So maybe they think she told me. Over the phone, maybe. That's an encouraging idea. Lockhardt and Val—how close were they?"

"I *think* she'd finally have left the Order and married him. He was a good man. He represented everything she needed: access, freedom to write and research, power. He was a little scary but—"

"What do you mean by that?"

"Oh, so much influence, all the secrets he knew. I find that kind of scary. Val didn't; she loved it. He was a big help to me, too. He provided me with an apartment in Rome, got me lots of introductions . . . even Cardinal Indelicato, who is very, very hard to reach. And, of course, he was so close to D'Ambrizzi." She held up crossed fingers. "Lockhardt, D'Ambrizzi, and the cardinal's shadowman, Sandanato. And Val. Whenever Lockhardt was in

Rome, the four of them hung out together. There was really only
one thing holding her back from marrying Lockhardt—"

"Father."

"Right. She didn't know how to handle it with him."

"She didn't need his blessing—"

"Ben, she *wanted* it!"

It was nearly two o'clock and the winds of the night were
hammering at the house like the last of the hobgoblins.

She said, "How did Artie Dunn get into this, anyway?"

"By chance." I told her about the meeting at the Nassau Inn
with Peaches. "What are you making faces for?"

"Dunn. He's a joker in any deck."

"You know him?"

"I interviewed him once in Rome. About his novels, how they
fit into his conception of the priesthood. He's very glib and well-
connected. He does this I'm-just-an-everyday-kind-of-guy routine
and then D'Ambrizzi sends a limo for him. He knows all those
guys. Including the Holy Father. It's just hard for me to believe
Artie Dunn does anything by chance—"

"Believe me, I met him by accident—"

"I'm sure you did. I just mean there's a whole lot more to him
than meets the eye. And I've never met a soul who knows what he
actually *does*."

"I know. I asked him that very question earlier tonight and
never did get an answer."

We were both exhausted. We cleaned up the kitchen and I took
her bag, led the way up to a guest room. I was standing in the
doorway when she came across the room. "It's good to see you,
Ben. And I'm so damn sorry." She kissed my cheek.

I closed the door and went off to bed.

After my first meeting with Elizabeth, the memory of Pete's
Tavern and Gramercy Park under the snow fresh in my mind, I'd
met Val for breakfast at the Waldorf. Elizabeth wasn't up yet. Val
wondered if I'd had a good time the night before. I said that indeed
I had. "Then why the long face?"

I shrugged it off. "Morning brings the harsh realities. Maybe I
had too good a time last night. Maybe I resent not being able to
keep it going, maybe I'm not crazy about getting older."

"You and Elizabeth seemed to get along well." She smiled

brightly. "I'm glad. Sometimes she and I are so close it's scary; we tune in on each other. She's the other side of me, Ben. We each might just as easily have become the other, exchanged lives."

"She's beautiful. Like you." I grinned.

"Men," she said. "Men are always falling for Elizabeth. It's not her fault but it's made her wary. She's the belle of the Rome press corps. Putting their best moves on a nun makes it all the more challenging and exciting for the boys. Drives her nuts. That's why I'm glad she just let herself have fun last night."

"Will she stay a nun?"

My sister took a long time before answering, nibbling at the crusty pointed tip of a croissant. "Will any of us stay? That's the real question, Ben. We're the first of the new nuns. No real connection to the old ways. We choose to live in the world but not by the world's rules. We're activists in one way or another and none of us really knows if, or for how long, the Church will find us digestible. We give all those bureaucrats in the curia ulcers. We're forcing the Church to change, we aren't subtle, we push hard . . . but the Church can always push back. If they get sufficiently pissed off, we'd better look out. Anyone who gets in the way of the grand strategy—whatever it is—had better look out."

"What about you? Will you stay?"

"Depends on the pressure, doesn't it? You got a bellyful and left. My gut feeling is that Elizabeth will stay. She thinks in terms of what is right, she believes in the essential goodness of the Church's aims—but me? I don't know. I lack her intellectual commitment, her philosophical involvement. I'm a troublemaker, an egotistical little twerp, a hell raiser. If they let me stay the way I am, sort of a squeaky wheel—well, then, I might stay a nun until I die." For some reason she reached out and took my hand, as if she were consoling me in some grief she knew awaited me. I told her to eat her eggs before they got cold because I was paying roughly ten dollars an egg. Later on I kissed her good-bye and went back to my office on Wall Street.

We give the curia ulcers. We're forcing the Church to change, we aren't subtle, we push hard . . . but the Church can always push back. If they get sufficiently pissed off, we'd better look out. Anyone who gets in the way of the grand strategy—whatever it is—had better look out. . . .

I came out of my dreams and memories of Val and Elizabeth, struggled back to the surface. It was six o'clock, dark, windy. Drafts everywhere. I pulled the covers up under my chin. I'd been half dreaming about Val, hearing her voice from the past, and it had pushed me back to the present. Someone had pushed back all right. The fear I'd heard in her voice when she called me made me think it—whatever it was—was even worse than she'd expected.

Were all the answers in the Vuitton briefcase?

If it was so damned important, and if she'd been afraid they— *they*—were after her, then why did she let them get it? Why didn't she make it safe somehow?

There was a logical inconsistency in my reading of Val's behavior. She'd known she was in danger. She must have known she had some kind of dynamite in her briefcase. Val was not an innocent in any sense of the word. She knew how the games were played. She must have discovered where the bodies were buried. . . . Yet she let them get the briefcase.

She must have left an insurance policy. In case of her death, her murder, the loss of the briefcase—

I sat up like a madman. Of course! She needed a hiding place, a place the bad guys would never look.

I was out of bed and into my old plaid robe, shivering, stubbing my toe on the bureau, fumbling for the lights.

The playroom!

It smelled musty and empty, the shades pulled down, a bit of wallpaper hanging askew. The door swung open like a portal to memory. I could almost see Val, in a short, high-waisted dress and Mary Janes and white socks, in the corner where she kept her books and paints. I'd have been there, too, messing around with my Official All-Star Baseball Game, spinning the pointer on the Joe DiMaggio card, telling her to stop bothering me. . . .

There was a rustling, skittering noise somewhere in the shadows. A squirrel shot across the floor, peered into the empty fireplace, then disappeared behind some boxes of Val's things in her favorite corner between the bookcase and window. I turned on the light overhead. The shadowy shapes were revealed as a pedal car modeled on the old Buick, a couple of bicycles, a blackboard, stacked boxes of books, the large bass drum which had appeared one Christmas. Val had beat hell out of it, an ungodly din. Then she'd found a better use.

I crossed the room, knelt on the dusty floor beside the drum. Someone had been there before me. She had left something in her old hiding place, where it would be safe.

The dust was thick on the edges of the drum but the side panel with the grinning clown had been wiped clean. I couldn't get my fingertips under the panel, so I used the sand shovel from a beach pail set, pried it loose, knocked the damn thing over, made a hell of a racket. But the panel came loose.

I stuck my arm in and felt my hopes take a nosedive.

The space was empty.

But it couldn't be. She'd been here. She'd knelt beside the drum, she'd left her smudged fingerprints in the dust. She'd used the old hiding place—

Then I found it.

It fluttered down from a crevice where it had been stuck. I nearly brushed it away, thinking it a relic of childhood. But I brought it out of the drum instead.

"What are you doing? Drum practice?"

Sister Elizabeth stood in the doorway. She was wearing baggy striped pajamas, rubbing her eyes, yawning.

"I'm starved," she said. She was peering into the refrigerator, conducting inventory. "Eggs. Ham, turkey, gorgonzola, onions, butter. This may add up to something. English muffins." She gazed around the kitchen. I'd given her an old robe of mine. She'd added a pair of Val's knee socks to the ensemble. She spotted the omelet pan hanging on a hook. "Ah, apples. I'll chop up some apples, too." She smiled at me. "Surely you know that breakfast is the most important meal of the day and no, I don't eat this way at home." She started cracking eggs. "It's all in the wrist. Like Audrey Hepburn in *Sabrina*. So what do you make of it?"

I sat at the kitchen table staring at the snapshot I'd found in the drum. Very old, yellowed and cracked, like something of my father and mother taken at Lago Maggiore in '36. Only it wasn't my father and mother. It was a photograph of four men. The tiny trademark on the back of the paper was in French. It was a memory from someone else's photo album.

"Doesn't mean a damn thing to me. Four guys at a table a long time ago. Looks like a club—brick walls, candle in a wine bottle, lots of shadows—a Left Bank cave. Four guys." She was chopping

onions and apples on the thick board. She was good at it. Fast. I
didn't see any bloodstains. She craned over to take another look at
the photo.

"Five."

"Four," I said.

"I'll bet another pal took the picture." She looked at me and I
nodded. "And you do know one of them. The one next to the
fourth man. No way to tell the fourth man, we get mainly the back
of his head. But number three, reading left to right, is in profile.
Take a close look. Recognize that schnozzola?"

She was right, it was familiar, someone I should have known.
But I couldn't quite place it.

"Well," she said, "I have the advantage of seeing him rather
frequently, a nose like that one doesn't change." She had finished
chopping. I smelled the butter in the pan. The boiling water was
dripping through the coffee in the Chemex, the aroma filling the
room. She was whisking half a dozen eggs and a shot of water in a
bowl. "It is an early version of Father Giacomo D'Ambrizzi."

"Of course! No mustache—he had a thick black bandit's mustache when Dad brought him home after the war. I'd never seen
anything like it outside of a Cisco Kid movie. You're so smart,
what's the point of the picture?"

"I'm only the cook." She was sautéing the onions and apples in
the butter. She had her back to me, working like a professional.
"But we know one thing for sure. It is one important picture. She
hid it from everyone in the world . . . but the two of us."

"Well, it means nothing to me," I said. "And she never knew I
knew about the drum, she couldn't know I'd look for it there—"

"You're wrong. Val told me a lot about you, about the time you
found the black powder in the basement—"

"You're kidding!"

"She told me about the famous feet of clay, she told me how
she'd hide your Christmas present in the drum, she told me that
you'd figured out the drum was her hiding place, but she never let
on to you that she knew you knew. She used to put stuff in there
that she wanted you to find—it was like a game, Ben. You were the
older brother who played tricks on her, but this was one she could
play on you—" She stopped short. "Ben, she put that snapshot
there for you to find in case anything happened to her. And you

found it. It's the key." She turned back to the stove, poured the eggs into the pan.

"A photo of D'Ambrizzi in the drum is the *key*?"

She was stirring the eggs as they set. This incredible creature was making me hungry again.

"Maybe D'Ambrizzi isn't what's important," she said.

"You think it's the other three?"

"Four. Don't forget the one who took the picture."

My father's secretary, Margaret Korder, arrived by nine o'clock and did what she did best: she took over, she fended off, she protected me from the claims of the outside world, just what she'd been doing for my father for thirty years.

Sam Turner arrived with Father Dunn's friend, Randolph Jackson of the NYPD, a black man who had once played tackle for the Giants. They stayed from noon until just past two. It was more a chat than an official interrogation. Jackson drank orange juice and wondered what might connect his murders in New York and Sam's in Princeton. I decided there was no point in wandering away from the beaten track of fact. I steered clear of the Church, of Val's relationship with Lockhardt; I didn't discuss the briefcase, Val's planned book, the fourteenth century and World War II, the priest who killed himself in our orchard so long ago. There was no point in dragging them deep inside the Church: they wouldn't know what to do about it and I wouldn't know where to begin the story.

When they got up to leave, with Jackson making conversation with Sister Elizabeth, Sam Turner took me aside and told me he couldn't find any files as far back as our hanged priest. "Name came back to me," he said. "French. Governeau. Father Vincent. I put in a call to old Rupe Norwich. He was mighty sorry to hear about your sister, Ben. Rupe said he took that file with him when he retired. I couldn't believe it—he was a by-the-book man, Rupe was. I told him that was against the law. He said maybe I should come down and arrest him! Quite a guy, old Rupe."

Jackson and Turner were barely out of sight when Sister Elizabeth and I were in my car and heading toward the Jersey shore, only an hour or so away. It was a gray, cold day. Ice had formed in patches on the road and the wind skidded vengefully out of the gulleys and across the fields which were stiff and brown with early winter.

Sand was blowing from the dunes when we found Rupe Norwich's frame bungalow. The salty gales had pitted the paint job but the house and lawn had the compulsive neatness you found in the residences of the old parties who had retired and didn't have enough to do. Norwich was eighty or so and glad for the company. He knew me from when I was a kid and he was sorry as heck about Val and asked about my father. He seemed almost guilty about Val's being dead and my father stricken while he was so spry.

"I'm not like your daddy, deciding the fate of the world and the Church," he said, hooking his thumbs into his suspenders and leading us into the living room which had too much furniture in it, too much heat. "But I stay busy. Got to keep your brain alert. Video games," he said, pointing to his IBM PC, "they're the key these days. Heck, I fly fighter missions, I play golf, baseball, never leave the house. PCs are the thing. I try to stay current, I listen to music, U2 and the Beastie Boys, 'course Springsteen, he's a Jersey boy. Then I get out my old Ted Weems 78's, too, with Perry Como singing. What you see here is a man of eighty-two trying to convince his twenty-eight-year-old granddaughter he knows what's going on." He was chirping along, glad to be talking. "Her mother got this Alzheimer's a few years back, passed away, but I'm just too damn busy with all my stuff here—but you notice what a gabby old fart I am, can't stop talking, always gotta get my two cents worth in. Sam Turner says you got young Vincent Governeau on your minds. Poor devil." He sat down in a rocker once we were settled on the couch. He was skinny and wore a sweatshirt and Reeboks. He was sizing Elizabeth up: he'd done a double take when I'd introduced her as a sister.

"Sam said you might still have the file," I said.

"I took it with me when I left fifteen years ago 'cause I didn't want it coming back to haunt Sam. Then I figured the hell with it, I didn't want it coming back to haunt me either. So I burned it up." He laughed abruptly. "Destroyed the evidence."

"Evidence of what?" Sister Elizabeth asked.

"Evidence of what you'd call a cover-up nowadays. I never got over it. Part of my education. Taught me where I fit in the scheme of things. Lots of folks more important than a Princeton cop.

Valuable lesson, all things considered." He smiled amicably at the thought. You could see nothing was going to get his goat now.

"And what was being covered up?"

"Well, Sister, it wasn't just what. It was also who was doing the covering up. Ben, I don't think your daddy ever knew all this maneuvering was going on behind the scenes. I felt kinda sorry for him, probably the only time in his life he wasn't in the know. I was deputy chief and Clint O'Neill, he was chief, and it all came down from on high and landed on Clint—he was a stubby sort of fella to begin with and he had a coupla beers one night and admitted he was just about buried alive on the Governeau thing. And he had to go along—you can't argue with the governor, a senator, an archbishop, more heavyweights than you see introduced at a championship fight—"

"All because a priest who taught art appreciation to teenage girls went off his rocker and hanged himself?" I was scowling at the idea. "What was the big deal?"

"Problem was, y'see, he didn't kill himself—unless he figured out a way to split the back of his skull with a hammer and then hang himself when he was already dead. Which was how it must have happened. Unless it was murder, which is what it was, natch."

"And this story never came out?"

"Never did." He grinned, rubbed his hand through his white butch haircut. "Never will. It was never investigated. It became a suicide after the fact. Like I say, your dad got stuck with a body in the orchard and the rumors, you know how people talk, and he got pretty damn sick of it, but what could he do?"

"What kind of rumors?"

"Begging your pardon, Sister, you can imagine, I'm sure—"

"Pregnant nuns stashed away in convents," she said. "Like that?"

"Sure, sure," Rupe Norwich said, "what else? Folks just insist on being folks, don't they?"

"They didn't think a nun killed him, surely?"

"No, Ben. Some folks thought he got a student pregnant and a daddy killed him. All just talk. We never found a weapon—damnation, we never looked for one. Am I gettin' through to you? It was a *suicide*."

"Well, no wonder my father would never discuss it. The gossip would irritate hell out of him." The idea amused me. "So why would Val be asking questions now?" It was a rhetorical question, but Rupe Norwich had an answer.

"Makes you think she already found out something," he said. "Or had a good idea, eh? Had a theory, a suspicion, maybe. Still darned near fifty years . . . Long time. Cold trail." He shrugged his square, bony shoulders. "Seems like yesterday to me. Poor bastard. Bad luck, I'd say, getting yourself murdered and nobody ever looks for the killer and you go down in the books as a suicide. Lousy luck, wouldn't you say? And him a priest?"

When we got home Margaret Korder had everything well in hand. Several friends of the family had called and she'd attended to one and all. Funeral arrangements were in progress: the body would be released tomorrow, burial the next day. The man from the funeral home was coming by to show me photos of caskets. I told Margaret something simple and solid would be fine and she could handle it all. She'd arranged my mother's funeral. It was just another thing she knew how to do.

Father Dunn had called from New York and would call again. Peaches had called. There were two messages from Cardinal D'Ambrizzi's office in Rome and they'd get back to me. There had been one call from the Holy Father's office but, having expressed sympathy, they hadn't sounded like they'd be calling again.

"You don't have to do a thing," Margaret said. "Everything's logged, I've hooked up the answering machine and referred after-hours calls to my room at the Nassau Inn. I've moved in for the duration. Your father is resting comfortably in intensive care. He was awake for a while, pretty groggy, and he's sleeping now. They'll call if there's any change. And that's about it."

"Margaret, you're a wonder."

"I'm paid to be, Ben," she said with a wintry smile. She'd been through the wars between my father and me and she'd never taken sides. She'd also never given me anything but good advice. "The important thing now is to keep our spirits up and pull your father through."

"And find out who killed my sister," I said.

"But let's make sure of the living first," she said, turning to Sister Elizabeth. "Would you like a cup of tea, Sister? I sent the Garritys home. They were fussing too much for my taste. Too lace-curtain, I fear. And she kept bursting into little fits of sobbing. Frankly, I couldn't take it anymore. Tea might revive me."

"I'd love some tea," Elizabeth said, and they went off to the kitchen. Elizabeth, in her slacks and penny loafers and heavy blue sweater, was reminding me more and more of Val, which was good and bad, I guess.

I went upstairs and soaked in a hot tub for an hour, thinking about the snapshot Val had hidden in the drum and the fact that our suicidal priest's murder had been covered up. Was the snapshot as old as the murder? Why was it French? Who were those guys— D'Ambrizzi and who else? What had prompted Val, in what was virtually her last act on earth, to call Sam Turner about the hanged priest? What had she wanted to tell me? And who knew that killing her wasn't enough, that her briefcase had to be stolen as well?

When I came downstairs, Margaret had left for the inn and Elizabeth was watching Dan Rather sign off the evening news. She looked up. "The pope's office called you? I don't know whether to be impressed or horrified. Val couldn't have been one of his favorite people."

"No, but my father is. More or less. Are you hungry?"

"I assume that's a rhetorical question." She stood up and took the teacups to the sink. "But first, they've unsealed the chapel. Would you mind if I spent a few minutes there? I won't be long, but let's face it, I need some help—the kind I'll get there."

"I guess that's what it's for. Would you like me to walk you out?"

"No, I'll be fine. We'll have some dinner when I come back, okay?"

Father Dunn turned up while she was still in the chapel.

"I called earlier," he said, "but you were out. I understand you have a houseguest. Remarkable girl. Where were you?" It was cold outside and he was warming himself before the fire in the Long Room. He gave the drinks table a yearning glance and I uncapped the Laphroaig. "Good idea," he said. "I'll have mine in a glass, thanks."

"Doing a little research," I said.

"Into the life and times of Father Governeau?"

"Just his death." I handed him the drink and poured my own. "Dredging up the past."

"*À la* your sister—and? And?" He gave me the crinkly Barry Fitzgerald look.

"It wasn't a suicide," I said. "The man who was deputy chief back then says it was murder. And a cover-up. Governor, senator, archbishop, the works. So there was no investigation."

Dunn stared at me across his scotch. He pursed his lips and sat down, sipped. "This damn thing gets worse and worse. I feel rather as if someone is laying out the pieces of a story and our job is to build the plot. D'you mind my talking like a writer? Writing's a mug's game, but it's a good deal harder to do than an amateur might suspect." His flat gray eyes were still, as if they were waiting for something, someone. "I've been in New York. No good news there either, though what would qualify as good escapes me. But if we had any doubts, we can forget them . . . the same gun was used on your sister, Lockhardt, and Heffernan." He drank again, looked up, grinned, but the eyes never changed. "If I weren't so brave, I might be starting to feel hot breath on the back of my neck."

"Well, I'm glad you're so brave, Father. But a murder conspiracy stretching across half a century and killing my sister forty-eight hours ago scares the daylights out of me. And by the way, what does this mean to you?" I fished the snapshot from my shirt pocket and handed it to him.

He took the picture, gave it a quick look, then took it over to the table and held it under the light. "Where in the world did you get this?" I told him. He shook his head, and with admiration in his voice said, "She hid it in the *drum*. Women are amazing creatures. Resourceful. I wonder where she got it. . . ."

"Does it ring any bells?"

"Sure. The fella with the banana for a nose is Giacomo D'Ambrizzi, of course. It's printed on French paper. I'd say it's forty years old, anyway. World War Two at a guess. Paris."

"You get a lot out of a beat-up old snap—"

He shrugged. "D'Ambrizzi was in Paris during the war. I was in the army, the boy chaplain. I was there after the Liberation. That's where I met D'Ambrizzi. But it stands to reason the picture goes back to that period, doesn't it? I met him just that one time . . . and then not again until many years later. These other men? They could be anybody."

"So why was the picture so important to Val?"

Dunn handed it back to me. "Beats me, Ben."

The front door opened and Elizabeth came into the Long Room. Her face was flushed from the wind and cold.

"Sister Elizabeth, my dear!" Dunn went to her. Several emotions crossed her face before he got there, and she settled for a very small smile. "I'm so sorry about Sister Valentine." He took her hand in both of his.

"Father Dunn," she said coolly. "Of all people."

"Sexually obsessed," Dunn said, munching on a ham sandwich. He looked at the last of the scotch in his glass, burped softly, said, "I'm switching to milk. Possibly for the rest of my life." He went to the sink, rinsed his glass, and poured milk. "Yes, sexually obsessed, and that's a quote. No way out of it, Sister. There it was in black and white. I'll bet you missed her review of my latest, Ben, but authors read them all—"

"And never forget the bad ones," I said.

Sister Elizabeth was leaning forward with her elbows on the kitchen table, her chin resting in her cupped hands. "Would you call it a bad review, Father?"

"Good gracious, no. I'd call it a review that sold books. Couldn't have done better myself. And I fancied some of my colleagues were looking on me with freshly minted respect."

"My colleagues, too," she said. "You're very big in convents, I suspect. Sex is good business. So, you owe me one."

"But did you mean it, Sister?"

"Sexually obsessed? Really, Father, would I lie? It seems to me the question is, was I right? You *seem* well versed in the area of literary sex." She shrugged provocatively. "Perhaps you only have a vivid imagination." She winked at me.

"Imagination helps, don't you suppose? For instance, you mentioned convents—but what, I wonder, do you know of convent life?"

"Enough, Father." She grinned. "Just exactly enough."

Inevitably we talked about the murders, concentrating on Val, trying to avoid the emotion. Just as inevitably Elizabeth fixed Dunn with one of her appraising stares. "I don't quite understand how you've gotten so involved in all this. Did you know Val? Or is it the Princeton connection?"

"I never met Sister Valentine, and Ben here is my first Driskill. No, I'm here by accident. Just a random blip on the screen but, as it turned out, I know the man in New York investigating those murders. I thought I might be helpful to Ben. Of course I did know Curtis Lockhardt slightly—"

"Excuse me, Father, but do you have a parish? An office? You must be assigned somewhere—"

"Oh, officially I'm connected to the New York archdiocese. Cardinal Klammer, God rest his soul—no, don't look so concerned, he's only *brain* dead, Sister—Klammer has the benefit of my counsel. He needs all the counsel he can get. Perhaps I should write a sitcom." He smiled genially at her. "Look, Sister, I'm not a particularly easy person to have around, but our masters make the best of it. I live here in Princeton and I have a condo in New York. I'm an inconvenience in some ways, but I also have the kind of mind the Church can always use—"

"And what kind of mind is that?"

"Devious? In the present instance you might say that I am acting as Cardinal Klammer's eyes and ears. Have you any other questions, Sister? Might as well trot them out." He was smiling, but he'd had about enough.

"I'm just curious," she said. "Leading two lives, priest and novelist, must be exhausting." She wasn't backing off just because he was a priest, a man. Together, she and Val must have been the scourge of Rome's male chauvinists. The Church barely tolerated women with influence and the prestige to speak out. But Dunn was enjoying the parry and thrust.

"I bear up as best I can," he said. "I study the Church rather like a scientist studies a section on a slide—"

"But the scientist is not dictated to by the goo on the slide."

"Ah, point to you, Sister. But still I do study the Church, how it reacts to pressure. First, there is my own case. I've observed how the individuals and the mechanism dealt with me. Then I watched it deal with the activists, from the Berrigans on through Sister Valentine and the gay rights activists. . . . The Church is a huge organism. Poke it and it squirms, challenge it, threaten it, and it fights to preserve itself. In the last few days the Church has gotten poked pretty hard." He raised his eyebrows, bushy gray thickets. The flat gray eyes blinked. "And here I am. Watching. Studying. It's a life's work."

"The Church has gotten poked," I said. "Presumably Val was doing the poking, making the organism squirm. And in that case haven't we been seeing how the Church strikes back to preserve itself?"

Sister Elizabeth shook her head. "God knows I'm no apologist for the Church, take that as a given. But I cannot seriously believe that the Church sanctions murder. Not in the twentieth century. The Church did *not* dispatch a killer to do these horrible things—"

"What is the Church?" I asked. "Men. Some of whom have a lot to lose."

"But there are so many other ways to deal with problems—"

"Oh, come on, Elizabeth! The Church has always murdered people," I said. "Friends and enemies. Our evidence indicates it was a priest who—"

"It could have been anyone," she said, "dressed like a priest—the nun's testimony notwithstanding. We mustn't be so gullible! There's always someone trying to blacken the Church, tear it down—"

"But," I said, "who else could have it in for Val? Who was she bugging but the Church?"

"That's just it—*we don't know, Ben!*"

"Look," Dunn said, "I've been trying to treat this like one of my plots. Let's take the time now to do it right. What do you say—will you humor me?" The Regulator clock over the refrigerator ticked loudly. Sleet had begun again, blowing against the window. "Let's just see what we've got."

I said it was fine with me and looked at Elizabeth. Dunn bothered her and she had reservations about taking him into her—our—confidence. But I sensed she was fascinated by his role and how he functioned within the Church's power structure. I realized also that she was looking on the two of us, who shared our love of Val, as a team. She didn't want Father Dunn leading me down strange, treacherous paths. She didn't want him breaking up the home team.

"Sure," she said at last. "You want to play games, I'll play." Dunn's iconoclastic attitude was forcing her into defending the Church. She sensed it and she was off balance.

We adjourned to the Long Room, where there was a fire and a long table with captain's chairs and a record player. I put the Elgar cello concerto on the CD spindle and pushed the repeat button. With the haunting music filling the room, we drew our chairs to the table: a lawyer, a journalist, a novelist, three people who lived by their abilities to organize awkward bits and pieces of information.

We began with Val's itinerary. Paris. Rome. Alexandria, Egypt. Los Angeles. New York. Princeton. She stayed with the limousine after dropping Lockhardt at the Rockefeller Center ice rink. Records showed that she had been delivered to the house at 3:45 that last afternoon.

She made two calls, the one to Sam Turner about the hanged priest and the other to me in New York. By which time both Lockhardt and Heffernan had been murdered by the lethal "priest." Sister Elizabeth insisted on the quotation marks.

At some point while she was at the house Val hid the photo from Paris during the war—at least that was Dunn's placement of it—in the drum, presumably so that I would find it if anything happened to her: she knew she was in danger even in Princeton and she was counting on me to do something once I found the photo. The picture showed four men, one of whom was D'Ambrizzi. A fifth man took the picture and Elizabeth included him in the group. What in the world made this snapshot so important? Would D'Ambrizzi remember it?

Val then went to the chapel—roughly five-thirty or six o'clock— where she was killed by the same gun that killed Lockhardt and Heffernan. Certainly by the same man. Who left behind a shred of his black raincoat: Dunn said it was a priest's raincoat.

The killer then returned to the house, found Val's briefcase, and took it with him.

And finally Rupe Norwich told us that the hanged priest had in fact been murdered in 1936 and a cover-up from on high dictated that it be ruled a suicide. What were they scared of? And who was being protected?

By the time we finished we may have had the known facts clear in our minds, but as Father Dunn observed, they could tell a thousand stories. The fire had burned low, the guard was on duty outside, and there was nothing left to do but try to get some sleep.

5

DRISKILL

He looked the part.

That was my first thought upon meeting Monsignor Pietro Sandanato. He looked the part, as if by an accident of physiognomy his life's course was dictated forever, as if free will had been denied him by the simple fact of his face. He looked like a tortured Renaissance saint painted on countless canvases, hung in countless museums, an artistic convention. Of course, on the other hand, he looked like a Mafia hit man I once met. Sensitive, troubled, tired, with permanent purple smudges beneath eyes that glittered like anthracite under heavy, dark lids.

He had the look of a Giacometti statue, emaciated, but with a boyishly smooth, swarthy face, straight black hair, a single pockmark on his left cheek like a brand marring an otherwise perfect hide. He wore the collar, a black topcoat draped over his shoulders, a soft black Borsalino, black kid gloves which he removed when Father Dunn led the way into the foyer and introduced us. It was past noon and Dunn had met him at Kennedy and made the long drive to Princeton.

"Mr. Driskill," Sandanato said softly, his voice husky with jet lag, "I bring messages of the deepest sympathy from your sister's dear friend Cardinal D'Ambrizzi, as well as from His Holiness, Pope Callistus. Our sorrow at this tragedy is profound. I, too, knew your sister, of course."

I took them into the Long Room and Sister Elizabeth came in from Margaret Korder's command post. Sandanato turned to her and they shook hands. "Such a tragedy, Sister," he murmured.

Mrs. Garrity served coffee and, after Sandanato refused the offer of lunch, I sat watching the three of them talk, Church professionals. I wasn't really paying attention to what they said. Sandanato was going to be my houseguest for a few days and I was trying to size him up. I couldn't recall ever having seen anyone drawn quite so taut. The face, the carriage, the haunted eyes, set off a chain reaction of references in my mind, ecclesiastical and Roman, and now so utterly foreign to my life. I kept coming back to the agonized saints in the galleries, the face of Christ with the crown of thorns and the blood running down his forehead that I remembered from the dark end of the hallway at school, to the strained Giacometti statuary, but I was also reminded of the sort of perfectly cast minor characters Fellini used to dress the set, to create in a stroke or two the world of the Vatican. His hair shone like glass. In the time I watched him he smoked three cigarettes. His hand shook slightly, giving the impression of someone wound so tightly that there was the risk of a broken mainspring, a disaster.

Eventually Garrity took Sandanato's bags up to his room and my guest followed, a dark wraith wearing Gucci loafers. I said to Artie Dunn, "Don't you ever sleep?"

"Four hours a night suits me fine. The sleep of the just. I also catch the odd catnap, which reminds me of Hairball. I must be going."

"I beg your pardon?" Elizabeth said.

"Hairball," Dunn said. "My cat. Her name is Hairball. She didn't have a name for two years—then it came to me. My cat is synonymous with hairballs. Besides she sort of looks like a hairball. Very irritating animal. But don't get me started—"

"Believe me, I wouldn't have," she said, "if I'd known. It's disgusting."

"That's what I say." Dunn smiled at her. "I must go feed the little wretch."

When he'd gone she turned to me. "What a remarkably weird little man! He has an agenda of his own—I'd give anything to know what it is. There's something about him that scares me."

"Speaking of weird, or scary, or *something*," I said, "tell me about Sandanato. What's his number?"

"I've never seen him without D'Ambrizzi—I mean, he's D'Ambrizzi's creature, he owes his career to D'Ambrizzi. D'Ambrizzi picked him out of an orphanage, brought him along, now depends on him every single day. Sandanato is his second in the ongoing battle with Cardinal Indelicato—"

"What are they fighting over?"

"The future of the Church, the nature of the Church. They've been at each other's throats all their lives, fifty years of sniping, or so people say. And now—well . . ." She shrugged and began rearranging a spray of dried flowers in a copper pot on the sideboard.

"And now what? I know I'm not in the Catholic inner circle, I've lost my membership card, but you can trust me—"

"I only thought you wouldn't be interested in shop talk—"

"Just try me, Sister."

"I was just going to say that it's odd how the two of them have come fifty years, through all the battles, wins and losses and draws, to this point—two old men, both within reach of the final triumph, the papacy."

"Aren't they awfully old? Neither one of them could get the Church to the next century—"

"They're both very vigorous," she said, "and age isn't really all that important. The job is to set the priorities, get the Church on track. And, frankly, we're a little weak on younger candidates. Federico Scarlatti maybe, but he's too young, only fifty."

"So would you call Sandanato D'Ambrizzi's campaign manager?"

"You know it doesn't work that way, Ben—"

"The hell it doesn't. The party line is wasted on this old Jesuit, Elizabeth."

She gave me a tolerant smile. "You're impossible, but I suppose you take pride in that. In any case, Sandanato wouldn't be the man. He's more like chief of staff. If you insist on a campaign manager, I suppose it might have been Curtis Lockhardt. That's only a guess on my part, but with Heffernan and Lockhardt meeting, it seems a good guess."

"What conclusion does that suggest? That someone who didn't want D'Ambrizzi to win—"

"My God, you don't *win* the papacy, it's not a ball game!"

"Of course you do, and of course it is, Sister. So somebody killed Lockhardt and Heffernan to derail D'Ambrizzi's chances? Does that sound possible?"

"It sounds absurd! Really, Ben, this isn't one of Dunn's thrillers, no matter what he says!"

"Absurd? I think it's absurd that three people have been murdered in cold blood. But I don't think it's so absurd that they were killed without a reason . . . now, *that* would be absurd. There was a motive, Sister. Believe me. And I'm damned curious about it. I want the man who killed my sister to pay—but he won't be found until his reasons are known. And in the world of the Church, the papacy may well be worth killing for."

I was wound up and had run on longer, more vehemently, than I'd intended. My anger was showing through and it took even me by surprise. It was like catching a glimpse of the red-eyed thing behind the mask of sanity.

She gave me a hard look, her arms folded across her chest. The wheels were going around in that regal head and finally she gave the tawny mane a shake. She'd assessed the situation. Her face softened as if she were going to give me another chance.

"Nevertheless," she said, "it *sounds* absurd. I know these men. They are not murderers, Ben. I don't pretend to have any idea what's been going on here. But I'm not jumping to the conclusions that seem to fascinate you and Artie Dunn. Let's say I'm trying to keep an open mind."

"Just so it's not empty," I said.

She laughed, giving up on me, reminding me so damned much of Val. "You *are* spoiling for a fight."

"You're right," I said. "I goddamn well am."

"Well, I guess I've been warned. You're Val's brother all right."

"And my father's son. Don't forget that. There's one ruthless son of a bitch inside me." I sank into a chair and willed the tension away. "I've just got to work my way through this situation. I haven't even begun to face her death—you see, Sister, I don't know yet what it is I'm going to do about things. I think I know but I'm not quite sure how—just humor me awhile. Just talk to me, tell me some more about Sandanato, and then I'll tell you something I noticed about him. Talk to me, Sister."

She sighed. "Well, I'm of two minds about the good monsignor. Some days I think he's the total Vatican insider, the perfect techno-crat, cold and calculating, the man who knows how it works and can play the system like a Stradivarius . . . but the next day I'll decide he's the complete religious, practically a monk. He's fasci-nated with monasteries and maybe that's where he belongs. Either way, for Sandanato the Church is the world, the world is the Church. That's the difference between him and D'Ambrizzi. The cardinal realizes there is a Church *and* a world and, most important, he knows the former must exist within the latter. Cardinal D'Am-brizzi is probably the most worldly person I have ever met."

"They sound like an oddly matched pair."

"In the end," she said, staring out the window at the chapel sitting bleakly on the frozen turf with the white frosted roof, "I think Sandanato is D'Ambrizzi's conscience. Of course, Val thought Sandanato was a zealot, a maniac." She laughed at the memory.

A silence settled across the room. It was gloomy outside, and shadows were gathering like the enemy. I was thinking about Val, imagining what kind of man could kill her. I was thinking about what I might do if I could find him.

She snapped on a lamp, then another. A gust of wind whistled down the chimney and ashes puffed out across the hearth.

"You were going to tell me something you noticed about him," she said softly.

"Oh—sure. He's in love with you, Sister Elizabeth."

She opened her mouth, closed it, and slowly blushed. For a moment she was speechless. "Now, that *is* absurd, Ben Driskill. And ridiculous! And insane! I can't imagine how you could come to such an idiotic—"

"Sister, be calm. It was just a passing observation. It's perfectly obvious. He couldn't keep his eyes off you for more than five seconds at a time. I thought it was sort of cute."

"Oh! Val told me how irritating you could be, but this—"

"Sister, I didn't say *you* were in love with *him*. Relax."

She rolled her eyes, still flushed. "You've got a lesson or two to learn, buster." Then she walked all the way down the room, stopped to look back at me before leaving. She couldn't think of anything to say at the last minute and just stalked off. I heard her going upstairs.

My own anger was gone for the moment. I went back to thinking about the killer. Whoever he was, wherever he was.

My father lay quite still on the crisp white sheets, his face gray as putty. His eyes were closed but the lids were fluttering softly, like tiny beating wings. The room looked like something from television melodrama, right down to the monitoring machine making faint beeping noises, background music. It was a private room, spare and utilitarian, but the closest thing to a presidential accommodation the hospital offered. Even hooked up to the machine and looking more dead than alive, he was a hell of a specimen. Massive, solid: I must have expected him to look old and frail and weak, the way he'd looked and felt in my arms at the bottom of the stairs. But I was wrong. I suppose he was in much better condition now than he'd been then.

It wasn't the sight of my father that bothered me. It was the black-robed nun bending over him, whispering to him like the angel of death making a pitch.

The nurse who'd brought me down the hall was a large, solid, florid, no-nonsense type. She went to the bedside, did some whispering, and the nun, an older woman, nodded and swept past me with a whiff of the clean, soapy smell I remembered from the nuns of my childhood. As she passed me, her habit swishing, I thought I heard her speak my name, just *Ben,* but she was gone and the nurse was speaking to me in a low, well-practiced tone.

"He's resting very comfortably. No longer comatose but he's doing lots of sleeping. He's hooked up there"—she motioned with her hand toward the beeping machine—"and we can monitor him out at the station. There really wasn't any need for keeping him in ICU any longer. Dr. Morris will be getting him up in a day or two. The doctor will be sorry to miss you, Mr. Driskill. Well," she went on, checking the leads attached to my father, plumping the pillows with a reflexive gesture, "I'll leave you for a few minutes."

"Nurse, you saw the priest with me? He's going to want to speak to my father—"

"Oh, it's only members of the family, I'm afraid—"

"Then perhaps you can tell me how I'm related to the nun who was hovering over my father here before he's altogether cold?"

"Oh, well, I'm sure I don't know. She's been here every day, morning and afternoon. I just assumed, I don't know, she was given permission by someone—"

"The priest with me, you see, is a personal emissary from Rome, sent by Pope Callistus. I don't think we should ship him back to Rome empty-handed, as it were—do you?"

"Of course not, Mr. Driskill."

"And I'd appreciate your checking out that nun."

"Of course, Mr. Driskill."

"Now leave me with my father, please."

She closed the door behind her and I stood with my back to the window, watching him, my shadow across his face.

"That's telling the old busybody. Good lad, Ben." My father's left eye opened slightly. "Never have a heart attack, that's my advice. Feels like an MX missile hit you in the chest. Don't do it unless you do it properly and cash in your chips."

"You sound pretty fit," I said. "You scared hell out of me."

"Falling down the stairs?"

"No. Speaking up just now. I didn't expect—"

"It's all an act," he said.

"What's an act?"

"My chipper act. I feel dreadful. Lifting my arm is the work of half a day. I don't talk to the doctors much. They'll have me up and running in place, blasted sadists." He was breathing with a raspy noise, the intakes of air shallow, quick. "Ben, I keep dreaming about Val . . . you remember the day Gary Cooper sketched her, the two of you?"

"I was thinking about it just the other day."

"My dreams are full of the dead, dammit. Val, Gary Cooper, your mother . . ." He coughed softly. "I'm glad you're here, Ben. Give your father a kiss."

I leaned over and pressed my cheek to his. He felt warm and dry and had a bit of stubble which may have explained some of the grayness. "Take my hand, Ben," he said, and I did. "You're a difficult chap, Ben. You know that. Difficult. Always will be, I suppose." I leaned back and told him I looked upon my nettlesome nature as part of my charm. "You would, you would," he said.

"You'll be delighted to know that the pope's emissary is waiting outside."

"Oh, my God, am I that bad off?"

"He's come for Val, too. A doubleheader."

"Ben, you're a sacrilegious man. A sinner, I'm afraid."

"He won't go away until you see him, you know."

"I suppose. Well, Ben, have you satisfied yourself that I'm still alive and kicking?" I nodded. "Don't be such a stranger. I've been wondering when you'd come by."

"They told me you were in a coma." I smiled at him. "So you're lucky I came at all."

"Just my luck." He grinned weakly.

"So who's this private, personal nun you've got hanging around?"

He shook his head. "Water, Ben. Please."

I held the plastic pitcher while he sipped through the straw. Then he said, "Let's get the pope's man in here. I'm damn tired. Come see me again, Ben."

"I will," I said. I was almost out of the room when he spoke again.

"Ben . . . is there any word on the killer? Val, Lockhardt, Andy—they catch anybody?"

I shook my head. "Same gun, though. Same killer."

He closed his eyes. I went back to the waiting room.

Sandanato was smoking a cigarette, staring out into the court-yard of the old redbrick building. Rain verging on sleet was falling again, and lights had come on in the gathering darkness. He had napped but didn't look any more rested for it. He was a long way from Rome and looked every mile of it. "He's awake," I said. "You'd better grab the chance."

He caught my eye, nodded, stubbed out the cigarette, and headed down the corridor.

Elizabeth came back to the waiting room, the elderly nun from my father's room beside her. The contrast was striking. The older woman, I was sure, could not imagine being a nun and living Elizabeth's life. Elizabeth looked at me, spoke to the nun. "So you must know this badly lapsed specimen."

"Oh, yes," she said. Her face was so fine in bone structure and texture, she might have been a piece of old porcelain whom age had made only more valuable. Her hair was hidden, of course, her face framed with white. She was so handsome now, I thought how beautiful she must once have been. It was always my luck to find the pretty ones. Those with warts on their noses and beards on their chins I seemed always to forget. "I've known Ben for forty years." There was mischief in her eyes. "But he seems to have forgotten me."

It came to me in the nick of time, a flicker of memory.

"Forget you? Sister Mary Angelina? The very idea! Sister Mary Angelina got me through my very first crisis of faith."

Elizabeth said, "Too bad she couldn't have followed you around for the rest of your life, picking you up each time you stumbled." She smiled sweetly, eyes flashing.

"Whatever do you mean, Benjamin?" Sister Mary Angelina fixed me with a look of utter curiosity. "What am I forgetting?"

"One day at school I got fed up with the whole business. You took a ruler to my knuckles and I ran away, hid in the school yard, then I made a break for it and you nabbed me. I figured the jig was up and I was really going to get it . . . but instead you put your arms around me, patted me, and told me everything was going to be all right. I've never quite gotten over it. And I've never quite understood what was going on. So, you may be sure I won't forget you, Sister."

"Isn't it odd," she said, "I don't remember it at all. Not a bit of it. Still, I'm nearly seventy, and maybe I'm beginning to lose a marble or two."

"I suppose it was all in a day's work for you."

"Well, one does have so many pupils over the years."

"I didn't know you knew my father so well."

"Your father and your mother. Yes, we were always friends. I was visiting Mrs. Francis the day your father was stricken and you brought him in—it was such a shock. Your father, well, one just expects men like Hugh Driskill to go on and on and on." She searched my eyes, then turned to Elizabeth. "Some men are like that. It's as if they lack the mortality gene . . . but of course we're all in the same boat when it comes to that, aren't we?" She sighed through a nice fixed nun's smile. "Ben, it's good to see you. And you have my deepest sympathy. Sister Valentine, she was such a dear child. But at least your father is coming along very nicely. You will, all of you, be in my prayers."

Sister Elizabeth tugged at my sleeve when we were alone, and when I looked at her she was smiling at me shyly. At just that moment I wondered what I'd be doing without her there.

"Val used to tug at my sleeve," I said.

"I'm sorry." She dropped my sleeve.

"No," I said. "I liked it. It felt . . . right."

"Are you going to behave yourself now?" Her voice was so soft.

"Why start now?" I said. "It's much too late for that."

We were in the car when a thought crossed my mind.

"Sister Mary Angelina," I said. "I wonder if she knew Father Governeau? If she was around back then and if he liked the ladies, she might have known him. Or is that stupid?"

"I wonder," she said.

She wouldn't let me sleep. She burned a hole in my night, in the darkness, in the very idea of rest. I closed my eyes and there she was, her face, almost as if she were coming to me in a dream. But it was no dream. I was wide awake and that was just the way Val wanted it.

It was as if she'd given me the days to weather the shock of her death. Now she was coming to me and meaning business. So much for grieving, she as much as yelled at me. Now, big brother, what are you going to do about it? Some miserable bastard blows the back of my head off, what are you going to do about that? In my mind she wasn't taunting me, she wasn't playing games: she wanted an answer. She was a creature full of action, ready to go. And I've done my part, she was saying to me, I've taken the risks, I've gotten myself killed for my trouble, and I've left you enough clues to stock a mystery story. . . . I've raised the issue of Father Governeau and I hid the picture in the drum. . . . Now, for God's sake, pick up the ball and run with it. . . . Oh, big Ben, why can't I get through to you, you're such a goof. . . . Be brave for me, Ben, raise holy hell!

Along about midnight, with the house asleep, I'd had just about enough of my dear dead sister. Even her ghost was noisy. I should have known it would be. In death she was alive as ever, insistent, determined. I got up and slipped into a robe. She wasn't going to leave me alone and I was talking to myself when she interrupted me. You're burying me tomorrow, Ben, you're burying me . . . then I'll really be gone, gone, gone for good. . . .

"Don't pull that on me," I muttered. "I'll never be free of you, little sister, and we both know it and wouldn't have it any other way." I could hear her calling me a goof, fading away.

I needed some brandy. Maybe it would help me sleep, or put Val to sleep, if she were—as a ghost—some projection of my own psyche. I went downstairs, hearing the house creaking and moaning in the wind, all the ghosts scuttling about.

There was a light on in the Long Room.

Sandanato was sitting in one of the mustard-colored leather chairs, turned with its back to the cold fireplace.

"It's freezing in here," I said.

There was a bottle of brandy on the table beside him. A snifter held in both hands rested on his chest. A cigarette burned in the ashtray. He slowly looked at me. His eyelids drooped low and his face was haggard with sleeplessness. He showed no surprise at my appearance. "I couldn't sleep," he said. "And I'm afraid I found the brandy. Did I wake you?"

"No, no, I couldn't sleep either. Thinking about the funeral tomorrow. It's going to be crazy around here. Half the mourners are expecting my sister to rise from the dead and proclaim salvation for all good Catholics, the other half are figuring she had a pact with Satan and has gone directly to eternal hellfire. More or less. My nerves are on edge."

He nodded. "You sound as if you have nearly as many problems as I—may I offer you some of your own brandy, Mr. Driskill?"

"Indeed you may." He poured a generous measure and I suggested he pour some more. "And . . . when." He stopped pouring and handed me the snifter. "Thank you, Monsignor. May sleep find us in due time." We drank to that.

"May I ask, are you the painter? It is a remarkable work. Quite remarkable. True feeling. Spirituality."

For a moment I hadn't the vaguest notion of what he meant, then he took a drag from the cigarette and waved his hand toward the end of the room. Then I saw it.

He'd removed the sheet from the easel. There was no way, of course, that he could have known of my father's prohibition against the viewing of his works in progress. I strained to see the canvas through the dim light cast by the table lamp.

"My father. He's the painter."

"A fine sense of theatricality. As well as a grasp of Church history. Has he ever painted any of the great monastic ruins? There are some incredibly dramatic vistas. . . . But this, this is very fine. You haven't seen it before?"

"No, actually I haven't. He never shows us his work before it's finished."

"Then it will be our secret. The vanity of the true artist." He unfolded himself from the chair, his profile against the light. His nose had a slightly aquiline aspect. There was a faint patina of perspiration on his face though the room was so cold. "Come, take a closer look. You will, I believe, find it particularly fascinating—if you still have an eye for Catholic things." He exhaled, a cloud of smoke obscured his features.

"Still?"

"Your sister once mentioned that you had spent time as a Jesuit. And then"—he shrugged—"you fell away."

"How delicate."

"Ah. I must say she put it more in the patois of the street. Your sister has—had—a very colorful grasp of idiom."

"I'll bet she did. I *know* she did."

"Tell me, why did you leave the seminary?"

"A woman."

"Would you say that she was worth it?"

"Isn't that in my dossier?"

"Come, come. What do you mean? There is no dossier—"

"Forget it. Just a middle-of-the-night remark—"

"So, was this woman worth it?"

"Who knows? Perhaps someday I'll find an answer."

"Do I hear the trumpet sound regret?"

"I think you've got entirely the wrong end of the stick, Monsignor. I left because of the Virgin. I couldn't buy her and all the rest of the act anymore—"

"And you wonder now if she was a good enough reason to leave?"

"My only regret is that I used her as an excuse. There were so many better reasons."

His smile had lost the edge of remoteness. "So much for autobiography. Come, look at your father's painting."

We went to the easel and I turned on another lamp and there was the Emperor Constantine seeing the sign in the sky. In his forceful, primitive style, a storytelling style, my father had captured the moment that changed the history of the West for all time. Monsignor Sandanato regarded the canvas, his chin cupped in his hand, squinting through the smoke, and he began to talk as if I were no longer there, as if he were informing a heathen of what had happened a long time ago on the road to Rome. He was talking about the blood red Church. . . .

The history of the Church had always been a cluttered tapestry, full of screaming faces and flayed flesh, soaked in the gore of unbridled ambition and greed and corruption, scheming and plotting and armies on the march. It had always been necessary to balance the worldliness, the evil, and the power, against the goodness, the selflessness, the faith and the hope it held out to man, the hope and promise that made an otherwise intolerable existence somehow endurable. No matter whom the Church was torturing and killing at a given moment, it was men who were doing it, men and not the faith for which the Church stood. Men were always good and bad, but the faith in the idea that Christ had died for our sins, that man in his weakness and frailty was redeemed eternally in Christ—the message of faith always tipped the scale. The good was always greater, that was what they taught us, but sometimes the issue was in doubt. More often than not, it seemed to me.

"Until the twenty-seventh of October in the year 312," Sandanato was saying, "it was a relatively simple, if not altogether pleasant business, being a Christian. You might be fed to a lion, or spend your life bent double shackled wrist to ankle, a pack of Roman toughs might beat you to death in an alley for the sheer sport of it, or you might find yourself crucified at the side of a Roman road to serve as an object lesson, but you certainly knew how things stood between you and the rest of the world. Wealth, power, and pleasure were evil . . . and poverty, faith in God, and the promise of salvation were what your existence consisted of." This might be Sandanato's idea of a midnight bull session, but I had to admit it carried me back. I felt strangely comfortable with it, there was no point in denying it. It was making me begin thinking like a Catholic again.

27 October 312.

Constantine, a German, thirty-one years old, fluent in six languages, a pagan warrior-king who ruled the West from Scotland to the Black Sea, was preparing for a crucial battle at one of Rome's great bridges, the Milvian. As dusk came, knowing that the morning would bring the ferocity of battle, Constantine had a vision . . . and the world ever after was an utterly different place. In the sky, reddish-gold in the glow of the setting sun, he saw the cross of Jesus and he heard a voice, just as Paul had heard it on the road to Damascus. "In this sign you will conquer." In the morning he joined the battle with his soldiers' shields and their horses' heads painted with the sign of the cross. And the battle was won. Rome was his and he had no doubt as to why. The power of Jesus had carried him to victory.

28 October 312.

Still drenched in sweat, spattered with blood, and caked with the muck of battle, he demanded to be taken to the Trastevere section of Rome, where a terrified little brown man was brought before him. Miltiades, the pope. Miltiades had spent his life in hiding, ever fearful of capture and the inevitable execution, and he feared the worst. He was so unlearned that he required a translator to understand Constantine's perfect court Latin. He trembled before the tall, blond Teuton. But the message was clear. He nearly fainted as he listened.

From now on everything would be different, new, better. Rome would be Christian. The emperor would wear a nail from Christ's crucifixion in his crown, another would be turned into a bit for his horse so it would always be with him in battle.

The next day Constantine and his family rode with Miltiades and his first priest, Silvester, past the stadium of Caligula and the temples of Apollo and Cybele to the cemetery atop Vatican Hill, where Constantine knelt in prayer over the bones of Peter and Paul. As the party strolled the cemetery grounds, the emperor sketched out his plans: a basilica in the name of Peter would be built here, over his remains, and Paul's bones would be removed to that place on the road to Ostia, where he had been killed, where another basilica would be built. But that wasn't all. Constantine was now a man with a mission. The party went to the Lateran Hill, which was covered by the palaces of the ancient Roman family of Laterani. Constantine flung open the gates: "Henceforth, this is the House of Miltiades and of every successor of the blessed apostle, Peter."

Fifteen months later Miltiades was dead and Silvester was pope, crowned by Constantine. Silvester, the first truly secular pope, grasped, with an acuity far beyond that of Miltiades, the new and undeniable future of the Church. It was Silvester who forged the bond between Church and empire, thereby guaranteeing the first worldwide Church carried forth along those straight Roman roads to every corner of the vast domain. It was Silvester who heard Constantine's confession. It was Silvester who saw that the triumph of Christ need not wait for the Second Coming. Jesus Christ could reign with the power of Rome throughout the world, governed through the offices of Peter's successors. The Church seemed unlimited in its scope.

"For three centuries we had barely existed in the world," Sandanato said, "hunted and martyred and in hiding. Now Silvester had the great chance to make the Church *of the world*. Jesus had spoken to Constantine, converted him, and Constantine was the means of converting the rest of the world. Spiritualism was now wedded for good to wealth and pomp and force. With Constantine behind him, Silvester could now harken back to what Jesus had once said to Peter at Mount Hermon." Sandanato stopped, looked at me, as if waiting for my Catholic memory to supply the quotation. Somehow, from the subconscious depths, it did.

" 'I give unto you the keys of the Kingdom of Heaven,' " I recited. " 'Whatever you allow on earth will be whatever Heaven allows. Whatever you forbid on earth will be whatever Heaven forbids.' "

"Exactly," Sandanato said. "For the first time in history the successor to Peter had some firepower anyone could understand. And of course he, along with his Church, fell prey to it. More than ever, in the centuries to come, violence haunted us, has never left us in peace. . . .

"It's the price of Constantine," Sandanato was saying. "Once we accepted the secular power, we had to pay the secular price. With the power came the power seekers, the challengers, those who would have stripped us of our military alliances and the vast wealth at our disposal. Our history is a history of the threats made against us, the compromises we've had to make. But, until now, Mr. Driskill, we've always known who our enemies are. Even when the challenge was most drastic, we knew what was happening. You'll of course remember that ungodly hot August of 1870 . . ."

As it happened, I remembered it well, as many a seminarian was bound to. It was when the secular world finally turned against the Church. But what occurred that long, agonizing summer a bit over a century ago had really begun in 1823 and stretched twenty-three years through the pontificates of Leo XII, Pius VIII, and Gregory XVI: twenty-three years of papal oppression and dictatorship in the city of Rome and throughout the Papal States, where the pope-kings reigned. Nearly a quarter of a million citizens had been put to death, or sentenced to life imprisonment, or exiled for committing political offenses—that is, for incurring the displeasure of the Church. Books were censored, people were forbidden to congregate in groups larger than three, travel was strictly curtailed, and tribunals were in session everywhere to sit in severest judgment on the accused. The trials were conducted entirely in Latin; consequently, rare was the man who understood of what he had been accused. Justice ceased to exist under these popes, and was replaced by violent caprice, the restoration by Leo XII of the Inquisition and its inhuman tortures, and popes who would not listen to the pleas of the people they ruled. Every town square was decorated with a permanent gallows, always in readiness to receive those who ran afoul of the Church.

Secret societies proliferated. Assassinations became a way of life. And when the people of Bologna, for example, revolted, they were brutally suppressed. Austrian troops seemed always to be responding to a pope's call, crossing the borders of the Papal States to practice the arts of war on the rebellious citizenry. But the tide of history was running against the old ways, and in 1843 the people—the *mob,* in the eyes of the Church—took over the city of Rome.

Pius IX was elected pope in 1846 and the world he inherited was a desperate one, at least as viewed from the papal palace. Garibaldi and Mazzini were in full cry and, not long after ascending to the Throne of Peter, Pius fled Rome by night in the open carriage of the Bavarian minister, didn't stop until he got to Naples, then scurried from one hiding place to another as the Romans proclaimed a republic, symbolically dispensed with the pope, murdered clergy, and despoiled the churches. He was finally able to return to Rome four years later, when the French Army took the city and Mazzini fled to Switzerland and Garibaldi returned to the mountains. Pius IX was back, it was true, supported by the might of a foreign power, but the fact was—and Pius knew it—that the handwriting on the wall of the Lateran Palace was finally indelible.

Pius IX had begun his reign on a wave of popularity and had

responded by trying to give his people what they wanted. He expelled the Jesuits, gave the okay for publication of a popular newspaper, razed the ghetto, saw to the first use of a railway in the Papal States: he proclaimed a civil constitution—all in an effort to undo the evils of the past quarter century. But it came to nothing. History, like a runaway coach and six, ran him down. The people wanted the future, not the past, and the future lay not in being owned by the pope but in belonging to the new Italian nation.

A climax had been reached with the assassination of the pope's prime minister, Rossi, an elegant aristocrat, on the steps of the Quirinal Palace. A crowd had gathered as Rossi left the main doors at the top of the famous steps. Halfway down, the flash of a young man's dagger, the blade in the throat, then Rossi tumbling and the blood spurting across the steps, the mob growling with pure hatred . . . and above at the window of his study, Pius watching. That was an image which haunted all my years of study and which has remained, engraved on what was once my Catholic conscience.

In the past, when things of the world had encroached on the power of the papacy, there had always been worldly recourse, an army to be summoned. Silvester I, Leo III, Gregory VIII, Clement VII—they had all withstood the secular challenge by calling for one soldiery or another, but in 1869 there was nowhere left to turn, no army to call upon to save the papacy. A de facto decision had been made in the capitals of Europe: the papacy was through. The *Times* of London referred to "the final passing of this venerable institution." When I first studied the period I can recall thinking in amazement, could my father know that things had ever been so bad for the Church? It didn't seem possible that such a situation had existed without his telling me, warning me, but of course he was simply doing all he could to make sure it didn't happen again.

Never in all the centuries since the vision had appeared to Constantine had the situation been so grave, but still Pius had a hole card and no choice but to play it. He turned to the power Jesus had conferred on Peter, the power of the spirit. In July 1869 the principle of infallibility was declared by the bishops, as well as what the Church called primacy. The pope was now incapable of error in matters of morals and faith; he must be obeyed. And as primate, his teachings and jurisdiction could not be superseded or replaced by any man or group in all Christianity. The Church had declared the man at its head the ultimate spiritual leader and authority on earth and dared anyone to deny or ignore it.

There was a hollow ring to this claim, however, and no one knew it better than Pius. While the spiritual battle might have been won, in a secular world the secular battle had been lost.

It was not merely a matter of metaphor. The battle was a fact and the French, falling back before the Prussian advance in August 1870, were leaving Rome that day, the nineteenth. General Kanzler's army of fewer than four thousand was all that stood between the integrity of the last pope-king and General Cadorna's Italian national army of sixty thousand men less than a day's march from the walls of Rome. Pius, with nowhere to turn, ordered only a token resistance, then surrender.

King Victor Emmanuel, leading his new nation, had won. Rome would be capital of all Italy. On the twentieth, at sunrise, the Italian cannon commenced firing.

Fewer than five hours later the white flag flew from the dome of St. Peter's.

In October a plebiscite was held throughout the Papal States. The votes cast in favor of joining the Italian republic numbered 132,681. There were only 1,505 against. In the spring of 1871 the Italian parliament guaranteed the pope's sovereignty over his reduced world, which would henceforth consist of the Vatican, the Lateran, and the summer home at Castel Gandolfo. Pius bitterly responded then and for the rest of his life: "We will be a prisoner."

Not until 1929, when Pius XI reached his accommodation with Benito Mussolini with the signing of the Lateran Pacts was the Church free once more to operate at will in the worlds of power, finance, and politics.

Sandanato's tiny gold lighter flared; I smelled the Gauloise, felt the blown smoke brush my face.

"Violence is nothing new," he said, "we both know that. Violence in the Church exercised considerable fascination for your sister. Or so I was told by His Eminence. We've always suffered it, but now it's running amok, isn't it? And we can't identify the enemy. You see, we've always known in the past who the enemy was. But now we have three freshly dead and we're afraid and there's no army to call upon to come crashing in to save us . . . those days are gone. Here we are, all alone, unarmed, in a darkening world." I sensed that despite the somber words he was smiling sadly. He seemed to relax when the subject was violence. Maybe he just wanted it out in the open. We were in the middle of murder. He lifted his brandy glass. It was nearly four o'clock, the morning of my sister's funeral, and I was finally tired, ready for sleep.

"Confusion to our enemies," he said.

I looked at him sharply. "You can say that again, pal."

My sister's funeral passed me by in a foggy blur of activities I performed by rote. It was all happening at one remove from me. I played my part, and rather to my surprise I carried it off all right. Not bad, since I was up to my eyeballs in eagle-eyed Catholics and precious ritual and their half-cocked celebratory mass. I'd always wondered what it really was they were celebrating at the funeral mass. Of course I got the stock answer, all about celebrating the life of the late departed guest of honor. For nearly a quarter of a century all that had struck me as a crock of the best. Never more so than at my mother's funeral. Not my idea of a cause for celebration, poor and lonely and ultimately demented wench she was.

Val's funeral was different. Hers was a life worth celebrating, a death worth avenging.

Peaches said the mass at the little church over in New Pru. We'd kept the crowd down, maybe fifty or sixty, most of them drawn from the ranks of the mighty, mightier, and mightiest. The President's representative, a couple of governors, three senators, some cabinet members and lawyers and fixers and all the rest of the riffraff who are determined to believe they make the world go round. There were five or six television crews held at bay by the state police. We did our best, Margaret and Father Dunn and Sister Elizabeth and I, to keep it under control, but it was still tinged with the stains of the "media event."

I'd never seen Peaches at work before, and I was impressed. It had to be an ordeal for him. The smell of the incense—so well remembered across the years—filled the place. The casket gleamed dully, like burnished gold, and they went through all the rigmarole I recognized from years before. I received communion, first time in all those years, and it was all different—no kneeling at the altar rail the way it used to be, and receiving not only the host but the blood of Christ as well. Maybe the differences made it easier. It didn't seem real. For God's sake, it was my little sister up there.

I delivered the eulogy: the surviving brother and all. From the occasional sniffles and at other moments the smiling, nodding heads, I judged it a success. I kept my remarks at arm's length from my own emotions. Val would have enjoyed it, my kind and sanctimonious words, a joke between us, like so many others. I couldn't have managed it any other way. I would not have chosen this particular crowd to view my bared soul. When it was over, there was a hymn and the mourners were filing out and the show was pretty much done for.

Val was buried in the graveyard attached to the little church. The gravestones went back a long way. And there was a Driskill family plot. My mother lay there, my father's parents. Now Val. There was plenty of room for my father and me. No big monuments for us: just stern headstones. Our work, my father used to say, would be our monument. It always made me think of the poem, "Ozymandias," which I'd memorized at school. Look on my works, ye mighty, and despair . . .

The wind was angry and cold, cutting through us, and I was damned if I'd stand there with my teeth chattering and tears freezing on my face while I watched the box disappear into the earth. I was already bothered by the irrational hatred of her being laid to rest, buried: the hatred coming from the childish but nonetheless powerful notion that it was in fact the conscious, living Val stuck out there in the cold, dark nights to come. I left the small group of close family friends who'd hung around for the final act of the day's drama and strolled away on my own. Sister Elizabeth and Margaret Korder were stuck with them.

I found myself under the dark gray clouds standing at the black iron railing marking the edge of the cemetery proper. But beyond the railing was a small cluster of overgrown markers. I opened the gate and went through. I'd never noticed those sorry little gravestones before, but now something—my subconscious, or maybe fate—drew me toward them.

Father Vincent Governeau's grave was covered over with thistle and crabgrass, the stone flat on the ground, his name and the dates small, hardly visible—1902–1936. He wasn't allowed a grave in consecrated ground.

I must have been standing there longer than I'd realized because Sister Elizabeth had finished up at the graveside and come to join me. She knelt down to inspect what had caught my attention. She was wearing a modified version of the Order's old traditional habit, one she'd found in Val's closet. Seeing her in it had thrown me at first. She looked like someone else, someone in costume. When she saw the name on the marker her hand flew to her mouth. "Oh, my God!"

"Poor son of a bitch," I said. "You can imagine the kind of burial he got from the good fathers of the Church. Swept his whole life under the rug, dropped him down a hole, and pretended he'd never lived at all. Because he was a suicide. When in fact he was murdered. Sister, he belongs inside the cemetery, not out here in the nether regions. . . ."

Walking back across the graveyard, she took my arm. "You were very good up there, Ben. Val would have been—"

"In stitches. Don't kid yourself."

"You were very good, nonetheless. She'd have been proud."

"You want to hear something funny?"

"What?"

"I don't even remember what I said."

"Oh, Ben. If you were half as tough as you act, I'd hate you."

"Then don't look too close, my dear. Val knew the truth about me. That's why she left the snapshot."

"I wonder . . ."

"Val spent her whole life fighting for what she believed was right. Get on her wrong side and you'd find out she was an avenging angel. She was a whole lot tougher than I am."

"Maybe I never really knew her—"

"You knew her. You *knew* her. Better to admit that to yourself. Now, you'd better prepare yourself for all the hoopla at the house."

"Did you see Sister Mary Angelina?"

"I didn't see much of anything."

"She said she came directly from your father. He wanted her to come back and tell him how it went—"

"What is this, Sister? A November and December romance?"

The house was packed full of people I knew vaguely. I doubted if Val would have known more than one in ten: they were my father's friends and cronies. The banking community, the CIA pensioners list, Princeton University, presidential aspirants of both then and now, the Church, the law—they were all wolfing down turkey and ham and liquor like refugees from welfare. The Garritys had laid on extra staff. The whole thing was impossible.

Father Dunn was leading the immense Archbishop Cardinal Klammer from group to group like an elephant in the early stages of training. Peaches, Sam Turner, some other locals, were trying not to gawk at all these veterans of *Meet the Press* and *Face the Nation*. Sister Elizabeth was assisting Margaret Korder, a pair of ringmasters keeping the circus going.

But the man I was looking for wasn't there.

The library was off limits for the day. I knew that was where I'd find him.

Drew Summerhays was standing by a window in the book-lined room, thumbing through a first edition of *Ashenden* that Somerset Maugham had inscribed to my father. Summerhays had introduced them one summer at Cap d'Antibes and they'd hit it off, two of a kind.

He looked up from the book when I came in. He smiled at me with his thin-lipped, bloodless mouth. He was spare as a hoe handle and wore a charcoal-gray suit and vest, a Phi Beta Kappa key on a gold chain—Harvard, of course—the scarlet thread of the Légion d'Honneur in his buttonhole, highly polished black cap toes from Jermyn Street, a black knit tie, a white shirt, a signet ring on the little finger of his right hand. *The* lawyer. He was a man who played in a league of one anymore.

"Did I ever tell you that Maugham is my favorite author, Ben?"

"Why, no, I don't believe you ever did."

"Willie had quite a stammer, y'know. I had a similar affliction as a boy. I cured mine, he cured his. Effort of will. Good a reason as any to make him my favorite writer. Your father was fond of Willie. They used to swap spy stories. Two different wars, of course. What's the latest on your father, Ben?"

"Putting up a good front. He's going to make it, Drew. Quite a scare."

"Your father's a hard man to scare."

"I meant me. I was scared. I'm very easy to scare."

"You and your father," he mused, then let the phrase drop. He believed my father and I were, beneath it all, birds of a feather, more alike than either of us cared to admit. He'd said so frequently in the past. "So you're easy to scare. You sound like a man indulging in false modesty. Or a man trying to set me up, you rascal."

"Just a curious rascal. I was looking for you, Drew."

"I came in here to get away from the crowd. Funerals and the gathering that follows—I'm too much aware that I'll be the main attraction someday soon. Poor darling Val. What a sorry day this is—"

"Were you one of her supporters?"

"I know too much to support anyone in the sense you mean. I wished her well. I respected her views. And on occasion I raised money for her work."

"So who killed her, Drew?"

"First you have to find out why, Ben. Then who follows."

"I've been thinking the same thing. Why did someone kill my sister? Did she die for her views on the Church?"

"I shouldn't think so—not for her philosophical attitudes, nor even for her attempts to implement them. But that's only one man's opinion. One would have to take an extraordinarily close look at Val's life . . . looking for the *why*. It's there for the one who looks assiduously. But you must have given all this rather a lot of thought over these past few days. You look at things like a lawyer, you've no choice, have you? Gathering evidence, building a case, rebuilding the elephant." He saw the puzzlement on my face. "You know what Rodin said when they asked him how he would sculpt an elephant. He said he'd start with a very large block of stone and remove everything that wasn't an elephant. Well, what you have is a floor covered with the chips of Val's life. Fit them all together and you'll see the outline of a killer. Val will be gone but you'll know the killer." He turned and replaced the book on the shelf.

"I want to know about Curtis Lockhardt. And Heffernan. They were singled out to die along with Val. Val was thinking about leaving the Order to marry Lockhardt—"

"Forget Heffernan, Ben. He got killed because of Lockhardt. By himself he was exactly what he liked to call himself—just another mick priest on the make. Get me my coat, Ben. Let's take a walk. Let's talk about the late Mr. Lockhardt."

He wore a soft homburg straight on his head and a black cashmere scarf and black gloves, a black chesterfield with narrow, high-cut arms and very square shoulders. He could have slit a man's throat with the crease in his trousers. His narrow face was pink in the wind that rustled leaves across the frozen lawn. We headed out past the chapel toward the orchard and the pond beyond where we ice-skated in years gone by.

"Curtis Lockhardt," Summerhays began as soon as we were clear of the babble of the house, "saw himself in a great many roles, like an actor moving on from one play to another. But at bedrock he knew he was an old-fashioned fixer with a lineage that ran back to Boston in the years following the Revolutionary War. You might say that Lockhardts had always been fixers, the way other men might work with their hands and could build a shelf or a stair or a chicken coop or a lobster trap. . . ."

Summerhays described a man who would always be among those composing the "secret government," the "government within the government," and the "Church within the Church." Lockhardt had learned his lessons at my father's knee.

"But," Drew Summerhays was saying as we stood among the leafless trees in the orchard where my father had found Father Governeau dangling from a limb, "Curtis always reckoned his greatest accomplishment was taking little Salvatore di Mona and turning him into Pope Callistus IV. You had to hand it to Lockhardt, you really did. He set out to buy a pope and, by God, he did."

It had come about because he sat on the board of the Conway Foundation in Philadelphia. Lockhardt had watched in curious wonder as Ord Conway, known as "the old fart" by his employees, concluded that he wanted his own personal pope. In the end Ord had turned to Lockhardt and Lockhardt had acquired a pope for 5.8 million dollars and change, fifteen million less than it cost Nelson Doubleday to buy the New York Mets. The fact was, only a very few people even knew you *could* buy a pope. Ord lived two years into the reign of Callistus IV, but then, it was common knowledge that life positively abounded with amusing ironies.

For a time Lockhardt had thought Ord Conway a somewhat dim, conventional old Fascist, the weak tail-end to a great family line. Ord simply liked the Church the way it had been when he was a kid working on his catechism. Lockhardt watched the process, sensed the man's degree of commitment to undoing a few reforms and reversing the trend toward what he called "a democratic Church." Ord had always said that democracy was all right in its place, but, goddammit, the Church wasn't the place. "Catholics," he used to say, "ain't supposed to vote on what the fuck they're gonna believe! They ain't got a say in it—that's the whole damn point!"

Lockhardt was working on a plan. The realization that Conway was only trying to bring back the old days and make peace with his own psyche made him the perfect tool. There was a lovely symmetry to the elements. Conway wanted to believe he would see a return to the Church of his boyhood. Monsignor Andy Heffernan wanted to get on the inside track to a cardinalate. And Lockhardt wanted to preserve the status quo, more or less. It would take some money, but that was no problem: Ord Conway was begging to be separated from some of his. And there would have to be a deal made: the nature of things demanded it. Curtis Lockhardt was in his element.

The birth control clinic in Bolivia was the perfect vehicle. It was liberal but not *too* liberal. That was a sign of how much things had changed. A lot of Catholics in positions of power, if not in that bastion of bureaucratic conservatism the Roman curia itself, believed the clinic was a strong, socially responsible step. It no longer was in opposition to the great subtext of Church teachings, not since Pope Paul's commission, which had been the pivotal event of the Church's recent history.

Curtis Lockhardt loved nothing more than putting these puzzles together. Give him just a few oddly shaped pieces and he could put his flair to work. He could fix it. Not for nothing had Cardinal Salvatore di Mona, on the eve of his subsequent election, told Lockhardt that he had missed his calling. "You belong in this scarlet robe, my dear Curtis, this robe and this biretta. There'd be no stopping you."

Lockhardt had been pleased. "But there's no stopping me in any case, Eminence."

But that moment came long after Lockhardt had seen a way of using Paul VI's poor battered soul as a lever in what he'd come to think of as the Conway affair.

It had begun with John XXIII. It had been his birth control commission to begin with. Then it had passed to Paul, who increased its size, removed it from Vatican Council control, and thereby made it hugely important. The world's Catholics had been turning to the pill all through the sixties, tens of millions of Catholics ignoring the official teachings of the Church. Now Paul's commission had a mandate from the pontiff himself to find a loophole in official doctrine—to find a way to make honest Catholics once again of all those practicing birth control. Obviously, if Paul had wanted no change in doctrinal interpretation, he'd have "dropped the commission in the Tiber," as one cardinal observed at the time.

When the commission's report was complete, they had indeed found the loophole, concluding that as long as a whole marriage relationship was open to the bearing of children, then each individual act of intercourse within it did not have to be open.

That was it, the crucial doctrinal breakthrough that might have brought the Church, in Lockhardt's view, fully into the twentieth century. And might have returned so many of the faithful back to the fold.

But Paul's conscience—and the backstage maneuvering of Vatican conservatives playing on that conscience—had caused him, miraculously, to ignore the commission's report. His encyclical, *Humanae Vitae,* utterly rejected the commission's findings and delivered the Church a blow from which it had not yet recovered. There was always a turning point, Lockhardt believed, and in his view *Humanae Vitae* had marked the end of the old conservative Church. It was now going to go one way or the other, backward or forward. Either the Church would remain in the hands of the conservatives and crumble to dust, or it would be seized by the moderates and liberals who had a vision of a new future and a changing, adapting Church.

The issue was far from decided—the turning point might, after all, last for years, decades—when the Conway affair began. Lockhardt had seen it all at once, the beginning and the middle and the end, one afternoon at the Conway Foundation board meeting. It must have been akin to the moment when I'd suddenly grasped the pure essence of football. Lockhardt had had his game and I mine.

"It was at this point," Summerhays said as we stood looking out across the shallow iced pond toward the gray horizon, "that Lockhardt turned to a couple of fellow board members—your father and me—and suggested a drink once the meeting was over. Lockhardt modestly believed that Hugh Driskill and I were his only equals at fixing things on earth."

The three of them met at a club Lockhardt used in Philadelphia. Hugh Driskill had listened quietly, then said, "The question, Curtis, is simply this. Can you convince Ord Conway that you can trade a birth control center in Bolivia and six million bucks for his idea of a fairly conservative pope?"

"I can."

"All right, Curtis," Hugh Driskill said, cocking an eye at Summerhays. "Tell us how."

Like so many great ideas, it was essentially simple.

Conway would present six million dollars to the Church, via the good offices of New York's Monsignor Heffernan. It would be earmarked for the birth control center, which would co-opt some moderate, progressive third world cardinals, some European intellectuals. But the money would in fact be used to collateralize a loan from a Roman bank to a bank in Panama and then shipped on to the Bolivian government. Conway's six million dollars would exist both on that piece of collateral paper and in another guise as well— would in fact become twelve million dollars. Or more. The point was, men like Lockhardt and Hugh Driskill and Summerhays and Cardinal D'Ambrizzi, who oversaw for the pope *L'Instituo per le Opere di Religione*—the Institute for Religious Works, as the Vatican Bank was euphemistically called, understood how you had to do business when it came to the Vatican.

"What was the second six million for?" Summerhays asked rhetorically. His eyes were fixed on a dog testing the ice of the pond, venturing out carefully, shaking each forepaw as it went. "To buy a pope. Your father and I agreed, Ben. It bore the stamp of a master."

In those days Octavia Cardinal Fangio presided over the Sacred Congregation for Bishops, which was located in a small square called the Square of Pius XII, the Savior of the City, just off St. Peter's. Fangio was a moderate, pragmatic, relatively greedy man who had more influence in the naming of bishops than any other man in the world. Popes took his advice and he was good at his job. From the ranks of his favorites came not only the bishops and archbishops but the cardinals as well. Fangio had let it be known that he was a candidate for the papacy—one of the *papabili*—but he was too young and he knew it. In another ten or twenty years, Fangio would no longer be too young and he would have made a lot of friends.

Hugh Driskill tumbled to it first. "You want to make the six million available to Fangio?"

"In a way," Lockhardt said. The fact was, Fangio's brother

Giovanni was a failed lawyer in Naples. Substantial investments had bottomed out for him. The villa in the mountains, the ancestral home, might be lost. Some of the six million would save the villa and set poor Giovanni back on his feet once again.

"And," Hugh Driskill murmured, "you suggest a small quid pro quo from Cardinal Fangio."

The pope had recently announced a new consistory—the selection of twenty-one new cardinals to replenish the dwindling supply. Lockhardt suggested that he, Hugh Driskill, and Summerhays might discuss these prospective cardinals with a couple of curial friends and Cardinal Fangio, arriving perhaps at the names of fifteen mutually acceptable candidates. For his efforts Fangio would salvage his brother and simultaneously create a hard core of support for his own papal candidacy when somewhere down the long road, when Lockhardt's present candidate had passed from the scene, his own candidacy would arise. And in the meantime the fifteen would vote as Fangio suggested. Monsignor Andy Heffernan could gain in Fangio an enormously valuable friend on a very fast track which led toward a cardinal's red hat for himself. Everybody would win, including Ord Conway, who would have in effect named the pope, at Lockhardt's suggestion, of course.

Summerhays turned and stared back through the naked orchard to the house. Darkness was drawing in on us. "Lockhardt spent a year or so putting this all together. And Fangio's men had proven good soldiers. And so it was, Ben, that Sal di Mona, an organization man, a good listener, a moderate, had become Callistus IV. And now Curtis Lockhardt was coming to New York to meet with Andy Heffernan while Callistus lies dying in Rome. Curtis knew the game was afoot again, don't you see? But now he won't know how it all turns out. Still, as the English would say, Curtis had a good innings." He sighed and looked at his watch. "Time to be going. Well, Ben, a word of advice in your ear. Get past all this as quickly as possible—Val's death, I mean. She's gone and she had a good innings, too. Don't you see? There's dangerous business here, serious players. Just step back and make it easy on yourself. Don't try to make sense of all the chips on the floor. You'll never succeed, you'll never see the outline of her killer. Speaking as one, to a man who once was one, let me say it's the Catholics, Ben. Best leave them to their own devices. Life's too short as it is."

He took my arm. He felt nearly weightless. Almost as if he'd begun to depart already, preparing for the final exit.

On the way back to the house I showed him the snapshot Val had left behind. He shook his head, said it meant nothing to him. He did identify D'Ambrizzi but his mind was on other matters. What difference could an old photograph make?

6

DRISKILL

The day after my sister's funeral was clear and cold and bright. I'd finally gotten to sleep the night before, but it hadn't been easy. My circuits were overloading and in the courtroom of my mind Drew Summerhays had been the last witness. Before I fell asleep I'd decided what I had to do. Only then had I realized—there had never been any doubt, none at all.

Monsignor Sandanato was in New York paying a courtesy call on Archbishop Cardinal Klammer. Sister Elizabeth was leaving for Rome that afternoon. I wanted to tell her my plan and if possible enlist her help. I wasn't prepared for it all to go wrong.

We were waiting for Father Dunn to pick her up. He said his car knew the way to Kennedy. The house was quiet and in the Long Room bowls of fresh flowers brightened things a bit. Sun streamed through the windows. There was a glare from outside and it was bitterly cold, the ground frosty and white. We were approaching a record low. I'd sent the Garritys home at noon and Margaret was attending to business at her HQ at the Nassau Inn. She handled the press and television people there. Sam Turner had kept the lone guard on duty outside. Sam was planning to keep him there until, in his words, everything blew over.

"Ben, it's been good seeing you," she said. She was dressed for travel, as she'd been when she arrived on Halloween night. "I wish I didn't have to go back now . . . everything seems so unfinished. But I've got to get back to the office. Callistus could die at any moment and then everything in my world will hit the fan—I've got to be there. But"—she put her hand on my arm, looked into my face with her searching green eyes—"I'm worried about you. I've been thinking about what you said, how you're ruthless, your father's son, and I'm wondering." She dropped her hand and stepped back from me as if she were suddenly embarrassed at having come too close, figuratively and literally. "So, I suppose you'll be going back to work yourself—" The sound of her voice had changed, grown remote.

"Not for a while," I said. "I'm taking a leave. I was on the phone to my partners this morning. You're right, Sister. It's unfinished. It's barely begun. I'm going to see it through. I'm going to finish it."

She looked up at me, startled, as if I'd cried out. "What do you mean?"

"I'm going to find out who killed my sister."

"How? What can you possibly do?"

"She would have wanted me to try. That's why she left me the snapshot, remember? I'm not going to let her down. That's all."

"You're wrong, you know." She dropped the words on me with precision. "Val would never have wanted you to put your life in danger. Oh, it sounds fine and I don't blame you—you're going out there and avenge her death. But face it, Ben, you don't have any real chance. The man is gone, there's nothing to follow. . . ."

"Look, I know what I'm doing—"

"Oh, Ben! Please just leave it! I've been thinking, too. I was up all night thinking, and it really hit me for the first time that Val was *killed*. Three people have been killed . . . and maybe all of it had to do with whatever Val was doing. Killing you would mean nothing to them at this point. And you know nothing about them, but they're watching you—don't you realize that? They could kill you anytime they want." She looked at me, perplexed, as if I were a backward schoolboy. "If you get too close, Ben, do you think they'd hesitate to kill you? Try to understand, this *is* like one of Dunn's novels. . . . Please leave it, Ben, just leave it!"

"I'm not going to argue with you, Sister. I'm going to see this thing through. Let's not quarrel."

"All right, suppose you do—what then? You learn what's going on, they kill you. Look, Val *knew* what she'd gotten into, she knew the risks but she believed it was worth it. Ben, for God's sake, you don't even know what she thought was so important—"

"You're wasting your breath," I said.

"I wish you'd just leave it to the authorities—"

"They haven't a hope in hell and you know it. You seriously think Val would have wanted me to walk away from this?"

"Val's dead, Ben. She's out of the game. Listen to me. Val . . . was . . . rash. She was brave but she was foolhardy—and I'm not. I hope to God you're not. She was out manning the barricades while I was observing, writing about it. Just because she pushed something too far and was killed—that doesn't mean we are honor bound to follow in her footsteps. . . . I know myself and I know I wasn't cut out to die for my principles. Were you? Really?"

"I'm not doing this because of my principles. I don't give a damn what my sister found out about your damned Church—"

"A madman in the Church—maybe. But not the Church itself! I won't listen to that, Ben, I just won't—"

"All right! Christ! Somebody killed my sister and somebody's going to pay! Why can't you see that, Elizabeth? It's simple enough."

"And why can't you see that the person most likely to pay is you?"

"Then you've made up your mind," I said. "You're going to just walk away from it."

"What do you expect me to do?"

I shrugged.

"Yes," she said, "I'm going to walk away from it—they're not going to carry me away from it. And I'm going to get on with my life—real life. The police can handle this, and there's the Church itself. . . . In Rome, when Sandanato makes his report, when they hear what Dunn's got to say, they're bound to do something."

"You could write about it. You were Val's best friend. You have a magazine—"

"Write wild suppositions about killer priests and torn pieces of raincoat and tattered snapshots and even a best-selling priest at the scene of the crime . . . you think I should write this? Ben, come on! There's a time to be realistic and this is it. It's one thing to sit around a table in the middle of the night making up a plot. It's something else to—"

"You simply don't care anymore, do you? It's become inconvenient for you—"

"That's a hateful thing to say, Ben. The truth is, I've had time to think, time to get things in perspective."

"Then," I said, feeling cold and sick to my stomach, betrayed, "we have nothing more to discuss, Sister." I told myself it was just the Catholics being Catholics. I'd let myself get too close to her. I'd let myself trust her. The old seduction.

Father Dunn had insisted on taking her to the airport. When he came by to get her it was not a happy parting. Tight-lipped, curt nods, and she was gone. It may have been that everything she said was true and inevitable. But I didn't want to hear it.

If I had let her convince me, if I'd let it all end there and allowed my sister's murder to go unquestioned, like Father Governeau's half a century before, I could not have lived with myself. It wasn't a question of what I wanted to do. I was facing what I had to do.

If I didn't, who would speak for the dead?

I spent the rest of the afternoon working myself into a truly rotten mood. The argument with Elizabeth had whipped me: it was so sadly fundamental. I believed in the reality of what had happened to Val; for Elizabeth reality was all the rest of life—her life in Rome, her commitment to the way things were, the reality of the Church. I had hoped—hell, I had *assumed*—that our shared love of my sister would make us natural allies in the search for her killer. I was convinced she had led me to feel that way: I knew I hadn't been imagining it. But I should never have assumed, not with a nun, not with one of *them*. Because when it came to the Church, brave talk was cheap: when the Church seemed to be involved in murder, then Sister Elizabeth had backed away.

When Sandanato got back from New York he found me sitting looking at my father's painting while the light slowly faded from the afternoon. I looked up as he dropped his coat on a chair and went to warm his hands at the fireplace. I told him he looked a little the worse for wear which was ridiculous coming from me. It was an English idiom he'd missed so I explained it and he nodded, slumped down in a chair with a doleful smile on his dark, haunted face.

"Klammer," he said, "certainly does wear one down. I don't know how Father Dunn stands it. It's difficult to have a conversation with the man. Nothing he says seems to follow logically from anything that went before. My brain is tired. And I'm cold. I've been cold ever since I got here. He made me go for a walk with him. Fifth Avenue, Rockefeller Center, the ice skaters. Beautiful. But cold." He shivered, leaned toward the fire. "And you don't look so wonderful yourself. . . ."

"Lousy day," I said. I needed a friend, a pal. I felt comfortable with Sandanato, which surprised me. Feeling easy with Dunn was simple: everything about him encouraged it. But the aura of tension Sandanato carried with him had kept me at a distance until now— I don't know, maybe it was the fact that I'd been sinking back into thinking like a Catholic. Maybe I recognized that tension because I'd carried it around for so long myself.

"Where's Sister Elizabeth? I've been looking forward all day to the cocktail hour, the three of us." I remembered what I'd said to Elizabeth. Now I wondered: did he love her?

"She's gone." I saw the smile fade. "Dunn took her to Kennedy. She's on her way to Rome."

"Ah. She must keep to that schedule of hers. The tyranny of her Filofax."

"She's what made my day so rotten."

"Really? I thought the two of you were great friends."

"Well, not after today, I guess." He was curious and I wanted to talk to someone, so I told him what had happened between Elizabeth and me, how she'd reacted to my determination to find out why Val had been murdered. He listened patiently, sympathetically. When I ran down and finally sat quietly staring at the fire, he took his time replying. He made us a couple of scotches with water and paced the length of the Long Room, where he stood contemplating my father's painting of Constantine.

"Women," he sighed. "They do see things differently, don't they? We are the avengers, they are the healers. It is as it should be. Sister Elizabeth wants life to go on; she sees your sister's death as a terrible aberration. Not to be dwelt upon. You see? But a man, he

must do something if his sister is killed. . . . I am Italian, I know
how you feel . . . but, but, but—"

"But what?"

"Reason is on her side." He shrugged expressively, resigned.
"You must see that. They could kill you, that's obvious."

"They? Who are they?"

"Who knows? I think it is possible we may never know."

"You're wrong. I'm going to find out."

"You are very much like your sister. I can see her when I look
at you, my friend. I can hear her when you speak. And like her,
you are both wrong and fearless. It is a dangerous combination.
She was like a keg of dynamite with a fuse lit. You are the same."

"You'd feel the same way I do."

"Yes, and you'd be telling me I had no chance. Your emotions
are killing you. Think—*they* know you, you don't know *them*.
That's really all that matters, isn't it?"

"My need is greater than theirs."

"Ah. How do you know this? You have no idea what stakes they
are playing for, do you?"

I brushed the implications aside. Logic was the last thing I
wanted to hear. "What do you think about Dunn's theory? That a
priest is the killer."

"I confess I do not know what you Americans get up to. It's
always guns and shooting. Maybe it is some crazy priest." The idea
seemed to exhaust him.

"It's not a crazy priest," I said. "There's something bad going on
inside the Church. A pustule has burst and killed three people—
the Church is in trouble and somebody's trying to solve the
problem with a gun." I decided to let my curiosity run. Elizabeth
had said Sandanato was either a Vatican insider or a monk. I
suspected he was both. She'd also called him D'Ambrizzi's conscience. "What is going on inside the Church? You must know it
all. The pope is supposed to be dying . . . you've got three fresh
murders. Is there some connection? Is the Church tearing itself
apart? Is it civil war?"

"The Church is always tearing itself apart." He was smoking a
Gauloise, his fingers nicotine-stained, his eyes in their customary
squint. A comma of black hair had fallen across his forehead and
he brushed it back. Was he thirty-five? Forty? I wondered how long
he would last. He looked the type to burn himself out. Elizabeth

had said Val thought he was a zealot, a maniac. It didn't seem likely: what Val had meant, no doubt, was that he disagreed with her. I was wondering what he thought of my sister when he began talking about her.

"Your sister is a case in point," he said. "No one could question the sincerity of her beliefs though many doubted her wisdom. But she had become a runaway train. The publicity, the books . . . by her nature she was the sort of person who rips and tears at the fabric of the Church. She was committed to the idea of changing the Church."

"I take it you doubted her wisdom."

"Your sister and I approached the Church differently. I was fascinated by the work of the Church, the systems of faith, by the Church as it was, as it had always been. Your sister was in her heart a humanist first, a Catholic second. I knew the Church was by nature a closed society. She believed that Church positions could or should be determined in some democratic way. I was concerned about man's soul and the means to his salvation. She believed in the Church as a kind of mighty welfare agency, devoted to the lives of its children on earth—"

"And you figure it's every man for himself?"

"The Church can do only so much," he said, smiling, refusing to take the bait, "and foremost it must deal with questions of eternal salvation. That is, after all, the point of the Church's existence, isn't it? Secular governments are supposed to deal with the living conditions of their citizenry. But not the Church. And to the extent that it involves itself in such pursuits it weakens its role as moral center. The Church is not about *now*. It is about *forever*. People are prone to forget that these days; they want life better now, they want a vote . . . You turn to the Church with a prayer, not a vote. There are other places to vote."

"So you and my sister were in fundamental opposition."

"Don't make too much of it," he said. "I sometimes find myself in disagreement with my boss, Cardinal D'Ambrizzi. These days disagreement is the standard within the Church—"

"Then you don't think my sister was killed for her beliefs?"

"I have no idea why she or Lockhardt or Heffernan were murdered."

I was thinking about Val, Sandanato, and Drew Summerhays's description of Lockhardt at work. How could they all have been so deeply, utterly, totally involved in the *same* Church? It seemed to me that they were each dealing with very separate Churches of their own.

"I'm going to find out." I sounded like a broken record. Maybe I meant I was going to discover whose Church was the real Church . . . or whose Church was destined to prevail. Maybe I could stop the kaleidoscope, freeze it long enough to see the pattern clearly.

"I must tell you then, my friend, my advice is the same as Sister Elizabeth's. Think twice, then make yourself think again. You'll be out of your element. And if you let it be, it will sort itself out. You're getting into something you really have no chance of understanding." He ground his cigarette out. "But if you're determined, why don't you come to Rome, fly back with me? Ask some questions, talk to Cardinal D'Ambrizzi—I understand you knew him when you were a child. I'm sure he would enjoy seeing you."

"Maybe my search will bring me to Rome," I said, sounding ponderous and unable to do anything about it. "But not now. I don't want the entire power structure of the Church telling me to butt out and mind my own business."

"I'm sorry," he said. "You know how it is. The Church is very jealous of its secrets."

"I'm sorry, too, but I'm committed to this—"

"We're all involved in seeking the truth of what has happened—"

"That's the difference. It's like ham and eggs. The pig's committed. The chicken is only involved."

The implication dawned on him, bursting through his formal command of English, and slowly he smiled, nodding that he understood.

Sandanato let you know where he stood. He wasn't afraid of telling me how and why he and Val parted company. I appreciated his willingness to put me in the picture as he saw it. He was, I decided, truly a Vatican lifer. He could keep his view of the Church's role apart from his personal relationships, yet when it counted, I was sure he'd back the Church to the hilt. The rest of the time he was happy to debate, conduct the intellectual exercise. He could blend theory and practice, balance them. After all, he was not only D'Ambrizzi's conscience: Elizabeth had said he was also the cardinal's chief of staff, and the cardinal was a worldly man. And in the end you could bet the house that he'd bring theory and practice together for the greater good of the Church as he saw it. Talking with him in the wake of my quarrel with Sister Elizabeth calmed me down, gave me a clearer set of bearings. I knew where he stood. But nothing changed my mind and I left Monsignor Sandanato in no doubt of that.

We went into Princeton together and took Margaret Korder to dinner at a little French place and talked primarily about the dogged efforts of the press to get to my father and me. At least they had the murders in New York City to occupy them. Sandanato bade her farewell in the lobby of the Nassau Inn, saying he hoped he would see her next in Rome. I told her I'd see her at the house in the morning.

It was a clear and frigid night. The moon was a silver stage prop. The stars were twinkling in the limitless depths of blue-black sky. Sandanato was leaving the next day. When we got to the house he went upstairs to pack. I was planning to visit my father the next day and tell him that I was going to track back through Val's last weeks—that my first stop was Alexandria. I had to know what she'd done those last days in Egypt. I was contemplating my itinerary when Sandanato came back downstairs.

He stood before me with a sheepish smile, an old pair of ice skates dangling from his hand. "I found these in the closet. I learned to skate once. I was ten and my father took us to Switzerland for a holiday. I haven't skated since. Do you think we might go out and try it?" He looked at his watch. "Ten o'clock. I'll probably never get another chance. And I could use the exercise. I'd sleep better."

It was so silly and unexpected that I jumped up and told him we could, indeed. The pond in back which was fed by the stream that circled and curled all through the countryside was frozen. I'd even noticed a couple of kids skating when Summerhays and I had taken our walk. For the first time in days I felt positively light-hearted. I found a pair of skates in a heap of old outdoor gear in the back hall, and we struck off toward the pond. This was something Val would have understood. As we walked across the crisp lawn together I could almost hear her laughing at us.

The moon was bright, nearly full, and the pond lay like a shiny silver dollar past the black silhouettes of the orchard. The chapel looked like an old-fashioned painting with the moonlight draped over the steeple. But I tried to ignore all the associations, my sister crumpled behind the wooden pew, the tree from which a killer had hanged Father Governeau.

We sat on the frozen ground changing from shoes to skates, laughing at ourselves, making jokes about who would be the worse skater. There was a sprinkling of dry snow blowing. My fingers were ice-cold as I fumbled with the laces, pulling them tight. The pond was relatively smooth, showing signs that the kids who'd skated the stream over from New Pru had had the foresight to bring a broom.

We staggered upright, holding on to each other as we edged onto the ice, two ridiculous figures, him in his black overcoat and me in my trench coat, pussyfooting across the slippery smoothness, testing our ankles. Muscle memory took over. I pushed off and glided a bit, wobbly, but without falling. In a few minutes I was sweating from the unfamiliar exertion, hearing myself grunting and panting, hearing in the back of my mind Val's distant laughter. The basic skill was coming back to me, and when I finally coasted to a stop I saw Sandanato swooping along, suddenly teetering, arms waving comically, and then he sat down hard and looked toward heaven as if pleading for divine intercession. He was slipping and sliding, trying to get up, and I tottered over to give him a hand and like two men in a silent movie we were both trapped in our clumsiness and collapsed together, sitting with our legs stretched out before us, gasping for breath, laughing. We finally managed to right ourselves. Moist white clouds were billowing from his mouth and nostrils. "Mother of God," he muttered, "whose idea was this?" He fumbled in his pocket, brought out a pack of cigarettes and, panting, lit one, dropped the little gold lighter back into his pocket. He gave me a determined, stern-jawed look and pushed off again, managing to stay upright as his outline grew dim against the dark background.

The dry snow was biting at my face, and I felt the sweat drying, cracking like ice. I watched him for a few moments, hoping it was as much fun as he'd expected. Then I went back to concentrating on my own endeavors, feeling my muscles stretching and relaxing, getting into the rhythm of my movements. My God, Val used to get hysterical watching me skate. She called me a trained bear. I was dripping with sweat when I chanced to see another fellow who'd come out that night to inaugurate the skating season.

Sandanato and I were at opposite ends of the oblong pond. I could just make him out. He wasn't so much skating as slowly, methodically, keeping from falling.

I was skating where the mouth of the stream entered our pond. The other fellow was fifty yards away in the moonlight, skating downstream toward me, his arms gently swinging as he came. I slowed as he approached, watching him, envying him his grace. I skated some big lazy circles, proud of myself for not crashing in an ungainly heap, though I wobbled rather badly when I modified my balance to wave to the newcomer.

He raised a hand casually in greeting. He was a much better skater, coming on steadily, the wind catching his coat and swirling it behind him. He was wearing a black fedora, and as he skated up to me I saw the moonlight flashing on the lenses of his glasses.

"Nice night," I said as he came close. I was breathing hard. His face was reddened by the wind. He was an older man, his face etched with deep lines, a strong face with a strong nose, and a wide, thin mouth.

"Yes, nice night," he said, and I couldn't understand why he wasn't stopping, why he was coming at me. Stupidly, I thought maybe he didn't know how to stop. And then in the last split second I knew there was something wrong.

He was holding something in his hand, low against the folds of the black coat. It was gleaming in the moonlight.

I turned away, toward Sandanato, who was still struggling to stay afoot a good fifty yards in the other direction, willing my legs to move, to get me some room, to get away from the man, but I wasn't going anywhere, I was slipping and sliding like a man caught in a nightmare, overcome with terror and soaked with freezing sweat and unable to get away, and I felt his hand on my shoulder, oh God, oh Christ, he wasn't knocking me down, he was trying to steady me . . . oh shit, steadying me for the gleaming blade. . . .

I tried to cry out to Sandanato, may have actually done so, just as I felt it, the pain arcing across my back from under my right arm. It was a sliver of cold, clean pain, like an icicle sliding under my skin, and I felt myself falling, saw the ice rushing up to meet my face, trying to brace myself, wanting to thrash my legs, hoping to trip him, and as his hand was trying to hold me up, I heard his voice muttering under his breath, *just a moment, Mr. Driskill, steady, steady,* and I heard the swish of his arm as he made another sweep with the blade and I heard it ripping through the fabric of my trench coat and then I was on the ice, trying to turn over on my back but suddenly robbed of the strength to do so. . . .

My face hit the ice hard and I felt my nose go, tasted a gush of blood, one eye against the ice, and with the other I saw the blades of his skates beside my face. I struggled to turn my head and I saw his face again. I was staring into the flat glass lenses, which seemed bottomless, empty, and while I looked up at him, feeling my back growing warm and wet, I saw his black fedora tip from his head in slow motion, slowly settle onto the ice, revealing silver hair combed straight back, wavy, incredibly silver in the moonlight.

Then he picked up the hat and he wasn't there anymore. I heard the silky whisper of the blades as he skated away. It had all taken ten seconds, and I couldn't seem to make myself move, and then poor Sandanato was panting and struggling toward me, reached me on his knees. I saw a tear in the trouser knee, and I heard him saying *Can you hear me, can you hear me?* and I kept answering him and he couldn't seem to hear me at all, and then his voice was growing fainter and fainter and then it was gone and I felt my face freezing against the smooth ice. . . .

PART TWO

The blues.

That's what her mother had called them. Elizabeth had never been one for falling prey to them—she was too active for that, too busy with the external world—but when they reached out and grabbed her on the 747 back to Rome she recognized them for what they were. The blues.

They had nothing to do with the shock and sorrow of Val's death. You could do your best to deal with all that. Your religious training helped you fight that. But the blues got under your skin, seeped into your bloodstream in a way that the Church and faith and discipline couldn't stop them, got hold of you when you weren't paying attention, and then it was too late. Then there was hell to pay.

It was the little girl on the plane who gave it a shape she could identify. The little girl in the seat ahead of her, six or seven years old, peering over the top of the seat at her in the darkened cabin.

They might have been the only two passengers who weren't asleep. The little girl with huge shining dark eyes and a short broad nose and a very solemn mouth and a blue and gold ribbon tied around her ponytail: it was the middle of the night, somewhere over the Atlantic, and Elizabeth felt the eyes staring at her.

Elizabeth smiled into the solemn face which came alive. She rested her chin on the back of the headrest. "My name is Daphne. My father calls me Daffy. I'm whispering because I don't want to wake my mother. What's your name?"

"Elizabeth."

"My mother is a light sleeper. So I have to be quiet and tiptoe and stuff. Why aren't you asleep?"

"I was thinking."

"Me, too." The little head nodded knowingly. "I was thinking about my friends. I'll see them tomorrow. What were you thinking about?"

"Friends, same as you."

"Will you see them tomorrow?"

"No, I'm afraid not."

"Do you live in Rome?"

"Yes. Do you?"

"We have a house in Chicago but my daddy works in Rome so we live there, too. Where's your house?"

"Via Veneto."

The little face brightened. "I know where that is. Via Veneto. Do you have a little girl? She and I could play together. . . ."

"Oh, I'm sorry, I don't . . . I wish . . ."

"What? What do you wish, Elizabeth? Do you wish you had a little girl?"

"Yes, Daphne. I wish I had a little girl. Just like you."

"Really?" She giggled behind her hand.

"Really."

"You can call me Daffy if you want."

That did it all right. The blues. It was a long night for Elizabeth.

She felt as if Val's spirit were overtaking her on the plane that night. Something was nagging at her, Val trying to tell her something, but it wasn't quite getting through. She put the headphones on and slipped one tape after another into her tape player. Billie Holiday, Stan Getz, Astrud Gilberto, Moody Blues, Jefferson Airplane, Mozart's "Jupiter" Symphony, Gustav Leonhardt's recording of Bach's concerti for harpsichord in F and C, one tape after another from her bag, her pen scratching at the pages in her Filofax while her mind dashed on elsewhere in search of Val. . . .

Val. She was trying to pull in her signal like some distant station's, but she couldn't do it. There was something Val wanted her to remember. It would come back, she told herself, it was bound to come back to her.

That was all bad enough, but when her thoughts turned to Ben it was even worse. She felt lousy about the way they'd left things between them. She hated the way she'd behaved, the argument. The fact was, he was right, absolutely right, and she wondered how and why she'd screwed everything up. She *had* wanted to work together to find out what had happened to Val; she'd been excited by the whole business, it had helped her cope with Val's death: finding the retired cop down at the bleak November shore, hearing about the murdered priest so long ago, theorizing late into the night with Ben and Father Dunn—

So why had it ended so badly, with her sudden sanctimonious defense of the Church? What had gotten into her? Maybe it was plain, simple fear catching up with her. It had hit her hard, with the clenched fist of realism, that Val was dead. Murdered, as if the truth that she'd sought had turned against her, struck her down.

Fear. Fear for herself if she pursued the inquiry, fear for Ben if he insisted on going after the killer. Her dearest friend was dead and she herself was sick with cowardice and she hated herself for it. She'd been a coward and . . . and she had trouble in the final instant quite believing that the Church could have reached out and killed Val to protect itself. She could believe so many things about this battle-scarred old Church, but not quite that.

Yet she'd never been the Church's tame little spokesperson, its apologist. No more than Val had been. She'd never been what Ben had accused her of being. And it wasn't fair that he should think that of her . . . *not fair!*

Then Daphne had poked her head over the chair and they'd had their little chat and Elizabeth had recognized the blues. And no, it had nothing to do with Val, nothing to do with the Church. Well, not exactly, anyway.

Daphne had set her thinking about little girls and love. Looking into the shining saucer eyes, she saw herself full of eager hope and

expectation so long ago in Illinois, her life before her like an endless
circus. She had looked into the child's eyes and felt the quickening
pulse, the flutter of the heart, the glimmer of love. The pang people
were always writing songs about. Daphne. The little hand over the
giggling mouth, Mother was a light sleeper, wishing Elizabeth had
a little girl . . .

Love.

Love was a problem for Elizabeth. When her guard was down,
it could waylay her, fill her heart, start a tear of longing in the
corner of her eye. The thing was, it always came from nowhere,
and when it started—not often, she was adept at staying busy,
fighting it off, declaring to herself that it was a complication she
neither wanted nor needed—but when it started it was like an
illness, a fever, that sapped her vitality, could hang on for days. The
pit of the stomach, ache in the heart longing for the warmth, the
touch, the dependency of another human being . . . What was it
but a longing for love, what was simply denied her by her vocation?

There were times when the longing took hold of her. Looking
into Daphne's eyes and thinking that she'd never have a Daphne of
her own. Talking at the kitchen table, cooking up a storm in the
coziness, watching Ben Driskill sitting there watching her . . .

Watching Ben Driskill watching her.

It had been good sharing the snowy night in Gramercy Park
with him, drinking beer at Pete's Tavern. And it had been good
these past few days, sharing time with Ben even in such unhappy
circumstances. In the house together, knowing they were under the
same roof, hearing him moving around even when they weren't in
the same room, talking to the old policeman together, sitting
together before the fire, finding the picture in the drum . . . sensing
Ben's irony and pain when it came to the Catholics, even feeling
the weight of his anger directed at her . . . He was life, he was out
there in the battle, he was willing to take the risks—

Damn! Her imagination was running wild, but, but . . .

She had led Ben on, she had wanted them to team up, there
was an inevitable male/female component to the time they spent
together: how could there not be?

But there wasn't supposed to be. No getting away from that.

But she'd enjoyed him so much. And been so furious when he'd
suggested that Monsignor Sandanato was obviously in love with
her. Her face had caught fire at that because of what she'd been

thinking about Ben and she'd wondered, was he laughing at her? It had been such a crazy thing to say. . . . He *had* been laughing at her, damn him, the nun as love object, ha-ha, that's a good one!

And she'd had those edgy little sensations a nun wasn't supposed to have and she'd thought Ben had sensed them, was laughing at her lack of experience, her self-consciousness.

Was that why she'd turned on him at the end?

Was her defense of the Church, her denial of the attitudes in him she'd been encouraging all along—was it because she had felt humiliated by him?

Or was it simply because she feared she might be falling in love with him?

Another woman—not a nun—might have thought an evening spent together in the past and a few days cloaked in the sorrow of a loved one's death hardly added up to an opportunity to fall in love. But another woman's relationship to men would have been entirely different. A nun was attuned to dealing with men, most of them priests, in a certain way, a very special way, that canceled out the romantic, the sensual. If you had any sense.

Her feelings for Ben weren't like that.

So she'd turned on him and made him despise her.

Nice work, Sister.

She arrived in Rome red-eyed and exhausted, her head pounding. Daphne gave her a good-bye hug with her mother looking proudly on, and Elizabeth felt again the magnetic pull of the huge, glistening eyes. Neither Daphne nor her mother, of course, could have guessed she was a nun.

In the taxi she rummaged through her Filofax, checking the notes she'd made during the flight, then had the driver take her to the tower on the Via Veneto. She changed into running gear, slipped the Beatles's *White Album* into her tape player, and went for a hard forty-five-minute run, working up a sweat, ridding herself of the night's stiffness.

After an ice-cold shower she stared unhappily at her reflection in the mirror over the sink. No makeup, hair soaking and bedraggled, face drawn, eyes dull. The face staring back at her reminded her of Sister Claire during her novice year. It was Claire who had summoned the Revlon representative to visit "the rookies," as she always called them, to instruct them in the subtle yet effective uses of cosmetics. "How can you expect to go forth and carry the word of God," she would say, "if you go around looking like Absolute Hell?" You could hear the capital letters when she spoke. And the lessons had worked. Well, there was no doubt she looked like A. H. at the moment, but ten minutes later she'd repaired the damage of a sleepless night and was ready to face the world, if not the Flesh and the Devil.

Hours later, as the busy reentry day wore to its conclusion, she sat alone in her office, the accumulated crises of the magazine at least momentarily laid to rest, and took her first break just to think. She sipped at a cup of cold coffee, put aside a stack of copy waiting to be proofed, and closed her eyes. Her subconscious had been puffing away all day, trying to excavate Val's passing remark which had eluded her memory.

Suddenly she opened her eyes. She'd heard a voice in the room with her. It took a fraction of a second, then she realized she'd been talking to herself, no, that wasn't quite right, she'd been talking to Val, and what scared her was that Val was answering. . . . It was a memory, of course, just a little time travel. They'd been waiting in the office one evening, Curtis Lockhardt was coming by to pick them up, the three of them were going out to dinner, one of his favorite fancy nightspots, somewhere new, and Val had been excited, her adrenaline pumping overtime. Elizabeth had asked her what was going on and Val had shaken her head, grinning, had said she couldn't tell her, but she was about to burst with the news. At dinner Lockhardt had mentioned someone he knew who'd died recently, someone who had something to do with the Church— damn, Elizabeth couldn't recall the name, had it been an Irishman? That seemed to stick in her mind—and Val's eyes had caught hers for just an instant and Val had said, "That makes five," and Lockhardt had stopped short and said, "What was that?" and Val said, "That makes five in a year," and Lockhardt had said something about this being hardly the time or the place and Val had mimicked Gilda Radner on the old *Saturday Night Live,* said, "Never mind . . ."

Five in a year . . .

Then the exhaustion hit her full on and she woke up hours later still at her desk and got home just in time to collapse in sleep for ten hours straight.

*   *   *

Work consumed the next several days.

She followed her normal routine which meant she had to chisel at each day to find seven or eight hours for sleep. There were interviews, editorial and production meetings, printers to schedule, last-minute copy to deal with, translators to pacify into working overtime, press conferences, visiting dignitaries to join for tea at the Order's headquarters at the top of the Spanish Steps, dinners with one delegation or another from Africa to Los Angeles to Tokyo. From all over the world they came to the Holy City, tirelessly, unceasingly, all the pilgrims, the rich and the impoverished, the saints and the cynics, the selfless and the greedy, bearing the hopes and prayers of their Church, hoping for the best or aiming to line their pockets or determined to work their will upon the immense sprawling creature that was the Church of Rome. And Elizabeth reported, interpreted, and recorded their comings and goings. And she listened; she never stopped listening.

In the days following her return, everywhere she went they were talking about the pope's health. The journalists had set up pools, predicting the timing of his death. The interest in the betting ebbed and flowed with the rumors. The word was always making the rounds that His Holiness had taken a turn—but whether for better or worse depended on your informant. The stock of the various *papabili* rose and fell like mercury in a series of thermometers. D'Ambrizzi and Indelicato were the favorites, but others had support as well. Everybody was a handicapper.

And there was the subject of the murders of Sister Val, Lockhardt, and Heffernan in far-off America, where such things might happen on any street corner. Still, even for America it was quite a triple. She was besieged with questions. She fended them off as best she could. She played dumb. She told no one about the killer-priest theory: in Rome that was a fuse she knew better than to light. Not a word had appeared anywhere, and she wasn't going to be the source of such an incendiary rumor. Consequently, alone with the killer priest ricocheting around in her brain, she began to feel claustrophobic, trapped alone with what she knew perfectly well was the truth.

She needed to talk to someone about it. It was so strange not to have Val. . . . And she wanted to know about the five in a year. Five *deaths* in a year . . .

She almost put in a call to Ben, wanting to hear his voice,

wanting to make an apology, but whenever she reached for the telephone she drew back; no, she'd do it tomorrow. Tomorrow.

It was a bad dream and he knew it well, the way you might grow used to a terrible running sore, something for which there was no cure, something which stank and infected the rest of your life and left you half mad, obsessed, impotent.

In the moments before waking, in the gauzelike blur of approaching consciousness when a man could almost control the beast within, Sandanato had believed himself to be wandering in the dark place that waited for him every night. Sometimes he managed to give it the slip. Sometimes not. He was moving soundlessly from room to room, but beyond some of the doorways and archways he passed through lay not rooms but chambers floored with burning sand, coppery walls of stone rising all around him, a thousand steps carved in the cliff's face, a disc of fiery white in the blue far above him, seen as if by a man trapped forever at the bottom of a poisoned well. . . .

In his dreams he was always at the bottom of a pit, unable to find a way out, alone and in pain, stumbling in the darkness with the mocking sky inexpressibly far above, out of reach. His dream was always faintly scented with incense and the peculiar odor of burned and blowing sand and scrub brush that had never known rain. In his dream it was always a nameless and dark place, throbbing with its own power, pulsing with black blood trickling forth from springs cut into the cliffs like wounds.

And then the unaccountable would happen. The miracle.

The floor of the valley would tremble underfoot, the black blood would gurgle and foam from the burnished walls of stone, and the stone would be wrenched apart before him and he would see a way out, a pathway cut through the mountain and a vast openness beyond . . . a desert in gaudy bloom and on the horizon, bathed in a mist of sun and moonlight, inexplicable because it was a dream, a castle, an immensely safe and holy place. . . .

And in his dream he was no longer alone but flanked by hooded brothers whom he somehow knew, whom he would lead from the prison at the base of the blowing cliffs. He had been made whole and new, baptized in the hot black blood, made a warrior at last, a gladiator of some atavistic order setting forth on a holy mission.

The Valley of Tears, that was the name he gave the hellish place from which he'd escaped.

And then all the images faded, the place of the black blood would recede into the subconscious, and he would open his eyes, his body and the sheets soaked with sweat, and the day would begin.

It was four o'clock in the morning of the first full day Monsignor Sandanato had been back in Rome.

Giacomo Cardinal D'Ambrizzi had conducted most of his life in secrecy, and four o'clock in the morning was a very secret hour.

From behind the wheel Monsignor Sandanato studied his old mentor's face in the rearview mirror. The cardinal was slouched in the backseat of the least conspicuous automobile registered in Vatican City—a blue Fiat with a rusty scrape on a rear fender. His mania for secrecy was in full flower. Four o'clock in the dark gray of a cool autumn morning, the back streets of Rome tilting sluggishly, the ancient buildings reaching across toward one another like very feeble old friends. It was like driving through a tunnel.

The cardinal reflexively took a black Egyptian cigarette from an old leather-backed case, stuck it on his lower lip, and lit it. He inhaled deeply and Sandanato, watching through the thick latticework of his eyelashes, saw the cardinal's fingers, short and stubby and tobacco-stained, the fingers of a peasant. The face staring intently into a volume of Sherlock Holmes bore the stamp of a lover of pleasure, a Borgia. His lips were thick, the teeth uneven and discolored from the constant nicotine, his eyes clear and blue when you glimpsed them behind the hooded lids.

The cardinal wore civilian clothing. It was his obsession with secrecy, but Monsignor Sandanato understood. Even now, sitting quietly in the back of the little car, the old man in the ancient Borsalino, part of his camouflage, wouldn't speak aloud. It was the fear that the car was bugged. In a high-stakes game, he would say, anything was possible. Loose lips sink ships, they were right, you see.

The hat was pulled down low on his head. Beneath it the once-thick black hair was now white; it lay tight against the massive skull like a cap. His nondescript gray suit was a bit small for him, was boxy, as if passed on to him by a Russian. He was squat, powerfully built, beefy, and intimidating even in his mid-seventies. Growing up in Trieste he'd had a reputation: quick brain, quicker fists.

Through the years Sandanato had had plenty of time to observe the man, the natural disguise he used to such advantage. He had the misleading loose jowls and lips of a garrulous old gossip. His natural posture was a slump. He was somehow always rumpled, no matter how significant the occasion. It was inconceivable to imagine him pressed and starched and neat, even when he was precisely that. But it was all a false front. A fierce intellect gleamed behind the sybaritic old face. Shrewd with instincts as precise as computer logic. Giacomo Cardinal D'Ambrizzi, one of the most secret of men, had few secrets from Monsignor Sandanato.

From the very beginning, Sandanato knew, the cardinal had been involved in the most worldly affairs of the Church. He had the canny, calculating, game-playing kind of mind required, and those in positions of power had recognized it in the young man from Trieste. Money had always been what he did best. He had begun by raising it and went on to investing it. More than any other single individual in his time, he had built and directed the wealth of the Church.

Along the way the cardinal had learned how malleable the Church itself was, how responsive to a lover's touch. Like people, the Church could be made to do what the cardinal wished. More than anything else he wanted to preserve the Church, to defend it against the evil and the enemies within and without its walls. It was an overwhelming task, but he had always been the man for it. And Pietro Sandanato had been at his side through the maturity of his power.

The cardinal had often told him of the time when he had recognized his calling, how best he might serve. It had been in a run-down office he'd visited in Naples some fifty-odd years before. Peeling linoleum, the smell of sweat, plates encrusted with pasta stacked on the corner of a cluttered desk. The office of a homely, unlettered tycoon whose hopes for the Church had dovetailed with his own. Father D'Ambrizzi had managed to pry a hundred thousand dollars from the grubby little man in the sweat-stained shirt. That was how it had begun and D'Ambrizzi had known where to channel the money.

Many years later, referring to Cardinal D'Ambrizzi's control over the Vatican's vast portfolio of investments, and the almost oppressive security surrounding his movements and actions, an American cardinal had said: "It goes with the territory, plain and simple. You smile at the wrong banker in Zurich or have dinner with the wrong counselor in Paris, and the New York Stock Exchange and the Bourse go into shock. But, my friend, have you ever wondered where the hell God fits into all this?"

It was true, of course, the cardinal had told Sandanato. His life was bounded by secrecy and security and, indeed, it did go with the territory. But it was also an aspect of his own nature. And so far as God's work went, the cardinal had long since ceased theorizing. Someday it would doubtless all become clear.

Monsignor Sandanato pulled the Fiat into a half-hidden alley-way and parked in the cul-de-sac, where anonymous, ancient trash was stacked helter-skelter, and doused the headlights. It was the back entrance of a hospital so obscure that it seemed to crouch, a pile of bricks one step from becoming rubble. The clientele was poor and undemanding and no one would suspect that a cardinal would set foot within it. Which was why D'Ambrizzi had chosen it, of course. Just three weeks before, a politician had been kneecapped by the Red Brigades less than fifty feet from the front entry and had still been taken by car to another hospital twenty minutes away. It was the perfect hospital for the cardinal's purpose.

The dim hallway was empty but for two men in gowns covered with blood. No one paid the slightest attention to the handsome priest and the stubby old man who walked slowly and with a slight stoop. They entered a small room around a dark corner and sat down on the rickety wooden chairs. The cardinal took a copy of Sherlock Holmes stories from his pocket and began reading, his lips moving as he read the English. Sandanato sat upright, waiting.

Dr. Cassoni came in quietly, making apologies. His lined face was grave. He and the cardinal had known each other almost all their lives, which was why he had over the past few months gone along with the covert game the cardinal was playing. Dr. Cassoni's normal venue was as elegant and moneyed as the little hospital was down-at-heel. Cassoni shook his head dispiritedly.

"You look terrible," the cardinal said softly. "You could use a doctor." He chuckled ironically, lit a cigarette from the gold lighter held by Sandanato.

"Ah, Giacomo, I feel terrible." Cassoni slumped down on the

edge of the old wooden desk. "And it's not entirely this ungodly hour, either."

Guillermo Cassoni was Pope Callistus's personal physician. It was D'Ambrizzi who had recommended Cassoni to the Holy Father when the headaches had begun two years before.

"You've mixed up someone's X rays?" the cardinal inquired with a smile.

"Far worse, Eminence," Cassoni said. "I have *not* mixed up the X rays, the brain scans, and all the rest of it." He shifted on the edge of the desk and frowned at the cardinal. "Our gamble, *yours* . . . we have lost, my friend. The Holy Father cannot possibly last much longer. The brain tumor"—he shrugged—"it's out of control. He should be in the hospital by now. It amazes me that he has not begun to act . . . well, erratically. I know, I know, he must remain where he is. He must endure as long as possible. We must increase the medication . . . but we are talking in terms of weeks now. A month, six weeks, Christmas maybe . . ."

"This is inconvenient," the cardinal said.

Dr. Cassoni laughed harshly. "It's not my fault, Giacomo. You're in charge of the Department of Miracles. His Holiness needs one—"

"Everybody dies, my friend. Death is nothing. But *when* you die, that can be important. There is so much to do before—"

"And so little time," the doctor said. "It is a common complaint. I hear it every day. Death so often comes at an inconvenient time."

The cardinal clucked softly, nodding.

Monsignor Sandanato heard them going on and on about pain, degrees of incapacitation, names of drugs, side effects. He wanted to scream. But he listened. The three of them in the little room, in the run-down hospital, were the only three men in Rome so close to the truth of the pope's condition. Not even the subject himself had heard it quite so straight. At such a time, to know could be an immense advantage. Time was so desperately short. There would be a new pope soon. It had to be the right man.

On the way back down the hallway they passed the men in the bloody surgical gowns. They were talking about tennis and didn't bother to nod at the priest and the old man. Monsignor Sandanato smelled the blood as he passed.

The morning was still gray but colored by a faint, light-refracting mist hanging in the air when they left the little hospital.

A puffy black cat sat on the roof of the Fiat and left only after determined urging by the cardinal. The flat wet tracks dotted the hood's paintwork.

"Take me to the country, Pietro," the cardinal said. "Take me to Campo di Maggiore."

The cardinal always enjoyed the sight of Rome at first light. This morning they passed the Castello Sant'Angelo, where Pope Clement VII had taken refuge from his enemies in 1527. The cardinal always felt a certain sympathy for poor old Clement, beset by French armies and who knew what else. All that Clement was trying to do was hold on to his power. It was all that any pope ever tried to do and now the Church was beset yet again, enemies scaling the ramparts, pikes in hand. The murders were on his mind, culminating with the three Americans. God's plan? he thought bitterly.

From the backseat the cardinal saw Sandanato watching him in the mirror. He smiled and folded his hands in his lap and watched the countryside flashing past, not really seeing it. He knew it, he could see it with his eyes closed. But now he was thinking, and he thought best with his heavy-lidded eyes drooping and his mind disengaged from the surroundings. He had put Sherlock Holmes aside.

The cardinal trusted Sandanato more than any other man he knew. And he took some degree of personal pride in the younger man, like a sculptor might take in a statue which was wholly his own creation, which had turned out just as he had hoped in his dreams it would. Yes, Monsignor Sandanato was the cardinal's man. And if the old man didn't trust him completely, it was simply that he knew there was no such thing as perfect trust. Never. Men who trusted too much came to early graves.

It had been a long climb from the roadside.

Everything—the car, the trees, the road, their clothing—was covered with a fine patina of dust, which reminded the cardinal of time spent years before on Sicily. Only there the dust had been ochre and red and the sun had left the old dogs dying in the streets.

Sandanato took the cardinal's arm when he stumbled on a stone and together they climbed out of the bright sunshine into the shade and sat beneath a gnarled tree as old as Christendom. It was cool in the shadow of the woods, and the valley below swept away in the day's brightness, a stream flowing cold and blue, on either side a clean green carpet studded with the odd bit of livestock. A sheep or two, some cows grazing, a man moving slowly as if in a dream. The opposite slope was rock-strewn. The entire scene waited for a landscape painter to do it justice and, the cardinal reflected sadly, justice would no doubt be a hopelessly ordinary daubing sold cheaply to a tourist from a roadside stand.

They sat beneath the tree.

"Would you like some of the wine? A bottle of beer? Anything?"

"Nothing, thank you," the cardinal said. "Just sit down and relax. You need to calm down—you've been under quite a strain." He was referring to the American trip. "You should always carry a mystery novel with you, Pietro. It passes the time better than your missal or contemplation of the eternal verities. The stories are not demanding, and one can think and read simultaneously. But then, I've told you that before. And now"—he looked casually around the hillside—"we are alone. Out of the range of microphones, aren't we? Now I must hear everything about your trip to Princeton."

They had come there first twenty years earlier, this lovely spot where a sixteenth-century diplomat from Naples, Bernardo di Maggiore, was ambushed by Aragonese sympathizers and accused of siding against them in a conflict with the pope. Despite his forthright explanations, he was disemboweled while alive during a daylong ritual and nailed to an olive tree to serve as a warning to those who would oppose the House of Aragon. For his final services to the papacy, he was canonized, made a martyr, and subsequently forgotten.

Behind the breeze rising from the valley, Sandanato almost heard the cries of Bernardo di Maggiore, imagined the twisted faces of his tormentors, the victim's final willingness to be slaughtered and rendered and drawn and left a mere scrap of what had once been human but was now something more, something immortal. He might even have died for something important, an idea with meaning, but no one now recalled. . . . Immortality required no great ideas, after all.

The cardinal listened to Sandanato's report. While he took it in he opened a bottle of Chianti and split off a chunk of bread from a fresh loaf. Sandanato talked quietly while they munched and drank and ate cheese. The cardinal kept himself well within check, but the story angered and frustrated him. Death was robbing him—

murder was robbing him and he hated it. His own death would have troubled him less; but he was unable to accept the death of his hopes, the commitment he'd made so long ago to the Church. He took a deep swallow of the wine which was so pure it could never give you even a headache. He wiped his mouth. He would have to work fast before the machinery jumped the rails, went hurtling into the darkness. He turned to Monsignor Sandanato.

"All right," he said, making a steeple of his hands before his Borgia face. "Now tell me about this Ben Driskill . . . and what part our Sister Elizabeth is playing in this dangerous game. It's no place for a woman, Pietro."

"I don't understand what you're telling me—he was stabbed by the priest while you were just standing there?" She couldn't keep the incredulity out of her voice.

The breeze across the piazza snapped at the fringe on the umbrellas over the tables and patted at the leaves of the palm trees. The exhaust fumes hung like old mourning lace over the traffic. The lunchtime sun was warm for autumn, glowing in a painterly manner behind the haze. The outdoor café was busy, but its restrained quiet was an oasis in the buzz and blur of Rome.

Monsignor Sandanato had called her the day before from his office at the Vatican and she'd been eager to accept his luncheon invitation. Now she sat with her mouth open, shocked at the story he'd blurted out. He was looking very crisp and calm, but the eyes gave him away, deeper than ever in the purple sockets, and he'd consumed half a bottle of wine by the time she'd arrived. He was choosing his words with care, as if he were carefully editing himself as he went along. It was always the same with the priests: they watched themselves in her presence—she was a journalist and a woman, two of the most dangerous things in the world.

"No, no, I was way across the ice. I didn't notice anything until it was too late, then all I saw was someone else out for an evening of skating—it's a small river or stream that broadens behind the house and the orchard . . . it must have been the first skating of the season." He broke off a bit of the herbed fish with his fork and nibbled. "He was gone by the time I reached Ben. . . . Ben was down on the ice, bleeding. I helped him to the house. So much blood—"

"But he's all right now? You stayed in Princeton to make sure—"

"Yes, yes, of course. He's recovering; it was a bad wound." He pointed awkwardly to his back and side. "Luckily it didn't touch any of the crucial organs . . . and his father is recovering, too, but he's an old man, it's harder."

She met his eyes staring determinedly into hers when she looked up. Something about his emotions lay close to the surface, as if the touch of a fingertip might cause him a kind of paralyzing agony. What was he seeking in her eyes? What was he leaving unspoken? She remembered again what Ben Driskill had said: he loves you.

"So it was a priest who stabbed him?"

"I can only repeat what Driskill said. I wasn't close enough to see. He said it was the priest, the silver-haired man who was seen at the Helmsley Palace. Driskill says it has to be the same man." He shrugged. A Vespa snarled nearby and sped away into the traffic. The white-jacketed waiters moved elegantly among the tables, above it all.

"But you didn't see the priest for yourself?"

"How could I, Sister? I was too far away at first and then I was trying to keep from falling down getting to Driskill—"

Sister Elizabeth sighed and put her cutlery aside. The delicate slices of veal lay almost undisturbed on her plate. She sipped the Orvieto, keeping her eyes disengaged. He had a way of holding you with his eyes. Martyr's eyes, suffering.

"The whole thing grows more and more insane," she said. "Whose bright idea was it to go skating in the first place? Ben told me he hates skating—"

"I admit it was *my* idea. It seemed—"

"I know, it seemed like a good idea at the time. But aside from that, Mrs. Lincoln, how did you like the play?"

"I don't understand," he said.

"Forget it. Bad joke. So it was your idea."

"I thought it would be good exercise. A way to clear our heads. How could anyone know this could happen?"

"What bothers me, Monsignor, is how did the priest know that Ben Driskill was going to be out there skating?"

"Surely he couldn't have known, Sister. No, I've thought about that. He must have meant to attack Driskill in the house . . . Then he saw him, the golden chance, and he took it. Getting the skates was a simple matter—they were just inside the back door to the house, and he had been that way before, after all." The sun had moved, was striking the top of his head, polishing his thick black hair, making a triangle across his forehead like a birthmark.

"When he broke in and stole Val's briefcase—yes. That must have been what happened. But, God, the luck!"

"Good or bad?" Sandanato mused. "Well, maybe there's a silver lining. It was a bad wound. He might have died, but he didn't. Maybe surviving will change his mind."

"Change his mind?"

"About going after the killer himself—that's the real insanity."

"Is that what you think, Monsignor?"

"He wouldn't stand a chance. Only another killer might have any chance at all. Maybe a close call will change his mind."

"I wonder . . ."

"Well, I would certainly think again if someone stuck a knife in my back."

"I wonder if that's the effect it will have on him. He's a stubborn man, very determined. Have you thought that it might just strengthen his resolve?"

"My God, I hope not. He'll die and he'll never know why or who killed him. He'll never know if there was a reason—"

"What kind of reason could there be? For murder—"

"And the way it is now," he continued as if she hadn't spoken, "his father's going to need him at home. He told me you tried to convince him to give up the idea of going after the killer, to leave it to the authorities."

"I tried—with highly counterproductive results."

Sandanato shrugged, resigned to the madness of others. "I hope he thinks it over."

"Look, the authorities in Princeton and New York aren't going to unravel all this—it's just not going to happen. They're not going to be able to get inside the Church to find this man—"

"You're assuming he *is* a priest, then—"

"Just listen to me. The Church is going to get the wagons in a circle and keep them there. It won't let the cops inside if the killer *is* a priest. So what's going to happen? We both know that. The Church is going to do its own investigation its own way, and if the evil ones are inside the Church we could have a case where the evil ones are investigating themselves." She sat back and took a long drink of iced mineral water. The pollution had dried out her tongue and settled in her throat. The autumn wind was growing cool in the piazza.

"You are needlessly cynical," he said.

"Oh, I am, am I? Well, you're on the inside. What kind of investigation are they going to conduct?"

"Wait a moment, Sister. I cannot simply assume a real priest, someone within the Church, is doing the killing—"

"But maybe that assumption is right. Then where are you? Who is this priest? Who knows his identity? Who gives him his orders? Or does he act alone, pick out his own victims? The questions are terrifying—"

"You can't believe that, Sister! The Church is the victim here, our people are being killed!"

"Next you'll be telling me that Cardinal D'Ambrizzi isn't all that interested in what's happened—"

"Believe me, he's busy enough with everything else. We're not likely to run short of scandals these days."

"That," she said, smiling, "qualifies as very, very old news."

Sandanato cleared his throat. She knew what was coming. "And speaking of news, you aren't planning to write about any of this in your magazine—"

"I can't pretend Val's alive and well, can I? She's one of our official heroines, Monsignor." She watched him shift uncomfortably in the white metal chair. "But I don't *know* anything. So what could I write?" She watched him relax. She was enjoying the opportunity to toy with him. "But I do have a question. It's from Val, really."

"And what could it be?"

"What did Val mean when she was talking about the death of a prominent layman, I believe it was a layman, the name just won't come back to me . . . but Val said, 'That makes five in a year.' What does that mean to you? Five deaths? What kind of deaths? Five Catholics? Which five? What did she mean?"

"Sister, I have no idea."

He answered quickly, interrupting her, giving himself no chance to think. She'd seen it all before. He didn't need or want to think. His eyes clouded over, erasing her once she passed a certain point. As a woman she would always be an outsider when it came to certain kinds of things, *serious* things, things within the Church.

* * *

His Holiness Pope Callistus IV was still capable of having good mornings. He knew the supply was running low so when one came he tried to enjoy it, so far as enjoyment mattered anymore, but more important he tried to get something done. He might have only an hour or two before the pain began, either in his chest or in his head. Then more pills, eventually the loss of consciousness. So he had to make time count. This morning was one of the good ones. He had summoned the men he wanted to see and now he waited, tried to relax.

Standing at his office window on the third floor of the Apostolic Palace, he watched the sun rise over the hills of the Holy City, over the swirling currents of the Tiber, cresting the dusty mounds at the horizon. He had often in years past wondered what a pope thought about as he surveyed the world from his pinnacle, but never had he imagined the state of mind in which he found himself. He was not a particularly emotional man: he had never chosen engagement when the role of observer was available. Which was probably why he'd emerged from the pack to become *il papa*. He had for many, many years been immune to confusion, fear, passion, ambition, and even the more extreme encroachments of faithlessness. All that was different now, in the last act of his life. Watching the beauty of the sunrise, he wondered if any pope before him had ever been so scared of what lay beyond his window. Of course he knew it was an idiotic question. He knew perfectly well that he was merely the latest in a lengthy procession of terrified pontiffs.

He was dumbfounded by the killings. Murders. This latest horror in New York . . . and the troublesome, irritating nun. Where the hell would it stop? Where was it leading?

He sighed and poured a cup of thick black coffee from a silver pot. A plate of rolls sat untouched on the desk. From his window he was able to see the section of Rome where he'd lived as a young student. It was unsettling to realize that from one of those anonymous hillside buildings a man with a rifle decked out with all the accoutrement of modern technology could sight in through the window, wait for Callistus IV, Bishop of Rome, to stop his pacing and stand still, mesmerized by the view of the rising sun, and blow his brains all over the office.

But he was being melodramatic. Nobody was shooting anyone with rifles. Not yet.

He finished the coffee just as the alarm on his custom-made Piaget wristwatch—a gift from a famous movie star—went off, reminding him that his first visitor would be waiting in the anteroom.

He took an antique cloisonné pillbox from his pocket, musing on the ironies of men's behavior. He was always contemplating ambiguities, ironies, absurdities: it went with the job. Not for the first time he supposed he'd have been better off—more resigned to the unexpectedly absurd nature of his role as pope—were he a pious man. Piety, however, was not a requirement in the pope's job description in this latter part of the twentieth century.

The coffee was a stimulant, tended to exacerbate any anxiety he might be feeling. The pills in the exquisite little box were propranolol, a beta-blocker. They slowed down his heartbeat, kept his hands from sweating and trembling, kept his voice steady and authoritative. They arrested any stage fright that might assail him at crucial moments. He took a pill, washed it down with cold water from a cut-glass tumbler on his breakfast tray, and made a check mark on a list he kept in his pocket. He'd taken his heart pill, his blood pressure pill, and his beta-blocker.

He reflected that, had he been granted a slightly longer lifespan, he might have become the first synthetic pope.

He picked up his telephone and said to the secretary, "Have His Eminence come in now."

Manfredi Cardinal Indelicato always intimidated the little man who had been simple Father di Mona when Indelicato had already been moving up the Vatican ladder back in the forties and the austere figure of Pius had perched atop it. Some people thought he had modeled himself on Pius, but they were mistaken. Indelicato was of truly noble birth, a family that must have gone back to the Ice Age; he was immensely wealthy with the full run of a spectacular villa and staff; he lived, however, the life of an ascetic. Intellectually, morally, genealogically, physically: he seemed the better man. Better than Pius, better than di Mona. But Sal di Mona was the pope, so nothing else mattered. If only the pope could keep that in mind.

He looked up at Indelicato's pale white face, the black hair which he probably dyed, the eyes like those of a patiently waiting bird of prey. A long-legged bird, waiting, watching, ready to dig its beak and spear something small and furry and fearful. "Holiness," he said softly, making the word sound somehow threatening. He could make anything sound threatening. In a way it was part of his job.

"Sit down, Manfredi. Don't loom so." Callistus always tried to establish their relationship by using his first name, by gently belittling him. Indelicato sat down, crossed his immensely long, thin legs. "Your friend Saint Jack will be here in a few minutes. You've been doing as I asked?"

The long, narrow head inclined slightly, as if the question hardly needed to be asked.

"Then I would hear your report." The pope leaned back, folded his hands in his lap. He wondered if it was too late now to train Manfredi Indelicato, the most feared man in the Vatican, the Chief of Vatican Intelligence and Security, to kiss his ring from time to time. Of course, it *was* too late. But it would have been amusing. So seldom was it given to one to bully the Bogey Man.

"I have kept the individuals in question under surveillance, Holiness. Dr. Cassoni is a paragon of discretion, of course, in all ways . . . but one. Yesterday morning he arose in the middle of the night and drove to a spectacularly unfashionable hospital in the depths of a slum. There he kept an appointment, and I am afraid it is reasonable to assume that you were the subject of the conversation."

It was important that the status of the pontiff's health not be revealed except in the exact manner the Vatican—Callistus and the curia—chose. It was Cardinal Indelicato who had suggested a watch be kept on the private physician.

"I am not seeking suspense here, Manfredi. I want information. With whom did he keep his appointment?"

"Let me ask you, Holiness, how did Cassoni come to be your physician?"

"D'Ambrizzi recommended him."

"I should have expected that," Indelicato murmured, a faint self-reproach.

"Not even you can be expected to know everything."

"Perhaps not, but it was with Cardinal D'Ambrizzi that the good doctor had his meeting."

The pope could think of nothing to say, but when he looked up from his cold coffee he wondered if he'd seen what passed for a smile in Indelicato's repertoire flicker at the corners of the wide, thin mouth.

Cardinal D'Ambrizzi came in, and after greeting the pope he turned to Indelicato. "Fredi, Fredi, why the long face? You think you've got troubles . . . ha! What I could tell you!" He stood back and looked at the tall, thin man in the immaculately tailored suit of an ordinary priest. D'Ambrizzi grinned, reached out, and rolled the lapel between his fat fingers. "Nice suit, very nice. Your usual tailor? Me, I don't have the figure for it. A good tailor would be wasted on me. The more voluminous the garment, the better I look, eh, Fredi?"

Indelicato looked down from his great height. "Giacomo. We must see more of each other. I miss your fabled wit." He turned. "And Monsignor Sandanato, how good of you to join us this morning."

More coffee and rolls were brought in while the pope waited for the two cardinals to stop pissing on each other's shoes. It was like watching Don Quixote and Sancho Panza, unless you knew them. Indelicato sat barely sipping his black coffee while D'Ambrizzi filled his with sugar and cream. Sandanato merely stared into his. All through the years Indelicato and D'Ambrizzi had been linked in the minds of the Vatican watchers—opposites, adversaries, colleagues with but one aim . . . to serve the Church.

"Eight," the pope said in the silence, and watched all the eyes turn toward him. "We are faced with eight murders. Eight murders within our Church. We don't know why. We don't know who is doing the killing. We don't even have a pattern . . . we cannot predict the next killing. But we may be sure there are bound to be more." He paused. "We have considered the possible killers . . . our friends, the Mafia. Extremists . . . Opus Dei. Propaganda Due."

Indelicato was shaking his head. "My investigators have uncovered nothing to indicate the involvement of any of these organizations. They say no, there's nothing there for us."

"No one teaching us a lesson?"

"No, Holiness. Not among these groups."

"The fact is," D'Ambrizzi growled, "all these people are always angry about something. The Jesuits are angry because they think you, Holiness, are slighting them in favor of Opus Dei. Opus Dei is fed up because they wanted autonomy from the bishops and control of Vatican Radio and you, Holiness, won't give them either one. The Marxists look upon us as capitalist tyrants operating out of the Vatican. And the conservatives look upon us as a hotbed of commie bastards destroying the Church. God only knows what Propaganda Due thinks, but He should be ashamed of Himself—they scare even me. But when it comes to murdering people within the Church . . ." He shook his head. "For one thing, they seem to kill indiscriminately, regardless of philosophical orientation. Have I left anybody out, Holiness?"

Callistus made a gesture of resignation. "Put three priests together on a street corner and you've got a new faction that's unhappy about something. But killers? No . . . but tell me, what is this I hear about a *priest* killing the three in America?"

D'Ambrizzi's eyes widened beneath the deep furrows carved across his forehead. "May I ask, Holiness, where you heard such a thing?"

"Giacomo, please. I *am* the pope . . ."

D'Ambrizzi nodded. "Point taken."

"Well? Is it true?"

D'Ambrizzi said, "Pietro?"

Sandanato recounted what he knew, and when he was finished Callistus thanked him with a noncommittal grunt. "We must get to the bottom of this. It must be stopped."

"Of course, Holiness," D'Ambrizzi said. "But it presents problems."

"But, but, but . . ." Indelicato appeared to be working up a contradiction but finally proved unequal to the task. "He's right. We can but try—"

"I want it stopped. If it's coming from somewhere inside the Church, it must be stopped, and every trace eradicated. I'm not overly concerned about exposing the killers . . . we will deal with them at the proper time." He was squinting, fighting the pain that had begun in his head. "More than anything, I want to know *why*." He took a deep breath. "And there must be no outside authorities turned loose inside the Church . . . here in Rome, in America, not anywhere. Do you understand? This is a *Church matter*!" He winced uncontrollably, clutched his head.

"Holiness," D'Ambrizzi said, getting up, going to him.

"I'm suddenly very tired, Giacomo. That's all. I must rest."

Leaning on D'Ambrizzi's great bulk, with Indelicato at his side, Callistus stood and slowly allowed himself to be led away.

Sister Elizabeth cursed herself for being too busy to have thought things through properly. Ideas kept coming to her that should have occurred to her days before. Now she'd thought of Mother Superior, the nun in late middle age who was the chief executive officer of the Order. She lived and worked in the peach-tinted gray building, part Church, part convent, part castle, at the top of the Spanish Steps. She was French. She had been fond of Sister Valentine. Elizabeth had known her reasonably well for nearly ten years. The mother superior could show warmth and affection, but she always reverted to protocol if you returned it in kind. She controlled the show, the world in which she lived, and you could raise hell all over the world if you were a lady when you presented yourself at the home office.

The mother superior's office was decorated in peach and cream and a soft art deco pearl-gray. There was a very modern crucifix that seemed to float two inches from one wall, casting a dramatic shadow, lit by a recessed spotlight. It looked like a wall in a small private museum. The bowls of flowers and shiny green leaves were the perfect complement. Beyond the window people moved in the sunshine on the steps themselves. The mother superior stood with her hands folded, looking out the window, then turned to face Elizabeth. She bore a striking resemblance to the actress Jane Wyman who had once been Mrs. Ronald Reagan. "You want to talk about dear Valentine?"

"I should have come days ago," Elizabeth said, "but there's so much going on at the moment, I get caught up in details. But I just wondered if you saw much of her during the past six months?"

"Why, yes, of course I did. She was living here, my dear."

"But she was mainly in Paris."

"I don't know about mainly. She seemed to be dividing her time. She was her usual rather ebullient but secretive self." She smiled fondly at the memory. She was rearranging the flowers in a cut-glass vase. "I gave her one of the big bedrooms here and we moved a desk in. She was working hard. As always."

"Have you emptied the room yet?"

"Not yet, Sister. It is such an unhappy task, I haven't had the heart for it. In fact, I've been intending to call you about the disposition of her things . . . the papers, books, she always collected quite a jumble, didn't she?"

"I had no idea she was staying here," Elizabeth mused.

"Well, you mustn't feel left out. She was so wrapped up in what she was doing. She was always so single-minded, wasn't she? She spent a lot of time in the Secret Archives. She still had so much influence—what is the American expression?"

"Clout?"

"Of course, *clout.* She still had clout in high places."

"You mean?"

"Cardinal D'Ambrizzi, of course. He greased the skids—an Americanism, right?—so the Secret Archives became her personal preserve."

"Might I see her room?"

"Of course. Now that I've got you here, I wouldn't let you leave otherwise. I'll take you up myself, my dear."

The mother superior left her alone in the sunny room. There was a lavish splash of bougainvillea outside the two narrow windows. For half an hour Elizabeth sat in an overstuffed chair sifting through notebooks, folders, loose papers. Everything seemed to relate to previous books, articles, even speeches Val had made. She sighed despondently and picked up a stack of folders and notebooks held together by three rubber bands.

The folder on top was marked with a felt-tip pen. Two words. THE MURDERS.

2

DRISKILL

I flew New York/Paris/Cairo popping pain pills and drinking champagne and losing track of time, closing my eyes and seeing that nightmare with the silver hair and the gleaming blade in his hand and so much for sleep. I was counting not in terms of hours but in days, and it had been nine days since my sister's funeral. I'd been in the hospital getting a hundred stitches sewn into my back and side and somehow it seemed, fast forward, the next thing I knew I was in the airport in Cairo waiting to connect to the Egyptair shuttle to Alexandria. It was hot and crowded and the jostling didn't do my back any good. Then, a pain pill and a sliver of bad dream later, I was dropping out of a clear sky toward Alexandria's undersized airport which they'd had to rebuild after the altercation with Israel in 1973. On one side of the aircraft I'd seen the desert stretching away into an infinity of burning sand, on the other the flat blue Mediterranean, and now the desert was sliding away out of sight

180

and I saw the long thin string of the city, narrow, greenish, arcing around the curves of the two huge harbors on the north and Lake Maryut on the south.

I took one of the busy little red and black taxis which squirmed its way through the traffic on the Delta Road. Four hours on that same road in the other direction lay Cairo. Four hours past Alexandria to the west lay El Alamein, then Matruh, then Libya and Tobruk, the ghost of World War II. The sense of timelessness—not simply history, but the utter timelessness of the shifting dunes and rolling surface of sea, so impervious to man and his cities and empires and momentary cultural blips—was overwhelming, even in the throbbing traffic and the comparative newness of the city of four million people.

My driver swung onto Suez Canal Street, then onto the scenic Corniche circling the Eastern Harbor, the *old* harbor, where the cooling breeze kept the city temperate and relieved the light-headedness I was feeling. He dropped me at Sa'd Zaghlul Square before the Cecil Hotel. Across the street, by a patch of green grass in the glaring sunshine, the Cairo-bound bus was loading up. Emerging from the cab, I was again revived by the gentle sea breeze. The hotel faced the Eastern Harbor across the gently curving sweep of the wide Corniche. Beyond that the Mediterranean sparkled. Just then, for a few moments, suspended between what had already happened and what was going to happen, it seemed like heaven.

Alexander the Great had taken Egypt from the Persians three and a half centuries before the birth of Christ. Having enjoyed a tumultuous reception at Memphis, he was proceeding along the coast toward the Siwa oasis to visit the Oracle of Amun. He had the notion that the oracle might inform him that he was the son of the god Wiwa. He stopped for rest at a charming fishing village with an exquisite natural harbor. As he did on many such occasions in his brief lifetime, he ordered a city to be built around the harbor. As was his habit, he ordered the city named for himself. Leaving a team of architects behind, he went on to chat up the oracle. He never saw the new city of Alexandria.

He died nine years later. His body, according to his last wishes, was on its way to Siwa for burial when his great general Ptolemy waylaid the procession and instead, with fantastic ceremony, buried the great man's remains at the new city's main square. Now, of course, all of Ptolemy's work is obliterated, buried somewhere beneath the modern Alexandria, beneath all those scurrying red and black taxis.

Euclid invented geometry in Alexandria. Ptolemy built the nearly unimaginable Lighthouse of Paros Island, four hundred feet high, one of the wonders of the ancient world. Later the Romans couldn't resist the lure of what had become the economic center of the East and along came Julius Caesar, Cleopatra, Marc Antony, and Octavian, who became Augustus Caesar. And later still St. Mark brought Christianity to Egypt and founded what eventually became the Coptic Church. And later still the Persians returned as conquerors. And then the Arabs. It was a long, long story and in the twentieth century the Brits with Lawrence Durrell and E. M. Forster had their say, and then the Egyptians themselves . . .

And then my sister had come to Alexandria. I had to find out why.

The floor of my room was polished hardwood, gleaming dully as if it had been endlessly massaged with beeswax. The furniture was old, slightly shabby in the genteel, aristocratic manner. A balcony jutted out with a view of the Corniche and the harbor. Breezes filled the room, cooling my burning, jet-lagged eyes. There was a telephone but I wasn't ready for that yet. There was a television, but I couldn't cope with the idea of *Dallas* or, more likely, an ancient *Wagon Train* in Arabic. And there was a refrigerator with a plentiful supply of ice. I ordered a bottle of gin and several bottles of tonic and limes from the bar. I got the prescription bottle of Tylenol and codeine out of my briefcase. I was loaded with painkillers and aspirin. My doctor in Princeton had told me not to count on finding aspirin in Egypt.

I went to the bathroom and peeled off my shirt. Gingerly I checked the dressing on my wound. It was hopeless, so I gritted my teeth, pulled it off, and built a fresh one. Damned awkward. I hated looking at the wound. The same doctor told me it reminded him of an old-fashioned kidney-removal incision. The flesh puckered along the two flaps that were sewn together. He told me I was crazy, asking for trouble, setting off on so long a voyage with it so fresh. He was probably right. One of the problems was that it always felt as if it were leaking buckets of blood, spilling blood down my back. It was an illusion, but it was disconcerting.

I made a gin and tonic that was mostly tonic and carefully lay down on the bed, my head propped against two hugely puffy pillows. I could see the pale blue pane of sea stretching away to the milky horizon. It looked as if a stone thrown from my balcony might crack it. I was terribly, awesomely tired. It occurred to me that I was a very long way from home.

The ice on my face had kept me from going all the way out.

Sandanato hadn't known what the hell to do. At first he hadn't realized what had happened, then he saw blood seeping out of me like motor oil from an old clunker. I could barely hear him muttering, partly to himself, partly to me, should he leave me there and go to the house and call for help, or should he start yelling and hope Sam Turner's cop on guard heard him, or should he try to get me up and help me back. Then I must have said something and he knelt down and I grabbed him and began pulling myself to my feet. I wasn't in much pain but I was losing a fair amount of blood. I was edging into shock but I knew for sure I didn't want to pass out on the ice, in the cold.

Finally, with my arm over his shoulder, he helped me up and we staggered the hundred yards to the house which seemed to take hours. Turner's man on duty helped get the skates off; it just went on and on and on. He called the hospital and Sandanato sat on the floor beside where I lay on the couch and kept talking, which was the last thing I remembered until the late afternoon of the following day.

The next several days produced a good deal of pain and passed in a kind of blur, mainly a blur of people telling me I had to put the idea of going to Egypt entirely out of my mind. It was amazing to me how they'd missed the point.

The silver-haired priest who'd been killing people, who had murdered my sister while she prayed, had come out of nowhere, out of the dark and cold, and tried to kill me. He'd gotten a lot of knife into me and another inch or two would have finished the job. The doctors kept telling me how lucky I was. Luck, I supposed, was a relative thing.

Peaches came to see me every day. His face always wore the same expression of puzzled innocence, as if each succeeding disaster struck him with greater force. His faith was being tested. The attack on me seemed to convince him that we were deep in the twilight zone without a map, with only God for a friend. When I was up and around he shook his head as if expecting me to come apart. He said that for himself he was doing everything he could to stay busy, anything to avoid dwelling on what had happened to Val and me. He wanted me to stick around once I got out of the hospital. He was for the first time since arriving at St. Mary's in New Pru beginning to go through the contents of the parish house attic and storage rooms, sifting through the accumulated junk of fifty or sixty years. He thought I could come watch, talk, keep him company. But I told him I couldn't do it.

Father Dunn stopped in at the hospital several times. The last time he was on his way to the airport. He was going to Los Angeles to meet with a producer who was making a film from one of his novels. "I make Klammer nervous as a cat," he said. "He's glad to get me out of his hair. As for you, Driskill, what can I say?" He tried a spoonful of my luncheon tapioca. "I suggest you take it easy. It's a miracle you're alive. Take that as a warning. You're not a supercop. You're neither James Bond nor Superman. You are lacking what you need most . . . a stunt double. Go to Antigua or St. Thomas or Hobe Sound, where you will frolic with others rich as yourself; they will teach you the blessed joys of indolence. You will not be murdered . . . you're a fool to pursue this, a fool to give your life. And you surely will if you persist. Do you understand, Driskill? Something horrible is going on, far worse than anything in my books . . . you must let the authorities do what they can. And the Church is bound to look into it. Try to understand—this is a Church matter." His pale eyes had gathered fire, like frozen jewels with heat at the center. "Stay out of it, Ben. You're no good to anyone if you're dead. And you can't bring Val back to life."

I smiled at him. "I'm going to make someone pay. They can't do this, to me, to my family. It's simple, really."

"You are growing very tiresome, Ben. You are not a hero. Believe me."

"Ah, Artie, remember Driskill's Law. Desperate times make heroes of desperate men."

Father Dunn was not impressed. "You're wrong to pursue this. Monsignor Sandanato agrees with me—"

"And Sister Elizabeth, don't leave her out. Can you imagine where I rank the warnings of two priests and a nun?"

He laughed aloud. "Well, since I can't dissuade you, I'll wish you well." As he was leaving my room he turned back and gave me one of his leprechaun looks. "Incidentally, I've been stopping to see your father these past few days. He's had a rough time, Ben. He won't last forever—"

"Yes, that's exactly what he'll do."

"I've dropped off a couple of my books and dared him to read them. They'll get his adrenaline going." Then he told me to think twice about my plans and put on his hat, gave a salute, and left.

Sandanato pleaded with me to remove myself from the whole ungodly mess. "You saw what they can do, they can strike at you from nowhere." His dark eyes were sunk deep in the purple sockets and he smoked incessantly. "You've given a sister—"

"Nobody gave her. Somebody took her—"

"Your father's on the critical list and you've been laid open like a rabbit—basta! It's not your battle. You're not even a Catholic!" Finally he left for Paris, where Curtis Lockhardt was being buried because of some family connection. He was so burdened by the outbreak of murder and the attack on me that he seemed much closer to breaking than I. But I'd seen his type before. They could take an almost infinite amount of stress. They fed on it. As it was, he told me at least to wait until he found out what Rome was doing about the killings. I told him I didn't care what Rome was doing. Rome was the problem.

My father was something of a surprise. He wasn't bouncing back the way I'd expected him to. The doctors told me he took a turn for the worse when he got the news of my misfortune, as if it had been the last straw. They said it seemed to draw the incentive to recover right out of him.

His reaction puzzled me: it would have been different had he gone under with the grief of Val's death weighting him down. But me? And anyway, I was still alive. . . .

But when I saw him I knew the doctors were right. He was parchment-pale, quiet, and Father Dunn's novels stood untouched on the table by his bed. When I got him to talking I wished I hadn't. "Sometimes I think I'm going to die after all, Ben. I feel lonely all of a sudden, out of step—"

"Dad, that's ridiculous and you know it. Besides the army of friends waiting for your call, you've got faith—remember? Isn't now the sort of time when faith is supposed to do the job?"

He didn't seem to hear me. "You're wrong. Loneliness isn't a matter of *people*. They don't matter . . . I'm tired, I don't have control of things the way I used to, I don't understand what's going on—oh, I don't really know what I mean. I'm trying to convey something intangible but so damned real. I've never felt this way before." He didn't say a word about faith. Maybe he didn't want to discuss it with his son the infidel.

"Look, you've had some rough shocks. You can't just expect to sail through."

"Well, Ben, I hope you're right, I hope I make it. I'll be mighty glad to have you around. We can recuperate together. I'd like to have you stay out at the house for a while, just hang around, welcome me home. The firm can give you a leave of absence for six months . . . maybe we could take a cruise or go to London and settle in for a bit once I'm fit again . . ." Just talking about it perked him up. The rest of the conversation didn't go so well.

He didn't want me to go after Val's killer, he didn't want to know what Val had been doing, why she'd been killed. He said I was a reckless fool, that I was not only wasting my time but risking my neck. Didn't I have enough sense to know I'd been warned? Didn't I know how lucky I was not to have been killed? Didn't I realize I was turning my back on him when he needed me?

I'd never heard my father ask me a favor, let alone beg. I felt as if I'd never met this man before. That made it easier to walk out on him. Not easy. Just easier. I was my father's son: I had learned how to turn my back. I saw a tear squeezed out of his closed eye. "I'm sorry, Dad. I've got to go. But I'll be back—maybe then we can—"

"You're obsessed, Benjamin. You're one step from madness and you don't even know it. You won't be back, Ben." He swallowed hard, looked away. "You won't be back," he said again.

The tears were running down his gray cheeks. Who was he crying for? Himself? Or Val? Maybe even for his black-sheep son? But no, that was impossible. I'd given in to sentiment for just an instant.

In the welter of religions you find in Egypt, the Muslims, naturally, are vastly predominant, and of course the Copts are the main Christian denomination. But, as everywhere, there was in Alexandria a Roman presence. There were the Jesuits and the Order, priests and nuns, caring for a small but determined enclave of Catholics.

After a sixteen-hour sleep interrupted by two plaintive calls to

Muslim prayer, sounds audible in every corner of the city as well as strong enough to seep into my benumbed brain, I telephoned the Order's office, which turned out to be a school they operated. I was referred to a Sister Lorraine, the mother superior, who quickly acknowledged that she'd seen Sister Valentine during her visit to Alexandria. Indeed, my sister had stayed at the Order's guesthouse. There was a quick competence as well as a smile in Sister Lorraine's French-accented English, and she said she'd be glad to see me as soon as I could get to her.

I grabbed a cab outside the hotel and fifteen minutes later I was shown into her office. Through her windows there was a view across a playing field swarming with uniformed children whose cries and laughter floated upward, happy accompaniment to her day. The playing field was ringed with palm trees.

Sister Lorraine was a small, dark-haired woman, fiftyish, petite, with huge eyes and beaky French nose. She wore a blue suit with a boxy open jacket like those Chanel made famous and a cream silk blouse with a bow at the neck. On the way in I had noticed some nuns wearing the traditional habit. The boss, however, was clearly a modern administrator. Like all the Frenchwomen I'd ever known, she was attractive by some kind of alchemical reaction, an instinct. The whole was so much more appealing than the individual features.

She had read about Val's murder and been particularly shocked because of their recent meeting. She leaned across the desk, toying with a gold pen, and listened while I told her that I was simply trying to reconstruct my sister's last weeks.

She nodded her small, dark head knowingly, before I was finished. "Yes, yes, I understand. I only wish I could tell you everything that was in her mind but, alas, one can never know that, is it not so? But I was drawn to your sister, I admired the work she'd done, I was very sympathetic. She, this dear sister of yours, was obviously preoccupied when I met her. She was tense, wary .... there is a phrase I've heard—she was watching her back. Do you understand my meaning? *Watching her back?*"

"She was afraid?"

"*Oui.* She had a . . . specific fear. Of something, or someone. Understand, please, this is my *observation.* Your sister did not speak of fear. I observed, I thought to myself, yes, she is watching her back. As if she expected to turn and see a follower. My curiosity was piqued, you know?"

"What did she want from you? Only a place to stay?"

"Ah, more than a bed. She had come here to find a man named Klaus Richter. She gave me no reason beyond mentioning some research she was doing. For a book. Finding Herr Richter was no problem. I know the man myself. A good German Catholic, a regular churchgoer." She allowed a mocking smile to wrap itself around the description of the German. "He owns an import-export firm, a large warehouse down on the western harbor front—very different from your harbor at the Cecil. He's a well-known businessman, well liked from what I've heard. An avid golfer, getting his picture in the press. And of course he's *très, très* German, a slap on the back, a foaming stein, all that. He's quite prominent in the German Old Guard—veterans of the Afrika Korps who came back to live in Egypt. They visit the cemeteries out in the desert, lay wreaths on the graves of both their fallen comrades and their brave enemies. Richter is much admired by the Egyptian government going all the way back to Nasser. I believe Richter was helpful to him as a go-between in some armament deals years and years ago."

"And Val came all the way to Egypt to see him."

"So it would seem." She looked at her watch. "I must attend to an appointment, Mr. Driskill. But if you have any other questions—" She gave a small Gallic shrug. "Or if you just want to talk, please, call me."

She gave me the address of Richter's office. As soon as I'd left her office I missed her. I found myself hoping I'd come up with a question or two.

The dingy gray warehouse of Global Egypt Import Export squatted among others of its ilk, one in a flotilla of froglike structures minus any indications of lilypads, jammed against the commercial harbor. Cargo ships, scruffy and nondescript, sat pierside amid the rusty shafts of motorized cranes. Loading, unloading, shrieking gears, belching smokestacks, the smell of oil and gasoline, dissonant Arabic shouts, the sounds of German and English and French, all yelling. If you closed your eyes it might have been any industrial waterfront in the world. And then someone would begin screaming in Arabic and it would all come back into focus.

Klaus Richter must have been in his early sixties but was built like a Mercedes—to last. He wore his thick white hair in a brush cut probably no different from the old days in the Afrika Korps. He had a dark golfer's tan, bleached-out yellowish eyebrows, a gold Breitling wristwatch that told everything but the World Series scores, and on his feet Clark's desert boots. He wore an old, immaculately laundered bush coat and a pale blue chambray shirt open at the neck with wiry white hair poking over the top button. His khaki slacks had a sharp crease. When his secretary showed me in he was lining up a putt on his green carpet. She and I stopped short, he sank the putt into the little tin device. When he hit it there was a clicking *ping* sound I'd heard before.

"Julius Boros putter," I said.

He looked up, smiling broadly. "Julie gave me the putter twenty years ago. I bought him in an auction, some tournament or other. He won, gave me one of his putters. Best I've ever owned." He was still smiling but his eyes were growing inquisitive. "Do we have business, my friend? Or shall we just talk golf?" He had a German accent but I'd have bet he spoke several languages. I introduced myself, said my call was personal, and he nodded to the secretary to leave us.

He crossed the large paneled office to his golf bag and slid the putter into its tube. "I've played golf everywhere, even at Augusta and Pebble Beach. All the great links in Scotland. And where do I live? The world's biggest sandtrap!" It was a well-practiced line and he smiled at it. He looked out the window for a moment at the ships and the cranes and the forklifts and the workmen, then turned back to me. "What may I do for you, Mr. Driskill?"

"I understand my sister came to see you not long ago. A nun called Sister Valentine—"

"Oh, my God! She was your sister! Oh, my dear fellow, I read about her death—"

"Murder," I corrected him.

"Yes, yes, of course. What a tragedy—simply unspeakable! I had seen her, right here in this office, only a week or so before and then, there she was on television and in the papers. A remarkable woman. You must be proud of her." He sat down behind his desk which was stacked with sales slips, bills of lading, catalogues, golf tees, golf scorecards, colored brochures. His office walls held hundreds of photographs as if memorializing each of his life's events. I quickly picked out large shots of a very boyish Klaus

Richter standing in the brilliant sunshine with his tank in the desert, another with a pyramid in the background, another holding up a silver tray at a golf club. There was a gold frame on his desk that contained a shot of what I assumed were two sons.

"My heart goes out to you, Mr. Driskill. Truly. The sands of time are always running, are they not?" As if to illustrate his point, he picked up an hourglass nearly a foot high from the corner of the desk, turned it over, and watched the sand begin sifting to the bottom. "I have seen my share of death. Out there in the Western Desert. Valorous men cut down in their youth. On both sides. We die soon enough in the best of times, don't we? This sand, it is sand from the Western Desert, Mr. Driskill. Always here so I will never forget the fallen." He looked up from the hourglass. "Yes, I saw your sister."

"Why did she come to see you?"

He raised his eyebrows, wrinkling his forehead. His sunburned scalp shone through the close-cropped white hair. "Well, let me think back." He sank into his high-backed leather chair and stroked his rocklike chin. "Yes, it was my dear friend Sister Lorraine who called me about her, then sent her over. I must say I was surprised—and yes, flattered, to be frank—by your sister's interest in this very ordinary old soldier. Did you know she was writing a book about the Church during those trying years of the war?"

"She had mentioned it to me," I said. The sound of a jackhammer began outside along the docks. It sounded like a heavy machine gun. "Did she come to interview you? Was that it?"

"Yes, but I got it all wrong to begin with. I was an aide to Rommel, you see, very junior but still close to the great man. Naturally I thought she had Rommel on her mind—the field marshal, my claim to fame. But no, she wasn't interested in the desert war, not at all. It was Paris! Paris. When I think of my war, I never think of Paris. Paris wasn't like a war, you see. No one was shooting at me! We were an army of occupation, Paris was ours, not a city in flames . . . at least not for a long time. It was what you Yanks called good duty—I could have been sent to the eastern front! But your sister was collecting material about the Church in Paris during our occupation. She was using Bishop Torricelli as a central character. And I had known him during the course of my administrative duties—the Church and the Occupation HQ had need of normal liaison, just doing daily business. Trying to keep the churches free of Resistance cells." He shrugged.

I remembered Torricelli, the old man with the candies Val had loved. I remembered his story about my father emerging from a coal cellar somewhere—probably a church—looking like a minstrel. It was odd, at a distance of forty years, imagining a man like Torricelli trying to maneuver his way through the middle ground between Nazis and the Resistance, knowing both Klaus Richter and Hugh Driskill. Well, no one better than a Catholic bishop to do the maneuvering. If my father were to meet Herr Richter now, would they sit in club chairs and trade war stories?

I was watching Richter as he reminisced about the old days and then my eyes were refocusing on a photograph behind him on the wall: the youthful but by then battle-hardened Klaus Richter standing with a couple of buddies on a gray Paris day with the Eiffel Tower behind them. The face leapt out at me. Turned slightly to look at the landmark, shadows filling in his eye sockets. The face.

"Tell me," I said, "did you ever run into a priest in Paris called D'Ambrizzi? Swarthy fellow, big nose, strong as an ox. He is a cardinal now—"

He interrupted me with a note of surprise in his voice. "Really, Mr. Driskill, I am a Catholic—there's no need to tell me who Cardinal D'Ambrizzi is! He is one of the most influential men in the Church today . . . yes, I know *who* he is. And I would surely remember if I'd ever met him. But no, I never did. How does he come into this? Is this significant?"

"Not at all. Just curiosity. My sister mentioned him to me once. I wondered if you'd been in Paris at the same time."

He spread his hands inclusively. "We might have been, of course. There were a good many clerics and a hell of a lot of German soldiers. It sounds strange now, but we tried not to make a nuisance of ourselves. No more than was absolutely necessary. We understood how they loved their Paris. We loved it, too. Had we won the war, I can tell you one thing. Paris would have changed us, we would not have changed Paris. But the Boche was stuffed back into his cage and the result? We've all been Americanized!" His laughter cracked, his eyes waiting for a response.

"Sometimes I think that's an all-purpose excuse for the rest of the world."

"Perhaps." He nodded. "Well, to return to your sister—I'm afraid I was a great disappointment to her. I knew Torricelli but only in passing and I never kept any journals or diaries or letters, all the things historians love—"

An intercom on his desk buzzed and his secretary said someone was in the outer office to see him. He looked up at me, said, "Will you excuse me for just a moment? My dock foreman needs a word with me. Please, stay right where you are. Try out my putter if you like, I'll be with you in just a second." He grabbed a stack of yellow sheets and went out to the secretary's office.

I went to look at the photographs more closely. The walls contained an incredibly detailed account of his life. I followed them from one wall to the next, and in the darkest corner of the room there was a gap, just a small space where a picture was missing. In the corner—with a long library table covered with manuals and notebooks and price lists and dictionaries in half a dozen languages and file folders and a couple of withering plants tied to stakes, with this cluttered table drawing your attention away from the photos above—the gap could have gone unnoticed for months, years. You'd have had to be looking at the photographs closely to notice it. And I was looking. And there it was. Something missing from the story of Klaus Richter's life. And I knew where it was.

I was admiring the Julius Boros putter when he came back. He sat down on the edge of his desk, holding a stack of white sheets, said something about the endless technicalities of running an import-export operation. He was watching the sand running through the hourglass. "Where were we?"

"Paris."

"Yes, yes. Well, I was no help to your sister. She came so far . . ."

"Maybe you were more help to her than you thought."

"Dear old Torricelli, now, there was a man the historians dream about. He was a pack rat. He kept everything, every menu and every laundry list, every memo. I would bring him papers, he'd file them. Organized, alphabetized, utterly amazing. I always thought it took a tremendous ego, don't you agree? A man would have to believe in his own importance to preserve everything." He sighed at the thought. It seemed to me that a man who turned his entire workplace into a photographic history of his own life had an ego of his own. But it was always easy to judge others. I thought I could find my sister's killers. Ego was everywhere. "Your sister was so patient with me that day. I was running in and out, carrying on a telephone negotiation—she was so understanding but I'm afraid I was a great disappointment to her."

We went on for a few more minutes but I'd mined the vein for all I was going to get. He said he had a golf date and I thanked him for his time and left.

I nodded to the secretary. She was receiving a package from a delivery man. It was small and flat and wrapped in brown paper, tied with string. Outside in the crowded street I saw a blue and white truck standing with the motor running. There was blue lettering in several languages on the side panel. In English it said: The Galleries of E. LeBecq.

The banana-nose profile. D'Ambrizzi leaning forward as if listening to what someone was whispering, the bandit's mustache drooping darkly. A young, hard-faced man next to D'Ambrizzi: was he wearing a uniform? Something Wehrmacht about the stiff collar . . . The man next to him, thin-faced, harsh lines slicing his face vertically and shadows filling them in, a face of a man who passed harsh judgments, an eyebrow like a crowbar, a single thick smudge over his eyes . . . Then the fourth man, who had at first looked to be out of focus, indistinct . . . but there was something, *something* about him . . . two candles on the table, wine bottles, the picture taken with a flash attachment, casting odd shadows on the wall of painted brick behind them . . .

I was sitting in a fly-specked, grimy little cantina where workmen were drinking coffee and Cokes and I was trying to keep an eye on the front and side doors of the Global Egypt warehouse. I was drinking thick hot coffee and glancing back and forth from the warehouse to the photograph Val had left for me in the drum. I smoothed it flat and thought about those four men. And I could hear Sister Elizabeth saying *no, five, five men.*

Klaus Richter seemed to be a mighty swell guy. He undoubtedly played to a very low handicap and damned if he hadn't understood how much the Parisians loved Paris. He loved all those snapshots of himself, a life of which he was proud. And Julie Boros gave him one of his customized putters. Sister Lorraine said he was a pillar of the Catholic community. Nice sense of humor, called Egypt the world's biggest sandtrap . . . Helluva swell fella.

And a liar.

He knew D'Ambrizzi in Paris and he'd lied to me about it.

I knew he was a liar because I'd found a picture of him in my sister's toy drum. He was sitting next to D'Ambrizzi in the snapshot. Young, expressionless, a face that had already seen too much by the time he got to Paris. And I was pretty sure where my sister had gotten the picture.

Val had come to Alexandria looking for a man in the picture and she'd found him. And then the man with the silvery hair had killed her.

Klaus Richter . . .

Sitting in the canteen with the sun shining bright as a new half dollar, I realized for the first time since it had begun that I was truly afraid. I was alone, thinking my own thoughts, no Sister Elizabeth or Father Dunn or Monsignor Sandanato to share them with me. The sun was shining and I was drinking a cup of high octane java and nobody had tried to kill me all day. And I was having chills because I was so damned scared. It just came over me all of a sudden. When I realized Klaus Richter was one of the men in the snapshot . . . and it was important enough to lie to me about. The chills made my flesh crawl. The fear was making me feel like my back was leaking, like I was soaked with blood.

I just hated that.

I hated being afraid. Val had been afraid . . .

Klaus Richter came out of the side door an hour later. He was carrying his golf bag. He put it in the trunk of a black Mercedes four-door parked in the alleyway, got in, and drove away with the wind swirling dust and sand in his wake.

I put the snapshot into my pocket and walked back across the street. I found the secretary away from her desk and the door to Richter's office open. Somebody was pounding up a storm in his office. I went to the doorway. The secretary had a hammer and was leaning over the library table flailing at the wall.

I knocked on the door and said, "Excuse me." She jumped back, turned around with the hammer in her hand, mouth open in surprise. "Didn't mean to scare you," I said.

"I hit my finger," she said, shaking her hand. "But"—she smiled with wide, dark red lips in a dark face—"I would have hit it even

without your help." She recognized me. "You just missed Herr
Richter. He won't be back now until tomorrow."

"Golf, I'll bet."

"Of course. Is there anything I can do for you?"

"It's not so important, but I thought I might have left my pen
behind me." It was weak but what the hell? "Here, let me do that
hammering for you."

She held out the hammer and pointed to the nail. It was right
where I'd hoped it would be. "What kind of pen?"

"Fountain pen. Big old Mont Blanc." I leaned over the table and
pulled the bent nail from the wall, steadied another one, and drove
it in with two quick blows. "And the picture?"

She was unwrapping the brown paper package. She folded the
paper back and held up the small framed photo. It was a twin of
the one in my pocket. I took it from her and she smiled again,
shyly. "I'm so glad you weren't Herr Richter," she said. "He's very
particular about his photographs, and I wanted to get this one
replaced before he noticed it was gone. I put plants and stacks of
things over here hoping he wouldn't see—"

"What happened to the original?" I'd hung it on the nail and
straightened it, filling the empty space. I knew Val had taken it, I
could see her spotting it and while Richter had been running out
of the room conducting his negotiation slipping it into her Vuitton
briefcase. *But why?* What was so damned important about that
picture?

"I'd never say this to Herr Richter," she said, dropping her voice
to a whisper, "but I'm sure the woman who comes in and cleans
the office knocked it down while dusting. The glass was cracked,
probably, and instead of admitting it, she threw it away— She
claims to know nothing, of course. Fortunately Herr Richter had
another copy in his photo files. So it's been a race to get it framed
and back on the wall before he noticed." She was following me
around as I pretended to look for my pen. Finally I got down on
my knees, slipped it out of my pocket, and "found" it under the
desk.

She saw me out, thanking me for the help. I told her I'd enjoyed
every minute of it. I could almost feel Val beside me, patting my
shoulder, calling me a goof.

But what was the big deal about the snapshot?

It tied Klaus Richter, a legitimate businessman in Alexandria, to

D'Ambrizzi forty years before in Paris. During the Occupation. But what made that so important? Why did he lie about it? And why had Val left it for me? What did it have to do with murdering her?

Back at the Cecil a message was waiting. Sister Lorraine had called, wanted me to call her back. I went up to my room, washed my face, inspected the dressing on my back, and made a gin and tonic, light on the gin. I washed down a couple of pain pills. Stood at the window watching late afternoon settle over the water and the square with the huge statue in the center. The sound of the trams and the buses at Ramli Station, the cool wind blowing steadily off the sea. I finished my drink, staring out over the harbor, watching the shadows lengthen and the lights come on along the Corniche. To my left a yacht club glowed like the promised land where we could all go and have a wonderful, perfect night. *So why did Richter have to lie to me?* A simple truth and I might have shaken my head at the mystery of Val's quest and maybe, maybe I might have given up . . .

I was way out at the edge of the circle. I was still out there where it was gray and the lights of safety beckoned. I could still say the hell with it and go home. I had one lying German and nowhere else to turn. Egypt wasn't yielding up much. I supposed I could go back to Richter, confront him about the photo. . . . I could keep pushing toward the darkness at the center of the circle, the black hole that had swallowed my sister. . . . That's where the secrets were, where the answers were. How much did I want to know the answers . . . would they bring me happiness and peace? And a gentle eternity for my little sister?

I called Sister Lorraine.

She asked how my researches were going. I allowed as how I seemed to have fetched up against a wall and was beginning to watch my back. She gave a Gallic laugh, rather on the world-weary side, and said she'd remembered something else I might be interested in hearing. I interrupted her. "Sister, could I prevail upon you for the name of a restaurant?" She began to speak but I went on. "And might you be the guest of this poor stranded wayfarer? Without your help I'd have come a long way for nothing." It seemed to me I'd done just that anyway, but I was in no mood to spend an evening alone with a bottle of Bombay gin and memories of the silvery hair and the blade in the moonlight. Thanks be to God, she said she'd be delighted, so I thanked God again for small favors, for the Order, and the modern age of the sisterhood. Brave new world. She gave me the name of a restaurant, told me how to get there, and said she'd meet me.

The Tikka Grill was situated next to the El Kashafa el Baharia Yacht Club, whoselights I'd seen from my balcony. The dining room was on the second floor. Our table looked across the harbor at the white yachts with the glow from their deck parties. It was like a scene from a Humphrey Bogart movie. The music was playing softly and my nun was smiling at me through the candlelight. I had the feeling that the only women I knew anymore were nuns. I mentioned it to Sister Lorraine and she tilted her small, sleek head to one side, her eyes wide. "God's way of saving you from your base self, do you think?"

"I wish God weren't quite so worried about my base self."

"Shame on you," she said. "God is everywhere, concerned with everything. Alexandria is no exception." She sipped a French white and recommended the fish kebab. As we ate we talked and I felt myself letting down, relaxing. The walls were white stucco. The room was pleasantly crowded. The tablecloths and napkins were a gentle pink, the wine dry and cold, the fish superb. A soothing oasis of reality where I was at least for the moment safe. I told her that Richter had been pleasant enough but hadn't really told me anything about Val I didn't know.

She put her silverware down. "Mr. Driskill, I can't believe you came so far without a real reason. I'm not a detective, but the whole world knows your sister was murdered. You've come here because your sister was here . . . I have the feeling you have decided to— what do you say in English? Take the bull into your own hands?"

"Matters, not bull. Or by the horns, not into your own hands—"

"Whatever. May I be frank?"

"Everyone else seems to be when it comes to this."

"I think you are being a little foolhardy. I have thought about it since yesterday and I nearly decided to put you and whatever you're up to out of my mind . . . but then I thought about your coming so far. And your sister was so—so significant a woman. Such a credit to the Order. And"—she made a small dismissive gesture—"I couldn't stop you from doing whatever you intend. I am correct, am I not?"

"Tell me what you remembered, Sister."

"Sister Valentine saw another man while she was here. Or, rather, she intended to. She mentioned it to Sister Beatrice, who mentioned it to me—it had slipped my mind, then I thought of it last night." She sighed expressively, as if she knew she ought to have kept the name hidden forever. Sister Lorraine was a natural flirt.

"Give me the name," I said.

"If I do, will you tell me what you're doing?"

"Sister—" My back was killing me. It had come out of nowhere, like the man with the knife. "I . . . don't know what I'm doing."

"Are you all right?" She leaned forward, her huge eyes narrowing. "You are so pale . . ."

"I can't tell you." I was thinking as Val had when Sister Elizabeth asked her what was going on. I was protecting Sister Lorraine from what I didn't know. "But I need that name, Sister."

"LeBecq. Etienne LeBecq. He owns a gallery. *Très chic.* Cairo and Alexandria. He's the sort of man who has his own plane. One of my countrymen, I'm afraid. His family has been in the art business for generations. In Paris. With people like Wittgenstein and Duveen Gobelin, the tapestry people. LeBecq apparently came to Egypt after the war, a young man . . ." She made a face. "The LeBecqs were, you know . . . Vichy, I believe."

"Do you know him?" I needed a pain pill. I needed a new life and a day without fear. The chills were shaking me.

She shook her head. "No Catholic nun, not even of the Order, can move in Monsieur LeBecq's circles."

"Is he one of Richter's pals?"

"I don't know. A Frenchman with a Vichy background and a soldier of the Occupation?" She shrugged. "Why do you ask?"

"My sister connects them. And one of LeBecq's trucks was delivering a package to Richter's office this afternoon." I moved gingerly in the chair, trying to ease the pain. My back felt wet.

"What's the matter? Mr. Driskill? Do you need a doctor?"

"No, no, please. I've got a bad back. And maybe a lingering touch of jet lag."

"I think it's time to get you to bed." She called for the check. She was trying to pay the damn thing, but I managed to force my credit card into the waiter's hand.

She was driving a Volkswagen convertible and the cold air off the water revived me. I got out at the Cecil, reassured her that I was all right, thanked her for her help, and tottered up to my room.

In one of Father Dunn's novels the bad guys would have searched the room or been waiting for me with guns, or the gorgeous blonde who'd sat next to me on the flight from Cairo would be naked in my bed, but the room was quiet and undisturbed and I was very much alone. The bed was turned down, the curtains were furling slowly in the breeze.

I got to the bottle of pills, checked my back, which was fine, lay down wondering if I'd better start saying my prayers.

The LeBecq Galleries faced the sea, plate glass windows on two floors with palm trees swaying in front, reflected above and below. The gallery was sterile, chrome and Plexiglas and glass and white walls, some huge paintings alone on vast stretches of whiteness. I spotted a Rauschenberg, a Noland, a Diebenkorn looking pale and cool and exquisite. In the ground floor windows, flanking the doorway, were two large Hockneys on chrome tripods, lots of water and sunshine and flat reflecting surfaces and inviting shadows. A couple of well-dressed customers strolled before the pictures inside, then climbed the open stairway which seemed to float like a dream of great wealth just above the floor.

I called from a restaurant five minutes away and said I'd like to see Monsieur LeBecq personally about the Hockneys that afternoon. The girl had a soft, limpid, soothing voice and wondered if she might be of assistance. A couple of minutes later I had an appointment with LeBecq for three o'clock. I ate my lunch and sat on a bench outside and read *Leave It to Psmith* by Wodehouse, which I'd picked up in the lobby of the Cecil. I showed up at the gallery a few minutes early and had a look around. It was all very spare, remote, cool, airy, devoid of any of the richer emotions. Art for the summer homes ranged along the beaches where the rich from Cairo maintained their retreats from the heat of the Nile delta.

The woman who showed me into LeBecq's office was short, compact, precise, with a face of sharp edges and rounded, female shoulders and hips. She was the one with the voice. She wore a tobacco-colored pleated skirt that swung from her hips when she walked. She had a deep tan, an oval face, a slightly tilted nose, rakish cheekbones, and a lot of gold against her flesh. She reminded me of just how long it had been since I'd truly wanted to touch a woman: you could always be driven to some kind of need, but wanting was something else again. She murmured something and left the office and Monsieur LeBecq entered a few seconds later. There was a soundproof double-paned glass wall overlooking the main two-story gallery. When I'd climbed the steps to LeBecq's aerie the damn things had swayed like a rope bridge over a chasm with the answers on the other side. I turned back from the view when LeBecq made a polite little cough, and when I saw him I had to do a quick double take.

He was pale, as if he'd just climbed out of a coffin full of earth from his native land, and he wore a black suit, a white shirt with French cuffs and onyx and gold cuff links, a black and gray figured tie. He was oldish but indeterminately so, tall, thin as a mop handle. His face was narrow and lean. He had an Old Testament look, a hanging judge, all severity. It was hard to imagine him sucking up to the rich and filling their need for something with pale green in it to match the stripe in the couch. He wore heavy black glasses and his eyes swam like huge waterlogged beetles behind the thick lenses.

"You were calling about the Hockneys, I believe," he said. "They are, of course, choice pieces, Mr. Driskill."

"I lied. I own two Hockneys and while I like them very much, two is a lifetime supply."

"I don't understand, m'sieur. You called about the Hockneys in the window—"

"So I did. I just wanted to make sure I saw you personally. I saw Klaus Richter yesterday. He didn't call you by any chance, did he? A word of warning, perhaps?"

"Herr Richter? No, he didn't call me." He was standing with his back to that big glass wall. His suit was cut tight, making him look like a stork in mourning. "Now I must ask you to state your business, if any . . . or—" He pointed to the door. I heard some Vivaldi start up, coming through hidden speakers.

"My sister came to see you and a few days later someone killed her. I want to know why she came—"

"What are you talking about? I know of no sister of yours!"

"Her name was Sister Valentine. She came to Alexandria to see you and Richter. I'm here to find out why."

He looked as if someone had snipped the wires holding him together. His limbs gave a nervous jerk, he ducked his head. He was wearing a black hairpiece that jutted away from the nape of his neck when he leaned forward. He stalked awkwardly to his desk, fumbled with the back of his chair, spun it into position, and sat down. He seemed to have gone whiter still. He steadied his hands on the desktop.

"Sister Valentine," he said tonelessly. "Yes, I read about her murder. . . ." He was talking to himself. "What do you want of me? What do you expect—"

"Why did she come to see you?"

"Oh . . ." He brushed his hand weakly across his face. "Nothing. She was digging up the past. I couldn't help her."

"What was your connection to the Church?"

"The Catholic Church? I had nothing to do with the Church. You see me—I am an art dealer. I have always been, my family has always been." He was struggling to get a grip on what he remembered about composure. He reached out and straightened a framed photograph on his desk. In it he was standing on a runway, one arm on the wing of a light plane. He wore a black suit then as well. "I have nothing for you, m'sieur. Please leave me, I have much to do." The beetles were darting restlessly behind the lenses.

"I'm not leaving without some answers." I leaned on his desk, staring down at him. "I've got a picture of you, LeBecq." I slapped the worn snapshot down on his desk. He jumped at the sound, drew back. I was scaring him but I didn't know why. "Take a look," I said. He turned away. I reached out, grabbed his arm, yanked him back in his swivel chair. "Look at the goddamn picture!"

He slipped his spectacles off and cautiously leaned forward as if he thought I might smash him facedown on the desk. I held the photograph flat on the desk and he blinked at it, then lowered his head farther, squinting. It was hard to imagine him flying the plane with eyes that bad.

"D'Ambrizzi, Richter . . . and you," I said. The thin man, cadaverous, the single black eyebrow. Forty years ago, but it was the same man. "Tell me about that picture. Tell me who was the fourth man." I paused. "And who took the picture." I waited. "Talk to me!"

"How can I help you?" He was muttering, plaintive. "How do I know who you are?"

My fist came down on the desk. The framed picture toppled over.

LeBecq shrank back. His lips were moving but nothing was coming out. Then he croaked: "Maybe you killed her . . . No, no, don't hit me! Don't touch me!"

"Tell me about the meeting in that picture. You, Richter, and D'Ambrizzi . . . You are going to tell me. The sooner the better."

"Maybe you've come to kill me," he said hopelessly, finally staring up at me as if he were contemplating his cruel fate. Those big wet eyes were speaking to me. They were saying I wasn't the only one having a bad day. "Maybe you'll kill all of us . . ."

"What are you talking about?" I eased up on him. I had to get him talking. "Kill all of you? Who?"

"She came here, your sister, she was asking about those old days. . . . I knew it would come to this sooner or later. The past always catches up with you. . . . Who sent you?" The eyes swam up in search of mine. His hand was feeling for his heavy black-framed glasses.

"I told you why I've come."

"Was it Simon? Did Simon send you?"

"Who the hell is Simon? The fourth man? Or the man with the camera?"

He slowly shook his head. He was having a lot of trouble coping with what was happening to him. "Have you come from Rome? Is that it?" He licked his dry, cracked lips. "For God's sake, don't kill me now . . . not after all these years. . . . Your sister is dead . . . my brother is dead . . . that's enough, isn't it?"

"Your brother? What's your brother got to do with this?"

"Your photograph," he said. He cleared his throat, trying to dislodge the fear. He was growing drastically older before my eyes. "That's not me in your little picture. It is my brother . . . Guy LeBecq. *Father* Guy LeBecq. Ten years older than I. A priest. I know nothing of this photograph. . . . Please, you must believe me." His personality kept shifting. Now he was morose, not fearful. "Like your sister, Mr. Driskill, he, too, was murdered . . . a long time ago in Paris. During the war. Murdered in a church graveyard, he was found propped against a gravestone . . . his back broken, the life crushed from his body . . ."

I took a step back from the desk, still holding the snapshot, bumped into a chair, and sat down. "I'm sorry," I said at last. "How could I know?" He was breathing heavily while the Vivaldi played on. "What do you mean about my coming to kill you? Who's

Simon? Why would Rome send me? I don't understand what's happening here—"

"Listen to me," he said slowly. He fitted his glasses into place, gripped the arms of his chair. "They will kill you, too. Have no doubt of that. You are far from home and you're meddling in something that is no concern of yours. It's the past, you'll never understand any of it . . . so go home, Mr. Driskill, forget us, for the love of God, forget us . . . and maybe they'll let you live—do you understand what I am saying to you? Go home, mourn for your sister—survive. You are an innocent—and your innocence is your only protection! Wrap yourself in it, hide within your innocence. Now, please leave me. There is nothing more I can tell you. Nothing!"

He sat silently staring at his hands while I left.

On my way down the floating stairway the beautiful girl who had shown me in passed me going up. She smiled and asked me if all had gone well. I shrugged and felt her eyes on me as I went on down.

When I got to the main large gallery I looked back up at the thick glass wall of Etienne LeBecq's office. He wasn't visible, but I saw the girl go in.

I left, walked slowly back to the Cecil.

His *brother*?

Jesus H. Christ. Everybody's a comic and there's always an extra little spin you didn't expect. I made a straight line through the lobby of the hotel toward the bar. The lobby had seen better days but those days must have been something. Now the opulence was faded and getting on but the memory, like that of an old rake, was keen. The bar looked out on the Corniche and the water. The rays of the lowering sun were turning the vista gold.

I eased my back into a comfortable position and downed a gin and tonic, signaled for another. I'd blown off some steam with LeBecq and had begun feeling a little better about things when he said the guy in the picture was his brother. And his brother was dead. So what was so upsetting? He had me coming from Rome, being sent by Simon Somebody, coming to kill him . . . *to kill all of us*. He must have told Val some of it. *Your innocence is your only protection.* Did that mean he could tell that Val had known things I obviously didn't? Somehow I couldn't have remained in his office hammering at him. But I was going to have to see him again. He was all I had and he was going to have to explain himself. Of course, there was Richter, but he was a much tougher customer.

I asked myself why I hadn't bugged Richter about the snapshot—and the answer was that I'd realized Val had stolen it from him. No point in opening that mess to view unless you knew what you were going to see.

Why hadn't I mentioned to either of them the silvery-haired man, the priest, who had killed Val and tried to kill me? I didn't have an answer to that, not one I was proud of. Maybe I was afraid they were all part of the same terrible conspiracy . . . maybe I was afraid he would come for me again.

"Mr. Driskill, telephone for Mr. Driskill." A bellhop was moving through the bar calling my name. I waved to him and he told me to take the call at cabin one in the lobby.

When I said hello I was hoping it was Sister Lorraine taking me under her wing for another dinner. But it wasn't. It was a woman but she was whispering. I couldn't tell if she was trying to disguise her voice or simply ensuring privacy at her end.

"Mr. Driskill, I must see you this evening."

"Who are you?"

"Later. Meet me at—"

"I only meet strangers in nice safe places, lady."

"At the statue of Sa'd Zaghlul in the square. Just outside your hotel. Safe enough?"

"How will I know you?"

"I'll know you. Eight o'clock."

She hung up before I could answer with any more dazzling repartee. I went back to the bar and took two pain pills with a third gin and tonic. Then I went up to my room, took a very careful bath, changed the dressing on my wound, sat by the window trying to make notes about what I'd learned in Egypt. It wasn't a bad list but when you started adding it up it was a disappointment. Just an accumulation of what might be truths without enough connective tissue. Maybe my mysterious caller could provide some.

A few minutes before eight I put on a pair of soft corduroys and a heavy sweater and went outside into the chilly, steady wind. The massive statue dominated the square. She must have been watching for me because she intercepted me right away as I crossed the street. She was still wearing the tobacco-colored skirt with all the pleats, the matching suede pumps, and a leather jacket. I told her she was a pleasant surprise but she found my attempt at charm immensely resistible. She was very pretty but her face was a solemn mask. The wind couldn't mess her cap of dark hair. She wore a gold necklace with a heavy amulet.

"Why all the mystery? How did you find me?"

"The Cecil was the first hotel I called." She shrugged. "I was afraid you wouldn't come if you knew who I was."

"So, who are you? You work at the gallery and you're the prettiest girl in Alexandria—what else?"

"Gabrielle LeBecq. It is my father's gallery." She stopped with the statue looming over us. She must have had a very beautiful mother.

"At least you're not a nun," I said.

"What is that supposed to mean?" She walked on with her hands jammed into her jacket pockets. "I am not even Catholic. I am Coptic."

"That's fine."

"I don't understand." She gave me a perplexed, sidelong look.

"It doesn't matter."

"I am Egyptian. My mother was a Copt."

"All right. It really doesn't matter." Her mouth was finely formed, delicate little ridges edging up and forming her lips. Gold earrings. "What are we doing here?"

"I must speak seriously with you. Come, have coffee."

We went across to the Trianon Coffee Shop.

She was quiet, watching me, unsmiling. She didn't say a word until we had our coffee.

"You must leave my father alone. You must. You must not torment him. He is not well." She watched me sip the hot, powerful brew. "Say something."

"I came here to see two men. Your father is one of them. I'm sorry for upsetting him but—"

"I don't understand what you want from him. He was . . . sobbing when I got to his office. He's had one heart attack. He must not have another. He told me who you are. He swore to me that he told your sister everything he could—"

"And what was that, Miss LeBecq?"

"I don't know. He told me he did what he could."

"My sister was murdered after she talked to your father. I want to know what he told her."

She was shaking her head. "My father is a decent man. Her questions had something to do with—I don't know, forty years ago. What could it matter now?"

"Something mattered enough to somebody that my sister died because she knew. The bottom line is I can't worry about your father."

"But my father was an art dealer, he had nothing to do with the war, you must understand." She bit her lip, near tears. "His brother, the priest, he was older. He died a hero's death in the war. He was in the Resistance, I think. Something like that." She brushed at her eyes, long lashes. "My father and his father operated the LeBecq Galleries. My father left France and settled here once that war was over—"

"Why? Why didn't he stay in Paris?"

"What difference does it make, Mr. Driskill? He came here, eventually he married my mother, and I was born in 1952. He's a respected man, and you have no right to hound him!"

"What's his connection to Richter?"

She stiffened. "They are friends, they have done business together, they are good Catholics—but this is not relevant. No, not relevant at all. First your sister comes, then you—"

"Listen to me carefully, Miss LeBecq. Think—how could something *irrelevant* upset your father so dramatically? Why would he ask me if someone called Simon has sent me to kill him? Why would he ask me if I've come to 'kill us all'? Those are *his* words. Doesn't sound irrelevant to me. Honestly, does it to you? My sister's dead and your father is scared out of his wits. . . . Why is your father so afraid?"

"I don't know. All I know is that he is afraid of . . . of you! We do know that, don't we?"

She stood up abruptly.

"Look—"

"Please, I'm begging you," she said. "Leave him alone. Just go back where you came from and leave our lives as they were."

She was gone before I could really protest. By the time I'd paid for the coffee and gone outside there was no sign of Gabrielle LeBecq.

*   *   *

I woke the next morning groggy from a handful of sleeping pills. I was running a fever, nothing terribly dangerous I told myself, and my back didn't seem any different. But I kept checking it as the afternoon wore on. It was slightly inflamed along the stitching, draining a bit. I had the right pills for that, so I added them to the mix and put the gin on hold.

It was an empty, pointless day, wasted. I tried not to think about the scattershot information I'd picked up from Etienne LeBecq. He was obviously a crucial source, but how was I going to get anything out of him if he didn't want to talk? I had hit another wall and I wasn't thinking very creatively but, as they say, even a blind pig occasionally finds a truffle.

I put in a call to Margaret Korder in Princeton. She told me that the story of the murders at the Helmsley Palace and Val's murder were falling out of the news. No headway was being made by the police and there just wasn't any news to report. She said that my father was depressed, slept a good deal, and didn't respond much when people tried to speak with him. He seemed to miss me, and the fact that I'd set off on my quest was the one thing that could get a rise of anger or frustration out of him. I took all that in and placed a call to the hospital. But my father was resting and they didn't think he should be wakened. I told them to let him know that I called, that I was fine, and that he shouldn't worry.

As night was falling across Egypt and the cold wind was getting a little uppity outside my window, the telephone rang. It was Gabrielle LeBecq and she wasn't playing any games with her voice this time. She was upset and it showed in her breathlessness. She said she'd thought a long time about calling me but then realized I was part of her problems and therefore the person to call. I told her to slow down, keep it all in English since my French was pretty rudimentary, and explain what she was talking about.

She said her father was missing, hadn't been seen by anyone since he'd left the gallery shortly after he'd spoken with me. He hadn't come home, had left no message for her. "I'm afraid something very bad has happened to him. He was so distraught after his talk with you." She took a deep breath. "You're the reason he's gone . . . I only hope that's all he's done . . . if he's done away with himself—" She choked back a cry of anguish. "Why did you come here? What is all this about—really?"

"That's what I'm trying to understand . . . why my sister had to die—"

"Then I must speak with you again. Come here . . . I'm at home. There are things I must tell you, show you . . . you are, I'm very much afraid, what my father has been waiting for all these years. Please hurry, Mr. Driskill, before it's all too late."

She gave me the address and I went downstairs, my fever and back forgotten for the moment, got a cab, and took off. I didn't know what the hell she was talking about, did I? The fact was, it was something to do, to create the illusion of getting somewhere.

The house was low and off-white in the moonlight. It looked as if it had grown out of the crest of the dune with a nod to Frank Lloyd Wright. I walked up the long stretch of driveway from the gates, past lots of palm trees and shrubbery and flowers. The house was dark when I reached it. I looked behind me, thought I heard a noise which wasn't part of nature. Sister Lorraine was a prophet: I'd started watching my back and that made me think of Val, who hadn't watched her back quite closely enough there at the end. I listened, watching for moonlight on silvery hair or the knife blade, but I heard only the surf on the beach behind the house and the wind shaking the palms, and I saw no signs of life at all.

The front door was actually two doors, an inner slab of wood, then a separate layer of filigreed black ironwork. I was staring at the doors looking for a buzzer when the wooden slab swung open and I levitated about a foot and felt like I was going to be sick. The iron filigree opened and Gabrielle said, "I didn't mean to startle you."

"Well, you made a damn good job of it."

There was a dim overhead light shining down on her face. When she looked up at me I saw that her eyes were red from crying. "Please come in." She stepped back and for just that fractional instant I had the feeling I was being set up. Then it passed.

She led me through the dark rooms toward a light at the end of the long, wide hallway. In the shadows we'd passed through I saw a Rouault, a Byzantine icon, a pair of Monets with a wall to themselves. There were mounds of low, heavy furniture, potted plants, some tapestries on the walls, thick rugs: everything subtle, understated, made more so by the dim light which came only from the moon at the windows.

"In here," she said. "I've been trying to understand what my father has been thinking. I've made a mess." She looked around his study at piles of papers. The drawers of the desk were open. Three table lamps were turned on. There was a Degas on the wall opposite his desk, which was a heavy, carved affair with gilded corner figures and an inlaid leather top. She straightened a couple of the piles, then leaned her hips against a library table, brushed her dark hair back from her forehead, and lit a cigarette with a heavy table lighter. "Tell me everything you said to my father—there had to be a reason for his . . . his going away." The cigarette trembled between her fingers.

"I showed him a photograph taken a long time ago in Paris. During the German Occupation. Then he just seemed to crack up, started talking about my coming to kill him. It made no sense. He was afraid of someone he called Simon and asked me if Rome had sent me. . . . I agree with you, he was afraid, scared to death. But then he clammed up, asked me to leave."

"This picture," she said. She wore a V-necked cashmere sweater and skirt. The sleeves were pushed up on her forearms, gold bracelets clinking. Her face was drawn, tired, faint circles etched beneath her shiny dark eyes. She was close to cracking: it was more than her father being missing for twenty-four hours, it had to be more than that. She was thirty, a grown-up, but there was something going on now she couldn't handle. "May I see this picture of yours?"

I stood beside her, put it on the table in a pool of light, and she bent over to study it. A pair of glasses hung on a chain around her neck. She put them on to study the picture. "Richter," she murmured. "And is this my father? I don't think—"

"He said it was his brother Guy. A priest."

"Yes, yes, it isn't my father but there's a strong resemblance." She pointed at one of the figures and looked at me inquiringly.

"D'Ambrizzi. He's a cardinal now. He could become pope soon."

"And this one? He looks like Shylock—"

"That's it!" I was whispering because it was so quiet in the house. "I knew there was something about that profile . . . it's Torricelli! Bishop Torricelli. It was right at the edge of my mind— he was a very big man among Catholics in Paris during the war. I met him once when I was a boy. Father took us all to Paris after the war. He'd known Torricelli . . . I remember someone calling him Shylock, a nickname, and my little sister asked what Skylock meant. Torricelli laughed and turned his profile to her and pointed to his nose, an incredibly hooked nose—more like Punch, to my way of thinking. Like the dancing man Lautrec painted." I stared at the photograph. "My God," I thought aloud, "now I know them all . . . Monsignor D'Ambrizzi, Klaus Richter of the Wehrmacht, Father Guy LeBecq, and now Bishop Torricelli."

"Is there some point to this picture?" She let her glasses fall to her breasts. "Why show it to my father?"

"I thought he was in it. My sister had this photograph with her when she was killed. It's all I have to go on . . . I've got to find out what it meant to her. Why did it set your father off and running?"

She was quiet for a long time. I stood looking out at the Mediterranean washing up the shingle of sand. My mind was racing, getting nowhere. I needed help, someone with a mind clearer and more agile than mine. When I turned back to her she hadn't moved, stood smoking the last of her cigarette, staring at me.

I nodded toward all the papers she'd been going through. "What's all this?"

She went to the desk. She moved gracefully, swaying elegantly on her high heels. She looked tired and tense and beautiful. I wanted to smash the moment to bits, reconstruct it as something romantic. I wanted to touch her. I tried to force the idea out of my mind. It was a hell of a time to lose my concentration.

"I've been going through whatever papers I could find. I've been looking for something that would tell me why your sister upset my father so . . . he hasn't behaved normally since she saw him." She pushed some of the debris to one side. "I found his diary. He came home yesterday when he left the gallery—I didn't know that until I found the diary . . . when I got home he was gone. He made some notations—this was *after* he talked to you. Here, see for yourself."

It was a spiral-bound datebook and agenda. He'd written something in French. I wanted to get it exactly right. "Translate," I said.

" 'What will become of us? Where will it all end? In hell!' " Her voice cracked. She bit her lip, turning to me. There were tears on her cheeks and her mascara was smeared. "My uncle died a hero's death . . . now my father forty years later . . . I know something terrible has happened. . . . I know you didn't mean it to happen—"

"No, Gabrielle, I didn't. I'm just wandering in the dark." I put my hands on her shoulders, felt the softness of the cashmere slide against her skin, and she came to me, her head buried on my chest. I held her, felt her quaking against me. She was small, her bones made her feel breakable, and she clung to me, a stranger, in her time of fear, and I kissed her sleek hair, inhaled her scent. I wanted to tell her that it would all be all right, that her father was safe, but I couldn't. Too many people had died. So I held her and let her cry it out. Maybe her father was right. Maybe he was in hell already. There was no comfort in false reassurance now.

With her head still on my chest, she said, "Why do I trust you?"

"What have you got to lose? You know damn well I'm not here to kill anybody. And I'm cute for an older man, maybe?"

She grinned and sniffed.

Then I took a shot in the dark. "Because maybe you know things you haven't told me . . . things you know I should know. You trust me because you want to trust me."

She pulled slowly away. "Here, there's something else in his diary." She was flipping through the pages, then stopped. "Here's the day he saw your sister. He makes no mention at all of her by name . . . but here, you see, he has written a list of names."

Simon.
Gregory.
Paul.
Christos.
Archduke!

She looked at me as I read the names aloud, then she said, "Are they real names, Mr. Driskill? Or are they some kind of code names? Archduke . . ."

I nodded. "And what does that big exclamation point mean? What makes Archduke so important?"

She said, "There are four men in your little photograph—"

"And I am reasonably sure my sister showed this same picture to your father. He sees the picture, he doesn't make a note about my sister—but he writes down these names—"

"But it doesn't match, don't you see? There's one name too many!"

"No, it fits. The fifth man took the picture."

We stood staring at each other, confusion registering. She said,

"Mr. Driskill, would you like to walk on the beach? Maybe the fresh air will clear our heads."

"Why don't you call me Ben?"

She was picking up a suede jacket from the back of a chair. "Then you must call me Gaby. Okay?" I smiled, nodded. "Come." She slid a glass door open and the cold air and the smell of salt filled the room. She kicked off her high heels.

We walked down a wooden stairway to the firmly packed sand. The surf rolled in, shining silvery in the moonlight. The lights of Alexandria glowed off to the east. We reached the point where the sand was damp and packed hard, then set off walking just out of the surf's reach. For a time we spoke of personal things, my life as a lawyer in New York, the death of the man she was planning to marry in the 1973 war with Israel, my own failure to cope with the Church and the Jesuits, her life as an only child with her father after her mother died. She had known only a couple of American men and she laughed when I said I'd never known an Egyptian girl.

"Everyone expects Cleopatra," she said softly, putting her arm through mine. The wind was blowing salty spray across our faces when we turned and began the walk back to the house.

I asked her if she thought her father might have called his pal Richter if he'd needed someone to talk with after I'd left him yesterday.

She laughed harshly, a bitter sound in contrast to her normal tone. "Richter? Believe me, he is not my father's 'pal' . . . he is my father's jailer!"

"What's that supposed to mean?"

"Let's go inside. I'm cold. I'll make coffee and tell you all about Herr Richter and the LeBecq family."

When we were settled in a room with wall hangings and old Persian carpets and low couches and bowls of flowers and heavy, squat lamps casting gentle pools of light, she told me a remarkable tale she said she'd pieced together over the years and never told anyone else.

Jean-Paul LeBecq, the father of Guy and Etienne, had been a very conservative Catholic and a sympathizer with the Nazi puppet government set up at Vichy with Marshal Pétain as its figurehead. Guy was a priest. Etienne was working at the gallery, heir to his father's business. Under the elder LeBecq's gaze, he had no choice but to echo his father's political sentiments. Early in the war Jean-

Paul was incapacitated by a stroke and Etienne, in his mid-twenties, took over the gallery completely. And discovered that the old man had been acting as a kind of diplomat without portfolio moving to smooth the relationship between the Nazi force of occupation and the Catholic Church in Paris. It was important to keep the channels of communication open because each of the great monoliths needed the other. It was during this time that Etienne had met Klaus Richter, who was working the same side of the street, connecting the army of occupation with the Church. Everything she said was fitting with the tidbits of information Richter had given me. She knew very little of Father Guy LeBecq's involvement in any of this during the war years, only that she'd always been told he died a hero's death—that phrase again—during the war. Nothing more.

By keeping her ears open while working as her father's closest assistant, and while hearing him out when he slipped into one of his fits of depression, Gabrielle learned that old Jean-Paul had been handling the art treasures looted by the Nazis from private art collections, most of which were owned by Jews. Once Jean-Paul's health removed him from an active role in the business, his tasks feel to young Etienne.

"But what did the Nazis need a dealer for?" I asked. "They were simply *taking* what they wanted."

"Yes," she said, "but don't forget the Church. They wanted their share of the loot . . . in return for their cooperation with the Nazis."

"But what did this cooperation really amount to?"

She shook her head. "In time of war—who knows?"

"But the rest of this you're telling me, you know it to be fact?"

"Don't be such a lawyer! I wasn't there, if that's what you mean. But I'm sure of it, yes." She was impatient with me. "It's been eating at my father all these years—why would he make it up? Yes, that's the way it was—"

"But how can you be sure?"

"Because of what came later—because of what I saw my father go through! I've tried to put it out of my mind, but first your sister and now you, you've brought it all back to life. I'm ashamed of what my father has done. . . ."

"Gaby, the Church and the Nazis in bed together during the war isn't a very pretty picture, but it's not exactly a scoop either. The Church did a lot of things during the war it couldn't be proud of. Your father, you can't be too hard on him. It sounds to me like he was caught in the middle, the agent moving looted art from the Nazis to the Church—Gaby, there was a war on, who knows what pressures they put on him . . . he was a young man, following in his father's footsteps."

But I was thinking: was this it? Was this what Val had discovered? No, it was just too much a part of the past, the distant past. One point in an old indictment. Who would care now? How could anyone be hurt by accusations forty years old?

"But it didn't stop when the war ended," she said. "That's the point! That's the worst part. My father became *their* creature! They set him up with the galleries in Cairo and Alexandria after the war so he could continue to ship artworks without anyone taking notice . . . they kept the whole thing going!"

"They? Who? The war was over—"

"It is so simple for an American to be naive! Not us, not here, we can't afford your view of the world—not when Germans with newly minted past lives began showing up in Cairo, rich, powerful, advising the government. The Nazis, Ben, the Nazis—they'd hidden away millions and millions of dollars worth of art treasures, of gold and jewelry and precious stones of every imaginable kind . . . but all the loot was useless to them. What could they do with it? They had to have money—some way of converting it into money. There were Nazi survivors everywhere—the Condor Legion in Madrid, Die Spinne, all the old SS men who were getting out of Europe to Africa, to Egypt, to South America, to your precious righteous United States, the old guard who dreamed of a Fourth Reich—it wasn't just Mengele and Barbie and Bormann, there were hundreds and hundreds of men we've never heard of, and they all needed money. One way of funding them, setting them up in businesses and fat investment portfolios, was by selling off the art. But it wasn't easy finding a buyer they could trust—so they had to turn it into a kind of blackmail, too, don't you see?"

"You're telling me they sold the stuff *to the Church*? And that's how they've been funding themselves—"

"The surviving Nazis had the Church in a tight spot. Buy this stuff from us or else . . ." She watched me, waiting for the penny to drop.

"Buy it or we tell the world how we supplied you with looted treasure *during the war*! There's the blackmail . . . but they were actually giving the Church something for its money!" I sighed, sank back on the low couch, careful of my back. "I will be goddamned. The Church had made a pact with the devil."

"It was—*is*—a delicate balance," she said. "The Church isn't powerless—they could reveal the hiding places of a lot of men who were once war criminals. So the Nazi survivors fear the Church, too—it's a compact of mutual fear. And my father was caught between them . . . and he, too, got something out of it. He got rich for his complicity, for his sins. I don't know the mechanics, but they used my father to sell, buy, smuggle, and distribute out of Europe and eventually into the Church's possession. And he funneled the payments to the Nazis—"

"By way of Klaus Richter," I said.

She nodded. "I think that's the way it worked. I can't prove it, but my father told me enough so I could fill in the rest of the picture. That's what my father has been afraid of all these years— that he would be found out. My father is a weak man. He has no stomach for these games. Richter looks on him as a weak link. So Richter is the man who held my father's leash. Richter was the watcher . . . and now I'm afraid my father has cracked under the pressure of his own . . . guilt. . . ." She was crying softly.

I went to her, knelt beside her. She reached out to me and I held her. She couldn't seem to stop crying, and she was trying to talk but the words were muffled. Then she looked up at me, her face glistening, and she kissed me. A little later she led me to the bedroom. We made love in the hungry ways strangers do, each of us doubtless searching out the momentary hiding places we needed. When she was asleep I got up, put some clothing back on, and went to stand at the top of the wooden stairway leading down to the beach. The cold wind dried the sweat on my face. I couldn't quite remember if the exertion of the past couple of hours had hurt my back. The dressing still seemed to be in place and I was none the worse for wear.

I watched the moonlight on the water and in the stillness, with only the throb of the waves against the shore, I tried to reach my sister, Val, tried to ask her if this was it . . . if this was *all*. . . .

Perhaps she'd stumbled on this ring of art thieves dating back to the war in the way that I had: some clergy, some old, unrepentant Nazi rogues stuck away in odd corners of the globe with their ill-gotten paintings and statuary and Fabergé eggs, with their tattered dreams of a world in their hands. Not nice, but not enough to bear upon the choice of a new pope, not enough to kill Val and Lockhardt and Heffernan for: it didn't compute. No. I'd found an ugly detail in the corner of the huge tapestry that was the Church . . . but that was all.

But there was the photograph. And Richter had dealt with the Church, and there sat three clerics, two of whom were dead and one who just might be elevated to the Throne of Peter very soon. And I had Gabrielle's word that this was all still going on—this flow of artworks and money. And if she was right, then there were men within the Church today who were involved in continuing the old game of mutual blackmail. . . . There would be someone within the Church who was the Nazi master—

Maybe someone from long ago. Or someone new, carrying on the tradition.

D'Ambrizzi was the surviving link on the Church side.

How could I be sure that a revelation now might not destroy Cardinal D'Ambrizzi's chances at getting that top job? D'Ambrizzi, my marvelous playmate that summer and fall of 1945 . . .

Val had been close to him. Sister Elizabeth knew him well.

The facts bounced around in my head, and I couldn't seem to hold them still. Where did Paris in the present day fit in? Val had spent much of the last several months of her life in Paris digging at something buried there . . . but what? And Paris *then*? Hell, everybody had been in Paris back then!

I was wondering where Etienne LeBecq might have gone, thinking of how much I wished I could ask him a few questions, when I heard something behind me. Gaby had wrapped herself in a heavy robe and was standing in the doorway.

"I think I know where my father is," she said. "He and Richter used to talk about a place, a Catholic place, where they could go if they ever wanted to get away from it all. They'd laugh about it. Richter said it wasn't necessarily the end of the world but you could see it from there. . . ."

"A Catholic place? What does that mean? A church? Or a monastery? A retreat house?"

"I don't know. But I know what they called it."

"What, Gaby?"

"*L'inferno.*"

3

1. *Claude Gilbert 2–81*
2. *Sebastien Arroyo 8–81*
3. *Hans Ludwig Mueller 1–82*
4. *Pryce Badell-Fowler 5–82*
5. *Geoffrey Strachan 8–82*
6. *Erich Kessler*

The folder Elizabeth found among Val's belongings had been disappointing because it derived its thickness from twenty-odd blank pages. Only the top sheet contained the list of names followed by dates. All but Erich Kessler, for whom there was no date. Whatever background information she'd gathered was gone. Probably she'd carried the lot with her in the Vuitton briefcase which had been taken when she was killed.

One other sheet in the folder was just short of utter blankness. There was a mixture of capital letters that conveyed nothing to

Elizabeth. A code of Val's impervious to interpretation. It didn't look breakable. But she took it with her anyway.

At the office, madness reigned, but she found a moment the next day to take Sister Bernadine aside over two cans of Coke and give her the list.

"Here's a special task, Sister," she said. Sister Bernadine was having a cigarette, the one she allowed herself in the afternoon, and she always looked more grown-up and intelligent when she smoked. It was all an illusion since she was admirably grown-up and intelligent whether smoking or not. Elizabeth handed her a Xerox copy of the sheet with the names. "You will recognize one or two of these names, as I did. I'm betting they are all dead, probably died on these dates. Covers roughly the past eighteen months. What I want is the obituary data as it appeared in their hometown papers, as it were. And render it in English for me, just so I won't make some dumb mistake. Okay?"

"Good as done, Sis. But it could take a bit of time—"

"Well, bring the mighty jackboot of the Mother Church down on any necks that require it. It's important. And keep it to yourself."

Sister Elizabeth knew that there was nothing else in the world like the Secret Archives of the Vatican.

Twenty-five miles of shelving. Thousands upon thousands of volumes too heavy for one person to lift.

She knew that it was nicknamed "the Key of St. Peter" by historians. Without that key there would have been no meaningful history of the Middle Ages.

Somewhere within the Archives were the answers to questions that have perplexed scholars through the ages.

Did the Orsini prince strangle his wife Isabella on her marriage bed in the sixteenth century . . . or did he hire someone else to do it?

Who was St. Catherine? With her long blond hair was she, in fact, Lucrezia Borgia?

What secrets are hidden in the seven thousand weighty volumes of indulgences? What was the payment required for the absolution of sin? For the necessary exemptions from ecclesiastical law? Money and treasure of all kinds, yes. But what in the way of personal services to the pope and his princes?

What was the plot behind the theft of the Petrarch manuscripts?

Was it a last-minute improvisation because the golden seals themselves were out of reach?

And was the answer to the question perplexing the twentieth-century nun Sister Elizabeth also somewhere in the Archives? What had Val been working on? And why did she have to die?

Perhaps the answer lay in one of the nearly five thousand papal registers, beginning with Innocent III's letters in 1198, all bound in volumes the size of world atlases with the ink having turned golden with the passing centuries. . . .

Of all the *fondi,* as each collection of documents was called— and no one even knew how many *fondi* there truly were—there is one *fondo,* called the Miscellanea, which alone fills fifteen rooms. Its contents remain uncatalogued, a grab bag.

It had been said countless times and with good reason, God only knows what reposes within the Secret Archives.

All the records of Galileo's trial.

The correspondence of Henry VIII and Anne Boleyn.

The personal letters of Pope Alexander Borgia and the women who loved him—Lucrezia, Vannozza dei Cattanei, and Julia Farnese.

The records of the Sacred Rota involving the most intimate testimony relating to annulments.

The archives of the Congregation of Rites, the deliberations leading to beatification and canonization, including all the reports of the Devil's Advocates.

The complete records of the trial of Monaca di Monza, which revealed the most intimate details of the life of the Nun of Monza and the others of the convent.

The *fondo* relating to the nunciature of Venice which came to the Archives in 1835 following the fall of the Republic of Venice and contained the stories of three religious institutions suppressed rigorously in the seventeenth century.

It was all part of Sister Elizabeth's—and even more particularly, of Val's—background, knowing what kinds of material could be found in the Archives. And Elizabeth had heard all the stories from Val about the near impossibility of finding, by plan, what you wanted to find in the vastness of books, parchments, *buste,* or folders.

She knew about the tiny room opening off the Meridian Chamber in the Tower of the Winds. In that square room was a bookcase which contained nine thousand *buste.* Uncatalogued, unstudied, unknown. To inventory those nine thousand folders would require two scholars working on nothing else but their contents for nearly two centuries. One bookcase.

The only meaningful index to the Secret Archives was devised long ago by Cardinal Garampi and collected in many volumes. It is incomplete, inexact, and altogether frustrating. He also wrote it in his own code.

She also knew about the gambler's chance. It was what made the Secret Archives worth the effort.

She knew about the hundred-years rule—that the archives relating to the past century are closed. Absolutely closed.

And she remembered Curtis Lockhardt talking to them about the hundred-years rule. "Without the rule," he had said, "half of the men who run the world would have to kill themselves. Thank God for the hundred-years rule. We Catholics know how to handle these things. Saints be praised."

The Secret Archives of the Vatican were served by a total staff of seven men, overseen by one of their own number who is called the prefect.

Elizabeth was meeting Monsignor Petrella in half an hour in the Court of the Belvedere, home of the Secret Archives. Monsignor Petrella was the prefect. Monsignor Sandanato, who had spoken with him on her behalf, was the closest thing to a friend Petrella had, but even Sandanato did not know what she was going there for.

In half an hour she would begin trying to learn what in the Secret Archives had so fascinated Sister Val during the final months of her lifetime.

St. Peter's Square lay in cool, bright early morning sun and shade as she crossed it, passed along the Leonine walls, and entered Vatican City through the Gate of St. Anne, strode purposefully past the *Osservatore Romano* building to the Court of the Belvedere next to the Vatican Library.

All her papers were in order, including the letter from the pope that had come with her job and her identification card with her photograph. But it was Sandanato's emphasis on the Curtis Lockhardt connection that had speeded everything up, smoothed the way. And because of him she was also given browsing privileges in certain areas, and browsing was *never* allowed. Curtis Lockhardt had personally raised millions to aid the Secret Archives in preservation technology. "Someday," he had joked, "I'm going to walk in and find that Petrella has named the Xerox room after me."

Monsignor Sandanato was waiting just inside the door, in the jarringly modern room with the floors of light marble and a big table where she would sign in.

"I was in here about a month ago to have a look at Michelangelo's letters," he said as they walked to the reception room. "Petrella's an arrogant man, but he'd met his match. He told me I couldn't see them just now and I wanted to know why not. Turned out the Holy Father had checked them out a while back and Petrella was afraid to nag him about returning them. Of course, no one else gets to check anything out. Ah, there he is. Tonio, my friend!"

The large reception room was furnished with antiques Callistus had sent over from the papal apartments. On a low table there was a tapestry of St. Peter sailing on stormy seas, not a bad warning for anyone about to begin working in the Secret Archives.

Monsignor Petrella looked like an elegant courtier with an invulnerable duchy of his own. He was tall and blond, wore a long black cassock, and his face was well preserved, vain, disturbingly unlined for a man in his fifties. He welcomed her with a thin smile and a firm handshake. Having delivered her, Sandanato excused himself to get back to the cardinal, and Val was alone with Petrella.

"As you are well aware, Sister," Petrella said in silky English, "there are certain problems of organization here. The fact of the matter is simply this—the contents of the Archives will never be successfully catalogued. There is too much now and it is growing too quickly. Life has cast me in the role of Sisyphus and I can only do my humble best. I hope you are prepared."

"I think I know the *fondi* I'm most interested in, but you can probably help me—that is, I'm finishing up some researches that Sister Valentine was working on—"

"Such a tragedy." He sighed. "Such a mystery." He raked her with his gossip's eyes, eager for a clue.

"Do you by any chance recall where she was doing most of her work? It would be a help—"

"Ah. Yes. The Borgias, I believe. Very popular always, the Borgias. The nunciature of Venice . . . she spent many days in the Miscellanea. Some of the *buste* in the Tower of the Winds." He made an openhanded gesture, as if to say, there is so much.

"I think I need to get a feel of the place. I know what a long shot it really is. But I owe it to her to try to find some footnote material."

Petrella nodded. "Good. A realistic approach devoid of impatience is the key to retaining your sanity. This is all terra incognita. Come with me and I will show you just a bit of what you're getting into. But you've been here before, have you not?"

"Only in a very limited way when we ran a piece in the magazine about the Archives. I was a tourist, you might say. Today I'm a worker."

He smiled, nodding, leading the way.

They began in the study room with its huge black desks and bookracks for volumes too heavy to hold, the great clock, the throne on which the prefect nominally sat overseeing the room. He was usually too busy to be there. "But it's the idea that matters," Petrella explained. Through windows she could see the patio and the glorious red oleanders, orange trees, some students already taking a break for a smoke.

She followed along through darkened corridors lined by huge metal shelves two stories high, where the lights are timed and go off automatically as you proceed along your way, moving always in a bubble of light upon a sea of darkness. She saw the Hall of Parchments, where the ancient documents have been turned vaguely purple by a fungus that will eventually destroy them. In the oldest part of the Archives she saw the poplar cabinets built by the greatest cabinetmakers of the seventeenth century for Paul V Borghese, still bearing the coat of arms of the Borghese pope. Within those cabinets, the papal registers.

They climbed the narrow dark stairs to the top of the Tower of the Winds. Far below, the gardens of the Vatican lay like a miniature green map. The Room of the Meridian at the top was empty. Two of the walls were covered with frescoes depicting the winds as gods with wind-whipped robes. The room was designed as an astronomical observatory—"One can't help hoping that Galileo, whose signed confession is stored downstairs, draws some consolation from this fact," Petrella remarked—and the floor was laid out in a zodiacal diagram oriented to the rays of the sun coming through a narrow aperture in the frescoed wall. From the ceiling above hung a wind indicator, moving gently.

"The Gregorian calendar was created here," Petrella said. "There are no lights in the tower for a very good reason. Since no artificial

light is ever seen here, the presence of even the slightest flicker
would indicate either fire or intruders. Clever." He laughed softly.

In the afternoon Val settled down into the incredibly uncomfortable chair at her huge desk in the study room and sent for her
first materials. She began with the *fondo* relating to the nunciature
of Venice.

She hated everything that intruded on her time in the Archives
but the fact was she had her job to do. For the next few days she
could at best spend three hours a day in the study room and even
that meant that Bernadine had to take up the slack at the office.
Which meant her researches into the six names slowed down. But
finally Bernadine had enough to warrant a report. Elizabeth, growing punchy from all her searching combined with the magazine
work, decided to reward them both with a lunch out at a favorite
trattoria near the office.

Even though she'd discovered nothing she could connect to Val,
she'd begun to lose herself in the Archives. She had come across
some fascinating things in the nunciature of Venice *fondo* and some
rather juicy bits from the Borgia material, hints of this and that, sex
and violence and treachery—all the hallmarks of the period. She
had read notes on the backs of letters and seen tiny obscene
drawings in the margins of documents, put there as doodles by
impertinent copiers dead these three and four and five hundred
years. She spent her days holding the history of the Church and
the civilization in her hands, felt herself being drawn seductively
down paths she oughtn't to have spent time on . . . and she couldn't
help it. And now, having been truly bitten by the archival bug, by
the past, she had to bring herself back to the twentieth century and
go to lunch.

Bernadine had found an isolated table in a corner and was
waiting for her. They quickly ordered lunch and Bernadine opened
her attaché case. "Preliminary report," she said, "with real biogra-
phies to follow. But I've tracked them all down and you were right,
those were death dates. What we seem to have here—if it's a pattern
you're after—is some very unlucky Catholics. I'll run through them
chronologically.

"First, Father Claude Gilbert. A French country priest, seventy-
three years old. He was what you might call an underachiever,
spent his entire life in the Church in a village not far from the coast
of Brittany. A champion of the preservation of the Breton language.

One supposes, a good and harmless man . . . in the fifties he even wrote a couple of books, diaries of a country cleric in Breton, you know the kind of thing—"

"He must have been in France all through the war," Elizabeth said.

Sister Bernadine nodded. "Yes, I suppose he would have been. Right age for it. Well, he was killed in Brittany, walking along a country road, hit-and-run in a rainstorm. The driver didn't stop and was never located. A couple of farmers saw it, said the driver never slowed down . . ."

Elizabeth nodded, dipping a piece of bread in her hot, newly arrived soup. "Next?"

"Sebastien Arroyo. Spanish industrialist, retired but served on several boards, seventy-eight years old. Big playboy before the war, liked to race fast cars, very big art collector. Became a major fundraiser for the Church . . . very devout, lots of good works, same wife for nearly forty years. Lived in Madrid and on his yacht. He and his wife were shot down on a dark street in Biarritz with his yacht in the harbor. Nobody saw it happen, nobody heard anything . . . very professional job and the general feeling was it must have been Basque terrorists though they didn't actually claim it.

"Hans Ludwig Mueller was a German scholar and amateur theologian. Seventy-four years old. Fit the mold of the conservative Catholic intellectual. He fought for the Reich during the war but was implicated in an anti-Hitler plot at one time, survived some Gestapo torture. Clean bill of health from the War Crimes Commission people after the war. Confined to a wheelchair in his later years with a bad heart. On a visit to his brother's home in Bavaria he came to grief—everybody else went out one evening to the theater, when they got back to the house there he still sat in his wheelchair . . . but someone had cut his throat."

By this time Elizabeth had lost interest in her food, was picking at it without tasting it. "A nice, quiet killing," she said. A knife like the knife in Ben Driskill's back. "Go on."

"Pryce Badell-Fowler, an English Catholic, historian, seventynine years old, widower, had a couple of strokes, lived in the country near Bath. Still working, writing, but not all that spry anymore. Working on some magnum opus, but then something very unpleasant happened that last night at the farm. He worked in a barn that had been converted to a library and office. Fire got started, the whole building went up, the old man, too. But when they found his body, thinking he'd been overcome by smoke, they got a surprise . . . bullet in the back of the head. Nice? Nice." Sister Bernadine stopped to take a bite of her lunch and sipped red wine.

"So the fire had nothing to do with killing him." Sister Elizabeth nibbled at a thumbnail. "Therefore the fire was intended to destroy something . . ."

"Mmm." Sister Bernadine looked up. "That's good. How did you think of that? Detective stories?"

"I just have a nasty mind. What about the next one?"

"Geoffrey Strachan, pronounced 'strawn.' He was eighty-one years old, visiting his castle in Scotland. Career civil servant and a Catholic, too. Sir Geoffrey. Knighted in the fifties for his wartime career. British Intelligence during the war, MI-5 or MI-6, I never can remember those. He always drove his own Bentley, patrolling the perimeters of his land, apparently knew his killer—people in the village swear they saw him driving one Sunday morning with another man in the car, but when the Bentley was found pulled off to the side of the road he was slumped over the wheel—"

"With a bullet in the back of his head," Elizabeth concluded for her.

"Guessed in one!"

"It was no guess, Sister," Elizabeth said.

Sister Bernadine sighed, looked up in surprise. "Oh-oh."

"And what about Erich Kessler?"

"There was no date." She shrugged. "Maybe he's still alive. I'm still looking for him."

"Sister, I have a feeling you'd better hurry."

Elizabeth had trouble sleeping that night. She lay in the huge bed hearing the whine and rumble of Rome from the street below and the impressions of the day tumbled through her mind at a dizzying pace. She had returned to the Archives after lunch but her thoughts had kept returning to the list of the dead, to the one who presumably wasn't. Val had pieced together the five violent deaths and the pattern had been sufficiently persuasive for her to predict a sixth. But who was Kessler? Why would he be next? What tied him to the other five? Indeed, what did those five have in common that got them killed? Inevitably, why were Val and Lockhardt and Heffernan added to the list? Val knew about the five already dead

. . . Curtis Lockhardt knew Val . . . Heffernan was with Curtis . . . was that it?

Unable to sleep, she threw on a robe and went outside onto the balcony overlooking the busy street below. Rome glittered at her feet. The breeze was chilly. She pulled the robe tighter, conscious of the loneliness she couldn't shake, the memory of the little girl on the plane, all her memories of Val. . . . My God, how she missed her! What, she wondered, watching the lights making patterns far below, would Ben Driskill say to the list of names and what they implied? He was the only one she felt she could talk to about any of it, and he was almost as distant as Val. Once again she wished to God she hadn't been such an ass with Ben. How to undo the damage? Or would she never get the chance? She wondered if he knew what he was getting into . . . and would he have gone after the killer if he'd known about Val's list of the dead?

For the next few days she shut out the problems of her relationship with Ben Driskill, her sense of desolation and isolation at the loss of Val, and tried to keep her mind on business. She went back to digging through the nunciature of Venice *fondo,* trying to find something she'd seen earlier, in her first day or two in the Archives. It was infuriating to search through the bits and pieces, looking for it, trying to remember just what it had been. It hadn't seemed of any particular interest at the time, her eyes had just flickered across it, but something about it had stuck in her mind. Dammit! Once she'd lunched with Sister Bernadine it had begun to seem important to find it again. But she was lost in the maze of paper.

Fed up, she went to the curiously modern Coke machine and took the can out into the courtyard. Two priests were chatting in one corner on a bench, smoking, letting the warm sunshine stroke their pale faces. She was wearing slacks. No way they could know she was a nun. They watched her, smiled, she nodded back. She had not seen another woman in the Secret Archives since she'd begun her work. A man's world. Still, one of the murder victims was a nun—one of eight. She wondered if the two comfortably fleshy, middle-aged priests across the courtyard could imagine the things filling her mind, the things going on within their Church.

Back on the trail, searching for hints of what Val had been after, she knew she was on the verge of losing it entirely. She had nearly decided to give it up by midafternoon.

And then she found it.

The bell rang. The penny dropped. It kept her going.

A single word.

Assassini.

By some small trick of the nervous system she had registered the written word without knowing it, without realizing she'd seen it. But it had been there. And somewhere in her cortex the connection had been made.

Assassini.

She found it scribbled on the back of a menu. A very grand menu, for a dinner given by a very grand personage, no doubt. But there was no clue to the host's name, nothing to give it away. In fact, the menu might have been something other than an official menu, perhaps a note for a chef. In any case, what she had been searching for was scribbled in Italian on the back of the menu. The word had leapt out, stuck.

She set to jotting down a translation.

Cardinal S. has applied for permission to engage Claudio Tricino, of the Tuscan assassini, to resolve the matter of Massaro's violation of his daughter Beatrice who is the cardinal's mistress. Granted.

Thus, Tricino had doubtless pushed a blade into Massaro, who had apparently made two big mistakes. He had committed incest with his daughter and cuckolded the cardinal, all in one stroke, as it were.

The scribbled, faded note certainly had nothing to do with any of the material in which it was embedded, nor did the obscure menu. No references in the surrounding material to Cardinal S., no Massaro, no Tricino. Yet she had noticed it. Now she wondered, *had Val?*

Odd, how the word triggered her memory. *Assassini.*

Assassins. Thugs. A casual word for a fact of life in the Middle Ages and Renaissance. Anyone with enough power and money could hire them to do what needed to be done . . . to protect the power and the money. A nobleman set upon by his enemies, a prince with a rival, a rich man with a faithless wife or a mistress who was making trouble . . . a brother with a sister who knew too much . . . the hints found in letters and documents of the time were endless. But always just hints.

And when it came to the Church . . . well, the Church had specialized in spilling blood. Some said the *assassini* did the pope's killing for him. But it needn't have been a pope. A cardinal, a rich priest, you paid up and somebody died. It had been a fact of life.

Elizabeth had even asked one of her Georgetown professors about the *assassini*. Father Davenant had smiled and shaken his head, as if to say, what does a pretty girl want with such information? She had held her tongue. And he had said, "Of course they existed, they were commonplace whenever life was comparatively cheap. Which accounts for the paucity of commentary about them. Crime was not much studied then, it was simply one of the dark parts of life. Unsavory. Unglamorous. My grandfather came from Italy at the turn of the century. He always referred to all villains as *assassini*. He used to tell me that it was with the first *assassini,* hired out of Sicily, that the Mafia was born. And then of course there are all the other legends. . . ."

Father Davenant had taken a dim view of the legends but not such a dim view of Elizabeth. She had persisted. What legends?

"Sister, are we not historians? What are we talking about here?"

"Look, you're the historian. I'm just taking the class. A lot of things started out as legends—"

"That sounds good but is not quite accurate."

"Humor me, then, Father."

"Just old legends. The hidden monasteries, the pope's own army of *assassini* . . . you can imagine the kind of rubbish people dream up. The Church has always been an inviting target—"

"But surely this is verifiable rubbish—I mean, either it was true or not."

"There were such people. But beyond that, where would you propose to do the research?"

"The Secret Archives, obviously."

Father Davenant had laughed. "You are very young, Sister. You cannot imagine the confusion in the Archives. You simply cannot imagine. They have a special way of hiding things in the Archives. You know how archivists are, they can't throw anything away. So when they find things of, shall we say, a sensitive nature, they can't bring themselves to throw it away . . . so they hide it. In plain sight. It's really quite diabolical."

Father Davenant had never bothered to discuss the *assassini* with her again. But he had explained how the archivists hid things. He was quite right. It was diabolical.

She might have spent a year looking. Or she might have turned to the next of the seventeen thousand parchments and documents in the *fondo* and found what she was after. But in fact some organization had been done and the next day she located the documents relating to the suppression of monasteries ordered by the pope, carried out through the offices of the nuncio of Venice. The fate of the monastery of San Lorenzo made chilling reading.

The suppression of this Tuscan monastery in the mid-fifteenth century involved a story that might have served as a subject for one of the period's infernal tapestries, which have remained hidden in private collections ever since. It featured witchcraft, incest, desecration of the Church, murder, torture, carnal possession of an entire convent of nuns, the worship of pagan idols, tyranny of every imaginable kind, treachery, arson, and politics. The tapestry, had it existed, would have been rich in detail, if not actually cluttered with horrors.

It would have had at its center a Florentine nobleman, Vespasiano Ranaldi Sebastiano, who had himself made a bishop of the Church, paying a wagonful of ducats for the honor. The pope's family needed money, it was that simple, and no one particularly cared where the money came from.

As a bishop, Sebastiano chose to mock the Church, despoil in every way its dignity, its mission, its holiness. As an officer in Sigismondo Malatesta's private army, he laid waste to Church lands, raped nuns, pillaged and plundered Church treasure. He took to wearing his bishop's vestments and regaling his flock with obscene jests concerning the unlikelihood of the virgin birth. In his castle he practiced the oldest kinds of witchcraft with modern twists of his own devising. He turned a nearby convent into a personal brothel for himself and his hired guard. Examples of torture and degradation were commonplace, but the tales of the occasional escapee were discounted as ravings of the mad.

Sebastiano also provided a haven for *assassini* at his castle. When their number grew too large—he hired them out at a considerable profit, a kind of death league—he turned his attention to the monastery of San Lorenzo, only a day's ride from Castel Sebastiani, to house them. It was a logical idea, since many of his *assassini* had been recruited from among the monks: after all, Sebastiano was charming, profligate with his hospitality, extraordinarily well educated, possessed of considerable wit and debating skill, and was as well a bishop. His views on the Church were not to be blithely ignored. While little of his writings on the state of the Church survived his own destruction, it was recorded that his arguments were viewed by the Tuscan nobility, the priests and nuns and monks and learned observers, as well reasoned and persuasive, if utterly heretical.

Concluding that what the Church needed most was a cadre of dependable killers, he took over the monastery, murdered those who chose not to be included in his plans, and set up his own Tuscan *assassini,* loyal to Bishop Duke Sebastiano but, nevertheless, available for hire.

The pope knew of the bishop duke's activities but had no particular desire to take him on. The pope believed that it was simply more prudent to let him make his own bed: one of the *assassini* was bound to put an end to him sooner or later. What had Sebastiano actually done? was the question raised at court. He had taken over a run-down, primitive monastery; he'd murdered a few illiterate monks, raped a few nuns who were of little consequence. He practiced some witchcraft, but that was probably just to add spice to his sex life. And he commanded his own army of mercenaries as well as his own jealous *assassini.* Better to leave him alone.

However, such an overweening megalomaniac as Sebastiano was bound to overstep the perimeters of the pope's noblesse oblige. Sebastiano took umbrage at a remark made by the cardinal-nephew at the time, a twenty-nine-year-old bon vivant posted to Florence, who was reported rather widely to have made an improper suggestion to Sebastiano's sister Celestina . . . a suggestion which she had accepted with alacrity.

Being a highly practical maniac, the duke demanded a fitting tribute in return for whatever of his sister's often shredded honor might have remained at the time of her capitulation. He suggested possibly an equestrian statue of himself cast in gold. The cardinal-nephew declined the opportunity and the duke dispatched Brother Scipione, his most expert and trusted killer, to make a point. The cardinal-nephew was slain in his bedchamber, in his bed, in fact, which he was sharing with Celestina, who unhappily tasted the good monk's blade as well.

Now that Sebastiano's evil had struck within his own family, the pope had no choice but to exercise harsh measures. First, he named another nephew, twenty-one years old, cardinal. Second, he raised an army of his own mercenaries, nominally in the employ of the new cardinal-nephew, who sought to avenge the murder of his brother, and sent them to Castel Sebastiani. The monastery was attacked first. All but nine of the *assassini* were put to the knife. The duke, bereft of his most trusted friends and defenders, tried to make a deal. He proved to be as unsuccessful at diplomacy as he had been successful at debauchery. The inhabitants of the castle, less the duke, were herded into a dungeon and burned alive.

The duke himself had his limbs ceremoniously removed. The still-living torso and head were left to die alone in a stretch of sandy, flyblown wasteland.

The pope was pleased at the outcome of the campaign but for the matter of the nine *assassini* who escaped. They were said to have fled toward Spain. Rumors abounded that they had taken refuge in a mountain monastery that had been long deserted, its exact location unknown. In any case, it was just a story.

The pope troubled himself no further.

The story of Sebastiano and the Tuscan *assassini* left Elizabeth exhausted and depressed. But she couldn't stop wondering.

What was the difference between what had gone on in the fifteenth century and what was going on now?

She walked back to the flat that night, the horrors of the *assassini* and their masters too vivid in her mind. She had a hellish headache and went to bed early, worn out, confused, bedeviled by the fact that she had no one to discuss it all with over midnight snacks and cups of coffee.

Was there any real point to her researches? She felt as if she'd forgotten why she'd delved into the Secret Archives in the first place. She'd been warned about their power. But no one had warned her about the *assassini* who hovered in the darkness of her room, the ghost of Val, the remembered hurt and anger in Ben Driskill's face. It was a familiar litany by now. Soon she would have to tell someone.

Soon . . .

Father Peaches O'Neale of St. Mary's in New Prudence got along
as best he could following the death of Sister Val, the only woman
he'd ever loved. He wore his habitually smiling mask as he made
his way through the bright, brittle days of an early winter. It was
getting dark early, and in the evening, when the winds whined in
the eaves of the old parish house and the fire had burned low in
the grate, Peaches would occasionally wake up in his easy chair, his
brain numbed from good single-malt scotch and David Letterman
grinning sourly at a stupid pet trick on the television screen. The
scotch was one way of coping with Val's death, but he was
determined not to overdo it. Too many parish priests had gone
missing down that lonely road.

So he stayed busy with the youth groups at the church. He
worked with the ladies' aid group. He accepted every dinner
invitation and stayed in touch with Father Dunn. He visited Hugh
Driskill in the hospital every day. He watched the old man's strength
fighting to reassert itself. He watched the awesome will exerting
itself on the huge, uncooperative body. Undoubtedly Hugh Driskill
was slowly but surely coming around. In a way Peaches came to
feel that he was becoming a substitute son, a stand-in for Ben,
who'd taken off for God only knew where. He knew he wasn't what
the old man wanted, but he was better than no one, nothing.
Peaches was someone to talk to about Ben and Val, too, for that
matter. Peaches saw the old man thinking, deep in concentration,
going over Val and Ben in his mind, but what he was thinking
remained a mystery. Another man might have been helpless, but
not Hugh Driskill. He'd had no experience at impotency. He was
keeping his own counsel while he chatted superficially with Peaches
and remembered better days.

Peaches also visited Val's grave in the little cemetery, mourning
not only for her but for what his own life might have been.
Sometimes he went outside the fence and stared for a while at
Father Governeau's grave, wondering about that story, thinking how
Edna Hanrahan and her girlfriends had had such crushes on the
handsome, doomed priest. Peaches tried hard to draw on his faith
to survive this period of his life. It was a hell of a test.

Nothing, however, kept him busier than cleaning out the basement, the attic, and a variety of storage cupboards that contained

the accumulated junk of his predecessors' very long lifetimes at St. Mary's. The men had been hopeless pack rats.

Boxes of letters going back to the thirties. Diocesan reports, financial statements, dozens of scrapbooks crammed with clippings, both pasted in and loose. Enormously heavy boxes of books. Religious tomes, inspirational treatises, best sellers, travel books, the classics bound in leatherette. Even heavier boxes containing thousands of magazines. *Life, Time, National Geographic, The Saturday Evening Post, Collier's, Harper's, The Atlantic, The Saturday Review,* on and on and on. Golf clubs, tennis racquets, croquet mallets and balls, badminton gear including nets and moth-eaten shuttlecocks. Reams of paper, notebooks, pads, pencils, pens, stamps from a time when two cents bought you a first-class delivery. It was unbelievable. Edna Hanrahan spent hours helping him. There was enough old clothing to stock a rummage sale. Or clothe a club of thespians. They couldn't throw it away. There was nothing to do but prepare a rummage sale, in fact, and Edna got into the spirit of it.

One evening Peaches settled down in front of his fireplace and his television, a bottle of Glenfiddich at hand, and began digging through a box of scrapbooks dating back to the end of the Second World War. Beneath the top two scrapbooks, however, he came upon a manila envelope, sealed with electrician's tape, tied with stout twine. The temptation was irresistible. With a Swiss Army knife he cut it open and withdrew some forty-odd pages, handwritten in ink that had faded on the brittle lined paper.

He began reading. He read it through twice and during that time got up twice to pace the room. He also consumed half the Glenfiddich and sat staring at the television while trying to calm himself down. What to do?

He laboriously read it through a third time.

All the times he'd heard the story from Ben and Val, how Hugh Driskill had brought the Italian priest, Giacomo D'Ambrizzi, home from the war, how D'Ambrizzi had locked himself in Hugh's study doing some kind of work or other that the children were absolutely forbidden to interrupt . . . Now he, Peaches O'Neale, for God's sake, knew what had been going on in the study.

He held in his shaking hands the testament of Giacomo D'Ambrizzi, who might any day now become the leader of the Roman Catholic Church. . . . Here it had lain all through the years, secure in its hiding place, forgotten. Forgotten? He turned back to the first

page, the title. *The Facts in the Matter of Simon Verginius.* He turned
to the last page, looked at the faded signature, the date.

Then, well past midnight, he picked up his telephone and gave
Father Artie Dunn a very big surprise.

Father Dunn had spent several days sequestered in his apartment in one of the mid-Manhattan towers, high above the city,
sealed off from the aftereffects of the murders. He ignored Archbishop Cardinal Klammer's occasional bleats from the general
vicinity of St. Patrick's. He ignored calls from his agent and from
his publisher. He worked on the murders as if they lay at the center
of one of his novels: he plotted backward, forward, and sideways,
trying to capture the story line in just the right light—so that it was
visible in its entirety. Of course he failed, but it was not time
wasted. He thought about Val and Lockhardt and Sister Elizabeth
and Ben and Hugh and Peaches and D'Ambrizzi and Sandanato and
the pope, and he made some notes, tracked down a variety of
unknowns, hoping that familiarity would breed understanding. He
thought about Val's travels. What the living hell had the girl been
on to? Well, whatever it was, the Driskill family seemed to be
involved no matter where you looked. . . .

The murdered Father Governeau hanging from a tree in the
orchard and it was *their* orchard . . .

World War II and who was dashing about Europe for Wild Bill
Donovan's OSS but Hugh Driskill . . .

The war is over then, and who should turn up in Princeton but
D'Ambrizzi, brought home by Hugh Driskill . . . but does anybody
know why? Artie Dunn wanted to know why. Hell's bells, the man
could become pope anytime now . . .

Sister Val had been making trouble this past year, scaring hell
out of somebody . . . and somebody finally killed her to stop
whatever she was doing. But what had she been doing?

And Ben Driskill simply wouldn't give up. His approach wasn't
to go off and think about it until it made some kind of sense. He
was more of a bull-in-the-china-shop type. It wasn't the behavior of
a lawyer showing through: it was a throwback to the football
player. . . .

What a bunch!

Finally Dunn settled on an approach that wouldn't have occurred to many other men. Having looked at his notes and found

them too complex, too confusing, he decided to go back to the start, back to the orchard, as it were, with Father Governeau swinging in the cold wintry gale.

He left Manhattan on a sunny windy morning and drove to a convent located off the main road between Princeton and Trenton. It was a gray stone building, once a mansion, surrounded by a green lawn going brown with frost. All the snow was gone but the freeze of the early winter ran deep. He was used to the unearthly stillness. It came with religious installations. He'd felt it a thousand times before.

He waited in the reception area while the old nun at the desk went to fetch Sister Mary Angelina. She came at last with a warm, welcoming smile. But it wasn't a smile that gave anything away. Sister Mary Angelina came forward, shook hands, and led him into the sitting room which was hung with several reproductions of religious paintings. The room was dry and cheerless, but the nun's beautiful face, bright and alert, lit it up.

She had retired to the convent after teaching at the elementary school where Ben and Val and Peaches had been students; eventually she'd become principal. She had met Dunn at Val's funeral.

"And you knew Hugh Driskill and his wife, Mary, back in the old days, isn't that right?"

"Of course I knew them. Seems like yesterday."

"You must have known just about every Catholic in the area in those days."

"Why yes, I expect I did. It comes with being a teacher, don't you think?"

"So you must have known Father Vincent Governeau, too."

"Yes, I did. I was here for all of that. Youngish, I was, in those days."

"I just wonder . . . what do you remember about Father Governeau?"

Another nun arrived with a silver tea service and set it on the table before the couch where they sat. Sister Mary Angelina moved forward, her habit rustling, and poured. Father Dunn took milk and two lumps. She turned the angelic professional smile—which Ben Driskill had once found so seductive—on him.

"Is that why you've come to see me, Father Dunn?"

"Yes, it is, Sister. Father Governeau."

"Well, I must say I've been expecting you."

"I don't understand. How could that be?"

"Well, you or someone like you."

"You don't say."

"It has been my experience that we, most of us, always have to pay the piper. Don't you agree? I didn't have the character to pay when the bill was presented—I speak metaphorically, you see? But I've been waiting nearly half a century for some man who would come to ask me about Father Governeau—"

"So I'm that man. Why is it you've been waiting?"

"Because I know why he died as he did. Once she died, I was the only one . . ."

"She?"

"Mary Driskill. She knew, too . . ."

"Why he killed himself?"

She smiled again, full wattage. "Please have a cookie, Father Dunn. Settle back, drink your tea, and I'll tell you the whole story about Father Governeau, God rest his soul. . . ."

4

DRISKILL

The rented Dodge gave up the battle after three hundred hot, dusty, windy, sandy miles, some of it along the Mediterranean and the long rest of it striking inland toward this place called The Inferno. I pulled in at a wide place in the road where a couple of gasoline pumps stood like the remnants of the Lost Legion, forgotten, but still on guard. There were a couple of sand-colored hounds, one watering a pump, four Egyptians who seemed to be just hanging out, and an attendant who said my transmission sounded like shit to him. He wore a New York Yankees baseball cap and a blue Ford coverall. Behind him was a building like a mirage if you don't expect too much from a mirage, a hotel of sorts baking like a big biscuit in the sun. Two stories, drooping shutters, no name.

While the man in the Yankees hat took a look at the source of the noise and the smoke, I went into the cooler darkness of the hotel. The desk was unmanned, the lobby was empty but for a

237

couple of ancient overstuffed chairs and three-legged tables. Shabby with a patina of sand on the floor. A stairway led up to a balcony and a few rooms. A radio was playing music I didn't understand. A tin Coke sign with Arabic lettering was nailed to a wall. It was late in the afternoon. My car was mortally wounded. I was out in the middle of nowhere looking for a man who might not be there even if I managed against all reason to get where I was going. I was hungry, thirsty, and the wound in my back was killing me. Maybe it was time to go home.

What, I wondered, would Val or Sister Elizabeth say in my place? Sister Elizabeth, damn her and her two-faced phony camaraderie, doubtless having cocktails at the Hassler with a papal nuncio up to his collar in intrigue. . . . I, too, was sunbaked, a little mad with the heat and discomfort. Well short of my best.

The dogs were barking and the guys standing around the Dodge were laughing at something. A woman in a second Ford coverall came out from a doorway under the stairs and looked me over. In English she asked me what I wanted. I pointed at the Coke sign and said I wanted some with lots of ice. And something to eat. She went away and came back ten minutes later with two hamburgers and a glass of Coke with ice. And so it was that my life and sanity were saved and I didn't pack it in, didn't go home.

The transmission was indeed shot. It would be two or three days before they could get the car going again. I discovered that they knew where the ancient monastery called The Inferno was, though they all seemed to feel that going there was an act of lunacy. But, if I was determined, a trucker called Abdul would be coming through in the morning and for a price would doubtless deliver me. For the night I could have a room upstairs. I didn't have the energy to stay up chatting with my new friends. They weren't interested in discussing my itinerary so I had a couple more Cokes and went to bed.

Sleep was slow in coming. I did what I could for my back, cleaned up, and lay down on the narrow bed, feeling gritty sand between me and the mattress. I pulled a blanket up to my chin as the desert cooled down. But I couldn't quite get to sleep.

I went over and over what Gabrielle LeBecq had told me about her father, the Nazi loot, the men in the picture—all the hopeless jumble of lives lived over four or five decades. It was all too complicated. I couldn't make it come together and result in the murder of my sister. Which was why I was trying to find LeBecq. I felt deep in my weary bones that he was a man on the edge and that I could crack him, push him over, and then dash around and catch him . . . and make him tell me more. Someone had to tell me more. Somewhere along the line I would have heard enough and I would know why my sister had been murdered. LeBecq was what I had to work with. If he hadn't run to the desert I might have written him off. Might have. But once he ran, I had to go after him.

The road had been built during the North African campaign forty-odd years before, had lain in the sun and wind ever since, and every year's hardness was being driven like stakes into my wound. I clamped my jaw, left my fingerprints in the rusty, dusty dashboard, and prayed for deliverance. Abdul's truck had been left behind by the retreating Italians. They knew what they were doing then and age had done nothing to improve the old heap. The ride reminded me of something that had made me throw up all over my uncle at a county fair once. But it was the only way to get to the monastery of St. Christopher unless you wanted to walk. As the man said, I might be dumb, but I'm not crazy. The back of my shirt was sticky. I hoped to God it wasn't blood.

"How much farther?" I screamed over the clanging, but Abdul merely hunched over the steering wheel, grunted, and chewed on his soggy, long-deceased cigar. I squinted through the flies mashed on the cracked windshield, but the road was hidden by blowing dust and sand. Even behind dark glasses I felt my eyeballs getting sunburned. Windburned. Sandburned. I picked up the canteen from the bench seat between us, burned my fingers on the shiny aluminum, sipped the scalding water to keep my lips from splitting. I'd been trapped in the truck for seven hours. I wasn't quite sure how much longer I could last. And I wondered what kind of men came to a place like this of their own free will.

The fenders up ahead flapped at each swerve and bump, at each chasm in the road and each time the bald tires slipped off into the sand and had to be yanked and wrestled back. The truck was so pitted by sand whipped off the dunes that it looked like a testament to a Chicago gangland war. If it made it to the monastery and came apart for the last time, how would I get back? Or would I have to join up, once in and never out? Or maybe the silver-haired priest was waiting for me with his blade and I wouldn't have to worry about getting back.

And then I saw it, like Brigadoon gone horribly awry, taking shape behind the blowing curtain of sand. It loomed, squat, close to the earth, jagged-edged, the color of the dunes beyond, gray and dirty brown. And then it was gone again.

As the truck ground on, Abdul pointed ahead, grunted some more, then applied the remnants of his brakes, metal screeching on metal, and the bouncing and slamming stopped. Very slowly I let go of the dash, wiped my eyes with an oily rag he picked up from the floor, and put my glasses back on.

"Road ends here," Abdul observed, peeling a wet brown tobacco leaf from the corner of his mouth. "You walk now, buster." He laughed enigmatically and spit through a hole in the truck where there should have been a window. "I be back tomorrow. I don't wait. You be ready, buster. You pay now for me to come back. Abdul born long time ago, not yesterday." He laughed again at his display of quick-wittedness, and I gave him a handful of money.

"Abdul," I said, "you're a hell of a buster yourself."

"You can say it one more time." He fired up the truck. I grabbed my bag and looked back up the faint pathway. His wheels spit more sand and dust all over me when he took off, but it didn't make a damn bit of difference. I'd arrived at the absolute asshole of the world and I was perfectly attired for the occasion.

The monastery was a ruin. Guarded by the ghost of a tank.

It sat, sand over the bottom treads, at an angle to the main gate leading into the compound. It bore the markings of Rommel's Afrika Korps, faded, paint-chipped, the long cannon commanding a wide arc of the road as if it bore one last shell, one last hurrah, like an ancient veteran of the Kasserine Pass waiting to greet Patton with one last, deadly muzzle flash. It was like a dream, a bad dream, with the stench of guns and blood clinging to it. But the cannon commanded an emptiness, a desolation of sand and weary, lank, windblown palms. The enemy was long gone. History and time had claimed them all, leaving this old derelict sadder than the last Christmas tree on the lot.

An exhausted dog hauled his bones out of the shadows of the low wall surrounding the monastery buildings. He wobbled to a halt, looked at me with a doleful expression of disappointment, and went back to the shadows. He sat down like a folding chair, slowly shaking his head at the buzzing flies. They were as big as my thumb and thought he was playing a game with them. They sounded as if they might eat him then and there, or just possibly carry him back to the wife and kids as a treat, but a few dozen peeled off and followed me into the grounds of the monastery, sensing bigger game. With the flies bouncing off my head and the fiery red heat billowing at me from all sides, I felt like I'd taken a long, mean ride to find refuge inside a light bulb.

There wasn't a soul in sight. A palm tree drooped over a puddle of muddy, sandy water where another dog lapped between deep breaths. Through the gritty sound of sand sifting against the walls of the main building, past the steady whine of the flies, I could just hear something else. A low rumble, voices, caught on the wind and blown this way and that. I walked toward the rumble and came to the back wall. It was louder, some kind of chanting that stopped as I came to another weathered gate hanging limply from a hinge of rope. I went on through, stopped short, stood in the shade watching the monks.

They were burying somebody.

I stayed in the shade, squinting, watching the shapes being distorted by the shimmering heat waves. I tried to snake my arm around to touch my back, to feel for blood. I knew it was all in my mind. I knew it was just sweat. But I couldn't reach it. It was too stiff, too tight, and it was hurting like hell. And it was sticky. So I leaned against the wall, watching the monks, trying to make them out clearly, one at a time. I was looking for a tall monk with silver hair and eyes like the business end of that tank cannon.

But, of course, he wasn't there. They all seemed small and skinny or potbellied or shrunken or stooped. There was one off to the side, bearded, harsh-featured like someone from the Old Testament who believed in fighting fire with fire. He had a ramrod up his tail and I caught him, alone of the assemblage, taking notice of me. The guest of honor was reclining in a sealed wooden box beside a hole yawning in the spongy, sandy earth. The little graveyard was punctuated by plain wooden crosses, sticking up at irregular angles, speaking for the past, marking the closings of chapters. While I watched, the bearded firebringer went to the grave and began speaking. I was too far away to hear what he was saying, which was just the way I wanted it.

Funerals. The dead passed before me, mirages in my heat and

pain. My sister . . . Lockhardt . . . I felt the sweat drying on my face, the winds drying it, leaving a salty crust that cracked again and again. I felt myself cracking all over, like something very new or very old thrusting out of its cocoon, being born or emerging from a crypt.

When the casket had been lowered into the grave and the monks had covered it over, I watched them come toward me. They came slowly, like extraterrestrials in a movie. They wore rough robes, a couple in patched trousers, one in jeans faded almost white. Ageless, deeply tanned, or sepulchrally gray, bearded, smelling of sweat and sand, which has its own peculiar scent.

The harsh one who had spoken last passed close to me and stopped. "I am the abbot here," he said softly, surprising me with a voice that didn't go with the forbidding face. I tried to speak but my mouth was too dry. "You're bleeding," he said. He was looking past me.

I turned. The wall where I'd been leaning was smeared with blood. I wanted to swear but my tongue was stuck to the roof of my mouth.

"Come with me," he said. I followed him into the dim halls of the monastery of St. Christopher, the saint who wasn't anymore.

A big, lumbering monk I hadn't noticed at the gravesite got me down on my belly on a table in the abbot's rough-hewn office which was cool and dark, slashes of light entering through narrow windows in walls three feet thick. His name was Brother Timothy and he had about a seven-day stubble, the bloodshot eyes and wrecked nose of a lifelong boozer, and the touch of an angel of mercy. He peeled the stiff, sticky shirt and bandage away, bathed the wound, and said he'd seen worse. Then he laughed under his breath: "But they was dead!" The abbot was standing near the table, watching. "Brother Timothy," he said, "is a great wit. He brightens our days." I lay still, wishing I could take a nap, while a new bandage was fashioned and set in place with thick bands of adhesive. Brother Timothy surveyed his handiwork. He helped me into a sitting position, then busied himself with putting his medical supplies back into a cracked leather doctor's satchel. He blew his nose on the sleeve of his faded cassock.

The abbot sat down in a wooden chair upholstered with a frayed, thick cushion, laid his hands palm down on the plank table. "Water for our guest, Timothy."

The big monk shuffled off and the abbot's eyes came to rest on me like the twin searchlights of curiosity and wariness. "No one ever comes here by chance," he said, "so I must assume you have some reason for this visit. You've come a long way. It shows in your face. You have been the victim of a murder attempt, judging by the looks of your back. And the fact that you're here at all proves you are a very determined man. What do you seek at the monastery of St. Christopher?"

"A man."

"I am not surprised. Only a manhunter is likely to overcome the obstacles you've faced. What sort of man? And why?"

"A man called Etienne LeBecq. You may know him simply as a man who comes here on retreat . . ."

"If I know him at all."

I took the snapshot from my bag, handed it to him. His face showed nothing. I pointed out Guy LeBecq, hoping the resemblance might trigger something in the abbot's mind. Brother Timothy came back with a pitcher of water and a bottle of aspirin. I gulped down four of them, swilled the cool water around my teeth, washing the sand away.

The abbot stared at the face in the snapshot, carefully smoothed the sheet flat on the table. The only sound was the sand scraping the walls outside and the strange singing that came from the desert, wind whistling in the sand. He leaned back in the chair and regarded me steadily. "I wonder who you are," he said obliquely.

He was as unyielding as the landscape. I couldn't avoid the sense I had that he was suddenly the most important man in my life. I was helpless in such a godforsaken place without his sufferance. All the flesh had tightened back against the underlay of bone: his face looked as if the surroundings had sandblasted it a long time before. He was waiting for me to fill in the blanks, so I did. He took it in, my name, the flight to Egypt. But how had I known where to come? He wasn't going to let me stonewall him. It was his monastery and his attitude was one of a commandant, though maybe that was what an abbot always was, in the end. I told him about my sister's murder. I told him LeBecq was someone she had seen shortly before her death. I told him I didn't have a hell of a lot to go on but LeBecq was something.

"This man, you say he talked with her before she was murdered." He seemed to have a Belgian accent, if I knew what that was. Maybe French. "What will you do if you find him?"

"Talk to him." I shrugged, felt the calm, distant eyes regarding me with an almost academic interest, as if nothing were meaningful enough to truly engage his attention. "Can you help me?"

"I hardly know the answer to that, Mr. Driskill. Help is not something we deal in here. Help and hope, abandoned within these walls. Let me tell you who we are, let me talk to you, Mr. Driskill, so that you will know what you have found here at St. Christopher." He drummed his fingers preparatory to an explanation I knew better than to interrupt. "We are a kind of foreign legion of monks, only nineteen of us, who never leave, who will . . . *never* . . . leave this place, and a few who come and go from time to time. We pray, we wait to die, we are ignored by Rome. Sometimes a man like your Etienne LeBecq will come here on retreat, to purge the evil he senses in himself. All of us here have faced the evil in ourselves, perhaps like the man you seek. Many of us are dying—incurable illnesses of one kind or another, illnesses we choose not to treat . . . maybe of pure despair at man's condition. I am the abbot of the dead, Mr. Driskill, and of the forgotten."

The monastery had been founded during the twelfth century, or so the story went, and in the abbot's view it might well have been so. Founded by the Cistercians, or more accurately by a radical bishop who felt that the Cistercian reaction against the lords of Europe—the monks of Cluny—had not gone far enough. As the Cluniacs had grown more and more worldly, had seen their political and economic power multiply, the Cistercians had sought to flee that world of privilege. A monk pledged to poverty was not intended to live in a world of riches, so the Cistercians withdrew. But their credo—to work—frustrated the need to remain impoverished. Under their tillage, remote and barren valleys and hillsides flourished. The conundrum was impenetrable. Work and poverty seemed incompatible. In 1075 Brother Robert and seven monks from the monastery of St. Michele de Tonnere fled to the forest of Molesme. But by 1098 their efforts had produced a kind of earthly success that frustrated his hope to create a true monastery. Shortly thereafter another group made the perilous journey to Africa, into the silence of the northern desert, where no crops would grow, no wealth and power could possibly accrue, and built this monastery, calling it St. Bernard. Why it had become St. Christopher, and when, the abbot did not know.

There in the heat and the rankest poverty, far from any of Europe's worldliness, the asceticism of the monks flourished. Fanaticism, self-denial, an almost unprecedented zeal for the rejection of the flesh, became the rule by which they lived. And they did not live long. Seldom did one reach the age of thirty. More often they failed quickly, were dead in their mid-twenties. "Leave your bodies without these gates," they importuned the young. "Only souls enter here. The flesh is good for nothing." Likewise, nothing that was welcomed in the world was welcomed within these walls. No knowledge, no art, no literature, nothing that might normally give a man's life meaning. No work. Nothing. Nothingness. They waited in the desert for the world to end, believing that only through their own sublime goodness, prayer, and irreducible emptiness might the world of man possibly endure.

"In the end—it was less than half a century, not a long time, Mr. Driskill, in the end they were all gone, dead, bleaching in the sun, not mourned, not even noticed by the Europeans. After all, there was no one left to carry back the tale . . . it was generations before anyone from Europe came here again and found what bits of record-keeping survived." The abbot swatted at a fly. Brother Timothy seemed to have fallen into a doze on a stool in the corner. The abbot had been talking for a long time, as if he couldn't pass up the opportunity to communicate with someone from the outside world. Beyond his initial questions he seemed devoid of curiosity about my life: he was far more intrigued with recounting his own story, savoring it, taking its measure, evaluating its madness as he spoke.

"The monastery stood empty then, preserved by the heat and the lack of humidity, for hundreds of years. Think of it, Mr. Driskill . . . centuries without a prayer, without a single monk, cleansed of all humanity by the passage of time and God's own elements." He smiled thinly, wet his lips, went on, a born storyteller trapped in a world without an audience.

Finally the lost monastery—Hell's Monastery, or, The Inferno it had become in legend—came under control of the papacy. It was used as a remote place where inconvenient monks or priests might be sent with the relative certainty that they would die in the attempt to get there. In any case, they would never come back. Some of them—the real hermits who wanted the supreme test, who wanted the satisfaction of renouncing everything—begged to come here, came on their own, just wandered off in hopes of reaching the place somehow. They came to die in a kind of ultimate spasm of arrogance, a complete, contemptuous rejection of the world.

The darkness was seeping in at the narrow windows, along with the chill of the desert evening that seemed to come rolling across the wastes like a cloud of mist. The abbot had stopped talking. I wasn't sure how long we sat in silence. He was watching me as if expecting a reaction. But he was prepared to wait a long time.

"So why did you come here?" I asked.

I thought he hadn't heard me, until he leaned forward, braced his elbows on the table, and made a basket of his fingers. He watched his hands as if proving to himself that they were steady, without a tremor. Still in control.

"The only discipline we have here," he said almost in a whisper, "is that we impose on ourselves. We have a few hermits who stay in the desert much of the time. Most of us speak, a few don't. But the fact is, we're a very thin strain, weak links, we are all hiding from something here, we have no illusions about perfecting our relationship with God. We have no illusions about the states of grace. No questions about being justified. We have just stopped short of the one last sin of murdering ourselves. Why? Mainly, I suspect, because we are afraid of what awaits us on the other side . . . or wherever. We hide, we hide in fear and shame because that is what we have become, creatures of fear and shame."

His tone lacked any emotion that might have laden the words he spoke. The chill I felt made my flesh crawl and my back hurt, and it had nothing to do with the dropping temperature. I felt as if I had found the geographical equivalent of the emptiness I saw yawning in the silver-haired priest's eyes.

"I came here," he said gently, "because I deserve this place. I earned it. I saw evil in my monastery, years ago in the Dordogne, sodomy and corruption of all kinds, so I took God's sword into these hands. I had a vision in my cell . . . I watched them from the corner of my eye when we were in the chapter house reading the Rule. They befouled the place. I went to their cells in the middle of the night, found them locked together, and I put an end to their corruption with my own hands. My cassock was stiff with blood. . . . I left on foot—in a daze—and no one came after me. . . . Two years later I had made my way to this place. . . . Unaccountably, years later, Pius XII took notice of me, letters were sent and received, and I was named abbot."

He didn't say a word about LeBecq until we had concluded a sparse dinner in the dining hall. I was too tired to press the issue or even to notice much of my surroundings. The aspirin on an empty stomach had provided me with at best a fuzzy perspective. But my back pain had eased and the hole in the dike had not come unplugged, thanks to Brother Timothy.

"Come," the abbot said, "the night air will do you good. Then an early bed. If you don't mind sleeping on a dead man's pallet." He almost winked at me.

"What is that supposed—" But he had stood up and was leaving the table. I followed him.

It was cold outside. We walked in silence beneath the pop-art moon in a black sky. It looked like a hole seen from the inside of a great metallic orb.

"I know your Etienne LeBecq, of course," he said.

"I thought you might."

"He's come to us from time to time for many years, a rather reclusive man, but I've spoken with him in reflective moments. A strong faith, made me feel a weakling. We would speak of the Church and its role, how each of us has a job however unexpected it might be. He never knew it, but he was a great comfort to me when I have questioned my faith . . . his belief in our Church abided, Mr. Driskill. But somewhere deep inside himself he carried a terrible secret. What? He never told me." One of the dogs had followed us out into the night and had begun to sniff and dig at the sand in the valley between two of the rolling dunes. "He was here a few months ago, only for a night or two—I forget. Time means nothing here. He came and went, he didn't ask questions. Sometimes he seemed to try to hide from his soul. . . . As for information, I cannot help you, Mr. Driskill. If he had a past or future, I know nothing of them. We have no worldly goods here, nothing to call our own . . . nothing, that is, but our individual pasts. Most of us have no future but what you can see. But our pasts, we guard them most jealously. If a man's past has been a happy one, then why would he be in this place? And if it has been unhappy or wicked . . . no one wants to speak of it."

The dog had dug with increasing fervor, had gotten below the top layer of sand.

"He smells death," the abbot said, going to the dog, gently shoving him away with his foot. He saw my quizzical expression. "Here is where we found the body of one of our older men. I spoke with him only briefly, but he was a talkative man, a bit of an old woman. Then one morning he was nowhere to be seen. A few days passed, I'd known he was near the end, I wanted to give him time to die as he chose . . . alone in the desert. He was babbling of green fields the last time we spoke. I'm sure in his mind that's where he died, in those green fields. Then the dog found him . . . apparently he had walked over the dune, composed himself, and just let go. His choice. We respect a man's choice. The dog found him half covered with sand, his hand sticking up, looking like a tiny gravestone. So we buried him today, as you arrived." He scratched the dog's floppy ears, rubbed his thin, moth-eaten hide. "Why did he die as he did? God's will, that's all we'll ever know . . . he was the lucky one, he had a good death, Mr. Driskill."

As he led me to the cell where I would sleep, where the late monk, fleeing from whatever secrets lay in the darkness of his past, had slept, he lit a candle. The shadows flickered against the walls of the tiny cell. A wooden cross above the narrow bed, the pervasive smell of sand and night. A blanket lay folded at the end of the bed. He surveyed the bare room. "Serviceable, if not luxurious, Mr. Driskill."

When he turned to leave, I said, "One more question. Just a stray thought. About another man who may have come here and then gone. Maybe returning from time to time—"

"Yes?"

"I don't know his name. I don't know if he's a priest or a monk or even a layman like LeBecq. But you would remember him . . . tall, very fit but in his seventies I suspect, round gold-framed glasses, silver hair combed straight back from a point in front . . . remarkable eyes, no bottom to them . . ."

The abbot stood in the doorway, the shadows playing across his harsh features. He shared some of the fitness I'd just described and he must have been as old. But he, too, was timeless. I waited, watching him, watching a spider make its way up the wall and stop, as if to listen.

"Yes," he said at last. "I know such a man. Brother August . . .

but I know nothing of him. If he is the same man, he lived here for a long time, two or three years, impervious to the toll this place takes. Said very little. Attended to his prayers. Then—it was quite astonishing—the bandit who drives the truck to bring us supplies, this scoundrel brought a letter for Brother August . . . this is an unheard-of event, do you understand? A letter from Rome . . . and then the next day he was gone, rode away with the bandit in the truck." He shrugged.

"I wonder, do we have the same man in mind—"

"Striking to look at," the abbot said. "How can I say this? He was not like the others here. He wasn't punishing himself, he was simply going about his business, as if he were conditioning himself for something. Amazingly strong man but with very gentle manners. An educated man. Sometimes he would go into the desert for days at a time, then return, without discussion, fit as ever . . . sometimes he seemed indestructible . . . no human frailty . . ."

"Yes. Brother August," I said. "He is the man, I feel sure." The abbot had the effect of making me talk in an unnatural manner. I couldn't help it. I felt like a man reading lines. The news of Brother August had caught me unawares. I was struggling with the idea. Now I knew something about this man and it had come from out of nowhere. "When did he leave here?"

"Time," the abbot mused. "Two years ago. That would be my guess." He shrugged again at the idea of time and its measurement.

I lay awake for hours, thinking, now I know something about *him*. The mystery is not quite so deep and dark. Brother August. Two years in this hell, then someone in Rome had summoned him . . . sent him on his mission. Two years later my sister and Lockhardt and Heffernan are dead. A two-year journey from The Inferno to New York and Princeton. I was bone-tired but I kept turning over bits of information, looking up from the heavy work and seeing a glitter of the knife blade, a clue, a bit of unforeseen evidence. I was too tired and too amazed at the threads of the story, too curious as to what the threads would result in, what kind of tapestry—I was too weary and too excited to sleep but too weary to sort through the mountain of facts and implications that had been accumulating all around me. I finally slept an empty sleep and came awake slowly, shivering under the thin blanket. My back was pushing uncomfortably against the wooden frame of the bed. I twisted slowly around, trying to settle myself without pulling my bandage loose, refusing to open my eyes and admit I was awake. First I thought I heard something, a scuttling sound on the packed-earth floor. What kind of creatures roam the desert at night? The nervous reaction crossed my mind: if I had to get up, what might I step on? The scuttling stopped as if something knew I'd sensed its presence. It was nearly pitch-dark in the cell. A narrow slash in the wall let in a blade of moonlight which proved inadequate once I forced my eyes open. A curtain hung at the door with the night beyond.

Then I smelled something. Someone.

And the hair on the back of my neck began to rouse itself.

Someone was in the cell with me.

As my senses began to click in, slowly, too slowly, I heard the breathing, someone trying not to make a sound. The man-smell of sweat-soaked garments moved closer. The breathing quickened. He was closing in on me. The bit of moonlight was blacked out by his shape coming closer. I saw flat on my back, I saw in memory and nightmare, the blade plunging downward at me. . . .

"I've got a gun on you," I croaked, hearing my voice shake. Everything stopped: the shuffling, the breathing, everything but the smell. I was afraid of something nameless and faceless, but I knew it was the priest, come to finish me off. He'd been watching me the whole time, had followed me. "Touch me, you bastard, and you die—" I was bluffing for my life. It was all a bad joke.

"It's Brother Timothy." The voice was soft and high-pitched. "I bandaged your back . . . you have nothing to fear from me. Please, put down your gun. I have a candle. May I light it? I must speak with you."

I heard a match scrape across a striker; the flame flared a few feet from my face. The large shape came into view. Brother Timothy smiled, his double chins cascading like falling pastries. I took my hand from beneath the blanket, pointed a finger at him and said, "Pa-choo, pa-choo."

He giggled like a man trying to prove he hadn't forgotten how, then the smile faded. The candle glowed. I longed for the warmth of a real fire. "What can I do for you," I asked, "now that you've scared me half to death?"

"I had to see you alone. The abbot wouldn't approve of my meddling, but I must. What I have to tell you—I haven't told even him. But I heard you telling him the story about this man you call LeBecq and I saw his picture . . . and I knew I had to tell you what I saw. . . ." He was panting hard, his face glistening with sweat even in the cold. He licked his lips, went back to the doorway and stuck his head out past the curtain, ducked back in again. "He's everywhere," he said apologetically, "always noticing things. There are stories about the abbot, stories of second sight . . . nonsense, of course, but I do wonder who he is," he mused almost dreamily, then lurched back to the present. "We must not waste time." He wiped his brow on his voluminous sleeve, looked at me with his bright little eyes.

"Go on," I said, pulling the blanket tight.

"The man LeBecq, I have seen him. He is out in the desert now. You can see him. I'll take you to him. You can see for yourself."

I followed his immense bulk out of the monastery compound, past the cells where the monks groaned and snored and muttered in their sleep. The moonlight might have been coating the scene with ice. The whole thing had the look of a road company Fort Zinderneuf. The wind kept a steady shifting of sand nipping at you, swirling up into your eyes. Outside the gate the huge Panzer tank loomed ghostlike, casting a strange moonshadow with its long snout of cannon barrel.

Timothy set off at a brisk pace, keeping to the hard-packed sand. I couldn't judge the distance, just kept my head tucked down and followed my guide and tried to pretend my back didn't hurt. We passed straggly palm trees, crossed between rolling dunes, always making good time. After a half-hour march Timothy stopped, plucked at my arm. "Just ahead in the flat beyond the next rise. I'll take you straight to him."

Next thing I knew we'd crested the ridge of sand and I was looking at the airplane I'd seen in the photograph LeBecq had kept in his office at the gallery. It looked frozen and silver, glistening with condensation in the moonlight. I didn't see LeBecq. What was he doing staying out in the desert when he could have stayed at the monastery? Timothy had slogged down to stand beside the plane, leaning with one hand on the wing. He beckoned to me, called something which the wind tossed away.

On my way down the dune I saw LeBecq. He was sitting on the sand, leaning back against the nosewheel. He wasn't paying any attention to us. It was the middle of the night. He was sleeping and whatever sounds we were making the wind was blowing away.

When Timothy went to stand in front of LeBecq, pointing at him, urging me to hurry, I realized something was wrong.

When I circled around the wingtip I saw that LeBecq's head was angled oddly. There was a black hole in his temple, a small inward-turned crater. A small .22-caliber pistol lay on the sand near his hand. His mouth was open, making a tiny circle. Sand insects were crawling in and out of his mouth. Then I saw the hole in his temple appear to move, but it was more insects drawn to the blood. He was beginning to swell. Sitting out in the sun for a day or two doesn't do a corpse a bit of good. His toupee had come slightly askew from the jolt of the slug.

I bent down, scooped up the gun, and dropped it into my jacket pocket.

Timothy had found him earlier in the day, but when he'd gotten back to the monastery there was the other funeral and then I had wandered in and the rest of the day had gotten away from him.

"Your friend put an end to his troubles," Brother Timothy said. "They must have weighed very heavily on his mind. For a good Catholic, too. . . . It's too bad. I must bring him back now." He leaned down and began to tug at the lapels of LeBecq's jacket.

"I'd go easy with that," I said. "He's pretty ripe. You'd be better off to come back tomorrow, a couple of you, put him in a bag or something so he doesn't sort of all run out."

"You're right." He nodded his huge round head. "Then we'll bury him."

"What about notifying his daughter?"

"He has a daughter?" Brother Timothy looked up at the moon. "The abbot will know what to do."

We walked back to the monastery more slowly than when we'd been coming the other way. One of the hounds had wakened and was wandering around sniffing the night air. He seemed glad to see us. That was the level on which I was noticing things. In my mind I kept seeing the hole in LeBecq's head . . . the blackened, singed hair that belonged to my sister Val. . . .

"Brother Timothy?"

"Yes, Mr. Driskill?"

"I killed that man back there."

"You did?"

"I murdered him just as surely as if I'd pressed the gun to his head. I was his personal nightmare, all his sins coming back to haunt him, and I wouldn't go away. I was all his fears and sins wrapped up in one neat package. . . . I was nemesis dropping in out of the blue and he ran like a crazy man into the desert . . . and then he sat down and looked his fate straight in the eye and knew there was just the one way to get free of all of it. . . ."

"Was he a terrible man?"

"No, not terrible at all."

"Now he'll burn forever in a fiery pit."

"Do you really believe that, Timothy?"

"I was taught that."

"But do you really believe it?"

"Do you really believe you killed him?"

"I killed him. Yes."

"Well, I believe he'll burn forever in a fiery pit."

"It's a question of faith, then?"

"Faith. That's right. A man who kills himself burns forever."

I may have slept later on. The night was endless. I thought about everything all over again and no matter how I worked it out I came up with the same result. But for me the poor bastard would still be alive. Maybe it was my Catholic conscience. I thought about Sister Elizabeth, about how she'd betrayed my trust, but that didn't seem like such a deal breaker now. *She* hadn't killed anybody. My last thought that night was about her, and then my dreams, too. I wanted to tell her what I had done.

I wanted her to hear my confession.

I was waiting for Abdul, saw his dust cloud, then heard the shrieks of his infernal machine before I actually glimpsed the thing itself. The sun was burning straight down, leaving no shadow where I stood with my bag, shielding my eyes with a hand for a visor. The past twenty-four hours had taken forever. I felt like a leper. No one had said good-bye, not even Brother Timothy. I knew it was just their way, nothing personal, but it made for a lonely departure. I took one last look at the forgotten place, shimmering insubstantially in the heat, looking as if it might just evaporate one day and no one would mourn it or its company of the damned. Then I climbed into the truck where Abdul, my deliverance, waited for me, grinning with his uneven, sand-colored tooth stumps and the soggy cigar jammed into the corner of his mouth.

As we parted the blowing dust and sand like a sinking tugboat in stormy seas, I asked him if he remembered a man he'd picked up and described Brother August. He nodded, spat, told me that nothing was free, most certainly not information. I gave him some more money and he stuffed it into his shirt pocket, told me I was a damn good buster. He was wearing a ratty old safari shirt and a straw hat with what looked like a bullet hole in the crown. He laughed like the bandit he was and scratched a wet armpit, nearly losing control of the truck.

He remembered the silver-haired man. But he'd driven him to a village on the Mediterranean and left him there. He hadn't seen him since. I'd paid for nothing. But it didn't really matter. I knew what I needed to know about Brother August. He got his orders from Rome.

Having worked her way through the horrors of the House of Vespasiano Sebastiano and the suppression of the Tuscan monastery of the *assassini,* Sister Elizabeth dreaded returning to the nunciature of Venice *fondo.* It was claustrophobic, oppressive with the evil and the bloodletting.

She was, therefore, contemplating how next to approach the problem of the Secret Archives when among her own papers she found the sheet from Val's folder that was inscribed with what looked like a simple, impenetrable code. She'd never really paid any attention to it before, but now she did.

SA TW IV SW. TK. PBF.

Elizabeth doodled on another sheet, copying the cipher again and again, trying to think with Val. What had she meant? She slept on it, woke up turning it over in her mind. She couldn't shake it from her memory. It was like the phone number of a lover, imprinted on your brain, which made her smile at the memory of a long-ago college-boy lover. He might as well have been a contemporary of those Renaissance princes she'd been reading about. All a long time ago, long gone. History.

She began to figure out the code during the walk to Vatican City.

Let's say SA meant Secret Archives. Then she thought she knew what TW meant.

She went to Monsignor Petrella, the prefect, and asked him to take her to the Tower of the Winds.

When they'd reached the elegant room with the zodiac on the floor, Petrella cast an anxious look about the contents. "You realize how unusual it is to leave anyone to browse through the *buste* here. It is, to all intents and purposes, never done. But for Sister Valentine an exception was made. A friend of the late Mr. Lockhardt . . ." He shrugged and that said it all. "He was such a friend to us here at the Archives. The same exemption will be made for you, Sister."

"I am in your debt, Monsignor. Val spent a good deal of time up here, did she?"

"Yes, she seemed to have—let me see, what did she say? Ah, yes, she said she'd 'struck a vein' here."

"Then I will mine it, Monsignor. If I can find it."

Monsignor Petrella nodded, smiling thinly.

Alone she surveyed the room, trying to understand the remainder of Val's code. Maybe it had nothing to do with the Tower of the Winds. But then, maybe it did.

She couldn't find a Roman numeral IV that seemed relevant. That stopped her for a while. The fourth bookcase? Fourth from where? You had to have the location of the first to find the fourth. . . .

Stymied, she spent several hours searching fruitlessly through the folders, leaving her sweaty, dusty, and discouraged. Maybe she was on the wrong track altogether. She wondered if Driskill was having this much fun poking around Alexandria in search of another of Val's trails. Fun! She wondered about his wound, then forced him out of her mind.

But she did keep pushing her way through the material, randomly searching for something, anything. *Assassini.* That was her goal, had to be, it was all she had to go on. *Assassini* and five dead men on Val's list. Five dead but one still left alive. Erich Kessler. Why had Val thought he'd be the next to die?

She continued picking through the folders aimlessly, doubtful now about the point of what she was doing—combing endlessly through bits and pieces of papers, hoping for another reference to *assassini*. In her heart she knew it was a fool's job. But she wasn't ready to quit yet. She might as well get it out of her system. A few more wasted days, so what? The world wouldn't stop turning.

She stood up, brushed herself off, as Val must have before her, and went to the window, gazed out over Vatican City, suddenly unsure of what day of the week it was, uncertain as to whether she had attended mass a few hours before, or had that been yesterday? In this unguarded moment she was disconcerted by recognition of a quality she'd shared with Val—the special ability to submerge herself in a job to the exclusion of the outside world. It had always been her way, from the time she was little. Work had always taken precedence over the rest of her life. Val, however, had been able to encompass more. She'd submerged herself in a career even more demanding than Elizabeth's, but she had also found a way to cope with Curtis Lockhardt. But that was Val's way, Val's life. Elizabeth felt the breeze on her face at the window, the warmth of the sun. She wasn't Val and she couldn't live her life as Val had lived hers. But she had to face the limitations she'd imposed on her life—what they had kept her from. . . . Suddenly she thought of another way of looking at Val's code.

Forget IV. Go on to SW. The only SW she knew was the abbreviation for southwest. And the tower room was based on the zodiac and the compass. She got her directions straight and turned to the southwest corner. There, crammed between bookcases, was a small leather-strapped trunk reminiscent of a man's fancy hat box of the nineteenth century. TK. Trunk. *Val!*

PBF.

She undid the straps and carefully lifted the hard leather lid.

There, neatly packed in its own carton, was the original type-script of Pryce Badell-Fowler's 1934 manuscript, *Ecclesiastical Power and Policy*. It had apparently gone uncatalogued for half a century, had slipped through the nets of the hundred-years rule, had been stuffed into the inconspicuous little trunk, left to gather dust and be found in some distant future by a scholar or an attendant yet unborn.

She knelt beside the trunk, picked up the manuscript, stared at the name. Pryce Badell-Fowler. PBF. Murdered in his converted barn near Bath only six months before. One of the five . . .

Clipped to the title page were two sheets of the author's stationery, his name simply engraved at the top, under it *Bath—England*.

The first sheet was dated 4 January 1931, a letter to Pope Pius XI, essentially a bread-and-butter letter thanking His Holiness for arranging "access to certain materials heretofore untapped by scholars."

The second letter, dated 28 March 1948, addressed to Pope Pius XII, observed that the author had only to take "one or two final steps before completing at long last my second volume. As you know so well, I have had to confront the issue of the Church's use of professional assassins to further policy in the past. I appreciate your reserve in discussing such matters for attribution, but I am also grateful for your candour in our less formal conversations. I need hardly add that I fully appreciate the sensitivity which arises when we pursue this matter into our present century, as in the matter of the late Benito Mussolini. I can only hope that you, Holiness, in your great wisdom, can understand equally my need to press on in my researches."

The letters were a window into the past. Mesmerized by the almost palpable presence of the Englishman in the room, she began reading, skimming, fluttering the pages, hoping. Near the end of the manuscript she found it. . . .

Little is known, or can be fully documented, about the assassini (Badell-Fowler wrote). *They lope through the darker chapters of medieval and Renaissance sub-history like the misshapen wild dogs who prowled the outskirts of Rome and were known at times to feast on the flesh of the unwary, the infirm, or slow of foot, or those whose fearlessness was born of a mistaken belief in their own invulnerability.*

Some of these scoundrels and bravos were pledged until death to the popes: these men were the pope's assassins, according to what little written evidence has survived the Church's determined efforts to erase them from history. While rumors continue to persist that documentary evidence exists hidden deep in the dank recesses of certain remote monastery chambers, none has come to light within living memory.

The pope's assassini *reportedly came into being during that period when the Church, in obsessive secrecy, built and then solidified the power of the Papal States. During the extraordinarily corrupt and bloodstained reigns of Pope Sixtus IV, Pope Innocent VIII, and finally Pope Alexander VI, the father of Cesare Borgia, the assassini flourished, torturing and murdering political enemies of the papacy, not only in Rome but throughout the more far-flung city-states of Italy, as well.*

They did their heinous work by means of poison, the dagger, strangulation. Among their many victims, the Colonna and Orsini families of Rome, who sought to undermine the Church's authority so that their own power and influence might grow, come most readily to mind. Both families were decimated by the assassini and finally forced to flee before the lines were wiped out entirely—men, women, and children.

It has been argued that a more terrible and more fanatically dedicated secret organization has never existed within western culture. The assassini risked everything in the service of the pope. They must not be confused with the everyday street ruffians of the day who ran nearly unchecked throughout Rome, nor with the killers-for-hire who were employed by all but the lowliest of families needing murder done in their behalf. The assassini were cut from bolts quite different in quality: they were often highborn, sometimes even dukes and members of the clergy who had bought their offices with awesome, arrogant ease, and sometimes clerical zealots who saw their work as the ultimate service one might render the Church.

One of the foremost of the assassini is said to have been none other than the bastard son of Ludovico Sforza, senior statesman of Milan. As the various city-states aligned themselves with Rome and participated financially, the list of those contributing to the treasure of the assassini grew . . . always in absolute secrecy. Very often the assassini drew from the ranks of the illegitimate sons, or the second and third sons of a great house, and frequently they called upon members of the clergy to carry out specific tasks. Apparently their numbers grew quickly. The Papal States had to be protected at any cost.

Not only did Cesare Borgia roam the streets at night with his armed guards in a kind of blood lust, carrying out vengeance in the name of the Church, but others like him followed his example.

During the reign of Pope Julius II, a benign and unifying pope, the presence of the assassini began to fade. They went into a kind of eclipse, slipping between the cracks of history. For several centuries they were heard of only sporadically, then only at times when stresses threatened to pull the Church apart.

During the Jesuit Inquisition in central Italy the assassini resurfaced, and for a time the mere mention of the word was enough to cause fear and trembling among the enemies of papal policy.

But then, the Inquisition having ended, they were gone. They had slipped away again, disappeared into the pit of darkness from whence they had come, where they lay still, in the blackness and stench, waiting.

There was nothing more about the *assassini,* only that brief teaser for what Elizabeth presumed the second volume would have dealt with. Badell-Fowler's evaluation was certainly open to question, but then, what Church historian's were not? Church history was a welter of contradictions by its nature; stories were twisted by the fires of jealousy, vengeance, and long-held familial hatreds. Elizabeth had a tough time imagining Cesare Borgia roaming through the streets in a drooling blood lust since, in her view, he was one of the most able and civilized men of his time. It sounded to her as if Badell-Fowler had been badly taken in by the bad press the Spaniard had gotten in the Italian press of the day. Better to look at Cesare as what he was, the model for Machiavelli's prince.

But that hardly mattered.

It was the continuing thread of the *assassini* that fascinated her.

Following the final page of the manuscript, she found a sheet of Badell-Fowler's notes, handwritten in black ink, in a firm, bold script. They were cryptic but the subtext was there.

1949.
How many of them were there? All dead? NO!
Wartime activities.
Simon the leader?
Pius Plot . . .
Betrayed by . . . ?

Elizabeth tried to sit quietly and make her heartbeat slow down. She didn't know what most of it meant, not specifically, but she felt as if she were somehow among them, the *assassini.* Val had read this: now they were sharing it.

The trick now was to stay alive. She had been sucked into a maelstrom where the clergy could be recruited to do murder— Dunn may have hit it right on the button when he'd held up that piece of torn black raincoat. The man who killed Val, who came out of the night to try to kill Ben—he could be a priest, not a man in fancy dress! Badell-Fowler had believed that, Val must have known it, and now Elizabeth could almost feel them beside her, urging her on, offering what help they could. The sense of kinship was real, something almost sanctified.

She copied the handwritten list Badell-Fowler had made.

She sat quietly, listening to the soft, insistent mutterings of the ventilation system, the ancient currents of dry air rustling the countless pieces of paper, the pulse of the Secret Archives.

Badell-Fowler had been killed because of what he knew about the *assassini*. The work of a lifetime had been destroyed in the fire. No, good sir, they were not all dead, not in 1949, and not now. Something *now* had made it imperative that this old man, survivor of so many years, must finally be killed. . . .

Slowly a reflective smile spread across her face.

She had no idea what Ben Driskill had accomplished, wherever he might be. But she had dragged the *assassini* back through the centuries where they'd been buried. She had placed them in the twentieth century, where they had gone back to work.

Now, dammit, she could wrap it up and present it to Ben Driskill. She could prove to him that she wasn't what he thought she was, that she wasn't a disloyal, mindless party-line papist who swallowed her nun's theology and cared for nothing but the Church, the Church, the Church. She'd make him understand that she wanted to find Val's killer as much as he did. It was her quest too, wherever it might lead.

If it was a petty reaction, a petty feeling of triumph, then so be it. She could live with that. So long as she could prove to him he was wrong about her.

She had to tell someone. Who better than Val's closest ally in the hierarchy of the Church? If Val were still alive, if she'd built her case to her own demanding satisfaction, she would inevitably have turned to Saint Jack himself.

She had called Sandanato, told him she'd made some real headway on what Val had been doing, and needed to discuss it with Cardinal D'Ambrizzi. He'd gotten back to her at the office within the hour. His Eminence had cleared his evening schedule and would be delighted if she'd join him for dinner in his private Vatican apartment.

The intervening hours were spent going over the presentation she wanted to make. In such a masculine world she was at a marked disadvantage: she could wreck her case before it was half made if she didn't watch her step. All it would take would be a hint of female gushiness, any kind of sloppy, breathless enthusiasm. They'd love to write her off, not because they disliked or mistrusted her, but because it was a part of them, instinctive: she was a woman, a nun, and therefore no one that really mattered, not in the end. The attitude didn't even make her angry. It was a given. She had to live with it. So she'd gathered her findings, got her shit together, as Val would have said, and imposed a cool, analytical order on her story.

Now the cardinal and Sandanato had heard her out and the dinner dishes had been cleared. D'Ambrizzi had been attentive throughout her recital, watching her quietly from beneath his heavy, wrinkled eyelids. Sandanato had been equally quiet, barely eating any of the excellent fare provided by the cardinal's favorite chef. He always gave the impression of running on nerve and cigarette smoke. When she finally came to a full stop and picked up her coffee cup, the cardinal shifted his massive girth and spoke.

"It seems to me, Sister, that I remember a certain amount of controversy about this Badell-Fowler of yours, long time ago. After the war." He was slowly rolling the cognac in the snifter, inhaling the fumes. Sandanato had lit a cigar, was rubbing one tired eye with his knuckle. "He'd written something tying the Church to Mussolini's intelligence service. Hardly a secret! But what can you expect from an Englishman? Wasn't he also critical of Pius XII's German connections? Handholding with the Nazis, rumors of plundered art treasures? Some people found it all rather explosive at the time and he became rather unpopular in these hallowed precincts." He chuckled deeply in his chest. "Then?" He shrugged his heavy shoulders. "Silence. These gadfly fellows have a way of just fading away. In any case, it all seemed such old news today. Nothing deader than an old scandal."

Sister Elizabeth leaned forward intently. "But laying aside what people thought and did then, Eminence, Badell-Fowler was murdered only months ago and his work, all of what might have gone into his second book, the *assassini* book—it was all burned to ashes. He was an elderly man, but they couldn't wait for him to die. They had to kill him *now*." She took a deep breath, looking for any hint of condescension in his face. Seeing none, she went on. "And the old scandals become part of accepted truth sometimes. No one would deny now that some of those less than honorable stories were quite true. The Church was up to its ears in that stuff during the war—"

"My dear," D'Ambrizzi said gently, "the Church has always had one foot in the muck, along with everyone else. And has always had its great and good men. Sometimes the good and the bad even coexist in the same man." He looked at the monsignor. "Nothing more interesting than such cases, don't you agree, Pietro? We've all known such men . . . and the Church is always only the sum of its men. And women, of course."

"No one actually knows what was lost in the fire," Sandanato said. "Why would he have waited so many decades if he'd had something as dramatic as you suggest, Sister?"

"I have no idea. I'm just working with what I do know. We *know* that Badell-Fowler was seeking to learn the whole story of the *assassini*. We *know* he was one of the murder victims . . . and we *know* his work was destroyed. I believe the work was as much the target as the man himself. Don't you both see this? Or am I crazy?" She shook her head. "No, I'm not making this up . . . all these people including Sister Val have definitely been killed. In less than two years. Is it possible they are not connected?"

"It would seem on the face of it to be unlikely." The cardinal seemed content to continue the discussion. He wasn't shutting her up. "It's this *assassini* idea that makes one skeptical."

"But," she said, "*someone* must have known Badell-Fowler had a barn full of dynamite . . . explosive because it pointed at *them*. Is that so farfetched? Why else kill him and destroy the evidence? Val was so much smarter than I am—if I'm this far into it, where was she? She was killed for the same reason Badell-Fowler was . . . more or less. What I'd give to see whatever he'd compiled!" She pulled at the reins of her enthusiasm, not wanting to blow it now. "If he traced the *assassini* deep into this century . . . if he named names, names of killers within the Church—" She sank back in her heavy, ornately carved chair. "Well, just think of it! Murderous operations within the Church, directed from within the Church. Which brings us to the ultimate question, doesn't it? Directed by whom?" She put her coffee cup down and carefully lifted her cognac to her lips, took a sip just to shut herself up.

"The poor old *assassini*," D'Ambrizzi mused, shaking his huge head. "A sturdy old bugaboo. Whipping boy of Church history. Frankly, I admit to doubting the existence of Badell-Fowler's second volume. I've been around this place a long time, I think I'd have heard of such a book—I do have my sources, too, you'll agree? No, Sister, it's ancient history and rather questionable at that."

She didn't want to engage in an argument with the cardinal, but she was damned if she'd just let it drop. "But what about this Simon Verginius? Who was he? And when? Are you saying Badell-Fowler was just a fool?"

"Gullible, Sister. He was gullible. Finding what he wanted to find. It's not an uncommon failing among a certain kind of historian. Or journalist, for that matter. As for this Simon . . . let me tell you about him. I was there, you see. Simon was a convenient myth, a kind of Robin Hood in those Nazi days in Paris. He had a dozen identities, hundreds of deeds attributed to him, an all-purpose hero who couldn't have been responsible for a tenth of what they said. He wasn't one man, he was many men. Some brave, some probably criminals, all anonymous . . . men who did things that are sometimes done in wartime . . . Your Badell-Fowler came across the stories and fell for them. Many have done so over the years. Believe me, Sister. I was there."

"You were there, of course," she said meekly. "And the *assassini* is a myth?"

"So long ago it hardly matters." He smiled benevolently.

She bit her lip, clasped her hands in her lap. "But there are murder victims *now*," she said softly, figuring she might as well get it off her chest since she might not get another chance. "They're not mythological. If, I say *if*, there were something to the idea of the *assassini*, then wouldn't these killings be their sort of thing?" She sensed Sandanato looking away, studying his plume of cigar smoke, not wanting to be associated with her irritating theory. "Doesn't that square with the idea that the killer in New York and Princeton was a priest? Coming from inside the Church?"

"Yes, yes," D'Ambrizzi barked, momentarily losing the facade of tolerant calm. "But if it comes from inside the Church, it would be coming from so high, with so much authority . . . I cannot believe it, Sister."

"But isn't it just as likely some kind of splinter group? Based on the old *assassini*? Zealots? Someone bent on a reign of terror would simply need men willing to kill—"

"Where, Sister?" Sandanato asked. "Where would one find such people? Why would one ask them to kill? Why would they be willing to do it? It seems to me too fanciful an explanation—"

"There's nothing fanciful about the murders of eight people," she went on doggedly. "Somebody killed them. Somebody dressed like a priest killed at least some of them if not every damned one—"

"But say that Badell-Fowler *was* killed because of his work on the *assassini*," Sandanato said. His eyes reached hers through the smoke. She felt almost as if he were touching her. "What about the other four men? They had no *assassini* connection. Why were they killed?" He frowned, stroking his lips. "You're constructing an enormous plot of some kind. I ask you, what could be worth it? What could it have to do with this Simon Verginius and the *assassini* forty years ago? What could be so important?"

She sneaked a peek at the cardinal.

"Who knows?" She thought she'd risk it: "Maybe the election of a new pope . . ."

Silence dropped over the table like a thick fog. Dammit, now she had gone too far! It was remarkably gauche to have made the remark with D'Ambrizzi himself, perhaps the leading papal candidate, staring at her.

The cardinal's face finally broke into his characteristic grin. "Just like Val," he said. "Sister, I must say you're a thinker. A real Machiavelli—I mean that as a compliment, by the way. I can see why Sister Valentine valued your friendship so very much."

Sandanato poured more espresso into the tiny cups. Candle flames flickered in the drafts from the open windows. The conversation swerved away from Elizabeth's mission and she knew the moment had passed. She didn't know quite what to make of their reaction: obviously their skepticism about Church-centered conspiracy theories was part of the drill. But to what extent had she piqued their interest? As the conversation turned, went its own way, she viewed her surroundings again, trying to focus clearly on something, an *idea* nibbling at the back of her mind. The cardinal's apartment in the Apostolic Palace was positively baroque, full of priceless antiques, paintings by several of the Italian masters. A

Tintoretto which Pius had given him for his service during the war dominated the dining room.

The tension brought on by Val's tale from the Secret Archives had ebbed and the cardinal dipped into history, his mind running along tracks of her laying. He let his mind drift over some of the bloodier aspects of Church history, drawing on a vastness of anecdote. As she listened she thought he'd been right about the Church's duality, always in the mud, always looking to the stars. The Janus face, Val had called it, the Janus face of the Church of Rome.

D'Ambrizzi spoke of Cesare Borgia and the *assassini* he had used once, then again, until he succeeded in having Lucrezia's husband strangled in his bed in the late summer of 1500. He sounded as if he'd been there, an intimate of the Borgias. The murder had been a stroke of policy, aimed at freeing his sister from one marriage so that she might enter into another immensely important marriage, this with Alfonso d'Este, the heir to the dukedom of Ferrara. The alliance that ensued was successful, and Lucrezia had been given an extraordinary going-away party at Halloween of 1501 by dear Cesare.

"Quite a party," the cardinal said, eyes closed, as if leafing through his recollections. "Fifty naked courtesans dancing about, picking up chestnuts from the floor with their teeth, while the men had them on the spot. All in all, things worked out quite well. Except for the dead husband, of course. Cesare managed to seize the lands of the Colonnas, slam the Orsinis into prison, and marry into the d'Estes of Ferrara." His eyes opened slowly. "Not a man to be taken lightly."

Sister Elizabeth was thinking about the naked courtesans and the chestnuts while she listened and heard that last phrase. *Not a man to be taken lightly . . .*

"The priest who killed Val and tried to kill Ben Driskill," she interrupted, forgetting entirely to mind her manners. "The man with the silver hair and the glasses . . ."

D'Ambrizzi turned to face her, indulgent. "Yes, Sister?"

"He's the right age—very fit but the right age. He's one of them. . . . He's always been one. I'm sure, I feel it . . . all this talk of Badell-Fowler and the wartime *assassini*—don't you see? It all fits . . . this Simon Verginius that Badell-Fowler thought might be their leader? He's our silver-haired priest! He's Simon Verginius! And that's not all. The Pius Plot in his notes? Think about Pius—what a scoundrel he was, or may have been, all those Germans in his life, the wrong kinds of Germans . . . Well, it was Pius who was using the *assassini* during World War Two—probably to aid the Nazis with what you were talking about, Eminence, the plunder of artworks! It fits, doesn't it? It's worth thinking about, isn't it?"

She sat there smiling at them, well across any boundaries of propriety she'd set for herself and not really stopping to worry about it. Not for a minute or two, anyway. D'Ambrizzi and Sandanato stared at her, then at each other, stymied for the right response.

Val would have been so damned proud of her!

Callistus came out of a restless sleep well past midnight and lay in the damp sheets, sweating, his head aching slightly, nothing he couldn't handle, thanks be to God. He watched the moon through the window directly before him and realized that its white, cool remoteness, its utter lack of involvement, made him think of death. Nowadays it was difficult not to think about death. But even before this illness of his, death had been a constant in his life as a priest. As long ago as he could remember he had always been going to some clerical funeral. Part of the job.

Thirty years ago he'd been a bright, ambitious monsignor in the Vatican Secretariat of State, right at the epicenter of the Church's convulsion when Pius XII finally died. Now, there was a colossal, cataclysmic death for you! In the silence of the room, lit only by the moonglow, Callistus heard himself laughing. My God, what a time that had been!

Pius had been the last of the old-fashioned popes: arrogant, autocratic, contemptuous of what others might have called simple decency or the common touch. Monsignor Salvatore di Mona had found him morally rigid, in a peculiar way morally bankrupt, and quite possibly insane. Despicable, in light of his behavior during World War II, which the very youthful Sal di Mona had spent partly in the occupied city of Paris. Insane in terms of the "visions" Pius claimed to have in his later years.

Upon the old bastard's death Monsignor di Mona, as a rising curial presence, was close enough to the laughable horrors of his funeral arrangements never to forget them. It was quite enough to convince him that you never knew when you might have to pay for your sins. In Pius's case the bill came late, presented a few hours after the last gasp.

Pius was well known within the Vatican to have lived beyond his normal span due to the ministrations of the Swiss gerontologist Dr. Paul Niehans, a Protestant for heaven's sake, who numbered King George V and Konrad Adenauer and Winston Churchill among his patients. All of them were treated with Niehans's living cell therapy which involved injections of finely pureed tissue taken from the newly killed lambs. When Pius was in his last hours at Castel Gandolfo in the early autumn of 1958, the Jesuits at Vatican Radio had miraculously surmounted normally obsessive curial secrecy by actually broadcasting live the death struggle, including the bedside prayers for the dying. Monsignor di Mona had listened in his office that night, since everything at the Vatican had ground to a halt anyway. He and three fellow priests had established a betting pool on the time of death, which came at four in the morning on October ninth. Di Mona didn't win the pool but the departure of Pius was prize enough.

Then the theater of the absurd took over.

The corpse of the late pontiff was embalmed at Castel Gandolfo by his personal physician, Galeazzi Lisi, and a specialist, Oreste Nuzzi. It was then transported to Rome in a municipal hearse decked out with four gilt angels stuck to the top, festoons of white damask more appropriate to a wedding, and a tacky wooden replica of the papal triple crown which threatened to slip off the roof at each bump in the road.

Monsignor di Mona was waiting at the Lateran Basilica when this peculiar vehicle arrived. It had never been truer than at that moment: he and a similarly minded friend hardly knew whether to laugh or cry. Then, incredibly, they heard what sounded like a pistol shot. His first thought was to cry out to the assassins, You're too late, you imbeciles! He's already dead! But it hadn't been a shot after all. Something had gone wrong inside the hearse. *Inside the coffin.*

The Lateran services went quickly and the hearse was quickly dispatched across Rome to the Vatican, where the coffin was hurried into St. Peter's. Monsignor di Mona, representing the Secretariat, arrived to find out just what was going on and retired, shaking his head in bewilderment. With the weather unusually warm, Pius XII had apparently begun to ferment, building up pressure until the lid of the casket had actually blown off. Lisi and Nuzzi consequently went back to work, laboring through the night to ready their subject for the public lying in state which would begin at seven o'clock on the morning of October twelfth. As it turned out, their problems were just beginning.

As the day progressed—the visitors streaming past, candles flickering, the remains of Pius encased in a red chasuble with a gold miter on his head—it all began to go wrong again. It was hot in St. Peter's. Too hot. The deathly pallor of Pius's face turned green. Everyone was noticing a sickening odor. *The real man finally showing through,* di Mona thought to himself. Common sense prevailed and the coffin was closed, encased in a leaden casket, and removed at last to a tomb in the grottoes beneath St. Peter's.

The reason given for such calamitous events was dazzling, revolving around Lisi's explanation that he and Nuzzi had used ancient embalming methods—no injections, no surgery, no evisceration—which had been good enough for the early Christians and were surely appropriate for this saintly pope. Lisi went on to sell his story of the papal death agony to the press, and the cardinals governing the Church during the interim between popes banned him forever from setting foot on Vatican soil. In every imaginable way Pius's end had been a messy one.

Appropriate in Monsignor di Mona's eyes then and, now, in Callistus IV's eyes. The passage of time had done nothing to soften his views. He was smiling both at the recollection of his young self caught up in the ridiculous events of that long-ago October and at the friendships that had taken root even before that, in Paris during the war, when he'd realized what a monster Pius truly was.

Paris. The very word transported him back in time, brought back memories of old friends and of causes worth dying for, worth doing anything for . . .

Callistus rubbed the back of his neck, massaging the dull throb, and got slowly out of bed. The most recent painkiller was wearing off. Dr. Cassoni had told him it was essentially the same thing as heroin, and Callistus had told him to keep any further lurid bits to himself. But D'Ambrizzi had been right: Cassoni was a good man.

He was wearing a dark blue bathrobe over scarlet pajamas and velvet English slippers. He dumped another pill onto the tabletop, washed it down with a sip of tepid water. He lit a cigarette. The evening breeze sucked the smoke out past the draperies. He pressed

a button on his tapedeck and out came *Madama Butterfly*. Poor
Butterfly, 'neath the blossoms waiting . . .

He took his cane and left the sitting room, nodded to the male
nurse sitting reading by a dim desk lamp, and went out into the
hallway. The tapping of the cane sounded like a metronome. Since
the crisis of the murders had heightened the tensions in Vatican
City, since he'd given Indelicato and D'Ambrizzi their marching
orders, Callistus had taken to prowling the corridors of his domain
in the wee hours, as if by surveying the calm and quiet of the night,
the guards, what he called the night shift, he could put his mind at
ease. If only he could believe that somehow all would be well.

He rapped softly on a door in shadow, loud enough to be heard
only if the man within were still awake.

"Come in, Holiness." The voice was raspy, animal-like.

Callistus entered hesitantly. "I didn't wake you, Giacomo?"

"No, no, I'm a night dweller these days, I'm afraid—like an old
marmoset. Come in, I'm glad for the company. You'll keep me from
thinking."

It had not always been quite so comfortable between them. For
a time years earlier Giacomo had also sought the Throne of Peter,
though they'd never really discussed it. Too many of their fellow
cardinals had believed D'Ambrizzi was too useful down in the
rough and tumble of the real world . . . and money had been
passed around, palms crossed. Irreplaceable, they'd said, D'Ambrizzi was simply irreplaceable, whereas Cardinal di Mona was,
indeed, easily replaced. That was the "official story" back then.
Well, D'Ambrizzi had read all the signs and thrown his support to
di Mona, the younger man he'd known so long. Ironically, D'Ambrizzi had lived to see the brass ring come around again.

"The pain is bad?" D'Ambrizzi's face was shadowed, giving him
a sinister aspect.

"Not so bad. I did some praying before sleep. Then an hour or
so later I woke up and began thinking about the death of Pius."

D'Ambrizzi smiled. "Black comedy. Some blasphemous young
fellow could write a very funny play."

Callistus gave a small, hollow laugh. "What do you think of
prayer?" He lowered himself carefully into a well-padded armchair.

"As our friend Indelicato would say, I don't see the harm. But
it's out of character for you, isn't it? What drove you to prayer,
Salvatore?"

The sound of his old name cheered Callistus. "The same thing that produces most prayer. Fear. These killings . . ." He shrugged helplessly. "Where can we start? How do we begin to stop them? Why are these people dying? Why? That's the important thing." He shifted in the chair, seeking a more comfortable position. The painkiller was beginning to work. D'Ambrizzi seemed to have no comment. "When I first met you in Paris during the war, you were habitually insubordinate. No, please, hear me out. That was what impressed me so, probably because I knew that insubordination was beyond me. I heard people talk, I knew what they said about you. You had contacts in the Resistance, you were smuggling Jews out of Germany, you hid them from the Nazis—"

"Only with the assistance of Reichsmarshal Goering," D'Ambrizzi said. "His wife, the actress, she was part Jewish—"

"You even hid them in the coal bins of our churches!"

"Infrequently, Salvatore."

"My question is this, Giacomo. Were you ever scared? So scared that you couldn't imagine anything worse? Did your faith see you through the fear?"

"In the first place, there's always something worse. Always. When it came to dealing with fear—faith never entered my mind, Salvatore. I was always too busy figuring out how to make my escape. Fear . . . With age, of course, the memory fails. Was I ever scared? Perhaps I was young and strong enough to believe I was invincible, immortal—"

"That's sacrilegious, Cardinal."

"How true! But the least of my sins. Look at old Pius and all his injections, doing all he could to cheat death. . . . Of course I was afraid. There was a German officer, he had been an acquaintance of Pius's before the war in Berlin. Young fellow, no influence, but I had reason to go to his office from time to time. He had known Pius and he kept telling me how he had personally introduced Cardinal Pacelli to Herr Hitler and now look, D'Ambrizzi, he would say to me, Pacelli is pope and Hitler remembers who introduced them. He found that hugely satisfying. Every time he called me to his office—from his window we could look out at the Arc de Triomphe—every time he called me in to see him I had to vomit. Before I went and after I got back. He scared me."

"What did you think he'd do to you, Giacomo?"

"I had it in my head that someday, just for sport, young Richter might take the Luger out of his huge holster and shoot me. Plant a weapon on me and say I'd tried to kill him. Yes, I was afraid Klaus Richter might kill me." The cardinal sighed, coughed. "For sport. You know, they suspected me of certain activities—they would have had to execute a priest! Never a popular thing to do at such a time, when priests represented sanity in an occupied country. . . . I got to thinking later that young Richter must have been a terrible liar, he seemed much too young to have introduced Pacelli to anyone. Perhaps he was trying to impress me. In any case, yes, I was afraid, Salvatore."

"Then you understand how I feel. I feel as if we are all on some terrible list, suspected by someone of certain activities—I'm at a loss, Giacomo, I don't know where to begin to find our way out of this . . . eight killings . . ."

D'Ambrizzi nodded. Callistus seemed so small beneath the long robe, so sick, so vulnerable. There seemed to be less of him each day. "You can't help being afraid. You're only human."

"I'm afraid for what is happening to the Church, certainly. And I'm afraid for myself . . . I'm afraid to die. Not always but some of the time. Is that shameful, Giacomo?" He waited in the silence. "To think—there was a time when you wanted this job of mine."

"That's not actually true," D'Ambrizzi said. "My supporters, I admit, were vocal. Eleven votes. That was my high-water mark in the enclave. Then talk of my 'indispensable gifts' arose and my support began to fall away. I didn't mind, you know. I have a good life, Holiness."

"How did you vote, Giacomo?"

"For you, Holiness."

"What on earth for?"

"I thought you deserved it."

The pope laughed aloud. "That, my old friend, can be taken two ways."

"At the very least," D'Ambrizzi said, smiling.

"Tell me honestly," Callistus said after a moment. "What is this Driskill up to? What *can* he do? Does he know about all the other victims?"

"No. The less he knows, the more likely he is to survive, don't you agree?"

"Of course. And we can't have outsiders turning the Church upside down. He'd have to be stopped if he persisted—"

"Exactly."

"Perhaps he'll get tired after a time and give up."

"That is my hope. But I'd have thought that the attack on himself might have dimmed his enthusiasm for the chase. I'd have been wrong, as it turned out."

"Where is he?"

"Egypt, so far as I know."

"We don't know where they will strike again, do we?"

"No."

"I feel as if history is standing still and we all hang in the balance. What is the pattern, Giacomo? Why these eight?"

Cardinal D'Ambrizzi shook his head.

Callistus turned away and looked out over the moonlit Vatican gardens. "Do you fear death?"

"I once knew a woman who was dying young. We spoke of what awaited her. She comforted me, Holiness, took my hand, told me I must believe her when she said that when the time comes you recognize death as your last best friend. I have never forgotten that."

"The woman was a saint! She had wisdom . . . why have I none?"

The pope stood slowly, his mind already elsewhere, lost in memories of another time. The cardinal wrapped his arm around the smaller man's shoulders, guided him to the window, where they stood staring into the night. There was no need to speak. Below them in the serenity of the gardens a lone priest walked the pathways, slipping in and out of the shadows, there one second and gone the next, like a phantom, like a killer . . .

Back in his bed Callistus's mind turned restlessly, relentlessly, back to the past, as if it were a magnet too powerful for his steadily decreasing strength to deny. Paris, it was always Paris, too much for him to resist anymore. For so many years he had kept the memory at bay, refused to acknowledge that any of it had ever happened. He had effectively erased the past, but now it was as if his resources had slipped, the situation falling from his control, and, like magic writing, those days and that story were all reappearing at the end. He wondered if the others had forgotten. Had D'Ambrizzi forgotten? And old Bishop Torricelli, had he repressed it all only to have it return as he lay on his deathbed? And what of the taut, austere man from Rome who had come and knocked on

his door in Paris, the man with pain and punishment in his eyes
. . . Indelicato, the inquisitor, did he now remember it all or not, as
he stood only one step from the Throne of Peter himself?

He tossed and turned, trying not to remember but unable to
fight the impulse, and he was back in the small churchyard on the
wintry night, crouched shivering by the black wrought iron fence.
There were three of them, Brother Leo and the tall blond priest and
Sal di Mona, and while they watched there was murder done in the
tiny graveyard among the tilted, antique headstones. They had held
their breath and tried to keep their teeth from chattering and they
had watched one priest kill another who had betrayed them all, kill
him with his bare hands, snap him like a matchstick, they all three
heard the crack of the bones.

Monsignor Sandanato was also having a bad night.

The dinner conversation with Sister Elizabeth had been upsetting though he'd tried not to show his feelings. What did she think
she was doing? Who had told her—given her the authority—to
complete Sister Valentine's work? Work that had gotten Sister
Valentine killed. What did she think she would do with the results
of her digging? So she had identified the eight victims the Church
had tried to keep unconnected in the public mind. So she had dug
up all the old *assassini* stuff—who out there cared, in a time when
scandals within the Church bank and potential schisms were
cropping up more or less constantly? So she thought she was
putting two and two together, eight murder victims and the idea of
the *assassini*. What then? Judging from the way things were going,
she was asking to get herself killed and he desperately didn't want
that to happen. The Church couldn't afford to lose an Elizabeth.
And besides that, there were all the other feelings he harbored
toward her, feelings with which he was increasingly uncomfortable.

Then there was the problem of Ben Driskill.

Before leaving his Vatican office for dinner in the cardinal's
apartment, he'd received a call from Father Dunn in New York.
Dunn wanted to know if they'd heard anything about Driskill's
travels.

"No," Sandanato had said, losing patience, "and I must tell you
I resent wasting time having to worry about him. We have enough
to worry about without Ben Driskill in Egypt irritating the people
who may have killed his sister. He must have a death wish! And he

has a wound in his back two feet long and two weeks old—Father, is he mad? Doesn't he realize this is Church business? Why can't he let the Church handle it?"

"You mean the way the Church is handling it now? That's a question I wouldn't raise right now if I were you." Dunn was chuckling, increasing Sandanato's annoyance. "And I'll tell you— Church business-as-usual doesn't impress Ben Driskill a whole lot. And he is rich, he's spoiled, he gets his own way, all the Driskills do, they always have. He's not grabby about it, he's just sort of relentless. I've been asking around about our friend Driskill, and I'm getting a picture of this guy—you know what I think? I think he may just kill somebody himself. If you're worrying about Driskill, my advice to you would be to start worrying about the other guys."

"You mean, he's out of our control, loose, and there's nothing we can do about it?"

"You seem to have grasped the essential message, Monsignor."

"I'm afraid, whether you are or not," Sandanato said coldly, "that he will indeed get himself killed."

"I'm as worried about him as you are. That's why I'm calling you, to find out if you've had any word from him or about him—"

"Well, as I said, the answer is no. And you're telling me he can't be stopped?"

Dunn chuckled dryly. "Not by me he can't."

"What do you suggest we do, Father?"

"Whattaya say we put prayer to the test, my friend?"

Alone in his spartan apartment, less than a ten-minute walk from the Gate of Saint Anne, Sandanato sat at a small, rickety desk by a window overlooking a quiet back street two floors below. He poured three fingers of Glenfiddich into a jelly jar, swirled it, watching it bathe the glass. He had once attended a seminar in Glasgow and been introduced to the single-malt whiskies. Italians were not scotch drinkers but a Vatican monsignor could lay his hands on most things. The Glenfiddich was one of his few indulgences. He let the first swallow warm his gullet and belly and closed his eyes, digging his knuckles into the sockets and kneading them slowly. Things were going wrong, and getting drunk just might be the only rational response. He was listening to the great recording of *Rigoletto*. Callas, di Stefano, and Gobbi. Callas was soaring in the

"Cara nome" and he waited, marveling at the body she brought to the highest, most rapturous notes.

He was fighting a constant battle against the armies of depression he had known all his life. He was losing. Everywhere he looked the darkness seemed to beckon. What he saw happening to the Church burned in his belly like a torturer's poker. The shadows seemed to be closing in unless, somehow, the Church could be saved in time. He had seen the fear in the pope's eyes, the confusion, the inability to take hold. Someone else would be pope soon. . . .

Sandanato opened his eyes, watched a neighborhood prostitute sidle up to a man in the street. She laughed, a harsh sound like glass breaking or a cat in heat, and linked her arm through the man's, led him away to the stained sheets and the smells of sweat and dried semen and perfume like garbage. He remembered it, the whore he'd visited once, and he gulped at the scotch to burn away the memory.

He dribbled more scotch into the thick-lipped jar, stared at his reflection in the glass. He needed a shave. His mouth tasted like a toilet, and he felt as if none of the dinner had been properly digested. *Where was Driskill and what was he doing?* He slammed the chair back against the wall and stood up, paced the small room. The loneliness was overwhelming. He ought to have spent the night in the Vatican. It was his only real home. His only life lay there, inside the Church.

He knew where his thoughts were taking him, but his resistance was paltry, a weak-willed thing. Out of his loneliness and frustration, he came to think of Sister Elizabeth.

He wasn't entirely sure why and didn't suppose it really mattered.

But he was sure he had never known such a woman before. He could identify in her appeal the quality of her mind, the freshness of her candor, her strength. She appealed as a human being, as a representative of the Church, on so many levels. He sat alone, wanting to be with her, in some other room without the pain and longing and frustration that seemed to festoon these four walls like remnants of a madman's delirium.

He wanted to hear her talk, to argue with her, to match wits. He sensed that rarest phenomenon, a true meeting of minds. He knew she thought the way he did, that the Church must always come first, that she had the same strength of inner commitment that he did.

He was sure Sister Valentine had been Lockhardt's mistress. Cardinal D'Ambrizzi had left him in no doubt of that. But what about Sister Elizabeth? He knew he was being irrational, but he had managed to drive himself half mad with thoughts of Ben Driskill and Sister Elizabeth. There was not a single piece of evidence: it was all in his head and he knew it. But he'd seen them together, he'd watched them. . . . For a moment he'd been delighted when Driskill had related the unpleasantness of their parting. It had momentarily put his mind at ease. And then he'd begun to see how Driskill was taking it, how badly it had hurt him, how angry he'd become. It was the reaction of a man who cared and it reminded Sandanato of the looks he'd seen pass between them.

It was evil the way it tormented him. It grew in him like a malignancy. Could anything have happened between them? Driskill had told him how they met before, how much she and Val had liked, loved, each other. . . . Could she take her vows so lightly, could she have done with Driskill what Val had done with Lockhardt?

Christ, he hated himself for even thinking it! It was so absurd. Val was murdered, Elizabeth flew to Princeton, and he was suggesting that they immediately fell into bed with each other! An adolescent fantasy, a paroxysm of fear from a lonely man who was a priest . . . and who had fallen into a mad infatuation with a nun who hardly knew he existed! What a classic performance, the behavior of a dunce—he'd seen it before in priests he held in utter, total contempt.

She could set his mind at ease. It would be so simple. But he could never ask. He wanted so badly to see her, to learn that she was true to all that gave her life—his life—its meaning. He wanted to trust her, to join with her. He needed her to help him climb out of the dungeon of his dark solitude.

But was she worthy?

The very question was hateful, but he couldn't deny it.

Finally, with his glass drained, he could restrain himself no longer.

He picked up the telephone, dialed her number, waited while it rang and rang and rang. . . .

* * *

Father Artie Dunn stood at his study window staring down at the top of Carnegie Hall and Fifty-seventh Street and Central Park South slumbering under a gray morning fog. The trees in the park were leafless and the lakes looked gray, and every so often brown and gray ducks would take off or land and float toward the reeds. He sighed, put down his binoculars, and poured himself another cup of coffee from the thermos on his desk. He'd dozed off for only three hours and he yawned mightily. The desk and coffee table were cluttered with pieces of paper full of his scrawl. Plotting the "Driskill affair." The family was everywhere. Everywhere! What an extraordinary bunch!

The whole *business* was extraordinary, amazing: it far surpassed any novel he'd written. He'd never have gotten away with it, that was the bottom line. For instance, there was this wild Gothic story Sister Mary Angelina had told him, this little old nun with the big eyes, safely tucked away in her convent, the last stop for Sister Mary Angelina. She'd poured out this story so calmly—more or less calmly, anyway—that she'd been sitting on for nearly half a century. After hearing her out he'd thanked her and what the hell else could he say? A bit of a conversation stopper, not your everyday item of family reminiscence. For one thing, he didn't know whether or not to believe her. She seemed perfectly sane, but you never knew. In his experience there weren't a great many wholly sane people who could have kept such a secret for so long a time and then have trotted it out at the end like a prize pet. He hadn't known what to think, so he'd thanked her and stopped off in Princeton at the Nassau Inn for a burger, the place where it had all started that foul night almost a month before. He decided he needed some kind of confirmation of her story. Which was going to be difficult since Mary Driskill was long dead, Father Governeau was longer dead, and he couldn't quite picture himself toddling into Hugh Driskill's hospital room and running through Sister Mary Angelina's trip down memory lane.

So, how could he dig up a second opinion? There had to be a way.

When he got back to New York it was dark and cold and he sat down and began trying to factor Father Governeau's death into the mass of plot he'd worked out. It was an unholy mess, it needed weeding, but he didn't know where to start. He longed for the order and control of one of his books.

He'd eventually tottered off to bed and slept a dreamless sleep, awakening three hours later at seven o'clock when the timer turned on the *Today* show. The NBC correspondent in Rome was reporting on two Vatican stories: the continuing scandal at the bank which seemed to be resulting in a rash of suicides and, almost as an afterthought, the rumor that Pope Callistus IV might be in ill health since his public appearances, which had decreased markedly during the summer, had come to a complete halt during the past month. The official story—a stubborn upper respiratory infection—seemed to provoke a jaundiced response from the NBC man. Dunn groaned sleepily but couldn't help grinning. He enjoyed the prospect of the Roman curia having to hotfoot it around the land mines and start dealing with real life. It was surprising that they'd kept the lid on so long.

Once he'd had his coffee he nudged his problems around with a freshly activated collection of brain cells. And he came up with at least one answer. He needed someone to confirm Sister Mary Angelina's story. The name came to him.

Drew Summerhays. If he didn't know the truth, then no one was going to. He was Hugh Driskill's mentor, adviser, friend.

Dunn got the number of Bascomb, Lufkin, and Summerhays and spoke with the great man's secretary. No, he wouldn't be in today but tomorrow at two o'clock would be fine. Dunn agreed.

Making the call, he noticed for the first time that he'd been so preoccupied the previous evening he'd ignored the messages waiting on his answering machine. The only one that mattered to him that morning was one that had come in from Peaches O'Neale in New Pru two nights before. There were two follow-ups during the day when Dunn had been off visiting the convent near Trenton. Peaches was growing exasperated by the conclusion of the third call, so Dunn wasted no time in calling the St. Mary's parish house.

Peaches made it to The Ginger Man, a restaurant across the busy intersection from Lincoln Center, for a one o'clock lunch. Father Dunn was sitting at a table in the glassed-in sidewalk café sipping a dry martini when Peaches came in from the cold rain that had blown in across the Hudson. Rain was slapping at the windows like an angry housewife who's caught up with her bastard of a husband at long last. It bounced on the sidewalk, puddled. Peaches came in shaking his raincoat and sniffling, red-nosed.

"There is," Dunn said, leaning back, "a sense of urgency about you, young Peaches."

"Ha! An understatement if ever I've heard one. You ought to pick up your messages more often. I've been going crazy." He ordered a Rob Roy and opened the rain-spattered black briefcase on his lap. His face wasn't quite so boyish. He had a cold and looked every day of his age for the first time since Dunn had known him. "Artie," he said, "hold on to your hat. I think we've got something here but I'm damned if I know what. Since you try so steadfastly to give the impression that you are truly wise, here's your chance to prove it. Take a look at this."

He handed the manila envelope with its remnants of electrician's tape across the table to Father Dunn, who carefully opened it and slid the handwritten manuscript out.

The Facts in the Matter of Simon Verginius.

"By none other than one Giacomo D'Ambrizzi." Peaches O'Neale smiled. "I hereby officially make it your problem." He was looking better already.

Eleven hours later the New York Giants and the Philadelphia Eagles were entering the fourth quarter, the midnight quarter, of a football game conducted in a soggy swamp of half-frozen mud. Peaches was slumped wearily before the television set in Father Dunn's study. Perhaps, he thought, hell is an endless football game played in a mud where you can't tell which team is which and nobody knows the score and nobody cares anymore anyway. He balefully regarded the remains of a pizza, the empty cans of Diet Coke.

Dunn looked up from the manuscript and grinned at Peaches. He tapped the manuscript. "This would make a helluva movie."

"Sure, sure. What do you make of it? You've read it enough times to memorize it—"

"I was memorizing it, in a way. Tomorrow morning I want you to put this thing in your little black briefcase and take it back to New Pru and put it where you found it. If this thing were to start floating around—well, perish the thought, laddie." He pointed to his forehead. "I've got all I need up here."

"So, who was this Simon Verginius? And Archduke? All these code names? Who were they?"

"I don't know, and that's the truth. But I'm going to find out, one way or another. D'Ambrizzi was sure as the devil close to this Simon and all the rest of them."

He made a plane reservation for the following evening, first-class, to Paris.

There was one man he had to find.

Erich Kessler.

Sister Elizabeth was working late, although magazine work had nothing to do with what was really on her mind. Word of the pope's illness, which had been privately known throughout the Roman press corps, was beginning to dribble out, first by way of Roman newspapers and then on television. It could only mean that the disease, or diseases, was not responding to treatment. Things were bad enough that a signal had been passed from somewhere within the curia: it was now time to begin to prepare the world for the death of Callistus IV, whenever it actually came to pass.

She was looking once again at her notes on D'Ambrizzi and Indelicato, trying to put her finger on the prime dark horse who would join them as the favorites, when Sister Bernadine came bustling in, closed the door, and let her facade collapse. She threw herself down on the couch and blew out a long sigh. She'd just finished a major struggle with the printer and the color separator and was worn out from the constant arguing.

"I've gotten together the next installment of your hit-list bios." She leaned forward and pushed the folder across the desk toward Elizabeth.

She opened it and leafed through the sheets. "Anything of special interest?" Her eyes flicked through the material, looking for something, but she didn't know what.

"They're all pretty much of an age—"

"We knew that."

"They were all Catholics."

"We knew that, too, Sister."

"They were all murdered—"

"Come on, Sister! Tell me something I don't know!"

"And," Sister Bernadine said with a smile, "they were all in Paris during the war."

Elizabeth's eyes clicked open like a cartoon character's, and she blinked several times at her colleague.

"Ahhh . . . now, that's something I did not know, Sister. Anything about Kessler?"

Sister Bernadine shook her head. "Talk about a mystery man!"

Brother Jean-Pierre had come to the village not far from the Hendaye border-crossing with Spain during the summer of 1945. Those were confused days in France, in both cities and the country-side, and he'd taken advantage of the confusion that came with the arrival of the postwar world to leave Paris and everything that had gone on there. On foot he'd come all the way to the coast of Brittany, then worked his way down that rocky edge of France and come to rest, where he'd remained ever since. Considering what might have befallen him as a result of a very strenuous war, he felt fortunate. He had made himself useful as the handyman for the priest at the threadbare country church. He would blush when they called him by his title, sexton. He tended to the bell, to the polishing and repairing, all the jobs that made him indispensable. And for nearly forty years he had passed largely unnoticed, which wasn't easy when you thought of how he looked.

When he'd left Paris they'd been looking for him, led by the priest who'd come from Rome to conduct the investigation. Simon had told him they'd been betrayed and he'd have to go to ground. Jean-Pierre had felt his world shatter. Simon had calmed him down, reminded him of how brave he'd been when they'd been trapped by the Germans and taken to the barn for interrogation. Jean-Pierre had nodded, and when he left Paris he had kept moving, his fear seeming to render him invisible. He was merely one of the walking wounded trudging the back roads of France.

A couple of weeks after leaving Paris he crested a rocky hill and saw below him a gentle stream, a village large enough to have a church. The steeple drew him like a magnet. He waited under cover of brush until after dark, watching the villagers moving deliberately about their business. When the lights had come on in the small houses and the church seemed deserted, he waited longer still, until the moon was high, lurking in and out among the clouds. Finally he crossed the stream, curled around the village's outbuild-ings, and approached the church from the rear. The door was padlocked. With his bare hands he slowly pulled the fittings from the door itself, leaving the lock secure.

Inside he heard someone snoring. The priest, an elderly man, tall and fat with a full head of fluffy gray hair, had fallen asleep at his kitchen table. He bypassed the tiny kitchen, searched the hallway for the door he wanted. It was easy to find. The nearly empty clothes closet. Yes, the cassock . . .

Five minutes later, the bundle under his arm, he crossed back over the stream and faded into the darkness.

Now, almost forty years later, he still dreamed about the days in Paris, the good times and the bad, as well. He remembered how the end had come—how Brother Christos had been killed and they had all been betrayed and Simon had sent him away in order to save him. He remembered and dreamed, dreamed of the day when he might be called upon to serve again. But the summons had never come and the years had passed and he had worked for the little church in the little country village and that had been all right, too. Simon had said that it was all over and he'd been right.

Sometimes he dreamed about the weeks he'd spent with Simon hiding in a basement with the cold smell of coal dust thick in the air that last winter. Simon had saved him, Simon had nursed him while his eye had healed. . . .

It had been his own fault. He'd been careless. And they'd caught him with the nun who had been the Resistance courier. He'd held them off with the revolver until she'd escaped up the road on her bicycle and then they'd stormed him and taken him and Simon to the barn. It was in the barn that the Germans had gone to work on him. On both of them. They whipped Simon until he collapsed, until the flesh of his back was flayed to the bone, and then they'd turned their attention to Jean-Pierre.

They'd had at him for two days, trussed up like a side of beef and hung from a hook, they'd finally thought he was done for . . . yes, when the Gestapo interrogator had heated the knife in the flame and they'd held him down and the interrogator had sliced his eye through and through, yes, they thought he was done for and they'd cut him down and left him in the bloody hay where Simon lay almost dead. . . .

But Jean-Pierre had roused himself and taken the pitchfork from the wall and when they came back, he'd done them, first the corporal, then the Gestapo man, he'd done them again and again, hearing the ribs separate and the backbones break, and he'd wakened Simon and together they'd dragged themselves away, had gotten to the little church where they'd met for their orders, and there the two of them had hidden beneath the false floor of the coal cellar. . . .

Sometimes he still dreamed of those days.

Forty years later. He was polishing the wooden benches in the church and heard the door creak open and saw the light from outside flood across the warped wooden floor. He stood up, turned, and saw the man silhouetted against the light.

"Jean-Pierre . . ."

He took a step toward the figure and shielded his one good eye against the glare.

Then he saw him, the tall man, his hair now silvery, his eyes clear and pale behind the round lenses. Slowly he saw the man smile.

"August . . ."

The sexton went to him, threw his arms around him, recapturing the past, his own past.

"Jean-Pierre, Simon needs your help."

PART THREE

1

DRISKILL

I was too damned tired to care what kind of plane I was boarding, as long as it was headed for Paris and I was on it. Coming back to the real world from what I'd found in the desert was more than a change of geography. Mentally, morally, and philosophically everything changed. The blades inside my head, like some fiendish Cuisinart, altered their pitch, mashing my brains in a different way. Of course, I still wound up with mashed brains.

It was like trying again and again to score from the one-yard line and failing. They wore you down and finally you had the feeling that you'd never get in again, never put another point on the board. I had seen Gabrielle LeBecq briefly, told her what had apparently happened with her father, and she had called the authorities. She knew I had to go, she understood. I didn't feel good about leaving her to cope, but I had no real choice. She reassured me that she would have the gallery to run, that she had friends who would see her through. She wasn't the sort of person who needed three days worth of explanations.

I tried to get hold of Klaus Richter but was told he had departed for Europe on a buying tour. His schedule would be so erratic that there was no way I could call him, but if I wanted to leave a message for him he called in almost every day. Any message I could think of for Richter just wasn't the kind you pass through a secretary. Hell, I wasn't sure what message I had for him . . . other than to ask him why he'd lied to me and what he'd had to do with Church skullduggery forty years ago—and I'd undoubtedly get just the answer such an overreaching question deserved. I had to remember I was a lawyer. Never ask a question unless you already knew the answer. Lesson one.

I slept like a dead man the first hour of the flight and then I woke up needing to organize my thoughts, feeling like an intellectual slob for not keeping everything in order. But there was so much to remember, so much happening for which nothing in my life had prepared me. One thing my life as a lawyer had prepared me to do was scratch out acres of notes on legal pads. A lawyer knew he couldn't keep it all in his head and all this had turned out to be as complicated as anything that had ever floundered through the doorway and flopped hopelessly on my desk. So I got out the legal pad and went to work. I had to know what the hell I was doing by the time I got to Paris.

My sister had gone all the way from Paris to Alexandria to find Klaus Richter . . . and maybe Etienne LeBecq, too. I wasn't clear about that: when she'd come up with LeBecq, that is. But she'd obviously found references to Richter in the papers of Bishop Torricelli in Paris. Richter—I could see him now, sitting behind the desk with his hourglass full of sand from the western desert so he'd never forget the fallen: he'd told me he knew Torricelli, that he'd been a liaison between the Church and the occupying army conducting daily business and trying to keep the Church free of Resistance cells. He'd told me he hadn't known D'Ambrizzi but the snapshot made a liar out of him. And he'd naturally neglected to tell me he'd been a player in the art deal between the Nazis and the Church, the mutually beneficial looting process that had led to the state of mutual blackmail: We won't tell about you if you don't tell about us. And the whole black business was apparently still going on: the Nazi survivors funding some current operations by selling to the Church of Rome . . . that much seemed simple. Improbable, yes, but simple. Maybe it had degenerated by now into mere blackmail minus the formality of selling the art, but that seemed *too* simple. No, secrets of forty years ago weren't enough: something had to be going on now. Maybe, just maybe, it was the approaching election of a successor to Callistus. Maybe, just maybe, across those forty-odd years, it was still all connected. . . . Fine, Mr. Learned Counsel. But how?

Then there were the LeBecq brothers. I had one dead LeBecq, strangled, crushed, back broken in a Paris graveyard during the war. Then, briefly, I had a live LeBecq talking about Simon Somebody he feared had sent me—*me*—from Rome to kill him . . . "to kill all of us." Well, all of that had come by express from left field. Simon who? Kill all of whom? Richter and Etienne LeBecq? I was lost in a wallow of confusion. What was it LeBecq had told me? My only protection was my innocence. He said I should hide within my innocence and they still might let me live. . . .

Then there was Simon again in the list of names, or code names, Gabrielle and I had found in her father's diary. Simon. Gregory. Paul. Christos. Archduke!

Would I ever know who they were? And why there was that enigmatic, irritating exclamation point? What did it say about Archduke? Were they the code names of the men in the snapshot? Plus one?

And when it came to that snapshot . . .

Bishop Torricelli in street clothes, Klaus Richter in his Wehrmacht uniform with the collar open, D'Ambrizzi, Father Guy LeBecq. And the man who took the picture. What the hell were they doing? Had it something to do with Richter's concern over Resistance operations within the Church? Surely it was Torricelli's business to keep the Germans from deciding the Church was shielding Resistance fighters. Maybe that was it. Or could it have had anything to do with the dividing up of looted art treasures? Guy LeBecq's father and brother were involved, maybe the priest was, too. But what was D'Ambrizzi doing hanging around with these characters? And who killed Father LeBecq in the graveyard and why?

It was driving me crazy. All of it.

And there were the results of the trip to the monastery.

One man was dead. As a result of me. Nothing I could do about that, no absolution in stock.

But I'd given the silver-haired priest with the knife a name. *August*.

And I knew he got his orders from Rome.

It was one thing to suspect something, altogether different to have it spoken aloud, a fact. It chilled me clear through.

August. Sent from Rome. To kill.

Who was he?

And, for God's sake, who sent him?

Hours later I woke from an exceedingly troubled sleep, soaked with sweat, my eyes burning, my throat dry, my face greasy with the recycled filth common to the cabins of aircraft. Overheated, recycled, sweating filth, compounded by ritual dehydration, too much in the way of sub-ordinary food and drink that you really didn't want anyway but it helped pass the time, on and on. The result that night was bad dreams, particularly my old bad dream that I'd spent most of my life repressing, only tonight it had a new spin, making it even more horrifying, the addition of a remembered face—a second remembered face—Etienne LeBecq's face. In my dream he was still propped up against the nosewheel of his little plane and bugs were crawling in and out of the bullet hole in his forehead and his dead, gaping mouth. He was filled with gases, about to explode like an overinflated doll, but that wasn't what bothered me most. It was the angle of his head and the hair sticking up and the fact that he was staring at me through bloodshot eyes yet was so obviously dead. The problem was that he, in my dreams, looked like, or reminded me of, or in some other way brought very clearly to mind, the subject of my old recurring dream.

He looked like my mother.

It was just that kind of night, when things couldn't get worse and then they got a lot worse, a bad plane trip, my brain mulched to thin gruel by all the questions and doubts, bad dreams taking on foul new dimensions, and a gun in my baggage just for good measure. Brave new world that has such a creature in it!

When my mother went over the balcony railing of our place on Park Avenue I'd heard the noise of her landing from my room. It was a three-story apartment, a triplex they call them now, twenty-some rooms and the carved balcony railing was too low, everybody

always said it was a danger, someone was going to take a header
one day, and I was in my room listening to a New York Giants
football game on the radio which, of course, made it a Sunday. My
father was off somewhere and Val was visiting a friend from her
school and the staff was having one of their Sundays and I seemed
to be there alone except for Mother.

I heard the sound: not a cry, not a scream, just the sound of
what turned out to be breaking glass and her head hitting the inlaid
parquet floor of the foyer. Foyer? Actually more of an entry hall,
something from a castle somewhere in mythology. A couple of
huge paintings, one a Sargent, and some trees in grand embossed
pots, a Persian carpet of uncertain provenance, a couple of busts,
not so terribly au courant, and Mother dropping through space,
through the still air, through dust motes and traces of the smoke
from thousands of cigars, dropping like a stone wrapped in one of
her filmy things, a nightgown, a robe like gossamer, a martini glass
dropping along beside her—no, still clutched in her hand—by
God, she wasn't going to spill a perfectly good drink just because
she was committing suicide, not while she still had the strength to
hold it as she hurtled down to smack into the inlaid parquet.

Well, we never admitted she'd died by her own hand. It was an
accident, that goddamned low railing. That gin. That vermouth. An
unfortunate and unexpected turn of events. Nobody said a word
about suicide. Christ, no! Not a Driskill. But I knew, I knew . . .

Smack onto the parquet, still holding the delicate Baccarat
crystal all the way down because you never knew when you might
want a good stiff one, a last stiff one, and then I came running
down the hall, racing down the stairway, and I found her with the
glass broken, the jagged stem driven through the fine-boned pale
hand like a spike, a tiny nod to Catholicism and its symbols,
crucified by the stem of her martini glass. I must have heard the
glass breaking, the shell of her skull cracking, splitting, the accumulated mechanical sounds of my mother's death. When I arrived
she was leaning with her back against a massive hand-carved
sideboard in the manner of Grinling Gibbons. Sotheby's subsequently auctioned it off for a nice round fifty thousand, the pocket
money of an Arabian gentleman. She was incredibly dead, as if
there were gradations of death. Perhaps there are. Blood was
smeared across the floor, her hand looked like a clot of hamburger,
there was blood running from her mouth, nose, and scalp. Her hair

was matted with blood. Her skin had acquired a faint bluish tinge. Her eyes were open. Some blood vessels had burst in the whites and she seemed to be looking at me from the remote other side of all that blood. This entire awfulness had befallen her—yes, literally, befallen her—in a matter of seconds. Somehow she'd had enough motor control, instinct, whatever, to hit the floor at X miles per hour, gather up the remains of her component parts—already dead, my poor mother—and pull herself into a sitting position so her son wouldn't see her all sprawled with her legs this way and that and her gown hiked up, ungracefully dead.

Mom. Dead. And there she was in my dreams again, first that ghostly scene in some hallway, Princeton or Park Avenue—this was what I'd well and truly repressed, right from the beginning, knowing so well it must contain the reason, more horrible than I could face or imagine—why she took a dive off the balcony. First that ghostly scene in some hallway, with her reaching out as always, trying to tell me something, her face obscured in shadow or a kind of fog that is known only in Hollywood and in dreams, with the smell of her cologne and powder enveloping us, my straining to hear her, failing, as I've been failing all my life, knowing how important it was to both of us and still I couldn't hear it . . . and then, years later? months later? she's going over the balcony railing, the sound, the bloody eyes, the puddle of gin and vermouth and still the smell of her scent mingling with blood and martini and death. . . .

And she and poor Etienne LeBecq, my personal victim in this story, were changing places in my dreams, I couldn't keep them apart in my dreams, it was all mixed up and unforgiving.

But then, from some prisons there is no escape, there is no freedom ever. It was true that night, it had always been true.

The Driskills knew all about the prisons of the mind.

I'd always stayed at the George V but I'd undergone a sea change. Like my sister, I'd begun to watch my back. So when I arrived in Paris I ignored my regular stop and found a tiny, anonymous hotel on the Left Bank, on the Boule Miche. I climbed a narrow flight of stairs next to the tobacconist and on the landing checked in and got my key. There was a small makeshift breakfast room off to the right and a dwarf-sized, rickety cage of elevator. My room was long and narrow and clean, and smelled of furniture polish. It was situated on a corner with one of those insufficient French balconies overlooking the Boule Miche and another, in the large triangular bathroom, looking out on the side street with the bright red lights of a pizza restaurant below. It was a chilly, damp evening with an accompaniment of rolling thunder. The night sky was pink with light. The traffic moved restlessly along the boulevard as if the population had grown itchy and nervous waiting for the rains of November. I knew that by morning the fakery of the night's cheap lighting effects would be gone and Paris would be wet and gray, as it should be, all its charm and antiquity unchanged.

The sheets were stiff with starch, the pillows heavy with down, and I was too tired to think. I fell asleep with Wodehouse's *Leave It to Psmith* on my chest. Maybe I would always be an innocent. I could hear Val laughing from far, far away at her big bad brother.

I woke up late to the sound of knocking at my door. I heard the key turning and the girl who had checked me in came in, smiling, carrying a tray with a basket of croissants and brioches, butter, a jam jug, silverware, coffee, milk, sugar, everything I needed to sustain life. I sat in bed munching away, watching the rain streaking down the long French windows I'd left open through the night. The sky was a perfect pearl-gray. I had the window open in the bathroom and the breeze was cool and bracing on my back while I contemplated my haggard face with its scraggly stubble and eyes that looked like they might be tired and worn out from now on. I stood at the sink trying to repair the damage. It was still thundering, thudding, and reverberating above the soft, steady rain. I changed the dressing on my back after standing under the lukewarm shower. Unless my wishful thinking had gotten the better of me, my back seemed to feel a little better. I swallowed some pain pills for good measure. Standing at the balcony in the bathroom, I felt the cool mist on my face, looked down on people in raincoats walking their dogs, and picking up the morning papers, and standing in the doorways of cafés, smoking their ever-present cigarettes and staring out at the cars hissing along the wet paving with headlamps reflecting in the rain's slickness. By noon I was ready to go.

I knew the first move. I knew the place to start.

It had been ten years since I'd seen Robbie Heywood, whom everyone had always called "the Vicar" according to my father, but

I figured he was the sort of tough old bastard who just wouldn't go off and die on his own. He was probably seventy by now, but his type lived forever. What type was the Vicar? Well, he was a twisty old Aussie newspaperman who'd covered Europe from Paris and Rome since the mid-thirties. Half a century, he'd say, but what's time to a pig?

My father had known him for a long time, since 1935 when Father had been working for the Church in Rome. He introduced me to the Vicar in Paris on that same trip when Val and I had also met Torricelli. So my father was the common ground Robbie Heywood and I had shared on my subsequent trips to Paris when I'd looked him up to say hello and treat him to an expensive dinner. My father—we always talked about him—and the Church, that, too, was common ground. Robbie Heywood had always found my adventures among the Jesuits tremendously amusing. He was probably the only person who could have laughed at all that and not provoked me to punch him out. When he thought it was funny, I too, saw that it was indeed funny. He was, I supposed, a kind of sophisticate that only the Church could breed, a Catholic who never got overheated about the Church, pro or con. Dispassionate, amused, with what he called "a leaven of purest malice." Robbie had covered the Church extensively, was what my father called a Vatican watcher, an old Vatican hand, and I'd begun thinking about him on the plane ride to Paris.

I suppose he should have come to mind earlier, once I'd begun thinking about Val having been in Paris doing her research. I'd never heard her mention him, though he'd always been full of questions about her, but that had been a long time ago. I doubted if she'd ever seen him after we first met him as children. For one thing, he wasn't a woman's kind of man. And for another, she was a scholar and Robbie was a gossip monger, an outrageous journalist straight from an Australian amateur theatricals production of *The Front Page*. So, it wasn't until I was half asleep in the dried-out, pressurized tube rocketing through its own little time warp that the Vicar popped into my head and stuck there, making me wonder if just maybe Val had looked him up.

The thing that had occurred to me, of course, was that Robbie Heywood was another link to the past.

He'd been in Paris during the war.

I called his number but there was no answer. I almost called

Tabbycats but then decided to drop in unannounced and surprise the old boy. The walk in the cool rain would do me good. I couldn't seem to get the feeling of the desert out of my mind, eyes, and bones. You can have the desert, just give me a city huddled in the rain and people everywhere, the smell of gasoline and oil and wet streets.

Robbie's apartment was in one of the crumbling, mouldering old buildings in the Place de la Contrescarpe, where Rabelais used to hang out almost five hundred years ago. The Vicar loved the area for its seedy toughness, its antiquity, its history. He'd once shown me the place, 53 rue Mouffetard just down from the Place where workmen found 3,351 twenty-two-karat gold coins in the well in 1939. Louis XV's money man had hidden them there a long time before. He had just moved into his rooms facing on the Place and recalled the excitement of the discovery as if it had been yesterday. The Vicar could make the past come to life: now I was eager to bring him the kind of story he'd appreciate most. Dirty work, blackmail, and murder, all inside the Church of Rome.

I set off from my hotel, relaxed by the familiar surroundings, flipping through assorted memories and coming back to the per-plexing question of my mother, her death, what had driven her off the balcony—but as I say, I could feel Paris releasing the tension built up within me. I could think about my mother's death, and my sister's, but for the first time in a while none of it was making me crazy. I crossed the Boulevard Saint-Germain at the Place Maubert, which I knew—thanks again to the Vicar—had a nasty history as a public execution ground. In 1546, in the reign of Francis I, they had taken the humanist philosopher and printer Etienne Dolet and put him to the torch as a heretic there in the Place Maubert. They used his own books as kindling. The Skid Row crowd, soaked with *gros rouge* and screaming with excitement, must have been the last sounds Dolet heard. Robbie Heywood never passed through the Place without a small salute to the statue of Monsieur Dolet. "Times change," he would say, "and Paris never lets you forget it." In the rain the open market that had replaced the stake was in session, bustling.

I followed the rue Monge until I turned right into the rue du Cardinal Lemoine and followed it into the Place de la Contrescarpe. There was no wind there and the wet leaves stuck like footprints to the sidewalk. The mighty dome of the Pantheon floated like an

apparition, a peculiar spaceship either landing or making its get-
away in the fog and rain. I was out of breath, stood looking at the
second-floor windows of Robbie's apartment. They were shuttered
and streaked with rain that dripped steadily from the eaves. Contrescarpe always looked like a movie set left over from a Jean Gabin
tough-guy picture. There was a small grassy patch with trees in the
center. The trees looked downcast, wet and black and leafless. The
clochards, the tramps and drifters who'd been gravitating to this
particular place for centuries, were there, a gray quorum discussing
the day's affairs. They might have been there waiting for my return,
unmoved all these years. They were clustered beneath the trees in
sweaters and raincoats. A couple of umbrellas glistened like shiny,
wet, smooth stones. A few huddled under a lean-to made from a
leftover packing crate.

Tabbycats was still there, a bar and café looking out on the
square with a low-slung eyebrow in the form of a faded green and
white striped awning. The canvas was swaybacked to begin with
and was collecting rain in heavy puddles. The awning wasn't going
to see its way to another summer. The white paintwork looked
grimy and in spots had bubbled and burst. I crossed the square,
the *clochards* watching this stranger among them, and went into the
shabby old joint the Vicar used for an office.

The immense slothful tabby lay in posh arrogance at the end of
the polished bar, its eyes squinting, staring at me, its tail slowly
flicking to and fro like the tongue of a grandfather clock. It was
either the same cat who'd always been there or an identical
replacement. It seemed never to age. Claude was behind the bar,
talking to a balding man with a bullet-shaped head and a large
nose that seemed to take up the whole front of his skull like a
mole's. Black-framed glasses straddled the breadth of nose rather
uncertainly. He wore a black suit, white shirt, and black tie. The
bartender was still Claude but his mustache and hair were gray.
"It's a dive," Robbie had said the first time he met me there, "it's
my office, Claude the barman is an Aussie, so I can trust him, not
one of these fucking Froggies. It's an honest man's dump, Your
Grace, only dump in this town worthy of the name."

Claude came down the bar toward me, the cat waddling along
beside him until it stopped abruptly and hissed at me. "Mr.
Driskill," he said. "It's been a while, sir."

"Almost ten years," I said. "You've got a good memory. But the cat doesn't seem to remember me."

"Oh, you've not met Balzac before. He's only in his sixth year now. Randy bastard he is, too. His only job is to water the banana tree there by the door." It was a new addition. It towered, its girth was awesome. "Balzac here tends it for me. Pisses on it. Twice a day, makes it bloody well grow. Out of fear." He sighed and I ordered an Alsatian *bière*.

"The Vicar been around today? Thought I'd surprise him." It was thundering again and Balzac cocked his head. Claude set the glass before me.

"Oh dear," he sighed. "Oh dear, oh dear, oh dear." He looked down the bar at the man with the mole's face, nodded to him. "Clive, come over here. This is Ben Driskill, you've heard the Vicar spouting off about him."

The man came toward me, put out his hand. I shook it. He had a limp and a cane. "Clive Paternoster at your service. Robbie was very upset at the sad news of your sister's death. Just god-awful, I'm sure you can hear him saying it. He'd seen her several times this past summer, you know. That was how I met her. Ah yes, the dear old Vicar . . ."

"Where is he?" I asked. "Don't tell me he's working." I smiled but they weren't smiling back.

"You're three days late, my friend," Clive Paternoster said, blinking at me past his enormous nose. "The Vicar crashed in flames the other day. He is no more, Mr. Driskill. A comparatively young man. Seventy on the button. I'm sixty-three myself." He pushed the heavy black frames back into place. "The Vicar is dead, Mr. Driskill, cut down in his prime."

"I'm sorry to hear that," I said, shock in my voice. "He was a good fellow." I was thinking: he *had* seen Val! But why? What had they talked about? Had it mattered? He'd been in Paris in the old days. . . . "What was it? What carried him off?"

"Oh, it was quick," Claude said bitterly, stroking the cat. "He didn't linger." He looked sorrowfully at Paternoster.

"That's what I meant . . . cut down in his prime."

"I don't understand—"

"Street violence," Clive Paternoster said softly. "Somebody took a knife to him." He looked at his black digital watch. "You might as well come along to the funeral. We're putting the Vicar in the ground within the hour."

The Vicar was buried in a small, out-of-the way cemetery in a dreary quarter of the city, not far from a convergence of railway lines. The coffin was plain, the priest not terribly interested and coming down with a cold besides, the grave dark and muddy. The gravel path was brown and wet, the grass cut too short and the color of the gravel. There were six of us mourners, nobody crying or wringing their hands with grief. There was a double row of evergreen trees flanking the path that led to the grave, the extreme symmetry seeming very Parisian. That was how the Vicar made his exit, and it only went to show you that what mattered was the living, not the dying.

Walking away from the cemetery, Clive Paternoster lit a Gauloise and plunged his hands deep into the pockets of his black raincoat. His shoulders were hunched and he gave the impression of pushing his nose on ahead of him, like a man pushing a giant peanut across Paris with his nose. Rain was dripping from the brim of his hat. "Robbie and I were roommates these last five, six years. People called us the odd couple, y'know, but we got along fine. Two old farts facing up to the end—I lied to you before, I'm nearly seventy myself—two old farts remembering what it was like to be young and full of mayhem. Hard to believe he's gone. Between us we covered more than our share of wars, murders, scandals, elections . . . I got the gimpy leg courtesy of a Mongolian sniper during the Korean fracas." He pronounced the word *frah-kah*. "But it was the Church, that's what you might say brought us together. Became an obsession. Interesting mechanism, the Church. Perfect refuge for scoundrels, of course."

"Tell me how he died. Everything you know."

He looked up at me curiously, then gave a little mental shrug. He couldn't resist a good story. "Somebody mugged him about five minutes from our place. I found him on the landing in front of our door, he was sprawled facedown in one of his loud, horrible tout's jackets, all plaid, y'know, and he'd fallen with his face pushed up against the slats of the railing, you remember what that looks like, and when I came in the downstairs door there was this funny sound, like a clock ticking, steady tock-tock-tock it went, and I'd never noticed it before. . . . I stood there in the dark stairwell, then

I thought I smelled something I'd smelled before—in Algeria in a cell where they'd tortured blokes, lots of that going on in the Algerian fracas"—that word again—"and what I smelled was blood. And when I took that step forward, something dripped on my hat, tock-tock-tock, and I felt it, took my hat off, and it was all sticky, then a big fat drop hit me in the head . . . blood of course, blood dripping from the landing, and when I got up there, old Robbie was gone, well, almost gone, he was babbling o' green fields like old Falstaff, y'know . . . talking about summertime, that's where he was, I suppose, in some sunny summer afternoon. . . ."

He lit another cigarette from the stub of the first one and we kept walking. He made good time with the cane. We were somewhere in Clichy.

"Well, I followed the blood like an old Indian tracker, Robbie had been knifed in the belly and in the chest, it was a miracle he'd gotten more than ten feet . . . the Vicar was a strong man, very strong . . . so I followed the blood, thank God it was a dry day, wasn't much to it. Blood stopped at the corner of rue Mouffetard and rue Ortolan, which is where it must have happened . . . probably some *clochard* from the Place, knew who Robbie was, went round the bend, had a go at him with a paring knife . . ."

"Was he robbed?"

"No, that was funny. Made me think it was a fellow who went psycho—"

"Yes, I suppose so." There was nothing else to say. Maybe he really had been killed by a maniac, maybe there was no connection to any of my troubles, and maybe the moon was made of green cheese. And maybe I was off the edge with my suspicions.

We finally caught a taxi and went back to Contrescarpe. Clive Paternoster showed me the corner where Robbie was knifed. We followed the path he took trying to get home and went inside, stood in the stairwell, climbed the stairs to the landing where he finally bled to death. Paternoster's charwoman had scrubbed the stained carpet and most of the blood had come out. Now there was an even more obvious trail of bleached-out spots marring the tatty old carpet.

He took me inside the apartment and I saw the place where the two crusty old bachelors had made their home among all the mementoes of two long careers. There were so many bits and pieces. A wooden propellor from the Battle of Britain, crossed oars

from a Henley regatta, a cricket bat from a match at Lord's, a photo
of the Vicar and the Fuehrer, the Vicar with Pope Pius, Clive
Paternoster with Pius and Torricelli, de Gaulle having dinner and
Jean-Paul Belmondo smoking a cigarette and Brigitte Bardot on
Paternoster's lap and Yves Montand and Simone Signoret and
Paternoster, Hemingway and the Vicar with their arms around each
other's shoulders beneath the Arc de Triomphe. Quite a pair of
lives, once wide ranging, once part of the history of their times, but
now drawing in, tightening, growing smaller. Paris, Place de la
Contrescarpe, Tabbycats, the bloody street corner, the bleach spots
on the carpet, the little apartment with the souvenirs that would
someday wind up for sale in an odds and ends flea market deep in
a side street . . .

The *clochards* had a fire going and were clustered around it,
ignoring the evening's cold drizzle. There were two huge frying
pans, black cast iron with toweling wrapped around their handles,
full of sizzling garlic sausages and onions and peppers and chunks
of potato. Bottles of cheap red wine, long crusty loaves of bread, a
kind of *clochard*'s picnic. It smelled wonderful, mixing with the
smell of the rain and the autumn fading into early winter. As I
watched, one of the tramps doused the contents of both skillets
with wine. It sizzled and steam puffed away in a cloud.

Clive Paternoster and I were sitting at the one table in the
window. Balzac was contemplating the banana tree. We were having
dinner, *pot au feu* after a coarsely grained garlicky pâté with
cornichons, a very nice Margaux. "I'm not saying the Vicar didn't
have his faults," Paternoster said, dipping bread into the thick
gravy, "but I miss the man. We knew all the same things, we could
talk. We could remember. You get a little older and it's not so bad,
sitting around on a rainy evening, remembering. He wasn't perfect,
but he wasn't half bad."

"What did my sister want to see him about?"

"All the old World War Two malarkey. She wanted to know
about Torricelli and—" He stopped himself, his eyes flickering up
at me from their crinkly sockets. His eyebrows were shaggy, like a
hedge in need of trimming.

"And? What? Don't stop."

"She was very interested in everything from that period. Anything we could remember. I was there, too, of course. Torricelli!

Now, there was a beauty! God, wasn't he the slick and slippery old devil. He knew the facts of life and the way of the world—a twisty old heathen! But then, he had to be, didn't he? Man in the middle and not wanting to be odd man out. Nazis on one side, the Church on the other—talk about the frying pan and the fire! Particularly after D'Ambrizzi got here from Rome. He was a pistol, that one." He shook his head, recalling those days. "He drove Torricelli crazy."

"What all did you tell my sister?"

"Oh, she met with the Vicar on another occasion when I wasn't available." He shrugged. "So I don't know—but the main thing was he called Philippe Bloody Tramonte about the papers—"

"What papers?"

"Tramonte's the old bishop's nephew, a runty little git, poofter if you ask me, but he's very grand indeed. He's the chap in charge of Torricelli's collected papers. Calls it 'the Archive.' I mean, really! If you want to know what your poor sister was up to, you'll have to take a look at the rummy old Archive." He laughed disparagingly. "I'll call Tramonte in the morning if you like, set it up for you."

We were having our second cups of coffee when I asked him the question that had been knocking so insistently at the back door. "Do you know if the Vicar had another visitor recently—a priest, tall man, roughly the same age as you two? Distinguished-looking man, silver hair, very fit—"

Paternoster wrinkled his mole's nose, his eyes widened. "You do get around! I commend you. How, may I ask, did you know?"

My blood was running cold, but every lawyerly instinct I had was up and saluting. It was coming together, another connection. "A shot in the dark. He was one of the last people to see my sister."

"A bringer of bad luck, then."

"What did he want from the Vicar?"

Paternoster shrugged. "He just showed up one day. Robbie and I were standing right outside here, one morning last week. Dammit, it was the day before he was killed. This silver-haired priest was suddenly standing there . . . introduced himself to the Vicar . . . said he was, let me see, it was Father August Horstmann, I think that was it. Yes, August Horstmann. And the Vicar did a bit of a double take, then he said a funny thing . . . he said, 'Bless me, August! I thought you'd been dead these forty years!' And then he introduced me and I went on about my business and the two of them went off together . . . old pals."

"Old pals," I said.

"That night I asked him about this fellow and the Vicar didn't have much to say about him. I gathered that Father Horstmann was someone he knew during the war—"

"In Paris," I said softly. "During the war."

And the next day the Vicar was dead. Four days ago.

I had the feeling that Clive Paternoster was a very lucky man.

And August Horstmann had known I'd find my way to Robbie Heywood.

After another of my routinely hellish nights—hellish because I couldn't stop being scared anymore—it was a relief to see the anemic gray light outside my window above the Boulevard Saint-Germain and notice a couple of swallows sitting on my balcony railing staring at me. I was tired and the tension that came from being afraid I was being watched by Horstmann had jammed the hot poker into my back again. Still, being up and awake was better than being in bed with my dreams.

By midmorning I was standing only a ten-minute walk away from my hotel, pressing a button next to an ancient, warped wooden door with hinges like anchors. A long wall stretched away on either side, blocking any view of the house within or its interior courtyard. It could have been any of a thousand such arrangements in Paris. I rang the bell again after a five-minute wait. An old caretaker who looked like original seventeenth-century equipment pulled the door open. It needed oil. The day was gray and misty. Splotches of dampness spotted the stucco walls. Wet gravel in the courtyard crunched underfoot, reminded me of the little cemetery in Clichy the day before. The caretaker clanged the door shut and spit through his mustache and pointed to the doorway in the foundation. He walked away, hunchbacked, a rake in his hand, and when I looked back at the darkened doorway a man in a crimson velvet jacket with some shiny, worn patches was standing there waiting for me.

Philippe Tramonte looked like he'd been designed by Aubrey Beardsley: thin, pale, tall, the velvet jacket, pearl-gray slacks with creases that might have been laid on with a pen, black tasseled loafers. The hooked Shylockian nose with its bony bridge proved the genetic linkage to his uncle, the bishop. A huge amethyst ring set in gold on his little finger: it looked as if it were intended for kissing. His voice was high and thin, his English heavily accented but expert, and his sighs—gargantuan, expressive, overwhelming—accompanied us on our way to the Archive much in the manner of Maurice Jarre background music. He wanted me to understand that his role of archivist was a hugely taxing one. I sympathized. Things were tough all over.

He led me down a long hallway to what had once been a very grand drawing room, now somewhat in decline. The ornate molding was chipped. A frayed carpet about the size of Atlantis but infinitely older filled the center of the room. Two long trestle tables with chairs and lamps were centered on the carpet. An enormous easel stood at one end beneath a tapestry of your typical knight slaying your typical fire-breathing dragon caught in the act of making off with a blonde. Some things, across the centuries, never change. The easel was empty, but my mind flashed on the painting my father had done of Constantine having the vision that reshaped the Church and the western world forever. My father always preferred the large themes. No knights, dragons, or blondes for him.

Tramonte showed me to a wall of glass-fronted bookcases and explained that he understood I was interested in the papers my sister had inspected. He was, of course, much too burdened with his own concerns to express any sympathy about her death. He pointed languidly at the matching boxes on the shelves. They were labeled 1943, 1944, and 1945. Those were the ones. He sighed, his narrow chest quaking, and asked me to please be careful, keep the material in the order I found it, and replace each box as I finished with it. I told him he was too kind. He nodded, receiving his due, and pattered away, leaving me alone. I took the first box of papers to one of the tables, long and dark and highly polished, and got out my notepads and went to work.

I spent two and a half days digging through the old bishop's papers, most of them in French and Italian, a few in German, some in Latin, some in English, and when I finally threw in the towel and sagged back in my uncomfortable straight-backed chair I had a migraine and a major brain cramp. I had fought my way through several bushels of paper and I wondered what I had, what it all added up to. It was the third day and the November rain was still slanting against the high French windows.

There were diaries, memoranda, casual notes to himself and to others, letters he sent and letters he received. It was like putting a mosaic together when you had no idea what it was supposed to look like when finished. I kept thinking of Val, trying to understand what she'd been after, but what had she *known?* I was beginning to realize that I was almost certainly never going to understand what had been in her mind. Bits and pieces, yes, but never the whole picture. My perception of her thought processes was further confused by the fact that I was tracking her backward, back toward where she had for some reason begun her quest—but I doubted I would ever reach that point. It was like tramping around the jungle looking for the source of the Nile.

What I read showed that there had been an ongoing struggle between Torricelli and the determined upstart priest, Giacomo D'Ambrizzi, over the issue of the Church's support of *le Résistance.* D'Ambrizzi had offered aid and comfort to Resistance saboteurs, and it was driving Torricelli crazy since he was the one who had to keep from slipping off the tightrope while dealing with the representatives of the German army of occupation. Torricelli had to deal with the Abwehr, the Gestapo, the casual errand boys, everybody. In the bishop's view D'Ambrizzi had gone rogue, was an impetuous hothead consumed by the morality of the situation rather than by the realities; he clearly felt D'Ambrizzi was risking the wrath of the Germans which might come crashing down on the Church in Paris, maybe even all across Europe. Torricelli had even taken his worries to Pope Pius, and the pope had replied that the bishop had better make damned sure that neither D'Ambrizzi nor anyone else within the Church did anything to help the Resistance. There was no doubt in my mind as I read the documents that Pius had been very, very serious. My sister must have been ecstatic at unearthing such extraordinary source material.

There was reference to Richter, the LeBecq family, the matter of the art treasures and where they might be going. Richter was apparently involved in collecting art from the dispossessed Jews for Goering's private galleries and also in dealing off some to the Church. So this was obviously how Val had been led in search of the contingent that finally surfaced in Alexandria. Torricelli also mentioned someone called "the Collector" coming from Rome to go through artworks to decide what exactly the Church wanted for itself. Who, I wondered, was this Collector? Add that to the list of questions.

And there were tantalizing references to Simon.

Etienne LeBecq had been afraid that Simon had sent me from Rome to kill him . . . so afraid that he'd finally just gone off and killed himself. Simon, one of the code names. And here he was again. Simon this, Simon that. All in 1943 and 1944. Paris had been liberated toward the end of August of 1944 and life had changed, the Germans were gone.

I had trouble translating much of the stuff about this Simon. There was the language problem and Torricelli's penmanship had gone to hell as well, as if whenever Simon's name came into his mind he got very nervous and hurried and flustered. The story seemed to be that in the winter of 1944–1945, while the Battle of the Bulge was raging in the Ardennes, Torricelli had come unglued in a major way by discovering "a plot so heinous that there is nothing left for me to do but summon Archduke to a secret meeting. Only he can control Simon! What else can I do? He might kill me if I get in his way. I can only tell Archduke and pray he can stop it. Will Simon listen to him? I cannot commit another word to paper. . . . Whatever my political convictions—and in a world such as this, do I even have political convictions anymore?—I cannot countenance what Simon intends. A miracle I learned of it . . . What will Archduke say? And Simon—is he good or evil? What if Archduke is behind all this and Simon is only his tool? Will Archduke turn on me if I turn against Simon? But I *must* or the blood of our victim will be on my hands, too!"

I went out alone that evening and had dinner at a little pizza restaurant where the pizza was good, with a couple of fried eggs and anchovies floating in a thin slick of olive oil on fresh tomato sauce with garlic and oregano. I was trying to concentrate on the food because the only other course was to face the brutal conflict between information and intelligence. I inevitably came across the same dichotomy in my practice of law. Somebody working for you would come in and dump a ton of information on your desk—everything from yesterday's depositions to precedents from seventy-five years ago. What you had to do was somehow turn it into *intelligence,* become your own intelligence agency. You had to push all the pieces of information around in your mind until you began to see the interpretation that would make sense. You had to sift out the irrelevancies, peer for days, weeks, months at the information

until you saw the hints of an outline—like the image on the Shroud
of Turin or that face on Mars everybody was talking about not long
ago. Just a hint could get you started. A hint.

Well, I had lots of hints. Lots of information right on the verge
of taking shape.

So it was time to have a pizza and plenty of Fischer beer and
walk along the fences enclosing the Luxembourg Gardens and let
November rain on you. There was no point in thinking about what
I knew. It was time to let it percolate on its own.

Later that night my mood changed. I was sure that August
Horstmann was following me, trying to pick the safest moment to
kill me. I was doing what Val had done. He'd killed her. He'd killed
Robbie Heywood once he'd decided I was bound to follow Val's trail
all the way back to the old journalist. He must have hung around
to finish me off, too.

But maybe he figured that with Robbie Heywood dead the case
was closed, the trail dead as my sister. Maybe I was safe. Maybe he
hadn't counted on Clive Paternoster knowing so much. . . .

And what was this about Horstmann and Heywood being such
old pals?

I called my father at the hospital in Princeton.

His voice was weak but distinct. The slurring I'd heard before
was gone. He wanted to know where I was, what I was doing, who
I was seeing. I told him I was following in Val's footsteps, that I'd
found people left over from Paris during the war: Richter, LeBecq,
the nephew who was the last remnant of Torricelli, Clive Paternoster. I told him Robbie Heywood had been killed by the same man—
somebody called August Horstmann, a priest the Vicar had once
known—who had killed Val, Lockhardt, and Heffernan.

My father spoke softly, sorrowfully. "Oh, not Robbie, not the
Vicar . . . Goddamnit . . ."

"Look, you were in and out of Paris during the German
Occupation. Did you ever hear of these code names?" I told him
about Simon and Archduke. It was easy to forget that my father
just might be a source of information. He'd always stayed so close-
mouthed about those OSS years. But now he might remember
something and open up.

But for the moment he just punched out a sharp laugh that was
distorted into a cough. "Son, what I mainly remember was being

afraid of getting my tail shot off by some trigger-happy Jerry. I was afraid of making a mistake and having to chew up my cyanide pill before I spilled the beans. I'll tell you one thing, Torricelli was certainly right about D'Ambrizzi working with the Resistance. It drove Torricelli up the wall. It was none of my business, but I'd hear things—that's how I met D'Ambrizzi, through my Resistance contacts. All I was doing, Ben, was in and out, usually in by parachute, sometimes by fishing boat along the coast of Brittany— do my job, try to get out to Switzerland alive—"

"I remember the movie," I said.

"Movie!" He coughed again. "Come home, son. Please, Ben, your life's on the line, whatever the devil's going on—"

"I'll be careful."

"Careful," he said numbly. "Don't you understand, careful doesn't matter a tinker's damn!" He began coughing again and I couldn't get him to answer for ten or fifteen seconds. Then I heard a nurse's voice explaining that he was all right, that he had just a touch of pneumonia in one lung. I wasn't to worry, everything was under control. His coughing had stopped in the background. I told her to tell him I'd be in touch again soon.

"You said my sister wanted to know about Torricelli and something else. And what? What was that other thing?"

I was sitting in a deep Morris chair between the wooden propellor and a table full of framed photographs and I was working on a glass of Clive Paternoster's scotch. My host was leaning on the mantelpiece, smoking a venerable pipe he kept polishing against his nose.

"Oh, really, old boy, there's nothing there for you." He sniffed and downed some of his scotch, his prominent Adam's apple bobbing.

"No, no, I'm quite serious. It must have been something—you held it back. Let me be the judge. She was my sister."

"It's just that it's the land of fairies and sprites and little men with green hats and pointed slippers . . ."

"What the hell are you talking about?"

From the window by the chair I could look down through the bare tree limbs at the weary awning and the lights in the window of Tabbycats. Down there Horstmann had arranged casually to bump into his old friend Heywood, who'd thought he was dead these forty years.

"Well, your sister comes to the Vicar and she's full of questions about the war years, about Torricelli and, and—"

"And what?"

"And the *assassini*! There, you satisfied? Old Clive sounds a fool!" He puffed nervously on the pipe, the woodsy smell filling the room.

"*Assassini*? I don't get it. What's the problem? It's Italian for assassins. What's the big thing here, Clive? I just read the word in one of Torricelli's diaries—"

He stroked his immense nose with the pipe for a moment, burnishing the dark brown bowl. "You read it in his papers, did you—now, that's rather interesting, I must say. Evidence to support the Vicar's theory, at any rate."

"Enlighten me," I said patiently. He wasn't the kind of old duffer you could hurry. You'd miss the cream of the jest.

"The *assassini*, man! You tell me you're a Catholic, yet you profess ignorance of the *assassini*—you astonish me. Your education has been sadly neglected." He was shaking his head, running his bony hand through the long gray hair that thinned out over the crown of his narrow head.

"Educate me, then."

"Simply put"—he grinned with the big stained rabbity front teeth—"the *assassini*, my son, were the blighters who did the popes' killing for them back in the old days, the Renaissance, the Borgia days when poison rings were all the rage. An instrument for carrying out papal policy. Now, the salient point has nothing to do with the Renaissance, as you might have guessed . . . no, the salient point that your sister had gotten her teeth into was that the *assassini* were rumored to have been brought back to life . . . here in Paris during the war. A rumor. I never put much faith in it myself, there were always rumors everywhere you looked, but the Vicar, oh, he was much closer to all that sort of thing than I was. The Vicar was a devoted "intrigue man," he was in Vienna when they made that picture, *The Third Man*, he never tired of seeing it, never missed a revival. He loved intrigue, believed it, you see—a conspiracy behind every loose brick—that's why he loved covering the Church, it never let him down! He used to say it made the Reichs Chancellory or the Supreme Soviet look like a child's idea of the real stuff, said the Church was all intrigue, all conspiracy, whispers in darkened doorways, voices in empty rooms and plotters gathered behind the closed shutters . . . well, he thought this *assassini* business was too good a fit to pass up. . . . The Vicar told me at the time that somebody had brought the *assassini* back to life, that they were operating in Paris . . . as if we didn't have enough going on in Paris back then . . ." Paternoster laughed at the memory, tamping the ash down in the pipe's bowl. "He said they were doing the Church's dirty work but damned if he knew what the work was! Who were they killing? The Vicar couldn't figure it out. Or he never told me if he did. But he knew they were on the job and he was bloody sure he knew some of them—"

"Personally?" I asked. "He knew them personally?"

"Yes, *knew* them. They were all men of the cloth as I understood it, these *assassini*. So when your sister asked him about the *assassini* she was right up his alley—got him right on his old hobbyhorse! He told me all about their conversation . . . I can't blame him, can you? For telling her? He didn't see what harm it could do to tell her now, forty years later . . . so he told her about another old friend of his, Brother Leo."

"And who was Brother Leo? I need a scorecard."

"Well, I never met him, but the Vicar said he was one of them . . . one of the *assassini*." He sniffed again, blew his nose on a large, soiled handkerchief. "I don't know if your sister, poor dear, went in search of him—it wouldn't have done her any good, but the Vicar thought it would interest her for her book—"

"Why couldn't she see Brother Leo? Is he dead?"

"Oh, not so far as I know. But he's at some godforsaken little monastery on the coast of Ireland . . . St. Sixtus, I think it's called. I daresay your sister wouldn't have been welcomed . . . " He looked at me expectantly, rubbing his enormous, broad nose once again with the kerchief.

"It's funny, Clive," I said when I'd thought about it for a few moments. "What harm could telling her about the *assassini* of forty years ago do? None. None at all. But I'll tell you what happened. I think it just might have made her think the *assassini* were still around. I've tried to think what she could possibly have known that meant she had to be killed. And I just couldn't imagine what it was—how could something from forty years ago have decided her fate now? Well, finding a coven of *assassini*—or just one of them, maybe—that might have done it. That might have been enough to get her killed. That goddamn Horstmann!" Paternoster was looking at me uncomprehendingly. "Horstmann's one of them, Clive. The Vicar did know him forty years ago, just as he knew Brother Leo. But Horstmann's still on the job. He killed the Vicar, he came all the way back to Paris for him because he was afraid I'd learn whatever my sister had learned. So he came back from killing my sister and from damn near killing me and he killed the Vicar. But he fucked it up, Clive, he didn't think about you." I stood up and slapped him softly on the shoulder.

"I say," he muttered, trying to cope with the flood of new information.

"My sister somehow found out about the *assassini* and somebody didn't like the risk in that, so she had to die before she could get the word out . . . that's why Horstmann tried to kill me—"

"I don't quite follow you, old bean."

"And the beauty part is . . . Horstmann takes his orders from somebody in Rome."

"And he tried to kill you? You've lost me—"

I went on explaining myself to him and drinking his scotch and most of what I said turned out in the end to be quite wrong. But it sounded good that night and I was partly right, too.

Before I left him, Clive Paternoster fetched his old atlas of the British Isles down from the bookcase. There, with a dirty, chipped fingernail, he pointed out the monastery of St. Sixtus.

Father Dunn got a personal call from Drew Summerhays the next morning, the day of their two o'clock appointment. "Am I right," Summerhays said in his thin, reedy voice, "in suspecting that you have personal—or at least not strictly professional—matters on your mind?"

Father Dunn chuckled, standing by the windows, trying to see the ducks in Central Park without the aid of his binoculars. "Let's say I don't expect a bill at the hourly rate."

"Well then, let's say it's personal and you might indulge a very elderly party and drop by my little house—would that be possible, Father?"

"My pleasure."

"Good. Just come down Fifth all the way to Washington Square. I'm in the little mews off Fifth." He mentioned the single-digit number. "Till two o'clock, then."

Dunn got out of the cab and crossed Fifth to the cobblestone mews that was blocked to automobiles by posts set in cement. Bright cold sunshine threw the scene into sharp relief. The little house was pristine yellow and white and olive and looked as if it had been freshly painted the day before. The yellow flower-boxes were now planted with miniature evergreens that poked up out of the black potting soil like the tops of huge trees. He tapped the doorknocker which was a reproduction in brass of one of the gargoyles of Notre Dame. It seemed to be smiling, a gargoyle of welcome.

Summerhays's man, Edgecombe, answered the door and ushered Dunn into a skylit sitting room, cheery with yellow and white slipcovered couches and chairs. Bookcases, a small formal fireplace with a neatly stacked rack of logs, bowls of flowers freshly cut, and through the French doors at the far end of the room a tiny, carefully maintained garden prepared for winter, still in the sunshine. A recording of one of Erik Satie's *Gymnopédies* was being dispensed through hidden speakers, each note dropping like a precious stone into a reflecting pool of perfect stillness. Dunn wondered how anyone got such a complete, perfect handle on things; maybe it was this environment that had helped keep Summerhays alive such a long time. It seemed to Dunn that dying, leaving such a world behind, would give death an extra sting.

He was looking out at the garden when he heard the thin, precise, clipped voice behind him. "Father Dunn, how very nice. You found your way."

Summerhays stood ramrod straight and trim, sleekly barbered and smelling of a hint of bay rum, and turned out in a gray herringbone suit, starched white shirt, red and olive club tie, shell cordovan shoes. It was so absolutely perfect that Dunn smiled, jotting down a mental note. This would find a spot in his next book.

Summerhays sat in one of the slipcovered chairs and Dunn, who felt uncharacteristically self-conscious, perched on the end of the couch. On the white brick wall behind Summerhays was a large painting by Jasper Johns. American flags, reminding you, if you thought about it, that this was the home of a patriot.

Edgecombe brought a silver coffee service, left it on a low table, and shimmered away.

Drew Summerhays said, "Father, I am very pleased to see you, but I admit to extreme curiosity. My assumption is that what may connect us at the moment is the Driskill family. Would I be far wrong there, Father?"

"Direct hit. Look, I don't want to dance around the edges of this. Shall I plunge right in without even a passing comment on Jasper Johns?"

Summerhays's eyes twinkled. "Mr. Johns will never know."

"All right, then. Am I right about your long friendship with Hugh and Mary Driskill? You go back a long way?"

"About as far as there is," Summerhays said.

"This isn't easy."

"You're a priest. You are experienced in discussing delicate matters. So am I. Between us we've been talking about the hard things for a century. Let's just do it, Father."

"I have recently heard a remarkable story," Dunn began. "It is the sort of thing that could be true but needs verification. It's a farfetched story in terms of the ups and downs of everyday life—"

"In our businesses there are no farfetched stories." Summerhays smiled frostily.

"Well, I'm not altogether sure of that anymore. This one's about a priest who's been dead fifty years, a woman who's been dead thirty years, and one of your closest friends. . . ."

Summerhays smiled with a hint of resignation. "I'm not altogether surprised that this should have come up. But it has been a long time." He leaned forward and carefully poured two cups of coffee. "Cream?"

"I'll have mine straight today." Dunn burned his tongue on the strong black brew. "It's funny . . . that's what she said. She'd been waiting for someone to come to her about this for half a century."

"Who could this be?"

"An old nun, a friend of the Driskill family. Taught Ben and Val. She was close to Mary Driskill. Sister Mary Angelina . . ."

"Ah, yes. Of course. I've met her. Strikingly attractive woman."

"Tell me—I've wondered about this, what did Mary Driskill look like?"

"Mary. Lovely woman, tall, stately, a woman of great natural dignity. Light brown hair, fair complexion, a sense of humor that could sneak up on you. She didn't make friends easily. That was Mary. She had only one real weakness, that old debil rum . . . she was so proper, so very well-bred, so restrained, some might even have said Mary was a little on the remote side." He sipped coffee, held the Spode saucer with his other hand, then placed both cup and saucer on the broad arm of his chair. "In many ways Hugh and Mary were a good match. Not exactly overflowing with emotion."

"But they were in love?" Dunn asked.

"Well, love is not always essential in marriages between such people. Theirs was more a friendly alliance, a great fortune— Driskill's—absorbing a somewhat smaller one. I'd say it was a sound marriage—"

"Like a takeover or a merger?"

"Any way you want to say it, Father. You're the wordsmith. But where is this line taking us? Sister Mary Angelina was expecting someone to come to her about this thing—what was it?"

"The death of Father Vincent Governeau."

"Ah. That."

"Sister Mary Angelina was very close to Mary Driskill, a confidante. Something like a female confessor. Someone she could talk to intimately."

"Many women these days prefer the services of a female gynecologist, I'm told. I suppose the principle is much the same."

"Mary Driskill came to Sister Mary Angelina several years after the death of Father Governeau who was, you recall, found hanging from a tree in the orchard out by the skating pond."

"Indeed, I remember well. I believe, as Hugh's attorney and adviser, I was the first person he called." He offered a wintry smile. "A kind of unindicted co-conspirator."

"Did anyone ever offer any explanation of why Father Governeau killed himself?"

"The same weary old reasons," Summerhays said. "Depression, crisis of faith, alcoholism, all the reasons why priests occasionally slip off the edge."

"You bought the suicide story, then?"

"What are you saying, Father Dunn?"

"You were satisfied with the suicide conclusion."

"Well, he had apparently hanged himself from a tree—"

"Why do I have the feeling that you know perfectly well that Father Governeau was murdered?"

"I can't imagine, Father. Was it something I said?"

"No. It's just that you're too much an inside man not to know. Father Governeau was murdered and strung up afterward . . . and because Hugh Driskill was and is Hugh Driskill, the truth never came out. I've spoken to the cop who investigated the case. There's no doubt that it was murder. When Sister Valentine came home, the day she was killed, she called the present chief of police just full of questions about the Governeau matter. Think of that, Mr. Summerhays—she's been doing research in Europe for months, her mind is full of a thousand other things, she's running for home, she's just hours from her own death . . . and she calls the law about Father Governeau! Amazing, isn't it? Why? I'll tell you why—I'll bet you a quarter that Sister Valentine didn't believe he'd killed himself either. Now, you're just too much in the know to still be chewing on the old suicide story. . . ."

"For the moment, Father," Summerhays said, smiling thinly, still interested, "let's say you're right about Father Governeau's death. I have the feeling we'll never get off the dime, otherwise, so far as this conversation goes. Which should be bringing us back to the vicinity of Sister Mary Angelina."

"Ten years after Father Governeau's death, after the war, when she had two children and a husband who was on the cover of *Time* and was the inspiration for a movie—when her life should have been at its absolute high point, Mary Driskill was drinking herself to sleep every night, she was in all probability undergoing a long-drawn-out nervous breakdown. Is that the way you remember it?"

Summerhays inclined his head slightly. "Hugh was very worried about her. Mary was so fragile. It was hard on the children—a succession of nannies, poor Mary would babble on to the children, frighten them . . . she was very unstable, then, and of course not long after . . . ." He gave a nearly imperceptible shrug of his shoulders. "She died."

"I'd bet that really *was* a suicide," Dunn said.

"No, you'd lose. She was intoxicated, she fell, it was poor young Ben who found her. He was fourteen or fifteen, I believe. It was an accident. They couldn't refuse to bury her in consecrated ground."

" 'They' being the Church?"

"Who else?"

"All right, back to Mary Driskill. When she was going through this breakdown, this severe depression, she felt unable to turn to the Church. At least not officially. She couldn't simply make her confession to a priest, not with what she had on her mind. But there was her friend whom she knew she could trust with anything, a woman *and* the Church—Sister Mary Angelina. She made an arrangement with Sister Mary Angelina, they met at the house in Princeton, the kids were in bed, Hugh was out, and Mary Driskill told the nun about what happened to Father Governeau."

"And now," Summerhays said, "Sister has told you."

"That's right. And I want to know if what she told me could possibly be true. You're the only person I know who might be able to verify the story. Will you hear me out?"

"Try and leave without telling me." Summerhays seemed disconnected from his smile, his eyes distant and clear and icy.

"Mary Driskill said that she had met Father Governeau back before the war when Hugh was still in Rome working for the Church. Governeau came out to the house to say mass at the chapel a few times. He was a decent, serious, honorable man, a man of God. Mary trusted him. But he fell in love with this pretty young woman who was so alone . . . it's 1936, '37, whenever, I'm not great on dates—"

"It makes no difference, Father. Go on."

"In short, they became lovers. Obviously they were both consumed by guilt. But they were also overcome by sexual passion. It was a desperate affair, midnight visits to the Princeton house, all pure John O'Hara, two devout Catholics tearing themselves apart. And then it was time for Hugh Driskill to come back from Rome— what was going to happen with Mary and Father Governeau? They decided it was time for their relationship to end, it was the only thing to do. Somehow they would remake their lives . . . it wouldn't be easy, but it was the only way. Well, it wasn't easy . . . it was impossible. For Father Governeau anyway. He called her, she wouldn't talk to him. He wrote her notes, she wouldn't answer them. That pushed him a little too far.

"He came to the house one night when Hugh was out somewhere—Hugh was always out somewhere—and Mary tried to make him leave, she told him it was over, they talked back and forth through the evening, and finally Father Governeau had had enough. He threw Mary Driskill down on the floor, tore her dress off, and raped her . . . it went on for a long time, too long . . . it was a snowy, windy night, Hugh's meeting ended earlier than it was supposed to so people could get home—well, Hugh got home all right. He walked in on his wife being raped by a man he knew as a priest. . . . Hugh saw red. He grabbed the closest thing, a silver bear from Asprey in London, and he cracked Father Governeau's head open with it . . . killed him. Together, Hugh and Mary came up with the suicide thing, Hugh hung him in the orchard . . . and the cover-up ensued . . . and the crazy thing about it, the thing that drove Mary Driskill almost all the way to crazy, wasn't the fact that her husband had quite unnecessarily killed Father Governeau, no, no, what bothered her was that Governeau had been buried as a suicide, outside the Church . . . she couldn't bear it, so she told Sister Mary Angelina, who waited all these years." Dunn finished his coffee. It was cold. "Now, Mr. Summerhays, all I want to know is, is that the way it happened?"

Summerhays stared at him for quite some time. Then at last he sighed and shifted slightly in the chair.

"No," he said softly, "that wasn't the way it happened. No, she's got it all wrong. Let me have Edgecombe bring us some fresh coffee and then I might as well tell you what really happened. . . ."

Another night spent in the small, anonymous room with its narrow bed, the single bookcase, the two old brass lamps, one with a dead bulb that had burned out two months earlier. Another night alone in the room with its smell of priest and scotch. The tiny refrigerator hummed loudly in the kitchen nook. Thick clouds of cigarette smoke hung in the damp air. The window was open. A steady rain beat the paving in the narrow street and rushed down toward the Tiber, gurgling in the gutters. The regular whore stood on the corner in a doorway, peering listlessly into what was going to be a slow night.

Monsignor Sandanato stood at the window staring into the night but not seeing. He had left the cardinal's office late, long after D'Ambrizzi had retired to his quarters. He'd come back to the apartment through the dripping night, wanting to sleep but afraid of what he might see once he closed his eyes. So instead he opened the bottle of Glenfiddich, filled his glass, and took up his place at the window.

He didn't know how many times he'd replayed the conversation from the night Sister Elizabeth had come to D'Ambrizzi's for dinner. But he couldn't keep from going through it again. Her mind was so volatile, so questioning: it excited him, listening to her cut through the tangle of possibilities and construct a theory. A theory of the murders which Sister Valentine had "discovered," a theory about the identity of the silver-haired priest, whom Elizabeth now believed was "Simon." And there was her theory explaining the meaning of "the Pius Plot" Torricelli referred to . . . a plot engineered by Pius to revive the *assassini* for use in aid of the Nazis during their occupation of Paris.

It all made sense, of course, or she wouldn't have thought it all the way through, as she clearly had. But when he'd asked her *why* . . . why were people being murdered now, why had Val been on the list and all the others Val had discovered, then she'd lost her confidence. *The election of the pope* . . . What else could be worth the spilling of so much blood?

He poured himself another couple of fingers of scotch, sighed. He rubbed his eyes which were already badly bloodshot. Where the devil was it all going and where would it end? He wanted to go outside: somehow he felt safer in the street, among the tourists and the men in pursuit of girls and the constant flow of priests murmuring among themselves. But safer from what? The dark corners of his mind, he supposed.

He was also beginning to feel less at home within the walls of the Vatican itself as the problems—the murders, the fear, the indecision and helplessness and confusion—tightened like tentacles about the heart of the Church. And he had grown to hate his apartment, its smell of loneliness and struggle and regret. He was running out of places. He wished he could go away, retreat to one of the quiet old monasteries where all that mattered was the old way and you knew what was going on and what it meant. . . .

He shook the idea out of his mind, like rattling a child's toy. Later. Time for all that.

The telephone jarred him back to life.

He shuddered when he heard the voice.

Sister Elizabeth had been sitting up late working when Monsignor Sandanato called her and she'd said, sure, come on over, but she warned him it might not be for long. She was tired, she said, and couldn't guarantee how long she'd last.

He wanted her company too much to be polite and tell her he knew it was late and she should go to bed. Now, sitting on the couch, watching her, how she'd curled herself in the chair, how she sipped from a glass of wine with her notebooks and file folders spread across the glass coffee table before her, he heard *Rigoletto* from the large speakers in the corners of the room. The doors to the terrace were thrown open and the rain spattered on the metal furniture. The draperies moved in the breeze. Sister Elizabeth was wearing corduroy jeans and a heavy woolen sweater.

"So you were having a bad night," she said sympathetically. "Well, I know the feeling. I've been having a lot of them myself lately. And you've been under a lot of pressure. They must be going crazy over there." She nodded in the general direction of Vatican City. "Who's in charge of murder investigations?" She smiled impishly.

"Guess," he said.

"D'Ambrizzi?"

"He's one of the faithful investigators. But it's Indelicato—"

Elizabeth slapped her palm against her forehead. "Of course, what was I thinking of? This is his kind of *thing!*"

"There's just so much frustration," he said. "No one really knows what to do . . . or if anything even can be done. Not even Indelicato. But he's the man they naturally turn to. The problem is that there's no consensus on the size of the problem." He frowned. "Don't be taken in by the way D'Ambrizzi talks about it—he knows there's something going on and he knows it's got to be coming from within."

"Well, the number one question must be—how will it affect the election of the new pope?"

"You're ahead of yourself, Sister. His Holiness could last another year—"

"Or he could be gone tomorrow. Don't kid me, my friend."

"What can I say? There's a growing fear that this has been a permissive pontiff, that he could have used more iron . . . there's a sense of a boil breaking, that all this has come to a head as a result of liberal rot within the Church. Some are saying that matters are simply out of control and we need order restored—" He shrugged. "You can imagine."

"Then it's accepted fact that Val was right about all those killings being part of some kind of plan. Why won't D'Ambrizzi just admit it to me?"

"Come on, Sister, he's from another generation. And you are a nun . . . he'd think I was insane, if not something much worse, to be talking all this over with you. You're too much of a—" He fumbled, at a loss.

"How about 'nosy bitch'?"

Taken by surprise, he gave her one of his rare laughs. "You're too perceptive, that's the word. You're too smart and he knows you're a reporter, remember."

"What am I going to do? Print scandalous theories and accusations in the magazine? Or run to the *New York Times*? Come on, get serious!"

"And he's worried about you. You are too perceptive and too persistent. So was Sister Valentine. He can't forget what happened to her."

"But what was she supposed to do? She discovers that mass murder is being done inside the Church—that devoted Catholics are being killed, that the *assassini* was alive in the Second World War and might still be alive—what's she supposed to do? Forget it? Because it might prove inconvenient?"

"She ought to have come to us. To the cardinal. And told us . . . she should have left it to us and we would have taken steps. It was a Church matter, Sister, and she'd still be alive." He'd been speaking with confidence but ended with a dying fall. "Anyway, that's one view. D'Ambrizzi's."

"And yours?"

"I don't know—"

"Oh, give us a break! All the paternalism is cute and cozy and horribly out-of-date. Women think and write and act and gosh, we're just like real people. Val finds people getting slaughtered wholesale and she's supposed to run tell the teacher! The idea makes me sick!"

"Well, Sister, she didn't go to the police—isn't that what your 'concerned citizen' should do? But not Sister Valentine—she decided she was going to find out what was happening . . . and why did she do that? Because she was a nun, because she was part of the Church—she was not like people on the outside. Well, I don't see how what she did and what she should have done—telling the teacher, as you put it, Sister—are so different. Either one tells the police and opens up the Church to some deeply troubling investigations . . . or one keeps it inside the Church. She naturally chose the latter . . . but she should have taken it to someone in power. Or the head of your order—she'd have known what to do." Sandanato was moving forward to the edge of the seat. "I suppose I can see your point, but you're missing the larger point—the Church is not the world. The world changes more quickly. What she did proves she knew the difference between the world and the Church . . . but if she'd followed something like the chain of command, she'd be alive and well and continuing her work."

He stood up, ran his fingers through his rain-wet hair. His soaked raincoat lay across the back of a chair. He shook his head, threw up his hands in a gesture of his own confusion and frustration, didn't trust himself to speak. He was simply afraid that if he began talking he wouldn't be able to stop, that his fears and dreams would come tumbling out in a swirling cacophony, screeching and sobbing. She had a way of cutting through to the heart of things unexpectedly, even when she had no idea what she was doing. He needed time to think, but there didn't seem to be any. How much could he dare tell her?

She watched him pacing, said, "Look, I'm not trying to bug you about all this. You've got your job and Val had hers and I've got mine. Everyone has to make his own decisions and take the consequences."

"I know." He was looking out at the rain falling on the Via Veneto, his back to her. "You're being a willing friend. I've imposed on you tonight and you're very kind to put up with me. As it happens, Sister, I have few friends. I have my work, my masters. I'm not used to dealing with friends—so I take advantage of you this way—"

"You and Ben Driskill seemed to hit it off well enough," she said. "Have you had any word from him? I wish we knew—"

He shook his head. "No, no word. He'll turn up." He brushed Driskill away. "Don't you see, Sister? My only friends—no, I am not a man with friends. I deal with Vatican people. You know it's an authoritarian place, relationships prescribed by form. And—one must be honest about oneself—I am a solitary man. We priests, whatever we may appear to be on the outside, are solitary creatures in the deepest sense. It must be true of you nuns as well—"

"Really, I think not. For many nuns and priests, too, it seems a very collegial life. Ready-made friends, you might say—"

"For some perhaps." He gave a brief Italian shrug.

"Priests have always struck me as an essentially gregarious lot, except for the complete assholes, of course."

He laughed again at her profanity. "You've heard the old wisdom, we are so gregarious in public because we sleep alone." He came back into the center of the room. He was looking into her lustrous, intelligent green eyes, returning his stare. "Like most old sayings, that one has survived because it's true. We are different . . . and I find myself ill equipped to deal with some of what I've been feeling lately. And now I have to ask myself, why have I turned to you? You have no obligation to share my burdens, Sister, yet I come to you with them. . . ."

"I'm a sucker for a sob story, maybe?" She grinned at him. He was so intense all the time. Somebody needed to push his off button once in a while.

"I came to you knowing you'd listen to me."

She nodded, her eyes wide, her face open to his needs. And her face was what did it. He began to talk, not worrying about the hour, not worrying about what she might think of him. He talked about the pope's weakening condition, about the closeness of his own relationship with D'Ambrizzi, as well as D'Ambrizzi's with Callistus. He talked about the murders and Driskill's blind determination to leap into the fray and all the costs that might entail. He knew he was working himself into a fury of frustration, the way it was playing itself out, and then he felt her hand on his arm and he looked at her as if he'd forgotten she was in the room, and she led him back to the couch, murmuring small comforts.

"You're exhausted," she said. "It's breaking-point time. You'd better get some rest. You need it."

He sat with his head in his hands, willing himself to go no further, to reveal nothing more. No more, not another word. She'd think he was mad if he kept talking. She brought him a glass of brandy which he gulped gratefully.

"Forgive me," he said. "Please. You're right, I'm overtired . . . worried. Forget all this."

"Of course. It's none of my business anyway."

"But like a fool I've made it your business. You must try to forgive me."

"Believe me, it's all right."

"The murders . . ." He grimaced behind his hand. "They're coming from inside the Church. They *are*. No point in pretending anything else." Why couldn't he just let it go, get up, and slink away? But he looked at her and smelled her fresh, newly bathed scent, shampoo and powder and bath oil, and he didn't leave. He sat quietly listening to her talk about Sister Valentine, about how close but how very different they'd been, how odd that now she,

Elizabeth, had taken up Val's work. She spoke about how sorry she was she'd left on bad terms with Ben Driskill, and at the sound of Driskill's name Sandanato felt an internal cringing, a fear of what she might be feeling about Driskill, and he fought not to show his fear, envy, jealousy.

Later he said, "But the Church must do what is necessary to preserve itself. Is that right, Sister? Isn't the greater good what matters? Is the long run the key to the story of the Church?"

She nodded thoughtfully. "The Church is good. That is a given, of course. Anything else and *our* lives are irrelevant, we—priests and nuns—have been tricked. . . . Therefore, the Church is good."

"Then, if these killings are coming from within the Church . . . and they are . . . then the possibility exists that the Church could be cleansing itself with these murders. *Possible.* It is possible, Sister, is it not?"

"Strictly logically," she said coolly, "the Church could sanction such acts to preserve itself. Logically. In the abstract. But you have reduced the principle to an absurdity."

"Have I? Are you sure?"

"In reality, in the world, it would be utterly monstrous . . ."

"But the Church is not the world—"

"But how would the killing of these people—of Val and Curtis Lockhardt!—how would that be cleansing the Church? The idea is diseased, you must agree. Monstrous."

"Yes, yes, monstrous, of course . . . but . . . but I ask myself, if the murders come from within the Church, sanctioned by men who put the Church first—well, what if they are in that sense justified?" His eyes were on fire. He felt the sweat on his forehead, the constant fever that kept him going, searching for an answer.

Sister Elizabeth shook her head vigorously. "It's not on, it's just not defensible. Not murdering Sister Val. Not her . . . how can you even imagine such a thing?"

"Sister, I admit the questions are strangling me, choking me. I mean the possibility that the killings are a kind of purgation, one we cannot understand . . . but part of a greater good."

"If I cannot understand it, then I say the hell with it!"

"You know that can't be true, not for a nun—"

"It's true when it comes to murder!" She fixed him with her hardest stare. "Your subtext is showing, Monsignor."

"It is?" He smiled at her and passed his hand across his brow.

"You're saying that such things have happened before. The cleansing, the purging of dissenters, troublemakers . . . all to preserve the Church, of course." She couldn't keep the sarcasm out of her voice.

"Well, it was Sister Valentine's field, wasn't it? Violence as policy—it fascinated her—"

"She discussed it with you?"

He nodded.

"That doesn't mean she approved of it," she said. "And neither Val nor I would have tried to justify violence as policy, a means to an end. Val was a historian, not an advocate. Most particularly not a devil's advocate."

"You know she was an advocate. Advocacy was her life—"

"Not of that!"

"Still, I wonder . . . the moral dilemma. Evil in the service of good." The tension was going. Being with her, talking to her, even being at odds with her, made him feel human again, put the bad things out of his mind.

"I find it an entirely impenetrable moral contradiction. I haven't anything like the wisdom to set it right."

"But you may someday *have* to solve the contradiction. Don't you see? You're following in Val's footsteps, in her shadow, doing her work . . . what if you were confronted with the choice, Sister?"

"What choice?"

"If the Church, in the person of a killer, says to you, 'Cease your work, forget what Sister Valentine was doing . . . and live. Or persist and be purged, for the good of the Church.' You would have to choose."

"In the first place, what's the point in frightening me?"

"To keep you alive."

"And in the second place, I will try to avoid the confrontation."

"I understand, Sister. I sincerely wish for you that luxury. But my wishes and prayers may not be enough. Evil in the service of good—does it become good? We may still need the insight of the Magus—"

She laughed. "You must mean D'Ambrizzi!"

"Magus," he repeated. "The man with the Janus face, looking both to the future and the past. Maybe he has the answer, after all. So much of his life is a mystery." Finally he stood up. "Well, the *assassini* of long ago may have served their purpose—so now in new times, who knows what our problems may force upon the Church? This is truly the heart of darkness, Sister."

He was putting on his raincoat. She was up and holding it for him. He stopped when she put her finger to her lips, motioning for him to listen to the tape of *Rigoletto*.

The most beautiful scene had just begun, the duet between Rigoletto and Sparafucile. The melody was both somber and wicked, sinister, rich with the colorings of the solo cello and the double bass.

Sparafucile describes himself to Rigoletto.

One who for a slight fee
Will free you from a rival—And you have one.

Sparafucile unsheathes his sword . . .

This is my instrument. Can it serve you?

Sparafucile was one of the *assassini*.

The pain visited Pope Callistus in the dark of night, as it so often did. He roused himself, got out of bed, and paced the bedroom with perspiration popping out on his face, his teeth grinding, waiting for it to pass. Sooner or later there would be an occasion when it didn't stop and the end would follow quickly. But, he wondered, could he wait for fate to exercise its cruel sentence.

Then it began to lessen and he relaxed his muscles, slowly, fearful that it might return, that it was tricking him. He stood by his desk and picked up the exquisite Florentine dagger he'd been given by Cardinal Indelicato upon his election to the Throne of Peter. He customarily used it as a letter opener, and now that he spent more time in his bedchamber it had found its way to his small desk. The dagger was a costly piece, gold and steel, very old. He watched the blade catch the dim glow from the lamp on the table. He saw his reflection, a blur of features, in the surface of the blade. He wondered how many men the blade had killed.

As the pain faded he rubbed his eyes, then took the towel that lay across the foot of the bed and wiped the sweat from his face. He lay back down on the bed to wait for sleep to return. He knew it might be a considerable wait. He was surprised to notice that he was still holding the dagger. That was happening more often lately, this business of having no recollection of performing some activity. Where had the dagger come from? He must never have replaced it on the desk. . . . He examined it, remembering Indelicato telling him how it had been in his family for a long, long time, centuries, how it represented courage and ruthlessness, both qualities he would need as Cardinal di Mona ceased to exist and Pope Callistus was born.

He was thinking more and more of Cardinal Indelicato lately, how he would have been sublimely at home in the KGB or the CIA of MI5 or—he smiled bitterly at the memory—the Gestapo. The tradecraft of the intelligence business was in the man's blood, at the heart of his nature. And now he was keeping his old enemy D'Ambrizzi under surveillance. Callistus wondered, does Giacomo know he's being watched? Callistus had to admit Indelicato was getting excellent intelligence from his acolytes. Indelicato had known D'Ambrizzi for so long: he was clearly the man to do the watching. But whom did that leave to watch Indelicato? The pope's mind was wandering. D'Ambrizzi had always been a match for Indelicato, all through the years, a match and then some.

They were such opposites on the surface: Indelicato so cold-blooded, reptilian with his flickering gaze and expressionless face, and D'Ambrizzi so gregarious, warm, and full of life. But both so merciless when the time came, so unforgiving, so brutal . . . each hating the other so deeply. They were both so much better equipped to be pope than he, yet he was the one who had been chosen, proving once again what people were always saying about God's mysterious ways.

Callistus was discovering the error in another old saying. He was discovering that your whole life does not pass before your eyes as you are about to die. No. All that was passing before his eyes was that time in Paris, that night when they crouched by the iron fence and watched what happened in the little graveyard. The night when they crouched shivering in the cold, watching the tall, thin priest with the unsmiling triangular face and the single thick, unbroken eyebrow, Father LeBecq, Father Guy LeBecq, whose father was the famous art dealer in the rue du Faubourg-St.-Honoré . . . it was Father LeBecq who had betrayed them. Now they were only the ragtag survivors, the others all dead by the tracks, and it was Father LeBecq's doing . . . LeBecq the traitor among them . . . it all came down to the Pius Plot, as it became known later in certain quarters, everything hung on the Pius Plot, Simon's plot, Simon, whom no one ever saw, Simon, who guided them in their

work, Simon Verginius, the leader who would never forsake
them. . . .

Through half-closed eyes he saw the dagger, turned it slowly in
his hand . . . sometimes when the pain was truly intense, when all
his eyes could see was a red rippling curtain of pain with a tightly
wound black hole at the center—at such times he thought about
the dagger, how sharp its point, sharp as a Jesuit's twist of logic,
how like a razor its blade . . . and he thought how easily he could
end the pain, an icicle drawn across his throat, his wrists, or driven
into his heart, and then peace at last . . .

Ice . . .

There was ice in the cemetery that night, all Paris was in the
grip of an arctic chill, there were frozen puddles of ice in the
graveyard, a patina of ice on the gravestones . . . the stocky,
brutishly constructed man in the cassock waiting in the graveyard
for Father LeBecq, one priest waiting for another, and outside the
fence, crouching, holding their breath, Sal di Mona, Brother Leo,
the blond Dutchman . . . then the two men in the graveyard, the
huddled conversation among the headstones, suddenly the stocky
man with the long, powerful arms leaping at the tall man like a
huge, misshapen hound, grappling with him, encircling him,
crushing the life from him, dropping him like a broken marionette
. . . and the killer standing still, his lungs pumping clouds of vapor
into the freezing night, the light of a streetlamp illuminating his
face, his profile . . . the face he would come to know so well, the
face that would be so near for the rest of his life . . .

The next day His Holiness Pope Callistus felt well enough to
call a meeting in his office. It was the same group—D'Ambrizzi,
Indelicato, and Sandanato, with two of Indelicato's young aides
waiting in the anteroom. The latter two had been taken into
Indelicato's confidence and were working on certain aspects of the
investigation into the murders. In the corner of the office nearest
the desk was a rolling oxygen tent with shelves for a variety of other
medical paraphernalia. There were now no risks worth taking.

The pope's weight loss was beginning to show in the face which
already bore new, deep worry lines, giving him something of the
visage of a sad clown. His face, known so well throughout the
world, was changing irrevocably, caving in. He was wearing his
contacts for a change, and one of the lenses was giving him trouble.

He kept pulling the rim of his eyelid away from the eyeball, making little apologies as he did so. Giving it up, he slumped back in the desk chair, toying with the Florentine dagger he'd found he was carrying with him.

"Well," he said, "let's get on with it. A progress report." There was no need to define the task. He was interested in only one thing now.

Cardinal D'Ambrizzi took a file folder from Sandanato. The sunlight streaming through the windows increased the impression of pallor, the dark hollows of Sandanato's cheeks. He seemed to have been drawn even tighter than usual. The pope's hands were shaking until he dropped them, still clutching the dagger, onto the desk before him. D'Ambrizzi himself looked tired and old, like a man with too many ugly secrets hidden behind his huge, bulging frog's eyes. Anxiety filled the room like a noxious gas.

"We've been looking at Sister Valentine's final weeks, Holiness," D'Ambrizzi said. "Where she was, what she may have been doing, trying to pin down the events leading up to her murder. We've discovered that Ben Driskill is tracking backward from her murder. He was in Alexandria a week ago, give or take a few days. While there he had a meeting with our old friend Klaus Richter—"

"You're joking," the pope said abruptly. "Richter? Our Richter? From the old days? You told me he was the one who frightened you!"

"None other, Holiness. And he did frighten me, I assure you."

"Your candor," Indelicato murmured, "becomes you, Giacomo."

"And," D'Ambrizzi continued, "he saw another man who subsequently killed himself."

"Who was that?"

"Etienne LeBecq, Holiness. An art dealer."

Callistus's eyes widened, he felt an adrenaline rush. His heart was beating erratically, leaping in his chest. Thinking: LeBecq, the brother of Father Guy, who haunted his dreams: now forty years later they were both dead, all the sins coming home to roost. Was that it? They had all been deep in the Pius Plot . . . did that make them all sinners, now called upon to pay up at last?

D'Ambrizzi went on, flipping through papers. "We also have a report from Paris that a journalist, an old chap by the name of Heywood—"

"Robbie Heywood," Callistus interrupted softly. "You remember him, Giacomo. Terrible loud jackets, he'd talk your arm off and drink you under the table, given half a chance. God's love, I remember him . . . how does he come into this?"

"Dead, Holiness," D'Ambrizzi said. "Murdered by an unknown assailant. The authorities have no clues, of course."

Callistus was trying to remember the last time he'd seen Heywood. "But what has he to do with any of this mess?"

"Sister Valentine saw him in Paris while doing her research. Now he's dead. There may be a connection—"

"You'll have to do better than that, Giacomo," Indelicato said. His voice sounded mechanical, uninvolved. "I'll send someone to Paris and check this out."

"Good luck to him," D'Ambrizzi said dubiously. He shrugged massively. "Perhaps it's merely a coincidence. Knifed on a street corner. Such things happen."

"Nonsense." Indelicato frowned sourly. "The Church is under attack and Heywood was a victim. It's obvious."

"It all comes back to Paris," Callistus whispered. He was slowly turning the dagger in his hands. "And where is our friend Ben Driskill now? And how is his father holding up?"

"His father is on the mend. A slow process. And we seem to have lost Ben Driskill. He flew to Paris. His habit was to stay at the George Cinq but . . . well, he's not there. He's somewhere in Paris. Unless he's left already." He turned to the pale, cadaverous cardinal sitting quietly with his legs crossed. "Fredi, Fredi, you are too quiet. I worry when you are so quiet."

Indelicato leaned back, tapped his fingertips together across his chest. "I am in awe of your resources. The good monsignor here"— he nodded at Sandanato—"is responsible for this outpouring of information?"

"Not this time. Poor Pietro is overworked as it is. No, I've simply unleashed my private army—oh, don't look so worried, Fredi, I'm only joking. I've sent out some feelers, asked a few questions—"

"The silver-haired priest," Callistus said. "And who is he?"

D'Ambrizzi shook his head.

"Your network is still an astonishment to me," Indelicato said. "But where is Driskill?"

"You're good at watching people," D'Ambrizzi said. "Maybe you've been wasting too much time watching me, Fredi." He laughed deep in his great chest.

Indelicato smiled slowly. "Not closely enough apparently."

Callistus spoke, ignoring the byplay. "So now we have nine murders . . . and a suicide?"

"Well, who knows, Holiness?" Indelicato said. "It's a reign of terror. Who knows how many more there are . . . and how many there will be."

Suddenly Callistus stood up, his body stiffening in a kind of bone-jarring rictus, fingers curling, his mouth pulled out of shape and into a ghastly scowl, saliva white on his pale lips, and without uttering a sound he pitched forward across his desk.

Jean-Pierre, the man August Horstmann had found in the Spanish village working as the sexton, wore a long black cassock, a bit frayed at the hem, and the old flat-crowned, broad-brimmed hat so common among the rustic clergy. He carried his lunch in a brown paper sack which had been rolled, creased, and grease-spotted many times. No one had paid him any attention on the train. No one, that was, except a little blond girl with her hair in braids who seemed transfixed by his eyes—the white milky remains in one socket, the other one so blue it nearly matched hers. He smiled at her and she stared, sucking her thumb, and he wished he could leave the train before it reached Rome. But, of course, he couldn't.

Rome was hot at midday when he arrived. Too hot for the season. He was sweating into his thick undershirts. He had grown used to the cool, windy Spanish countryside, the mountains and the brooks and the gentle pace of his work.

Now he stood outside the railway terminal unsure of himself among the tourists, the crowds pushing and hurrying. He wondered fleetingly if he would ever see the little country church again. Would he ever see the silver moon from the window of his small room and smell the fresh clean air and the breeze that carried faint hints of the ocean on it. Would he ever hear the rushing brook below the village, feel it on his feet?

He went in search of a telephone. It was a Vatican number.

Once he made his contact and received his instructions, there was time for a long walk.

He could even visit the Vatican gardens. It had been such a long time since he'd seen the gardens. He'd been little more than a boy when he'd last visited Rome.

Yes, with the call behind him there was plenty of time to stroll through the city.

He wanted to forget for the moment why he'd come to Rome.

3

DRISKILL

nother rented car, another rain-blown afternoon with low, disgruntled clouds scowling down, draped across the rugged mountaintops tracing the northwest coast of Donegal. The mountains seemed to be pitching me downward, closing me off from behind, funneling me toward the rage that was the Atlantic. Donegal was one of the desperately beautiful and poverty-stricken corners of the Irish sorrow, the coastline a place God might have designed for the express purpose of hiding—the wide-mouthed bays created by the drowning of the valleys between mountain ranges, rocky cover and darkness everywhere you looked. The land could no longer support the population that grew older and smaller with the passing of each decade. It was a place of breathtaking natural beauty but also the very heart's core of all that had gone wrong with the country—the core of denial, the fist shaken in the face of fate. Pure Catholic. Naturally.

Still, the day's drive was quiet, calm, and my back wasn't hurting all that much. What lay ahead was a mystery, but I was being driven by the potent combination of fear and irrevocable anger. To my chamber of horrors I'd now added poor old Robbie Heywood, set up and butchered by Father August Horstmann, presumably under orders from someone, something in Rome. I was as ready for whatever lay ahead as I was going to get.

I smelled the peat, cut deep into the earth, and the heather and the honeysuckle. I'd have given almost anything to forget for a moment the killing and the *assassini* and the Roman intrigues. It was so pleasant to watch the solitary road, the puddles shimmering in its depressions, to smell the wet earth, to find a kind of peace in the sighting of the infrequent whitewashed cottage and the faint orange glow of the sun behind the blue and purple rain clouds.

But I was past all that: I had the uneasy feeling that this mysterious landscape which could transform itself from gentle fields to threatening ocean-racked cliffs with a turn of your head— I had the feeling that it was swallowing me, might never let me go.

Again and again during the long lonely drive, Sister Elizabeth had filled my thoughts.

Why? It made no sense, my thinking about her, wishing as I did that she were beside me, talking and thinking and reassuring me that I was doing the right thing. I had to keep reminding myself that she was nothing to me. My last image of her, the argument in the quiet house, held nothing for me. Yet I had to force myself to remember the essential truth: she was one of *them,* a nun, someone you couldn't trust. Everything for her was filtered through the prism of the Church, either its secular rules or the mumbo-jumbo. Either way you couldn't win, not with them.

Look back at Torricelli, I told myself; now, there was a case in point. Poor Torricelli, the quintessential churchman, caught in a vise of Nazis, Catholics, Resistance fighters, and no clear choice for the old bishop. For him it was always a question of tiptoe, tiptoe, along the line, being neither one thing nor the other, ignoring or refusing to acknowledge right and wrong. If you couldn't decide right and wrong in a world run by Nazis, then you had a problem. Didn't you?

Yet Sister Elizabeth would have understood the old bishop's dilemma. It was like an amputation you underwent upon entering the Church: the Church cut away your morality and replaced it with something of its own, something unnatural and contrived and prescribed. There was no room for simplicity anymore, no room for right and wrong. Expediency was the new morality and you accepted it.

I looked back at Elizabeth and it seemed forever since I'd seen her. Back then I hadn't been sliced open by Horstmann, I hadn't faced the idea of myself-as-murder-victim, I hadn't yet turned into a hunter, I hadn't gone to war. Back then I hadn't carried a gun. It *had* been forever since I'd seen her. I'd almost died myself. I'd caused the death of a scared little man in Egypt. I'd put a name to the silver-haired priest. I'd visited the monastery in hell. I'd found another murder in Paris. I was a different man from the fellow who'd said good-bye to Elizabeth. But she wouldn't have changed. She was still the creature of the Church, owned by it, instructed by it, purveyor of its official stories. She wanted to believe she was something better and finer, more like my sister, but she was wrong. She thought she knew so much but she knew only the party line. She was caught in the web from which Val had miraculously freed herself, that was the difference.

I knew all of that, but none of it mattered when I remembered how I'd laughed with her and made vast inroads into the contents of the refrigerator and unraveled some of the ominous riddle Val had left behind and gone to see the old cop on the shore and learned that Father Governeau had been murdered and the murder covered up. . . . All that had been so good. And then the performance had dropped away and I'd butted up against the real Elizabeth.

She was a nun. And that was the last thing in the world I wanted to let myself in for. I couldn't win, not in a struggle with the Church, with her vows. I couldn't risk it. I knew all about nuns. I always had, from the day I found the dead bird hanging on the school-yard fence. . . . You could never know what they thought. You trusted them and depended on them and all of a sudden they were telling you they weren't women, they weren't human, they were nuns. But I'd been lulled by Sister Elizabeth. She'd blurred the lines, blunted the warnings I'd learned by heart, smudged the distinctions between herself and other women. Then I'd let her hurt me.

Hurt. That was the second reason, the bad one, that made the whole idea of Elizabeth so wrong. I'd loved my sister and the Church had killed her. If I let myself fall in love with Elizabeth, I knew the Church would somehow kill her, too. Another innocent would die. I knew it.

Of course, she would think me mad even to contemplate her in such terms. After all, she'd proven it, she was a nun. She'd betrayed my trust.

I was driving through a sudden squall, rain spitting out of the thick mist. I felt the wet cold sweeping at me from the ocean and then I saw the first low beehive cells, a thousand years old, and the broken ruin of stone walls and the gray, moss-speckled shape rising from the cliffs. . . .

The monastery of St. Sixtus.

I'd read about such places but I'd never seen one, never seen anything like it. I felt as if the earth and the weight of centuries were slipping away and I was plummeting backward through time and space to the sixth century, when St. Finian had prescribed the kind of asceticism that went with the desolation of the scene stretched out along the barren, rock-strewn bluff and shoreline before me. It was a beehive monastery, St. Sixtus, a creation native to this Irish coast with its fury of frothing, pounding, ceaselessly slamming ocean breakers. The beehives of piled stones were dwarfed by both the sea and the cliffs, as well as by the later additions to the monastery which had probably been built over a period of more than a thousand years.

St. Finian and his successors had ordered an almost inhuman kind of ascetic endurance for the monks who were expected to survive on a minimum of sleep and food, hideous scourges, and interminable masses. The monks were forbidden from using any beasts in the tilling of their stony fields. Instead, they harnessed themselves to the plows. The asceticism pervaded the orders, whether a monk chose the life of a hermit or vowed eternal wandering. It was all a uniquely Irish kind of severity. Never before in history had even the traditional monastic refuge been thought to endanger true self-abnegation.

St. Columban had always been one of my special favorites. His penitential—the table of punishments for even the slightest carnal stirrings—was the kind of thing that made you wonder about saints in general, Irishmen in particular. The ideas of sodomy and masturbation drove him into paroxysms of sadism. One image had stuck with me from the first day I researched him as a seminarian. The naked monk, standing alone up to his neck in the rough seas along just such a canker of coastline as lay before me, dawn to dusk, dusk to dawn, singing psalms until his vocal cords ruptured, until his blood ran cold, until he gave up the struggle and slid beneath the water . . . For what? What was the point? Was it simply that they were all crazy, had nothing better to do with their dementia? Sometimes an enemy of the Church would be caught among them, an infidel, a sodomizer, and he would be crucified on the sandy, rocky shingle and the cross driven into the sand upside down so that the tide would just possibly drown him before he died of suffocation or loss of blood. . . . I couldn't forget those old stories a quarter of a century after reading them, now that I set my eyes on this dying place for the first time.

I drove off the narrow, rutted path and got out of the car, felt the sting of the wind and the scythe of the damp, salty, acrid spray filling the air. The Irish coast was the perfect place for these red-eyed, maniacal monks who could never scourge themselves unto satisfaction. Rocky, barren lumps rose from the bay and the crumbling cliffs of the shoreline were split as if by hammer blows. Ravines angled away from the water like fistulas, crags and promontories bearing crippled, stunted trees crumbled wetly, and a wilderness of thorn and gorse crowded through slots in the rocks. Someone I'd read a long time ago wrote that the uninhabited and the uninhabitable seemed to these monks "as so many invitations to the pain they sought for their earthly lives."

Maybe it was an atavism harbored deep in my genetic matrix. The fact was I had to walk among the relics of that other world, had to see what it all looked like from the vantage point of some benighted pilgrim washed ashore five hundred years before by capricious fate and unmanageable gales. Behind me now the sea thundered, shuddered up along the stretch of uneven rocky beach that lay pale and helpless between the angry, brooding cliffs that threatened it as well as me like a giant pair of jaws. Caves, dark fenestrations, peered like impenetrable black eyes down upon me. The poor long-ago bastards had made monasteries, surrounded by the implacable sea and the barren, unforgiving marshlands, as if what they really wanted was to hide not only from the world but even from God, hoping somehow to be overlooked, forgotten, if not forgiven.

The sprawling monastery's single large building was made of packed, unshaped stones, the lower reaches painted with a damp dark-green beard of moss, the upper with moss and lichen dried to a sickly brown. A tower capped by a cross against the lowering clouds, no sounds but the chill wind and the surf pounding like a wildly amplified water torture, a nervous breakdown demanding possession of your soul.

I walked among the beehive huts, avoiding the loose stones that had come free centuries before and rolled off by themselves. I looked inside, into the darkness, but there was no sign of life, only the smell of birds and the sea. How could they have lived in such places and at the same time created the ornamental art at which we still gaped, goggle-eyed, the books, the work of the goldsmiths, continuing the work of Germanic and Celtic prehistory? What sort of geniuses were they? I didn't know the answer, couldn't even begin framing an answer, which probably helped explain why the wheels had come off my faith so long ago.

Eventually I went back to the car, breathing hard against the sucking power of the constant gale. I knew why they had never been able to add anything to the noble history of monastic architecture. It was the Irish in them. They distrusted whatever it was that endured, anything that might presume to beauty or eternity. Better to wander, or to hide away in a cave, and disappear eventually, return to the past, like the Latin words scraped from the vellum, erased, to make way for the new that must then in its time be scraped away, too.

I drove on up the narrow path, dragging the past behind me like a huge corpse.

I had to get moving. I had work to do.

I found Brother Leo in what passed for a garden, a patch of vegetables and a few flowers at the top of a cliff, just outside a wall of stone that had crumbled away many centuries ago. He was kneeling in the wet, dark earth, and he looked up at me as I leaned into the gale and pushed my way toward him across the close. He waved cheerfully, as if he knew me, and went back to his weeding and planting. I climbed over the remains of the wall, slipping on the wet moss, and found I was winded once more. He looked up at me again, said something blown away out of earshot, and smiled. His face was old and round and wizened, rather distracted in an amiable way, earnest in his determination to finish whatever he was doing. He wore black trousers wetly crusted with mud, a black turtleneck sweater up around his thin, wrinkled neck and jowls. His hands were bare, caked with mud, and there was a streak of mud on his cheek where he must have scratched an itch. At last he finished the job, patted the earth flat around some rather weary-looking stems I couldn't identify, and stood up. He wiped his hands on a muddy bit of toweling.

"Brother Leo," I said. "My name is Driskill. I've come to see you from Paris. Robbie Heywood gave me your name."

He blinked at me, one of those innocent faces that always looks surprised. He pointed a grubby finger at me as if I'd said the magic word. "Robbie," he said. "And how is Robbie?" He didn't sound Irish. His intonation and pronunciation were indefinable. Probably Irish at birth, a life lived elsewhere. I told him that Heywood had died and left it at that for the time being. He listened, busied himself with a gunnysack full of fertilizer, tying it shut, gathering up some trowels, a small spade. He nodded intermittently. I couldn't tell how much sense he was making of what I told him.

"Paris," he said. "You've come all the way from Paris. So Robbie's dead. Used to call him 'the Vicar.' He sent you to see me? I am, I admit it, frankly amazed. I cannot quite believe it. After all these years. We're rather off the beaten track here. But," he argued with himself, "do I not have the evidence looking me directly in the eye? Amazed, I am. The Vicar! I would have enjoyed seeing him again." His eyes popped wide, innocently, and he seemed to have known what I was thinking earlier. "Oh, enjoyment is no longer outlawed here. Such a relief. A blessing. An obstreperous, nosy man, but a good companion during some dark days. Good Lord." He shook his head, bushy eyebrows catching the wind. "Dead. Old time is on the wing. The shadows are gathering, deepening." He smiled at me happily.

"He didn't live out his span," I said. "Robbie Heywood was murdered in Paris a week ago—"

"But who would do such a thing?"

"A man who came through time, from forty years ago, a man he trusted . . . a man who tracked him down and didn't give him a chance. Less than a month ago my sister, a nun, Sister Valentine,

was murdered by the same man. Robbie Heywood believed that you
could shed some light on this killer . . . who he is, where he came
from, why he is killing. Again."

"May I ask," he said calmly, "why he killed your sister?"

"Because she was researching a book that apparently dealt in
some detail with what was going on in Paris during the war.
Torricelli, the Nazis, the Resistance, something he called 'the Pius
Plot.' And a man, a phantom, called Simon—"

"Stop, please." He smiled at me so gently, as if he were beyond
earthly matters, guilt and sin and murder. "You seem very well
informed about very ancient, very secret matters. I hardly know
what to think of you, Mr. Driskill."

"I've come a long way to hear your story. People have died—"

"How well I know," he mused enigmatically.

"—beginning with Father LeBecq in a graveyard in Paris forty
years ago—no, of course, he wasn't the beginning. Who knows
where it began? My sister, your old friend Heywood, they were just
the most recent additions. It began long, long ago—and I have code
names you might be able to identify." The words and questions
and ideas were tumbling out of me too quickly and he was drawing
back. I was too much for him to handle. I saw it in his eyes,
dimming for a moment as I spoke. I broke off, allowing the surf to
drown the words.

His eyes swept out across the distant sea, where it might lead
you to believe it was tranquil and quiet. "I am rather afraid of you,
Mr. Driskill—if Mr. Driskill is in truth your name. You see," he
went resolutely on as I began to object, "I've known there would be
someone and there would be a due bill of sorts. Because there were
things happening then, things that could never be forgotten as long
as any one of us survived, any of us who knew the whole story . . .
or even parts of it. I'm afraid I knew as much as any of us. Surely
too much to be allowed to live if someone wanted to cover up the
past, erase it. Someone would remember Leo someday and they
would wonder if he was still alive and then they would have to find
out." He cupped his chin in his hand, arms crossed on his chest.
"It's taken rather longer than I'd thought it would. And now I
wonder, are you that man? And if you are, which one of them sent
you?"

He lowered his gaze, seeing the waters grow more troubled as
they swarmed toward the base of the cliffs. I called his name but

the wind and the pounding waves drowned it out. I reached out, grabbed his arm. Harder than I'd intended. He turned gently and the innocence of his face shone on me like God's grace.

"I need your help," I said. I wasn't much of a salesman. I was too far gone to make a pitch and the wind was sucking my breath away, making me feel weak. This little man was one of the keys I had to have. "I must hear you, in your own words . . . the truth—"

"You want to hear my story. I understand." He spoke softly, as if amazed by a secret revelation, one I couldn't know, but somehow I heard him, made out every word. "It was all so long ago." He cocked his head and gave me a fatalistic, philosophical nod. "You will have to convince me—I may have lived the useful years of my life, but I have no desire to die sooner than is necessary. Do you understand? I have said you make me afraid. If you have come to kill me—if you have truly come from *them*—if you've come from Rome to kill me . . . then there's little I can do to stop you. But if you have come, as you say, in search of the truth, then I will tell you my story. So, come walk with me and tell me again who you are. Let us exchange stories, yours for mine." He smiled again. He said he was afraid but he wasn't. He didn't have a fearful bone in his body. "And if you have come from *them,* maybe I can convince you I'm nothing but a harmless old man, no danger to you and your masters—who knows?"

"Them," I said. "Who are they?"

"Young man, whoever you really are, you know perfectly well who *they* are. Why else would you come so far? Come, come, we'll walk on the cliffs. We'll not dissemble. I'll give you a chance to kill me." He chuckled to himself as if the joke were somehow on me. I fell into step beside him.

During the Second World War the Catholic Church was as concerned, indeed obsessed, with survival as any other European institution. Conduct of affairs had to be designed and executed with extreme care and diligent attention to the state of the war, to the shifting balance of power, to *realpolitik.* Further complicating matters was the issue of individual morality coming into conflict with the somewhat less luxurious morality of the organization, as Brother Leo's story was destined to prove. The role of the Church was rendered increasingly ambiguous by the fact that in the twentieth century it had no army of its own, no means of forcing its policies or its independence from outside interests. In the first place, the course the war was taking at any given moment had to be taken into account; in the second place, some attention had to be paid to the overt horrors being systematically perpetrated by the Nazis—they were simply difficult to ignore no matter how much one might wish to; and in the third place, there was the fact, with its uncertain consequences, that the Church was led by Pope Pius, whose ties to Germany were strong, deep, and basically mystical.

Exemplifying this confusion of morality, aims, and effects, there arose a curious response: a cadre of Paris's activist Catholics—priests, monks, some laymen—were recruited by a priest who would be known to them as "Simon Verginius"—that is, Simon. He bound them together by a sacred oath of secrecy that would last a lifetime. They would never reveal their brotherhood's existence, nor would they ever reveal their identities to anyone outside the group. As long as the oath was intact, they were safe from discovery.

But, of course, there were problems even from the institution of these first principles, Brother Leo assured me with a weary shrug. "I will simply raise the questions for the moment, providing no answers," he said. "First, whose idea was it, this cadre, to begin with? Not Simon's surely. There were orders coming from someone in Rome—at least that was my assumption as a young man caught up in events and wanting to play a part in things. Someone, somewhere was guiding the hand of Simon . . . because there was an inner proof. Conflict. Simon rebelled against some of the orders, and that was our undoing."

The aims of this group were to protect the Church from the misfortunes of war, to enrich the Church from the spoils of the war, and to keep the Church strong and beyond the conflagration, the firestorms of ambition and insanity that were, in fact, the war. In a nation, in a great city ruled by Nazi invaders, the implications such aims carried with them were obvious, but inevitably at odds with the morality of some individuals. Brother Leo let me think that one over as he went on with his tale.

The men in the group were known to one another by code names. Leo said he'd forgotten them, the result of trying very hard to bury them in the distant past. He insisted that he'd forgotten how many of them there were and he wouldn't budge on that point. Christos, yes, there was the one called Christos, he admitted remembering that name, and I'd soon find out why. At the time they were, he said, a perfectly Catholic group: totally authoritarian, nobody daring to openly voice questions, not even thinking about questions as such, except in the quiet of one's own mind when the defenses were down. Orders were given, orders were carried out. Decisions were left to others. These men saw themselves accurately as weapons in the service of the Church. It was a time of war and the Church had never cowered before secular armies: well, not *often*. Historically it had raised its own armies, sent its own soldiers to the battle, to die if necessary, to kill if killing was called for. Now, in Paris, the Church had raised a new army to call its own and it would do what had to be done. Brother Leo wouldn't look at me just then but I understood: killing had been called for all right, and killing they had done.

"It was a time for carrying out orders," he said. "Any orders. All orders. Don't say it, Mr. Driskill—I agree with you . . . following orders is the last pallid excuse of the murderers of those days. A concentration camp guard at Treblinka, a priest stalking a victim in a Paris slum . . ." He shrugged, staring at the sea with the shadows lengthening and the wind getting colder. "I am not excusing myself, nor any of us. I am telling you how it was, that's all. Sometimes the order was to kill a man. For the greater good, of course. It was always for the Church. We believed we were saving the Church, didn't we?"

But more often than not it was something else. Usually it was a matter of trading. Back onto the tightrope they went. Trading loyalty, trading actions the group could perform, trading for the good of the Church. Trading with the Nazis, with the Wehrmacht, the SS, the Gestapo. And in return the Church benefited: a not unreasonable share of looted art treasures which made their way by this means and that back to Rome, the spoils from the rape of the Jews who were simply never seen again. When it was necessary, Simon's little band, with Christos often in charge of the mission, kept tabs on the Resistance and seemed to have no choice but to betray their French friends, to throw bones to the Nazis, to maintain the fragile balance between working *with* the Resistance here, *with* the Nazis there, but always *for* the Church which as an article of faith they *knew* must outlast the Resistance fighters, the Nazi invaders, and the war itself.

But there were times when it was not simply trading, not the simple act of betraying the Resistance on one hand or sabotaging

the Nazis on the other. There were times when the Nazis wanted a
man to die. Why didn't they kill the offender themselves? Brother
Leo had pondered that one at length. Was it a test of the cadre's
willingness to work with the occupiers? Or was it the simple
imposition of their will?

Brother Leo remembered one occasion when the rift between
Simon and Christos came into the open. There was going to be
trouble, sooner or later, within the ranks, Brother Leo was sure of
that. It had boiled up over the matter of the Resistance priest. . . .

Father Devereaux was the priest who had gotten too good at
the Resistance business. An SS officer had been kidnapped and
subsequently found in the garbage dump serving a village near
Paris. The culprits were unknown but the village had seen some
Resistance sympathy, due in large part to the attitude of Father
Devereaux.

The SS required a symbolic response. The priest must die and
the Catholics led by Simon were given the job of killing him. Simon
reported to the group that it was not possible, he was going to tell
the SS the answer was no. But Christos, the tall, wraithlike priest
from Paris, argued that the preservation of good relations with the
Nazis was more important than the life of one trouble-making
priest. It was a war, he said, and in wars men died as a matter of
course. For the greater good, Father Devereaux must die as the SS
had ordered.

Christos argued the long view. A life here and there, put them
in the scale with the Church, with the existence of the cadre. "You
see, Mr. Driskill," Brother Leo said softly as the rush of the sea
calmed, said it casually as if it hardly mattered, "we were the reborn
assassini, back at work for the Church. . . ." A few murders didn't
weigh much. And they weren't even murders! They were battlefield
casualties. A realist, Christos called himself, a pragmatist. Some of
their little band found him brutal, ruthless. But he insisted and
they obeyed and Simon stayed his hand, didn't stop them, but
played no part in what happened in the village the night Devereaux
was killed. Christos bent some of them to his will, Brother Leo
observed. "But not Simon, not little Sal, not me, and not the
Dutchman. We took our lead from Simon. We stood with him, not
with Christos. . . ."

But there were other occasions, nasty jobs with deadly consequences, and they all did as they were told. Simon, all of them.

And no matter how the war ended, the Church had to be ready to ally itself with the winner. The Church must survive.

Did Rome know?

Did Pope Pius know?

Unthinkable, unaskable questions. But Simon had come from Rome to Paris. . . .

Brother Leo spoke deliberately, calmly, his hands rubbing his cheeks which were pink and chapped from the cold wind, or smoothing the wiry fringe of white hair against his skull only to have the wind pluck it, rearrange it at once.

Then came the final night, toward the end of the bitter winter of 1944.

The time had come again to kill a man.

But the Nazis knew nothing about it. Nor did the Resistance. Not a soul but the *assassini* knew that an important man would be killed.

For the good of the Church. To save the Church.

It was Simon's mission and the most elaborate undertaking they'd attempted. It required more planning, more transport for which they relied on the Resistance, more supplies which also came from the Resistance.

Dynamite. Two machine guns. Hand grenades.

They were going to change the course of history and save the Church in a single audacious strike.

They had to hole up in a woodsman's hut on a hillside overlooking a stretch of train track hidden from outside view by thickly wooded slopes. The train was bringing the great man to Paris for a secret meeting with high Nazi officials. Reichsmarshal Goering was rumored to be among the participants.

They were going to blow the track. And if the train wreck didn't kill the great man, they were going to shoot him and anyone who tried to stop them.

But it all went wrong.

The Germans knew. The great man was tipped off. Someone told them, someone inside the operation.

"The great man wasn't even on the train," Brother Leo said. "We were betrayed . . . it was a terrible mess, only a few of us survived. Several of our men were killed, tracked down and killed in Paris afterward when a man we called the Collector came to find us if he could. . . . Well," he said, shaking his head, wiping his hand across his mouth, "it was a long time ago. Simon knew everything was over but he also knew who had betrayed us. We were all so scared, running for our lives. Simon was going to take care of us—we didn't know how. We believed in him, we trusted him . . . we knew he'd take care of us. He did, he told us what to do, and then he went to meet the traitor . . . Christos, you see. He was the one . . . he was always more of a Nazi than anything else. . . . The Dutchman, little Sal, and I followed Simon that night, we wanted to be there if he needed us, we knew Christos carried a gun."

The night was cold, icy shreds of snow blowing on a cruel wind. February of 1944. A small, weedy cemetery in one of the drearier reaches of Paris, a run-down church attached. A loose shutter banging in the night. Ice like broken glass on tops of gravestones. Bent, withered weeds poking up through puddles of ice. Mice dying of hunger and cold scuttling underfoot.

Simon and Christos, in the dim light, across the gravestones.

Leo, the Dutchman, and little Sal crouching in the shadows outside the fence. Leo was afraid his button of a nose would freeze. Sal kept muttering prayers: his life as a priest had taken some unexpected turns, leading to the freezing graveyard in the middle of a lonely night, fear all around.

Christos was telling Simon that he'd betrayed no one, that he didn't understand what had happened, yes, there must have been a traitor, yes, there was still a traitor, but he didn't know who it was. . . .

Simon told him it was over, Christos was a Nazi, had always been a Nazi, and it was all coming to an end tonight. "You murdered the Resistance priest Devereaux, and you betrayed us to your Nazi friends—"

"Devereaux was a liability, a threat to us all. He had to die!"

Simon's voice was lost when he spoke but Christos shrank away from him, then Simon's voice came again. *You murdered a decent, honorable man.* The wind whipped at them. Leo turned to the Dutchman, who shook his head, put his fingers to his lips. A dim yellow light in the church refectory was extinguished. A cat leapt from behind a headstone, yellow chips in his eyes, and a mouse died.

No, said Simon, *it cannot be for the good of any Church. It cannot be God's work—*

And what you were planning for the man on the train, that was supposed to be God's work!

You collaborate with the Nazis, who are godless pagans, yet you say it is for the good of us all, for the good of the Church. All right—maybe it is. Simon was speaking slowly, into Christos's face, but Leo heard every word. *But killing Father Devereaux—that betrays the Church. Betrays God. Betrays us all. And now you have betrayed us again. The man on the train deserved to die . . . and instead we lost men. Because of you . . . and now it's over, this is the last night . . .*

Christos took a gun from the pocket of his threadbare overcoat which he wore over his cassock. Leo backed away from the fence, stepped on the cat.

Perhaps if the cat had not screeched and pounced on another doomed, glad-to-be-out-of-it little mouse, a blur of hungry eyes and moth-eaten fur, then perhaps Christos might have shot Simon dead on the spot and left the body to freeze hard as a plank, might have changed the world in his own way.

But the cat did screech and pounce, and as it did Christos's head turned a fraction of an inch, his concentration was tugged by surprise from its purpose, and Simon, with an agility surprising in so powerfully built a man, was on him with all the finality of the plague.

Immensely powerful arms were around him, clasped behind Christos's back, as if they were dancing among the headstones in an ungainly rite, among the cats and the mice, and they seemed to embrace for a long time, their faces almost touching, their faces shiny with sweat and racked with the passions of death, the old passion, and finally there was a grating sound, a cracking, a grunt of dispelled air, a man deflating.

And Christos was dead.

The killer was hardly winded.

He dragged the body over toward the fence and pushed it with his foot, wedging it in between a headstone and some dark, wet shrubs, kicked the feet out of the path, and calmly walked away, was swallowed by the darkness, the cold and windy night.

With Christos's death the *assassini* had died, too. So far as Brother Leo knew. In the summer Paris was liberated, the war's outcome was a foregone conclusion, though dark days for the Allies still lay ahead, between now and the end. But it was over for the little band of killers.

Leo stretched his arms out in the last of the day's sunshine like a man doing an exercise. The cloud cover, purple and blue and shading to black at the horizon, was closing down on the last rays.

"After the night he killed Christos I never spoke with Simon again . . . never saw him again."

Brother Leo moved among the gravemarkers, kneeling here and there to straighten a basket of flowers, or remove dead blooms which he called deadheads, or tug at dried-up, recalcitrant weeds. The sun was sinking, the wind stiffening, driving the temperature lower still. I shivered but not entirely from the cold. Simon was coming clearer in my mind, coming to life. And I knew about Christos now. Christos the Nazi priest. But I would always think of him by another name, dying in the night.

"What did you do then? After Christos was dead and Simon was gone, I mean. And by the way, I'm not entirely in the dark—for instance, I know Christos was a man called Father LeBecq, the son of the art dealer. But Simon . . . who was Simon?"

He ignored the question, just went on. He had his own agenda. "After that night, I went back to my regular work in Paris and that was the end of it. At least for a while. Until the Collector came from Rome, that is."

"Ah, yes. The Collector. What was his name when he was at home?"

"Don't be so impatient, Mr. Driskill. We have plenty of time here. Very little else, but plenty of time."

"You can't blame me for being curious," I said. "Who was the Dutchman you mentioned? And little Sal, the priest whose life was turning out so differently from what he'd expected? Whatever happened to them?"

"I suppose we all went back to our former lives, the lives we'd gone right on living during the days. At least for a while, that is—"

"I know, I know. Until the Collector came."

"Precisely. Came to collect us, you see." He levered himself to a standing position with his hand on one of the old stones. Dead, once-yellow flowers were scattered at the base of the stone. "Simon was the only great man I ever met. Do you understand? He knew no loyalty other than to God and to the Church. I may look back now and say that things were done that shouldn't have been done, but it was a bad time for everyone, a battle to the death. Simon, however, was like no other man—and even the saints themselves made mistakes, didn't they?"

"That's putting it mildly," I said.

"And so it was with Simon. But a great man. His courage was simply boundless."

"So who the hell was he?"

"Mr. Driskill, *please.*"

"But you knew him. I mean *really* knew him—"

"Let's say I observed him. We spent some nights hiding in barns together. He talked to me. He argued the point of what we were doing—was it right, was it truly for the good of the Church . . . He argued every side of the issue, and I listened. He was a far more intelligent man than I. He was a great student of the past, of all that we call history. It was Simon Verginius who told me about the Concordat of the Borgias."

He led me back out of the graveyard, strolled slowly down toward the cliffs.

"The what?" I was shouting against a sudden explosion of ocean against the rockface.

He leaned against a twisted tree, pushed his hands down into the pockets of his muddy trousers. He spoke again as if it weren't all that important, just a bit of distant wartime history. The sea took a rest.

"Simon said it was the concordat, the agreement made between Pope Alexander, the Borgia, with the society of men who did his— what did Simon call it?—yes, his 'heavy work.' His killing. Simon said we were the descendants of these men from five hundred years before, he said we were a living part of the history of the Church. He told me that he had personally seen and handled the concordat—" Leo stopped, looking down into the rolling foam, his face a model of serenity, an emblem signifying his accommodation with his past.

"Did he describe it? Does it still exist?"

He smiled, tolerating my latest impatience. "So many things disappeared during the war and in the aftermath. But Simon was obsessed by the fate of the concordat itself, the parchment on which it was written. You see, he said it contained the names of the faithful men who had served Pope Alexander. He said it contained as well the names of the unbroken line of descent, inked in as the centuries passed, of all the men since Alexander drew it up. I wasn't

so sure, it sounded so fanciful . . . but then, the history of the
Church is heavy-laden with secret documents, isn't it? It sounded
so very Catholic to me. Simon was afraid that it would fall into the
hands of the Nazis during the war—then he feared they would
forever hold it as a club over the Church."

"Are you saying he actually had this thing in his possession
back then?"

Leo nodded.

"How did he come by such an amazing document?"

"He never told me."

"Maybe he was lying, maybe he was just pulling your leg—"

"Simon? Lie? Never!"

"But how can you be sure?"

He looked at me from the corner of his eye, slyly, from the
distant towers of great age. "I know. I knew him, for one thing.
That's how I can be sure."

"Tell me the rest of it. You could be holding the fate of the
Church in your hands." A list of the assassini . . .

"I doubt that, Mr. Driskill. That's Jesuitical talk."

I wasn't going to impress him with my quest, with all I'd been
through. He'd been through more, and now his struggle with life
was over and I couldn't intimidate him or impress him or coax him
or force him into anything that wasn't on his agenda. He'd thought
it through a long time ago. "I was a Jesuit once," I said.

He laughed immoderately. "Driskill," he said, "what a piece of
work you are! Are you by any chance an honest man?"

"More or less," I said. In my world nobody asked you a question
like that. What were you supposed to say?

"Well," he sighed, "as for the concordat— When Simon left the
graveyard the Concordat of the Borgias was on his mind . . . as
history. And it was like a license, a charter—would you agree? Its
history validated it, didn't it? When the assassini are needed, when
they can serve the Church, they live again." He looked up at me,
round eyes wide. "I wouldn't want the responsibility of deciding
when, would you, Mr. Driskill?"

"Just tell me what happened to the concordat."

"Oh, he sent it north. For safekeeping. In fact . . ." His face was
pink, almost merry, like Santa Claus in the school play. "He sent it
north with me! He trusted me, you see." He showed me his teeth,
small and white and somehow fierce. "With me and another fellow.

The Dutchman who'd been there outside the graveyard that last night. He'd come to me with a letter and a packet. The letter was from Simon, it told me to take this packet, the concordat, and go with the Dutchman, make a run for the north country . . . oh, I'll tell you it was an adventure! We went as Breton fishermen, ran the Channel to England. Cloak and dagger. But we made it. God must have wanted us to finish Simon's job." He looked out at the darkening sea, reliving the moment of triumph.

"So," he went on, turning back to me, "we kept it out of the hands of the Nazis. It's here, you see. We brought it here to this place, St. Sixtus. Like so many of the Irish monasteries, this one has always been a repository of Church documents from the Middle Ages on. A tradition. Things preserved for centuries. Out of the way and safe."

"You're telling me it's here? Right here?" Blood was pounding in my head. *A list of assassini* . . .

"Yes, of course. The archivist, Brother Padraic—very old man, failing now, I'm afraid—he has it, it's hidden here, somewhere in the St. Sixtus archives. Through these forty years Padraic and I have become great friends. Now it's time for both of us to get the thing off our consciences. We had no plan to do so, but now you've come, you may be God's answer to our final doubts about what was done in His name back then. We will die soon . . . but you may be the answer to our prayers. We are just two simple old men." He sighed again but without a scintilla of sorrow for himself. "I suggest that I give you the concordat for your disposal . . . I mean, it is mine to give, is it not?" He spread his hands and shrugged. "The man who came north with me, the Dutchman, is long, long gone. Lost. And Simon? Well." He shrugged again.

"Is Simon alive? You know that?"

"Oh my, yes, Simon is still alive. And little Salvatore." A tiny grin played across his small features. "All very grand now," he said enigmatically.

"Why not just tell me, for God's sake?" My voice was trembling with frustration. And I was so goddamned cold. "Who was Simon? Who the hell *is* Simon?"

"If I don't give it to you, it will quite probably be lost forever. Padraic and I will die, the concordat will remain in our vaults here for a century, maybe two. But if I give it to you . . . tell me, will you do me, the Church, a service?"

"What?"

"I'll give you the Concordat of the Borgias if you will take it away and deliver it for me—could you arrange that?"

"Deliver it where? To whom?"

"To whom he says! To Simon, of course. It was his in the old days. Take it home to Simon for me."

"You'll have to tell me where—"

"Obviously. Who and where."

"You baffle me, Brother Leo."

"Do I?"

"You were all killers. All of you."

"I thought perhaps I'd explained the circumstances. The war, all that madness . . ."

"And now you're at it again."

"Not me, as you can see. The others, whichever of them may be left, they must answer for themselves."

"You're going to tell me who Simon is?"

"Yes. In due time." He looked into my eyes for a long moment. "Someone still killing," he mused. "Killing for the Church. Ah, Mr. Driskill, I worry about my sins." He stood still for what seemed like forever. "Still killing to save the Church. But Robbie Heywood? Your sister?" He turned back to me, his face suddenly tired and filled with worry. "Goodness," he said, "I am so out of touch."

I had to stay calm. I couldn't run the risk of scaring the old man. But I was coming apart inside from sheer excitement. So close now, so near some answers. Simon was alive, I'd have his name, I'd know where he was. . . . But it would all have to be done Brother Leo's way.

Which was why I found myself soaked to the skin and scrambling down the rough escarpment by means of a natural set of footholds. I'd been to two monasteries since this thing had gotten hold of me, and I longed for something else. Smooth green lawns, privet hedges, a birdbath in a courtyard, a gently tolling bell. That was what monasteries had meant to me. Peace and the time for quiet reflection. No more.

We were halfway down the cliff face when dark clouds scudded quickly in off the sea and let us have it, full force, pelting down for all they were worth, drenching us. Leo looked back at me, water streaming down his face, called something about "a spot of weather, we're used to it around here," and I ducked my head, followed. Down, down, through brush and sharp rock and slipping crumbs of cliff, down until we stood on a battered strip of sand invisible from the top. It was actually a small inlet, shielded by large boulders rising out of the water fifty yards away, with surf running up the sand and slipping quietly in among the rocks at the bottom of the cliff. He beckoned to me again and we went across the cement-hard, wetly packed sand, threading a path in among the rocks which were slippery and treacherous to footfall.

"Cave," he said, pointing.

We sheltered in its mouth. He took a tiny pipe from his hip pocket, along with a cracked oilskin pouch with a few shreds of tobacco gathered in the corner. He filled the little bowl, lit it, puffed, and rubbed his hands together. While the downpour blew wildly a few feet away, he explained that the cliffs were honey-combed with similar caves, all of which were part of the monastery, hermit hideaways for those who'd found the beehives of stone too luxurious. Some of the caves, including the one where we stood, led finally into the bowels of the monastery itself. There was a point, it turned out, to his showing me this particular cave.

He told me it led into one of the hidden chambers where the secret documents were stored in special caskets. The domain of the archivist, Brother Padraic.

"Can you find this place again?" he asked me, rubbing the bowl of his pipe against the cold palms of his hands. "Can you get down the cliff at first light? It can be tricky."

I said I supposed I could.

"Good. Be careful. First light, then. We'll have the world to ourselves then, and Brother Padraic and I will meet you here. We'll hand over the bloody concordat, some instructions as to what you're to do with it, and that'll be that. I trust you, Mr. Driskill. I trust the dear God who sent you to me. And then I'll be done with the whole business after all these years—I'll have rid myself of the memories. . . ." He puffed, watching the rain blow across the cave's entrance. "We all have sins, don't we? Some greater than others. All we can do is confess, repent, pray for mercy. We took lives in the name of the Church." He couldn't stop talking about it now that he'd started. I wondered if he'd spoken with anyone else about it once he'd gotten to St. Sixtus. He'd told Padraic, I assumed. But it must have built up in him until he began to tell me, this stranger he was betting on, for better or worse. "Is that one sin or two? We killed *and* we blamed it on the Church. Two, I think. Let me tell you something, Mr. Driskill. It is often argued that from our first communion onward we consume the Church. It is a lie, my friend. It's the Church that consumes us. It's like a riddle, is it not?"

The rain stopped, the storm clouds lingered, brought night to the monastery and its inhospitable shore, and he led me back along the spit of sand in the direction from which we'd come. He excused the surreptitious aspects of my visit but said he thought it far better that I keep out of sight. The fewer the questions, the better off we'd be. I pointed out to him that I'd already been seen by several monks in the main building while I was enquiring as to his whereabouts, but he shrugged it off. "I'll lie," he said happily, "tell them you're an American cousin and already gone. If anyone asks." The small sins didn't matter.

He told me I could spend the night in one of the beehives. He'd bring me bread, cheese, wine, and a blanket. While he went off to fetch these necessities I pulled the rented car farther down off the shoulder of the road, parked it behind and among a screen of stones, broken walls, and high weeds. Anybody who saw it, particularly in the darkness, would have to be looking hard for it. I waited for Leo's return, standing beside the beehive wrapped in my old macintosh like a coast watcher from another, less secret war.

He came back with the provisions as well as a couple of thick candles. We huddled in the center of the stone beehive. I tried not to think about the pervasive damp and the slipperiness of the walls. He uncorked the homely bottle of red wine and I swilled it down with chunks of fresh soda bread and sharp white cheese. He went over the plans for the morning, and just as he was about to leave I spoke a name.

"August Horstmann," I said.

He was ducking to get through the low-cut opening in the beehive, his hand up to brace himself against the archway. "What did you say?" He spoke, standing stock-still with his back to me.

"August Horstmann. Was he the man you called the Dutchman?"

He turned slowly, small mouth pursed, regarding me with an air of disappointment. "I don't like being made a fool of, Mr. Driskill. I expect a man to be square with me, not be leading me on and laughing behind my back—"

"What are you talking about?"

"You knew it all along and let me blither on like an old crock . . ."

"Nonsense. I was guessing." I didn't tell him about the Dutchman killing the old Vicar, Heywood.

"Horstmann's the man who came north with me. The Dutchman. We brought the concordat here, to St. Sixtus. He left like a shadow when night came . . . and I stayed. He was a brave man. Fearless, that Dutchman."

I was exhausted and the cold and damp weren't doing my back any good. It was wet and sticky, felt like the bandage was stuck to the flesh with wet, hardening cement. So the various throbbings and achings made sleep difficult to come by. I kept shifting in the blankets I'd wrapped around myself under the trench coat but there was no such thing as a comfortable position. The waxy candle guttered in the drafts; black smoke curled away. The sea thrashed as if it were at my doorstep. But I probably wouldn't have been able to sleep even in my bed at home.

The connections kept breeding among themselves. Horstmann and Leo. Together they had brought this concordat of the Borgias from Paris to the north coast of Ireland. Forty years ago. Simon Verginius had given it to them, to keep it safe, out of the hands of the Nazis. Paris. *Assassini.* Simon. Concordat. Horstmann . . . LeBecq in the graveyard, his brother propped against the nosewheel of an airplane in the Egyptian desert forty years later, the two deaths somehow connected. My sister Val . . . Richter, Torricelli, D'Ambrizzi, LeBecq caught by the camera so long ago . . . the Collector . . . Little Sal, the Dutchman, Leo crouching in the cold . . . Father Governeau on my sister's mind the day she died . . .

Leo. There was no point in telling him that his comrade on that long and perilous flight from the Nazis was still abroad in the land, like the spirit of evil.

But I couldn't keep Horstmann from invading my thoughts, finally settling in like another occupying army. I felt as if I were no longer alone in the ancient monk's beehive. Horstmann was there beside me. He'd been there in Paris, anticipating me, killing Heywood to keep me from finding out about the *assassini,* and he'd failed. And he'd tried to kill me in Princeton and he'd failed and I knew he'd keep trying to kill me until one of us was dead . . . and in the desolation of that night with the rain dripping through the chinks in the stones I wondered if I had any chance at all against him. Or would he just keep trying to kill me on through time, forever and ever and ever, as if we were both trapped in the inner precincts of hell.

I yawned, shivered, rolled myself ever more tightly in the blankets. I was safe in the beehive. He couldn't possibly know where I was. . . . Still, he'd been there, forty years ago he'd been there, right there, at old St. Sixtus.

I had to get hold of myself. I had to keep the fear of Horstmann from overtaking me and running me off. But he was so implacable a killer, so determined, so ruthless, killing to protect the secrets, Simon's secrets, and I could feel him, hear his breathing and his footsteps behind me. . . .

Could I turn it around now, I wondered, could I turn hunter and hunt him until he dropped? How could I hunt someone invisible? Could I hunt him and corner him and kill him for Val and Lockhardt and Heywood and Monsignor Heffernan? And for myself? Could I bring myself to kill anyone? If I could, I knew who it would be.

He was so overpowering in his madness, so far beyond my powers of comprehension, like all the great mysteries of the Church. I felt like a man pursued by a mythical beast that could render itself invisible whenever it chose, then reappear in a puff of brimstone, give me enough of a glimpse to keep me in the chase, then disappear once again as I rushed headlong toward my own doom. It seemed to me that I had no choices. I'd have to continue, press on until it was over.

My reactions to Leo were ambivalent. He bothered me. He was so clearly a kind, decent old man, yet I was repelled by his story of the *assassini* in Paris. The pragmatic betrayal of the Resistance in order to remain in the good graces of the Nazis—still, I supposed it was a fairly accurate microcosm of the Church's attitude in those days. Pius wouldn't even excommunicate Hitler! And there was Leo's reaction to Simon. Leo seemed to find him saintly. This Simon, who had by whatever means come to possess this concordat, struck me as a killer at the least, maybe worse. . . . But it all must have been terribly complicated and who the hell was I to judge anyway? I wanted to find a man and then kill him.

What had happened to Simon after the war?

Who was he? And was he still giving Horstmann his orders?

As I went to sleep at long last I was thinking of Sister Val, wondering what she and Sister Elizabeth would have made of all this. . . .

The first time I jolted awake it was with a peculiar realization, the subconscious ticking away. I was thinking of Val dead in the chapel and the way my father had spoken to me late that night, coping with his grief, and the sound of his body crashing down the steps come morning. Time was jumbling it all together and when I woke again I was cold, perspiring heavily, my stomach in a knot. I shook my head, trying to clear away the dreams. I saw Elizabeth in the doorway of the house when she'd arrived unexpectedly and I had thought she was my sister, Val.

Later on it was the knife flashing through the moonlight, the sting and the ice against my face and Sandanato calling to me from far away.

Jesus, what dreams!

I didn't sleep anymore and first light came early.

When I left the beehive a cold wind was whipping a palpable fog. It hit my face like a wet glove. It was impossible to see more than an arm's length ahead. In no time I was soaked through again, stumbling over the uneven landscape, working my way along the top of the cliff feeling like a fool trapped on Conan Doyle's deadly Grimpen Mire with the hound baying, where a misstep guaranteed eternity. I wasn't Sherlock Holmes and the hound of the Baskervilles wasn't after me, but my thoughts during the fitful night had left me tired and on edge and I was trying to keep my fears under control and my wits at hand.

I inched slowly along the cliffs, and wherever I looked there was nothing but thick fog. No monastery, no sheer drop to my left, no breakers against the rocks, nothing. So I went slowly and Eliot's lines kept running through my mind.

I have seen the moment of my greatness flicker,
And I have seen the eternal Footman hold my coat, and snicker,
And in short, I was afraid.

I came to the crumbling wall at the graveyard, frisked my memory for the lay of the land, felt for the slippery footholds in the cliff until I found them. I felt I'd been at it for hours already, clammy and wet and confused by the fog. In short, I was afraid.

I held on to the clumps of gorse and the bits of cracked ledge and the odd protrusion of root, praying that nothing came loose, and felt my way, step by step, down the face of the cliff. Fog acted as a buffer, muffling the crashing of the waves. It also blinded me, disoriented me, but heightened some of my other senses: the reverberation of the waves traveled through the sheets of stone, left my legs quaking, as if the cliff were about to split open.

Panic stopped me somewhere between the top of the cliff and the beach. I thought I was going to lose my footing and pitch forward into gray oblivion. I waited, hanging on the wall, until the worst of it had passed, then felt with my foot for the next step. Slipped. I grabbed hard at the tangled hook of root with my right hand and it pulled slowly from the crevice where it had taken hold. I heard myself cry out as I fell, twisting in the air like a cat, scraping my hands raw, reaching for some salvation, and there was none.

I landed on all fours, my head hanging like a whipped dog, choking on my own terror. At most, I'd slipped and fallen six feet before landing on the sand. I'd almost reached the bottom and I hadn't known it, hadn't sensed it with the enveloping fog. Fighting for breath, I sat back, leaning against the wet rocks, wiping the condensed moisture and sweat from my dripping face. I couldn't see a damned thing. I felt like throwing up. And I was sick of the whole bloody horror.

I'll never know what I might have done if I hadn't been able to penetrate the fog. I might still be sitting there, catatonic, an uninhabited body that had once contained a man. But unexpectedly the wind swirled in off the water, carrying with it gusts of rain, and blew some gaps in the fog and I caught a glimpse of the sand wandering away to my right and I knew where I was.

I stood up, knees on fire from the fall, palms bloody in patches, rain blowing in my face, and set off toward the cleft in the rocks where I would find Leo and Brother Padraic. I went cursing them both for making the job next to fucking impossible. Adrenaline was pushing me on. If I'd encountered the dark angel of my nightmares just then, I'd have ripped him limb from limb, his flickering blade notwithstanding, or I'd have died trying. Which was, I supposed, far more likely.

The tide was receding. I saw gulls flapping like ghosts, in and out of the fog banks. I got to the entrance of the cave, stood on the ledge inside its mouth where Leo had smoked his pipe and told me that it was the Church that consumed us, not the other way around. But Leo wasn't there now which didn't make any sense to me. I'd taken forever getting to the cave. He and Padraic should have been coming from inside the monastery: wasn't that what he'd implied, that some of the caves wound their way back into the cellars of the main building itself? They should have been waiting for me.

I couldn't see any point in standing, waiting. I headed back into the darkness of the cave, aware I could go only so far before the gloom stopped me. As it turned out, I didn't have far to go.

A man was waiting for me on a ledge. He looked like he was napping.

But his eyes were wide, sunken into sockets dark as walnuts. I saw the whites like two dim crescents of moon and I knew it was happening all over again and I froze in my tracks like a man who knows he's already dead, just waiting for the blow. Listening for the footsteps behind me, the figure wafting like a bad dream from the darkness, knife in hand, an end to it all. . . .

But no one came. I looked back, seeing the shape of a man in the luminous mouth of the cave. No one was there. No one came.

I stepped closer, looked at the old, old man in his cassock. The blood at his throat was still sticky, a scarlet ribbon. I felt it on my fingertips. Brother Padraic . . .

I leaned on the slippery wall. I swallowed the sourness of fear. I concentrated on the pain in my knees and hands and back. I tried to think, but the mechanism wouldn't kick in. I couldn't think. I wanted to get the hell out of the cave. But what was waiting for me outside?

I sloshed back through the shallow water and stood again in the grayness, blinking, trying to get my bearings.

Where was Brother Leo?

Where was the concordat?

I'd have to go back to the monastery . . . I wasn't making much sense. I staggered out onto the beach, wandered through the blowing fog, knowing I couldn't climb the cliff, knowing I had to head back down the beach.

The gigantic boulders suddenly materialized out of the fog and there was something, someone, standing in the water, between the boulders and me. The fog whisked it all away. I went closer to the water, straining to see. Trying to pick out the figure again. Something was all wrong.

I waded into the water, saw it again.

A cross, plunged into the surf, driven in like a stake. It was waving to me through the fog and rain, beckoning me like Ahab lashed to the whale. . . .

It wouldn't come clear in the swirling, blowing fog. The rain was blurring my vision, whipped across my face by the driving wind. Somewhere, in the distance beyond the fog and rain, the sun was glowing, whitening the vapor all around me.

Then I saw it.

Ten feet away as I stood in the frothing water that sucked at my shoes, soaked my feet and ankles.

A rude cross plunged upside down in the sand, tilting sideways as the sea swept back and forth.

An inverted cross. The oldest warning in Christendom.

Nailed to the cross, one hand hanging loose, flapping with the push and pull of the surf, was the waterlogged, already bloated and rubbery and blue-tinged corpse of Brother Leo.

There was no way to put a good face on it.

I panicked. Really panicked. I didn't try to think it through, I didn't rely on my reason and experience and come to grips with the situation. I just lost it. I didn't think about the gun in my pocket and go hunting for the miserable son of a bitch. I didn't go to the monastery to report a maniac's work. I didn't do anything that my life and training had prepared me to do. I ran.

I'd been doing pretty well, I thought, since I'd seen my sister Val's body at my feet. But with the sight of Brother Leo's grotesque crucifixion burned into my brain, I half ran, half staggered back along the beach, tripping and falling, a caricature of terror. Somehow I got to the beehive, grabbed my gear, threw it into the car, and scraped the fender against the jagged edge of a milestone, getting the car out of the muck and back onto the narrow road. I wasn't thinking. I was acting in a blind rush, speeding as if there were something gaining on me, something I couldn't elude no matter where I went. It was a rebirth of the worst fears of vulnerable childhood and I was, for a time, that child again, fleeing the monsters of darkness, an old rhyme from a book I no longer remembered repeating itself again and again in my mind.

. . . one that on a lonesome road
Doth walk in fear and dread,
And having once turn'd round, walks on,
And turns no more his head;
Because he knows a fearful fiend
Doth close behind him tread.

I drove hard for two hours before I'd calmed down enough to stop beside the road and finish off the bread and cheese left over from the previous night. It grew a little warmer as I drove inland but a thin rain fell steadily. I paid no attention to the countryside, nor to a village where I finally stopped for coffee. Then more coffee, eggs, sausage, broiled tomatoes, toast. My hunger was almost out of control, as if the act of eating would ward off the thing pursuing me. Finally I sat on a bench in a sudden shaft of sunshine and watched some children kicking a soccer ball around a patch of grassy park, watched mothers pushing bundled-up babies in prams, and my heart began to slow down and I began to recover the ability to think.

It had to be Horstmann, not some other phantom banshee. Horstmann. He had brought the concordat north forty years before; now he had come to leave slaughter in his wake. Surely he had come because of me. He had known I was coming to find Brother Leo. He had learned so much from Robbie Heywood before he killed him, then perhaps he'd waited, watched me, followed me . . . and killed Leo, who had been planning to tell me so much.

But why hadn't he killed me?

Horstmann had been watching, and having struck had disappeared in the fog. . . . The soccer ball rolled to my feet. I booted it back to a girl with pigtails, who thanked me through the space where her two front teeth had once been.

He had the concordat. So I could forget that. Unless I could discover to whom he would eventually give it.

But why hadn't he just waited in the cave and killed me, too? Why hadn't he finished the job he started? I'd have been so easy for him this time. But he'd let me live. . . . Was it because he now had the concordat? How important was it? Had the names of Simon's *assassini* been added to it? Had it gone beyond that? Were they adding names even now?

No. Crazy.

Did I no longer matter to them? Now that he'd killed the two old men who held the answer to the riddle of the *assassini,* now that he had the concordat, was I mere addendum, a useless, feeble appendage?

So why hadn't he lopped me off?

Could it be that someone was now protecting me? Had Horstmann been ordered by someone not to kill me? But who could that someone be? There was only one man so far who gave Horstmann orders . . . Simon Verginius. A long time ago.

Still, Horstmann had tried to kill me once. Why stop? Even if I were nothing more than a loose end, why not tie me up once and for all? Why not kill three in the fog as long as you've killed two?

Maybe I'd just been lucky. Being late, maybe I'd avoided another appointment with that knife . . . maybe he'd gone looking for me in the fog, perhaps we'd passed each other unseen in the fog and I had lived. . . .

Christ, I was getting nowhere.

And then I found myself thinking of Sister Elizabeth again, wanting to tell her the story of what I'd been through, wanting to see her face and her green eyes, wanting—God help me—to hold her and cling to her.

It was an idiotic line of thought. I had to be in shock.

I sat for a while in the park. Across the brown grass, where the children in puffy parkas played, I saw the railroad station. A small brick building, a shabby outpost of lonely travelers, grimy with age. I watched a train pull in, wait for no more than a minute or two, then clang scruffily away.

A man was coming out of the station, walking toward me. He strode through the kids, coming toward me. Me. He stopped in front of me and set his bag down.

"They tell me there's a bus to St. Sixtus stops here." He turned, looked down the road. "I must say you look worse than I'd have thought possible." He turned back, looking at me askance. "Your tailor should see you now. You are a disgrace to the idea of excessive privilege."

"Father Dunn," I said.

He sat in the first-class carriage, his grip full of damp clothing, and watched the blur of sunshine behind the rain squall cast shadows that brought out the texture of the landscape. The train was sparsely populated. Two other priests munched sandwiches, rattled their brown paper sacks, polished apples against the fabric of their black suits.

Horstmann watched them awhile, slowly turning his old rosary, blessed by Pius himself during an audience before the war. Then he put it away and peeled off his spectacles and pinched the bridge of his nose which bore a reddish crease, closed his icy eyes. It had been a long night, talking with Brother Leo, reminiscing about the old days, that long-ago, choppy night they had crossed the Channel in an open boat, clinging to each other for dear life and praying aloud against the howling gale.

Brother Leo had been understandably confused when his old, long-lost comrade had appeared unannounced at his room in the middle of the night. Confusion had been followed in quick succession by hesitancy and fear. But Horstmann had calmed the fears, told him a story about having been sent from the Secret Archives to finally bring the Concordat of the Borgias back to Rome, back to the place it belonged. Yes, he'd come from Simon personally, yes, it was safe now, after all these years. Horstmann had spun a tale that might have been true and Brother Leo had wanted to believe it. Horstmann had told him that a treacherous journalist from New York was on the trail of the concordat, had stumbled across the story of the secret brotherhood, and that it was now a race, the Church against the *New York Times,* which was bound to reveal everything in the worst possible light and create a great scandal and cause the Church a great injury. And then he had described the journalist. Ben Driskill.

Brother Leo's instincts had been to mistrust such a story, but his fear of Horstmann's ghostly materialization had made him want to believe it was true. But Horstmann, with something like regret, had seen the doubt in the little old man's eyes . . . *Little old man.* Chronologically they were almost the same age, but there was more to life than chronology.

That morning in the cave had been a sorry business.

Brother Leo's doubts had come to life again, he'd sensed something in his old comrade and it had proven his undoing. Brother Padraic hadn't seemed to be aware he was dying: he'd folded his arms and babbled a bit, as if he thought Horstmann were the angel of death, and had drifted off like a spaceman severed from his support system. Leo had been a problem. He had tried to escape, had cried out to Driskill, and Horstmann had cut him quickly, almost in anger, which was unlike him, and then he'd carried out the ritual. There had been an old cross left over from some service carried out on the beach long ago, maybe even another crucifixion, now worm-eaten and damp through, and it had struck him as an omen, finding it propped against the wall of the cave like timber bracing. Simon would have understood the gesture. Simon had done the same thing once in the French countryside with a priest who had tried to betray them to the SS. . . .

Brother Leo was no better, no better than the one who had betrayed them in the end and brought them to ruin and scattered them like ashes on the wind. Leo had known the secret of the concordat yet had been planning to give it to a stranger. Simon had long ago left no doubt in their minds as to the sacred need for secrecy. Yet Leo had urged it on Driskill.

Incomprehensible.

To die was not enough.

The ritual—so ancient, so brutal, so damning for eternity—had been called for, and God had given him the strength to carry it out. . . .

The fog had blotted out Driskill. Horstmann had not been willing to wait for him.

Driskill.

Horstmann had begun to think of him as a hound of hell. Driskill was the devil's work. The fog had saved him this time or he'd have taken Leo's place on the cross.

Why wouldn't he die?

On the ice that night in Princeton, Horstmann had killed him. But he would not die. It was as if he were being saved for some other fate.

But how could that be? And where was he now? What had he done upon finding Brother Leo in the fog, drained of blood and turning blue with the cold—

Had he been afraid?

No. He didn't think Driskill was afraid. Driskill was a merciless, godless man, and he was not afraid. He was not afraid to die, yet he was full of sin. He should by rights have feared death, the punishment for his sins, what lay in wait for him in the final darkness. But he was not afraid.

It made no sense.

Where was Driskill now? Was he following? Who, he wondered, was hunting whom? The thought perplexed him. But God was on his side.

Horstmann slipped his eyeglasses back into place and told himself that there was nothing to worry about. No man possessed greater vigilance than he. No man.

So he closed his eyes, holding the leather briefcase in his lap. The Concordat of the Borgias safe at last. It was for him a living thing, a kind of disembodied heart, pulsing with the blood and the commitment that would cleanse the Church at last. . . . He remembered the night in Paris when Simon had entrusted it to him and Leo and sent them on their mission, the mission that had turned Leo into a virtual hermit and himself into a wanderer, telling them to wait for the time when they would be summoned again to save the Church. . . .

*   *   *

The spools of audio tape whirled slowly and the voices filled the room, a little tinny without enough bass, but then, the quality of the fidelity had not been the point.

He was in Alexandria a week ago, give or take a few days. While there he had a meeting with our old friend Klaus Richter—

You're joking. Richter? Our Richter? From the old days? You told me he was the one who frightened you!

None other, Holiness. And he did frighten me, I assure you.

Your candor becomes you, Giacomo.

The draperies were drawn, shutting out the gray light of a cloudy morning. Across the pine-bordered lawn one might have seen the brown haze rounded like a lid over Rome. A gardener was trimming the hedges with something like a chain saw, judging by the sound of it. The angry whine penetrated the draperies hanging heavily at the open windows and French doors. It sounded like a monstrous wasp trying to decide upon a victim.

And he saw another man who subsequently killed himself.

Who was that?

Etienne LeBecq, Holiness. An art dealer.

There was a long pause.

We also have a report from Paris that a journalist, an old chap by the name of Heywood—

Robbie Heywood. You remember him, Giacomo. Terrible loud jackets, he'd talk your arm off and drink you under the table, given half a chance. God's love, I remember him . . . how does he come into this?

Dead, Holiness. Murdered by an unknown assailant. The authorities have no clues, of course.

"Antonio! This is a genius of sorts! How incredibly underhanded this all is! How did you get these tapes?"

In the library of the villa which was the home of Antonio Cardinal Poletti, whose brother was an Italian diplomat stationed in Zurich and whose other brother was in the business of making and distributing unsavory films in London for a small but demanding market, five men sat with cups of breakfast coffee and rolls and fruit close at hand. And a very large problem in their laps.

Poletti was forty-nine, a small man with a bald head and alarmingly hairy arms and legs, all of which was in full view since he wore his tennis costume. The other four included Guglielmo Cardinal Ottaviani who was sixty and widely regarded to have the most exaggerated "attitude problem" in the entire College of

Cardinals but was a man whose very irascibility rendered him powerful and persuasive: he was feared; Gianfranco Cardinal Vezza, one of the eldest of the elder statesmen of the Church, a man who carefully maintained his reputation for increasing balminess so that he might all the more easily spring the iron jaws of his traps on the unwary; Carlo Cardinal Garibaldi, a chubby "club man" among the cardinals, a natural politician who had learned much of what he knew best at the feet of Cardinal D'Ambrizzi; and Federico Cardinal Antonelli. They were arranged in a variety of dark red leather chairs and couches, surrounded by entire walls of books—several of which Cardinal Poletti had himself written. Garibaldi's question went unanswered as the tape played on.

But what has he to do with any of this mess?

Sister Valentine saw him in Paris while doing her research. Now he's dead. There may be a connection—

You'll have to do better than that, Giacomo. I'll send someone to Paris and check this out.

Good luck to him. Perhaps it's merely a coincidence. Knifed on a street corner. Such things happen.

Nonsense. The Church is under attack and Heywood was a victim. It's obvious.

Cardinal Poletti leaned across the coffee table and punched the stop button. He looked slowly from one face to another.

"The heart of the matter," he said. "Did you hear it? 'The Church is under attack.' That's what I wanted you to hear Indelicato himself say . . . he sees it for what it is, an attack." He frowned at his coffee which was cold by now. "It is better that we lay our plans now than try to accomplish everything at the last minute when we're up to our ears in foreigners—Poles and Brazilians and Americans! Give those people enough rope and they hang us all, they hang the Church. You know I'm right."

Cardinal Garibaldi spoke again without moving his plump lips, like a ventriloquist temporarily in search of a dummy. "You say these voices—Callistus, D'Ambrizzi, and Indelicato, eh? Well, there's a nasty genius to it, Antonio. How did you get these tapes? Where did this discussion take place?"

"His Holiness's office."

"How extraordinary. You put a bug in his office! No need to look so startled. I'm up on the latest terminology."

"It must be the influence of that brother of yours," Cardinal

Vezza murmured. He stroked the white stubble on his chin. He often forgot to shave these days.

"Ah, but which brother," Ottaviani said, striking one of his attitudes, his smile like a sickle wound, "that is the question. The diplomat or the pornographer?" He cackled softly under his breath, enjoying young Poletti's discomfort.

Poletti glared at him. "You're more of an old woman with each passing day." He stood up, bouncing on the balls of his Reebok-shod feet, his simian legs bowed, and picked up his American-made Prince tennis racquet. He practiced a few crisp backhands, presumably picturing Ottaviani's face on the imaginary balls. "Always disagreeable," he muttered.

Cardinal Vezza, who was a large, slow-moving man, struggled forward in his chair. As usual, he was having trouble adjusting his hearing aid. "I had reference to the diplomat, of course. Aren't embassies always being bugged by someone or other? So he should know about this sort of thing."

Garibaldi repeated his previous question. "Well? How did you do it?"

"I have a distant cousin on the Vatican medical staff. He attached a voice-activated device to the cart bearing His Holiness's oxygen supply." Poletti shrugged elaborately, as if to say such miracles were the stuff of his everyday life. "He is completely trustworthy—"

"No man," Vezza suddenly shouted, "is *that* trustworthy." He laughed harshly. He began coughing, a hacking cough that hadn't caught up with him in seventy years of smoking. He held his cigarette between yellowed fingers with cracked and split nails. He smoked each cigarette to the stubby end.

Antonelli, a tall blond man in his early fifties who looked ten years younger, cleared his throat, a signal for the others to lay off the childish bickering. He was a lawyer, a quiet leader among the College of Cardinals despite his comparative youth. "I presume there is more to the tape. May we hear it?"

Poletti threw his racquet into an occasional chair, crossed back to the table, and depressed another button. The recorded voices resumed and the cardinals fell quiet, listening.

The silver-haired priest . . . and who is he?

Your network is still an astonishment to me. But where is Driskill?

You're good at watching people. Maybe you've been wasting too much time watching me, Fredi.

Not closely enough, apparently.

So now we have nine murders . . . and a suicide?

Well, who knows, Holiness? It's a reign of terror. Who knows how many more there are . . . and how many more there will be.

Then there was a pause, a muffled crashing sound, a jumble of voices.

Poletti turned the tape recorder off.

"What the devil was all that ruckus?" Vezza looked up, shocked.

"His Holiness collapsing," Poletti said.

"And how," Ottaviani said, "is the papal health?" His own sources were utterly accurate. He was testing Poletti and Poletti knew it.

"He's dying," Poletti said, flashing an arctic smile.

"I'm aware of that—"

"He's resting, what can I say? We're not here to worry about the man's health—we're miles past that! It's too late for anyone to worry about Callistus, in case that detail has escaped your attention. We're here to discuss the *next* pope . . ."

"And," Ottaviani said—he was a small, narrow man with a slightly twisted spine that gave him the appearance of a caricature by Daumier and that Poletti interpreted as the mark of Cain—"I can only assume that you are gathering evidence in support of your candidate." He smiled crookedly, an expression that seemed to fit with his deformity.

Poletti surveyed the group, his mouth set tightly so that he might refrain from speaking long enough to avoid blurting out to Ottaviani his deeply felt opinion that he was an intolerable old cripple who'd be better off dragged out, stood up against an anonymous wall somewhere, and shot. Poletti saw himself reflected in a mirror struck through with veins of gold. It was lamentably true that with his small head, long upper lip and small chin and excessive hairiness, he did look like a kind of miracle: a tennis-playing prince of the Church who was also a monkey. He looked away from the mirror. A man could take only so many unpleasant truths in one morning.

"We *are* under attack," Poletti said, picking up the tennis racquet, pointing it for emphasis. "It *is* a reign of terror. This is the atmosphere surrounding us as we face the election of a new pope. It is appropriate that we never lose sight of this framework when we consider the man we will support—"

"You make it sound like politics," Vezza said a little sadly. He had stopped shouting and now could barely be heard.

"My dear Gianfranco," Garibaldi said patiently, "it *is* politics. What else could it be? Received wisdom?"

Antonelli said gently, "The truth is, everything is politics in the end."

"Well said." Poletti nodded. "Nothing wrong with politics. Old as time."

Ottaviani was tapping his fingers together. "My dear friend," he said to Poletti, "is this old woman"—he nodded at Garibaldi— "correct in saying that you are about to take on the role of campaign manager for some man you expect us to join you in supporting?" The permanently aggrieved smile seldom left his deeply lined face, a map of pain and the determination to overcome it, to use it.

"I have a name for our consideration, that's true."

"Well, go on," Vezza said. He enjoyed giving the impression that he had a short attention span and was easily bored. His attitude tended to prompt others into offering fresh stimuli. "Trot him out."

"You heard the tapes," Poletti said. "There was one voice full of command, one voice that was decisive, one voice that recognized the seriousness of the crisis we face . . ."

"But he already *is* the pope!"

"No, dammit, not him! Vezza, my old friend, I worry about you at times."

"He called it a reign of terror, Tonio—"

"That was Indelicato," Poletti said, straining to control himself. "Indelicato said we are under attack—"

"Are you quite sure?" Vezza persisted. "It sounded like—" He had begun fiddling with his hearing aid again.

"Gianfranco, believe me, it *was* Indelicato!" Poletti implored.

"Videotape would have been preferable to the thing you've got rigged up on the oxygen cart, I must say," Vezza grumbled. "I mean, these disembodied voices . . . could be anyone, couldn't it? Do you think we could rig a video camera? Now, then we'd really have something—"

"We *really* have something now. The last thing I expected here was petty quibbling—"

"I'm sorry, Tonio," Vezza said airily. "I didn't mean to be ungrateful—"

"Well, you sounded damned unappreciative of my efforts and I am frankly surprised—"

Antonelli interrupted smoothly. "You're providing us with invaluable information, Tonio, and we are all much in your debt. There can be no question of that. Now, am I to assume that you are suggesting we gather our support behind Cardinal Indelicato?"

"You understand me perfectly," Poletti said with relief. "And thank you for your kindness, Federico. Indelicato is the man for these times—"

"Are you suggesting," Ottaviani said softly, "that there is only one issue worth considering? That we are under some sort of siege? And nothing else matters, is that what you would have us believe? I merely want to explore the crevices of your mind, Eminence."

Poletti could never be sure whether or not Ottaviani was making a fool of him. "That is what I am saying."

Vezza said, "Indelicato? Isn't that rather like picking the head of the KGB to be premier?"

"You have some problem with that?" Poletti said, eyeing him warily. "It seems to me the proper response to the situation. We are at war—"

"If we are at war," Garibaldi, always the confident club man, observed, "shouldn't we choose a general? Like Saint Jack, for instance?"

"Please," Poletti sighed, "could we save the canonization for later and just call him D'Ambrizzi?"

"D'Ambrizzi, then," Ottaviani said. He grimaced with pain, arranging his back against the cushions. "He seems to me a man worthy of our consideration. A forward-looking man—"

"A liberal," Poletti said. "Call him what he is. Do you relish the idea of rushing about parceling out condoms—"

"What?" Vezza said, head snapping up.

"Condoms, French letters, rubbers," Garibaldi said from behind a small grin.

"Good Lord," Vezza muttered. "What about them?"

"If D'Ambrizzi were pope, we'd be passing them out on the steps of our churches after mass, we'd be up to our chins in female priests, queer priests . . ."

"Well, I've known plenty of queer priests in my day, but do you really think D'Ambrizzi would encourage that?" Vezza made a doubtful face. "I mean, I've heard Giacomo say things which make me doubt—"

Antonelli interrupted again, full of deference but implying that he would offer up the last word on the subject. "Cardinal Poletti was, if I may say so, indulging in a bit of hyperbole. He was merely pointing out a tendency in Cardinal D'Ambrizzi which could, if followed to its logical conclusions, lead to the idiocies he described. Am I right, Tonio?"

"Utterly, my friend. You have captured my attitude to perfection."

"Perhaps," Antonelli said, "we could take a sounding in light of this tape recording and what Tonio here has had to say. What do we think—in a preliminary sense only, of course—of Indelicato as our man?"

Garibaldi said with a diplomatic nod, "He could be just the man for a hard job. He's not afraid to take drastic steps, not afraid to make an enemy. The stories I could tell—"

"The stories we could all tell," Vezza said sleepily. "He doesn't have much of a sense of humor—"

"How would you know?" Poletti interjected, staring grimly at the old man ringed in smoke.

"—but he certainly takes his work seriously. I could live with him. Better than many of the criminals and nitwits I've seen wear the red hat in my time."

"And you, Ottaviani," Antonelli said. "What about you?"

"What about an African?" he said impishly. "Or one of the Japanese, perhaps? Or an American, if it comes to that."

"Oh, for the love of Christ," Poletti said, ignoring the smile spreading across Ottaviani's face, "don't be foolish!"

"I merely wanted to see if Vezza recognizes an attempt at clerical humor." Ottaviani smiled fleetingly at the old man.

"What?" Vezza said.

"On the whole," Ottaviani said, "I find Manfredi Cardinal Indelicato a cold-blooded, only marginally human machine, a kind of butcher—"

"Don't be shy," Antonelli said. "What do you really think?"

"I'd never turn my back on him. He would have been at home as the Grand Inquisitor . . . in short, he would be the perfect man for the Throne of Peter."

Poletti's head jerked about to stare at Ottaviani. "You mean you would support his candidacy?"

"I? Did I say that? No, I don't think so. I'd support his assassination but not his elevation. No, I'm more inclined to support D'Ambrizzi, a thoroughly corrupt and worldly man, a captive of his own pragmatism, who would emerge no doubt as a much-beloved world figure . . . something of a movie star. How could any true cynic not find it appealing?"

The preliminary meeting of the Group of Five was winding down. Eventually Ottaviani and Garibaldi had been ferried off by their drivers and Antonelli had waved good-bye from his Lamborghini Miura, glossy, in clerical black. Vezza leaned on his cane and stumped along the tiled veranda, listening to Poletti droning on about one thing or another. Vezza had kept his hearing aid volume turned low throughout much of the meeting because he already knew what everybody was bound by history and personality to say. He was seventy-four years old, a man with a long memory who had heard just about everything. Much of what he himself said he didn't bother to listen to because he'd heard it before as well. Indelicato, D'Ambrizzi: he really didn't give a damn which way it went because he believed that the group of which he had been a dues-paying member for forty years—the curia—always got its way. It always had, so far as he could tell. He'd never seen the pope who hadn't in the crunch knuckled under to the Vatican professionals. What he'd just half dozed through was a curia coven meeting. He'd attended a great many such gatherings, stared into many a boiling, bubbling cauldron of clerical desires. This one, because of Antonelli's involvement, carried some extra weight. If the name they finally came up with was indeed Indelicato's, then Indelicato stood an excellent chance. Vezza just didn't find himself terribly interested. He had learned three months before that his kidneys were failing him. The way things were going, even Callistus might outlast him. The name of the next pope was low on his list of concerns, but one question lingered persistently in his mind.

Vezza and Poletti were standing on the edge of the driveway in the cool hilltop breeze waiting for the black Mercedes to be brought around. Vezza turned up the volume on his hearing aid.

"Tell me, young Tonio," he said, "about that tape of yours. Somebody on it is talking about nine murders—did I hear that accurately?"

"It was His Holiness."

"Well, I am a very elderly man with a hearing problem, so I may have missed something somewhere along the way. But for the sake of clarity, let's try to remember the murders . . . there's Andy Heffernan and our old friend Lockhardt in New York, the nun Sister Valentine in Princeton, and the journalist Heywood in Paris. The suicide is the LeBecq fellow in Egypt, though I must say his name means nothing to me . . . four murders and a suicide. Now, help me out on this in case I've missed something. By my reckoning I come up five murders short. How do you figure it? Who were the other five?"

Poletti saw the black Mercedes nose its way past the high hedges bordering the gateway to the driveway. Thank God this conversation wasn't going to last much longer. Vezza had a way of asking the most irritating, most pertinent questions.

"Come, come," the old man said. "Help an aging colleague. Who were the other five?"

"I don't know, Eminence," Poletti said finally. "I simply don't know."

At the outermost edges of his mind Callistus heard the striking of the grandfather clock on the other side of the bedroom but it wasn't part of reality. Somewhere in the fringe of consciousness he knew he was stretched out on his bed, two o'clock in the morning, the night watch being tolled by that god-awful clock, a gift from an African cardinal, carved by a primitive tribe obviously obsessed with sexual duality. But he heard it striking, he felt the closeness of the night. He seemed to be more alive at night now, at home in the darkness. He sighed within the ninety percent of his brain that was asleep and he could hear it, he could hear the snow rattling quite clearly against the roof and the walls as the wind blew it down the mountain pass, through the pines that drooped with heavy, snow-laden boughs.

He, Sal di Mona, stood in the doorway of the woodsman's hut, a thick scarf wrapped around his throat and covering the lower half of his face. The mountain wind seemed never to stop. Looking down the moonlit defile, he thought his eyeballs would freeze. All the color had been bled out of the scene. The snow was white, everything else was black as coal. The trees, the outcroppings of rock, the shadows, the footprints stitched down the mountainside to the black ribbon of railway track that he and Simon had inspected an hour before. The stream ran along the tracks, moving like a twisting shred of funereal ribbon.

Back inside the hut the six others were either dozing, eyelids fluttering, or reading by candlelight. One was soundlessly saying the rosary. Simon got up from the primitive chair, put his book into the pocket of his coat, and lit a cigarette. He looked into Sal di Mona's eyes and smiled. "A long night," he said, brushing past and going outside where he stood solid as a boulder, staring out across the gash cut between the mountainsides, the smoke of his cigarette curling back through the doorway.

The woodsy, dank smell of the single room had been transformed by their arrival. Now it smelled of the grease on the machine guns, of warm, sweating bodies and the fire now reduced to banked embers. It was hot and cold at the same time. Nothing was normal, nothing real. The plan that had once seemed so heroic had drawn in on them: all the heroics were gone. Now they were a group of frightened men risking everything to kill another man coming through the pass on the early morning train. There was nothing heroic about it. There was just the apprehension, the fear, the knot in the stomach, the trembling in the knees, the sensation of looseness in the bowels.

Sal di Mona had never killed a man. He wasn't going to kill the man on the train. He wasn't being given one of the guns. His job was to handle the grenades, bring the train to a stop on the damaged track. The others—two of the others, the Dutchman and another man, led by Simon—were using the guns. Outside he could hear the sound of footsteps crunching in the snow as Simon circled the hut, then went off to the lookout post they'd set up on a shelf of rock, giving a clear view down the length of track. It would be more than two hours before they saw the telltale column of smoke from the train engine, but Simon, like Sal di Mona, couldn't sleep, couldn't quite sit still.

An hour later they were all dozing except for Simon, who leaned against the log wall smoking a cigarette, and little Sal, who stared at his missal by candlelight but saw none of it.

Suddenly Simon was crouching, moving across the room, quenching the candle's flame between thumb and forefinger.

"There's somebody outside," he whispered. "Someone moving."

He tugged at Sal's arm, pulling him toward the low door at the

back of the hut where the roof sloped down and almost touched
the rising hillside. The Dutchman was awake, too, and the three of
them crawled outside, poking out beneath the eaves, in the shadow
of a woodpile.

In the stillness the sounds of soldiers reached them. The
clicking sound of metal on wooden gunstocks and cold gun barrels,
the cracking of feet through the snow, the low whispers. They were
somewhere in the trees, a dozen of them slowly revealed as they
moved down to approach the hut from the front. They didn't know
about the door in the back. They seemed unhurried.

"Germans," Simon whispered. Sal di Mona saw the moonlight
reflect in the round lens of a soldier's glasses.

"But how . . ."

"How do you think, Father? We have been betrayed."

Simon ducked back in through the low crawlspace. He was
going back inside to wake the others, but the shadows had all
moved out of sight, around the front of the hut. Sal di Mona was
trying to understand what was going on, but it was all moving too
fast. He had two grenades in the pockets of his coat. The Dutchman
was holding the machine gun.

The Dutchman pointed up the hill toward the thick stand of
trees, pushed Sal's shoulder, whispered something. They had gotten
twenty yards across the moonlit snow and they heard more sounds
of metal clicking, clear in the stillness. Then the sound of something
smashing at the door of the hut. Shouts in German.

The crack of gunfire, the pop-pop-pop sound, and out of breath
they flung themselves into the shelter of the trees.

Everything, absolutely everything was going wrong.

Sal di Mona reflected for the thousandth time that he was not
cut out for this damn war stuff.

He heard an explosion, then another, shouts and screams of
confusion and pain.

The bulky figure of Simon appeared at the back of the hut,
scrambling in the snow. Then he stopped, turned back to face the
hut, his arm looping in an arc through the air, something bounced
on the roof, disappeared over the front. Then it exploded, more
shouts, and Simon came struggling up the hill.

He was panting when he reached them. "They're all dead and
dying by now," he gasped. "Some of the Germans, too." He took
Sal's grenades, pulled the pins, and launched them back down the

hill. "Come on, we've got to get moving." The grenades exploded, blew the back off the hut.

No one followed them, but they could hear German soldiers stamping about, calling to one another.

By first light they had reached the road, where they waited nervously for the beat-up old truck to pick them up. It was right on time.

Four men were dead and they were alive and it was all over.

He could smell the explosions, couldn't get them out of his head.

The next day back in Paris they learned that the great man they had intended to kill hadn't been on the train after all.

When he woke up in the papal bedchamber he was soaked with perspiration and chilled to the bone and he could still smell the grenades going off, could still see the moonlight reflecting on the glasses worn by a German soldier in the shadows, and Simon struggling up the hill toward them after he'd bounced the grenade off the roof. . . .

"Giacomo? Is that you? What are you doing here? How long have you been here?"

A gray dawn was gathering stormlike over Vatican City, but that was a carryover from the dream, the memory. It had stormed that morning after the night in the mountains and the roads had been slick with rain that was almost ice. Now, this morning, was just another morning four decades later, another morning in the death of Pope Callistus.

"I couldn't sleep," D'Ambrizzi said. "I need only three or four hours a night. Sometimes less. I came in here about an hour ago. I've been thinking about so many things, Holiness. We need to talk." He sat in the armchair by the window, wearing a striped silk robe, his slippered feet cocked on the bottom shelf of the rolling cart containing the various medical equipment now required for the pope's health. "How are you feeling?"

Callistus sat up in bed, slowly threw his legs over the side, sat on the edge, breathing deeply. His face was slick with sweat. His pajamas clung to his back, clammy. D'Ambrizzi watched him struggling to hide the pain. It was an agonizing process.

"How do I *feel*? How do *I* feel?" Callistus coughed, half a chuckle. He knew D'Ambrizzi was referring to his indecorous collapse, the fainting spell, whatever it had been, in his office a few days before. "Relieved that it wasn't a heart attack—though why I cling to life, as if there were some useful future, I'm damned if I know. . . . Probably precipitated by one or another of my medications. It's all so tiresome, Giacomo."

"Aha, the cure worse than the disease."

"Would there were a cure, my friend. That's what makes it all such a joke. On me. I don't ask many questions about my condition these days. Who cares? Do you understand? Who in the name of God cares? Who needs to know? Other than the sheeplike faithful, the unwashed, the believers in voodoo and thingamajig . . . it's just not important, not anymore." He smiled ironically. "Not important in the eyes of God and His plan, anyway."

"Oh, do you think God has a plan? No, I don't think so." D'Ambrizzi shook his massive head. "No, He must be improvising. Nobody, not even God wherever She may be, could have concocted such a lousy plan." He lit a fresh black cigarette with a gold band around it. "But that's what I've come to talk to you about—"

"God's lack of a plan? Or the matter of God's sexual identity? If any?"

"Amusing as that might be," D'Ambrizzi said, "the subject I have in mind has nothing whatsoever to do with sex. It is, Holiness, directly related to your continuing usefulness on Planet Earth, however long or short your remaining time. We do need to talk."

Callistus stood up, refusing to give in to the cane, and walked slowly to the window. He was, idiotically, he thought, glad to be alive. Thankful for that small blessing, however glorious might be the world to come. Glad . . . even though his dreams, his days, his every memory—they were all death-haunted, death-ridden. All the victims, all the dead from long ago, all those who were dying now, all nine . . . and how many more to come? Who best to bring it to an end? Who best to find out the meaning, crystallize it, smash the crystal? He would think and dream all night of the dead and then each morning he arose and prayed and struggled along to mass and attended—increasingly pathetically, he was well aware—to whatever business he could. The world was getting accustomed to the idea that he was dying. Well, why not? He was Callistus, but as he grappled with death he seemed to be returning from fantasy a little more each day, seemed to be turning back into the reality of Salvatore di Mona again. . . .

"So you want to talk," Callistus said. "Sometimes it crosses my mind that I actually sit around talking to and with Cardinal D'Ambrizzi, one of the great men of the Church, one of the great leaders of our time, Saint Jack . . . and I am frankly amazed. What business have I to take up the time, to divert this great man from all his pressing duties—don't smile, Giacomo. I am in absolute earnest. You are D'Ambrizzi . . . and I am—"

"The Boss," D'Ambrizzi said. "Yes, Holiness, I want to talk."

"Has it occurred to you, Giacomo, that we live in dangerous and cynical times?"

D'Ambrizzi laughed. "Not especially, Holiness. All times have been dangerous and cynical. And those were the good times."

"Ah, you may have a point. But I was thinking that I'd rather talk in your rooms, if it's all the same to you. They may have installed listening devices—bugs, you know—here. But I have decided they'd be afraid to bug you!" He laughed.

"They?"

"Guess." He took his own robe from across the foot of the bed, slid into it, and finally, grudgingly, picked up the cane. "Come, we'll go to your rooms."

D'Ambrizzi was about to follow him through the door into the antechamber when Callistus stopped. "Giacomo, I suppose we dare not leave my oxygen contraption behind." He nodded at the cart, the oxygen. "Can you wheel it along? It's boring, but I'm afraid it must be done. They'd kill me if I left it behind."

With Cardinal D'Ambrizzi pushing the cart, the two giants of the Church, the one old, the other old and dying, made a peculiar procession stumping along the Vatican halls in their elegant night-clothes, past priceless tapestries and wall hangings, past the functionaries and staff on duty through the long night or freshly arrived with the dawn.

Once the door was closed behind them, D'Ambrizzi stood beside the heavy, ornately carved dining table with the lions fiercely forming the legs, sitting on their tails, holding the great slab of burled, glasslike wood on their heads. He held a chair—the papal preference was for a straight back and arms—and Callistus slowly, with a constant tremor, lowered himself into its reassuring clutches.

The beginnings of watery sunlight were seeping into the room, lay in puddles on the Aubusson carpet, on the polished surface of the table. The paintings—among them a Tintoretto—added a degree of texture to the room that was absent in the papal apartments which Callistus had taken pains to unclutter.

"Giacomo, here I am, or what's left of me. Full of curiosity. What's troubling you? You seldom exhibit much concern over Church matters—"

"I'm not sure that is quite fair—"

"Or any other matters, so far as that goes. But now I read it on your face. What is it? Does it have anything to do with the murders? Is that it?" Callistus felt a flaring of hope. He didn't want to die without seeing an end to it. And how much longer did he have? He had a terrible fear of his mind losing its edge and beginning to wander, of roving in and out of memories and reality.

"Before I begin, Holiness—"

"Please, Giacomo, cut out the Holiness stuff. We know perfectly well who we are, a couple of battle-scarred veterans." He reached out and patted the cardinal's sleeve. "Now, go on. Talk to me."

"I'm going to speak of something you have time to deal with— something that can serve to cap your works on earth—so forgive me if what I have to say at first seems to have no purpose. We will come to it presently. But it's also important for you to know how I reached my present state of mind. Indulge me, Salvatore. Remember . . . it is you, *il papa,* to whom I speak. Remember who you are and all the weight and grandeur and power of the office you hold."

Callistus settled back in his chair, began to relax and forget the pain that was his constant companion. He had known D'Ambrizzi a very long time and knew what he was in for. They were going back, as if a master hypnotist were at work, back into the history of their Church with D'Ambrizzi serving as the guide. If Callistus was less than certain that it would be an enjoyable journey, he knew that it would be instructive. How it would lead to him, what he might be galvanized to do, he had no idea.

"You have long known of my love for the city of Avignon," D'Ambrizzi said. "I want to talk about Avignon but not that lovely city we both know. Instead, I want you to think with me of the fourteenth century, the removal of the papacy to Avignon. Our world was in tatters then, warring families surrounded us. Imme- diately upon his election in 1303, Benedict XI left Rome, literally fled for his life, wandered a bit, died the following spring in Perugia—not a natural death, let me assure you. Poisoned. A plate of figs, if his biographers are to be believed. Life in the Church was in those days comparatively cheap. Treasure, power, control—so much was at risk. The next conclave took a year. In 1305 Clement V was crowned in Lyons. But he dared not go to war-torn Rome. Instead, he settled in Avignon, driven there by the secular world because the Church had joined the secular battle.

"So, the papacy had passed to the French. It became an instrument of French policy, more secular than it had ever before been—the Church was now truly a political entity. Spiritually the Church had lost its way. Rome was Peter's see and the popes were Peter's successors, but now the Church had turned its back, abandoned Rome. And the Holy City had fallen into decay. It had been plundered and ravished by murderers, smugglers, kidnappers, thieves. The churches were desecrated, the marble and the carvings stolen. By 1350, fifty thousand people a day—pilgrims they were— were arriving to pray at the tomb of St. Peter and found cows grazing on the grass growing in the main apse, the floors covered with dung.

"John XXII, Benedict XII, Clement VI . . . Clement *bought* Avignon for eighty thousand gold florins! He built the Palace of the Popes, and the cardinals filled it and their lavish villas with art and accumulated vast personal fortunes. They were secular princes. . . . When Urban V died, his personal treasury contained two hundred thousand gold florins. The Church was no longer Peter's Church, it had been corroded from within. It was rotting with the lust for riches, with indulgence and decay and secularism; materialism had triumphed! The Church was now living as if there were no eternity, no judgment, no salvation, nothing but the eternal void and the infinite darkness."

The cardinal's voice had sunk to a whisper and he stopped, rested his chin on his chest. Callistus was afraid to speak and break the spell. Where it was all heading he had no idea, but the life of the Church at Avignon seemed to swirl around him. He watched the cardinal stir, reach for a pitcher and goblets on a silver tray. Carefully he poured a glass of water and handed it to Callistus, who wet his lips. The medication tended to dry him out.

"Petrarch," D'Ambrizzi said, returning warmly to his tale, "said Avignon was the fortress of anguish, the dwelling place of wrath, the sink of vice, the sewer of this world, the school of error, the temple of heresy, the false and guilt-ridden Babylon, the forge of lies, the hell of dung."

Callistus murmured, "The Babylonian Captivity."

D'Ambrizzi nodded, his lips dry, his eyes protruding like a frog's. "Petrarch said that Avignon was home to wine, women, song, and priests who cavorted as if all their glory consisted not in Christ but in feasting and unchastity. St. Catherine of Siena said she was assailed by the odors of hell at Avignon. . . ."

"Not that I don't appreciate the history lesson, Giacomo, but I wonder why you are telling me all this tonight?"

"Because time may be short, Holiness," D'Ambrizzi rasped. "And I refer not only to your health. The Babylonian Captivity . . . it's happening all over again. And you, *Papa,* are presiding over a Church that has led itself into captivity. A Church that has gone willingly, eagerly into the sink of vice!" D'Ambrizzi watched the pope's eyes slowly blinking, the dullness gone, now glittering from the bed of wrinkled, dying parchment. "Now it is up to you to lead the Church back to safety . . . and to the service of man and God." He grinned, showing yellowing teeth. "While you still have time, Salvatore."

"I don't understand . . ."

"Let me explain."

The pope swallowed a beta-blocker for his blood pressure. Unaware of the reflexive gesture, he withdrew the Florentine dagger from his pocket, began slowly turning it in his hands. The hands were wrinkled and papery and shook weakly, but his face was alight. When D'Ambrizzi offered a rest period, the dying man brushed the suggestion aside, anger coloring his voice.

"No, no, no, I'm perfectly able to continue. I'll have a long enough rest when I've finished with you, Giacomo."

"All right. Now, for some hard truth, then," D'Ambrizzi continued, his gravelly voice low, the words heavy with emphasis, as if he were sinking them into Callistus's mind. "Our Church is captive again, captive in thrall to the secular world—to the world of men and all the basest desires men, flesh, are heir to. Do you understand what I am saying? Truly understand? We are captives of the right wing dictatorships, of left wing liberation movements, of the CIA and the Mafia and the KGB and the Bulgarian secret police and Propaganda Due and Opus Dei and banks all over the world, of countless foreign intelligence services, of all the selfish interests of the curia, of all the endless investments we have in real estate and

arms manufacturers . . . in sum, we are captive of our own greed
and lust for power, power, power! When I'm asked what the Church
wants, I think back to a time when the answer might have been
complex, requiring judgment and a concept of right and wrong—
but now I know the answer before they ask the question . . . more!
We want more, always more!"

The pope felt a fluttering in his chest and glanced at the oxygen
equipment. It followed him everywhere since his collapse. Now
perhaps it might be useful . . . but the tiny, desperate beating
against the walls of his chest faded. False alarm. He wiped a bubble
of spittle from the corner of his mouth with a handkerchief before
he spoke.

"But, Giacomo, you perhaps more than any other man of your
time have shepherded the Church into this modern secular world,
the *real* world, where we must make our choices, where we must
compete to survive. You, *you* have designed so much of the leverage
we bring to the world's stage . . . in the West and in the communist
bloc, in the emerging nations of the third world. You, Giacomo,
more than any other man, have guided the financial fate of the
Church to these unprecedented heights. It's you who have dealt
with all the great powers in all the most delicate matters. This is all
unarguable. So—what am I to make of what you tell me now?"

A thin smile played on Callistus's parched lips. His face no
longer had color. It was becoming almost translucent, revealing the
skull beneath the skin.

"Call it an old man's hard-earned wisdom, Salvatore, the prod-
uct of spending so much of my life doing what you have just
described. You still have the chance to benefit from what I have
begun to learn now at the end of my career. . . . There is still time.
Therefore, you *must* listen and learn. We have had a sign, Salvatore—the first of my lifetime, a sign to warn us, guide us . . . and
we have ignored its true meaning!" His fist came down with a crash
on the shiny tabletop. Callistus watched with mordant curiosity,
fascinated by D'Ambrizzi's performance.

"The murders," D'Ambrizzi whispered. "I pray that you see it.
The murders—a sign like the cross that appeared to Constantine
engraved on the evening's setting sun. You have the greatest opportunity to shape the Church for good of any of Peter's successors.
You can return the Church to its purpose, its true purpose . . . if

only you recognize the sign, the truth of the murders, the truth *behind* the murders.

"They are not *holy* murders, Salvatore. They are not *Church* murders, not what they have seemed, not what we may have assumed. We have been fools, blind to what we might have seen, shrouded in our own cloaks of self-importance. These murders we have let terrify us are no challenge from within the Church—no matter who is behind them! *They are part of the world we have created for ourselves.*

"They were inevitable because we have handed ourselves to our enemies. . . . They are secular murders because we have become nothing more than another cog in the secular machine . . . and the murders, they are the payment extracted from us by the world. We involve ourselves in unprincipled financial machinations, in crime and politics and the endless accumulation of wealth, and we must pay the price!

"Oh, some may whisper of the *assassini,* but if we believe them, we delude ourselves. We have been blind and the *assassini* is nothing more than a symbol, a tool we have created to scourge ourselves. But you, Holiness, can become the opened eyes of the Church, you can stop it . . . only you. . . ."

"But how, Giacomo? What is it you are telling me I must do?" Callistus, hardly a mystical man, wondered if he just might be in the presence of some kind of maddened, divine messenger or prophet. Was God speaking to him? Was this old man who had once been his mentor somehow possessed of divine inspiration? Callistus had no time for miracles, divine or otherwise. His entire orientation was that of the bureaucrat and how was the bureaucrat supposed to deal with this kind of situation? Still, he had been a pupil of the cardinal's for so many years. . . . The power of D'Ambrizzi's personality was working on him. It lingered still in the old man's fiery shell, like the distillation of spirit, the essence of the man.

"Just remember who you are."

"But who am I, Giacomo?"

"You are *Callistus.* Remember the first Callistus and your mission will be clear. . . ."

"I don't know—"

The immense hand suddenly clamped down on Callistus's arm like a vise.

"Listen to me, Callistus . . . and be strong!"

Sister Elizabeth leaned back in her desk chair, pushed herself away from the desk, and put her feet up on the blotter. The magazine's offices were empty and dark. It was ten past ten, she'd forgotten to have dinner, and her stomach felt as if the coffee had finally burned a hole all the way through to China. Meltdown time. She was holding a cheap ballpoint pen. It was out of ink. She pitched it toward the wastebasket, missed, and heard the pen clatter away into a corner. Perfect. She just couldn't seem to get the hang of the three-point shot.

"Who the hell is Erich Kessler? Why was his name on Val's list?"

She spoke softly, distinctly, dropping the words into the silence with a little shove, as if she hoped to sail them across some troubled waters to the feet of an oracle. She'd done everything but ask a Ouija board or consult a mentalist. If the name of Erich Kessler had appeared anywhere but on a list created by Val, she'd have assumed there was just no such man. But Val was too accurate, too specific. The name meant there was such a man, that he was connected in some way to the others. The fact that no date had followed his name almost surely meant he was still alive, since the dates following the other names had been dates of death. But where the hell was he?

Meltdown. Dead-end time. What to do?

She woke up at midnight, still with her feet on the desk blotter. "This," she said, "is nuts."

She went back to the Via Veneto flat and couldn't sleep. Before she really knew it, it was time for a run and then the day began and she knew she had to make the call.

"Eminence, it's Sister Elizabeth. I'm terribly sorry about interrupting you—"

"Don't be silly, my dear. What can I do for you, Sister?"

"I need to see you, Eminence. I need only fifteen minutes—"

"I see. Well, this afternoon. Four o'clock at my place." He always called the Vatican "my place." Saint Jack.

He was waiting for her alone in his office. He was dressed in full ceremonial regalia. He saw her eyes widen at the sight, and a broad smile broke beneath his great banana nose. "A performance," he explained, "for the tourists. I was, I'm afraid, a stand-in for the Holy Father. Sit down, Sister. What's on your mind?" He opened a carved cigarette box, dug around inside with his stubby fingers, and came up in the end with one of his black cigarettes, slightly the worse for the search. He stuck it on the huge shelf of lower lip and struck a match on his thumbnail.

"It's the murders," she said. "The names of the men on Val's list, the men who we discovered had all been murdered."

"Excuse me, Sister, but we've already had this conversation. Unless there's something new at your end . . ." He shrugged massively, shifting the expanse of finery.

"Look, Eminence, think of Val. Think of how she gave her life, try to put yourself in her place. She really was close to something so important that they had to kill her . . . think of Val—"

"My dear young woman, you needn't instruct me on my feelings about Sister Valentine. I've been close to the Driskill family since before the war when I first met Hugh Driskill. He was in Rome . . . working for the Church . . . we used to go to concerts together. I was introduced to him at a concert. I remember it as if it were yesterday, Sister. Beethoven. Trio number seven. B-flat major. Opus 97. A particular favorite of Hugh's. It was the first thing Hugh and I ever discussed . . . but that's neither here nor there. The point is, I love this family, all of them. But let's admit it, they *are* a headstrong lot. Hugh and his OSS missions, parachuting and God only knows what else. Valentine and her digging around in things that got her killed . . . and Ben, whatever it is he thinks he's doing. I want to find the man who killed her. I am conducting my own investigation, in my own way, and frankly, Sister, I'd like to be left to get on with it. Without having to worry about your being murdered, or Ben Driskill's being murdered. . . . Am I getting through to you at all, Sister? Am I making sense to you? I want you to get entirely out of this thing. You have no business, no right, no reason to pursue it. None. None at all. Look at me, Sister Elizabeth, and tell me that you hear me."

"I hear you," she said softly.

"Ah, I hear a 'but' in your voice. Do I hear a 'but' in your voice, Sister?"

"With respect, Eminence, I don't understand why I have no right to try to finish the work Val had begun. I feel as if I not only have the right, I feel as if I have something a whole lot like an obligation. I . . . I . . . I can't help feeling as I do, Eminence."

"I understand about feelings, Sister. I've even had some in my time. What I don't understand are your actions. Leave this in the hands of others."

"But, Eminence, the others—they're the ones who are killing people! These others of yours are inside the Church—"

"You're guessing, Sister. Leave it. It's a Church matter, leave it inside the Church—"

"How can you say such a thing?"

He smiled at her, lit another cigarette. "Because I wear the red hat, I suppose. That's probably the best reason as far as you're concerned." He looked at his wristwatch.

"I really must be going, Sister." He was standing up, the elaborate costume seeming to slow him down with its weight.

"Erich Kessler," she said. "Who is Erich Kessler?"

D'Ambrizzi stared at her.

"His is the last name on Val's list. The only name without a date of death after it. But there doesn't seem to be such a person. Who is he? Is he the next scheduled victim?"

D'Ambrizzi was watching her through his closed alligator eyes. "I have no idea, Elizabeth. None. Now, please drop it! All of it!" His voice was low, little more than a whisper, but the exclamation points were all in place.

"If Erich Kessler is the next intended victim, then he must know why the others were killed . . . that would mean that Erich Kessler has all the answers." Her hands were shaking and somehow she was on the verge of tears. "I'm going to Paris. Val was there, she was working there."

"Good-bye, Sister."

He swung the door open.

Monsignor Sandanato was sitting at his desk in the anteroom. He looked up. "Sister," he said.

Then she had brushed past and was hurrying down the hallway and to hell with all of them, every damn one of them!

Cardinal D'Ambrizzi turned to Monsignor Sandanato.

"Pietro, have you had any luck looking for Kessler?"

"No, Eminence, not yet. Not an easy man to find, it turns out."

"Well, keep at it, Pietro."

*   *   *

That evening Sister Elizabeth kept a long-standing dinner invitation to join several fellow sisters of the Order. They dined in the grand dining room of the convent, off the very best Wedgwood and the heaviest, oldest silver. The atmosphere was collegial, exactly what her state of frayed nerves required. The candlelight shone in the crystal and the conversation flowed quietly, calmly onward, punctuated by genteel laughter. It was not a life Elizabeth much experienced anymore, nor one she often sought out, but when she found herself in it, caught by its spirit and rhythm, she enjoyed it and remembered one of the reasons that she'd become a nun in the first place. It was a haven from the cacophony of choices the rest of the world insisted on offering, like it or not.

The evening was a wonderment of relaxation, calm civility, gentle yet pointed wit peppered through with irony and sarcasm. These women were not easy on their Church: indeed, they were among its most demanding critics. And so they sat together, in their traditionally elegant black habits—for some, the only time in the month they wore them—and they talked. For Elizabeth the evening and the company added up to proof that there was a world beyond the Vatican and the hissing shadows of the *assassini* and the murders. Proof that there was a world of order and restraint and intelligence without the intolerable pressures operating on, crushing down upon the men who lived their lives within the Apostolic Palace. Sitting with the sisters, listening to the conversation ranging freely across the board, the recounting of experiences and feelings to which she could relate so easily . . . sitting with them she found an uncluttered oasis of peace, so far from calamity and blood and fear.

Sitting in the parlor with the old paintings in their gilt frames, with the aroma of espresso, she thought of Val, how often they'd sat in this room with the sisters drinking coffee after dinner. . . . Poor Val. What would she have done if D'Ambrizzi had given her such peremptory orders? It wasn't an easy question. And what, she wondered, would Ben Driskill have suggested? She bit her lip, tasted salt, forced a smile. Ben would have told her to tell him to go to hell. . . . But in the back of her mind she counted the dead. Finally the evening had drifted to an end and she made her goodbyes. The serenity of these few hours had faded already, as indistinct as a cracked, forgotten childhood photograph.

She arrived back at the tower on the Via Veneto, working at reviving her sense of calm and failing miserably. She still felt the sting of her confrontation with D'Ambrizzi. She had never experienced anything like it before: the flat anger, the disappearance of diplomacy in his style.

Somehow, she told herself, it would all work out, somehow she would see it through.

God, what foolishness! See it through . . . There wasn't a shred of hope anymore!

She undressed and drew a hot bath, sank slowly beneath it, watching the steam condense on the tile walls. She massaged herself with the bubbles, leaned back, luxuriating in the bath oil and the fresh clean smell.

She had left the bathroom door ajar. In a mirror in the hallway she could see the reflection of the night's breeze rippling the curtains by the sliding door leading to the terrace. Her eyes were drifting shut. She glimpsed the wrought iron table, the cloth fluttering. She'd planned to have a friend in a few days before and had made the preparations. Then, at the last minute, they'd gone out. Now she could see the crystal and the candlestick, heavy and silver and gleaming within its glass chimney windbreak. The terrace was lit by the lights from below in the street, from all the reflected lights of the rushing city; they flickered like a handful of jewelry flung at the curtains, clinging . . .

Her tired muscles were relaxing beneath the water. She felt the heat soaking the tension from her, nibbling at her hard edges. She felt herself slipping away and welcomed it, longed to drift off to sleep. . . .

From the edge of sleep she thought she saw something move in the mirror's reflection, a cloud moving across the trace of moon, the shadow of a bird on a sunny day, something moving in the almost darkened flat, a flicker.

Something.

When she looked again there were the curtains drifting in the night, the dull gleam of the candlestick on the glass tabletop.

She watched the mirror. Waiting.

A bat? She was terrified of bats. Had one blundered in from the terrace only to find itself trapped, banging against the walls?

And the shadow shimmered again in the mirror. Almost too

quick to see. A shape like a fleeting memory, out of sight and unidentifiable.

Something.

She felt the hair on her neck tighten, goose flesh rising. Slowly, locking her eyes on the mirror, she rose from the water, reached naked and dripping for her terry-cloth robe, stepped out of the tub, wrapped it around her shivering body. Her knees were shaking and her nipples had tightened with the chill. Her heart fluttered like the bat.

She thought briefly of barricading herself in the bathroom. No, no, she'd be trapping herself. The same was true of the bedroom across the hall. A child could smash through the flimsy door. And something told her it wasn't a bat . . . And it wasn't a child.

There was only one door out of the apartment. If only there were a telephone in the bathroom . . .

My God, she was fantasizing. It was all a question of her nerves, the worry, the *assassini,* the confessions she'd heard from Monsignor Sandanato in this same place, the fear about Ben Driskill and the memories of Val, the confrontation with D'Ambrizzi. It was all nerves.

Light switches? No, they were all in the living room . . . and did she want the lights on? Or not?

Imagination. Shadows? Death?

She moved down the hallway toward the living room. She didn't know what she could do to defend herself, but she didn't want to be trapped in the back of the flat . . . and the kitchen with its knives was all the way across the darkness.

The living room lay in a menagerie of shadows, lumps of furniture, lamps, potted plants, all hiding intruders. Nothing moved. She heard nothing but the breeze on the terrace, the faint street noises. But the shadows were deep and dark.

She went into the room, stood still, listening.

Maybe the mirror had tricked her. The curtains were still drifting softly. The wind was unexpectedly cold, icy.

Surely the room was empty.

She turned to the terrace. The door was still open, nothing had changed. It had been her imagination. The fear that dwelled in the reptilian brain . . .

She moved toward the terrace, slid the door open the rest of the way, hearing the sounds from the street increase. She breathed a deep sigh of relief. She went out onto the terrace. The traffic was thick far below. Crowds moving, pushing. Reality. There was nobody creeping around her flat and the reality was a million tourists and nighthawks staying up late and having a good time. She turned to go back inside.

He was standing in the doorway.

A tall man, motionless, watching her. Eight feet away.

He wore a black cassock like the countless thousands you saw every day in Rome. He stood quietly, as if he expected her to speak. Then his mouth moved, but no sound came.

Why was he giving her time, why hadn't he finished the job in the living room, while her back was turned on the terrace, while she was helpless in the tub? Now she could see him.

He stepped into the light. She saw the whiteness of one terrible eye. She screamed.

Instinctively they both moved at the same moment.

He came toward her and she stepped to the side, grabbed the heavy silver candlestick with the glass chimney.

His hand sank into the soft terry cloth. She yanked away from him, jerked free, and felt her robe pulled open. The eye fixed her unblinking. A dead eye—

Confused, scowling at the sound of her dying scream, distracted by the sudden sight of her nakedness, the man—this priest—stopped grabbing for her, aborted the lunge that would have pinned her against the railing.

In that fractional instant she readied herself for him, and when he came again she drove the candlestick and the glass chimney past his long arms toward the white eye, felt the glass disintegrate and the silver grind on bone.

He gave a muffled cry and she braced herself against the table and rammed her weapon home again, using her entire body to push, and he threw up his hands, the whiteness utterly gone, his face a mask of streaming blood, he groped for her, and she pushed and he staggered back, hit the railing and turned, and she saw that his face was red like a sea of rubies studded with glass like fake diamonds and his mouth was open but no sound was issuing forth . . .

She backed away from him, staring at his agony.

He rose again to face her.

His arms were spread as if pleading . . .

Then he slowly toppled over the railing.

She watched him go, arms out, cassock billowing in the wind, floating, turning slowly, but in the end all she could see was the single terrifying eye like a glowing red flare . . .

PART FOUR

1

DRISKILL

Father Dunn pulled me back to safety as surely as if he'd found me hanging off one of those crumbling cliffs by my fingernails and given me a hand up.

The sight of him coming across the park where the kids played under the watchful gaze of their gossiping mothers, the sight of him swinging along, pipe in the corner of his mouth, representing the real world of sanity, brought me up short, shocked me out of the downward spiral of my feelings about what I'd just done.

I had cracked like an egg freshly laid on a marble slab, I'd cracked and run and there was just no way to make it all right. I had personally led Horstmann to poor Brother Leo and the archivist Brother Padraic, and they had paid for my blundering with their lives. I was as responsible for their deaths as I was for Etienne LeBecq's, yet somehow I was escaping the consequences of my follies. A charmed life but everyone else was dying.

395

The experience of St. Sixtus had worked a humiliating transformation, had left me feeling as if I were a frightened animal, running and thrashing in a blood-spattered maze, unsure of the role I was supposed to play: hunter or prey. Hunter or prey, both would die in the end. There was always another hunter. My mood swings lurched drunkenly between the two and, either way, I'd even lost my gun, for God's sake. My gun, whatever good it might have done me.

If Artie Dunn hadn't shown up when he did, I suppose I'd have nursed myself along the crumbling edges of a nervous breakdown for quite some time. I might even have taken the plunge. I wasn't engulfed in anything as simple as self-pity. I was drowning in flop sweat, choking on my fear. No nightmare—not my mother with her hand reaching out for me, telling me something, not my memories of Val's head with the singed, blood-caked hair—no nightmare could compare with my morning at the beach. I was going to be seeing Leo nailed to that makeshift cross, feet in the air, the surf drowning him, turning him blue and rubbery, for as long as I lived. . . .

But Artie Dunn appeared out of nowhere, right on cue in the land of the leprechaun and, as they used to say in less introspective times, took me out of myself.

We drove my rented car back to Dublin and then took a plane back to Paris and we never stopped talking. It was like a radio game show I used to listen to under the covers, *Can You Top This?* What I heard opened my eyes. I'd had the feeling that I was so utterly alone once I'd left Princeton, like an astronaut left behind on the far side of the moon. Listening to Dunn, I was beginning to realize that the rest of the world had been carrying on without me.

What, I wanted to know, was Artie Dunn doing on the wild coast of Ireland?

Well, he'd gone to Paris looking for Robbie Heywood, news which brought me up short. It turned out that Dunn had known Heywood there at the end of the war when he had arrived as an army chaplain. He'd discovered Heywood was dead and had found himself talking with Clive Paternoster as I had. Paternoster must have begun wondering who'd show up next on the trail of one Driskill or another. Paternoster had told him about my coming through Paris, taking Dunn quite by surprise, and when he heard I'd gone to Ireland and why, he'd put aside what he'd come to Paris for and taken off in search of me. Why? Because Paternoster had told him about my knowing it was Horstmann who'd killed Robbie, told him about my interest in the *assassini*. Dunn figured I was in danger since Horstmann was still on the loose. I congratulated him on the quality of his insight and asked him why he'd come to Europe in the first place, why had he come looking for Robbie Heywood?

"I had to find Erich Kessler," Dunn said. "I thought about it and I kept coming back to Kessler. More than anyone else, he's likely to have the answers. Once I'd read D'Ambrizzi's testament—full of all those damned code names—I knew I'd have to find Kessler, assuming he was still alive."

We were on the road back to Dublin and a rain squall had blown up out of nowhere and the wipers were flipping raggedly across the windshield. There was a concert of Gaelic music on the radio and it made more sense to me than what Father Dunn was saying. Who was Erich Kessler?

"Robbie Heywood," he went on, "was a place to start looking for Kessler. He always seemed to know everything when it came to Catholics—"

"This Kessler is a Catholic?" I began.

"No"—he looked up, surprised—"no, not that I'm aware of—"

"None of this makes sense to me."

"Damn little of it makes any sense to me," he said, "but I'm working on it. We'll get it figured out sooner or later." He smiled reassuringly, but his flat gray eyes, set like stones in the pink cherubic face, were as faraway and remorseless as ever.

"D'Ambrizzi's testament," I said, "and this Kessler—what are you talking about? Next you'll be telling me you know all about the Concordat of the Borgias. . . ."

"The devil I will," he sighed. "We've got a great many blanks to fill in, Ben." He hunched down inside his heavy lined Burberry, pulled his olive-green felt hat down low over his bushy gray eyebrows. The eyebrows looked as though he'd pasted them on, an amateur's disguise. "Can't you do something about the heater in this crate?" He shivered, clapped his gloved hands. "Why don't you tell me your story since leaving Princeton? It'll bring me up to speed and it'll keep you from falling asleep. You look like a man who hasn't slept in weeks."

So I began to talk and I told him about meeting Klaus Richter and the photo on his wall that matched the one Val had left for me in the old toy drum—Richter, LeBecq, D'Ambrizzi, and Torricelli; I told him about Gabrielle LeBecq's story of her father's and Richter's involvement with the art smuggling and the mutual blackmailing of the Church and the Nazis by one another through the years. He interrupted me there with a sharp question.

"Who is the Vatican connection these days?"

"I don't know." What I did know was that he'd asked the question without a moment's hesitation about the subject matter.

I told him about my journey to the monastery in the desert and my conversation with the abbot, how he'd identified Horstmann for me, giving him a name, how Horstmann stayed there at The Inferno and how he got his marching orders from Rome, how that tied Rome and Horstmann to my sister's murder. And I told him how I'd seen Gabrielle's father, Guy LeBecq's brother, a suicide in the desert and I told him how I'd hounded the poor bastard to death, how he'd been so afraid I'd been sent by Rome to kill him, and I told him how Gabrielle and I had looked through his diary and seen his fear written practically in tears and blood, code names . . . all of it.

What will become of us? Where will it all end? In hell!

The code names. *Simon. Gregory. Paul. Christos. Archduke!*

The men in the picture. Richter and D'Ambrizzi remained alive. Was the picture enough to damn D'Ambrizzi's chances in the papal race? What were the four men actually doing? And who took the picture?

He listened intently as I went through all of it, on to Paris and how I'd just missed Heywood's murder and read through the Torricelli papers about Simon and the *assassini* and the "heinous plot," whatever it was, and how Paternoster had gone ahead and told me about Leo, how Leo had been one of *them*. I'd followed so closely in Val's tracks, learned all the same things.

"Which ought to make you just about ripe for the plucking," he said grumpily. "Good thing I found you. You need a protector, my son."

"It was this morning that I needed you."

"I'm too old for that sort of thing. You'll find I'm a far subtler man than that. I'll be there when you *really* need me and no one else will do. Bank on it." He yawned. "It's all quite mystifying. What a pity Leo didn't live to tell you just who Simon actually was.

What a help that would be—might lead us to Archduke, too. But,"
he mused, "they may all be dead and gone by now—" He cleared
his throat like a man with a cold coming on. "Has it occurred to
you, Ben, that someone in all this is lying? That's the problem. We
just don't know who it is. . . . Someone knows all of this, Simon
and all the rest of it, but he's lying to us. . . ."

"You're mistaken there, Father," I said. "They're all Catholics
and they're all lying. But each one is doubtless lying about his own
little patch, lying in his own interest. It's the Catholics, that's all."

"But I'm a Catholic," he said.

"That fact never leaves my mind, Artie."

"Well, you're a cheeky fellow."

"I understand Catholics, no rose-colored glasses. I was a Catholic once—"

"And you still are, dear boy. Deep down, you're one of the
flock. One of us. Always will be." He reached over and patted my
arm. "Just having a little crisis of faith. Not to worry."

"Twenty-five-year crisis of faith," I snorted.

Father Dunn laughed until he started to sneeze. He reached for
his handkerchief again. "Don't you fret. There's plenty of time to
be saved. You'll be fine. Now, before I begin my end of this tale—
you mentioned the Borgias?"

I explained what Brother Leo had told me about the peculiar
document which was, in effect, a kind of history of the *assassini*.
Names, places, the bloody trail through several hundred years of
Church history.

When I finished, he nodded. "Sounds a bit like stage dressing
to me. Probably a nineteenth-century fake to convince somebody
to do something awful." We were almost to the airport and the rain
had stopped and the jetliners seemed to skid past, low overhead.
"Still, it squares with what I know."

"You know about this concordat thing?"

"I read about it in D'Ambrizzi's testament. At least that's what
I'm calling it, his 'testament.' Does it sound too grand?"

"*What is it?*"

"It's what D'Ambrizzi was writing in your father's study while
you and Val were wishing he'd come out and play games." He
pointed at the car rental kiosk where I could return the car. "Let's
get on the plane for Paris, have a couple of drinks, and I'll tell you
about it."

"What the hell do *you* know about it?"

"Keep your shirt on, Ben." He flashed me an impatient glance. "I've read it."

"You've . . . read it . . ." I just sat there looking at him. It was tough, trying to get a handle on Artie Dunn.

D'Ambrizzi, locked up in the study that summer and fall of 1945, with Val and me running around outside making faces at the windows, trying to get him to come out and play, had for reasons of his own been indulging himself in some first-class reflective voyeurism. Maybe he'd wanted to clear his conscience of things he wished he didn't know but couldn't forget. Whatever his reasons, he had obviously felt compelled to put down the story of what he'd seen in Paris during the war. He'd been operating in that foggy gap between the Church and the Nazis and the Resistance: there'd really been no choice, no getting away from it. Attached to Bishop Torricelli's staff, he'd observed everything that was going on and he hadn't known quite what to do about it. So he'd written it all down in the home of his American friend—and what the hell was he doing in Princeton, with Hugh Driskill his pal and savior?—and then he'd disappeared. One morning he'd just not been there anymore and Val and I were left wondering what was going on. The old who-was-that-masked-man thing. But now I learned he'd had time to give the manuscript into the safekeeping of the old padre at the church in New Prudence, where it had lain stuck away and forgotten for forty years. He'd gone to the considerable effort of writing it, then hidden it, and presumably forgotten about it. What was the point? Why couldn't I ever see the point? I kept uncovering things, but they never seemed to give me the answers. Now I had this thing—the story of D'Ambrizzi and his lonely testament—but it only produced a harvest of new questions.

Monsignor D'Ambrizzi had already been on his way up the Vatican ladder when Pope Pius had sent him to work in Paris under Bishop Torricelli as the bishop's liaison to Rome. With the German Occupation came a whole new level of responsibility. Keeping a reasonable peace between Torricelli's force in Paris and the Nazis was a severe test for D'Ambrizzi's diplomatic skills. He worked hard at it and then one day it grew considerably more difficult.

A priest arrived from Rome on a mission from the Holy Father.

He would be a personal aide to Torricelli, but his mission was in fact the darkest secret D'Ambrizzi had ever confronted: he was drawn into it only because Torricelli had been confused and terrified by the new priest's story and had turned in utter confidentiality to D'Ambrizzi.

The new priest, whom D'Ambrizzi in his "memoir" referred to only by the code name *Simon,* had brought a document from the Vatican to establish the validity of what he was to undertake. A letter accompanying the document explained that it was the secret historical record or register of the Church's *assassini*—the Church's trusted killers, those the popes had used for centuries, dating back to the Renaissance and before. The document was known by the name it acquired when one of the greatest Italian houses produced a pope and reaffirmed the relationship with a cadre of killers drawn both from within and from outside the Church . . . the Concordat of the Borgias. It was, in effect, the license conferred by the popes to those who killed on papal orders for the good of the Church. It listed many of the names of ancient *assassini,* the names of the monasteries where they could take refuge in times of crisis (crises in which they'd frequently played an instigatory role, no doubt); and it had been updated as recently as the 1920s and 1930s when the Church was busy allying itself with Mussolini and serving as one of the central sources throughout the world for Italian Fascist spying and intelligence gathering.

The accompanying letter, bearing the papal seal, instructed Torricelli to re-form the *assassini* and use it to maintain a good relationship with both the Nazis, primarily, and the Resistance. The *assassini* was also intended to serve as a useful tool in accumulating certain plunder—treasure of various kinds, art objects, paintings, and so on—for the Church, in exchange for services rendered to the forces of occupation.

D'Ambrizzi wrote that he watched Torricelli's nervous compliance as Simon carried out the commission for both of them, watched as Simon recruited *assassini,* watched as Simon became increasingly disgusted—he loathed everything the Nazis stood for, everything they required him to do. D'Ambrizzi watched as Simon became increasingly aware of Pope Pius's sympathies for the Nazi cause, his hostility toward the Jews and all other victims of the Nazis, and his refusal to speak out with all the moral power his position conferred upon him against the satanic tyranny ravaging humanity. Inevitably Simon took control of the *assassini* himself, while Torricelli relievedly looked the other way. Simon cut the linkage between the *assassini* and Torricelli. In so doing, Simon cut the linkage between the *assassini* and Pius himself, between the *assassini* and the Church in any form. The priests and monks and laymen who'd taken up the cause for the good of the Church— they became Simon's personal army, to be used as he saw fit.

It was then that Simon Verginius turned them into a tough anti-Nazi group, only infrequently carrying out any Nazi requests whatsoever. Instead of their original aims, the *assassini* began killing Nazi sympathizers and informers within the clergy and working to hide Jews and Resistance fighters in churches and monasteries.

When the Nazis came to Bishop Torricelli with a direct order, backed by their typical ominous silkiness, to kill a priest who was causing the Occupation considerable grief, Simon and Torricelli came into open conflict. And Torricelli had to admit to himself that Simon was working and plotting against his and the Church's orders.

At about the same time, Torricelli somehow discovered that Simon was planning the assassination of a very important man. There was only one way so far as Simon knew that Torricelli could have discovered the plot. There had to be a traitor among the *assassini:* one of his trusted cadre had betrayed them.

Simon attempted to carry out the assassination: he had no choice, the timetable was exact, and the killing could not be postponed. The man was coming to Paris on a special private train routed through the Alps. Everything was ready. As it happened, the Germans had been alerted and they were ready, too. D'Ambrizzi's story of the disastrous attempted assassination was sketchy. Several of Simon's team were killed, the others escaped back to Paris, where Simon set about learning who had betrayed them.

Torricelli frantically convinced him that he hadn't done so wicked a thing, no matter how much he disapproved of the plot. Eventually Simon tracked the man down—he was the priest Leo had told me about in the frozen graveyard, LeBecq—and killed him. He disbanded the *assassini* at about this time because, D'Ambrizzi wrote, an investigator was rumored to be on his way from Rome. So far as D'Ambrizzi knew, Simon's final act as leader of the *assassini* was to dispatch one or two of his men north to Ireland, to the monastery of St. Sixtus, with the Concordat of the Borgias.

* * *

We were having an after-dinner cognac in the first-class cabin of the 727 when Father Dunn reached that point in the story of D'Ambrizzi's extraordinary memoir. Two questions stuck in my mind, lodged in among the welter of facts that seemed on the face of it to confirm everything Brother Leo had told me.

Who was on that train? Whose life was saved by the traitor Christos—or Father Guy LeBecq, as I knew him to be?

And, secondly, I had to wonder why D'Ambrizzi had committed the whole story to paper. Had it been another man I might also have been more curious as to how he could have come to know so much about the *assassini*. But that wasn't the case with D'Ambrizzi: he was so involved a man, so alert: he was there, therefore I understood how he could know so much. But what was the idea behind writing it down and then leaving it behind, forgotten?

I was amazed by the existence of D'Ambrizzi's testament at all, but I had to point out that it really didn't add much to what Brother Leo had told me, nor to what I'd learned from Gabrielle LeBecq. I didn't mean to put a damper on Father Dunn's revelations, but it was true. All it really did add was the fact that D'Ambrizzi had been able to observe the implementation of Pius's plot—to activate the *assassini*.

Dunn heard me out, then cocked his head and gave me one of his long, out-from-under-the-eyebrows looks.

"Listen up, Sunny Jim. Did I say I was done?"

D'Ambrizzi watched and waited as the drama pitting the Nazis and the Vatican against the renegade *assassini* played itself out. Spring turned to summer of 1944 and in August, Paris was liberated by the Allies and the German occupiers were gone, though the war itself was far from over. Life in the city was chaotic. Necessities were in short supply and a virulent bitterness ran like an epidemic through the population. Those who had collaborated with the enemy occupiers lived in fear of reprisals from vigilante groups bent on revenge. Murder invaded the precincts of Paris and would not be dislodged until its work was done. It was in this atmosphere that the Vatican's man continued his investigation into the murder of Father Guy LeBecq, the disobedience of Simon's army of killers, the attempt to assassinate the man on the train—that is, the manner in which the *assassini* betrayed the mission entrusted to it by the Holy Father.

The Vatican investigator, who came undercover and reported only to Bishop Torricelli (who must, we surmised, have confided to D'Ambrizzi) was a hard-edged, tough-minded, emotionless monsignor whom, D'Ambrizzi wrote, came to be known as "the Collector," presumably because of his policeman's mentality, intent on collecting evidence. In D'Ambrizzi's view, the Collector was no different from the *assassini* themselves, except that he was representing the Holy Father's disgust with their refusal to serve the Nazis. The contempt and scorn with which D'Ambrizzi treated the Collector, at least in his memoir, was deeply felt. Or so Dunn, who'd actually read the papers, told me.

For months the Collector interviewed everyone who had known Father LeBecq, asking his questions openly, by day, as it were; in the dark hours, in secrecy, he dug away at the nether world of people who knew, or might have had hints, of the *assassini* and their plot to kill the man on the train.

Simon proved a tough nut to crack, refusing to admit any knowledge whatsoever of the plot, and managing to slide away from that part of the investigation dealing with Vatican orders to work with the Nazis during the Occupation. The Collector pressed on and D'Ambrizzi could see him drawing the noose around Simon's neck. The Holy Father wasn't giving up, wasn't recalling the Collector and writing it off as something he'd have to accept.

D'Ambrizzi himself, because he knew so much about the *assassini* activities through his working relationship with Torricelli, was not immune to the Collector's attentions. A dozen times or more he was called in for sessions that lasted as long as six hours on occasion, going back and forth over the details of the war years in Paris. Along toward the late spring of 1945 it dawned on D'Ambrizzi that the Collector was under a great deal of pressure from the Vatican—the Holy Father—to find the killer of LeBecq as well as those who had planned the assassination of the man on the train. A scapegoat, if necessary, someone to frame. Then there would be the trip back to Rome, to God only knew what fate.

Simon simply disappeared, as if by magic, a puff of smoke, a conjuror's best trick. D'Ambrizzi never saw him again.

Thwarted, the Collector began casting long, hungry glances at Bishop Torricelli himself, who had been, after all, put in charge of the *assassini* by the Holy Father when Simon was sent from Rome. D'Ambrizzi knew the bishop was as crafty an old clerical veteran as you could imagine, crafty and suspicious with an almost superhuman ability to withdraw into his shell and ride out any storm, unharmed. And he wouldn't be overly concerned about *how* he saved himself, *who* had to pay the price.

D'Ambrizzi realized that when Torricelli began to look around for a patsy to take the fall, to satisfy the insistent yelping the Collector was hearing from Rome, he was bound to see his faithful aide-de-camp . . . D'Ambrizzi. Who had been his confidant, to whom he had revealed so many of his fears about the use of the *assassini* in contravention of Vatican wishes. D'Ambrizzi, the perfect fall guy.

So D'Ambrizzi made his own move before Torricelli could hand him over to the Collector.

He turned to an American intelligence officer the evening of the day he'd received the summons to return to Rome for "reassignment." It was, he reflected in his manuscript, like being called back to Moscow. A wise man knew better than to make that return trip. The American was an old friend who'd been in and out of Paris during the German Occupation: a man he could trust as well as a man with connections. With his help—D'Ambrizzi told the story in some detail—he was able to drop out of sight, escape the Collector's clutches. Like Simon, he disappeared, with the Collector sniffing the air like a prize hound, momentarily confused but not quite prepared to give up.

D'Ambrizzi's American friend got him out of postwar Europe with the identity of a dead priest and brought him back to Princeton, New Jersey.

His American friend was, of course, Hugh Driskill.

And in Princeton, Monsignor D'Ambrizzi set down his story.

When Father Dunn finished D'Ambrizzi's tale I sat mulling it over, trying to determine if it added up to anything more than an interesting sidebar to the main story as I saw it. The story was twisting and thrashing in my hand like a frantic living thing, as if it were still trying to mislead and maim, all to retain its mystery.

But it was clear that Cardinal D'Ambrizzi had a great many answers. How one could get him to dig up the past—particularly one in which the Church was using a team of killers sent to aid the Nazis—and relive it with names rather than code names was a hell of a question.

But it did strike me that we now knew from two independent sources, possibly three if a second hand one such as Gabrielle could be counted, a story about Paris which the Church would surely wish to keep quiet. And Val had found out about it.

Was there more? Was this enough to kill and die for?

And who were these people?

The Collector?

The man on the train?

What really happened to Simon?

And why had there been no mention of the shadowiest figure of them all . . . Archduke? He was important enough for Etienne LeBecq to have put that exclamation point after his name . . . important enough for Torricelli to turn to in the time of his greatest crisis. . . .

D'Ambrizzi had missed so little. But he had missed the shadowy one—

Archduke.

Paris was suddenly glowing brightly far below, and we were sinking swiftly toward it.

The next morning we found an outdoor café looking at Notre Dame and sat in rattan chairs at a glass-topped table with a Cinzano awning flapping overhead. It was a bright blue morning and warm for mid-November but the day seemed poised on the edge of danger, mirroring our own situation. High white clouds, stacked and folded back upon themselves, loomed like a mountain range behind the great cathedral. The glare of sunshine picked out the faces of the gargoyles grinning down on the rest of the world.

We breakfasted on soft omelettes damp and rich with butter and herbs and cheese. The café au lait was rich and sweet, and I leaned back to survey the peaceful scene while Father Dunn grunted occasionally from behind the morning's *Herald-Tribune*. I was glad for the quiet, the moment's respite. I couldn't quite believe that the previous morning, little more than twenty-four hours before, I was staring breathless and terrified at the dead figure of Brother Leo crucified in the surf and beckoning to me, arm flapping, and I was running for my life with a fiend, real or imagined, at my heels. At the thought, which had surfaced during the night like a beast rising from the muck, my heart would seem to freeze, the piston rods seizing up, refusing to beat.

Finally Father Dunn lowered the newspaper and methodically folded it. He blew his nose. "My cold is worse and I've picked up a sore throat. Did you sleep well?"

"Better than the night before. If I don't come down with pneumonia, it'll be a miracle."

"Suck one of these." He handed me a tin of raspberry pastilles. I popped one into my mouth. It was not perhaps the perfect accompaniment for café au lait.

"So, who is Erich Kessler?"

The morning had slipped away while we sat quietly. The breeze off the Seine was quickening, had grown sharper and colder in the past hour.

Dunn regarded me across his coffee.

"What makes him so important?" I asked.

"Ah, Erich Kessler . . . he was always the secret man. He knew the secrets, he kept the secrets, he was a secret. He was the boy genius of German intelligence during World War Two."

I hadn't expected anything like that, but what had I expected? What made him fit into the puzzle? "A Nazi?"

"Oh, I have no idea. His loyalty was surely to himself, first, last, always. But he was the whiz kid of what came to be known wherever the spooks gathered as the Gehlen Org. He was the personal protégé of General Reinhard Gehlen, the master spy." He looked at me, letting it sink in. "Gehlen served Hitler, the OSS, the CIA, and the West German Republic, in sequence. One very clever, slippery, opportunistic fellow—and Kessler learned his lessons well." Dunn waved to the waiter for more coffee, then warmed his hands on the cup.

"What happened to him?"

"Well, he was a survivor, that's certain. Like Gehlen, young Kessler foresaw how the war was bound to end. He saw it all laid out before him in the maps and in the charts of the enemy manufacturing and manpower estimates and petroleum production—he saw it as early as 1942 when Pearl Harbor still had America feeling around in the dark for its shoes. From '42 onward he knew the war was nothing but an ego trip for Hitler . . . a monument to psychopathology. Well, Erich was sure of one thing— Hitler's big finish wasn't going to take him down, too. So he made sure he was going to survive. All his intelligence expertise was aimed at getting him through the coming apocalypse. . . ."

Working with cunning and extreme discretion, he arranged a contact with the allied intelligence networks in France and Switzerland, deciding against the British or the French, both of whom were taking this Hitler war with considerable bad grace and might choose to be rough on one such as himself, and settling on the Americans. Through an old boyhood friend he sought out an OSS operative, one of Wild Bill Donovan's cowboys, as Gehlen called them. The OSS man accepted the legitimacy of Kessler's proposal, became his case officer.

From 1943 on, Kessler, working through the American, fed information about German intelligence capabilities and findings to the Allies; of even more interest, as the war wound inexorably toward its conclusion, was his expert information about the Russians, who were in fact very secretive in dealing with their allies: Kessler's American contact knew even in '43 that the godless commie bastards were the real enemy, knew that what the postwar world would require was massive intelligence about the East. Thus Kessler spent much of the war providing for his future, as did Gehlen, who himself became the preeminent intelligence expert on the Russians in the postwar world and served the CIA with distinction.

Once the war actually ended, Kessler became a deep-cover American agent, a rover moving easily throughout Europe. What set him apart from other German agents sucked up and put back to work by the victors was his special area of quite eccentric expertise: the Catholic Church. It was widely believed that he knew as much about the activities of the Church during the war years as any man alive. His files on the Church, known in some circles as the Kessler Codex, probably because it sounded like something in a movie, were the cause of a good deal of strife between the Vatican and the Americans. Kessler kept them safe in a Swiss bank vault, carefully reduced to microfilm and smuggled into Zurich in ladies' lingerie by a commercial traveler. There they remained for several years until he finally put them up for sale. Inevitably the Church was the highest bidder: they *had* to have them, while the Americans merely wanted them.

And shortly after the Vatican had acquired the files, Kessler's Maserati was forced off the Grand Corniche between Nice and Monaco. Only a miracle saved his life. Who had tried to kill him?

The Vatican, who simply wanted to ensure his permanent silence? Or the CIA, who had pretty well used him up and were pissed off at him for selling the stuff to the Vatican? Kessler was never quite sure. But he did deeply regret the fact that for some inexplicable reason he hadn't made an insurance copy of the codex for himself. Thinking about it later on, he'd have given himself a good swift kick in the hindquarters but the irony was that that was no longer possible.

The automobile "accident" had left him crippled, wheelchair-bound for the rest of his life. He spent over a year in a French hospital. Then he went to live in Brazil, trying to lose himself in Rio; then to Buenos Aires, where there were so many old Nazis living on the lam, as it were, that he grew intolerably depressed with all that talk of a Fourth Reich and the Teutonic Knights rising again. From there he went to Brisbane, Australia, but he felt as if he were visiting the moon. Then came a time in Japan.

He was, however, protecting himself. Each time he moved, he seemed to be moving more deeply into the haze of the past, becoming more of a legend, a colorful memory, losing his definition as time furled itself around him like a highwayman's cloak. But there were still people who would have preferred him rounded up and shot. Even they finally lost track of him, though it was said they were bound forever to keep looking for him. Maybe they believed that the stories of their determination to find and silence him were enough to keep him forever crouched in his hole. . . .

"I ran into him in Paris after the war," Dunn said, pushing another raspberry pastille around with his tongue. He pulled his scarf tighter around his throat and slipped into his double-breasted Burberry trench coat. The clouds had nearly obscured the morning sunshine. Notre Dame was looking gloomy all of a sudden, not so soaring. "It was hard not to if you moved about. He was ubiquitous. I'd see him, we'd have a few drinks. He intrigued me, he'd had an interesting look at the war, though you had to piece the little clues together to get anything like a picture. He took a liking to me, this irreverent priest, just a smart-ass kid really, and I struck him as a guy who couldn't take the posturing of the Vatican all that seriously. And I wasn't afraid to say so—so you might say I amused him. And I don't flatter myself into thinking *I* was picking *his* brains . . . it was Erich's game, he picked me clean as a Christmas turkey on the subject of the Church. In any case, I eventually lost track of him.

But he was the sort of fellow who was hard to forget . . . he stuck
in the mind, so I picked up passing references to him as time went
by. He was, after all, of particular interest to Catholics. The last I
heard, someone said he was coming back to Europe . . . then I read
the D'Ambrizzi manuscript, all of the *assassini* stuff, hot stuff the
Church would definitely kill for if it meant keeping it from coming
out, and I began to put the story together, Val and Lockhardt and
Heffernan dead, a priest the killer, at least so far as we could tell
. . . it didn't take a genius to make these connections, but what
stopped me in my tracks was the remarkable connection between
two entirely different eras divided by forty years. And the one
person I wanted to talk to about the old days was Erich Kessler. He
knew the most and he wasn't a priest, he wasn't a Catholic, he had
no ax to grind in keeping it all a secret . . . in fact he had a damn
good reason to want to stick it to the Church as hard and deep as
he could, if he believed they'd crippled him while trying to kill
him.

"But how the hell was I going to find him?

"Well, I'd heard the rumors about his coming back to Europe,
about his health deteriorating. Was it true? Or was it some kind of
disinformation campaign? That would, I had to admit, be just like
him. Well, I figured that the Vicar, Robbie Heywood, was as likely
to have a line on Kessler as anyone. So I came to Paris and I got a
hellish shock . . . the killer priest had finished off the Vicar . . . *and*
. . . and you'd been here before me. You could have knocked me
over with a shamrock. It was all getting worse and worse, there was
no hiding from murder . . . but God in His infinite wisdom had
spared old Clive Paternoster, who had known most of what Robbie
knew. I put Clive on the hunt for Kessler while I went in search of
you. . . . Laddie, I've never been so scared in my life—I just *knew* I
was going to find your bloody corpse in Ireland. . . ."

Rain had begun to fall. The glorious day had been an illusion,
had lost its promise. Reality had descended on Paris like the cap on
the parrot's cage. The city had grown muffled, subdued.

We walked along the Seine, stopping to leaf through picture
books and folios of old dog-eared prints and reproductions in the
open-air stalls. Rain was pattering in the orange and brown leaves,
dimpling the surface of the river.

We were waiting.

We stopped someplace anonymous for *pommes frites* that led to a *croque-monsieur* and Fischer beers. In the welter of narrow streets behind the huge Gibert Jeune bookstore serving the Sorbonne students we stopped to stare into the window of a toy shop. Featured there was what appeared to be a Smith and Wesson Police Special. Father Dunn exhibited some familiarity with whatever it was. I remember thinking how real it looked, not at all like a toy. You could almost smell through the pane of glass the linseed oil or whatever it is they use for packing weapons.

Dunn pointed at the toy gun. "Incredible, isn't it? Fellow could hold up a bank with one of those."

"I suppose so. Dillinger broke out of the Greencastle, Indiana, jail with a gun he carved and stained with shoe polish. People will believe anything."

"Yes, I suppose they will."

"Of course they will," I said. "You wouldn't have a job, Father, if it were otherwise. The Church proves the point."

"You are a cheeky shit, Ben."

"You sound like my father. And I'll tell you what I've told him. It takes one to know one."

"You say you lost your gun back there. Up north."

I nodded.

"This is all a tricky business."

"I know. People are lying. Everybody's lying. All I seem to know is that Horstmann isn't Simon. I'd thought he was."

"Tricky. Man ought to have a gun in a pinch."

It was all a game. We were playing a game to pass the time.

"Frankly, Ben, I think we should arm ourselves. What do you think?"

"I'd hate to depend on that gun," I said, nodding toward the window.

"Perfectly good gun, it seems to me. Can't hurt yourself with it."

"Perfectly good until you have to hurt someone else with it."

"Good Lord, no good ever came from firing a gun."

"Nonsense. There's an old saying, Father. Never draw your gun unless you intend to fire it. Never fire it unless you intend to put a man in his grave."

"You just made that up, Driskill."

"Famous saying. I'm sure of that."

"Sounds like Billy the Kid, then."

"Yes. Probably was Billy the Kid, now that you mention it. Yes, I'm sure it was."

"Bill Bonny."

"Right. William Bonny."

"Well, he was full of bilge and died very, very young."

"He'd have died much younger if he'd carried a cap pistol, Father."

"Nonetheless, Ben." He pushed open the door of the toy shop.

In the store he spoke passable French to the young shopgirl.

"We'll have two of those," he said, pointing to the display case.

"The revolvers?" she said in English.

He nodded. "Two of them."

"Do you wish a box of caps, too?"

"Oh, we don't want to actually fire them. Do we, Driskill?"

"I certainly don't."

"There you are," he said to the girl. "Just the guns. No ammunition." He smiled at that.

When we left the shop the rain had thickened. He handed me my toy gun. "Put it in your pocket. Just in case." He winked at me. I stuffed the gun into my raincoat pocket. "Now. Don't you feel better?"

"You baffle me," I muttered.

He put his hand into the trench coat pocket and squeezed the butt. A childlike grin spread across his pink face. He was smoking his pipe and had it upside down so the rain wouldn't enter the bowl. "The gun-toting padre. Suits me. Perhaps I'm the stuff of legend after all."

"It's a plastic toy."

"Well, it's all illusion and reality. We're just blurring the line a little." He glanced at his watch. "Four o'clock. Time to go see Clive."

The Peugeot taxi labored grumpily up the hill to the Place de la Contrescarpe. The rain was puddling in the square and the tramps had their fire going as they'd had a few days before. The lights of Tabbycats shone warmly through the window, like reflections of polished brass.

Clive Paternoster had settled into the table by the window. His glasses balanced precariously on his mole's nose which he was

blowing violently. It was the season for colds. His grubby old mac
hung on a hook by the window, and he got halfway out of his
chair, welcoming us.

We had cognacs all around. The two of them puffed their pipes,
filling the window cubbyhole with the woodsy, smoky fug.

"So, you found him in Ireland," Paternoster said to Father
Dunn.

"Brought him back alive," Dunn said.

"Tell me, did you find Brother Leo? Is he well?"

"Oh, yes," I said. "I found him." I paused, suddenly unprepared
to answer the most obvious possible question. "He's fine," I said at
last. "He's just fine." The lie came from a newfound protectiveness
I felt about Paternoster. I didn't want to draw him into the circle
any further.

"Well," Father Dunn said, "did you have any luck at this end?"

"It's magic sometimes, I reckon." Paternoster looked around
proudly, from Dunn's face to mine and back again. "Maybe I haven't
lost the old touch yet. The Vicar would have been proud of me. I
lit up the old network like a pinball machine. No, no, don't worry—
most discreet men in the world. I gave them a story, put all the
scraps together . . . yes, Father, in short, I know where Erich Kessler
is."

"Good work, my friend. The jackpot." Dunn's Irish eyes were
smiling. "Now, what's the story?"

"I know where he is and . . . I know *who* he has become."

Erich Kessler had taken the name *Ambrose Calder*.

He was living near Avignon.

He would see us because he remembered Artie Dunn.

He gave specific instructions on what we were to do.

Ambrose Calder wasn't taking any chances.

Father Dunn had had an idea back in New York that Curtis
Lockhardt might have kept a flat or house in Paris, that he might
have given the use of it to Val while she'd been working in Europe.
I don't know why it hadn't occurred to me: I'd assumed she must
have bedded down at the Order's Paris installation. Fortunately
Dunn had contacted Lockhardt's New York office, explained the
situation as persuasively as possible, and they had kindly arranged
for Dunn to pick up a key to a Paris address. The address, not
surprisingly considering Lockhardt's tastes, was as prestigious and

pricey as they come: just off the rue du Faubourg-St.-Honoré, a stone's throw, more or less, from the Elysée Palace, where the president of France lives, the American embassy, and the nearly incomparable Bristol. Long ago my father had had a falling-out with the management of the Bristol and we had switched our patronage to the George V; I'd always had a certain warm place in my heart for the Bristol, a hotel that could lose my father's business and totter on uncaring.

We didn't know if Val had ever used the place, but with key in hand we took a taxi through the rainy gloom across the river. It pulled over not far from the intersection with the rue La Boétie. I remembered an odd moment from the past: Bishop Torricelli had taken Val and me to number 19 rue La Boétie and introduced us to croissants. We had thought they were about as delicious as anything could be, buttery with fruit preserves slathered this way and that. We'd eaten them day after day, and had our first cups of café au lait, settled on just the proper color it should be, and the bishop had peered down his Shylockian nose and told us how a famous writer had, at the age of thirteen, consumed the croissants from number 19 as eagerly as we had, long ago. I had pursued the story, assuming it was some Frenchman I'd never heard of. It had been 1856 and 1857 when the boy had developed his taste for croissants and he hadn't been a Frenchman after all but an American I vowed to read later on. And I did. Henry James. Number 19 rue La Boétie. Croissants. It all came back to me in a flash, getting out of the taxi, turning my collar up against the rain and wind, seeing the street sign. Remembering a summer's day, the bishop, the croissants and the coffee and my little sister in a pink dress with a pale green bow at the back and a pink hat with a bow to match and now it was thirty-odd years later and she was dead and I was following her last footsteps and they were probably still selling the perfect croissants at number 19 and I'd given up on Henry James when I'd bogged down in the middle of *The Golden Bowl*. I missed my sister, that was the absolute hell of it. No more croissants with Val.

It was a quiet, gray building exuding dignity and money. The gated iron doorway should have guarded a crown prince at the very least, or secrets beyond price. The building looked impervious to change, death, and taxes. But of course Lockhardt was dead and Val was dead and maybe she had used the building.

There was a concierge's office and Dunn went in briefly after we'd let ourselves in the front door. He came back humming to himself and we ascended to the top floor in the rickety wire cage. The central core of stairway wound narrowly around the elevator. You could see the cables through the open grating of the floor. "Penthouse," Dunn said.

We stepped out of the elevator. There were flowers on an occasional table, thick gray carpets, a large mirror. Very subdued. Lockhardt's apartment was one of two on the floor.

Inexplicably, the door to his apartment stood six inches open. Dunn glanced at me and shrugged, put his forefinger to his lips. I pushed the door all the way open and led the way inside.

There was a cool breeze in the hallway, and you could hear and smell the rain. There was a window open somewhere. There was a faint gray light coming from a doorway all the way across the width of an elegant living room with chandelier, a rococo fireplace, gilt-framed mirrors, some understated drawings, low furniture covered in dropcloths. Halfway across the room I stopped and listened.

Someone was crying, low-pitched, deep sobbing. It was a haunting, incredibly sorrowful sound, matching the soft, insistent throb and drip of the rain on the roof and running from the eaves. Through the fog outside, through the darkness, I could just pick out the blurred lights on the Eiffel Tower.

Then I was standing in the doorway, looking into the small study where the windows were thrown open. A dim light was on in the corner and the curtains were twisting in the wind. Someone was sitting behind the desk, head in hands, quietly sniffling, oblivious.

I must have made some slight sound, because the face turned up to look at me. It wasn't a quick, frightened movement but slow, as if nothing really mattered.

For a moment I thought I was having a bizarre hallucination, the face was so unexpected.

It was Sister Elizabeth.

How can I explain the conflict of emotions that flashed past me in the instant of recognition? I had thought about her so frequently since I'd last seen her, had at times summoned up memories of her and at others willed them not to come. Now here she was at the least expected moment and the emotional range she'd put me through back in Princeton was replicated in a matter of seconds,

THOMAS GIFFORD

delight and warmth and affection giving way like quicksand to the plunge into the harsher realities of our parting.

She was wearing the suit the Order favored, and her long, tawny hair was held back with clips, revealing the width of her forehead, the wide, straight eyebrows, the wide-set eyes that I knew were green. The raincoat was thrown across the corner of the desk which was otherwise bare. Her face was streaked with tears.

I might so easily have relaxed my grip, gone to her, put my arms around her, held her regardless of who or what she was . . . *what she was,* that was the blade turning. . . . She was so desperately beautiful, so sad, and then her face drew itself together and she wiped her eyes with her knuckles like a little girl and she saw me and she smiled at me, the happiness on her face so palpable, so powerful in its emotional impact—I wanted to reach for her but I knew that if I did I would be utterly, irrevocably lost. She was as dead to me as Val. My whole life, all that I learned, was the proof.

I was staring at her when Artie Dunn came in, sized up the situation, said, "Faith and begorra, what next?"

Father Dunn was just the sort of priest who would know a perfect little restaurant nearby, this one in the rue St.-Philippe-du-Roule a little over a block's walk away. It was dark and heavily beamed and firelight threw shadows helter-skelter everywhere. The smell of garlic and full-flavored wine-scented sauces hit you right away. The baguettes were warm and fresh, the *vin du pays* full of character and vigor. It woke me up, wandered to my brain in record time, and coaxed me out of the surprise and discomfort I'd felt upon discovering Sister Elizabeth.

She said she hadn't eaten all day and looked as if she hadn't slept in a week. Her face had lost its pink-cheeked look of health, and her eyes were hollowed, red-rimmed. Neither she nor I spoke much in the immediate aftermath of our meeting, so Dunn carried the brunt of the conversation. It didn't seem to bother him. He herded us to the restaurant, got us seated, ordered and approved the wine, and set the agenda for what turned into a long evening's discussion. He suggested that she should tell us what brought her to Paris and so she did, though the story came in fits and starts and was punctuated by food: crusty onion soup, pleurote mushrooms with garlic, pâté thick with garlic and green pistachios, sweet butter, beef stew which was their own speciality, two and a half bottles of wine. The meal would have been memorable if the story had not been unforgettable.

As it was, I kept struggling to keep the pieces in place, kept trying to fit them into what I'd discovered. It was like trying to keep a delicately balanced kaleidoscope from shifting and creating a new pattern. But it did keep shifting and I had to keep refitting it into my own patterns. She was becoming the old Elizabeth, eating like a farmhand, getting her strength back, and I had to struggle to keep my heart from going out to her. That night in Paris she was everything I'd fallen in love with in Princeton and I had to hold all my feelings in check. The one thing I couldn't let her see was a hint of how I felt. Then, of course, I would be at the mercy of the nun. Behind that facade lived the Church.

Her story took a certain chronological form in my mind. It began with her finding the names of the five murder victims Val had listed in the folder. Claude Gilbert. Sebastien Arroyo. Hans Ludwig Mueller. Pryce Badell-Fowler. Geoffrey Strachan. All dead, all with a connection to Paris either during or after the war, and all involved in one way or another with the Church. And all of them important for some reason to Val.

Elizabeth had followed Val's footsteps and, like Val, had discovered the existence of the *assassini*. And she had pursued them through the centuries, as far as the rise of Mussolini in the 1920s. She had made a pretty sound connection to World War II with the five victims and their murders. Anybody could have poked holes in the theory, but they'd have run into murders and documents and circumstances that fairly begged to be linked. It simply made sense except for one blank: what motivated the murders so many years after the events of the war years?

Elizabeth nodded when I raised the question, and said that was the objection D'Ambrizzi and Sandanato had raised.

"And what kind of answer did you have for them?"

"Isn't it pretty obvious? What's happening in the Church worth killing for? What's the big prize? The election of a successor to Callistus . . ."

"But what had these five victims to do with a new pope?" Dunn smiled at her kindly.

"Look, I didn't say I had the answers." She was full of impatience. "I'm raising some questions that need answering—you're nowhere if you don't have the right questions. Val used to say that, over and over. It's all in the questions, she'd say. And I want to get back to Val's list. There was a sixth name on that list. And he doesn't seem to exist. We can't find anything about him. But there was no date of death following his name. Did Val think he was dead? Or did she think he was the next to die? Erich Kessler. His name is Erich Kessler—"

"You are kidding!" It just popped out of me. I looked at Dunn. "How in the name of God could Val have found out about him?"

"All that matters," Dunn said, "is that she did." He looked up at us from his wine. "I mean, you can understand why they'd want to kill him, too. Hell, Ben, he probably knows everything. . . ."

"Wait a minute—you know who he *is*!" Elizabeth's spirit was back. She gave us an exasperated look. "Well? *Who?*"

That's the way the evening went, our stories interlocking, and getting out of hand until Dunn would step in and pull it all back together again. But the articulated structure rising before us was worth the trouble, worth the interruptions and the leaps of imagination back and forth through time.

I told her we had to get through her story as best we could before we got to mine, and she grudgingly went along. She was just as she'd been back at the kitchen table in Princeton in the middle of the night, alive and determined and full of the excitement of discovery. It sounds sappy, but in the midst of the nightmare we were suddenly having a good time.

She had taken her findings to D'Ambrizzi, and his faithful shadow minister, Sandanato, had told them the whole story because the cardinal was the man in the Church Val had respected most and loved, the man she'd known the longest, since childhood. And—anger flashed in her green cat's eyes—they had refused to take her seriously, had refused to admit the idea of the *assassini* was anything more than an old anti-Catholic bogeyman. She tried not just once, but twice, and D'Ambrizzi had lost patience with her. Furious, she had decided to come to Paris. She had thought of the apartment Val must have used there . . . but then, everything had changed a few nights before. Then D'Ambrizzi had had to take her seriously.

I said, "And what so momentous happened a few nights ago?"

But Dunn interrupted. Wait. He wanted to know more about what D'Ambrizzi had said about this mythical beast, the *assassini*.

She said he told her it was all a fabrication based on some

glimmer of truth from hundreds of years before. Badell-Fowler was an old crackpot; no one had ever taken him seriously. He accepted none of it: the five murdered men, the destruction of Badell-Fowler's researches—those were all things that just happened, nothing particularly ominous in them. No connections, no shadowy implications. No *assassini*. And he'd never heard of anyone named Erich Kessler.

Dunn sighed, pushed his bowl of stew away, and dabbed at the corners of his mouth with linen. "I'm very sorry to hear all that. Very sorry, indeed. You'd say he took you seriously, would you?"

She nodded. "He takes me seriously. And even if he didn't, he certainly took Val seriously. And he knows I've been working on Val's agenda—"

"Could he be trying," I said, "to keep you from getting killed?"

She shrugged. "I don't know. That could be part of it. But I know him. I think he'd tell me the truth and *then* try to convince me to stay out of it. He wouldn't just lie, he respects me and what I do, what I am—"

"Sister," Father Dunn said, "I don't want you to take offense, but you're mistaken. D'Ambrizzi is a cardinal. It's the Church of Rome we're talking about here." He smiled gently, his pink face crinkling in his most avuncular manner. "I speak as a priest and as a student of the Church. D'Ambrizzi may like you. I'm sure he does. What's not to like? But he does not respect you, he does not respect your work. You are a woman, that's not good. You are a nun, that's worse. And you are a journalist, full of questions and principles and standards by which you like to measure people . . . and a lot of people won't measure up. That's when the red lights start flashing, Sister. And being an American just makes it worse—because Americans just won't listen to reason. He'd lie to you as a matter of normal precaution, he'd lie to you *reflexively*. Believe me, you are the enemy to guys like D'Ambrizzi. And I love the old bastard. . . ."

She didn't flinch, looked him straight in the eye. "I hear you. I really do. But—*lie* to me?"

"Sister, he already has."

"Prove it."

"Did you ever come across the name Simon? Simon Verginius?"

"Yes. In Badell-Fowler."

"D'Ambrizzi knows a great deal about the *assassini*. He was up close and personal with Simon Verginius in Paris, he was involved with the *assassini*. . . . Simon Verginius was the code name of a priest sent by Pope Pius—"

"The Pius Plot," she murmured.

"—sent by Pius to Bishop Torricelli in Paris to form a cadre of *assassini* to work with the Nazis, to help keep the lid on the Church's involvement with the Resistance, to help divide the art treasures of the Jews of France . . . and Simon, whoever the hell he was, balked at murdering people for the Gestapo and the SS, and—"

"How do you know this?" Her voice wasn't quite so steady now.

"Because D'Ambrizzi wrote it all down, back in Princeton after the war. He wrote it and he hid it and now I've read it. It's quite a story. We don't know why he wrote it but there's no question about its authenticity. . . . He wrote it and I read it, Sister. That's how I know."

She bit her lip halfway through the story of the night in question, then pushed on, not hurrying, not sliding past the details, but just telling us about the man, the priest in his cassock, the priest with the milky-white eye that turned into a liquid ruby when she drove the candle's glass chimney into it, how he'd tried to kill her and how she'd fought him and how he'd gone over the terrace railing at the flat on the Via Veneto. . . . She bit her lip just that once, that was all. No tears, no floods of emotion, not even any real anger. Just the story.

When she stopped she caught my eye for the first time. "All I could think," she said, "was, why hadn't it been Val? Why hadn't she been the one to survive? Why hadn't she sensed the danger and fought off the man in the chapel?"

"Because it wasn't the same man in the chapel," I said. "If Horstmann had come to your room, you, too, would be dead. Believe me." I swallowed against the dryness in my mouth. "You have no idea how lucky you were."

"Horstmann?" she said.

"By sheerest chance Monsignor Sandanato was in the street below—"

"The lovesick keeping watch is more like it," I said.

"I wish you wouldn't say that. This is too serious for joking."

"I'm not joking," I said. "But the hell with it, it's not important. Go on, go on."

Dunn said, "Try not to spat, children."

"Sandanato was down below when it happened. He was exhausted by everything that's been going on. He's got the world on his mind—the killings, the pope's illness, D'Ambrizzi and the pope meeting at all times of the night and day, all the jockeying for position among the *papabili*. He looks like death, sometimes I think he's ready to crack. That night he was just walking aimlessly, he found himself near my building, he thought he'd see if I was up and willing to talk for a while. He's taken to confiding in me some of his thoughts about the Church; we have these long discussions, the way Val and I used to talk late into the night—"

"Ah," I said, "I remember that . . . the life of the mind."

She ignored me. "Anyway, he heard this scream, he didn't know what it was, but a woman nearby was screaming, pointing into the darkness above . . . it was the priest, the man who tried to kill me, falling through the night. . . . He hit the top of a parked car, bounced off into the street. . . ." She shuddered. "Where two or three cars ran over him. Not much left. No identification on him . . . He may not even have been a priest. Sandanato came up to my flat, he was frantic—"

I shook my head. "I wonder how he knew the priest had fallen from your particular terrace?"

"I don't suppose he could have," she said. "He . . . just wanted to make sure I was all right. . . ."

"There's no hiding from them," I said. "I've been thinking it was just Horstmann out there, Horstmann getting to them and killing them before I can reach them. But now we know that they aren't watching just me, they're watching both of us—"

"Don't leave me out, old boy," Dunn said. "I'm in it as well. Maybe they're watching me, too." He emptied out another bottle of wine, shaking the last drop into his glass. He gestured to the waiter for coffee and cognac.

"So," I said, "are there more of them? And who gives them their orders? Who is telling them to kill? Who said Sister Elizabeth knows too much, she must die? Who benefits from your death? What does it have to do with the successor to Callistus?"

*   *   *

She wanted to know what we knew about her mystery man, Erich Kessler, and Dunn told her the story, told her we had run him to ground in Avignon, were about to go there. The Nazi connection again, and Dunn said, "But one of the good Nazis, my dear."

"Good Nazis, bad Nazis—" She shook her head, eyes closed. "I thought that was all over a thousand years ago." Her shoulders slumped.

By the time we'd lapsed into silence the restaurant was nearly empty, the waiters were clustered in a watchful group, yawning. The firelight had dimmed to a faint glow and it was midnight.

It turned out that Sister Elizabeth was staying at the Bristol down the street. It was arguably the most expensive hotel in Paris. She smiled distantly as if she had a secret. When we had drawn to within half a block of the hotel so gloriously located on the rue du Faubourg-St.-Honoré, a black and shiny limousine, rain beaded on its highly waxed paintwork, slid up to the entrance. "Wait," she said, motioning us to stop.

Two men got out of the back of the car while the driver held the door and the doorman hovered with a huge black umbrella. The first man wore a black raincoat and a black slouch hat. He turned back and offered his hand to the second man, who was squat and wore a cassock, heavy shoes. The light caught his face, the banana nose, the folds of his jowls. As he emerged he flicked a black cigarette away into the rain-washed gutter.

Cardinal D'Ambrizzi and Monsignor Sandanato.

I grabbed her arm, turned her toward me. "What the hell's going on here?"

"I told them I was intent on coming to Paris to see if I could turn up any more on what Val was doing before she was killed. D'Ambrizzi, angry as he was, suggested I accompany them since he had to meet with Common Market economists and finance ministers here. After the attempt to kill me, he insisted I get out of Rome while they tried to identify the dead man and . . . and . . . whatever. So I took him up on the offer. I'm staying at the Bristol; we all are."

"For God's sake, Elizabeth, be careful what you tell them. Dear old Saint Jack isn't quite the fellow we thought he was—"

"All we know," she said, "is that he may have lied to me about the *assassini* simply to protect me . . . to throw me off the track and make me give up. You're the one who suggested that explanation,

Ben. Then you"—she looked at Dunn—"you tell me about this testament he left behind in Princeton—that sounds to me like a man trying to expiate his guilt. Really, what was he supposed to do with what he knew? Run crying to the pope? According to him, the whole bloody mess started with the pope! So, big deal, he lied to me, he wanted me to drop it . . . and I would have if I could, I would if I had any sense, but I've gone so far with Val now—I can't just give up. And some miserable—*bastard*—tried to have me killed." She stopped short, cut off the torrent of words.

D'Ambrizzi and Sandanato had entered the hotel.

Dunn was flagging down a taxi, leaving us alone for a moment.

"I have a question for you," I said. "The last time we spoke you'd decided that enough was enough, it was time to cut out the horseplay and get back to reality. And your reality was that nothing like I suggested could be happening inside the Church, coming from somewhere near the top. . . . It wasn't a pleasant discussion, Sister. I wonder, do you still feel the same way? Is the Church still so pure, so far above all this?"

She looked around as I spoke, as if there might be someone in the night who could help her out. "I don't know. What do you want from me? I can't turn on the Church as easily as you can. . . . It's my life. Surely you can see that." She didn't sound very hopeful. "It looks like you were right. But try to understand how hard that is for me to say. We're still looking for men who have done these evil things, they may be inside the Church, but that doesn't mean I have to condemn the whole Church, does it? Ben"—her hand fluttered out to touch my sleeve and withdrew as quickly—"believe me, I don't want to fight with you. We both lost Val . . . now I have to try to think my way through everything you told me tonight. But please don't be angry with me, cut me a little slack. . . ."

The taxi pulled up to the curb. Dunn was climbing inside, left the door open for me. I turned away from her.

"Ben," she said as if she'd only just discovered my name and liked to use it.

"Yes?"

"I can't get Father Governeau out of my mind. Do you know any more about him? What happened to him, why he was in Val's thoughts that last day? How could he be connected to any of this other stuff? What was Val after?"

"I don't know," I said. "I have no idea whatsoever—"

"And your father—how is he?"

"He's . . . I don't know. He's recovering. I know him, he'll be all right. Too big a bastard to kill." I got into the taxi. Father Dunn folded his umbrella.

Sister Elizabeth stood watching us as we pulled away.

"What was she saying?" he asked.

"She wanted to know about Father Governeau. What could I tell her? We may never know about him at the rate we're going. Val was playing that card, and what does it really matter anymore?"

Father Dunn sat quietly, staring out the window into the breeze and mist. The Paris night.

"My throat is killing me," he muttered at last.

My mother came to me again in my dreams, as inconclusively as ever. She was reaching out to me, speaking softly, and I strained to hear her. It seemed that if only I could listen just a little harder, concentrate a little more, I could make out the words. It wasn't just a dream: I was sure of that much. I was remembering something that had actually happened. Why couldn't I force the issue, make myself remember? Why?

I woke sweating, shivering, my back stiff and painful. I'd fixed a new bandage that morning and it was wet with sweat. The room was cold, the window open. I got up and worked on a fresh bandage. The scarring was doing well, itched, didn't seem to leak anymore.

The next thing I knew the telephone was ringing and rain was slashing at the windows.

I answered the phone, wondering what the hell Dunn had on his mind that couldn't wait.

But it was Sister Elizabeth and she was downstairs in the lobby. She informed me that she was going to Avignon with us in search of Erich Kessler, aka Ambrose Calder. She said she had a prior claim. She'd been looking for him longer than I had. She wasn't taking no for an answer.

2

DRISKILL

A vignon lay in the slanting rays of sunshine beneath a fleecy cloudbank, the afternoon warm for November, the smell of a cleansing rain lingering in the perfect clarity of the day. The capital city of the Vaucluse, it was situated tight on the eastern bank of the Rhône River. The city itself seemed somehow inconsequential, dominated as it was by the eight-towered fortress built on a mighty rock two hundred feet above the rest of Avignon. It was the Palace of the Popes, dating from the Babylonian Captivity, squatting like a great sleepy despot, sunning itself above its subjects, a monster of legend watching over its loyal, terrified populace. It was colored a pale sandy beige in the glow from the dipping sun.

I'd visited as a tourist many years before. Now my mind was occupied by thoughts of the complexity of D'Ambrizzi's nature, the simplicity of Horstmann's, and the ambivalence of my own feelings toward Sister Elizabeth. But seeing the city again reminded me of what I'd learned about it the first time. It was difficult to imagine such a pleasant spot as the sewer of depravity and corruption Petrarch had described, but of course the Romans had hated the idea of the French popes in any case. Still, it must have been one of the racier stops on the tour back then. The Italians were fond of pointing out that the regular visitations of plague that swept the city during the captivity represented the vengeance of a wrathful God. When it wasn't the plague, it was the *routiers,* the private armies of mercenaries who would rampage in off the plains from the direction of Nîmes, requiring both gold, of which there was plenty, and papal blessings, which were if anything even more plentiful, in return for their retiring to pillage and raise hell elsewhere.

Upon our arrival there was a festive air, crowds milling in the streets. The ramparts built by the popes still circled the city, towers, gates, turreted battlements. The other famous tourist attraction was the Bridge of St. Bénézet, unfinished, sticking out into the Rhône, ending abruptly at the point where it was abandoned in 1680. The river had proved too powerful, so the four-arched bridge ended in midstream, going nowhere but into history, memorialized in the children's song every French kid knows.

It all came back to me, what I'd squirreled away about old Avignon. I even remembered that John Stuart Mill had written *On Liberty* while living in Avignon, had arranged to be buried there in the Cimetière de Saint-Véran. But I wasn't a tourist anymore, though the thought had occurred to me that I might wind up in the same graveyard if Horstmann was still watching.

I was returning as something other than a tourist. I hesitated to name what it was.

A hunter armed with a toy pistol?

A victim playing out the hand, waiting for the end?

Maybe it didn't need a name.

The three of us made our headquarters at a nondescript businessmen's hotel and Father Dunn made a call to let Ambrose Calder or his representative know he was in Avignon and following instructions. He came down to the lobby, where we'd been waiting, and told us that arrangements had been made for him, and only him, to see the man who had once been Erich Kessler. Dunn's plan was first to put his mind at ease and then get word back to us about joining them. "He's calling the shots," Dunn said. "All I can do is ask."

"Where is he?" Elizabeth asked.

"Not far from town was all he'd say. A car is coming for me. You two might as well kill time, have a look around town. Then check back here for messages." He took notice of the worried expression on her face. "It's going to be all right. Our man Kessler is one of the good guys." He looked at me with one of his crinkly grins. "Probably."

"Unless he's Archduke," Elizabeth murmured, but Dunn didn't hear her.

Sister Elizabeth and I made an uneasy pair. Flung together by Dunn and circumstances, I felt as if I'd wandered into the enemy camp. I knew how badly I was behaving, how cold and remote I must have seemed to her, but there was nothing I could do about it. It was a question of my own survival. I was afraid of her, afraid of the power she had to hurt me and afraid of my feelings about her. I barely spoke to her but couldn't stop looking at her. She was wearing a gray herringbone skirt with pleats riding on her hips, a heavy blue cable-knit sweater, leather boots, a Barbour field jacket. I knew we should somehow have kept her from coming with us. But she wasn't easy to stop. As with Val, you'd have to kill her.

Frustrated and breathless from the crush of bodies, we found ourselves in a crowded square below the massive fortress walls of the palace. The sun had dropped from sight and it was suddenly cold. The palace walls rose like sheer cliffs. Shadows covered the square. Lights were strung in varied colors, carnival style, and the press of the crowd was insistent and damp and oppressive. Menace seemed to fill their laughter, echoed in their innocence.

At one side of the square a stage had been erected. A commedia dell'arte performance was in ragtag, bawdy progress, il dottore and the other stock characters shouting and capering improvisationally before the packed-in audience. The laughter cracked and rolled, spontaneous, organic, earthy, but all I registered were the masks of the performers which gave them the otherworldly, predatory look of disfigurement. Giant torches flamed at the corners of the stage, shadows leaping and jumping like hidden murderers from another play gathering in the night. All my thoughts were dark and dangerous and sinister. I saw nothing to make me laugh.

Sister Elizabeth spotted a small empty table on a raised platform outside a café, beneath blue and red and yellow lights strung on wires between damp, leafless trees, ghosts of summer. We sat down, managed to get a waiter's attention, sat quietly while he squeezed through the maze of crowded tables. We got bowls of steaming coffee, sat warming our hands, staring at the players.

"You look so hopeless, Ben. Is it that bad? Or can we finish the job? Aren't we drawing close to the answers now?" She sipped the coffee with its froth of steamed milk on top. I knew it would leave a little mustache of foam on her upper lip, and I knew she'd carefully lick it off. She asked the questions innocently, her eyes shifting from me, surveying the shadowy crowds, all their heads turned toward the squawk and strut of the performance.

"I don't know. Hopeless? Jesus . . . I'm tired and I'm afraid. Afraid of getting killed and afraid of what I'll find out. I came apart up there in Ireland, really came apart. . . ." I was going too far, dropping my guard. "But there's no point in going into it now. It was bad, very bad. There's something wrong with me."

"You've been through too much," she said.

"It's not just that. You've been damn near killed and a man died . . . but you're not full of despair and fear. Something's gone wrong inside me. I can't get rid of the sight of Brother Leo . . . blue and rubbery and that arm, beckoning to me. The closer I think I'm getting to the end, the real heart of the darkness where all the answers are—Rome, of course, I'm talking about Rome—the more afraid I am. I don't know, maybe I'm not really afraid of getting killed anymore, maybe that's not it—but I am goddamned afraid of what I'm going to find out. Val found out, I know she found out everything—" I shook my head and took a scalding swallow of coffee. Anything to break the spell of the confessional. What the hell was the matter with me?

"You're exhausted. Mentally and physically. It's all catching up with you. What you need is rest," she said.

"He's here, you know. He *is* here. You do know that, don't you?" She gave me a puzzled look. "Who?"

"Horstmann. I know he's here."

"Don't say that. Please."

"But he is. That's all there is to any of this. Somehow he knows. You must see that. Somehow your precious Church is harboring him. Keeping him informed. He's not just lucky, Sister. He's being *told*. Oh, he's here, right now. Here."

She watched my outburst, then reached across the table for my hand. I felt her touch, pulled away from her. "So who's behind it, Ben?"

"I don't know. The pope, for God's sake. How should I know? D'Ambrizzi's a liar, maybe it's D'Ambrizzi . . ."

She shook her head.

"Sister, your judgment is suspect. Forgive me, but you're a loyalist, you're one of them." I was flailing in the darkness and I knew it. Just beating my gums. I didn't know what the hell was going on. I never had had the slightest idea.

We sat staring at the scene, locked within our own airtight compartments, unable to intersect or connect or communicate.

"Why do you hate me? What have I done to you other than love your sister and turn heaven and earth to find out why she was killed and by whom? I can't help wondering—just how have I pissed you off so thoroughly?"

She took me by surprise. I offered the standard coward's response. "What are you talking about? I've got more important things on what's left of my mind than hating you, Sister."

"I may be only a nun, like Dunn said, but I am not without a certain feminine sense of—"

"Okay, okay, spare me the details of your feminine intuition."

"Ben, what is going on? Don't you remember how things were when we were on the same team in Princeton?"

"Of course I remember. What's the matter with you? You're the one who quit the goddamn team! I remember our last conversations—"

"I remember them, too. And I remember the good times—"

"I treated you like a human being, a woman. That was my mistake. I suppose I should apologize—"

"What for? I am a human being and I am a woman!"

"You're just a nun. Nothing more. That's all that matters to you. Let's just leave it at that."

"Why? Why do we have to leave it? Why can't we clear it up? Your sister was a nun, do you recall? Did she cease being a person? What is your problem here? Did you hate her? Did she put that disgusted look in your eyes? You're so damned transparent—"

"Val was my sister. You're on thin ice here. Leave it."

She sighed, staring at me. Her eyes were potent green fires. Her wide mouth was set, full of intractable tension. "I want to talk. I want to get this cleared up now so we can see this through as Ben and Elizabeth . . . friends, two people who like each other. . . ." Her two front teeth bit into her lower lip. Her eyes were so wide, pleading with me. "Whatever we are to each other."

"All right," I said. "The problem is your Church, the fact that you are a nun, that the Church—however wicked it may be—is all that ultimately matters to you." I didn't want to have this conversation. It was pointless. I wanted her gone, out of my life, erased from my memory. "It's that simple. I can't begin to understand any of it. I learned the lesson a long time ago but I forgot it, you made me forget it, I forgot what you're like, all of you . . . it's like a disease, it gets inside you, the Church, the Church, right or wrong. How can you serve it? How can you give yourself up to it, body and soul? It's not noble, it's not selfless—it has an endless appetite, it feasts on your life, consumes you like a great institutional vampire, it sucks the life out of you and leaves the husks of men and women in its wake, demanding everything and never relenting. . . . How could you give your life to the goddamn Church when there's a real life out there, a place where you could be the person your instincts tell you you could be? I've seen that person and you're killing her in the name of your Church. . . ."

I don't know how she kept on an even keel during my tirade. For all I knew it may have been possible for her because she was a nun, one of God's little jokes on me. Maybe her Church had given her the strength to cope with me as I was just then. She had the good sense to wait it out while the little man brought us fresh bowls of coffee and sandwiches. Maybe she thought she was waiting long enough for me to feel foolish and possibly even apologize. I could have told her, in that case, that there wasn't enough time. Not if we waited for Gabriel's trumpet would there ever be that much time.

"I didn't set out to become a nun, of course. It just sort of happened. No, that makes it sound like an accident and it certainly wasn't that. On the contrary, it was almost inevitable given the circumstances of my life and my particular personality. When the time came I made a conscientious, conscious decision to devote myself to the work of the Church. I'm going to spare you some of the sappier details . . . just give you an outline of sorts.

"I grew up in the Eisenhower years—that's a code word, are you with me? And my parents were very devout Catholics, well off, a Buick Roadmaster and an old Ford Woodie station wagon, my father was a doctor and my mother gave every spare moment to the Church. My grandparents and all my cousins and friends and, well, everyone I knew—all Catholics. My brother Francis Terhune Cochrane, that's our family name, Cochrane, by the way—he talked about becoming a priest. All the boys did, naturally, and all the girls went through their nun phase. But it was usually just a phase. Naturally.

"When I was ten John Kennedy, a Catholic, was elected president. My God, what rejoicing! We lived in Kenilworth, near Chicago, and Mayor Daley had won—or stolen, they said—the election for Kennedy, and that made it all the better. It was as if we had won *our* civil rights battle. A Catholic in the White House—you and your family must have felt much the same way, though your father would have had a pipeline into the White House, I suppose, and mine was still just a doctor—but, you know, what a brave new world it was! But in what seemed like no time at all everything began to go to pieces. Everything changed . . . I was thirteen when Kennedy was murdered. The Beatles came along and turned all the music upside down—pretty amazing stuff for a thirteen-year-old girl. The Rolling Stones, rebellion and smoking dope and people dropping acid and *Hair* and Vietnam and having a boy spreading your legs and touching you when you were all wet for God's sake and the Catholic guilt! I'm telling you—particularly when you liked what the boy was doing and you liked to do things to him—my God, we are talking mass confusion! And then there was Bobby Kennedy staring up into the bright lights with blood seeping out of his head and Martin Luther King on the motel balcony and Kent State and Woodstock and Bob Dylan and the police riot in Chicago in '68 and I got a busted lip in the melee. . . .

"Maybe I was a dope or too sensitive or an adolescent at just the right, or the wrong, time. But the point is I looked back on my own life and it hit me hard that I liked security and faith and— forgive me for sounding like a nerd—I liked doing what can only be called good works. I loved the Church—I was a kid, guilt-ridden and disappointed in my pathetic little attempts at sexuality and I was confused by dope and the long hair and the fuck-the-world attitude I kept seeing all around me. . . . I look back now and what I see is a girl who watched in the sixties while everything she'd grown up counting on in the fifties got blown to bits without an apparent care. Some kids loved the change, the chance for rebellion, and some didn't. I just couldn't get into it . . . rebellion has never much appealed to me. Working for change is something else and I made little moves toward getting involved in the civil rights movement but Kenilworth wasn't exactly a hotspot on that score. So rebellion wasn't my thing, it was Val's thing, by her very nature.

"Me, I realized I loved the security of the first ten years of my life . . . what happened from 1963 on scared me. Oh, I'd never have admitted it then, but nothing could get in the way of my belief in the goodness of my parents, the goodness of the Church, the rightness of the way things were supposed to be. So many of my friends fell away from the Church, lots of them wound up in the drug culture, they ran away, decided all they wanted to do was raise hell and fling it all back in their parents' faces . . . but not me. It just wasn't me.

"What I saw was a world that looked like it was coming apart at the seams. All the values I'd been raised with seemed to be falling into some kind of disrepute, the 'normal' paths one traveled were all being closed off. . . . And then my brother Francis, the idealist in the family who'd gone off to war determined to serve his country, was killed in the Tet offensive and I had a hell of a tough time coping with that. Here again, another kid might have said such a pointless death proved there was no God and would have turned against the Church. But not me. I had to face it and explain it to myself, I couldn't, wouldn't, just shriek and scream and blame it on anybody handy or on Lyndon Johnson, I wouldn't say that Francis's death was evidence of existence without any purpose or meaning. Life does have meaning, there is right and wrong and there is punishment at the end for those who deserve it. . . . God gave meaning to life—and I went to the Church for the answers I needed. The Church just seemed to mean more than the available alternatives. And the timelessness of the Church—it just sort of overtook me, everything else seemed so trivial. Does this make me sound like a Jesus freak? I hope not. Because I'm not. But I could take the Church seriously and I just couldn't take acid rock or tie-dyed jeans *seriously*. I was against the war in Vietnam, I was for the

sense of responsibility and the willingness to accept the consequences of your acts. Oh, my God, I listened to the music and
bought the records and wore the clothing and my peace badge, but
it all seemed to be passing . . . do you see what I mean? The
Church had been there a long time, it *mattered.*

"I knew a couple of very decent priests, one extraordinary old
nun, an elderly woman with a mind so inquisitive and bright that I
was just in awe . . . my God, she was an Elvis freak, and she was a
truly happy woman, her life made so much sense, she enjoyed her
life. She was a teacher, a school administrator, she wasn't afraid of
being politically active and she was always telling the Vatican where
to get off. . . . She was just great, she inspired me, made me realize
that if everything else worked, then maybe I could go on and live
without the pleasures of the sexual life and keep from going nuts—
can you understand that? It wasn't going to be perfect, but it would
be good. . . .

"Well, either you understand it or you don't. The convent was a
haven, too, I don't deny that. What they say about nuns and priests
looking for a place to hide, sure, why not? Everybody wants a place
to hide, Ben, everybody—and most of us find one place or another.
I hid out in the convent for a while. And sure, my parents were
proud . . . you know that mixture of pride and sorrow you see all
over the faces of Catholic parents when their daughter chooses the
Church rather than husband and kids and mortgage . . . but they
were proud of me, proud, curious, doubtful. *Our little girl, O Mother
o' Mercy, does this mean our little Liz will never get laid?* Or words to
that general effect. My God, it's funny when I look back on it. . . .

"I wanted to serve God. To serve mankind. And have a life I
would enjoy.

"It looked as if the Church was moving toward a new definition
of women and their role in the Church, moving toward a more
liberal interpretation of things. . . .

"Well, you can't have everything can you, Ben?

"You know that, don't you, Ben?"

"The truth is you're something like aliens. Creatures from
Jupiter or thereabouts. You look like the rest of us now, and you
move around in the real world, you seem to be one of us. . . . But
it's all an illusion, it's a lie, and you play it for all it's worth. You're

like an odorless, colorless gas that numbs the brain and dulls the senses of the rest of us.

"It's an illusion because as soon as life comes close to you, you jump back and start putting the seven veils back on, you hide behind your sanctimonious bullshit, you use it to excuse anything, any kind of betrayal. . . . I'm a nun, you say, had you forgotten I'm a nun? The Church is my savior and I'll be goddamned if I'll think for myself, that's what you say. . . . I'm a nun, I'm made of purer and finer stuff, and I also know which side my bread is buttered on . . . and lucky me, you say, I don't have to deal with men! What a relief that is!

"Sister, you're afraid, you're a liar and a fake and a bullshitter—"

"And Val? Was she a fake and a liar and a bullshitter?"

"No, she wasn't. She was up to her ears in life, soaking it up, making her own judgments, risking her life—"

"If I'd died, if he'd pushed me off the bloody terrace, would that make me as wonderful as Val? Is that the problem? You hate me because I didn't die? How incredibly petty—"

"I don't hate you—"

"You've got some real problems, Ben. It sounds to me like you hate me because you hate the Church and you hate the Church because you hate yourself and you hate yourself because you think you failed the Church, failed your father, failed and failed and failed. . . . Well, you're nuts, far nuttier than I am. . . . You didn't fail yourself or the Church! It just wasn't for you. . . . But you've let it drive you crazy. And you take it out on me—why? Val was a nun, I was her best friend. Our styles were different, but we were on the same side. . . . What is it with you? Why can't you just give me a break? I've admitted I was wrong—so forget the last conversation in Princeton, for God's sake! Val . . . me . . . what's the difference? What's the big deal here? Grow up, it's not a black and white world!"

"I love you, that's what's wrong . . . I saw enough to fall in love with you. . . . You're right, Sister. I am crazy. And you're just not worth it. . . . You heard what I said that other time. You and Sandanato—there's the love interest. You sort of deserve each other, don't you?"

Furiously she stood up, knocked over the chair, glared down at me, her lips drawn back, whitened. "Fine! You're making a mistake and you're going to have to live with it for the rest of your life!

THE ASSASSINI 435

You've earned your mistake about me, you've been a real bastard. And you're welcome to it—you can dry up and die with your mistakes and your hatred . . . but you will have been wrong! Wrong about the Church, wrong about me, and saddest of all, wrong about yourself. . . ."

She whirled away from me, pushed her way blindly through the crowd which was applauding the commedia troupe. I could still see the back of her head when she stopped abruptly and screamed, trying to turn away from something or someone. I was helpless. The throng had closed between us.

Then Arlecchino, the harlequin from the commedia troupe, leapt out in front of her, posed wildly, grotesquely, his pelvis jerking, grinning lasciviously from beneath his masque. She turned away again, trying to push past him as he thrust at her. Finally, realizing she wasn't interested in playing, he made an obscene noise into her face. While the crowd laughed, taunting her, she pushed past into the darkness and was quickly gone.

Things were going fast, speeding up all around me, but I sat there like a statue, wondering if what she'd said about me was right. For all I knew she was dead on the money. Maybe I owed myself a damned hard looking-over, but psychological introspection can take you only so far. I could worry about what was going on in my head later, if I survived. As she'd said, I'd have the rest of my life to tighten my chain.

The commedia characters were working their way back toward the stage, where a brightly painted wagon of a sort used by such troupes centuries before had been drawn into place. Some of the lights illuminating the crowds were dimming and the clatter of conversation from the tourists, scholars, kids, townsfolk, and drunks began lessening. I looked out over the sea of berets and caps and clapping hands and popping flashbulbs. Spotlights were coming up softly on the wagon, and music came from somewhere. The next performance was about to begin.

I stood up and moved away from the little table, skirting the crowd, paying as much attention to my interior monologue as I was to finding Elizabeth. What an imbecile, blurting out my feelings, *I love you* . . . what idiotic blithering! And what a remarkably gallant fellow I'd been! There she was, taking me into her confidence in a remarkably intimate and unexpected way, telling me about how she'd chosen to become a nun, and I decided it was the perfect moment of vulnerability to blast my way forward, overrun her positions, score a point or two. . . . She was right. I was crazy. I had to find her and apologize and get her out of my mind. Give it up, old Ben, she's a nun, for Christ's sake. . . .

Such were my reflections as I circled the crowd, heard its braying and the yakety-yak of the actors, heard the breeze off the Rhône whistling damply in the naked trees. Somewhere, up above me in the palace another play was being performed, and the faint punctuations of laughter drifted down upon us. Where the devil had she gone?

At first I didn't realize what I was seeing, maybe because it was so utterly unexpected. I was looking for Elizabeth but . . .

Across the glut of people I saw Drew Summerhays!

It made no sense. What was he doing in Avignon? Summerhays should have been dividing his winter between that elegant house off lower Fifth Avenue, with his cats and his clutch of Catholic friends and the splashing fountains and the trays of perfect drinks, and his place in the Bahamas which over the years had earned its spot in the history books. Presidents had come on yachts to call on Summerhays.

But here he was, ramrod straight, in Avignon.

He turned his noble head and spoke to another man, shorter, wearing one of those Tyrolean green felt hats with a feather on the side, which was all I could see of him, that and a trench-coat collar turned up.

Drew Summerhays . . .

I was sorting out the possibilities of this being only a coincidence, and the odds were ridiculous. Summerhays didn't just happen to be in Avignon with Dunn and Erich Kessler and me. Coincidence was for the birds. So what was the point?

I began working my way through the crowd, wanting to get a closer look. What good did I think that would do me? And why didn't I want to reach him, speak to him, join him? Don't ask. Maybe I was hoping I'd see that it wasn't Summerhays after all, that I'd made a mistake, that it really wasn't getting more complicated.

Everybody was laughing and applauding, and I kept pushing past them and stepping on their feet and getting dirty looks. I got to within twenty feet of Summerhays and his companion and there wasn't any doubt. Summerhays was wearing a charcoal-gray chesterfield with a velvet collar. He wasn't laughing and he wasn't applauding. He was dry and cool and calm, as if deep within him lay the essence of death, eternal repose. He looked as if he'd gone beyond age and had become something other than a man. The guy with the hat was slowly, meticulously, scanning the crowd looking for something or someone, maybe a trail of broken twigs and moccasin tracks. On the spur of the moment, not wanting to question the impulse, I decided to speak with him. Hell, it was Summerhays, my trusted mentor. . . .

I'd drawn to within maybe ten feet of packed humanity, approaching from behind, when I stopped short, held my breath, and felt my determination sputter and die. The questions came to life again. What the hell was he doing here? Why should I trust Drew Summerhays? Why should I trust anybody anymore? There was just no end to the surprises. I felt as if I were standing in a tunnel watching a flood rushing and frothing at me, the sewer rats one step ahead, squeaking, and I couldn't move.

The man with the feathered hat was flicking it back and forth, fanning himself. The woolly metronome was moving at about the height of Summerhays's shoulder. I couldn't take my eyes off the feather splayed out against the dark green wool. Then the man turned and I saw his face. He wore glasses and had a mustache, an olive complexion. One cheek looked like it had been used long ago as a dart board. But you had to notice his throat, the horrible ragged splash of scar tissue puckered between his chin and his necktie's knot. Maybe the dart board had been a warm-up for the throat cutting. Jesus, Drew . . . This guy was standing there, pals with Summerhays, one of the lay princes of the Church.

Watching them from the end of my private nightmare tunnel, I felt again something of what had shaken me so badly on the beach in Ireland. A kind of preserved, freeze-dried fear injected into my veins. But something beyond fear. The beckoning arm of the old man . . . the flickering feather in the silly hat. . . . I couldn't see the sense of it, I couldn't see where it had been and where it might lead, but I didn't want to go there. . . .

I waited too long.

Summerhays turned. I saw his face head-on. And he saw me.

Our eyes locked in recognition. I saw the hat stop in midair, Summerhays's hand on his sleeve, his eyes still fixed on me. It all seemed to take forever. I was caught in no-man's-land again, watching the hand on the sleeve, the nod, while I tried to under-

stand. But I couldn't. Something was going on but I didn't know
what. Had Summerhays called my name? I couldn't hear. But I
knew I had to get away.

I came to life, hurling myself back into the dense crowd,
shoving my way past the same people I'd just disturbed moving in
the other direction. Someone swore at me, shoved me angrily with
a hand holding a bottle of wine that splashed my sleeve, but I was
past, already edging toward the darkness beyond the colored lights.

I had to get away. I took one look back over my shoulder, saw
a continuing commotion. The man in the funny hat was coming
after me.

I felt the bulge in my coat pocket. The gun.

It was plastic. It was a toy.

I had to get away.

Out of breath, heart pounding, I stopped in a narrow street,
then ducked into an alleyway, flattened myself against the crumbling wall. Even the side streets were clogged and streaming with
gabbling tourists, actors in a variety of costumes like refugees
through time from an old Hollywood back lot. I sagged against the
wall to catch my breath. When I looked up I was staring into a
man's glimmering eyes. A hooded face drawn close to mine. I
smelled rancid breath as he grunted and, like Death, held out his
hand. His fingers brushed my face and I pulled back, bumped my
head, swore at him.

He grunted again, jabbed the hand at me, a beggar dressed as a
monk. Not Death, not yet. I brushed the hand away and pushed
him backward. I must have frightened him. He stood his ground
for a moment, rocking back on his heels, then flinched, his face
still hooded by the cowl.

"Get the hell out of my way."

He looked back at the street. He hadn't come alone. There were
several more hooded figures watching us, like the chorus in a very
bad fantasy. We all stood still, then I realized that maybe they really
were monks, the *pénitents noirs* who were said to still maintain two
chapels in the town. I'd seen them years before, dark figures who
marched hooded and barefoot through the streets of Avignon,
dating back to the *pénitents noirs* of the fourteenth century, laymen,
flagellants, who had counted kings of France in their number. Now
they stood staring at me, either actors or monks or thieves, waiting.

I pushed past the one who'd confronted me and went toward the others who blocked my way. I said something angrily. They grudgingly parted for me in absolute silence. I looked down, realized I had a gun in my hand, just visible in the shadows. They backed away, watching me, the gun. Then I was past them, jamming the silly thing back into my pocket.

Back in the street, shouldering against the grain, past knots of street performers, looking for the little man. A fire juggler caught my eye, flames darting through the darkness. Where was Elizabeth? What was going on?

The man in the Tyrolean hat stood near the juggler, his face suddenly illuminated by the burning clubs flying through the air. He was straining to see in the smoky darkness, his eyes swiveling toward me.

I was sure he saw me just as I broke away, bumping into sidewalk tables where people sat with their wine and coffee, bundled up against the chill. I was past a flower cart, past yet another group of commedia players, their hook-nosed masques turning like malevolent birds to peck at me, draw my blood. Looking back past the onlookers gathered about the capering Arlecchino doing his shtick, I saw the man pursuing me stopped momentarily by the *pénitents noirs*. I ducked around another tight corner while he was trying to extricate himself, ran down the narrow street, turned again, slipping on cobblestones, trying to lose myself.

I had to think. I had to come to rest somewhere. And I had to find Elizabeth.

Summerhays, of all people . . .

What had brought him to Avignon? What did he know? What was his connection with the little man? Did Summerhays know about Ambrose Calder? Did he know someone had tried to kill Elizabeth? Did he know about Horstmann?

Drew Summerhays had always seemed to know everything.

That's what my father had always said.

From the doorway where I stood I felt the earth shake and heard a tremendous bang, saw an enormous pattern of comets and meteors, blue and white and pink, showering down from the black sky, casting a shifting patina of garish light. I jerked backward, cracked my head again, this time on a low, rough lintel, felt another shock and heard the bang and awed response from the streets.

They were merely the initial shots of an endless salvo of fireworks raining down from the heights of the palace. The *son et lumière* exhibition I'd noticed announced on handbills and posters earlier. The heavens seemed to twist and froth with gold, green, silver, red, orange, a continuing patchwork of lavish explosions.

I didn't know where the little man was, but I dreaded him as if he were another furious hound running me unceasingly through the tight, unfamiliar streets. Peering out from my shadowy cubbyhole, I saw yet another group of *pénitents noirs* clustered before a small church squeezed between cafés and shops across a compact square, a splashing fountain merry in the center. Children in down jackets stared intently, like the hooded monks, in the direction of the thunderous, wondrous cacophony unleashed overhead.

The square was packed. Everyone in Avignon was out for the night, viewing one of the countless performances, watching the fireworks, soaking up the sights and smells of a festival. The explosions battered the night like heavy mortar fire.

I couldn't see the little man, or the pointed crown of his hat, or the feather. Then I began looking for Sister Elizabeth, wondering where she could have gone. I was fighting the Irish panic, the sight of Leo's beckoning arm.

I set out across the square, heading for the little church. It looked sadly ignored for the moment, dark, unable to compete with the masked actors and the artillery whacking away from the palace.

I slid inconspicuously through the rapt observers and, moving from shadow to shadow, climbed the few steps and crossed to the heavy wooden door with its iron bands, pulled it open only far enough to slip inside, and stood sweating and panting in the darkness, holding the door shut behind me. It seemed larger inside than out and was both stuffy and cold, dry and damp, smelled of candles and wax and smoke and incense. There wasn't a hint of movement in the air. Candles burned, still, steady, tiny, and the reverberations of the fireworks seemed to snuffle at the stone walls, nudging them ever so slightly. I felt my way along the wall and down one side toward the altar. The pillars were seamed, heavy, thick. Finally I sat down in a wooden chair, of which hundreds were arranged in rows on the smooth stone floor, and took a deep breath. Damn. I was never sure, was I hunter or hunted? Tonight, anyway, the answer was easy.

I was out of ideas, stymied, soaked with sweat. I felt as if my soul had just given up the battle and melted. The toy gun in my pocket banged against the next chair. It sounded like a pillar falling down. Everything was out of control and I couldn't understand any of it. Who was chasing whom? Who was winning? No, better not ask that one.

I didn't know what to make of Summerhays, but the little man whose throat had been run through a lawn mower was enough to make me distrust the old man, mentor or not, enough to make me think of a secret world, an unholy coven of necromancers, plotting, plotting . . . as if Summerhays were served by a private curia of his own, as if he were a kind of homemade pope. What was Summerhays up to? He'd always been up to something, why not now? A pope was dying, the game was afoot. . . .

I felt as if I were watching the strands of a story as old as time being pulled tight, like a net, trapping me, strangling my life away . . . like a wire biting at my throat.

Had there been a sound behind me?

Something soft, stealthy, almost hidden by the explosions booming outside.

Christ, was I hearing things?

Could he have seen me even in the cramped, crazy crush of the little square? Was he here with me now? Why did I *know* the little man had a knife? Was it the mess that had been made of his throat?

The door at the front of the church was shutting. I almost felt the intrusion of air, like a sigh, from outside in the square.

There was someone in the church with me.

But the dead stillness returned. I felt for the toy pistol. Reflexive idiocy. It caught in the pocket, slid from my fingers, and clattered like the family silver on the stone floor. Damn thing sounded as if it were echoing down the centuries. I retrieved it, waited, dripping sweat from my nose. I was freezing.

Nothing.

I slid off the chair and moved back into the deeper darkness beside one of the pillars. The hair on the back of my neck was standing up, braced, dancing and singing a song. Somehow, through the inky streets and the throbbing crowds, the little bastard had found me, run me to ground in a church.

Perfect.

Wherever he was, he was damn good at being quiet. All I heard was my own breathing and the *crrrummmmmp* of the explosions overhead. The fireworks would go off, I'd see the glow, distorted beyond the stained glass windows. A ghostly angel seemed to be descending, coming down through the bursts of flak.

Then I heard a slight shuffling sound, a footstep or two, but they could have been anywhere, all the way across the rows of chairs or muttering along behind me. Sound slid along the walls, bounced among the pillars, like a children's ball loose in the street. Somewhere he'd been moving, quietly, carefully, looking for me.

"Mr. Driskill?"

I froze again, clutching my gun, flattening myself against the pillar. Where had his voice come from? All I had to do was reveal myself. And I'd be dead.

"Now, be reasonable, Mr. Driskill. We must talk."

He was moving on crepe-soled shoes, soundless, like the fog seeping in at night. I moved backward across the side aisle, feeling for the wall behind me. When I reached it, I let out a tiny sigh. A dim patch of grayness lay to my left, where something of the night sky with its flickering explosions, bursting colored lights, filtered through a broken pane or two of stained glass across the way. If I could get across the width of grayness, I could continue along the wall and try to find a doorway, a back door out of the trap I'd set myself.

What I needed was a way out into the night. Any way. How had he followed me? I'd been so sure I'd lost him . . . yet, here he was.

Who was he? And what was he to Summerhays?

The questions were going off in my head like the explosions in the night sky. I felt like the poor hopeless bastard who's fallen into the rattler pit.

I sensed a movement, a ripple of atoms and molecules, invisible, silent, but then figuring the hell with it, I took the risk, took the two steps across the faint bar of light, holding my breath, my hand in the pocket clutching the gun, sucking up against the wall, looking back the way I'd come.

The hand came from the darkness, clamping like a vise around my arm. He was breathing very softly beside my ear.

"Mr. Driskill, it's time for you to be careful . . . there is a very sharp knife right . . . here." I felt the point prick through the jacket and shirt and nip at my back. He pulled my arm slowly from the pocket of the trench coat. "Give me the gun, Mr. Driskill."

"Look, it's . . ."

"Shhhh." He took the gun from my fingers. "Oh, Mr. Driskill . . . this is a . . . toy." He handed it back to me. "Be careful," he said softly.

He pushed me gently into the bar of gray light and I turned very carefully to see him, to see the scar and the silly hat.

But I'd made a mistake. I had the wrong man.

The point bit at me again.

"Go home, Mr. Driskill. Go home and I will pray for you. Go where you can do some good. I do not wish you harm. You. The nun. Just go . . . away."

He fixed me with the bottomless eyes, the faint light shifting on the flat lenses.

Horstmann.

Then he was gone.

I was alone in the church.

3

DRISKILL

I stood at the end of a muddy lane, rutted and
slippery, listening to the dogs barking at the
moon glimpsed through running clouds. I'd
parked the rented Citroën on the wet, sucking
shoulder as Dunn had instructed me to do. His call
had come through not long after I'd arrived back at
the hotel.

"But how the hell am I supposed to know if it's the right muddy
lane?" I was trying to control my temper. It had been a difficult
couple of hours.

"Are you all right? You sound a little peaky—"

"You wouldn't believe me if I told you."

"Well, you've got to calm down and get this straight. Is Sister
Elizabeth with you?"

"Not exactly. Now, tell me again, which muddy lane?"

"Just park the car," he'd said, "and get out and hold your

breath. You'll hear the dogs. If you don't, you're in the wrong place. Wear your Wellies, my boy."

Now I could hear the dogs and I turned back to the absurd little car where Elizabeth sat quietly, staring out into the ground fog rising from the wet fields. We had spoken little since I'd found her in the hotel lobby. There was nothing to say. I owed her an apology and it was beyond me. I knew I was right about her and her Church and her priorities, how they would slash and wound me: I couldn't collapse in the face of the fact that she was also a human being who'd trusted me, talked to me. That wasn't the issue.

I wanted to tell her the story of what had just happened to me. Summerhays, the man with the throat. And Horstmann waiting for me, Horstmann with his hand on my arm . . .

Horstmann.

When I'd realized he was gone, it was too late to find him. There was no sign of him in the crowds in the square before the church. No sign of Summerhays and his companion.

It might all have been a dream. I felt as if there was just the outside shot that I was living in a dream, but of course it wasn't a dream. I felt like Basil Fawlty having a bad day, hoping it's a dream, banging his head on his typewriter, and concluding no, no, it's real. No, no, it was real. It had been Summerhays and it had been Horstmann and I wished I could have told Elizabeth but I couldn't.

I could deal with the fact of what had happened during the past two hours. What I couldn't understand was what hadn't happened.

I was still alive.

He'd had me alone in the church.

But I was still alive. I couldn't come up with an explanation that made any sense to me. The stage was littered with dead bodies. Why not mine?

What would Elizabeth have said? I wanted to tell her but the shot wasn't on the table.

So I stood in the mud, no Wellies, of course, looking up a hundred yards of very bad road to a rambling shape against the night and fog. We were thirty-one kilometers from Avignon and it was beginning to rain again. I was sinking in the mud. But I'd have trekked through considerably worse to have a chat with Erich Kessler.

Over the telephone Dunn had told me a bit more, including the fact that Kessler insisted on being called by his new name, Ambrose Calder. He was, all things considered, in good shape, more active in recent years than Dunn had expected. For years now he'd managed to run a shadow network of his own personal agents, like a CPA working on a second set of books, paying them out of blind accounts he'd set up in the old days at the CIA. He sent his agents, like electronic probes and sensors, into the darker, tighter corners of Europe. To a certain extent he made sure his former employers and persecutors and pro forma enemies knew that he was up to something. They just didn't know exactly what, and that not-knowing was what scared them, kept them in their cages. And every so often secret emissaries would pay him a visit, from Langley or the Vatican, for example, and give him a stern talking-to, but he knew, they all knew, he was perfectly safe. They lectured him and they consulted him for information, and his existence was kept a dark secret on a need-to-know basis and the fact was he was too dangerous to kill. Ambrose Calder could truly strike back and destroy you from his grave. I wondered: had Elizabeth put her finger on his third identity? Archduke?

No one knew for sure what he had stashed away in safe deposit boxes in Zurich, but neither did anyone want to run the risk of killing him and finding out. He was, therefore, thought to be one of the safest men on the planet. His death in a calm, peaceful bedchamber with a dog at his feet and the rest of them baying at the moon was more or less assured by several of the world's most elaborate intelligence services.

Only a renegade would want to kill him and risk spilling the beans. So why was he on Sister Val's list?

I went back to the car and tapped on the windshield.

"Come on," I said. "This is the place."

Ambrose Calder was a reedy man with a face and throat and hands of ropy sinew, a hatchet jaw, two days' stubble of graying whiskers, eyebrows like Brillo pads verging on flight. It was an outdoorsman's face, the effect of the dogs and their care, wind-reddened with a tracing of veins that seemed to have broken as they stretched across the high, pointed cheekbones. One of the house dogs watched him as if wondering whether or not he ought to growl and bark at the intrusion of all these strangers. Aside from the barking which had faded to an occasional yowl outside, you'd

never have known about all the Semoyeds. Calder was drinking
slivovitz like water, as if it killed some private pain.

"So," he said, "you come to me wanting to find out if I know
who's killing your Catholics."

"We want to know rather more than that," Elizabeth said.

"Yes, yes," he said, waving her away like a gnat. "You want to
know why. And you want to know who Simon was. Father Dunn
has made it all plain enough. And I say, what a curious lot you are!
And presumptuous! Why should I tell you any of this? Where are
the thumbscrews and the electrodes? Well, I'm going to tell you
what I can and the reason is simple enough—there is not a way in
the world you'd find out these things otherwise. And in my old age
I grow maudlin, I take pity on the children who have stumbled into
a game of grown-ups. Do you see? I help you because a fair fight is
always better—I wonder, I actually am curious as to just how much
havoc you will create! The Church and its self-importance amuses
me . . . so I place you, prowling cats in the lions' den. Will you
become lunch? Or will you set the pigeons flying, will you confuse
and even frighten the lions with their great bloody claws. . . .
Forgive me, I am indulging myself. And before you thank me, wait
and see what it benefits you." He held out his powerful hand. His
valet placed a cigar not quite so large as a baseball bat in the huge
fingers. Calder scraped a wooden match with his dirt-rimmed
thumbnail, watched the flame explode. He lit the cigar, sent smoke
billowing in thick clouds.

"Answers of the kind you seek are never plain and simple," he
said. "Oh, sometimes plainer and simpler than others, as when
you're dealing with dear old Moscow Centre. They always end up
operating rather primitively, try as they might not to. It's the
English you have to watch—they're the clever, crafty devils in this
line of country. Second best liars in the world. Go lie down, Foster,"
he said to the dog. "That's a good doggie. Named him after Dulles.
The dog is loyal, however. But not even the Brits, devious though
they are and thankfully blessed with that nasty ironic humor, can
match the Church, the Vatican . . . there you truly find yourself
among the liars, the plotters, the professionals. Their whole world
is a house of cards, one big wind of reason blows the whole damned
thing to kingdom come—yet by their will they hold it in place, give
it body and weight. It is the great illusion . . . it makes the mightiest
secular empires seem childish and feckless by comparison. I admire

them for the swine they are. All of us in the illusion business are bound to be swine in the end, at least professionally. We have in fact given the noble barnyard swine a bad name." His smile was very wide, very thin, and remarkably unamused.

"You have done an extraordinary job of homework. Torricelli's papers, putting up with that imbecilic nephew of his—he really ought to be put to the knife, he's an offense to good taste . . . old Paternoster, a grand chap . . . Brother Leo . . . and you, Sister, all that work in the Secret Archives, nothing short of miraculous, my God, how they hate women! And D'Ambrizzi's indiscreet memoir finding its way to Father Dunn—almost a proof, I submit, that you are meant by some higher power to press onward. Understand, it's all the work you've put out thus far that got you an audience tonight. Father Dunn was a most effective advocate. I drink to you. All three of you."

"Listen," I said. "It's my sister. Do you grasp that? That's why I am here. The Church is nothing to me. The Church killed my sister, she was one of its dedicated servants and it killed her, and I went looking for the son of a bitch who pulled the trigger. But somehow my sister's death has gotten lost in this ungodly swamp. . . . I've turned over the rock of the Church and it's just seething and pulsing and festering under there, I'm standing in all this muck—D'Ambrizzi and Torricelli and Nazis, you name it, I'm covered in it—but I want the man who killed my sister. His name is Horstmann and I . . . I—" I threw up my hands and stood up. The dog had decided that, though overwrought, I was basically okay. He came over and pushed his wet, cold nose into my hand. "How are you, Foster?" I murmured.

Ambrose Calder listened, watching me through the clouds of smoke. He was wearing a dinner jacket. He was confined to a wheelchair of the old-fashioned variety with a wicker back and side panels. It was pushed by a young man, also in dinner clothes, who looked like a state security interrogator. Once Calder had his cigar going, the young man slipped quietly away.

"I understand, Mr. Driskill. In your place I would feel much the same, I presume. But the fact is, by seeking your sister's killer you must suffer the consequences. You *have* overturned the rock. You *are* knee-deep in shit. Or look at it this way—it's like the genie in the bottle. Once he's out, there's just no getting him back in again. And when you've worked your way through the mess, *if* you get through the mess, then perhaps you will satisfy your original aim . . . who knows?" He drank from his glass of slivovitz. "There is no turning back now. Your life is poised in the balance, Mr. Driskill. But I'm sure you realize all that. The trick is to avoid tripping over the rock."

"That," I said, "is why I am here."

Calder began to laugh, turned to Father Dunn, and began to talk about World War II days, casually, as if Elizabeth and I were for the moment forgotten.

The house was immense, falling down in places like a folly of sorts, ancient, shrouded in pines. I couldn't quite imagine what it would seem in daylight. The central heating left the reaches of the room in cold, but there was a roaring blaze in the baronial stone fireplace that burned the chill from my bones. There was a casket of Davidoff cigars, a very old, dust-encrusted bottle of cognac, crystal snifters with heavy bases, huge cut-glass ashtrays. Calder clipped the end from one of the huge cigars, slid one of the ashtrays toward me, said, "There. I've done everything but smoke it for you. Now, to our friend Simon Verginius."

Kabalevsky's cello concerto was drifting romantically from immense speakers as we began to get to the point.

Elizabeth first described how she found Val's folder with the five names, the murder victims. Calder listened intently, his jaw clamped down on the cigar. He refilled his glass of slivovitz, smacked his lips.

"Claude Gilbert," she said. "Sebastien Arroyo. Hans Ludwig Mueller. Pryce Badell-Fowler. Geoffrey Strachan. They have all been murdered within the last two years. They were all involved, concerned Catholics. Men of distinction. They all spent time in Paris during or after the war. . . . But—what linked them? What else, I mean . . . and why did they have to be killed? And why now?"

"In the first place, it's a list of four plus a wild card not connected to the others—at least not in the way they are connected to one another. Badell-Fowler was presumably killed because of his work, his study of the *assassini,* as you have discovered. Put him to one side. He knew about the *assassini* and had to die for that reason." Calder's tone had grown more precise and businesslike, less jocular. He was tilling his own field now and he knew its every contour. "The other four—I'm rather afraid you've got the wrong

end of the stick so far as they go. Yes, they are linked but quite
differently from the way you assume. Catholics yes, but Catholics
with a crucial difference. The Madrid business tycoon, yachtsman,
big man in the Church—Arroyo. But did you know he was very
close to Generalissimo Francisco Franco himself? Oh, yes, very
thick, those two. An adviser to the generalissimo in many arenas.

"Mueller, the German. Scholar, served the Reich during the
war—in the Abwehr. I knew him reasonably well. But he was one
of the scary ones—a party man. For a time there was talk he'd been
caught in a plot against Hitler. He escaped being hung up on a
meat hook, however, survived the war, went back to his career as
Herr Doktor Professor. Catholic yes, of course. Had a stroke that
left him less than his best. The most interesting thing about that
plot against Hitler was that Mueller was an insert. Is the term
familiar to you? No? Let's see, how else to—ah, a plant! He was a
plant, a Gestapo plant in the midst of the real plotters—he was a
very willing free-lance, an Abwehr man in a Gestapo operation . . .
he betrayed the plot, of course, that was his job, and got a medal
for it. I was his case officer at one point after that. I knew of the
operation. And he spent some time in Paris during the Occupation.

"Let's see . . . Father Gilbert, the Breton priest. His loyal
parishioners bloody near killed him not long after D day. His
problem was, he wasn't a fighter. More of a lover. Figured it was
best to go along with the boys running things. Once the Hun had
packed up and fled, some of his fellow Bretons took rather a dim
view of his wartime activities. Collaborator, they called him, and
when they pointed it out to him they had a tendency to be holding
boat hooks and meat cleavers. He had a close call . . . some farmers
tarred and feathered him. He was a year recuperating in Rome, then
a somewhat safer constituency was found for him and he took to
writing homily-filled slender volumes of imaginary memoirs, diaries
of a country priest . . . with much of the money he earned flowing
to his protectors, the Condor Legion, *Die Spinne,* people like that,
the old Nazis.

"And Geoffrey Strachan, the MI5 man. Sir Geoffrey. Full of
honors, put out to grass relatively young, packed off to the family
castle in Scotland, not much heard from the last thirty years of his
life. Why the sudden retirement? some were heard to ask. Well,
there was a slight problem that was swept under the well-worn rug.
Strachan was in Berlin before the war, came back to advise Prime

Minister Chamberlain, accompanied him to Munich . . . the problem was merely that Strachan was an agent of the Third Reich, very close to both Doenitz and Canaris. He used to go boar shooting with Goering. The English discovered the truth in '41, used him for their own purposes, kept it all very quiet and eventually pensioned him off without a breath of scandal. Investigative reporting was not then what it is now, obviously. By the fifties they were so preoccupied with Red spies, an old Nazi seemed positively quaint, you see."

The ash on his cigar was two inches long and he regarded it affectionately, as if he hated to part with it. He gently rolled it across the lip of one of the heavy ashtrays, watched it fall.

"Now," he said, "do you begin to understand? Try to realize what a complicated world this is. These men were not simply important Catholic benefactors . . . they were part of a larger world, a world of conflicting goals and methods and motives. Yes, these men were all Catholics, they all floated in and out of Paris in the forties. Did they know about the *assassini*? Perhaps. Some of them did, I'm sure. But that is not why they were tied together in the minds of . . . someone. Someone who wanted them permanently silenced.

"The key, my friends, is that they were all Nazis. That is why they had to die. Catholics who worked for the Nazis. I know. I was in a position to know. Do you understand? Of course you do. You have discovered through LeBecq's daughter and through the Torricelli collection the connection that existed in those days between the Church and the Reich. I am merely adding to your store of information. These four men knew of the connection, they knew of what Miss LeBecq described as the mutual blackmail . . . and therefore they had to die."

Everywhere you looked, every time you looked, it was all changing. There was never time to get used to the situation as it appeared to be. The murder victims on Val's list had just been transformed from martyrs, slaughtered innocents, to cynical bastards who'd been on borrowed time too damn long. They were being erased. Another man was erasing his own past. Rewriting his own personal history.

"Surely you don't suggest that Curtis Lockhardt was some sort of Nazi." It was Elizabeth again.

"Of course not, Sister. He was devious enough, certainly, a great player of odds, a man who hated to back a loser, so he sometimes backed everyone just a bit. But I'd have thought the reason for Lockhardt's murder was perfectly obvious by this time." He inserted a finger inside his starched white collar, loosening it. The fire was hot. "He was too close to Sister Valentine. She had to die because of what she knew. He had to die because she might have told him . . . that was almost certainly the cause of the attack on Driskill here. Fear that she might have gotten the story to him. And you, Sister Elizabeth, were marked for your big fall because you were learning too much and weren't showing any signs of coming to your senses." His face was flushed from the slivovitz as much as from the heat, but he was enjoying himself. Every so often he winked at Father Dunn, who would smile back patiently.

"I wonder," I said, "about Val's list. Why was yours the sixth name? Your former name, I mean. You're the only one who doesn't share the crucial element—you haven't been murdered."

The dogs began barking outside. The wind had come up.

Calder wheeled himself over to the window, pulled the drapery aside, stared into the darkness.

"Sometimes they get nervous," he said.

I couldn't get the thought out of my mind.

Someone is erasing his past. . . . People are being erased, the past is being rewritten. . . . Someone . . .

Someone who wants to be pope.

Calder's valet came in to stoke the fire, bank the coals, bring a shawl for his master's shoulders.

"My circulation is not what it used to be," our host murmured, then turned to his servant. "Go tend to the hounds. Have Karl check the grounds, walk the perimeters. The normal drill."

"Could you address the question," I asked, "of Simon Verginius, the Pius Plot, the identity of the great man on the fateful train—"

"And the dog that barked in the night, eh? You begin to sound like Sherlock Holmes, Mr. Driskill."

"—and the identity of someone called Archduke?"

"I feel like a waiter taking an order. But, but"—he held up the rawboned hand, waving away my apologies—"what the hell are we here for if not to chat about the old days? What else is there, really, but the old days . . . those *were* the days, let me assure you. Where do you want to start? I'll tell you what I know . . . right, Father?" He looked at Dunn, who nodded.

"It all begins with Simon Verginius," I said.

"And ends with him, too, perhaps? All right . . . the debriefing of Ambrose Calder, late of the Third Reich, will continue." He suddenly slammed his palm down on the table. It was like a horseshoe landing. "Achtung!" For the first time he sounded like a German. There'd been no trace of an accent before, just a vague Europeanness, mid-Atlanticness, unidentifiable. "Vee haff vays uff making men talk. . . ." He laughed. "They used to have Germans in old American movies say that . . . I was one of those Germans." He sighed. "Long time ago. Well, to Simon Verginius . . ."

Dunn took one of the Davidoff cigars, no longer able to resist the temptation. Elizabeth sat by the fire, legs crossed, hands cupping her knee. Her eyes, green and intense, never seemed to leave Calder's extraordinary face. She was focusing all that wondrous energy, laserlike.

"You know, of course, about how Simon came to Paris on a mission from Pope Pius . . . to form a group of *assassini,* easier to do in those days than one might imagine in times of peace and calm. The Pius Plot designation was surely a reference to the Holy Father's plan to use the *assassini* to carry out covert Church policy. Simon Verginius worked through Bishop Torricelli, made his contacts with the occupation authorities—working in intelligence is how I learned all this, from the German side, of course—and we know he also worked with the Maquis, the Resistance. Pius was hedging his bets and he wanted the Church to get its share of the loot, particularly the art, as well as gold, jewels, whatnot. But art, that was the thing. The thought of Goering and Pius fighting over a Tiepolo always amused me somehow. Greedy men. They'd have ripped it in half rather than give way to the other.

"Simon subsequently had his falling-out with the Nazis. This we know, this *I* know. Frankly, I believe his heart was never in it. It wasn't in his nature to come to Paris and start doing the Germans' dirty work. Pius made a mistake—the old bastard didn't make many, but this one is echoing down the years. He merely picked the wrong man."

"Not so very mere, then," Elizabeth said.

"No so mere," Calder repeated. "The looting, the killing, the Nazi-Church ties . . . all that formed a perfect basis for the mutual blackmail. They could keep each other honest, or dishonest, if you prefer, down the dusty halls of time so long as some of the players remained alive and in place. Well, some of them are still in place and Simon knows them all—"

"Simon is definitely still alive, then?" Dunn cleared his throat to show he was still awake and in the game.

Calder smiled again. "Simon knew everybody in the old days, didn't he? Torricelli, LeBecq, Richter, Brother Leo, and August Horstmann, a great many more. Simon knew everyone but only a very select handful knew he was the legendary Simon, the Simon whom D'Ambrizzi said was many men."

I reached into the inside pocket of my jacket and took out an envelope, placed it on the table. That got Calder's attention. "You brought a prop!" he exclaimed. "Good for you, Mr. Driskill. I performed in amateur theatricals myself once. Long ago. Army days. I always said an actor was only as good as his props! Something in the envelope?"

I opened the envelope and took out the old snapshot with which I had begun. I smoothed it flat. I pushed it across the table toward Calder. His eyes followed the dog-eared scrap of paper from another age, another world.

"My sister knew she was in terrible danger," I said. "This is the one clue she left me."

"Nothing more?"

"That's it."

"She had much faith in you, Mr. Driskill."

"She knew me well. She knew I loved her. She knew I never know when I'm licked. She knew the picture would get me started—"

"And the rest was up to you." He picked up the snapshot.

"Torricelli, Richter, LeBecq, and D'Ambrizzi," I said as if reciting a litany. "All along I've wondered who might have taken the picture. It was Simon, wasn't it?"

Calder's thick wiry eyebrows went up, his eyes rose to meet mine. Then he began to laugh, a loud laugh, full of humor at last. He knew a joke I hadn't heard. I looked at Father Dunn. He shrugged.

"No, no," Calder said, calming himself. His eyes were watering. "No, Mr. Driskill, the one thing I can tell you for sure is that Simon Verginius did not take *this* picture."

"What's so goddamn funny?"

Calder shook his head. "D'Ambrizzi told the story of Simon in those papers he left behind in America—this is true? Yes. But he refrained from identifying Simon. And Horstmann killed Brother Leo before he could tell you who Simon was. . . . This leads one to believe Simon wishes to remain anonymous." He smiled broadly, seemed on the point of laughter again. "You really don't know who Simon is—"

"Cut all the bullshit," I said. "Who is he?"

"*D'Ambrizzi, of course*. Simon is dear old Saint Jack! The sly old bastard! Surely, you must see. D'Ambrizzi wants to be pope . . . and he was Simon . . . he's a murderer . . . and he collaborated with the Nazis . . . and none of it can come out now, so he must become a murderer again. Who better to be his instrument than a man who is used to doing his killing for him?" He sighed, the wicker in his wheelchair creaking under his weight. "A public relations nightmare, Mr. Driskill, if you see my point," and he began to laugh again.

"You tell me that there seems to be no success at all in the Vatican's investigation, Sister. Well, why should there be? It is a joke! D'Ambrizzi professes to believe that the *assassini* have always been a legend and Simon Verginius a myth—well he might, well he might! Simon, or call him D'Ambrizzi, is investigating himself. His job is to blur the lines of inquiry. The pope is dying—so how carefully can *he* oversee the investigation? D'Ambrizzi is in charge. When he succeeds with his own agenda, the killings will stop. The sleeper, Horstmann, will be put back to sleep. Think—when did the killings on Sister Valentine's list begin? When did D'Ambrizzi learn of the pope's illness! My reading of it is simple—the latter triggered the former! Let me be frank—if you find prayer efficacious I suggest that you pray for yourselves and you may yet survive all this."

"Archduke," I said. My mind was staggering here and there like a drunk on a late New Year's Eve, but I wanted to keep pressing homeward.

"Ah, yes, Archduke. Well, there you have me. I had good reason to know him—but only at a distance, only as Archduke. I never saw him, never spoke with him except once, in a bombed-out church in the outskirts of Berlin. I don't know how he got there, or how he got away. He needed to see me, needed to debrief me personally. He had a flair for the dramatic. He was in the priest's box in the confessional. I went in, couldn't see him, it was raining and cold, the roof bombed off the church, that awful smell of burned wood that's soaking wet and lasts forever . . . Archduke. What he may have had to do with Torricelli, why there was an exclamation point after the name, what LeBecq and the others may have had to do with him, I have no idea. Archduke. Who knows? In the end, he was one of the most secret men . . . more secret than I, by far. The sort of man who spends his entire lifetime in deep cover."

Like Drew Summerhays . . . Like Kessler himself, as Dunn had described him to me in Paris.

It had taken so long, but finally it was all taking shape.

Father Dunn said, "One last thing. I can't get it out of my mind, maybe it means nothing, but it's irritating me, not knowing . . . who was the chap on the train that Simon was setting out to kill? I've read D'Ambrizzi's account of Simon's career, and now you say that D'Ambrizzi and Simon are the same man—well, maybe, maybe not—"

"They *are* the same man," Calder said softly.

"But who was the Great Man on the train?"

Calder heaved his massive shoulders. "Could have been a Reich bigwig. That would be my suspicion. Goering or Himmler, someone along those lines. Or a prominent collaborator—but no, on the whole I'd bet on the high-ranking Nazi. But that wasn't in my area. In the end, what difference does it make?"

"Father LeBecq thought it was important enough to betray," I said. "Do you know where Archduke was headquartered?"

"London. Then Paris."

Sister Elizabeth said, "And the man the Vatican sent to Paris to find Simon . . . or to prove that Simon had refused to do what the Vatican wanted him to do—this man we hear called the Collector. Do you know who he was? Isn't he a significant figure, someone who must have known a great deal of the truth? And who had the trust of Pius?"

"He must have been all those things, yes," Calder said. "But by that time my life had grown exceedingly complex itself. The Gehlen Org was coming apart, the war was in its final stages, I was trying to stay alive, but arranging to surrender safely to the Americans was a complicated problem. I was looking for Archduke, figuratively and literally—I had to get word to him, I wanted to come over, preferably in one piece, but he was moving around, London, Paris,

Switzerland . . . I was sweating blood. And I wasn't paying any attention to what some renegade Catholics were doing in Paris. I have no idea who the Collector was. The Vatican had some enforcers who knew what they were doing . . . it was one of those tough guys, I suppose . . . he's probably dead, all things considered. Archduke may be dead, too, by now. All we know for certain is that Simon is alive." He looked up, taken by a fresh thought. "If Archduke is alive, then maybe Archduke is behind Simon's plan to become pope, maybe Archduke is still pulling some strings. Or . . . or, look at it another way—Archduke knows the truth about Simon, his identity. Maybe Archduke is the next to die. . . . And maybe Archduke is ready and waiting." The thought seemed to amuse him.

I drove the three of us back into Avignon. It was four o'clock in the morning when we reached the hotel. The streets were empty but for street cleaners sweeping up the debris from the previous evening's revelry. Sister Elizabeth spoke hardly a word. Everything about her was subdued, as if she'd had more bad news heaped upon her than she could handle. The D'Ambrizzi revelation had hit her hard. In the quiet of her solitude she was having to reinvent her world, her Church.

Father Dunn asked me if I wanted to join him in a nightcap. He took a silver hip flask from his jacket pocket and nodded to a deserted corner of the lobby. A table lamp cast a dim amber glow, and outside on the corner there was a streetlamp swaying in the wind. He took a swig from the flask, handed it to me, and I felt the brandy burning my throat. It hit my stomach like a depth charge. Immediately I felt light-headed.

I told him about seeing Summerhays in the crowd. His face played all the proper, startled reactions.

"Do you know much about Summerhays, Ben?"

"A fair amount. You've got a gleam in that gimlet eye."

"I was just thinking. He's like an older version of Lockhardt, isn't he?" Casually, as if he were hardly thinking about it, he said, "I wonder what he was doing during the war?"

"Which one? Civil? Spanish-American?"

"Yes, my son, he's old." His pink face was a mask of sour patience. "Your wit may work wonders with sheltered nuns, not with sophisticated old clerics."

"Why don't we find a sophisticated old cleric and ask him, Artie? I haven't had much to laugh about lately—"

"Oh, what a shame. We'll have to remedy that one day. I was thinking more about the Hitler war."

"Now you're thinking what I'm thinking. Yes, if memory serves, Drew Summerhays was—I don't know, in a strange sort of out of the ordinary way—one of Wild Bill Donovan's Knights Templar, y'know, a Catholic, a Yale man, a natural for OSS, but he was more of a strategist than an agent. Look, I'm not quite clear on this, he's led a life full of secrets, you'd always know you saw only a hundredth of his life. But he *was* in London during the war. My dad has let things drop about him at various times . . . he ran OSS men into occupied Europe, into Germany. He was my father's boss, I'm sure of that. He may even have recruited my father." I waited, letting it all sink in. "He knew Pius, he probably knew Bishop Torricelli. He's been in the game since the time of the Borgias— Artie, honest to God, he's still in the game and you know damn well what his code name was. . . ."

"Archduke," Father Dunn said.

"He's the only candidate," I said. "Unless Kessler was lying to us to keep us off his tail . . . In that case, Kessler is Archduke. Sitting in his wheelchair at the center of the web, spinning. . . ."

"So what the devil was Summerhays doing in Avignon this particular night?"

"Well, that's the hard part, isn't it? Summerhays is a better fit . . . But, the story of my night on the town is only half done."

"You amaze me," Father Dunn said.

"Sister Elizabeth and I had a problem tonight, a difference of opinion—"

"I detected a chill on that front."

"The point is, I was alone out there in the crowd when I saw Summerhays and his man. When they saw me I suddenly realized I wanted to get the hell out of there, there was something all wrong with that picture. Everything got confused and I was half running from, half looking for the weird little character with the chain-sawed throat and the feather in his hat . . . anyway, I was found by someone else, as if he knew where I was, as if I'd never been out of his sight, as if—I'm not kidding—he were waiting for me—"

"Give him a name, Ben."

"Horstmann! It was Horstmann, here in Avignon, all of us here in Avignon—"

"You mean you think he was with Summerhays?"

"Who the hell knows? Who understands any of it?"

"Holy Mary, what happened? How did you get away?"

"He told me to go home. He didn't kill me, he almost begged me to go home. Try to figure that one out."

"Let's just say that Archduke is Summerhays and Simon is D'Ambrizzi," Dunn mused. "Both men have deep-rooted reasons for loving and respecting your father, your family, you. And if they are behind all of it, then Horstmann is working for them. That could explain the warning. They want you out of it. . . ."

"But in that case they killed my sister," I said.

Dunn nodded slowly. "Maybe they did kill your sister. And if they did, they killed her to protect themselves. And that's all the more reason to save you . . . an expiation of their guilt. Your father saved D'Ambrizzi's ass after the war, brought him to America when the heat was on, and Summerhays was your father's patron on the road to power, God knows what kind of missions your father took for Summerhays during the war, so Summerhays owes him, too . . . so if they had to kill your sister, his daughter, for God's sake, can you imagine the agony they must be going through? They don't want to have to kill Hugh Driskill's son, too."

I hadn't prayed in twenty-five years, but it was a prayer that leapt to my lips in that awful moment.

"God grant me the power," I said, "and I will kill them all. . . ."

In the morning we left Avignon.

Three frightened pilgrims on the road to Rome.

PART FIVE

PART FIVE

1

The cardinals were playing boccie on the lawn of Poletti's villa. Ottaviani had just rolled the heavy, criss-crossed ball, and it sped across the perfectly manicured green grass with unerring accuracy, dislodging Vezza's ball and nestling up against the small, gleaming white ball, or "spot."

Vezza moved ponderously toward a wooden lawn chair and slowly lowered himself, like an old building that was still settling. He coughed and wiped spittle from his dry, cracked lips. "Whatever happened to the idea of letting the oldest man win? Where has decency gone?" He sank back in the chair with a heavy sigh. He fumbled in his baggy flannel trousers, brought out a pack of cigarettes and a cheap disposable lighter. "I've had enough of this game. You know, they say these things can kill you."

Poletti rolled his eyes, said, "Cigarettes are not exactly a newly recognized health hazard."

"Not the cigarette, you silly fellow. I *know* that. I have reference to these sleazy lighters. Explode, they are said to do. Engulf you in fire." He lit the cigarette. "God was with me that time." He nodded toward Ottaviani. "Guglielmo cheats. He has always cheated. Why don't I ever learn?" Vezza's socks had slipped down low on his ankles, revealing hairless, spindly ankles and calves, unsuitable, it would have seemed, for supporting so large a body. "He thinks he's allowed to cheat because of his crippled back. No sense of honor."

Antonelli, who had been partnered with Ottaviani, sat down on the grass. The sun was bright behind a cloud of pollution. "Gianfranco," he said to Vezza, "you can't cheat at boccie. No one can. In that way boccie is wholly abstract, unlike life in every detail."

Ottaviani said, "He doesn't bother me. He's a bad loser, always has been. He's had so much experience at it, you'd think he'd have mastered the decorum by now—"

"I lose only at games, my friend. I always win in the real world." Vezza's smile was full of oddly shaped teeth like yellow candy corn.

"The real world!" Poletti scoffed. "You haven't noticed the real world since the dawn of time! Why, the real world is as foreign to you as—"

Cardinal Garibaldi interrupted, his round little eyes in his round face glittering and alert. "Speaking of the real world, where does the matter of the murdered nun stand—"

"She wasn't murdered," Antonelli murmured. "It was the man clad as a priest who died."

"Ah, we're at cross purposes. I was referring to the murdered nun in America, but it's all the same, isn't it? So, what of the nun who was *nearly* murdered? What's the news?"

Cardinal Poletti was kicking the balls over toward the heavy gunnysack in which they'd brought them to the lawn. "There is no news. They haven't yet been able to identify the priest—if priest he was. He had only one eye, apparently—"

"I'm not surprised," Vezza said, "after that fall!"

"No, no, he had only one eye even before he fell." Poletti sighed wearily. "But he was badly disfigured by the fall—"

"No, actually you are in error there." Vezza waggled his ancient, wrinkled finger. "He was not disfigured by the fall. He was disfigured by the landing. And the truck or bus that then ran over him."

"The real question which interests me," Antonelli sighed from beneath the floppy hat that shaded his eyes, "is why did he try to kill the nun, Sister Elizabeth. We know of course that she was Sister

Valentine's dearest friend . . . which I presume ties her to Driskill and his lot. But why kill her? And the Americans are playing too big a part in all this. That always leads to no good."

"Oh, they're not such bad chaps," Garibaldi said diplomatically, "once you get to know them."

"My God, man!" Ottaviani said. The corner of his mouth twitched with the pain which seldom left him. "You're such an appalling innocent! How could you ever have reached your present station? Americans are the very worst. Bulls marauding in the china shop, no attention to tradition and the rules of the game . . . in short, I *like* them! They shake things up. And they think we're the crafty, devious, plotting bastards . . . they flatter us. I haven't known a truly crafty, devious cardinal in twenty years! We're all children compared with our predecessors. And the Americans have charmingly little self-knowledge. They don't quite understand what vicious, cold-blooded swine they are. Yes, I *do* like them."

"Then you'll be delighted to hear," Garibaldi said, "that Drew Summerhays, no less, is here in Rome."

"Good Lord," Poletti said. "The Holy Father may already be dead and Summerhays knows it before we do!" His face showed that he was only half joking.

"What's he sniffing around here for?" Vezza snorted.

"A professional vulture," Poletti said. He was kneeling in the grass, putting the balls into the gunnysack. The sun was warm for the end of November.

"And I suppose we're not?" Ottaviani smiled thinly.

Poletti took no notice of him. "A pope is dying, then Summerhays will not be far behind. He is bound to be here to force somebody's hand, push his own man forward. . . . Who *is* this man, by the way?"

Ottaviani shrugged for all of them. "We'll know soon enough."

Poletti said, "Indelicato is going to be asking me for a head count. Core support . . . people he can count on for votes and for rounding up others." He scanned the faces. The sun was shining in his eyes. He shielded them like an Indian scout.

"Well," Vezza muttered, "it's only common sense to hear what Summerhays has to say before we commit ourselves—"

Ottaviani grinned wolfishly. "Greed dies only with the man himself. It never lessens with great age. Exhibit A, our old, *very* old friend Vezza. I rest my case."

"I gather that Fangio is lining up the outlanders," Garibaldi said. Like a plump sponge, he always seemed to soak up a surprising amount of peculiar news. "He promises them access whether they be Marxists, Africans, Japs, Eskimos, South Americans, Trobriand Islanders, Methodists, or ax murderers. And, of course, D'Ambrizzi is very cool. He never gives a hint, says he hasn't really thought about it . . . but the fact is he knows a great deal and he can call in a lot of debts. Between the blackmail and the gratitude, the Throne of Peter may await him. And if Summerhays is behind him, then we know the money's there if it comes to that."

"Who's working for him on the outside? Do we know it's Summerhays?"

Antonelli crossed his legs, inspected his sneakers, flicked at a grass stain, sighed. "With Lockhardt dead, my guess would be he'd have the other Americans. Summerhays, Driskill—"

"Driskill is a sick man," Poletti said, "and Summerhays is two hundred years old. Maybe," he added hopefully, "they don't carry the weight they once did—"

"Money," Vezza said, "is always heavy."

"But Driskill isn't well, I tell you," Poletti insisted. "His daughter has been murdered. His son is apparently on the verge of madness—Indelicato remains our strongest choice. He will know how to deal with the crisis at hand."

"Driskill," Ottaviani said, "will give Summerhays his proxy and stay home. We need to know where Summerhays stands."

"The man's frail as a leaf!" Poletti said. "Do we actually *know* what he's up to?"

"Well, he doesn't wear a flashing neon sign," Ottaviani observed sourly. "Line up behind me if you support D'Ambrizzi, right this way for the latest thing in indulgences, step right up and claim your bribes. . . . It's rather more subtle than that. Summerhays was in Paris, by the way."

"D'Ambrizzi's just back from Paris."

"Precisely. They're plotting, take my word for it." Poletti looked away, out into the cloud of crud drooping over Rome. "How do we stand now, D'Ambrizzi or Indelicato? We each represent a great many votes."

"I won't commit myself," Vezza said, shaking his head. "Not with Summerhays in the game."

"Are there any clean candidates in the field?"

"What in the world are you talking about? Getting into the running gets you dirty. Don't be fatuous."

"But are they dirty enough to hurt them in the voting?"

"Well, now, nobody's that dirty!"

"How is the Holy Father?"

"Sinking," Poletti said. "But hanging on."

"Is he going to take a hand in this?"

"Who knows?"

"Indelicato's picked a wonderful time for a party."

"Perhaps it will cut the tension."

"Nonsense. He's turning up the heat. He thrives on tension. He'll never crack."

"Well, if he expects D'Ambrizzi to crack . . . he's going to have a hellishly long wait."

"The point is someone is going to have to start leaning hard on people."

"The point is either Indelicato or D'Ambrizzi is going to have to be forced out—or throw his support to someone else—or we're going to have a nobody sneaking in to win . . . we've seen that happen. And we know what had to be done."

"Start leaning on people? What are you talking about? Indelicato is already leaning on us. On *me*!" Poletti stood up. "I have another tape for you to hear. The second conversation between D'Ambrizzi and the Holy Father—"

"You know, I feel uneasy about all this taping—"

"Garibaldi, you are made of noble stuff. If it makes you uneasy, by all means stay out here, sharpen up your boccie, and don't sully your ears."

"My God, I only said *uneasy* . . . don't jump all over me this way! Relax." He shrugged his narrow, round shoulders. "Come. It is our duty—however disagreeable—to listen to these tapes."

"How adaptable you are, my friend."

In the darkened library the cardinals took up their customary positions around the low table. The coffee was served, they waited while Poletti fumbled the tape onto the spindles with his short, hairy fingers. Then he pushed the button and the voice of Cardinal D'Ambrizzi was among them.

You are Callistus. Remember the first Callistus and your mission will be clear. . . .

I don't know. . . .

Listen to me, Callistus! Be strong!

But how, Giacomo?

That Callistus, in a world where countless challenges to the Church sprang up like weeds, from cat goddesses of the Nile to the seahorse fairies of the Celts, that Callistus hewed to the true meaning of the Church. The Roman Empire was coming apart, chaos was encroaching from every side . . . but Callistus saw that the business of the Church was salvation . . . as Jesus made clear, the salvation of all sinners. All sinners. Even ourselves when we had sinned. There was time to repent and be saved, so said the first Callistus, and Hippolytus cried out against him, called him a whoremonger for decreeing absolution for prostitutes and adulterers who repented. Hippolytus, the first self-proclaimed antipope. But Callistus was right. Salvation was all . . . and when he was murdered in the street it was Pontian who carried on. . . .

What are you telling me?

Make salvation the work of this Church. Reclaim it from the secular world, withdraw from politics and money-grubbing and the wielding of secular power and pressure. Wield moral power! Offer eternal salvation, not riches and power here and now. Care for the souls . . . and the killings by which the secular world holds sway will cease and this Church . . . this Church, Holiness, will be saved!

Tell me how, Giacomo . . .

When the tape ended and Cardinal D'Ambrizzi's voice had faded to a faint dry whisper and was gone, the room was quiet. A breeze pushed at the heavy curtains.

Finally Vezza said, "Which one of them is crazier? That would seem to be the question, would it not?" He peered at the control of his old hearing aid, tapped it with a long fingernail.

"You can never be sure about D'Ambrizzi," Antonelli said softly. "Whatever his agenda—and I don't for a minute believe we've just heard him state it—you can be sure that he's not crazy. What he's pulling on the Holy Father remains to be seen . . . but remember this, no one is a better manipulator of hearts and minds than Saint Jack . . . Callistus is becoming Saint Jack's tool . . . but what job he intends to use him for is a mystery."

"We can be frank within these walls," Poletti said.

"Who says D'Ambrizzi or Indelicato doesn't have you bugged?"

Garibaldi's question stopped Poletti in mid-thought. Garibaldi smiled, the tip of his tongue tracing the line where his plump lips met, pressed.

"Now you've frightened him," Antonelli said. "It's all right, Poletti. Go on."

"I was about to say that the kind of talk we've been hearing is the sort of madness we heard in the old days from John XXIII. He was going to revolutionize everything. He was setting out to strip the Church of its worldly power and wealth. I need hardly remind you of the action we had to take. An unhappy task. Thank God, I was not a cardinal at the time—"

"Lucky man," Vezza muttered. "Murder, it was—"

"But I *was* here for John Paul I," Poletti said. "Poor misguided fool . . ."

"Old news, old news," Vezza grumbled from deep within his jowls. "What are you suggesting? Murder, I suppose. Blood, blood, always a cry for blood." He might have been talking to himself. "But Callistus is dying. . . . Why commit murder when you need only count the hours, when time will do it for you?"

The quiet stretched on for minutes, each man contemplating his own morality, his own agenda. Their eyes steadfastly refused to meet.

Finally Ottaviani's knifelike, bleak voice broke the stillness like an iron pipe on plate glass.

"All well and good for Callistus," he said, "but Saint Jack is in perfect health. . . ."

Peaches O'Neale arrived at the Driskill place in the fading gray light of late afternoon. Hugh Driskill had called him at the parish house. The great man's voice had been weak, yet stronger than Peaches had expected. He said he'd been home forty-eight hours and was about to go stark staring mad. He said he needed company and wanted Peaches to stop over when he could get away. He also had something specific on his mind, but he'd tell Peaches about that when he saw him.

Margaret Korder, Hugh's personal secretary and all-purpose shield from the world, opened the door. Behind her a large nurse in starched white hovered, torn between watching the door and peering down the length of the Long Room. She seemed to be straining at an invisible leash which kept her from going on through, into the Long Room.

"Oh, Father," Margaret Korder said softly, "he's not behaving very well, I'm afraid. I think he needs some male company, but all his regulars are so work-obsessed and, well, you know . . . you are just what he needs. Someone to *talk* to rather than run the world with, if you see my point. He won't let this poor nurse into the room. Literally. He's far from top shape, but he can still raise more absolute holy hell than any other dozen men I know." He was helping her into the mink coat she'd had no trouble affording on her salary. "I'm still down at the Nassau Inn. Practically permanent by now."

"You are a jewel." Peaches smiled.

"It's a vocation, Father. My life's work. Though I am worn down to a mere zircon tonight."

"Ah, Ms. Korder. You must know where a great many bodies are buried. I'm surprised you've never been kidnapped."

"Father!"

"A joke, just a joke. Is he going to give me a particularly hard time?"

"Just don't argue with him." She sighed. "A drink, a cigar, we can't stop him. When we did try he got purple and looked like he was going to explode—that's got to be worse than the drink and the cigar. If you need her, Nurse Wardle stands ready out here in the hallway or in the kitchen or somewhere. You know where to get hold of me. I'll be curled up with room service and a good book. Have you ever read Father Dunn's books?"

"Sure. He's a friend of mine."

"I love them. What a devious mind! How can a priest know so much about sex?"

Peaches blushed, looked sixteen. "Wondrous powers of imagination. What else could it be?"

"Well, you must be right, mustn't you?"

Hugh Driskill's face was drawn. The lines at the corners of his eyes had deepened. When Peaches approached the couch, he laid aside one of several photograph albums bound in dark green leather. Peaches saw a flash of Val's face, a color picture taken on the tennis court, her legs tanned and straight, the skirt flaring up in the wind to show her white pants. She was smiling, squinting in the sun, one hand shading her eyes. Twenty . . . oh, hell, twenty-five years ago. It was unspeakably painful for him to think that she was dead.

"Sit down, Father. Have a drink. Plenty of fixings." The Laphroaig and a pitcher of water and a silver ice bucket sat on the coffee table. "Go on, Peaches, fill 'em up. I'm going to keep you here for a while. You can listen to me complain about the turn things have taken here at the end. Top this off for me, I'm very dry." He watched while Peaches made a drink for himself, then refilled the other heavy, squat glass. "The doctors, the nurses, this incredible creature who's here now—they treat me as if I'm dying, and I say if I'm dying, what difference does it make which day it happens? Margaret is a life saver. But things, as you may have noticed, are not going well . . . the fact is, it's hardly worth being alive. But there are a few things I have to do before I go—my God, where did the time go, Peaches? The lament of every dying man, I suppose. Well, so be it. My daughter is dead, I'm led to believe the Church is somehow implicated, my son is off God knows where, inconveniencing the Church and making an ass of himself. . . . I have friends in Rome, you know, I still hear a thing or two. Ah, yes, I surely do . . ." His speech might have been just slightly slurred: Peaches couldn't quite be sure. But he'd never heard Hugh Driskill engage in such a stream of consciousness. He'd always been a man of a very few words and those markedly impersonal. The old man wore a bathrobe of dark scarlet with royal blue piping, his initials on the breast pocket. He gestured with his glass, ice tinkling, at the far end of the room near the foyer where Nurse Wardle still stood her ground. "She's afraid of me. She realizes who I am. Poor wretched girl. I was unkind. Told her she needed a shave. I don't know what got into me. . . ."

"Well," Peaches said, "she could use a quick once-over."

Hugh Driskill laughed, a weak, hollow sound. "Peaches, no offense, but I don't believe God exactly intended you for the cloth."

"Other people have occasionally reached that conclusion."

"You're an innocent. Bad priest material. But a nice man. You *are* a nice man. My daughter loved you . . . you were a good boy. Tell me, did you love Val, Peaches?"

"Yes, I did."

"Well, that squares. She told me you did. And she said you were a trustworthy man—"

"When was all this, sir?"

"Sir? *Sir?* Come on, Peaches. It was the last time we talked. Just before she died."

"Really?"

Hugh Driskill was staring at the girl in the photograph, squinting into the sunshine. He slowly turned the pages. Peaches saw so much of the family's history passing by, upside down. "Here you are . . . standing beside a Christmas tree with Val . . . happy days, long ago. We couldn't see the future, could we, Father?"

"Just as well," Peaches said. "Would have ruined those happy days long ago."

"Now here, this is my wife. There she is with Cardinal Spellman . . . not long before she died. She was an unhappy woman, my Mary, but of course you knew her, didn't you. . . ."

"Well, not really, sir. I was too young. I came along later."

"Of course you did. What was I thinking of? Well, you didn't miss much, to be honest. Mary was a distant sort of creature, or she could be. She was never very good with children . . . I don't know, the truth is I have trouble remembering her all that well—is that shameful? Well, my memory generally is not so hot lately. The truth is not always a welcome visitor. For instance, I'm told the Holy Father has all but kicked the bucket."

"You'd know more about that than I. You've got your contacts. Cardinal D'Ambrizzi . . ."

"Yes, I guess I would, even in my pathetic state. Old Jack has called me a few times. Well, Peaches, I might as well admit the ghastly truth. I've brought you here to put the screws to you, my boy. Look upon me as the Inquisition. . . ." He smiled crookedly. "Do you recall one of your predecessors over there in New Pru, Father John Traherne. You do recall him?"

"Father Traherne. Sure. Of course."

"Well, I got to know him pretty well. He was in his later years an obsessively curious old fart, was Father John. Let me tell you a story about him, Peaches. You play the part of my son tonight . . . the son I never had, the son who should have been a priest, not the son who turned to footballing and lawyering instead of—well, I won't blacken his name to an old friend of his. . . ." He held out his glass for a refill.

Peaches was squirming at the turn things were taking. From where he sat he could see the forecourt, which was under illumination. He saw his beat-up old car being spruced up by the snow which had begun falling since his arrival. The radio weatherman had said the first big snow of the winter was moving in from Ohio and the Midwest beyond. It was snowing hard but there was no wind and the scene was peaceful as a Christmas card. He filled Hugh Driskill's glass with Laphroaig, water, and ice.

"Father Traherne used to get pretty well loaded with me from time to time. He'd get a real skinful. He knew I paid his salary over at New Pru, he was an Irishman, so he naturally resented me all to hell. He was always looking for an angle, always wanted to be a bigger man than I, wanted to show me he didn't need me . . . you know the type, little men who resent their lives . . . he drank himself to death, no surprise there— You don't drink much, do you, Peaches?"

"No, sir. Never much of a drinker."

"I remember one time when Traherne came over, in his cups, Irish courage, and he told me how Monsignor D'Ambrizzi—that's as he was then—had come to see him one day over in New Pru. That's when D'Ambrizzi was a visitor here with us after the war in Europe. Well, Traherne was taking great pleasure in telling me how he and D'Ambrizzi had this big secret. Something I didn't know about and they did. Small mind, Traherne." Hugh Driskill's fist tightened around the glass as he sipped. He'd lost weight, not only in his face where the skin had taken on a slightly translucent quality, but also in his hands. The veins were like gnarled roots now, the skin ashy, sinking in upon them. "Well, he couldn't resist running his mouth, you know the type. Hard to tell the real thing from the whiskey and the blarney. Anyway, he tells me how D'Ambrizzi is this big old pal of his, how he came over to New Pru and gave him these papers, important papers, for safekeeping. . . . Traherne says he's to keep them safe until the time came when he'd need them. . . . Traherne says that D'Ambrizzi told him never to let anyone, *anyone,* see these pages. But old Traherne—this is years and years later, D'Ambrizzi's a cardinal practically running the Church—old Traherne's got a wild hair somewhere and he's drunk and he's got to come lording it over me!" He laughed, shaking his head. The nurse had given up, stomped off to the kitchen. The snow was falling thicker. Peaches wished he were somewhere else. Anywhere would have done.

"Can you believe it, Peaches? The old nitwit had kept his secret all those years and what does he do? He gets drunk and has to show me how important he is so he spills the beans about the manuscript . . . he kept teasing me about it, kept going on about how important it must be and wouldn't I like a peek at it, the silly

old boozer. I told him that D'Ambrizzi had written the whole thing
in my own home, if he'd wanted me to read it he could have asked
me to take a look at it then. Since he didn't, I had no intention of
reading it at Father Traherne's suggestion and I told him just that."
He sipped his scotch, pulled his robe tighter, as if a chill were
creeping upon him. His face was pale, his eyes sharp, quick,
restless. "But . . . things change. My daughter has been murdered,
a man she may have loved was also murdered . . . someone, maybe
the same man who killed them, also tried to kill my son . . . the
Church may be involved in some crazy way—how the hell should I
know? But the pope is dying, D'Ambrizzi is nearing the Throne of
Peter itself . . . it all seemed to be getting mixed up in my mind
while I lay in that damnable hospital bed and the funny thing was,
Peaches, I kept thinking about how D'Ambrizzi stayed here with us
for a while . . . how he'd worked in the study, writing and writing
. . . and then I got to thinking about Traherne, and D'Ambrizzi
giving him those papers for safekeeping and never coming back for
them or sending word . . . Peaches, you follow me on this?"

Peaches had gone to the window, stood watching the falling
snow, the way it drifted gently into piles and cast soft midnight-
blue shadows. He'd jammed his hands into the pockets of his baggy
corduroys but couldn't keep from clenching his fists. He wished
he'd never heard of the goddamned papers.

"Sure, I'm following you, sir. But—"

"But nothing, as they say. Come here, Peaches, I can't see you
over there." He watched him turn from the window and walk back
to stand before him. "Now, come on, boy. Did Traherne ever tell
you about these papers? Or Father Kilgallen, your immediate
predecessor, did he ever take you aside and say listen, sonny, there's
a little secret I've got to tell you about . . . ?"

"Absolutely not, sir." Peaches felt himself blushing, a hot flush
across his face like a passing shadow.

"Well, you found the papers on your own—is that the way it
was? You stumbled across them, wondered what they were, had to
take a look . . . was that what happened? It's no crime, you know.
He wrote it forty years ago."

"Mr. Driskill, seriously, I don't know what—"

"Father, Father." Hugh Driskill was smiling faintly, as if the
emotion caused him pain. "You don't have the first quality a priest

needs. You cannot tell a lie, never could. You're an honest man. You know about the papers, don't you, Peaches?"

"Mr. Driskill, it was an accident, honest to God—"

"I understand, son. Believe me, I do. Now, I've got some more questions for you. Just relax. You all right, Peaches?"

"I don't know, sir. And that's the truth." Peaches was wondering where Father Dunn was, what advice he'd have.

Half an hour later Peaches was back in his banged-up old car, wishing he'd put on his snow tires, heading for New Prudence. He had his orders. Go get the D'Ambrizzi manuscript and bring it back. Tonight. The hell with the snow. There was something about Hugh Driskill. There was damn near no arguing with him.

Her first night back in Rome, Sister Elizabeth went to the flat on the Via Veneto after paying a quick call at the home of the Order at the top of the Spanish Steps. Driskill and Dunn had tried to get her to join them for dinner at the Hassler, also at the top of the Spanish Steps, but she'd said she was tired and wanted to check in at the home office. They had watched her go, she'd felt their eyes on her retreating back. She'd also rejected Driskill's suggestion that he and Dunn accompany her to the flat for a quick look around the place, just a precaution against possible villainy. She was having none of that, either. She'd killed one man, she would kill another if need be: she tried to sound hard and indifferent and knew her performance was laughable. It would, however, have to do. She wanted none of their company.

But by the time she stood alone in the hallway outside the door her heart was beating a tattoo and inside the flat she was turning on lights as quickly as she could. Bright lights, no shadows, that was the point. And when she went to the bathroom door she knew a leisurely bath was out of the question. No stretching out in the tub, no dozing off with the steam rising around her, no loss of control. She showered instead with the shower door open, as well as the bathroom door, so she could see the length of the hallway. It was a very brief shower.

In her robe, she poured a glass of wine, boiled linguine and made a sauce, then settled on the couch in the living room with an Ennio Morricone film score on the turntable. But nothing could keep her from thinking, nothing could keep her from replaying the scene with Ben and the aftermath, over and over in her mind.

She'd been light-headed with anger and frustration when she had whirled away from him and knocked over her chair and made her dramatic, empty gesture, her exit. She was nearly blind with tears of humiliation as well as the anger and the furious, overpowering frustration with the man and his crazy, impenetrable hatred of the Church, its servants and, apparently—she had the evidence of her eyes and ears—of herself in particular. His hatred was so visceral, unforgiving, unreasonable: she was exhausting her supply of offensive adjectives. How, *how* could he hurt her the way he had? When she was vulnerable and had spoken of her life with such trust? What was the point? Simply to wound?

But, of course, if it were mere cruelty, Ben Driskill was a jerk and a swine.

And she knew that was not the case.

His hurt and his pain, hidden however deeply they might be, were greater. Greater than the damage done to her ego, the boot applied to her pride. The question was, could she in any case help him?

It seemed unlikely.

Yet he'd said—my God, had she heard him correctly?—he'd said he loved her. . . .

Where did she go from there?

Whatever she did, she always made everything worse. She thought she'd truly been offering her openness, her trust, and she'd been certain he would accept it, accept it as read. But whatever she did, she always made everything worse.

Nonsense! Not *everything*. Just when it came to this damned Driskill.

Driskill had looked pale and shaky and half broken during the meeting with Kessler. Dunn, however, was his usual unfathomable self. Whose side, she wondered, was he really on?

Ambrose Calder. Now, there was a piece of work. Dr. Strangelove's first cousin. How much of his rambling did Ben and Dunn take at face value?

D'Ambrizzi as Simon Verginius was preposterous.

But back to square one: who was behind the *assassini*? It simply couldn't be D'Ambrizzi because what they were talking about in the present—if not the past—was pure evil. She knew D'Ambrizzi. He couldn't be evil. . . .

Then, who could it be?

The curia? A cabal within the curia? Maybe someone, a single man in a position of great power: Indelicato? Ottaviano or Fangio? Someone she didn't know at all? Maybe someone outside the official structure of the Church, one of the lay princes, some twisted equivalent of Lockhardt? Archduke? Or the Collector? *Who were they?*

Could it, she wondered sleepily, be the pope himself?

Maybe it was an unseen hand, someone who could never be revealed, a kind of infection, a plague, a symbol . . . and maybe it would achieve its aim or run its course and the killings would stop and the mystery would slowly fade, generations would pass, until it was time for the *assassini* to strike again and keep the Church true to the needs of its secret masters.

Now she sat with her empty plate and her empty glass, staring at the terrace where the man had tried to kill her. She saw him again, the milky eye, felt the glass candle chimney in her hand, felt the impact as it hit his face. . . . How to kill the memory?

She'd screwed up everything so badly.

People didn't realize how important for a religious were the relationships you made outside the Church. They couldn't know what such things meant, what connections they implied, in some cases what hopes they could represent.

The fact was, she'd ruined things with Ben Driskill back in Princeton with her uncertainty and self-absorption and fear. She'd hidden in the Church, taken refuge from a world she wasn't sure she could control—but the world had reached in anyway, grabbed her, torn her from safety. She had admired and liked and felt drawn to him: she had turned on him not for anything he had done but for her own failures of commitment, her own doubts and fears about the course she had chosen for her life. She was making him pay for her own mistakes, making him pay while she indulged in an orgy of self-doubt and ran to hide in the skirts of the Order.

The Order had, in a way, asked too little of her, and she had given only what it required, unlike Sister Val, who had given so much more, had enlarged and defined the Order with her determination and commitment to make it something better than it had been. At the moment, she felt unworthy of Sister Val.

How could she ever explain her own twisted logic to Ben, who saw only her coldness and his own humiliation at her hands in

Princeton? She knew he was right: with his sister newly murdered, she had held out her hand to him and when he'd reached out to take it she'd turned away. Maybe now they were even, after Avignon.

Now, back in Rome, all she wanted to do was sleep. When she woke maybe it would all be over.

Sleep, however, proved elusive.

"Would you care to explain just what was going on with the nun?"

"Eminence, he was never intended to kill her, I made that clear to him, I tried to—"

"Not clear enough! The whole thing was a mess and it's just getting worse!"

"Horstmann said this man could be trusted—"

"Horstmann hadn't seen him in thirty years! Horstmann is an old man and a fanatic. He must have gone mad years ago. Maybe he was mad at the beginning. Anyway, it's not the nun we need to kill . . . it's Driskill—"

"But, Eminence, is that wise? Now that he's here in Rome?"

"Don't presume to tell me what is wise! And may I remind you that you are the one who has let Driskill get out of hand?"

"We need him now, he needs us . . . we must listen to him. Forgive me, but that is a fact—"

"Horstmann should have killed Driskill in Paris . . . or at St. Sixtus. . . . Time is running out. The Holy Father could die at any moment. We must be sure of the outcome before that—"

"Is there still any chance he might make his wishes known?"

"A two-edged sword, obviously. If I receive his blessing, it's one thing. If it's someone else, it couldn't be worse. Better he should just die. What now? What of Horstmann?"

"Eminence?"

"We may need him once more." He shrugged.

"Who? It's dangerous now, more dangerous than ever. Everyone has come to Rome. Whom do you have in mind?"

"You wouldn't like it. But it would solve everything—"

The name dawned on him. "Horstmann would never do it, Eminence."

"He will do what he's told. He was programmed a long time ago and by an expert. He's not a man. He's an instrument."

"Forgive me, Eminence. But he *is* a man."

"Don't be a coward now. We're almost there. Remember, the Church must be saved."

Pope Callistus paid no attention anymore to matters of night and day, dark and light. The darkness—the personal darkness—was encroaching, coming closer with each breath, each heartbeat. He sensed the systems shutting down. Life had been too short but, perhaps, just long enough. He wondered what came next. He was very tired. And very frustrated.

He was living more and more in the past, his mind drifting in and out of the shadows, remembering, seeing old comrades once more. Horstmann, little Leo, LeBecq dying in the graveyard, the night of waiting in the snowy mountain night, waiting for the train, Simon . . . they all seemed to gather around his bed, nodding, paying their respects, the living and the dead helping to see him out. . . .

It was too late now to become a new Callistus. Too late to follow D'Ambrizzi's plan. He'd told the cardinal that there was no time left and the great heavy head had bowed, nodding.

"Hold on a little longer," D'Ambrizzi said.

Callistus was dozing, muttering in his sleep, when his secretary gently touched his shoulder.

"Yes, yes," he said, his mouth dry and clumsily working its way around the words. "What is it? More pills?"

"No, Holiness. I have this for you."

Callistus saw the plain envelope.

"From whom?"

"I don't know, Holiness. It was delivered downstairs, by messenger."

"All right. Turn on that lamp." He nodded toward the table at bedside. "Thank you. I'll ring for you if I need you. Thank you."

Alone, he reached into the pocket of his robe and felt the Florentine dagger, pricked his finger on the razor-sharp point. He removed the dagger from his pocket, saw the drop of blood on his fingertip. He put it to his mouth, tasted it, then turned to the envelope. He slid the dagger's point under the flap and slit it open.

There was a single sheet of paper, folded across the middle. He opened it and saw the line of handwritten script. Before he put the words together he recognized the hand. Slowly, as he read, a small smile crossed his face.

You are still one of us. Do not forget . . .
                                                    Simon V.

2

DRISKILL

It was a curious calm, as if the world stood waiting for the second shoe to drop. Of course, the world knew nothing about it. But I had that eye-of-the-hurricane feeling. We were all waiting for the eye to pass and the heavy weather to hit again. So long as Cardinal D'Ambrizzi remained in camera with the pope, it seemed that the calm would persist. I wondered, is he really dying, the poor old man who presided over a Church that showed so many signs of tearing itself to pieces, or is it just another story I've fallen for that will have a surprise ending? Nothing was predictable. For years and years all of my life had been so routine, the matters crossing my desk and the faces of my clients and their inevitable concerns, the unceasing sniping between my father and me, my night sweats when I dreamed of the Jesuits and my leg flared up from my little problem with the chain, the occasional woman I'd meet at one or another charity function and with whom I'd conduct a moderately satisfying, short-term affair.

But now—now nothing was predictable anymore. I didn't seem able to foresee a goddamn thing. I'd never felt so naive and confused in my entire life. And I was up to my knees in dead bodies. And I was armed with a toy gun. And all I wanted to do—or more accurately, was *able* to do—was think about a nun.

Finally my resolve to stay away from her, to mind my own business, collapsed. I suppose it was inevitable. I simply could not leave things the way they'd been when we left Avignon. How could I? I'd told the woman I loved her. *What* had I been thinking of as I blurted it out? Well, I was thinking that I'd fallen in love with her. Obviously. First time in my life. A nun. And now I was suddenly forgetting all the fears that had kept me safe from her so far. Now I had seen the light. That was the only explanation. The fact of the matter was that when it came to two people thrown together by circumstance, nun or not, neither of their minds worked in blissfully ignorant isolation. The fact was, she was a living, breathing woman.

I called her, full of an unspoken apology, and suggested a walk in the Borghese Gardens. "I've got to talk to you before all of this goes any further," I said. "We'll go for a walk. And I'm going to ask you to listen very carefully to what I have to say. I owe you an apology. But there's more."

"All right," she said. I heard the doubt in her voice.

I felt safe—whatever that meant—in the Borghese Gardens, out in the open, with tourists who had never heard of the *assassini* strolling and laughing and consulting guidebooks, with women carrying babies and pushing prams. The villa had been built in the seventeenth century for a Borghese cardinal. The park spread away, immense and green, a topography of undulating slopes, small lakes, villas, gentle views, meadows. The great esplanade of the Piazza di Siena shone happily in the sunshine. The pines were everywhere.

We were walking on the grass, following the shoreline of one of the lakes. Children laughed happily. She couldn't help smiling at them. Children. Looking at all the dapper Italians in their tight-fitting suits, coats slung over their shoulders, sunglasses, I felt more than ever like a broken-nosed pug who hadn't won one in way too long. I'd seen the face in the mirror. Eyes dark-rimmed, my face drawn with exhaustion, as if it had been in trouble forever and had only now shown the full extent of the damage. What a gorgeous guy.

"Well," she said, "what's so important that I have to listen very carefully?"

"Listen, Sister, and you shall hear . . ." I tried smiling, and she looked off across the flat surface of the lake. "While I was going through the mess in Ireland, I ran headfirst into a couple of things that I've got to tell you. They affect both of us. It's not exactly the easiest thing I've ever done, deciding to tell you—"

"Maybe you shouldn't, then," she said. "Think twice, Ben."

"I've thought a thousand times. It doesn't seem to get any easier. So . . . first, I lost my nerve up there. I saw it happen and it was ugly, like I was watching some other poor, contemptible bastard come unglued. Only it was me. Old Ben Driskill was fresh out of guts. I've taken my share of beatings, one way or another, believe me, but this was something different, what happened at St. Sixtus. . . ." I wanted to confide in her as she had in me, something hidden from public view: something to make myself vulnerable. I wanted to put my faith in her. I wanted to show her I could trust her. That was my apology. "I was lost in the fog and the ocean was making the earth shake and I found that little old man with his throat cut in the cave and I was afraid to go back outside . . . but I finally went. I had to get out of there, but I was afraid he was waiting for me and out there in the fog I wouldn't be able to find him . . . Horstmann. He'd see me but I wouldn't see him and I knew he was going to kill me. I knew I was beaten. Still, I went back out there even though I knew I was going to die. I hadn't come apart inside yet, I could face whatever was waiting for me.

"Then I was wandering and staggering around in the fog and I saw Father Leo strung up on that cross, upside down, all blue and pink with blood and his arm beckoning to me, flapping, and I saw what Horstmann could do and I knew how overmatched I was. I couldn't stop him. And I was going to be next. . . . It wasn't just fear, Elizabeth. It was something so much worse. I was empty, I couldn't imagine fighting back anymore." I caught her eye for an instant. I wanted her to understand. I wanted her to absolve me of the unspeakable sin of terror. "I felt as if I'd become one with him, the killer and the victim, two signatories to the same agreement— he would kill and I would die.

"And I broke and ran. Like a child with the bogeyman right

behind him. He was inside me, we were the same being—I ran and ran and I didn't stop running until I was in the car, my heart didn't stop racing until I was miles and miles away—you see, I didn't know that kind of fear existed."

I kept walking, hands in pockets, staring at the ground, as if I were alone with my cowardice. Just then I was alone.

"I understand," she said. "You can't blame yourself. Yours was the only sane reaction." She very nearly touched me. But she drew back before the impulse had hold of her.

"I wasn't simply afraid," I said. "I had lost my hope and my will to survive. I didn't know if I could find it again. I didn't know where to look. I didn't know what good I'd be anymore. The fear is still with me, I can't shake it—"

"You'll find yourself," she said. "It's your nature. You'll be all right. You're like your father, unbeatable." The words were out of her mouth before she could bite them off. She knew better than to compare me with my father.

"That's the second thing I realized. I *am* like my father. He made me, you see. Created me, formed me. Not with love, not by setting me an example and encouraging me . . . but by despising me. He despised what he saw as my weakness and he turned me into a tough, unforgiving son of a bitch. I just can't help it. I *am* my father's son. I realized that after Ireland—I was sick of myself, but I knew what I wanted. I know what I want. I know what I have to do and I'll do it. . . . But there's nothing left inside me. And there's only one way to fill the void—"

"You see," she interrupted, "you've already begun to recover. You knew what you were doing, you knew what you had to do to put yourself back together." She tried to smile but it faded. She could see trouble ahead. I hadn't met with her just to apologize for the rough treatment in Avignon, a tidy return to friendship. She could see I hadn't finished making a mess at the edges of her life. I was going to be inconvenient and the nun was seeing all the warning signs. "You know . . ."

"I do know. That's the problem. There was only one place in the world I wanted to be—"

"Please, Ben, stop there." She took a few steps away, as if she could drift beyond the sound of my voice, blot it out. "Please, don't—"

"It was you," I said. "I wanted to be with you . . . I wanted to keep from dying and I wanted to be with you. Even more than I wanted to kill Horstmann. It was you, Elizabeth, and I'm damned if I know what to do about it. Everything between us had gone wrong but I remembered—I knew if I could get to you, I could make it all right. But I was so afraid of you, I keep making it worse, everything I do or say is wrong, it's the past I can't seem to escape, the Catholics. . . ."

She turned and walked away.

"Dammit," I said to her retreating back. I felt as if I were speaking an unfamiliar language. "I love you, Elizabeth."

She looked back at me for a moment. I thought she was going to cry. Her face was pale. But there were no tears. She, too, looked empty.

I followed her, reached out and touched her arm. She shook away from me. She wouldn't look at me. A solitary priest drew abreast of us, looked into our faces, nodded genially, and passed on, his heavy black shoes kicking the skirts of his cassock.

"Sister," I said, "you surprise me. I thought you'd have had this all figured out by now." I slowly released the breath I'd been holding.

A small boy stood before us, holding a black control box in both hands. Turning slowly on the lake was a large model yacht, trying to catch the wind in its lofty white sails. She watched the sails suddenly billow.

I sat down on the slope, took her hand, and pulled her down beside me. I knew I couldn't say anything. I'd said too much: I'd been in control only moments before, but no longer. I waited silently. She fixed her eyes on the white sails.

"I mean it, you know," I said at last. "There's no point in ignoring it. I can't explain it. I've fallen in love with you . . . I've seen myself lose my nerve, my will, and I've finally seen myself for what I am—my father's son. But I've found you. It's like finding hope. A treasure."

"You must stop," she said, her voice choked, trapped. "Please, Ben . . ." She blinked, eyes glistening. "It's all wrong, you shouldn't be saying these things. I'm not the woman for you, how can I be? And you're not the man for me. There can be no man for me. I am still a sister—" She was crying, wiped helplessly at a tear. "I am in so damn much pain." She couldn't go on.

"Listen to me—"

"No, I will not listen to you!" Her anger flared like a bonfire. "If you care about me at all, as you say you do, you'll stop this. You won't speak like this to me again. You will remember who and what I am . . . you will respect what I am!"

Her eyes met mine defiantly, the tears drying on her face. I'd had her for just that moment. An instant of the real Elizabeth at last. But now she was receding like a ghost. I'd done it all wrong, I'd driven her away just as I'd finally touched her. Her eyes were troubled, but her face was whitened with strain, her lips trembling. I didn't think. I took her shoulders and pulled her to me, kissed her, feeling her mouth so soft, salty with tears. It was all foreign to her: I felt the resolve leave her, felt her shaking in my arms as if anger and defiance were just words and this was something else. I kissed her mouth and her cheek, felt the softness, smelled her hair. *Elizabeth* . . .

Slowly, gently, she pushed me away, her hands between us, where I'd felt her breasts against my chest. I smiled at her, hopeful, and watched unbelieving as she shook her head. *No, no, no.* I read her face. Fear. She was afraid of me. She might have been a nun, a witch, facing her inquisitor, knowing she would burn, knowing the flames were crackling, knowing the end was at hand.

She was so deathly pale, staring at me, and I saw it all in her face. Her denial. And I felt it all festering inside me. *I might have known I couldn't trust you.* It was in her eyes, the set of her jaw. *You're one of them. I trusted you anyway, it's my own fault.* Her eyes stared at me, through me, as if we'd truly become part of some endless mutual nightmare of impossible, pointless love. *You are what you are, not a woman!*

"I didn't want to talk," she whispered. "You made me."

I could think of nothing more to say.

"Driskill . . ." I could barely hear her. "Please . . . don't look at me that way, Ben."

I stood up. "Are you coming, Sister?" I held out my hand.

She shook her head. I went away, moving through the clusters of tourists and priests. There were priests everywhere. The word was making the rounds. The pope was dying. Rome was filling.

The sails had caught the wind now and the little boy let nature take over. His father stood proudly to one side. "Good show, Tony! Good show, old chap!" The English at play.

When I looked back she was staring at the lake, her shoulders shaking. A priest was bending over, offering assistance.

Once I left her behind I struck off blindly and didn't give a damn where I went or what I did. I had to get myself under control and I had to try to deal with what had gone wrong in the idyllic setting of the gardens. And I had to remember what I'd come to Rome for. . . .

Reason told me I had no call to direct my anger at Elizabeth: she was what she was. Where warmth and desire lived she was cloistered, protected, empty. And I had been terribly wrong, made a sorry fool of myself. It was becoming a habit.

The odd thing was, having her pull the rug from beneath my silly hopes and emotions got the adrenaline going again. It got me back to the point where I'd been before she came to Paris. I was back to having nothing to lose. In a strange way, once I'd begun to recognize the feelings I had for her, I had begun to lose my way. I had given in to fear because suddenly I'd had all the reasons in the world to stay alive: I loved someone, unexpectedly, absurdly, but there it was. By slashing at me like a Horstmann of the soul, she had cut the cords tying me to life, to her. She wasn't alive inside, not to me, so I was cut free. Maybe she had saved me. I was back to wanting Horstmann, nothing else.

When I'd calmed the furies, realized I was lonely and needed to talk, there was only one place to go.

I found Father Dunn in his room at the pension which he preferred to the elegance of the Hassler, where I had taken a room. He said the hotel was part of the Vatican: "Can't you see the fog of deception that seeps under every door? No, Ben, not the Hassler for me, not this time." He was sitting at a plain table by a window where his bedroom overlooked the narrow street. He was smoking a cigar, staring at a large package wrapped in oilskin on the table.

"I saw you coming," he said through the smoke. "I hoped you'd stop."

I nodded at the package. "Get a bargain on a piece of the One True Cross?"

"Not exactly." He unwrapped the package, folding the oilskin back, then a cloth that was greasy and reeked of metallic oil.

A .45-caliber automatic, government issue, lay on the table. A heavy, dull presence in the small room. It was no toy.

"What kind of priest are you, anyway?" My mouth got dry when he picked it up, hefted it in his right hand. Nobody ever turned out to be what I expected.

"One who intends to get them before they get me. I've already told you that. People are getting killed out there. Horstmann wasn't impressed by your gun. He probably wouldn't have thought much of mine either."

Then he laughed quietly and wrapped the gun back up, dropped it into his open suitcase, looked at it, and slid it under the bed.

"Let's go for a walk," he said. "We need to talk. By the way, I don't like to bring bad tidings, but you look like a road accident. Maybe you'd better tell me why, my boy. When my life is in danger I like everything explained. Humor me."

He knew the mysterious geography of Trastevere like the Stations of the Cross. He almost breathed a sigh of relief when we crossed the bridge and were there, as if its secret corners somehow matched his own. He knew it so well that he told me about landmarks which no longer even existed.

"This is the Piazza San Apollonia. Over there, across the square, that's where the Church of San Apollonia stood. Gone now, of course. But once it was a home for repentant women. It was August of 1520 when a daughter of a baker, a girl called Margherita, came to them. Margherita . . . the whole world knows her now. She was Raphael's mistress, the girl in his great painting, 'Fornarina'—the baker's daughter. She was also the model for his Sistine Madonna. And the 'Veiled Woman' in the Pitti. Look at the pictures. Perky little breasts, nipples like rosebuds. She came to the nuns four months after Raphael died . . . even his final work, the 'Transfiguration' in the Vatican gallery, includes her, and he painted it right over there, in this same square." He walked on, pointing at one thing and another, and we passed on into the Via della Lungaretta. He was a masterful psychologist, soothing me, just chatting away while I kept reducing things to a more manageable perspective.

We stopped for a glass of chilly Orvieto at a café in the Piazza di San Maria. The fountain in the square tinkled and splashed and the kids were playing and the wine was bringing me back to life.

"You're so fond of telling stories," I said, "tell me the one about your gun."

"Oh, it's a kind of talisman, I suppose. Souvenir of my army days. I studied in Rome after the war, left it with a friend of mine here. I dropped by to see him yesterday, talked over old times. Thought I'd take a look at the old blunderbuss. And I discovered he'd taken good care of my souvenir." He shrugged. "Don't make too much of it, Ben." He signaled to the waiter for more wine. A breeze came up, ruffled its way around the square. The laughter of the girls was like a flurry of coins tossed, ringing, into the fountain. "Now you were going to tell me why you came to me looking like you'd just been hit by a truck. What's the problem?"

There was something about talking to Artie Dunn. Maybe it was that nothing ever seemed to surprise him. And he'd caught me when I needed to talk. So I told him about Elizabeth and me, the whole story, starting way back on that snowy night in Gramercy Park when my sister was still alive, what it was like when she turned up in Princeton, how she pulled me through Val's death. I told him how fresh and alive and bright she'd been and how it was she who'd isolated the *assassini,* given an identity to our enemy when it was only a fleeting shadow of an old man with silvery hair and a knife. She'd picked out the pattern in the ancient tapestry. She'd found the path to Badell-Fowler, she'd found the path into our own era. When it had all looked like a dead end, she had kept pushing ahead . . . and she'd been right. I told him all that. I told him that I'd fallen in love with her and I told him about what had happened in the Borghese Gardens.

He listened patiently, sipping wine as the breeze freshened, smelling a bit like rain. The water from the fountain splashed the kids.

"Cheer up," he said. "She's a woman. Lord Byron said the wisest of all things about women. 'There is a tide in the affairs of women which, when taken at the flood, leads . . . God only knows where.' That says it all, I'm afraid."

"But under all the up-to-date trappings," I said, "she's a nun and I'm a fool."

"Nonsense. Horse feathers. Our Sister Elizabeth is a modern woman. She happens to have chosen a career that makes certain unusual demands. Get anything else out of your mind. This isn't the Church of your childhood. Not even the Church of your Jesuit days. It's all changed. Almost beyond recognition."

"A vocation's a vocation," I said doggedly.

"My dear fellow," Dunn said blandly, "we're talking about an intellectually sophisticated woman here—not the child of illiterate peasants, not an unlettered bumpkin who saw Christ sitting in a tree and decided to consecrate her life as his bride. She has the full complement of doubts, not about her religion perhaps but about the conduct of her life, her own decision-making ability." He regarded me with a tolerant, reflective smile. "She's an exceedingly modern woman, which means she's confused, ambivalent, and a bit of a pain in the neck. That would be true were she a business executive, a professor, or a housewife—she's simply a nun, which is a little different. Not much, not anymore. She's not in the throes of a divine calling. Good Lord, the Order doesn't attract that sort. They want the cloister, those women. The Order specializes in activists and elitists and hotshots, that's just the way it is. Driskill, I really shouldn't have to be telling you this—you're a smart fella."

He lit a cigar which took a while and I kept trying to put what he'd said together with the Elizabeth I knew.

"The women the Order attracts, well, the Order knows it can't keep them all. The game is being played with new rules. And Sister Elizabeth is experiencing all the trials of her time. She's wondering about love, men, children, her personal commitment, her vows, her fear of her own weakness and vulnerability, the idea of failing in her own eyes as well as in the eyes of the Church. My goodness, Ben, you've been through a lot of this yourself. Think back. And face it, laddie, it's not easy being a woman these days. You're a halfway bright fella, you should be able to figure that out." He smoked, watching me like a professor waiting for a pupil's response.

"What, may I ask, makes you such an expert on women? It's like a nun telling people all about birth control and marriage and abortion. Just maybe you don't know what the hell you're talking about."

"You want a story? I'll tell you a story about priests and women. We've got to clear some of the cobwebs out of that poor old head of yours, my friend." He blew a perfect smoke ring and slid the cigar through the hole. "You'd better have another sip of wine."

He told me a remarkably poignant story about his postwar love affair in Paris with a married Frenchwoman. He had loved her and she him and she had had a daughter who meant a great deal to him. It had all ended very badly. Both women had died tragically and Father Dunn had a very tough time of it. It was all a long time ago and he told the story quietly as the fountain splashed and the wine flowed and his cigar burned down.

"Priests are far from perfect," he said. "Just men. We fight with all the same temptations. The acquisition of power, the loneliness, the bottle, women, lust in all its many guises. Salvatore di Mona solved his family's money problems when he became a cardinal, let alone Pope Callistus. It's perhaps not so amazing how many people want to come to the aid of a cardinal, any cardinal. The list of alcoholics, adulterers, traitors, no different from most groups of men under lots of pressure. We could both produce a lot of names . . ." He shrugged. "D'Ambrizzi is just one."

"D'Ambrizzi?"

"Don't tell me you're surprised at what Kessler told us. It's such a fit. He's the most worldly of men. Truly a *prince* of the Church. Power beyond your dreams, I assure you. Like Lockhardt, or your father or Summerhays, only operating from the other side of the fence. Birds of a feather. What D'Ambrizzi really loves is the intrigue, all the moves on the board."

"D'Ambrizzi," I said mostly to myself. Was it really possible he had ordered the murder of my sister, sent his old silver-haired weapon to kill her . . . to kill Lockhardt and Heffernan . . . to kill Brother Padraic and poor Leo. . . . And my gun was a toy.

We left the café. A fine mist had filled the air and the smell of fruit and flowers and restaurants was overwhelming, like an exotic bazaar.

He showed me the Church of Santa Maria, said to be the oldest in Rome because in the old imperial days Trastevere was a center of Jewish life. A meeting place for Christ's followers had been required and another Pope Callistus, the first of that name, had founded it. I followed him around a corner to the tiny Piazza di San Callistus— connected to Santa Maria by the Palazzo di San Callistus—which he told me is owned by the Vatican.

"Did the Holy Father take his name from this Callistus?"

"An infelicitous choice if he did." Father Dunn led me across the square to stand before the palace. "Where the palace now stands there stood the house where the unfortunate Callistus was finally imprisoned and tortured. He was eventually thrown out of the window into a well in the courtyard. That was all some time ago. The year was 222, actually."

We were standing on a bridge looking down into the Tiber. The mist had just barely turned to rain and it dimpled the river. He was talking to me about D'Ambrizzi and Simon.

"He really was in his element during the war," he said. "The man was designed for use in a crisis. Built by a firm that meant business, built to last. But I don't quite make him fit Simon now. I suppose that's the point though—not to be obvious, I mean. I don't know, Ben." He was staring into the black Tiber running in the rain. I heard thunder far away, over Tuscany. We began to walk. There was nothing left to do but wait for D'Ambrizzi and Callistus to finish their conference. Nothing to do but wait and wonder what to do when the waiting was over.

"Come," he said. "There's something else I want you to see."

Ten minutes later we stood across the street from a shabby building, part warehouse, part grocery store with an attached restaurant. It was dark and the wind from the river was cold. He said, "The Church owns this building. The whole block, actually. Not a bad *ristorante*. The owner used to be a priest in Naples. Come on."

I followed him down an alleyway, back around to the rear of the building. A single dreary automobile, well past its prime and showing it, stood by a metal door that was open an inch or two. "Come on," he said again. "Don't be shy." He pushed the door open and stepped into a narrow, dimly lit hallway that smelled of spaghetti sauce and clams and oregano and garlic. I heard a sound from a room at the end of the hall. Someone was pitching darts into a cork board. There's no sound quite like it. We stopped just short of the doorway. "Go on in," Father Dunn said.

There was a man pulling darts from the board. He turned, his hand bristling with the gleaming points.

I hadn't seen him in such a long time. Not since my sister and I had waited impatiently for him to come outside and play with us. He was wearing a dark gray suit with a pinstripe, a white shirt with a dark tie and a starched collar that sank into his jowls.

Seeing me, his face lit with a broad smile.

He came toward me, stood looking up into my face.

Then he grabbed my shoulders and embraced me.

"It has been too long, Benjamin. You were only little children."
He shook me like a giant doll. He was still very strong. "Benjamin."

He leaned back to look at me again and I stared into the eyes
of Giacomo Cardinal D'Ambrizzi.

Why had Artie Dunn delivered me into the hands of my enemy?

Sister Elizabeth sat at her desk in the empty office, eyes closed, hands clasped before her on a stack of layout sheets. She had come back to the office from the Borghese Gardens and Sister Bernadine had quickly and efficiently briefed her on the production status of the material ready for press. At the conclusion of the recitation, Sister Bernadine leaned against a file cabinet, pushed one of the drawers shut with her hip, and said, "Look, it's none of my business, but are you okay? You look a little chewed up around the edges—have you been crying?"

Sister Elizabeth had tilted her head back and laughed softly. "Ahhh," she said, thinking. "No more than usual, I guess." Seeing the concern on her assistant's face, she added, "No, no, I'm fine. But you're right, I am tired."

"And there's the aftershock of that nut getting into your apartment."

"Probably."

494

"You need some real down time, Liz."

"Don't worry. I'll be all right."

Now she sat alone at her desk in the quiet, darkened office with the portable Sony radio playing pop music, the volume turned low. She reluctantly opened her eyes to the green glow of the computer screen. She'd called up the D'Ambrizzi and Indelicato comparison she'd entered a few weeks before, stared at the stories of their lives reduced to a few lines of type, the paths they were taking toward the papacy. She wondered about the war years. There now seemed to be no doubt D'Ambrizzi had been up to something in Paris—how she'd have liked to get her hands on those manuscript pages he'd left behind in New Prudence!—but she was even more curious, at just that moment, about what Indelicato had been doing. Working in Rome. Close to the pope . . .

The image of the two men as two armies, gathering their supporters, grinding inexorably toward the one goal, stuck in her mind. A lifelong race toward the Throne of Peter. D'Ambrizzi and Indelicato, the peasant and the nobleman, linked together through the years, step by step, enemies and brothers of the cloth.

She fumbled in the dark in search of a half-empty, dried-to-dust package of cigarettes that was six months old. For some unfathomable reason she smoked two cigarettes a month, on average, and now was the time. Her hands were shaking and when she found the package it was empty. It lay among the paper clips and rubber bands and ballpoint pens by loose dried tobacco. Sister Bernadine had beaten her to it. *God, may I have your attention, please? I've been through a lot, am I right? So I want a smoke, just one cigarette? Too much to ask for? What they say about You? It could be true.* She pushed the drawer shut and saw her hands, couldn't take her eyes from the hands. . . .

Dry, bony, parchment hands, cold hands, blue-veined—the hands of an old nun . . .

She was sobbing.

She was remembering Val's hands, how they had always been strong and tanned and supple. Now Val would never be old, never be a dry and barren old woman, mourning the life and the children and the love she would never know. . . .

She was staring at her hands through the tears.

The telephone was ringing.

She wiped her eyes with a tissue, tried to shake away the tears and the depths of her mood.

She answered and heard a voice she knew and had half expected at the other end. Monsignor Sandanato.

"Listen to me, Sister. Stay where you are. Don't leave your office. Not with anyone. Wait for me. Do you understand what I am saying to you? You are in danger. I must speak with you. I'm leaving my office now."

Sandanato arrived in less than fifteen minutes. He was breathless, his face damp and glistening with a patina of perspiration. His dark olive complexion was blanched. He sat on the edge of the desk, his burning, fevered eyes searching her face. "Where have you been? You were in Paris and then you were gone—this is crazy. I've been very, very concerned."

"I'm sorry," she said. "I ran into Ben Driskill and Father Dunn in Paris—"

"Oh, my God," he sighed under his breath. "Go on."

"I went to Avignon with them."

"But why?"

"Why not?" There was no hiding the exasperation. "You have no business giving me the third degree! Remember, they're two of the good guys. You and the cardinal may not take the *assassini* theory as seriously as I do, but they had found a man who was able to throw more light on all of that—"

"What man? What are you talking about?" He reached across the desk and took her hand. "Sister, forgive me—I'm acting like a madman—but you've got to tell me the truth now. We're almost at the end of this terrible thing. We're going to cleanse the Church, Sister, and we're going to do it now. But you must tell me about the man in Avignon. *Please.*" He squeezed her hand, encouraging her.

She felt a sigh escape her, as if she were expelling an awful burden, and told him the story of the trip to see Kessler/Calder. When she reported his assertion that Simon Verginius was in fact D'Ambrizzi, she looked at Sandanato, waiting for the explosion, the denial.

But it didn't come. Sandanato's shoulders slumped. He stood up, pacing the room, hands in his pockets, shaking his head.

"Sister, you and Driskill have got to get out of this thing now. Listen to me. You're not really in it, you're not *players*, you're bystanders, and I don't want you to be the ones who get hit by the runaway truck. Do you understand me?"

"No. I understand almost nothing at this point. Not you, not Driskill, none of you. But I can't believe that Cardinal D'Ambrizzi is guilty of—"

"Promise me you'll stay out of this. Please!"

"I'll be damned if I will—who gave you all this authority all of a sudden? And why aren't you blowing your top about Kessler's story?"

"All right," he said, making theatrical calming gestures, controlling himself by an exercise of extreme will. "I'm not blowing my top because Kessler's story may be true. D'Ambrizzi may have been Simon. Yes."

"What are you saying? Is he Simon now? That's what matters— Pietro, you love this man—you are closer to him than anyone else on earth—"

"We're not talking about personal relationships, Sister. We've gone way beyond that. We're talking about the future of the Church . . . we're talking about the man who may be pope. Now we're very close to pinning this all down. The murders Sister Valentine tied together, her murder, the attack on you—"

"We? Who's we?"

"Cardinal Indelicato and I! Yes, just believe me. His Eminence and I have been working together to get at the truth—"

"You and Indelicato? My God, they're sworn blood enemies! They hate each other. What's going on? Since when are you and Indelicato together?" Her mind was reeling. One of the fixtures of the Church she knew was the pairing of Sandanato and his master, D'Ambrizzi. What had happened?

"Since . . . since I realized that D'Ambrizzi was leading the Church astray. Since I realized that he was doing nothing to carry out the Holy Father's wishes on the question of Sister Valentine's killer, the killer of all the others. D'Ambrizzi was in fact obscuring the truth, confusing the issue. . . . Because he—he himself—was behind it all. Indelicato and I both saw what he was doing to Callistus, isolating him, lecturing him, leading him because Callistus no longer has the strength to make his own way. We saw D'Ambrizzi's hidden agenda . . . and it terrified us." He looked at her, his face an agonized mask.

"But when? How long ago?"

"It doesn't matter, Sister. What matters is that you must realize that it hasn't been easy for me. You know he's been like a father to me . . . but the Church must come first. You and I, we agree on that. I have always known that I would have to tell you the truth sooner or later. That's why I tried to talk to you about the need to cleanse the Church . . . and how good might come from evil. There's no time to thrash it all out now, Sister. No time." The dim light threw his face into dark relief, the cheeks and eyes hollowed out and black. The spirit of agony, the martyr, willing to die for his Church right or wrong. He was drawn to the breaking point.

She was scrambling to assimilate what he was saying. Trying to reinvent the world on the spur of the moment. D'Ambrizzi had for so long been the one certainty in the Church, the one unfailing beacon of rationality, common sense, decency: the man who had it all in perspective. Saint Jack, the man who should have been pope.

"Kessler was right," she said softly. "Is that what you're telling me? That everything Ben said is right?"

"I have no idea what Driskill said, but I want you to stay away from him and Father Dunn. Driskill is perfectly capable of taking care of himself—"

"I thought you said he and I had to get out of this!"

"I don't care what happens to Driskill, Sister! It's you I'm—"

"I can't take care of myself? Is that it?"

He ignored her sudden petulance. "You have to deal with what's going on here. There's no point in our arguing. *You* are a terrible threat to D'Ambrizzi's plan. He'll remove you without thinking twice if you keep after him . . . you may still believe in him, but what you're actually doing, what you've been doing all these weeks—it can destroy him!"

"This is pretty hard to buy," she said.

"Think how it must have seemed to me."

"If you're right, what's his agenda? What's happening?"

Sandanato fished a cigarette from his coat pocket and lit it, the smoke swirling toward the light on her desk. She didn't want a cigarette anymore. He coughed, flicked a shred of tobacco from his tongue.

"D'Ambrizzi," he said, squinting at her, "is set to take over this entire Church . . . starting with the heart. He has centralized his power, he has a solid cadre of support among the cardinals and in the press, he has American money behind him, he has one foot solidly in the material and political world, the other in the Vatican. The press loves him, Sister . . . I love him, as do you, as did Val . . . but the man we love and trust has used us to further his own plans. He is the only man the Holy Father will listen to anymore. He has complete control over Callistus, over his mind, over access to him. He is arranging for the Holy Father to speak with enough cardinals to press D'Ambrizzi as his own personal choice as successor— Cardinal D'Ambrizzi intends to be pope and he has arranged to hide his past forever. He must be stopped, Sister!"

"And you and Indelicato can stop him," she said.

"If anyone can."

"Then you and Driskill are allies," she said, trying to see it all whole.

"No, no. Don't you see? Dunn has complete control over Driskill! He has had from the beginning. Dunn is a subtle man, a manipulator—"

"But what's wrong with that? Dunn is—"

"What's wrong with that? Elizabeth, Dunn is D'Ambrizzi's man! Don't you see? That's why Dunn has been in on this from day one in Princeton . . . he was with Driskill that night, he was the first to find Driskill in the family chapel with his dead sister. Ben Driskill never had a chance to react to Val's murder without Dunn at his side, guiding him, comforting him." He coughed again on the smoke, moving past her to look into the street from her office window. "Dunn must have known that Sister Val had to die . . . she was too close to the truth about D'Ambrizzi. . . . She had connected him to the Nazis in the past and she knew the past had to be wiped clean. And D'Ambrizzi wanted Dunn there to see Driskill through it—and to make sure the job had been properly done."

"But they tried to kill Ben when you two were ice skating—"

"Ben had convinced Dunn that he was going after Val's past, he was going to try to reconstruct what had led to her murder. . . ."

The words kept coming, one enormity after another, like time bombs triggered long ago and exploding now in the depths of her psyche. The Church was being blown apart. Dunn was a villain, D'Ambrizzi was a villain, the Holy Father was D'Ambrizzi's captive . . . all in the name of D'Ambrizzi being elected pope. Quite a journey, from *assassini* to the papacy, forty years.

Sandanato wanted her to come with him, he'd take her to the Order, where she should stay until it was all over. But she shook him off. He persisted and her anger and frustration bubbled over again, she flailed at him with words. It was all insane, you couldn't possibly keep track of any of it . . . and he'd tried to explain it all rationally, calmly. It was all D'Ambrizzi, all his own brilliant, perverted conception. The pope was terminally ill; the Church needed to be moved even further into the mainstream secular world and he was the master, the expert. As pope he could see the Church into the future as a world power. But there were men alive, and a woman, two women eventually, who knew too much about his past, what he'd had to do with the Nazis and the *assassini* . . . so he had begun to clear the obstacles away. It wasn't difficult to comprehend if you looked at it that way, the right way.

She sent Sandanato away and he left grudgingly, warning her to stay away from Driskill and Dunn and D'Ambrizzi until it was over.

Driskill. Alone, she could barely think of forming the sound of his name. Nothing in her life had ever gone so bleakly, desperately wrong. She was wrung out, all the options closed off when it came to Driskill. Hopeless.

An hour later she left the office and was struck by the cold wind of late November. It was dark and quiet in the street of shuttered offices. She set off briskly, but by the time she'd reached the corner a gleaming black Mercedes had pulled alongside her.

A priest in a black raincoat, his white notch of collar peeking out, stepped out of the front passenger side.

"Sister Elizabeth?"

"Yes?"

"The Holy Father has sent his car for you. Please." He swung the back door open.

"The Holy Father?"

"Please, Sister. Time is very short."

He took her elbow and she went into the black hole of the backseat. She was alone. The car pulled away.

"The Vatican is back the other way. Can you explain this, Father?"

He turned his face and nodded solemnly. "I'm sorry, but we have another stop to make, Sister."

"Where?"

"Trastevere, Sister," he said as they gathered speed, staying on back streets which were dark and empty, heading toward the Tiber.

The driver honked and a flurry of cats was caught in his headlights, dashing in a frenzy for safety.

4

DRISKILL

I was still trying to figure out why I was there
when they brought Sister Elizabeth into the
large, roughly finished room. It was chilly and
dusty and was mostly empty but for Dunn, D'Ambrizzi, and me. And a desk and some chairs haphaz-
ardly arranged around a long, scarred table. Nobody
had been saying much, and nothing helpful.

She was accompanied by a priest who ushered her in and left,
closing the door. She was wearing her belted trench coat, a bag
slung over her shoulder. She looked apprehensively at us, started
to say something, but stopped dead when she saw D'Ambrizzi. He
crossed the cement floor, smiling, looking up at her, guiding her to
the table. She hung back a moment but he was irresistible.

"Please, sit down," he said, looking so unlike himself in the
gray pinstripe. Everything about him seemed to have changed. His
posture—which normally found him rocking back slightly on his
heels with his hands clasped in an avuncular manner across

501

his broad girth—had an indecisive quality, as if he didn't quite know what to do with his feet and hands. It made him seem innocent and unsure, utterly disarming. A smile flitted across Father Dunn's face when he caught my eye. You bastard, I thought.

"I am prostrate, my friends," D'Ambrizzi said, "at having brought you here so rudely, without warning, without explanation. But time is short and you will discover my motives. These, I need hardly remind you, are—what?—unusual times. Calling for, at the very least, unusual measures. Please accept my deepest apologies." He stumped across the room once we'd all seated ourselves at the table and scraped the chair behind the desk across the rough cement. He seemed unaccustomed to being without his attendant. Sandanato was nowhere to be seen. "And you must further forgive me if I dominate these proceedings. I have much to say to you. I will try to anticipate your questions . . . as you understand, my time is unhappily limited. And there is so much to cover." He consulted a wristwatch self-consciously, like an actor with an unfamiliar prop. Sandanato was doubtless his customary time-keeper. He leaned against the back of the chair, staring down at the empty desktop. "All right. We begin.

"Father Dunn is a dear friend of mine, more so than you ever imagined. He has briefed me on your activities, Benjamin. Egypt, Paris, Ireland, Avignon. He has told me of the manuscript that was found in New Prudence. I know about your belief that August Horstmann is the killer. And, of course, he told me how Erich Kessler explained that I am this Simon Verginius who has played such an important part in the unfolding of this story. Yes, I believe I am quite well briefed.

"Now, I must tell you, I believe there are certain explanations you deserve. Why do I say *deserve*? Well, Benjamin, you deserve to know the truth because your sister is dead. And you, Sister, because you have nearly been murdered yourself. You both deserve the truth because of the determination you have shown, *foolish* determination, determination to a point near madness—all to discover the truth of events so deeply buried beneath the rubble and dust of time. Frankly, I wouldn't have believed such detective work quite possible in the circumstances. But you have persevered." He shook his head in mock sorrow, the banana nose dipping toward his chin, like Punch. "Making the riddles far more difficult for me to solve, making it more difficult for me to put an end to the killing, and in the words of my faithful Sandanato, 'save the Church.' "

He paused, as if looking for some answer that might satisfy us all, then gave up. He took a labored, raspy breath and lowered his bulk onto the spindly chair.

"Yes," he said from deep in the cavernous chest, "I was Simon Verginius. It was I who was sent by Pope Pius to Paris to report to Torricelli, to organize a group of guerrilla fighters to protect the Church's interests—to accommodate the Nazis, gain their trust and support, and acquire a share of treasure for the Church. It was no easy task, let me tell you, with men like Goering and Goebbels after everything for themselves. In any case, it was an ungodly, unholy task, I admit it, but you must try to understand the weight, the power of an order given personally by Pope Pius—the mission was the darkest secret possible. He told me that . . . he told me he was entrusting me with a job crucial to the survival of the Church. You—you truly cannot imagine the weight of that man's personality, his nature, like a laser . . . and as it happened he'd chosen a man capable of carrying out his orders. How it pains me to say it! But I was by nature a pragmatist and a student of history. History, you see, is not a very pretty place. History—if you want to survive a while—is the dwelling place of the pragmatic. Home of the secular Church. Well, I was a secularist as well. Not much of a priest, you say. Perhaps, perhaps not. But I was the man for the job. Whatever would benefit the Church, I was willing to do.

"Yes, well. Pardon me if I skip about. I'm trying to hit the important points—

"Yes, I killed Father LeBecq in the graveyard. I hardly remember his face, it was so long ago. And he was such an utter swine. Killing him was an act of war, the battlefield execution of a traitor, a man who had betrayed us to the Nazis." He looked up abruptly, his eyes heavy-lidded like a crocodile's but still inquisitive. "Do you wait for the priest's act of contrition? Then you wait in vain, I fear. As you have pieced together from all your varied sources, I—as Simon— had never been content with aiding the Nazis in any way . . . it was my job, I gave it my effort for a time—but it didn't take me long to begin working primarily with the Resistance, maintaining only enough of a relationship with the Nazis to keep them from coming down with their great hobbed boots on the Church. I was a terrible thorn in the side of Torricelli, poor fellow. He wanted to live and let live, survive, ignore reality. Everything I did and said seemed to frighten him. He was trapped among the Nazis, the Church as represented by me, and various American spooks who could drift in and out of Paris like dangerous viruses." He looked at his watch, clasped his hands before him on the table. His fingers were swollen like a fat lady's ankles.

"Yes, there was an attempted assassination of a great man, an *important* man. He was coming to Paris by train, yes. Father LeBecq knew about it, he'd been in on the planning, but he disapproved. It was not his decision, however. When the plan was betrayed and so many of us were killed there in the mountains, I felt sure it was LeBecq who had passed the word to the Nazis. So I executed him. In my own fashion." He cracked his bulbous knuckles for emphasis. "And yes, Pius sent a man from Rome to investigate, to collect evidence and build a case against me—if indeed I were the man who had killed LeBecq and planned the assassination of the man on the train . . . and generally failed to carry out the wishes of Pius insofar as the Germans were concerned. The man sent by the Vatican knew the latter charge was true. The truth was, Pius had just about had his fill of me. The Nazis had complained to him of my reluctance to comply with their wishes. And yes, this man sent from Rome by Pius was known in some circles by the name 'the Collector.' He was collecting information, evidence, who knew what else he collected, and it was a difficult job for him because I had disbanded the *assassini,* the few of us left alive, and no one knew who they were, anyway. No one but me and the men themselves, and I was the only one who knew them *all*—except for one other man, that is, his code name was Archduke. And yes, there was a document dating back to the time of the Borgias, a roster of names of men who had forsaken all, risked everything in the service of the Church—men who had killed for the popes, for the Church. I sent the document north to Ireland with two of my people, Brother Leo and my very best man, the most selfless, the man I trusted most . . . August Horstmann.

"Once they had left for Ireland, I heard no more from them. I had my own problems in Paris with the Collector, and when he was closing in on me—I sensed it, the hair in my ears stood on end, I knew he was meticulously building a case which would certainly have satisfied Pius, who might have done almost anything to me by way of punishment, *anything* . . . then, *in extremis,* I turned to your father, Benjamin, my old comrade-in-arms, one of those OSS spooks who moved around Europe like ghosts in those days, doing what good he could, getting information out to the Allies by whatever means were at hand. And it was Hugh Driskill who used all his considerable magic to get me out of Paris with the Collector, frustrated, furious, nipping at my heels. And Hugh brought me to Princeton while he and his great friend Drew Summerhays began negotiating with Pius for my return to Rome. My safe return."

He lit one of his black, gold-banded cigarettes, looked out tiredly from those hooded eyes which seemed to blink in slow motion. It was an extraordinary performance he was giving.

"Now, the manuscript. What was I doing all that time you and little Val wanted me to come out and play ball with you and work in the garden with you and your mother—why did I write it all down? I needed more than whatever your father and Summerhays could negotiate with Pius because Pius had a very personal reason to hate me, to fear me. I needed a very good insurance policy if I wanted to be sure of remaining in the Church and staying alive. So I was writing out my life insurance policy. Once I left it with the priest in the village I knew I was safe. I had a copy of it to show Pius—and I could tell him that in case of my death the world would be regaled with the story of his *assassini,* his determination to work with the Nazis in plundering the art treasures of Europe. Yes, I used code names in the manuscript because I had to guard against the old priest in New Prudence reading it and knowing too much, but the code names would not invalidate the details of the story. The details were all there, they were the internal proof, they could be checked, they had happened.

"Once the pages were written and your father and Summerhays had prepared the way for my return—and make no mistake, it was a bitter, bitter pill for Pius to swallow—I returned to Rome and I held my club over them and I made my way, my career, safe and sound. Now"—he looked at our faces—"that takes care of the past, does it not?"

I'd been listening for a long time, trying to make it add up. When D'Ambrizzi paused to shift gears, I spoke. The room was stuffy, the heat had been turned on, and now it was too warm, and

I could hear faint noises from the restaurant kitchen overhead. My voice sounded stilted, unnaturally loud.

"Whatever you may have done in the past is no business of mine. Whatever the Church gets up to, there are no surprises for me. A Nazi-sympathizing pontiff fits right in. If you're telling us the truth now, I say more power to you. Kill the bastard LeBecq. But that's an old story. Nothing to do with me. I'm here because somebody killed my sister—"

"You're here, Benjamin, because I sent for you. But do go on, son. I look at you and I see the little boy you were. Impatient, eager to play. The little boy still exists in you. You have not changed. You want to get things settled—"

"I want to know who killed my sister. Who was behind it. Horstmann pulled the trigger—your pal Horstmann, the best man you had—and he sliced my back open, but who sent him? You're looking like the number one candidate, and to me you're just a fat old man who's bucking for pope. You're not a great man, the fact that you're a cardinal cuts no ice with me. And you're sure as hell no Saint Jack!"

D'Ambrizzi was smiling, nodding gently, as if he were forgiving me. Dunn was studying a corner of the ceiling. Sister Elizabeth seemed hypnotized, staring at her hands in her lap. Waiting. Still.

"I realize," D'Ambrizzi said, "how suspect I must seem in your eyes. But remember this, I brought you here to talk to you, to explain what I am doing and what I have done . . . if I were the man you think I am, why not simply have you killed? If I have had so many people killed, why not a few more?"

"I can think of a million reasons," I said.

"Only one matters—I'm not killing anyone, Benjamin. I *was* Simon. But I have not activated Horstmann after forty years. I have neither seen nor spoken to nor heard from him since I last saw him in Paris and gave him the Concordat of the Borgias that Pius had given to me." He watched me through the drifting smoke, squinting like Jean Gabin in an old movie. "Which poses the great question, doesn't it? The question we must answer . . . who has sent him back to work?" He leaned back. The chair squeaked. He folded his arms, still watching me through slitted eyes.

"Who?" I said. "Who are we looking for? Well, first, it would have to be someone who knew how the hell to find him. Second, it would have to be someone who knew he had been a killer in the service of the Church. And third, it would have to be someone from whom Horstmann would take orders. Horstmann would probably take orders only from Simon. So it sounds like Simon Verginius to me, reactivating the old-boy network—"

"Indeed it does," D'Ambrizzi said. "You're a lawyer, certainly, building a case of your own. But wouldn't that be the point, counsellor? Making Simon seem the man in question? You may believe whatever you choose, Benjamin. You have always had an independent mind. But let me pursue for a moment another approach." He leaned forward, his elbows on the table. "Someone is guiding Horstmann, instructing him. This unknown man is the real killer. We agree—"

"Horstmann is not exactly off the hook with me. He pressed a gun to my sister's head—"

D'Ambrizzi nodded but went on. "Why are these people being killed? I'm predisposed to agree with Herr Kessler on this point. To remove people who knew the truth about what had happened in Paris during the war, anyone who knew the truth about the Church and the Nazis and the *assassini* and the involvement of our villain . . . these people who pose a danger to this man had to die. Now, who would be most hurt by all this history coming out?"

"Someone who was killing people in Paris," I said. "Brings us back to Simon Verginius. Someone who had the most to lose now, like someone who wants to make a stop at the papacy on the way to canonization. No one fits the profile like you, Saint Jack—"

"But," D'Ambrizzi said quietly, "is old Saint Jack the only suspect? What if there is yet another reason behind all this havoc? Think about the selection of a new pope. We are dealing with a very small electorate—the College of Cardinals. And the dying pope is a man of great personal influence. There are many ways of influencing this electorate. Money, of course, is one. The promise of power, access to the papal ear. And there is perhaps the oldest way of all—fear. Let me tell you what the curia and the Vatican and the Church establishment fear most, the ultimate anathema . . . the destruction of order. Give it another name. Chaos. There is nothing worse than chaos. They will respond to chaos, I assure you, and they are powerful men. They will want to stamp it out, crush it, and believe me, they will prevail. They will turn to a man with an iron fist, do you see? The Church will endure if it requires a journey backward into the darkness, back to repression of dissent, back even to another Inquisition—they will happily provide one. There are those who believe indeed that another Inquisition is long, long overdue. The dying pope hates chaos as much as any man alive—he, too, will look to the strongman, the brute, the grinding heel. We must ask ourselves, who will benefit most from fear and chaos and disorder? The answer, of course, is the man who is creating it. He is the answer to all of our questions."

Sister Elizabeth finally spoke, her voice brimming with frustration. "Why are you playing games with us? How do we find out who it is? How much longer does this madness go on? What if it *is* you? What if you are the man to benefit? You are the man with access to the pope. . . . My God, you make it sound as if this is no different from the Mafia, the KGB, the CIA—it's the Church! The Church is better than this!"

D'Ambrizzi listened with closed eyes, his massive head nodding slowly in apparent agreement. He cleared his throat, a raspy sound. "The sad truth is this—when the stakes are sufficiently high and when it comes to a fight for control and power, there is less difference among the organizations you mentioned than you might think. History tells us this. Your friend Sister Valentine understood this as well as anyone on earth. She understood so well the side of the Church that was not good works. She also understood that the aims of the Church, what it means to us all, are very different from the organizations you named.

"As far as how long this will go on—not much longer, I can assure you of that. We are almost at the end.

"And there are no games being played here. You see, I *know* who is behind it. But if I told you, would you believe me? Perhaps not quite yet. But soon, very soon . . .

"First, however, there is the matter of Cardinal Indelicato's very grand party. His sense of timing is audacious at the least. I urge you not to miss it."

"Party?" I said, reacting a little tardily. "What are you talking about?"

"Why, Ben, Fredi's parties are the stuff of legend. It's slipped my mind what he's celebrating this time, but it will be a splendid evening, I assure you. And I'm sure he'll want you there." The heavy lids lowered over his reptilian eyes. "Believe me, you don't want to miss it. I have a surprise in store for you—but only at the party."

He scraped the chair back. "Now my driver awaits me. I must get back to business—"

"A question," I interrupted. "Something you said—why did Pius have such a hatred of you?"

Sister Elizabeth was on her feet. "And who was the 'great man' on the train? And what was the Pius Plot? Was it the *assassini*, his plan to put them into operation again?"

D'Ambrizzi stopped, turned, squat and broad and powerful despite his years. He looked up at Sister Elizabeth, surprise flashing across his heavy features. "Why, that was all tied together. Pius had—I readily admit—a good reason to look upon me with considerable disfavor. You see . . . it was Pope Pius who was supposed to be on that train."

"You were going to kill him!" There was shock and disbelief in her voice.

"We intended to assassinate the pope, yes. Shocking, isn't it? But a grand old tradition, let me add. And naturally our plot came to be known as the Pius Plot. The plot to kill Pius. It's easy when you know the answers, isn't it? Lots of explanations make sense but only one is correct. Remember that as we draw near the end."

"Wait. Stop." Sister Elizabeth was frowning as if she were unable to quite grasp the situation. "You intended to murder Pope Pius?"

"It was just what he needed, Sister."

"And Father LeBecq blew the whistle, warned the Vatican, Pius didn't make the trip, so you killed LeBecq—"

"I have told you, I did kill him. He had, I believed, caused the death of my fellows. But there's a problem with that. I was told by a man who knew, some time later, that LeBecq wasn't the one who warned the Vatican. I had killed the wrong man. No great loss, however—"

Sister Elizabeth gasped. "My God . . ."

D'Ambrizzi went to her and took her hand. He refused to let her go. "Poor Sister, poor dear girl. You've had a bad time with all this. I'm deeply sorry. But all I can do is bring the nightmare to a conclusion."

"Who tried to kill me?" She was fighting off tears.

"Soon, it will be over soon. I understand your concern, your outrage. You're right, it is a kind of insanity. A priest who tried to kill the pope, who killed another priest with his bare hands . . . yet this priest is also the beloved old man you see before you, a man you've known for a long time and trusted. It's confusing. What are you to make of it? Well, I stopped worrying about the morality of it all long ago. I did what I needed to do, what I believed to be right. Not much of an attitude if you want to be a good priest. But I was never much concerned with being a good priest. I wanted to be a good man." He looked at his watch. "Tomorrow night at Indelicato's villa about this time—the last act begins. For now, good evening." He stopped in the doorway, looking back. "Be careful."

That night I sat in my room at the Hassler, alone, thinking about D'Ambrizzi's version. Father Dunn had gone off on business of his own without a word regarding just what his relationship with D'Ambrizzi involved. I couldn't imagine having another go at Sister Elizabeth. How big a fool could a man make of himself? Why go for the Olympic record?

So I sat and thought about D'Ambrizzi in the mountains waiting for the train bearing Pope Pius. The audacity of his plan was breathtaking. What might have happened had he succeeded? Would the Church have found a great man, a great leader who would have helped reveal the Nazis for what they were? Would the moral development of the Church have proceeded differently? Would it have emerged from the war prepared to lead? And if it had been a different Church, might I have been a different man? Might I have become a priest in a Church that—Pius having lived—never existed?

My life had not worked out as planned and I couldn't foresee a time when I wouldn't be paying one price or another. I had lost the Church and I had lost the love of my father, and somewhere along the way I had begun to hate both. What if D'Ambrizzi and his little band had killed Pius? Might I still have the Church and my father?

I decided that I couldn't afford to know the answer.

But I wondered, who did betray the Pius Plot?

My back was pretty well healed. The scar was puckered and joined. The occasional pain was more a dull throb when it came, not the searing poker. I filled the tub with water so hot it steamed the mirror. I opened a bottle of scotch Father Dunn had found at some joint catering to thirsty Brits. It had an almost sweet taste, yet still earthy and full of peat smoke, and I'd never tasted anything quite so good. E'Dradour, it was called, and Dunn told me it came from the smallest distillery in Scotland. I no longer had any idea where Dunn stood on anything else, but when it came to the water of life the man knew what he was talking about. I lay in the tub and kept dribbling E'Dradour over ice until there was only half a bottle left. Some of my worries were fading in the glow of strong drink.

I was very tired and maybe it didn't matter so much anymore that nothing was ever what it seemed. Rome, Roman angles, Roman intrigue, they were swallowing me whole and I knew I wouldn't be missed. It was an odd, disconcerting feeling, but comforting, too. Maybe I just didn't matter all that much. I wouldn't be much of a loss. . . . Well, they did things differently in Rome. When in Rome, you were supposed to do as the Romans did. But who could ever figure it out?

D'Ambrizzi.

How much was true? Was any of it true in the sense of actual truth? Did anyone even remember what truth was? I lay soaking, sweating, my mind wandering into delusion. . . .

I felt as if I were dying on the beach with a pretty girl crying in the shade of a palm tree and there was the colonel, his shadow falling across me, the sun shining past his head with its peaked officer's cap, shining in my eyes, the colonel with his stupid face, the glasses, and the gun. . . .

It was a Donald Fagen song running through my mind, jazzy and sad, and I knew perfectly well I was in the tub with the steam and the scotch and the melting ice in the Hassler's bucket and the fear about what might happen the next night knotted in my gut, but I was down and bleeding in the sand, too, the motor launch I'd hired from the skinny man in two-tone shoes had never come to take me off the beach and the girl had betrayed me and the colonel had betrayed me and I was going to die. I knew the plot, I'd read the book, I think I just got the good-bye look . . . my mind was wandering, I was half singing the song to myself, as if I had a fever that was going to kill me if the slugs I'd taken didn't. . . .

Christ. D'Ambrizzi had tried to kill the pope!

And he had succeeded in killing LeBecq—the wrong man.

And he simply didn't give a shit!

Who did such things?

Must have been the war, that was it. There'd been a war on and that had changed everything. The rules had no longer applied. . . .

I finally staggered off to bed, lay shivering, thinking about the warm, dark, rounded softness of Gabrielle LeBecq, knowing I would never see her again, wanting her to wrap her legs around me and draw me inside her, where I'd be safe . . . I wanted to be safe. It didn't seem like too much to ask.

I wondered if Cardinal Indelicato's party would be a safe place. It seemed unlikely. Our invitations had been waiting for us at the Hassler. He requested the pleasure of our company at his villa.

The next night.

My mother was once again waiting for me in my dreams.

It was the same old dream.

She was coming closer this time, though, as if some strange sense of urgency were compelling her toward me. She was still clad in the filmy nightgown or robe, it was the same old scene I'd grown familiar with through the years . . . the dream, the memory of her reaching out to me, her hair disheveled, the rings glittering on her long fingers with the painted nails, but she was clearer this time, as if a curtain or two had blown away from between us.

It was as if I felt an acute embarrassment, as if I were seeing her in a private moment when I shouldn't have been there at all, yet she knew I was there, she was reaching out, talking to me, and I could smell her perfume, one of those gardenia-scented numbers you smell as a kid and never forget, but I could also smell the gin, the martinis on her breath . . . all this for the first time, new to my dream . . . she was coming out of her bedroom, the light shone yellow behind her, it was night, I realized I was wearing my red plaid Pendleton robe and pajamas, I must have been ten or twelve, and I could for the first time hear her voice quite clearly. . . .

I'd never heard her speaking—words, real words—in the dream, yet I knew it was a memory, that I was remembering something that had happened but that I'd forgotten, repressed, and the words were coming from far, far away, she was calling on me, repeating my name, *Ben, Ben, listen to me, please Ben,* my mother's voice pleading with me, *listen to me* . . . and I was shrinking from her, not seeing her as my mother normally was, not perfect and pristine and right, this woman had been crying and drinking and there was a catch in her voice, almost a sob, a handkerchief clutched in one hand, she was pleading, she wanted me to come closer but there was something frightening about her, maybe it was just the *differ-ence* in her . . . her voice was ragged, raw . . . *Ben, don't run away from me, please, darling, listen to me . . .*

I was moving closer to her, so great was her urgency. I felt her hand closing on mine, strong, like a bird's talons, I saw the bird impaled on the point of the wrought iron fence so long, long ago, saw my mother's frightened eyes staring at me, it was all mixing together in my dream, the bird, the fence, my mother's raw voice, her hand like a claw, a collection of bones, on mine. . . . Then the bird was alive and wriggling on the fence, dying, jerking, its wings beating, flapping helplessly, its feet kicking, and then it metamor-phosed into another shape—why? why? Because it was a dream, I suppose. The bird was now a man, the feet dancing in midair. It was black, still black like the dying bird, and it, too, was dying, this figure of a man, black against white, and then I knew who it was . . . dying . . . already dead, swinging in the wind. . . .

Father Governeau.

Out in the orchard, a sight I'd never seen.

But I saw it then, in my dream. Why? I had no idea why. It was a dream, dammit! A dream and more, of course.

Then I heard my own voice. *The priest in the orchard—*

I'd never said such a thing before, not to my mother: it was an impossible subject, but there I was, blurting it out into my mother's face and the tears seemed to explode from her eyes, as if her eyes had burst, overripe, spilling her sorrow down her cheeks as if her face were melting, as if I were losing my mother there in the hallway . . . and I heard her voice . . .

You, you, it was you . . . you did it . . . it was all you, you did it, you from the beginning . . . you . . . only you . . . nothing I could do about it . . . it was too late . . . you did it . . . the poor priest . . .

Then she turned, staggered back to the bedroom, closed the door.

I stood in the hallway, ice-cold, it was dark. I was shaking . . . and I woke in my bed in Rome, wet with sweat, shivering, exhausted but full of dread and awe. For more than thirty years I'd suffered through that dream, for all those years I'd struggled to hear her words and see her more clearly and understand what it was all about.

Now I'd gotten through the whole thing.

I wished I hadn't.

It sounded to me as if my mother were telling me I was to blame for what happened to Father Governeau.

It was all tied together. Father Governeau and Val and everything else. Why had Val been so interested in Governeau at the end?

And how could I have been to blame?

The knocking at my door started at something past three o'clock and I lay there having trouble deciding whether or not it was in my dream. When I finally got to the door and swung it open, Sister Elizabeth was about to give it another hammering. I asked her if she knew what time it was.

"It doesn't matter. What time is it?"

"Three in the morning. Past three."

"You're tough. You can handle it. Come on, let me in." She wore her trench coat which was soaked and her hair shone with the rain. A black turtleneck showed and slacks and wet sneakers. She swept past into my room. She was acting like she was on speed, but I knew it was just the hyperactive side of her nature. Everything had finally gotten to her.

"What are you doing here? What's going on?"

"I cannot put up with the fighting and the uncertainty anymore. Between us, I mean. We've got to talk before this whole thing crashes in flames. It's my whole world, Ben—the wheels are coming off everywhere I look. No, no, don't interrupt. We'd just fight and then we'd be worse off than ever, so just let me tell you what's on my mind and don't say a word unless I ask you a direct question."

I nodded.

"I'm worried about my life getting away from me before I've lived it. I think Val was going to leave the Order. Marry Lockhardt. I know what she felt about him—I think I've felt it with you. I'm worried about that. And my belief in the Church has been shot to hell—what does it mean if the Church is involved in all this? What has happened to the Church?"

"I take that as a direct question. And the answer is it's the same old Church, just the part you've refused to notice. It's no better, no worse, than ever."

"So I don't know what to believe anymore. My Church is suddenly a mystery. I don't know if anyone in it can be believed.

D'Ambrizzi has more faces than the portrait gallery—and I'm looking for someone to believe. So I'm wondering about you—"

"Look, I—"

"That wasn't a question. Look, I'm normally a very organized person with my schedule and my Filofax and my orderly mind. You may think that's a lie but it's not. I've been a nun for a long time and I admit I've developed certain ways of thinking—about life, about myself, my feelings, my faith. I'm not about to bore you with all that, but you've got to understand it's powerful, the way I've learned to think and believe. Now I come across you—and you are some crazy ex-Jesuit novice who has more complicated motives and a more screwed-up set of defenses than anyone I've ever met. . . . But that doesn't mean I don't like you and care about you, even if you make a point of treating me like absolute shit whenever you can. Well, I look at you and I think, there's a fairly elaborate head case, but you could probably be fixed. . . . Now all I want from you is the answer to one question. Then you'll just have to sit and wait and think about not being quite so full of blind, mindless animal hatred for the Church which, God knows, is an imperfect institution—"

"Wait for what?"

"To find out what I'm going to do next, I guess."

"What's the question, Sister?"

"Did you mean what you said to me?"

"I've said a whole lot of things to you. Some I meant—"

"You know perfectly well—"

"Look, if you came here for another fight, I'm just the guy who can—"

"You told me you loved me! Now, I want you to—"

"I certainly did tell you that. You want to know if I've lost my mind, is that it? Well, I've asked myself the same question. Is it worth it? What's the point in sacrificing myself to the Church again? Who needs this crazy belief in mumbo-jumbo, right or wrong?"

"Nobody needs a wise guy, Ben."

"I never suggested you or anyone else needed me."

"I want to know what you meant when you told me you love me."

"Anybody ever say it to you before? A man, I mean?"

"Yes. But there's love in a convertible when you're seventeen, and then there's *love*. What did you mean by love?"

"Well, I'm a hellish long way from seventeen. Love, Sister. I meant *love*. I'm sorry, I hate to make it messy for you, but I meant I *love* you. Now, if you've got another question, I pray it's not *why*. I haven't any idea. . . . Love, *love* just happens, Sister. Maybe it's proof I'm crazy. Maybe it's proof that I can find someone I love after all, just when it looked pretty damn hopeless! What do you want from me? It's the middle of the night!"

"No more questions. I've got to think. It may take a while. Let me know if you change your mind."

She was gone before I knew what was happening. I stood there in my pajamas, staring after her.

What had I just let myself in for?

It was simply incredible, that was all.

A nun.

5

DRISKILL

There must have been a thousand candles flickering in the foyer, the ballroom, down the shadowy corridors of the Villa Indelicato, built in the sixteenth century and ever since the family seat of that noble family. Cardinals, statesmen, scientists, bankers, rogues, poets, lovers, generals, thieves—the Indelicato blood had produced all of them as the centuries had passed by in parade and the villa had seen the last bunch, the last three centuries' worth. It was immaculately cared for, staffed by thirty full-time attendants, and now home to Manfredi Cardinal Indelicato, who stood, in the eyes of Roman handicappers, a very good chance of becoming the first Indelicato pope.

Everything about the setting was absolutely right. The candlelight flickering on the peach marble, the strains of Vivaldi from the chamber orchestra, the gold thread tracing through the tapestries, the scent of pines from the open portals, the multitude of clerics in

517

full regalia, women in elegant designer gowns with acres of creamy cleavage on display, silver-haired men who could afford such women, film stars, cabinet ministers, the hum of conversation blending with the music, the heightened sense of drama that came with the knowledge that a pope might be dying in a secluded Vatican chamber, the tension that is so often sexual when a dressy and powerful crowd is on view.

Sister Elizabeth, Father Dunn, and I arrived by limousine, thoughtfully provided by Cardinal D'Ambrizzi. We climbed the long, gentle flight of stairs and were quickly absorbed by the flow of the party. Elizabeth was immediately approached by people she knew, Dunn was stopped by clerical acquaintances, so I wandered on alone. Champagne, elaborate food on long tables and from trays whisked about by waiters in evening dress. The light of the candles, only subtly enhanced by electricity, had a dreamy rose-lit quality.

The villa was a dwelling; on nights such as this it was a showplace; it was also a private museum. The walls forty feet high were hung with tapestries and paintings by the great masters, all of which were surely worth incalculable sums. Through the centuries the Indelicato family had produced many determined collectors, the fruits of whose labors were on view. Raphael, Caravaggio, Reni, Rubens, Van Dyke, Baciccio. Murillo, Rembrandt, Bosch, Hals, on and on. It was almost surreal, so much art, so much wealth concentrated in a single private dwelling. I walked slowly, caught in the crush, through one gallery after another, sipping champagne, half forgetting at times why I was there.

None of us knew what to expect. Why had we been invited in the first place? Dunn, who had said nothing by way of explaining his suddenly revealed relationship with D'Ambrizzi, said he believed we were there because Indelicato had, along with D'Ambrizzi, been entrusted by Callistus with finding Val's murderer. Since we'd been on the same search, Indelicato wanted to meet us. Why had D'Ambrizzi been so insistent on our attending? That elicited nothing but a shrug from Father Dunn. But obviously D'Ambrizzi was working to his own timetable: he'd said that it would all be over by the end of this evening. Something was going to happen. We just didn't know what or when or to whom. Every time I took a sip of champagne it stopped and dug in its heels about halfway to my stomach.

Sister Elizabeth was exquisite in a black velvet dress with a square-cut neckline, a cameo choker she said Val had given her, her hair tied back with a black ribbon. She smiled at me when we met at the Hassler, a smile I'd never seen before. It was as if there were no conflict between us anymore, as if the air had in fact been cleared. Our eyes met, and she took my hand as I helped her into the limousine. We had reached our truce in that brief middle-of-the-night conversation in my room. Now I, too, felt calm. We were at last on the same page, regardless of how our minds might be working, what resolutions we might be hoping for.

We found ourselves on a sweeping staircase, looking down on the ceaselessly surging crowd. She looked up at me. "Which story do you believe?" She had told me of her conversation with Sandanato, his claim that D'Ambrizzi himself was behind all that had happened. That D'Ambrizzi was reaching for control of the Church and would destroy it with his reaction against everything he himself had stood for. "D'Ambrizzi is either the good guy or the bad guy. The question is, how will we know?"

"I don't know. They're all bad guys. Okay—he fits all the criteria for the bad guy. We have only his own word he's the good guy."

"We also have Father Dunn's word," she said.

"How reassuring. What's it worth? I have no idea."

"But what does your gut tell you?"

"That I still want to spend some time alone with Herr Horstmann. Then I'll worry about who sent him to do the killing. It stands to reason it's Simon, the *real* Simon . . . D'Ambrizzi."

"But there's Val—he'd never have ordered Val's murder—"

"What about your murder? My murder? He could have ordered those?"

She looked away, said nothing.

A middle-aged priest with a smug, humorless face approached us from the stairs above. "Sister Elizabeth," he said, "and Mr. Driskill. His Eminence Cardinal Indelicato would like to meet you. Please follow me."

We followed him up the stairs, along a landing, then down a corridor lined with green and gold brocade occasional chairs and dozens of framed drawings and tables of green and gold with vases of cut flowers. He stopped at a doorway and pointed us inside. The room was long and narrow with high windows, heavy floor-length draperies, a carpet a thousand years old, an elegant escritoire, a

large painting by Masaccio dominating one wall. I had no idea there
were such works in private homes, villas however grand.

The room was empty. *"Momento,"* the priest murmured, and
disappeared through an ornately carved door behind the desk.

I nodded. My eye was caught by a small painting hung beside a
window above an ultrasonic humidifier that was doing its best to
keep things from crumbling to dust. In the painting a ghostly robed
figure seemed to float in the middle distance, a long arm extended,
pointing at the viewer, or the painter. On closer examination the
figure's face was revealed to be a skull, blanched and smudged.
There were leafless trees in the bleak background, black birds
turning in a faint red sky as if the fires of hell burned beyond the
horizon. I was struck by the picture because the pointing robed
figure might so easily have been a depiction of my dream-mother,
reaching for me, about to speak the incomprehensible words. I
heard a rustle of heavy garments and turned in time to see Cardinal
Indelicato shimmer into the room.

His face was long and sallow. His dark hair might have been
shellacked against his skull which was long and narrow. He shook
hands with Sister Elizabeth, then came to me and repeated the
gesture, very nearly clicking his heels. A heavy silver cross hung
from a thick silver chain draped around his neck. It was studded
with what appeared to be emeralds and rubies. He saw the way it
caught my attention.

"Not part of my normal costume, Mr. Driskill. A family heir-
loom—good for warding off the nimble vampire, I'm told—which
like this ostentatious attire I wear only on ostentatious occasions.
Of which this, I'm afraid, is one. The Church pays heed to the
modern medium of television. We're previewing an American television program which will reveal 'how the Vatican really works.'
How very American, eh? The inside story—I find that Americans
are fascinated with what passes for the inside story. And they will
believe—pardon my saying so—almost anything they're told. But I
am rambling, forgive me. I wanted to offer my personal condolences
regarding your sister . . . I did not know her well, but her reputation
made her known to everyone throughout the Church and the world
beyond. And my dear Sister Elizabeth, what a horrifying experience
you've had." He shook the sleek head, lifted a thin, long-fingered
hand, an eloquent gesture. "But we are nearly finished with our
investigation. I can assure you there will be no more killings. The

Church is back on the road to salvation." A smile so thin it must already have slipped between a million cracks.

"That's a comfort," I said. "The word seems to be getting around that we're all just about home free. Which is certainly going to do my sister Val a lot of good. And Robbie Heywood and Brother Leo and all the others who have died at the hands of Herr Horstmann—"

"Yes, yes, I understand how you feel." He turned from my rather bellicose outburst to Sister Elizabeth, who watched him from behind a veil of calm objectivity. She looked as if she were studying a particularly interesting specimen of *Cardinalus Romanus,* looking perhaps for signs of panic—of anything that would reveal guilt or innocence, the truth or falsity of Sandanato's version.

"But," he went on, "you must remember that this is a Church matter. It is not only that it is best handled from within the Church . . . it can *only* be handled within the Church. Very soon Horstmann and his master will be revealed and dealt with as only the Church is capable of doing. Until then, I must ask you both to refrain from pursuing this matter any further. The Holy Father has involved himself at last . . . you two must remove yourselves, whatever your personal feelings. May I assume I have your pledge?"

"You may, " I said, "assume anything you damn please."

"You only make it more difficult," he said. "You are precisely what I've been warned you'd be. But you are a free agent. And there is nothing you can do to affect the outcome now. Thank you for coming." He smiled again in a distant and pitiless manner. "Please, enjoy the evening. And don't miss the screening of the film. You may indeed learn something of how the Vatican really works. I believe it is portrayed as a disarmingly simple and cheerful place." He inclined his narrow head.

"So you say it's D'Ambrizzi," I said to him, standing my ground as he tried to move us toward the door. "You must think you can prove it . . . but to whose satisfaction, I wonder? Not to the Roman police. Not to the Princeton police. You want to keep it inside the Church. The pope is dying and may not even know what you're talking about anymore. So where is it you go with your case?"

Cardinal Indelicato shrugged, the tiniest elevation of his shoulders. "Enjoy the evening. Now, you must excuse me." He went around me, then stopped in the doorway, turned back to stare at me. He said nothing, rather to my surprise, and left.

*   *   *

The *papabili* were out in force. They were everywhere. There were also some other faces I recognized, men who were not in the running for the papacy.

Standing on a balcony, I saw them moving in the crowd below.

Cardinal Klammer was there, all the way from New York. Cardinal Poletti, the curia spin-doctor, and Cardinal Fangio, said by some to be an innocent in a viper pit, said by others to wear the mantle of innocence as camouflage so perfect it was nearly believable. There was Cardinal Vezza and Cardinal Garibaldi and hunchbacked Cardinal Ottaviani and Cardinal Antonelli with his long, still-blond hair. There were others whose names eluded me but whom I recognized: a Dutchman who walked with two canes, dragging his feet; a German with a famous trademark crew cut, a black man who must have been nearly seven feet tall, all faces familiar to the viewers of television or readers of newspapers. I also spotted Drew Summerhays and at his side the little man I'd seen with him in Avignon, the little man with the mangled throat. In an archway, with shadows playing across his face, was a surprise, a face I knew but hadn't expected: Klaus Richter in a dark business suit, sipping champagne, speaking to a priest. It was all still in place: the Nazis, the art, the Church. Richter. The old golf-playing Nazi, one of the men in the photograph Val had stolen from his office. I wondered, was he in Rome on the old master business, the blackmail business? He had to be.

Father Dunn drew up beside me, murmured something, and as I turned toward him I thought I saw from the corner of my eye a sleek silver head, round spectacles catching the candlelight, a man flickering past in the crowd below. I jerked my head quickly but the man was gone. Dunn followed my glance. "What?"

"I'm having delusions," I said. "I thought I saw Horstmann."

"Why should that be a delusion?" He smiled wryly. "Are you telling me you still have it in you to be surprised? *That* surprises *me.*"

"I never seem to learn a damned thing."

"Of course you do. You seem positively lighthearted given the circumstances. Let me guess. Détente with Sister Elizabeth?"

I nodded.

"Just remember," he said, "she'll never make it easy for you. Even when she tries, it won't be easy."

I nodded, wondering if I could possibly have seen Horstmann. Maybe he was waiting for fresh orders from Simon. So far as I knew, he hadn't killed anybody in a week.

"Look," Dunn said, pointing toward a flurry of activity at the far end of the hall below.

Cardinal Indelicato was greeting Cardinal D'Ambrizzi. Tall and thin and suave; short, fat, smiling. They might have been best friends. Other cardinals seemed drawn to them as if they were powerful magnets which, of course, they were.

"What a game it all is," Dunn said. "Tonight Indelicato stakes his claim for all the initiated to see. He's saying in their secret code, *I will be Pope!* And everyone here—almost—is trying to make sure they're on his good side. You just have to love it."

An hour later the crowd was being slowly herded into the ballroom, where the television program would be previewed for this select audience. Cardinal Indelicato was going to say a few words. He introduced the famous American anchorman who was the narrator; he would accept the praise once the lights went up. He was being swept along on the wave of the heady moment. It was not the sort of excess he often permitted himself.

D'Ambrizzi had slipped away and joined us in the shadows behind a grove of potted palms. Dunn turned. "Eminence."

The cardinal had Sister Elizabeth in tow. "This one"—he inclined his head toward her—"still maintains the belief that I am not Jack the Ripper. I hope to demonstrate that fact to you, Benjamin, as the evening goes on. As for my dear friend Indelicato, he believes he's putting an end to the career of old Saint Jack tonight." He shrugged. "And what if he does? Would it be such a tragedy? Well, yes, it might be something of a tragedy for the Church."

"What *do* you want for the Church?" I asked.

"What do I want for the Church? I suppose I don't want it to fall into the hands of the Iron Masters—my name for them. The old guard, the ultraconservatives. I don't want Indelicato to take it over and turn it back into a kind of baronial preserve. It's too late for that. That's the heart of it."

"Indelicato seems very confident tonight," I said.

"And why not? He has me under his heel, does he not? Horstmann was Simon's creature, everyone agrees on that . . . and I was Simon . . . I tried to kill a pope, I led a band of killers, and now I am supposed to have reactivated Horstmann. It all fits into the long, dark history of the Church and Indelicato thinks he can prove it. How in the world can I stop him from blackmailing me out of the picture? It would—if I may say so—take an act of God. Of course, I believe in God." He smiled beneath the broad, hooked beak, gently fingering an ivory crucifix on his chest. "And God is well known to help those who help themselves. But now, are you intent on seeing this television program?" We all indicated we weren't. "Neither am I. Come with me. Quietly. I have something to show you."

He led the way down a deserted corridor, down a flight of stairs that hooked around a corner into a dark, cavernous basement, lit only by occasional ceiling lights. He touched a switch on the wall and the great hulking shadows were revealed as wine racks. Thousands of bottles stretching away. Dunn said, "I've heard it's the finest cellar in Rome."

D'Ambrizzi shrugged. "I am no judge of wine. As long as it's rough and the color of blood I'm happy. A peasant." He was moving between the racks. "We will not be disturbed down here. I have something you must see."

Elizabeth said, "How can you be sure we won't be—ah—interrupted?" She was looking over her shoulder as if expecting a Swiss Guard S.W.A.T. team at any moment. "Isn't this off limits?"

"Sister, I have known Manfredi Indelicato for more than fifty years. There's nothing we don't know about each other. He always has his spies watching me. But he sees me as an unsophisticated bull in a china shop. About me, he believes what he wants to believe. In any case, he would never believe that I have my spies in his personal employ . . . members of his household staff. He occasionally uses something he could learn only from his spies. Thus, he gives himself away . . . and identifies his spy for me into the bargain. I, however, never use what I learn about him. I merely note it for future reference." He grinned like a crocodile. "I use it only obliquely, you see. I am the subtle one, not Manfredi." He beamed self-consciously. "He's prepared to kill me tonight. If he must, he will . . . or so he believes. But do I appear worried to you? Please, Sister, be assured—we are quite safe here. I have been here before. What I am about to show you I've seen several times, just to assure myself it was real. . . . Come, follow me."

The dust from the bottles, the smell of the wooden racks, the coolness of the cellar: I was inhaling all of it, wondering why we were there. When he came to the final rack against the wall D'Ambrizzi reached up and gently pushed the rack sideways. I heard a whirry, softly grinding sound and the rack, as well as the wall itself, slid away on invisible bearings, giving access to yet another room. D'Ambrizzi beckoned us to follow.

"Manfredi is an arrogant man. Another man with a secret room beneath his villa would install an alarm system, a series of television cameras—this is the age of technology. But then, the people who installed the system might leak and there could be nothing worse. . . . Manfredi is so certain of his inviolability, so deliciously egocentric, he believes himself to be utterly impregnable. No one could know about this crypt—no one could know what he has hidden here. But he is mistaken. Giacomo D'Ambrizzi knows . . ."

The room was deeper yet beneath the level of the ground and, in contrast to the vast wine cellar, it was clean and free of the trappings of great antiquity. There were two large humidifiers and an air filtration system, temperature gauges, automatic sprinklers in case of fire. Everything was in crates of all sizes and shapes. The room was the size of two tennis courts.

"This, my friends," D'Ambrizzi said, "is the loot of World War Two. All in Manfredi Indelicato's basement. Come, look at these crates. Come." He waved us down two flights of stairs onto the concrete floor, among the crates. "Look . . . look!"

The crates were stenciled in black with eagles and swastikas of the Third Reich. Some had names inscribed in more faded black ink. Ingres. Manet. Giotto. Picasso. Goya. Bonnard. Degas. Raphael. Leonardo. Rubens. David. There was no end to it. Scrawled in red on many of the crates was the word *Vaticano*.

"It's all very safe here," D'Ambrizzi said. "He has taken great care with the environment. Very fond of art, Manfredi. Runs in the family. And this stuff is going to have to be safe for a very long time. Because most of these pieces have rather detailed histories. Provenances. They may have to be kept in hiding for another century. If Fredi becomes pope, he will surely see that it all goes to the Church—"

"And if you become pope?" I asked.

"I have hardly thought about it. I would not be a free agent. I suppose I'd think of something. Maybe Indelicato will try to keep it in his own family." He sighed. "It's really something of an albatross, isn't it, this treasure? Since we're not supposed to have it at all. I thought you might enjoy seeing it, seeing what Indelicato was up to back then. If you inspected the crates carefully, you'd see that some of it was earmarked for Goering or Himmler or Goebbels or Hitler himself. But Indelicato took it . . . with my help, I admit, on occasion—"

"But why Indelicato?" Elizabeth asked. "He was in Rome during the war, he had nothing to do with the *assassini* in Paris . . . you were the one making sure the Church got its share of the loot—"

"Well, I had no heart for it, you see. But Fredi, he was at Pius's right hand when the whole *assassini* business was conceived. It wasn't only Pius who gave me the unpleasant job of going to Paris to do the dirty work. It was Indelicato that Pius turned to for a suggestion. And Indelicato saw a way to get rid of me. Even then we were natural rivals. He believed it was unlikely that I would survive the Paris assignment. He supposed the Nazis would eventually have enough of my contentious behavior and simply kill me. Oh yes, Indelicato monitored my work very closely."

"Did he know about your plan to kill Pius?"

"Oh my, yes, of course. It was Indelicato who was tipped off to the plot. It was Indelicato who further cemented his relationship with Pius by 'saving his life.' Pius never forgot."

"So, who told Indelicato? Who betrayed you?"

"Someone I trusted, someone who knew everything. For a long time I didn't know . . . at the beginning, of course, I was sure it was LeBecq. Now I know it wasn't."

"Who was it?"

He shook his head, wouldn't answer.

Elizabeth said, "But how did Indelicato wind up with all the booty?"

"Pius was a grateful man when it was convenient for him. He gave it into Fredi's keeping as a reward for services rendered. For saving the papal hide. For all I know, Indelicato may have blackmailed him." That thought made him smile.

"Well," Father Dunn said, "it was an appropriate gesture. The Indelicato family has always taken pride in its collections. They have always collected."

Then it hit me, better late than never.

"The Collector," I said softly.

D'Ambrizzi nodded. "Yes. It was Indelicato whom Pius sent to Paris to find me . . . that is, to build the case against me for catch-all disobedience, for killing LeBecq, for plotting to kill Pius himself. But we held firm, held silence in the face of his probing. Eventually I realized he was going to have me killed—he'd have been rid of me forever. Yes, Pius called him 'the Collector.' It was a little joke, a play on words. Fredi had been sent to Paris to collect *me*. In any case, as soon as the war was over, it was Indelicato who handled the Vatican end of what you referred to as 'the mutual blackmail' with the escaping Nazis. Fredi was a kind of clockwork spider, weaving his web of blood and fear and iron self-righteousness, the Nazis and the art and the Church. Those days are the key to his entire rise. The serious, ascetic figure, the King of the Curia. Indelicato has been a busy man. One of us, I suspect, is going to have to die so that the other might succeed—"

"Nonsense, Giacomo! Your various delusions, your sense of melodrama, have blinded you!" It was His Eminence Cardinal Indelicato in the doorway behind us. "What do I have to fear from you? Or you from me? And why all this talk of dying? Has there not been enough killing?" His dark eyes, so like Sandanato's, flickered from one face to another, a half smile on his thin lips. In that moment he reminded me of Sandanato, someone only a step from martyrdom and fanaticism. Elizabeth's story that Sandanato had defected to Indelicato's camp after a lifetime of loyalty to D'Ambrizzi made sense, if only in terms of Indelicato's face. Never had two men been more unlike each other than the cardinals in question. Except, perhaps, in their ambitions, their ruthlessness.

D'Ambrizzi turned to us with a tolerant smile. "I owe my friends here an apology. I knew you would have me watched, Fredi, and I wanted you here. They'd never have come if I'd told them—but I am trying to prove a point to them. A tour of the treasure chamber was in order."

"But I'm afraid you've given the wrong impression. These are the gifts bestowed upon the Church by various states both during and after the war. I lease this space to the Church for storage. It's all down on paper and perfectly proper."

D'Ambrizzi laughed. "Why tell this to me, Fredi? I'm the one the Germans allowed to steal it! You are an amusing fellow sometimes, in spite of yourself."

"As always, my friend, you are too kind. But you must realize that our rivalry—as you see it—is at an end. We are old men,

Giacomo. We must escape from the past. Surely we will live out our days in peace—"

"Do you think so, Fredi? Really?"

"Of course. The long war is over. I have your memoir now, the story you wrote and left in America so many years ago . . . at least, it will soon be in my possession. I will destroy it. And so your claws will be dulled. Whatever you insist on dredging up from the tragedy of the past will be irrelevant jabbering—"

"And forty years after the events we have our second Nazi pope!" D'Ambrizzi couldn't keep the laughter out of his voice. "What a joke! And who is it that procured my memoir, as you call it?"

Indelicato stared at him and then let the question slip away. "You see, you are hostage to the past. *Nazi* is no longer a word with any meaning."

"Perhaps that's one of the things that's wrong with the world. For me, it will always have meaning, I assure you."

"You are paralyzed in the past. For you there is always a war, always killing to be done. Well, Simon, your killing is over at last. Now you must contemplate the fate of your eternal soul. You have such a lot of blood on your hands. You have murdered so much of the past. But, Giacomo, you have not murdered me!"

"I assume this is all for their benefit," D'Ambrizzi said, turning slightly toward us. "Well, you may convince them. But I must say it's you, Fredi, you *are* the past. While you live, the evil of those days lives. You are the spirit of evil that infects our Church. Evil. Pure evil . . ."

"Ah, my poor Giacomo! Up to your chin in blood, the man who tried to murder the pope—and you call me evil! You should seek out your confessor if you still have one, my friend, while there is still time."

They stared at each other, all the smiles gone, like two prehistoric creatures, all but extinct, ready to thrash it out. After what they had been through and what they had done, extinction held no fears for them.

I broke the silence, faced Indelicato. "Who warned you of the plot to kill Pius?"

"I will tell you—"

"No!" D'Ambrizzi shouted. "There's no point!"

"Archduke. It was the man we called Archduke. He knew where the real hope for the Church lay. He knew then. He knows now."

Cardinal Indelicato led our peculiar little group back to the festivities. He walked side by side with D'Ambrizzi, their arms linked. Father Dunn and Elizabeth and I followed, watching them, outwardly two old friends engaged in a formalized ritual. Maybe that was all it was, a ritual, a gavotte they'd been dancing for half a century. Maybe their emotions weren't involved. Maybe their emotions had died long ago and what was left was sheer plotting. Whatever the truth, I wanted to see how the dance ended.

The viewing of the television show was just concluding as we stood in the vast foyer outside the ballroom doors. The applause was still rippling away as the footmen opened the doors and the crowd milled out upon us. The American anchorman was swept along until he saw Cardinal Indelicato. Then the two of them stood together while we moved away. Flashbulbs were going off, everyone was exclaiming at the brilliance of the show. Indelicato was giving his thin smile, inclining his head humbly, fingers touching the bejeweled crucifix.

I turned to Father Dunn. "Let's get the hell out of here. I can't keep any of it straight anymore. It was supposed to end tonight. The big flash of lightning . . . the truth. And what do we get? The villains decide it's old home week. And what did Indelicato mean about getting his hands on D'Ambrizzi's memoirs? You said Peaches found the damn things—"

I felt D'Ambrizzi's hand on my arm before Dunn could answer. "Don't leave yet. The evening has just begun."

Monsignor Sandanato had just appeared in the crowd, pushing his way toward the subject of the popping flashbulbs.

D'Ambrizzi drew me back toward Indelicato. "You see?"

Sandanato was breathless, his face gleaming and gaunt.

"Eminence, please, excuse me."

Indelicato turned slowly, magisterially, the thin smile fading. "Yes, Monsignor?"

"I've just come from the Holy Father, Eminence. He has sent me to you. He wants to see you now." Any tighter and Sandanato would have snapped right before us.

Indelicato nodded, turned away from the well-wishers and the television people. The anchorman said, "Eminence, does this mean that you are the pontiff's choice?"

Indelicato stared at the anchorman in amazement, whispered, "The Holy Father has no vote," and brushed past him, stopping in front of D'Ambrizzi. "You heard, Giacomo? Why not pledge me your support?"

"You'd better hurry, Fredi. He might change his mind."

"You find this amusing?"

"Good-bye, Fredi."

Sandanato, avoiding D'Ambrizzi's eyes, plucked at Indelicato's sleeve as he passed. "Do you wish me to accompany you, Eminence?"

Slowly Indelicato—as if passing some secret sentence—shook his head. "Not necessary, Monsignor."

The word had spread almost instantaneously through the crowd, a kind of electrical charge. The pitch of voices had risen with that special frisson that comes with being at the heart of a moment, a moment of history. Was the papacy of Callistus ending? In his last hours he was making known his own hopes about a successor? Would his last wish carry weight? What would the morning bring?

D'Ambrizzi's heavy hand was on Sandanato's shoulder. "You've done well, Pietro. I thought Callistus might need a messenger tonight. Well . . . so be it. Now, you must join our little supper party. I won't take no for an answer."

6

tanding near the double door through which she'd entered the private dining room, Sister Elizabeth reflected on just what Cardinal D'Ambrizzi might still have in store for them. The room was small and comfortable, cozy beneath two small chandeliers. The waiters were from the Hassler staff. Using the hotel seemed like a concession to Driskill and herself: he was a few floors from his room, she was across the square from the Order's headquarters. For some reason—it seemed rather sinister to her—D'Ambrizzi had made her promise to stay there overnight rather than return to her Via Veneto flat.

Now the cardinal was speaking to a man with a huge mole's nose, so vast the room for a moment seemed to revolve around it. Driskill stood listening to Drew Summerhays, whom Elizabeth had met at Val's funeral. Driskill's face was remote, emotionless, but there was a desolate look in his eyes: lost, tired, or puzzled nearly to exhaustion? She thought she alone knew him so well.

D'Ambrizzi as the Ringmaster was a remarkable sight. He had controlled, stage-managed, their entire evening—the whole time they'd been in Rome, if it came to that. But his arrival at the party, the mysterious descent into Indelicato's netherworld . . . she was still trying to cope with the room full of Nazi treasure. The dollar value had increased—what? Tenfold, a hundredfold, maybe a thousand times in forty years? Whatever, it was not surely a priceless collection.

Now Drew Summerhays was standing by a drinks cabinet with a glass of sherry and at his elbow a short stocky man who said nothing. Someone seemed to have taken a potato peeler or a sharpened rasp to his throat on some long-past occasion. A gray-haired man with broad stooped shoulders stood talking with Monsignor Sandanato: she was introduced to him, saw his large, moist eyes with purple bags beneath: he was Dr. Cassoni. As she circled the room she met the man with the mole's nose: an old journalist from Paris whose name was Paternoster. *Our Father . . .* Clive Paternoster.

She wondered if Archduke was among them at that moment: it would be so like D'Ambrizzi to bring Archduke the Betrayer to the center ring of his little circus. D'Ambrizzi, the death-defying high-wire aerialist. Working without a net.

Father Dunn was weaving among the guests, a word here, a word there, finally finishing up with a sherry in hand at D'Ambrizzi's elbow. The conversation was general. She heard herself joining him, the only woman, as always. There were pointed jokes about the television show and Indelicato's venture into self-promotion. There were speculations on the health of the Holy Father, as there were bound to be at every dinner that evening in Rome. There were comments on the circus that would begin when Callistus finally died and the cardinals journeyed from the corners of the earth to choose his successor. Father Dunn was unable to resist an observation on Archbishop Cardinal Klammer's ambition to be the first American pope.

Dinner passed in the same superficially untroubled manner, suspense gathering steam as the guests began to wonder just why they'd been chosen to share the cardinal's largesse. Inevitably the subject of Indelicato's departure for the Vatican was raised, and a nervous hush fell across the table. But D'Ambrizzi smiled broadly and said that there was no point in staring so hard at him, he had no idea what might be on the papal mind that night. He let a chuckle rumble deep in his chest and the conversation level returned to normal.

She had maneuvered herself into the chair next to Ben, who gave her a thankful smile. But his eyes bore that distracted look. He said next to nothing. Finally she asked him if he was all right.

"Yes, sure," he said. "No, of course I'm not. But—I don't know. Is this how it all ends? Is this what it comes to? Nothing?" He was speaking softly, his voice leaking tension. No one else was able to hear him. His face remained blank, emotionless. "So maybe there aren't any more murders. But is that supposed to satisfy us? What about Val? What about you and me? It's a goddamn miracle we're alive, either one of us, and now it just peters out, sputters to a halt . . . and that's the end of the story?"

She nodded, knowing how he felt. "They're keeping us boxed out. What more can we do?"

He shrugged. "I don't know. I want to know who gave Horstmann his orders. But everybody's a drinking buddy all of a sudden and maybe I'm not very sophisticated, but I still want to know who the hell took the brain dive off your balcony, who gave Horstmann the list of victims, who's the bastard . . . I want to kill Simon, whoever he is, and then I want to find Horstmann and I want to kill him. I know I sound totally nuts but some grudges are worth holding." She'd never heard bitterness so deep. "I am a payback man. I was as a football player. I am as a lawyer. And I am now. This just isn't fair. Everybody gets to try to kill us, but we don't get a shot at them. Well, bullshit. I want my shot." He grinned suddenly at her. "I've earned it."

She reached out and put her hand over his. It felt perfectly normal. Everything was different now that she'd screwed up her courage and visited his hotel room and cut through all their silly posturing and self-righteousness and pride. Now she could take his hand and give it a squeeze and not feel she had to launch into an awful lecture full of priggish nonsense about the Church knowing best. She'd believed all that back in Princeton, but now, in Rome, she no longer knew what to believe.

D'Ambrizzi was calling for attention, snapping his whip to get them all to jump up onto their boxes and mind their manners.

Supper was gone and she had not the vaguest notion of what she'd eaten. Across the table Sandanato was steadying himself, hands flat, bracing himself. His eyes didn't seem capable of focusing. His forehead had broken out in beads of perspiration. He wiped his deep, darkened eye sockets with the back of his hand. His gaze wavered across hers, moved on toward D'Ambrizzi. D'Ambrizzi. Sandanato's fallen idol.

"I thank you all for indulging me." D'Ambrizzi had risen and was speaking calmly, seemingly in excellent spirits. "You may wonder why I was taken with such a determined desire to be your host tonight . . . well, there is a point. Sister Elizabeth, you were Sister Valentine's closest friend. Ben Driskill, she was your beloved sister. Thus, Sister Valentine was your entry card. Father Dunn, my old friend, confidant, trusted ally through the years . . . in a time of crisis I would naturally turn to you for help and guidance . . . and the series of murders which began a year and a half ago qualifies in this old peasant's mind as a crisis. Drew Summerhays, fifty years I've known you, worked with you, plotted and counterplotted with you and against you in war and peace—and you are a good man in a crisis. Clive Paternoster, you have known so much for so long, you and Robbie Heywood, that it would have been grossly unjust to withhold from you the final chapter. . . . I only wish that Robbie could have been with us tonight—he'd have been hugely amused by all the melodrama. My friend and personal physician, Dr. Cassoni—you are also the Holy Father's doctor, you made no protestations about keeping me informed of his condition. And the pontiff's health has been at the very center of this whole business—only when his illness struck could the killing begin.

"And you, Pietro, Monsignor Sandanato, my faithful aide-de-camp through so many battles, so often my greatest strength . . . no man has a greater belief in the necessity of saving our Church from its enemies. So you must be included tonight." He smiled around the table, taking them all in.

Ben Driskill said, "You missed one of us. The little one over there. I've seen him before . . . he chased me through the streets of Avignon. But we weren't introduced."

D'Ambrizzi said, "Drew?"

Summerhays said, "Marco Victor. He is, not to put too fine a point on it, my bodyguard. He travels with me. Ben, I wish you hadn't run from me that night in Avignon. You know you have never had anything to fear from me . . . surely you know that."

"Sure," Driskill said. "We're all pals now."

Sister Elizabeth knew what he was thinking. Summerhays is Archduke, the cold son of a bitch. Wake up, Saint Jack, this is the man, the traitor—

"Now," D'Ambrizzi said, "we are all accounted for. And I will begin the story we all, each of us, have reason and right to know. Be patient, my friends, it is a story worthy of the Borgias . . . it is a story the likes of which our Church has survived before and will again."

It was the second lecture Elizabeth had heard from D'Ambrizzi in a very short time. She was an impatient woman. But she couldn't remember ever wanting to hear anything quite so much in her life. She whispered to Driskill, "Here it comes."

"Let's hope so," he muttered. "I've had just about enough buildup."

"We are all concerned here tonight with the Holy Father's condition." The customary smile that could take you off your guard had faded as D'Ambrizzi began to speak. "The next stage in the Church's history will soon begin. A new pope will be chosen to serve and take the lead in shaping the future, ours and the world's. But first our beloved Callistus will die. We are old friends, Sal di Mona and I, and now it seems that he—the younger man—will precede me in death. I knew about his illness even before he himself did. It was Dr. Cassoni who identified the tumor and the serious worsening of his heart condition. He came to me in simple human-ity, asking me what I believed he should do—how he should handle the news with the Holy Father. I gave him my opinion. Callistus is a man of great courage and perspective. Tell him the truth. This was two years ago. Callistus and I spent many a midnight hour going over the situation, talking about the old days, talking about the future . . . things we had done together, things we'd hoped to do, and those things which now we would never do.

"Most of you in this room know things about my work in the war, back in the days when I was carrying out a unique papal mission in Paris. I did things which a world at war seemed to require. Things that at another time I'd have found horrible, impossible to contemplate, beyond me. But I did them then.

Salvatore di Mona knew these things. He was with me in those days, long before anyone ever dreamed of little Sal's *papacy.* . . .

"Not long after I learned of his illness, something else caught my attention. Men who knew about my Paris mission—these men were dying. And I quietly investigated—*they were being killed.* It was no coincidence. Someone had a reason and I had to discover why. . . .

"Sister Valentine eventually came to me with her own discoveries—she alone had seen the pattern in the killings. She connected them without at first understanding why or how they fit together. But she was a prodigious researcher. She burrowed into the Torricelli papers in Paris, she saw Robbie Heywood, she attacked the Secret Archives for historical precedents, she pieced the story together, she followed the trail of looted treasure and Nazis and this 'Simon' she'd uncovered and she worked her way right to Alexandria and the Church's involvement in the mutually beneficial relationship with Nazi survivors. She had excavated four decades and more, and she found an old snapshot on Klaus Richter's office wall in Alexandria and there was her old friend Giacomo D'Ambrizzi. . . ." He clasped his hands before him, almost in prayer. "The past is always waiting for us, it comes alive and lashes out at us when we least expect it. One of God's little jokes. He keeps us humble.

"Sister Valentine laid it out for me, told me she believed the *assassini* were back at work, she had all the old code names, she had theories about who they were. Did she know I was Simon? She never said . . . but she wanted me to know she'd uncovered much of what had been going on during the war. Now it was all happening again, she said, the *assassini* were back and they were killing people again. She wanted to know why . . . and I had to be very careful. I had to deny everything, I had to tell her she had run astray of pure myth and sheer coincidence, much as I had to tell Sister Elizabeth later on when she followed in Val's footsteps. Of course I included my faithful Sandanato in all of this. And he backed me up in my misleading of these two remarkable detectives, though he knew a good deal of my previous exploits. He was my protégé, he was the young man I had educated in the ways of the Church, he was the one who received my living legacy, my knowledge, my experience. But I also turned to an old friend of mine to investigate in some detail the five recent murders as well as to check on what Val was doing—this delicate task fell to my trusted colleague, Father Dunn. And he concluded by backing up all of Val's contentions . . . but who was doing the killing? And why?

"It had begun not long after Callistus became ill. The more I looked at it the more I came to believe there was cause and effect. Sister Elizabeth put this to me, I ridiculed her . . . she knows she has my apologies, but Val had been killed and above all I didn't want Elizabeth to suffer the same fate. I decided that the choosing of the next pope was also deeply intertwined in all of this—but how? What held the murder victims in the pattern? The fact that they had all been in Paris during the Nazi Occupation. They were all men who knew certain things, or could have known . . . and they were all being killed. And, as Father Dunn said to me in his familiar puckish way, I was the obvious killer. I was inevitably a possible pope and I was cleaning up my checkered past—because, after all, I knew what had gone on and I hadn't been killed! An excellent, logical theory—but, of course, I wasn't killing anyone.

"Then came the murder of Sister Valentine and Father Dunn's report that it was a silver-haired priest, a description, and I suddenly realized that it must be my old comrade, August Horstmann, whom I hadn't laid eyes on since the end of the war. Where had he come from? I knew that at one time he'd gone to live in a monastery in his native Holland. But who else had known? And how had August—a peaceful soul—been turned back into a killer?

"There was only one answer to that last question—he would take his orders from only one man. Only one . . . Simon. But I knew I wasn't ordering the killings. Someone had ordered the killing of Sister Valentine, whom I had known from her childhood, the daughter of my old friend Hugh Driskill. . . . Who could have done such a thing? Who knew about Simon's past?

"Monsignor Sandanato knew much of my past, that's true. But someone else knew it all . . . someone who, in the time since Callistus had become ill, had taken my faithful, zealous Sandanato away from my side—no, Pietro, no protestations, it doesn't matter—"

Sandanato was suddenly on his feet, swaying, pointing a shaking finger at D'Ambrizzi. "You are the one! You are the destroyer of the Church! You, you and your Curtis Lockhardt, who whored with his nun, your precious Sister Valentine, your darling Sister Val, who ignored and despised everything on which the Church was built and which it taught . . . she had to die, you must see that, you must see that she was bringing ruin to the Church, standing everything on its head! She supported communist priests, she defied the teachings on birth control, she ranted against all that is sacred, she was a heroine in the eyes of the weak and the disobedient who would undermine and tear down the Church! She and her kind would destroy the Church! And, so help me God, *the Church must be saved!*"

Elizabeth felt Driskill's muscles flexing, straining, as if he might explode across the table. She held him back. "Wait, Ben, wait . . ."

A deathly quiet had dropped across the table. Sandanato stood staring at D'Ambrizzi, but his eyes might have been sightless. Tremors raced through his body like electrical charges shaking him, shorting out. He spoke again, as if he were alone, muttering to himself. "She was going to write a book about the Nazis and the Church—she would have destroyed you, Eminence! She would have brought it all down on us, a rain of fire and desolation! She had to be stopped, order had to be restored, I realized who the Church must turn to—"

"Pietro," D'Ambrizzi said quietly, "sit down now, my son." He waited while Sandanato sank into his chair. The tortured, sensitive face was working, tears streaming: he knew the truth, knew he was broken on the wheel of things so much larger than himself.

He hadn't understood. He had been used.

D'Ambrizzi looked away from Sandanato, as if he were sorrowfully casting him into darkness. "Who could have led my poor young friend astray? Only someone who knew as much of the past as I did. The man sent to Paris by the pope, the man who came to be known as the Collector. Indelicato. He was the man who had raked through the rubble of World War Two to uncover everything that he could of the *assassini*. He dogged my tracks, he interrogated me, he threatened me, but always only up to a point . . . because he knew I had an insurance policy. I knew what he and Pius had done and ordered done, just as they knew what I had done . . . what some of you have heard referred to as the Pius Plot.

"Indelicato wants to become pope. He perceived me as his greatest challenge. *He* needed to wipe out the past, the witnesses from the war, and his was an elegant, mathematical solution. He would remove the men who knew too much. But why not simply remove me? So much easier—an accident, a heart attack—so much easier except for one thing. The weapon he planned to use for the killing would be the man who had long ago killed *for me*. Horstmann. And Horstmann would never turn on me. But Indelicato was right—Horstmann would still kill *for Simon . . . for me*. Indelicato's task was then to find Horstmann, not a great difficulty for Indelicato since he had tracked down all the living survivors of the *assassini* after the war was over. But Indelicato not only had to find Horstmann—he had to convince Horstmann that it was Simon calling him back to do battle for the Church.

"So Indelicato had no choice—he had to seduce Sandanato. An intellectual seduction crafted to appeal to Pietro's zealot's soul. It was the one spot where Pietro was vulnerable. Pietro loved me, admired my capabilities, the riches and power I helped bring to the Church . . . but I am not a pious man, I have blasphemed in word and deed and Pietro has often prayed for my soul. Indelicato recruited him in the early days, once we knew the truth of Callistus's health, once we knew there would be a new pope in the foreseeable future. And so poor Pietro became a spy, an accomplice in bloody, bloody murder. Pietro became the voice of Simon for August Horstmann. Everyone knew Pietro was my 'shadow' and everyone knew that Pietro was the keeper of the keys to me. So Pietro could explain everything to Horstmann and Horstmann would believe. It was done by remote control. When Sandanato told me that Horstmann had nearly succeeded in killing Driskill in Princeton I was already almost certain that, yes, Sandanato was in the quicksand with Indelicato . . . and the other one—"

Driskill's eyes were burning into Sandanato, who sat slumped in his chair, as if his life were draining away. He hadn't moved since his outburst. And Ben Driskill seemed to be in a kind of trance.

Sister Elizabeth said, "Does Horstmann corroborate all this? Or is it simply speculation on your part?"

"You may be sure, Sister, I have spoken at length with August over the last two days. He told me the story . . . he told me everything he knew . . . including how he found the man who paid the late-night call on you, Sister, the poor creature who was intended to frighten you off and who went off your balcony instead. He was a simple man, he'd been a good man once who had saved my life long ago, a man who underwent the attentions of the Gestapo, a man who had found a home and who should have been left to live out his days in his backwater. Yes, Sister, that's why I was able to assure you that the killing would be over tonight—"

A terrible animal howl, a shriek of agony and despair, escaped Sandanato's lips, the cry of a man who has stared too long into the fiery pit, a man who had felt the stakes driven into his palms and was dying for a false god. He leapt to his feet, knocking his chair over, making a sound that was no known word, and staggered backward. His hand was at the door.

Driskill was on his feet, his face white with rage.

"Stay!" Driskill's voice filled the room. The others at the table sat frozen in place.

D'Ambrizzi waved his hand as Sandanato stopped, lurching. Spittle flecked his chiseled chin. His eyes seemed to roll, confused. All this was true, yet he was still Sandanato and his gaze settled on Elizabeth. She shrank inwardly but stared back, unblinking.

"You," Sandanato whispered, "you understand me . . . we have spoken, Sister . . . we were of one mind, the Church needed cleansing . . . evil in the service of good—we spoke, Sister . . . can't you make them see what had to be done . . ." His voice cracked. He wiped his mouth on his sleeve. His face glistened with sweat. "Tell them . . . for God's sake!"

"We never . . . not what you've done . . ." She shook her head, looked away. "No, this is your madness."

"Go, Pietro," D'Ambrizzi said.

The door closed softly. He was gone.

"So, Eminence," Drew Summerhays said, his voice papery, dry. "What would you have us do? What about Indelicato? He has set this bloody engine in motion. . . . Now he's with the Holy Father. Give us some guidance."

"All this speculation about the next pope is premature. The will of God and man will be revealed in time." D'Ambrizzi was suddenly bland, undisturbed.

"The hell with the will of God! Spare me all your sanctimonious garbage!" Driskill's voice cut through the obfuscation like a blow-torch. "God didn't put the gun to my sister's head. God didn't cut Brother Leo's throat. God is not taking the fall on this one. Man is answerable! The nutcase who just walked out of here free as the breeze and the psychopathic killer who pulled the trigger and drew the blade and this fucking megalomaniac chatting with the pope as we sit here—what the bloody hell do we do about them?"

"What do you suggest, Mr. Driskill?"

"Where is Horstmann? You spoke with him—"

D'Ambrizzi shook his huge head. "He is gone. I have sent him back to his anonymous life. I have absolved him as best I could, I have heard his confession. He was betrayed, he did what he had been trained to do. His torment and guilt are punishment enough."

"Maybe for you they are. But you don't speak for me. Nobody speaks for me but me . . . and you haven't told us about Archduke. What's the big secret about Archduke? Don't you have a tidy conclusion for Archduke? He betrayed you. . . . Like you and Indelicato, Archduke knew everything . . . and he betrayed you to Indelicato. Where does he fit in now? He wasn't one of the lads in the photograph and he wasn't killed—so Indelicato wasn't using Horstmann to kill him. You know what I think? I think Archduke is part of Indelicato's plan . . . I think Archduke has been an ally of Indelicato's and an enemy of yours ever since he discovered the Pius Plot. I think Archduke and Indelicato decided to band together to keep you from becoming pope because they don't like the way the Church is moving . . . they see you and my sister on the same side and they've had enough. A few lives is a small price to pay for scaring hell out of the curia and the Vatican and stampeding the cardinals in Indelicato's direction . . . so why are you so strangely silent on the subject of Archduke?"

Driskill finished out of breath, staring at D'Ambrizzi.

"I have nothing to say about Archduke," the cardinal said at last. "This is over. Let go, forget." He looked at his guests. "I have no more to say. You, all of you, I trust to remain discreet. This spasm in the history of our Church is over. Time will have its way with Callistus; the next pontiff will emerge. Life and the Church will go on and very soon, we and all this will be forgotten."

The end of D'Ambrizzi's supper party was subdued. There was nothing to add. No one seemed to know quite what to do. Did the cardinal expect them all to go off to bed and a sound night's sleep? He stood at the door, offering each of them a word, a handshake, men he had known for so long a time, through good times and bad. He was informal with them, as he always was.

Sister Elizabeth stood with Ben, who seemed lost in thought, his face an indecipherable mask. Father Dunn joined them. "You don't look happy," he said.

"Does that surprise you?" Driskill said.

"Of course not. But you may have to settle for this. You may have gotten just about all you're going to get. You *have* been brought deep inside, you know."

"Well, I don't much like what I've found."

"Did you really think that you would? I'd have thought your worst suspicions had been confirmed. Isn't that fairly satisfying?"

Driskill stared at him.

Dunn said, "Did you expect them to set up Horstmann and the others in a shooting gallery for you? Come on, my friend, get real—"

"Artie?"

"Yes, my son?"

"Shut up."

"Ah," Dunn said. "The reasoned approach at work."

"What about Sandanato?" Sister Elizabeth tried not to look overly concerned in light of what they had just learned about him. "I don't like the idea of his wandering around Rome in that condition."

"You're right," Driskill said, a muscle jumping along his jaw. "Maybe I should go find him."

"Forget him," Father Dunn said.

"He might do himself harm," Elizabeth said.

"He's a priest," Dunn said.

"Jesus, Mary, and Joseph," Driskill said. "He's a murderer. Hasn't that dawned on you yet?"

"He's not exactly a murderer," Dunn said.

"You're splitting hairs, Artie. He's an accomplice to murder. He obviously set me up that night on the ice. What was I thinking? He asked me to go skating . . . said it would be good for me! Honest to God."

"I think he's quite mad," Sister Elizabeth said. "I look back on things he said . . . I think he was trying to make me see . . . but it all sounded so theoretical." She saw D'Ambrizzi coming toward them. She was exhausted. She said, "I'm staying at the Order tonight. *His* request." She nodded at the cardinal.

"Thank you so much," D'Ambrizzi said, "for sitting through another of my long . . . confessions. I wanted the air cleared."

"So now you just forget Indelicato."

"Not exactly, Benjamin. Sister, I need a word with these two. I've asked Drew Summerhays and his keeper"—he allowed himself

a small smile—"to escort you." He took her hand and led her to
the door. "Sleep well, my dear. I will speak with you tomorrow."

When she was safely with Summerhays, D'Ambrizzi turned
back to Driskill and Dunn.

"I want you to come with me."

Dunn said, "All right."

Driskill said, "Why? Where?"

D'Ambrizzi sighed, looked at his watch. It was past two in the
morning.

"The Vatican. We're going to see the Holy Father."

Monsignor Sandanato went blindly into the night. It had begun
to rain softly but he didn't notice. His eyes were on fire. His ears
were buzzing, blood pounding as if his heart were about to burst.
He wasn't able to create a thought. His brain was nearly gone with
fever.

He stopped to catch his breath at the top of the Spanish Steps.
He didn't notice the tall man in the black raincoat standing in the
shadows, his hat pulled low so the brim hid his face.

And when Monsignor Sandanato set off down the long stairway
he didn't notice the footsteps behind him.

Callistus was wide awake when he was informed that Cardinal
Indelicato was waiting in the anteroom. "Bring him in. And then
get some sleep. I won't be needing anyone."

The cardinal stood before him, lean and gaunt and solemn. A
heavy, jeweled crucifix hung in the middle of his chest. Part of the
family jewels, Callistus reflected with an inward-turning smile.

"Holiness," Indelicato said. "I am at your service."

"You look so sad!" Callistus turned the smile outward. He lay
on the bed, propped up against an enormous monogrammed
pillow. "Do cheer up. The last thing a dying man wants to see in
the dark of night is someone with a sad face."

"Please accept my apologies, Holiness. What may I do for you,
Holiness? You need only ask."

"Well, Fredi, what's this I hear about you?"

"I don't understand . . ."

"I'm told you're the Antichrist, Fredi." The pope chuckled
softly. "Can such a thing be true?"

"I'm sorry, Holiness. I can't hear you."

Callistus was suddenly aware of everything in the room. The rain at the window, the letter on his bed, the heavy ancient document beside it, the low light from his bedside table, the silent flickering image of a soccer match on the television screen. He felt the texture of the sheets, felt his hand clenching beneath the sheet. With one part of his mind he was intensely aware of all that, the rustle of Indelicato's garments, and with another part of the brain which would soon be closing down forever, he remembered, saw and heard, that night in the snowbound cabin, the cold wind, the men waiting, with Simon encouraging them against the fear and the frozen gale, the smell of the weapons. . . .

"Come closer, Fredi, so you can hear. There's something important . . ." He held the parchment document between his fingers. It felt as if it might crumble away. "Here. I have something for you."

Manfredi Cardinal Indelicato came to the side of the bed.

He leaned across the body of the Holy Father to take the document. He saw the ancient seal.

The Holy Father moved, a shifting beneath the sheets, and withdrew his hidden hand.

7

DRISKILL

The bedroom of Pope Callistus.

This, in the heart of the Vatican, the Apostolic Palace, was not a place I of all people had any business being. It was ghostly as hell, the corridors quiet, the lights dimmed, our footsteps muffled. Some of the tapestries on the walls, scenes of history and violence and armies on the march and bands of angels wanting attention and God only knows what else—the tapestries seemed so full of sound and fury, battle cries and trumpets of the heavenly variety, but someone had turned the volume down. Or maybe they hadn't the strength to make noise anymore.

D'Ambrizzi led the way, all business now, and Dunn and I followed like courtiers. There was a priest on the night watch at a desk outside the bedroom. D'Ambrizzi spoke to him very quietly, forcefully, and he didn't move from the desk. We went into the bedroom. It was odd, no formalities, just through the door. No knocking. No announcement. Nothing.

Nobody would have answered, as it turned out.

Cardinal Indelicato lay sprawled facedown across the bed. He was utterly still. From ten feet away I'd have bet ten to one he was dead. The fact registered simply, directly. The implications dawned a good deal more slowly. Father Dunn crossed himself perfunctorily, sighed. "Jesus Christ," he said.

D'Ambrizzi said, "Hardly." He bent over the other man, whom I'd momentarily forgotten. Callistus lay under the blanket, Indelicato's body pinning him down. I went closer. D'Ambrizzi leaned down, murmured. "Holiness? Can you hear? Sal . . . it's Simon." He waited, listening, then placed the fingers of his right hand against the papal pulse. "He's alive. Unconscious, but alive. Help me turn this one over." Dunn stood watching while D'Ambrizzi and I shifted the body of the late Cardinal Indelicato onto his back.

The light was dim. The television was on, the sound off. The shadows seemed to have erased the walls. We might as well have been onstage.

D'Ambrizzi turned on two more table lamps in addition to the one beside the bed. He stood with hands on hips staring at the bed. Then he looked at me, then at Dunn.

"This man has died of a heart attack."

Protruding from Indelicato's chest was the ornate gold handle of a dagger. Dunn and I looked at each other.

"So he has," Dunn said. "In a manner of speaking."

"Yes," D'Ambrizzi observed sagely, "this man has suffered a fatal coronary." He slowly pulled the dagger from Indelicato's chest. He took several tissues from a box on the bedside table. He folded them around the blade and wiped it clean. He crossed the room and opened a drawer of the desk, placed the dagger inside. "Florentine. Fine workmanship." He closed the drawer.

"You don't often see a heart attack bleed like this."

"Benjamin, you're not a doctor, so don't pretend to things well beyond your understanding." He picked up the telephone. "Private line. Doesn't go through the Vatican switchboard." He dialed a number and waited. "Dr. Cassoni, this is D'Ambrizzi. Are you in your pajamas yet? No? Good. I'm with the Holy Father. He's unconscious, breathing normally. You'd better come have a look. And, Cassoni . . . I also have a corpse. Heart attack. I'll tell you when you get here. Do hurry. And don't bring anyone to assist you. Do you understand? Good fellow." He hung up and looked again at the body of Indelicato. "We may not know the man the Holy Father would prefer to succeed him. But his reaction to Fredi shows a marked lack of confidence, wouldn't you agree?" He stood looking at the long, gaunt face of his old enemy. "Well, no tears for Fredi. He was a diabolical son of a bitch here on earth and got just what he deserved. Now God can sort him out."

He dialed another number, turned his back on me as I walked around the bed, trying to make sense out of all this. Of course, I knew perfectly well that everybody was staying right in character. D'Ambrizzi, Indelicato, Callistus, who was once Sal di Mona, Horstmann, Summerhays, even Dunn and me. We fit our roles perfectly.

In the folds of the blanket I saw a piece of vellum or parchment with a bit of red waxen seal that seemed to be flaking away. I was just reaching for it when I stepped on something that had drifted off the bed. It was a single sheet of paper, handwritten, only a line or two.

I read it and of course it made the present charade take shape. I folded it and slid it into my pocket.

D'Ambrizzi said into the telephone, "My dear Cardinal Vezza, please accept my apologies for the lateness of the hour. Yes, Eminence, I'm very much afraid it is important. Fredi Indelicato is no longer with us . . . no, I mean to say that he is no more. . . . Dead, Vezza, quite dead. Yes, of course, a great tragedy. Well, yes, young perhaps, in your eyes." D'Ambrizzi chuckled softly. "I believe it would be wise if you joined us. We are in the Holy Father's bedchamber. I've called Cassoni. No one else knows. The sooner the better, my dear Vezza."

When he replaced the telephone I said, "Why Vezza?"

"An ally of mine. He's my man in the enemy camp. A member of Cardinal Poletti's little group of Indelicato supporters. Invaluable, really. Do you know, they even went so far as to put a tape recorder on the oxygen machine so they could listen to my discussions with the pope? No, so help me, it's true. Not only was I telling Callistus what would motivate him . . . but I was prodding them onward as well. It's a strange world, Benjamin."

While we waited, listening to the pope's breathing, D'Ambrizzi noticed the piece of parchment on the bed. He reached across the blankets and picked it up. "This has caused so much trouble." He paused, pursing his thick lips. "No, that's not true. It is, however, a kind of record of trouble. This is the Concordat of the Borgias. What might we call it? Almost the charter of the *assassini,* I suppose. Pius sent it with me to Paris, as if it were indeed a piece of the One True Cross. As if it validated me, gave me power, as if it would inspire me to do what had to be done for the Church. I sent it north with Leo and Horstmann . . . and now here it is. A list of names."

"How did it get here?" I asked.

"Horstmann gave it to me yesterday. I gave it to Callistus. He'd never actually seen it. I wanted him to see his name. Now—what to do with it? Hide it in the Secret Archives?" It was a purely rhetorical question. "No, I think not. It is a relic we can all live without, don't you agree?"

Casually he dropped it into an ashtray on the desk and produced his gold lighter. The flame leapt to life and he touched it to the edge of the centuries-old parchment. History went up in smoke, a matter of seconds. Dunn watched, shaking his head.

D'Ambrizzi looked up at him. "Who needs it, Father? Nobody. Little good ever came of it."

We sat in chairs staring at the tape of the soccer match on the television.

Then Dr. Cassoni arrived and set about making certain very special arrangements.

It seemed that Cardinal Indelicato had indeed died quite unexpectedly of a massive heart attack.

They planned to release the news of Cardinal Indelicato's passing thirty-six hours later. By then I was going to be airborne, bound for whatever might pass for sanity back in Princeton. Out of the confusion filling my mind, all I knew I needed was some recovery time. And I wanted to see my father. I'd learned a lot since I'd left, but there was precious little satisfaction in it. None of it had turned out the way it should have. There wasn't even a single villain at the core of the evil, least of all Horstmann, who was now painted as an unwitting victim in Indelicato's master scheme. Maybe it was Indelicato's and Archduke's scheme: I didn't know. I wouldn't have trusted myself with a gun in my hand and Horstmann nearby, but

Horstmann had been sent back to the darkness from which he'd come. I'd lost my chance even for base animal revenge.

And then there was the matter of Monsignor Pietro Sandanato. What to make of him? Well, he was, I suppose, your over-the-edge Catholic crazy, call him a zealot or just bloody nuts. What was he to do now? How could he live with himself, with the betrayal of his mentor and the death of his accomplice and new sponsor? I supposed that D'Ambrizzi in his wisdom and apparently Godlike power within the Church would paper over the relative disgrace of nurturing a murderous little shit at his bosom all those years and shuffle Pietro off to an obscure post in an even more obscure venue.

Perhaps I should have been more surprised or shocked or even amazed by Callistus's murder of Indelicato, but in a peculiar way— a way I could see was reasonable, on its own terms—it made sense. He'd been one of the *assassini,* he'd set off following his leader into the snowy mountains to murder a pope. So, forty years later, that same leader reminds him he was once one of the *assassini,* that maybe they hadn't gotten their pope back then but what was to stop their putting an end to a would-be pope now? I mean, once you've decided you can kill a man, it's surely only a matter of circumstance and proper motivation thereafter. Forty years went by and Callistus, once Sal di Mona, still had it in him. Well, he wasn't the first dying pope to have murdered. I said more power to him. The Church could undoubtedly benefit from more right-thinking murderers. Or have I lost the point somewhere along the path to Golgotha?

I was summoned by Cardinal D'Ambrizzi late that same afternoon. No one knew yet, at least in the public sense, of Indelicato's fatal heart attack. D'Ambrizzi left instructions for me to meet him in the Vatican Gardens and I was escorted there by a smiling, round-faced priest who enthused about what a lovely day it was.

The cardinal was strolling the path, the skirts of his plain cassock catching the chilly breeze beneath the palm trees. Gardeners were at work. His head was down, as if his eyes were fixed on the bulbous toes of his old-fashioned boots.

When I caught up with him he took my arm for a moment and we walked awhile that way. I felt curiously close to him, as if we were old and intimate friends, which was a fantasy, of course. I blamed the delusion on my exhaustion. He stopped and watched a workman with a wheelbarrow full of rich black earth.

"You see that man," he said to me. "Now, you might say he has dirty hands. But, Benjamin, I think of my hands today—in a very rare moment of conscience, you understand—and they seem a good deal dirtier. I've been dirtying them for such a long time. I think in terms of this kind of metaphor every so often and, by God, it's never, *never* a good idea. Dirty hands, clean hands, what difference does it make? But I'll tell you what makes a difference, Benjamin—would you like to know?"

"I'm not at all sure," I said.

He shrugged, grinning suddenly. "People make a difference, Benjamin. For instance, I already miss Sandanato . . . I'll never think of him the way he was during these past two years. He'll always be earnest young Pietro . . . faithful to me . . . yes, I'll miss him for the rest of my life."

"What have you done with him? A distant posting?"

"I've done nothing with him. My old friend August Horstmann killed him last night. I should have known Horstmann would strike back at him. For betraying me, you see. Once he knew Pietro had played the part of Simon—oh, it was an evil thing to do. August sometimes sent communications to me thinking they were reaching the Simon he knew from long ago. But Pietro read them first, led poor August to believe he was working for me. So August did what he does best . . . he killed Pietro. The police have just been to see me. A single bullet. Back of the head. I called you here at once."

"Just as my sister was killed."

"Well, it *is* over now. Horstmann is gone. Sandanato is dead. Indelicato is dead. Callistus is in a coma from which Cassoni tells he may not emerge. Benjamin, what would happen if we ran out of priests?"

"I'd sure as hell like to find out," I said.

His laughter rumbled across the silent expanses of garden. "Sounds like a good idea to you, does it? Now poor Pietro wouldn't have seen the humor of that." He looked at me sharply. "He had no sense of humor. Maybe that's what was wrong with him." He shrugged.

"There sure was something wrong with him."

"Agreed." There was a memory, a bit of sorrow in the old man's voice.

"Since I'm quite a heathen—"

"Agreed, once more."

"—and no respecter of clerics, I can ask you an impertinent question. The next time I hear about you, will it be your elevation to the papacy?"

"Maybe. If I want it, Summerhays will probably arrange to buy it for me. But I'm getting on. Does the Church need a long-term or a short-term leader? That's the question, isn't it?"

We walked to the place I'd entered. The penny had dropped: forgive Archduke . . . because he may just buy you the papacy!

"I think I'll walk awhile longer, Benjamin." He turned to face me, squinting at me from those hooded eyes. It was as if someone were living—had scraped along as best he could and then taken shelter—inside the aged hulk, peering out, plotting, occasionally feeling. "But let me give you one small bit of advice. When are you going home?"

"Tomorrow," I said. I didn't relish his advice, but then you never knew. He was a gnarly old bastard, he'd survived a hell of a lot more than I would ever see, maybe I should pay attention. The sun was sinking and the palm trees looked lonely against the dome of sky going gray.

"Forgive yourself, Benjamin."

"I beg your pardon, Eminence?"

"That's my advice. Forgive yourself. Take a leaf from my book, son. I don't know what it is you've done, but you should have learned recently that there is far, far worse. It's part of being alive, that's my guess. Bad things occur in one's life . . . one *does* things." He was trying to light a black cigarette in the wind, finally succeeded and took a deep breath. "Forgive yourself your deeds, your trespasses, your sins. . . . I'm not speaking as a priest, or even as a Catholic, but just as a man who has lived his life. Forgive yourself, my son."

Artie Dunn said he was staying in Rome for a few days, doubtless hatching some ungodly plot with D'Ambrizzi, so we had a last Roman dinner together. He seemed to have something on his mind but I couldn't shake it loose. Somehow we got to talking about my parents and Val's death and the suicide—Father Governeau, who had to sleep his eternal rest outside the fence, outside consecrated ground. By mistake, of course, since he'd been murdered. Ah, God is great, God is good. He told me to wish my father well and badger him about reading the books he'd left. I promised that I would. He said he'd call when he got back to New York.

We spoke only circumspectly about Indelicato's and Sandanato's deaths. He'd heard from D'Ambrizzi, too, and we knew we'd speak of these things later when the dust had cleared.

"D'Ambrizzi said something that struck me rather sideways this afternoon." We were walking back toward the Hassler, climbing the Spanish Steps. "I asked him if he thought he'd be elected pope—"

"You just asked him?" Dunn's fuzzy gray eyebrows rose. His eyes twinkled mischievously.

"It's what *he* said . . ."

"Which was?"

"He said if he decided he wanted to be pope, Summerhays was prepared to buy it for him. Summerhays."

"Not entirely a scoop, Ben. I mean, it's a growth industry, isn't it? Summerhays, your father, Lockhardt, Heffernan . . . and others, I'm sure."

"You miss the point. Summerhays. *Archduke.* Don't you see the . . . the amorality of it? Archduke betrayed him to Indelicato and the pope forty years ago . . . and now he says Archduke will buy him the papacy. I call that pretty damned astonishing."

"Sounds like excellent use of human resources to me," Dunn said. He winked at me.

I wasn't quite sure what saying good-bye to Elizabeth was going to be like: I was going to miss her but the door wasn't closing. That was the important thing. So I called her. The phone conversation was cryptic.

"I've got things to tell you before I go," I said. "Important things. Have you seen or heard from the cardinal?"

"Yes, yes, I have." She was cutting me short. "Look, don't say anything. I don't know who's listening—we have to meet. When are you leaving?"

I told her.

"All right." I heard her thumbing her Filofax. "Look, I can blow off my next two hours if you can. Are you at the hotel?"

"Sure. I'm free, whatever you—"

"Meet me at the bottom of the steps. Fifteen minutes."

I stood at the bottom of the Spanish Steps, waiting. Then she was calling to me, out of breath. I took her shoulders in my hands. "Stand still," I said. She looked at me expectantly. "It seems a month since I last saw you." She smiled and I kissed her softly on the mouth. It was the most normal thing in the world. She was wearing her blazer with the rosette of the Order in the lapel.

"Come on," she said, tugging me along behind her. "How much do you know?"

"More than I can quite believe," I said.

"You know Indelicato's dead?"

"Know? Elizabeth—D'Ambrizzi and I turned the body over . . . we saw the knife at the same time—"

"Knife? What knife? What are you talking about?"

"Florentine dagger, to be precise."

She was staring at me as if I were mad. She pulled up short, pulled at my sleeve, led the way into a small park. A crowd of children had gathered around a puppeteer's stage. It was a peculiar show with Pinocchio cast as a lying cleric in Roman collar, nose growing ever longer, as he boasted to a pretty girl about how brave he was. While he blabbered on of his mighty victories over evil, a huge black knight clad in armor and riding a horse with snarling lips was prancing up behind him. The pretty girl with blond hair didn't know how to interrupt him to warn him. It looked to me like Father Pinocchio was about to get it in the neck. The cries of the children, shrill and full of half-hysterical laughter and cries of warning, rose and fell with the action on the tiny stage. We walked off to the side and sat on a bench beneath trees with their crowns full of wind.

"Ben, Cardinal Indelicato died of a heart attack." She gave me a severe look. "D'Ambrizzi called me this morning. He told me Indelicato had a coronary while talking with Callistus, collapsed, and died, but they're saving the news until tomorrow—"

"Did he mention how Callistus is taking it?"

"No, but—"

"Look, trust me on this one. I was there. Cardinal Indelicato was murdered by . . . by—now, don't bail out on me here—murdered by Callistus."

"You don't mean—"

That's how the conversation went. Callistus the killer, now in a coma. Sandanato dead by Horstmann's hand. It wasn't that she fought the story: she knew so much, she wouldn't have wasted time fighting the truth. But it was rather a lot to take in.

When I had finished, Pinocchio and the black knight were gone and the uniformed schoolchildren and the younger ones with their mothers and nurses were slowly scattering. The sunny sky had grayed over. The wind was pushing a chill this way and that. Christmas was coming.

"I can't help thinking like an editor," she said, the flecked green eyes staring across the park. She raked her fingers through the tawny, heavy hair. Her fingers were long and slender and strong. "What a story it would be." She couldn't keep from grinning. "My God . . . what an ending. The pope killing a—"

"It was Salvatore di Mona who killed Indelicato."

"Yes, I suppose you're right. And now he's in a coma. So D'Ambrizzi lied to me." She stood up.

"One more thing. Simon told him to do it. To kill Indelicato."

"Simon . . . D'Ambrizzi?"

"Yes. He put it in a note reminding Callistus that he'd been one of the *assassini* and he had a job to do. I saw the letter. It was on Callistus's bed when we found him."

"D'Ambrizzi sees me as the press, I suppose," she said. "So he didn't tell me. But he must have known you'd tell me."

"Of course. And he knew you'd never violate the confidence."

"Well," she said, "what would be the point? How could I ever prove any of it? Where's the smoking gun?"

We were walking back toward her office, the traffic yapping and sputtering.

"Think of the toll in human life," she said. "I wonder how many there were? Ones we know nothing of?"

"Who knows? There must be the odd stiff tucked away in shadowy places." I blurted out, "My God, I'm going to miss you, Elizabeth."

"I should think you would. You *are* in love with me, Ben."

"Making light of my affections?"

"Making light of your sad face."

"I make no apologies for this face. It's been through a lot lately. Good reason to be sad, things taken all in all. And I *am* in love with you, now that you mention it."

"Then don't be sad. Love is happy. Val would tell you the same, you know."

"Not if it's a one-way love affair."

"What's that got to do with any of this?"

I smiled. "What, indeed?"

"Let's say good-bye here, Ben." We were about to cross a busy square.

"I keep wondering. About Summerhays. Not just buying the papacy for D'Ambrizzi, but . . ."

"What are you talking about?"

"Why was he in Avignon? He never explained that—what was he doing? Why did he have Marco with him?"

"Well, it's over. What does it matter?"

"But it's never over, don't you see? Not if Summerhays is Archduke . . ."

There was no point in going on, holding her there. "Look, Elizabeth, keep well—I don't know what else to say." It was time to go.

"Give your father my blessings at Christmas, Ben. And just stay steady-on, all right? I need—we both need some time to get it all straight. You do understand?"

"Sure."

"And we'll talk soon."

"When?"

"Not knowing, that's the point, Ben. Don't be impatient with me."

I gave her a look that said I hoped she knew what she was doing.

I watched her cross the square.

She waved her hand once over her shoulder without looking back.

I climbed aboard the plane for the flight home, sank into the seat, and my exhaustion hit me like a hammer blow. I hovered in that limbo between sleep and wakefulness and I had plenty of company. It was their presence that kept me from going all the way under, from diving down into the darkness where the ghost waited.

I was surrounded by all the faces, past and present, the photograph from the drum came to life but the figure holding the camera still in shadow, a mystery . . . and I saw Richter and I wondered who would partner him—and his interests—within the Church now that Indelicato was dead . . . and I saw LeBecq in his art gallery in Alexandria, his face frozen with terror as I pushed him, as my sister had. . . . The beautiful nun who had pointed me on my way and had had dinner with me, it seemed so long ago, and lovely Gabrielle, whom I would never see again . . . all the faces, the Torricelli nephew, such a snot, and Paternoster with his incredible nose and the tramps cooking dinner in the rain in the Place de la Contrescarpe . . . and Leo and the time in the fog on the rocky shingle with the surf shaking the world and my soul dying, drowned in fear . . . and Artie Dunn with his story of the D'Ambrizzi memoir, Artie Dunn appearing like a genie, almost in a puff of smoke, in Ireland . . . and Sister Elizabeth sobbing in Val's room that rainy night in Paris . . . Avignon, Erich Kessler, Summerhays and his little protector moving like dream figures . . . and Horstmann finding me in the little church, mocking my plastic gun, telling me to go home . . . Elizabeth confiding her secrets to me in Avignon and my anger and hatred of the Church disfiguring everything, everything I needed . . . and then Rome . . .

The shade was drawn on the plane window, shutting out the endless, bright day as we flew westward. A couple of drinks, something to eat, and finally I could no longer resist the plunge into the dark pool.

And she was there, waiting. The same tired old act.

My mother in the role of the specter from beyond never changed the material.

She was still calling to me, reliving a moment my conscious mind denied ever existed. She was still talking about Father Governeau, the poor bastard. . . .

You did it. . . . It was you! You, you, you did it. . . .

Her finger was pointing at me.

She was absolutely sure.

PART SIX

1

DRISKILL

The jack-o'-lanterns, the witches on broomsticks, and the hobgoblins in Nixon masks had all gone, replaced by merry, plump Santa Clauses, snowmen, elves, and reindeer with red noses. The campus lay under several inches of snow, crusty and windswept, and the big gate on Nassau Street was shiny with ice. It was an unusually early, oddly frigid winter. The street was rutted and frozen and the wind whistled nastily up your sleeves and you could hear the carols pouring from outdoor speakers. Shop doors tinkled happily, the gifts sparkled in the decorated windows. It was Christmastime, all right, time for the family to come together if the fates allowed, time to have yourself a merry little Christmas.

The house was empty when I pulled the Mercedes into the drive and went inside. It was clear that nobody had driven up from the road in several days. The house proved the point: chilled, echoing, empty. I wandered around aimlessly, wondering what

559

exactly was going on. No notes. Plenty of evidence that my father
had been there, home from the hospital. I thought about the
chances of a relapse. I called Margaret Korder at the office in
Manhattan and told her I was home and couldn't seem to find my
father.

"Why, Ben, you should have given us warning. He's up at the
lodge in the Adirondacks. And, if I may speak freely," she said
edgily, "he's being a damned problem. Just impossible, Ben. He had
a nurse up there these last few days, but she called me in tears
yesterday—he'd thrown her out. At his most imperious and impossible, from the sound of it. Now I'm not sure what we should do."

"How did he get there, Margaret? Is he well enough to be
alone?"

"Are you kidding? He thinks he's well enough, but he's no kid,
Ben. Of course he's not well enough. But try to tell him where he
can go and what he can do. He was just on an absolute tear. He
had that priest friend of yours, Father Peaches, with him—he drove
him up there and stayed several days but he *does* have a job. . . ."
She stopped for breath.

"I think I'll drop in on the old boy, Margaret. I don't like his
being up there alone. I'll go up tomorrow."

"Well, be careful. There's a big snowstorm headed our way.
Chicago got two feet—Ben, when did you get back? What all
happened over there?"

"Oh, Margaret, what can I tell you? But I got to New York
yesterday."

"Well, welcome home. Everything cleared up to your satisfaction?"

"Tell me the last time anything was cleared up to anyone's
satisfaction. It just never quite happens, does it?"

"Quite a shock, Cardinal Indelicato's death. Did you meet him?"

"Yes," I said. "And it certainly was shocking." I told her I had to
get a move on and she warned me again about the approaching
storm. I hung up the telephone, sat wondering how long it would
take me to get used to knowing so much I could never reveal, never
discuss. What a time Val and I would have had with it!

I ran into the same problem over lunch.

I called Peaches and we met at the Nassau Inn, in the downstairs
taproom, where we'd happened into each other on that other cold

and snowy occasion when Val already lay dead in our chapel. He
drove over from New Pru full of questions about what I'd gotten
into "over there."

I told him it was incredibly complicated, but when you got
right down to it, it really was a Church matter and I had been
excluded from any big conclusions. So on and so forth. He gave me
a funny look and winked as if to say he knew how they did things
in Rome.

"But tell me this," he said. "Did you find out who killed Val?"
There was that deep hurt, the open wound he would never outlive.
He figured I owed him this one. "Was it the same guy who attacked
you and that monsignor from Rome?"

"The same man. That seems to be the prevailing view, anyway.
A mad old priest. Who knows what happened to him? I don't
expect we'll ever find him or see him again. Look, Peaches, I'm
pretty worn out by all this. We'll have to talk about it later. Right
now—well, it's a maze, it all gives me a headache."

"I hear you, pal." He flashed the old grin from boyhood, but his
face was tired and lined. It was three o'clock and we were chewing
on cheeseburgers and fries. We were the lone customers. We could
hear the wind howling outside. "So how are you disposed toward
the dear old Church of Rome these days?"

I felt the laughter welling up at the odd question. "It's funny,
Peaches, it doesn't make any sense, but the Church has never
seemed more human to me than it does now. It's *so* imperfect—
you almost have to love the poor old thing."

I asked him what my father was up to and that led him into the
story of how he'd found the D'Ambrizzi manuscript, how he'd
taken it to Artie Dunn.

"I ran into Dunn over there," I said. "He told me about the
papers."

"You did? You saw him? God, what a piece of work he is! When
I found the stuff, Artie and I spent quite a night. You should see
this condo he's got. On a clear day you've gotta be able to see
Princeton . . . he says helicopters fly *below* his windows!"

"He took me through the basic content," I said. "It was all pretty
mysterious. I know it was D'Ambrizzi's insurance policy but it was
pretty old news." I saw no point in giving Peaches any reason to get
more involved. He was better off entirely out of it.

His eyes were gleaming, cheeks pink. "All those code names, all the cloak-and-dagger stuff. The odd thing—all the secrecy and hiding places aside—the odd thing was your dad knew all about it! He said it was none of his business and had never given it another thought . . . but he knew D'Ambrizzi had given it to the old blabbermouth priest. And now, ten days ago, he's suddenly got it on his mind. Weird, the way the mind works, Ben, weird."

Peaches told me the story my father had told him of the drunken, jealous, loquacious priest who'd held the D'Ambrizzi papers and taunted him with them. It rang all too true. I remembered the old nitwit with his gin-laden breath.

"So," Peaches said, mopping up the last puddle of ketchup with the last fry, "he just seemed to know I knew all about it. It was eerie as hell. He made me get it all out again—"

"Did you tell him about showing it to Dunn?"

He shrugged. "Well . . . gosh, I don't think I did. I didn't want to explain it all, I guess. Anyway, he had me drive him up to the lodge. He has that way about him—I felt like an employee. He can be a very domineering guy."

"You noticed that, did you?" I said.

"Well, I spent the better part of a week up there, neglecting hell out of my parishioners. I mean, it was great, I tramped around on the mountain . . . it's a great place, that huge bear standing in the corner—"

"What else?"

"I made a snowman! I stocked the larder from the supermarket in Everett. I puttered around, I read two novels, I cooked, fetched, and carried for your father."

"And what did my father do?"

"Read the D'Ambrizzi stuff a few times, didn't really have all that much to say about it. He brought a lot of records and some sketch pads with him. He played records all the time. We didn't talk that much . . . he kept to himself but friendly. It was fine. We talked about you and what you might be doing. He's recovering pretty well, Ben. But he was worried about you, thought you were asking for trouble digging around inside the Church. He said you just didn't understand the Church. I just nodded on cue and let him talk. He took Val's death very hard, Ben. I heard him crying one night. . . . I went into his room, asked him if he was okay and he said he was dreaming about Val and then woke up and remembered she was dead. I felt for him, Ben, I'll tell you that."

"I'm going up tomorrow," I said. "He got a nurse after you left but kicked her out. I don't want him alone up there."

"You want me to come along, ride shotgun? There's supposed to be a hell of a snowstorm headed this way."

"It's okay, Peach. I'll be fine. You tend your flock."

"My flock," he said. "Poor bastards."

Alone in the house that night, I couldn't get to sleep. Indelicato's death made the national news on television, primarily in the context of speculation regarding the health of the pope, who hadn't been seen publicly in two months. There was nothing else on the late news about the Church, other than Archbishop Cardinal Klammer's decision to stay in Rome for Indelicato's funeral. I sat in the Long Room sipping my third Laphroaig double on ice, listening to the wind outside and the sound of snow blowing off the crust, rattling on the windows.

I was trying not to dwell on what had happened since Val's murder, but it was a pointless attempt. I could think of nothing else: it was as if I'd come to life that day. Finally I finished the drink, slipped into my old sheepskin coat and a pair of Wellies, and went outside.

The cold air filled my lungs and cleared my head. I walked out toward the orchard where, maybe on a night much like this one, someone had strung up the already-dead body of Father Governeau. So long ago. It was the same walk Sandanato and I had taken with the ice skates. The ice lay beyond the orchard, shining in the moonlight. A couple of skaters moved silently like models for Currier and Ives. The blades caught and reflected silver across the ice.

I was drawn inevitably, irresistibly, to the chapel. It wasn't sentiment: I didn't know what it was until I was inside. The door was unlocked, the steps slippery with ice. The night was clouded with freezing mist.

I turned on the lights. What was I doing there? What did I expect? There was no ghost in the chapel, no voice from the darkness.

I sat down on the bench where Val had been sitting when Horstmann had pressed the gun's smooth snout to the back of her head.

And then I did something I hadn't done in twenty-five years.

In the house of God, I knelt, bowed my head, and prayed for my little sister's eternal soul. And in the dim light, my eyes shut, I whispered aloud, still a Catholic, confessed my sins and begged forgiveness from whoever might be dispensing it these days.

Later that night I lay in my old bed beneath the picture of DiMaggio, listening to the wind at the glass and feeling the draft, hearing the usual rustlings in the eaves. I was drifting in and out of sleep and seemed at one moment to be watching Val as she peeled back the side of her drum and left the photograph inside for me to find, at another I was in the hall at the top of the stair watching my father fall. . . .

I lay there wishing my mother would stay out of my face for just one night. It was getting to the point where I was half afraid to go to sleep. She'd be there waiting for me, full of her accusations.

And as I lay there, turning, banging my head against the pillow trying to get comfortable, I remembered Val coming into my room one night, that same room. She wasn't very old, she was wearing a red flannel nightie and she was crying, rubbing her eyes. She'd gotten up to go to the bathroom and our mother had been standing in the hall, had ambushed her, you might say, and had started in on her. I remembered the occasion now, who knows why, but there it was, the memory of Val, tear-streaked, sleepy, scared, while I asked her what was the matter.

She said Mother had been mean to her.

I asked her what she meant.

"She said I did it, Ben," Val had sobbed, "and I asked her what and she just kept saying it, kept saying I did it—"

"Tell me exactly what she said."

" 'You did it, you did it, it was you . . . out in the orchard . . . you took him, you did it—' " Then she started to cry again and said, "But, Ben, I didn't do it, I promise I didn't," and I put my arm around her and told her she could climb into bed with me for the rest of the night.

I told her that Mother had been having a bad dream, that it wasn't her fault and she shouldn't be afraid of her and I don't recall our ever talking about it again. Maybe because it had to do with the bad thing that happened in the orchard, the thing we weren't to speak of, the thing found hanging out there. . . .

Now, decades later, Mother's nightmare had survived.

Val hadn't, but the nightmare had, and now my mother's nightmare had become mine.

2

DRISKILL

The drive to the lodge was long and slow because of the dense mixture of fog and snow, all blown to hell by a strong, gusty wind that kept shaking the car. The snow was collecting thickly by the time I got to Everett and saw the detour sign. The bridge had failed a state check, and traffic was being routed off through another small town, Menander. I followed the markers and negotiated the long hill that led under a stone bridge and curved up and to the left. The ascent was abrupt. For a while I was afraid I might not get the traction in the ice and snow to make the climb. The forested hillsides made a maze of dark, leafless tree limbs which seemed hopelessly entangled with one another. Some kids from Menander were sledding among the trees. The tops of the hills were lost in fog. The snow on the road was getting deeper, far deeper in the gullies, and there was ice underneath. If I'd set out an hour later I might have had some real trouble.

Menander was outfitted for Christmas. Decorations hung on lampposts, and from a banner across the street, the church had a creche lit up by floodlights and snow had built up heavily on the roof of the manger. Joseph, Mary, and the Wise Men looked desperately out of their element. I pulled in at the drugstore which had once belonged to a brother-and-sister team called Potterveld. It was a Rexall now. I called the house and heard my father's voice. He sounded much stronger than he had on the transatlantic calls. I told him I was about to drop in on him.

"Well, it's about time," he said. "I should have known you'd get home for Christmas. Wouldn't want to miss your presents. I know you, Ben." He laughed to show he was kidding me rather than continuing the sniping war that had gone on so long. "You'd better step on it. It's getting dark up here and snowing hard."

"I'll be there in under an hour," I said.

For some reason, as I guided the car ever more carefully along the increasingly treacherous, twisty stretch of road—for some reason, maybe because my father's voice made me feel kindly toward him, I got to thinking about that day several centuries earlier when the sun was shining and Gary Cooper was sitting on the porch talking to my dad about the movie. The OSS adventures that came to life on the screen for me, seeing my dad's great, heroic escapades, running across the airstrip with Nazi bullets chewing up the dust at his heels. . . . The sunny day, little Val prancing around showing off, Cooper sketching for us . . . magic. Those days, viewed again through my mood, wore a perfect roseate glow. But Cooper was long dead, Val was dead, my father's heroic OSS days were just a memory . . . a story . . . a movie . . . it had all, as everything did, turned to dust.

The lodge sat on the rounded-off top of a mountain, the naked trees and prickly evergreens and firs and pines surrounding it. The light from the hidden sun was fading as I drove up the driveway from the road. The snow was deep on all sides, like frosting on a cake. Pristine, perfect flakes drifting through the branches, piling ever deeper. The lodge was a massive affair. It looked as if it were made of mammoth Lincoln Logs. Snow covered the pitched roof, nearly a foot deep. Smoke curled away from one of the fireplace chimneys rising higher yet. One slanted roof began at ground level, leaving one story of the main living room below ground at one end. That roof was mainly a skylight, faced to the north, for the benefit of my father's painting. There were lights in the windows, and when I pulled the car up to the flagstone walk the front door swung open and there was my father standing with the light behind him, waving to me. He was a little gaunt, but his broad shoulders were still square beneath the heavy dark blue sweater. I couldn't recall ever having been welcomed anywhere by my father before.

My father's manner was uncharacteristically warm, or at least not aggressive, that first night. Some of his piss and vinegar had doubtless been drained off by his illness, yet I wanted to believe that we were possibly entering on a new phase of our relationship. Better late than never: I'd thought all the same thoughts about him before.

We horsed around in the kitchen together and eventually ate a long, leisurely dinner of grilled steaks, baked potatoes, salad, and a robust claret and powerful coffee with chicory. The questions he had couldn't be avoided, obviously, but we started on them slowly, very careful when it came to Val's murder. But slowly I told him how it had all developed. It was the first time I'd tried to relate the story and it made for a long evening, through which his interest and energy never flagged.

Names I mentioned jogged his memory, tapped into his pool of anecdotes. Torricelli and Robbie Heywood and Klaus Richter, countless memories of D'Ambrizzi and the war and the adventures with the Resistance. He told me stories he'd never told me before, stories about dropping into occupied France from planes flying only high enough to make sure the parachutists didn't get killed by landing, or coming ashore by rubber rafts from submarines, eluding German patrols, connecting with Resistance cells, meeting with D'Ambrizzi in the damnedest places. It was all a game, I could hear it in his voice, scary most of the time, but everybody was younger then and there was a war on and you had to do your bit. . . .

"You knew Richter? He was a *German* officer—"

"Look, son, he was working with D'Ambrizzi in Paris and I was working with D'Ambrizzi. These things happen. I was having a fairly unusual war."

"But did Richter know you were OSS?"

"Of course not, Ben. What are you thinking of? D'Ambrizzi probably told him I was an American trapped in Paris when the war broke out. I don't know—"

"But you could have been betrayed by anyone who knew who you were."

"Well, not to Klaus Richter; he didn't give a damn about me or who was going to win the war—he had his own work to do. Everybody was engaged in their own little war. People like LeBecq, all the rest of them—"

"You knew LeBecq?" It was disconcerting, realizing that my father had been there then, that I had all these years later followed in his footsteps. "You knew D'Ambrizzi killed him for betraying the Pius Plot?"

"Sure." My father poured himself fresh coffee and clipped the end off a cigar, held a flame to it. "The Pius Plot, now, there was a crazy idea—" He puffed a couple of times. "If ever there was one. D'Ambrizzi was playing with fire on that one. He was way out of bounds."

"Was it really so terrible?" We'd moved into the long skylight room. Wind blew the snow overhead, across the glass. A fire blazed in the fireplace which was made of rough slabs of fieldstone. We sat across from each other in deep slipcovered chairs. In the distant corner beside the arch leading to the dining room stood the towering Kodiak bear, arms out to embrace whoever chanced near. "D'Ambrizzi made a pretty good case for Pius as a Nazi sympathizer, a kind of war criminal."

"The man wanted to murder the pope in cold blood. Doesn't that strike you as just a little bit crazy? Pius was no war criminal. He had to be very careful on a continent entirely dominated by the Axis . . . the fate of millions of Catholics was in Hitler's and Pius's hands. So, what if Pius couldn't make quite the moral choices D'Ambrizzi would have—so what? D'Ambrizzi was trafficking with Nazis every day." He stared into the fire.

"On Pius's orders," I said.

"Look, D'Ambrizzi was a great man, I'm not saying he wasn't. But he had a tendency to go off the deep end occasionally. Kill the pope . . . But it never happened, so . . ." He shrugged. My father had never conversed with me in this manner: he was taking me into his confidence, man to man, as he'd never done before.

"It never happened," I said, "because Archduke betrayed the whole thing. And all D'Ambrizzi's people died—"

"Not all."

"Did you ever have any dealings with Archduke?"

"Well, I wasn't there when that particular balloon went up, but I naturally heard things. Then the time came to get D'Ambrizzi the hell out of there. I liked the guy, he was a good man. The Vatican was on his tail, so I brought him out." He watched me through the cigar smoke.

"What about you and Archduke?"

"Never met the man."

"Do you know who he was?"

"Can't say as I do. It's all over now, what difference does it make?"

"It matters because it's still all tied up with what's going on now . . . the murder of Val—"

"You're confusing past and present, Ben."

"No, I *almost* understand the connection between past and present, Dad. I've just about got it . . . it's a man, it's a couple of men. Indelicato was one, tying past and present together. But there's another and it's Archduke. I think Archduke is still alive, that he betrayed D'Ambrizzi a long time ago and allied himself with Indelicato then . . . and I believe he was allied with Indelicato now, to keep D'Ambrizzi from becoming pope by making sure Indelicato did. Of course everything's up for grabs now, with Indelicato dead."

"You give this Archduke a great deal of credit," he said. "Do you have any idea who he is?"

"I'm sure I know."

"And?"

"You won't like it." I took a deep breath. "Summerhays."

"What?" He banged his huge palm on the arm of the chair. "Summerhays? Why in the name of God Summerhays?"

"He was your control out of London in the OSS days?"

My father nodded, a small smile of surprise on his broad, flat face.

"He had you and plenty of other sources inside both France and Germany. He had access to all the intelligence coming to London from Europe. . . . He had a long history of deep involvement with the Church, he knew Pius both before and after he became pope . . . he's a traditional conservative in Church matters . . . he taught you and Lockhardt how it's all done—face it, Dad, he's the logical Archduke, like it or not!"

"And you're telling me he's still at it. It's a hard one to swallow, Ben."

"It's hard to swallow what's been going on for the last eighteen months, tidying up the past. Dad, you can help me on this, you can help me prove it . . . Summerhays trusts you."

"Oh, now, Ben, I don't know about that. My God, Drew Summerhays . . . I haven't thought about all these things in a long time."

"But you've had your memory refreshed by reading the papers D'Ambrizzi left behind when he disappeared from Princeton."

He nodded, laughing softly. "Sure, sure, but Summerhays—you really surprise me there, Ben. You're on the wrong track, you must be. Yes, I read D'Ambrizzi's brief, Peaches told me about it—"

"With a little prodding, I understand."

"So you've been talking to young Peaches. He told you the story of that old padre who used to brag to me?"

I nodded.

"Well, I did badger poor Peaches and he finally admitted he'd found the papers. I read it all. Interesting stuff so far as it went, but what does it really amount to? I don't know. The Church sponsored something like a Resistance cell, there was some art theft involved, a little murder, lots of code names . . . all very old news, isn't it? What did you make of it?"

"It had a ring of authenticity," I said. "Did you ever get wind of the idea that Indelicato was the Collector? Did you know that Indelicato was the man Archduke went to with the Pius Plot story?"

"Maybe, Ben. Who knows anymore?" My father looked up at the sudden blast of wind smacking the side of the lodge. A draft whispered across the floor. "But yes, I found out that Indelicato was the man they sent after D'Ambrizzi. Of course. I'm the one who got him out of Europe with Indelicato in hot pursuit."

"Well, it was Horstmann who's been doing the killing. Did you ever come across him over there?"

The memories were wearing him out, but though his face was drawn his eyes were bright and he didn't seem to want to stop talking. "No, I don't believe I ever knew him. But that's not surprising. D'Ambrizzi had a pretty involved network—"

"*Assassini*," I said.

"Call them what you will, he had them. Most of what he was up to had nothing to do with me, Ben. I could use a brandy. Don't argue. It's good for my heart."

I poured us each a snifter and he sipped, rested his head on the back of the chair.

"Think about it, Dad. What if we could somehow reveal Summerhays for what he is . . . he's as much a killer as Indelicato, he was in on it, plotting, killing . . ."

"Ben, I'm mighty tired all of a sudden. We'll talk tomorrow. I really do want to hear all the rest of it. But I'm bushed." He stood up slowly, but I knew better than to help him. He stopped at the foot of the stairs that led up to the balcony and the second-floor bedrooms. The snow was rattling on the skylight. From the windows I looked at the snow building up. My car had a fresh layer of snow, six inches anyway. "Ben, I've had an idea. Tomorrow you're going to go out and get us a Christmas tree." He sighed. "I miss your sister, son. Dammit."

When I got up it was past midmorning and my dad was frying bacon and eggs. We sat at the dining table. I ate a prodigious amount. I reminded myself of Sister Elizabeth. He brought the coffeepot to the table and told me he wanted to hear the rest of it, how it all turned out.

I told him. I told him D'Ambrizzi's explanation as he'd presented it to our little party at the Hassler. I assumed that if D'Ambrizzi could pass on everything he did that night to all those people, I could certainly tell his old comrade in arms. My God, he'd even told Summerhays. So I told my father everything. I wanted his help, if we could come up with a way to land Summerhays. I told him everything but why Val had had to die: that she'd learned the truth, that she'd tied it all together and that she was coming home to tell her father and brother. . . .

I wanted to make sure he could handle all that, the rough stuff. So I waited. He didn't ask about Val, so I decided to wait some more.

But otherwise, I told him everything. How Indelicato died, how we found him, how D'Ambrizzi had—how could I say it to him? How D'Ambrizzi had spoken from the past, as Simon, and given Salvatore di Mona his last instructions . . . to kill Cardinal Indelicato.

My father looked at me over the rim of his coffee cup. His eyes were hollow, circled in purple, as if he'd been up all night. "Well, as a student of Church history, I must say that a pope committing a murder is not entirely unheard of. Even eliminating his most likely successor—it's all been done before. Nothing new under the sun or the dome of St. Peter's." The tired eyes bored into me. Something had changed from last night. We weren't enemies, but we weren't pals anymore, either. It was as if the world had come between us, by stealth, in the dark of night.

I told him how Sandanato had betrayed D'Ambrizzi by working with Indelicato and my father spoke up.

"They all believed they were doing the right thing, didn't they? That's the tragedy, Ben. That's always been the central tragedy of the Church. Indelicato and Sandanato and Archduke wanted what was best for the Church . . . D'Ambrizzi . . . your little sister . . . even Peaches, for all I know, wants what's best for the Church . . . Callistus was willing to kill for the Church in 1943 and he did kill for the Church now. That's the hold it has on people. Do you see what I mean, Ben? Have you ever believed in anything enough to kill for it?"

"I don't know. I've never killed anyone."

"Most men, I think, would ultimately kill for something. Not that they ever have to face up to it."

"The heart of the Church," I said, "is the heart of darkness. I've been there. I'm just back. And I don't believe it's full of great guys trying to do the right thing."

"You haven't been to the heart of darkness, son. You haven't even come close. I've been there. Your mother even got there. But not you. There is no worse place, and when you get there, there's no mistaking it. You'll know."

I told him how Sandanato had died.

My father went to the window, stared out into the steadily falling snow.

"Horstmann," he said, "is the kind of man who apparently believes in evening the score. All the way back to zip."

In the afternoon I bundled up in the old sheepskin and took a hatchet and a saw outside into the snow. It was still falling, large wet flakes, quiet, still. I passed by the huge skylight that slanted up from ground level and looked inside, down into the main room. The warmth of the house made the snow melt on the glass while it piled up all around. I saw my father standing at the turntable sifting through phonograph records in well-worn jackets. His shoulders were slumped, and when he'd placed the disc on the spindle he used a cane, walking slowly back to his chair by the fire. He lowered himself carefully and sat staring into the flames. Defenses down, he wasn't the same man. He looked like a man—suddenly too old, too frail—who hadn't long to live. I wished I hadn't seen him.

The wooded hillside sloped upward for perhaps a hundred yards, dotted with rocky outcroppings among the thick black-green clumps of evergreens and the spindly trunks of oaks and elms and poplars. At the crest it leveled off and descended slightly to a lake of no great size, where I'd first gone sailing and swimming. It was an inhumanly cold little lake. Now it would be frozen over. I set off climbing and discovered there was more breeze than I thought. The pillowy flakes seemed suddenly smaller and sharp-edged, designed to sting.

I noted a couple of potential Christmas trees as I climbed headdown toward the summit. I was drawn there by a sense of the past, I suppose. It had been several years since I'd been there last. Not since boyhood had I gone there with any regularity. Within twenty yards of the top I stopped, leaned against a tree to catch my breath. It was at just that moment that I got a whiff of something that surprised me. I smelled the remnant of a pungent fire made of branches and pinecones.

It didn't take long to find the source. Beneath one of the clusters of rock, tucked back under the shelf for shelter, was a damp, blackened pile of ashes, partially kicked over with snow. There was still the faintest wisp of smoke, only a dying gasp, and the aroma of wet, burned pinecones. But someone had warmed himself at that fire during the night. I looked down the eighty yards toward the lodge. Through the trees that dark gray afternoon the glow from the great skylight was plainly visible, a yellow blur of light. Smoke curled away from the chimneys. The wind blew snow down the back of my neck. I was perspiring from the climb.

Someone had crouched by the fire through the night, waiting, huddling for warmth close to the fire; but why? I could see nothing before me but a mountainside deep with drifted snow and our own lodge.

I began looking for some indication of arrivals and departures. There were footprints trailing off, but within only a few yards they blurred and were filled in and became indistinguishable from the rest of the landscape. I followed one such beginning that seemed to have come down from the lake. I tracked it back, watched it disappear, and then I was at the crest, looking down across the frozen surface of the lake. There was no one in sight, and the wind was cold, with teeth like the saw I was carrying. My eyes were full of tears and my face felt as if it were about to crack from the gale. I turned back and slowly sank into the deeper snow drifted among the trees.

The light was going.

I still had the tree to fell, whether someone else was on the mountainside or not, watching me or not. Who might find himself in such an isolated place, so far from the road, from *any* road, so late at night? The answer, of course, was no one. The idea was preposterous. Whoever had been there had intended to be there and nowhere else. But who? Why? Had they for some reason been watching my father? Or, for that matter, had they been looking for me? Waiting for my arrival?

Fighting the inclination to look over my shoulder, I settled on a tree, used the hatchet to hack away the lower branches, then got down on my knees and went to work with the saw. I half expected the faint crunch of someone's tread in the snow, heard too late, the clout to the back of my head. But none came. Too many movies clattering around in my head.

With the tree finally down on its side I took a look around again, unwound the heavy woolen muffler, and sat down on the stone the unknown camper had pulled near the fire and used for a chair. Below me, in the gathering darkness, the skylight seemed even brighter. And in the lodge my father listening to his music, trying to put on a front for me, wanting a Christmas tree, contemplating his own idea of the heart of darkness.

I sat on the stone for quite some time, thinking about that region where I thought I'd been but about which my father had disagreed. I never doubted that he had been there, at the deepest, darkest place, where hope and sanity were gone, but why had he mentioned the part about my mother? What would my mother with her life of wealth and ease and privilege have known about? But what could I have been thinking?

My mother had killed herself. Twice. Once by drowning her private pain in alcohol, then by going off that balcony. . . . Perhaps she'd gone deeper into darkness than any of the rest of us.

Why, I wondered, had she done it? It wasn't a question I'd ever given much attention to. She was my mother and some mothers did crazy things. Mothers of friends at school had behaved strangely, mothers and fathers. Alcohol, suicide, these were not unknown to children who were my friends and they were part of life, you never asked about such things.

"Mother . . ."

When I sobbed that word, almost without knowing it, I heard her voice again, as if she were there beside me. I was staring at the last of the footprints, now almost entirely filled with fresh snow, and she might have been alive in the shadows behind me. The footprints shouldn't have been there, neither should my mother, but I could hear her voice as I did in my dreams, only this time it was different, I heard her with utter clarity, no muffled voice in the hallway at night, this time I heard clearly what she'd said to Val and what she'd been saying to me for so many years, and it was different, it wasn't what I'd been hearing, it was different and it meant something else very, very unlike what I'd been hearing.

Hugh did it . . .

It was Hugh . . .

Hugh did it . . .

It was Hugh in the orchard . . .

Hugh. Not *you,* as Val and I had heard it.

We were kids. We'd thought we were catching hell.

And our mother had been telling us that our father had murdered Father Governeau.

Val must have remembered it, too. That was what had been on her mind when she got back to Princeton and started asking questions about Governeau. . . .

Family history, family lies.

Slowly, not knowing what the hell to do, I dragged the Christmas tree down to the lodge. Not until I was almost there did it occur to me to wonder if someone was watching.

I wrestled the tree into the big room. It was seven feet high and full, a perfect tree. My father had brought boxes of ornaments in from storage. Boxes of tinsel, a couple hundred electric tree lights in red and green and blue. He watched me struggling to get the tree into the stand, giving me encouragement, holding the tree straight while I screwed the damn thing into place. He was trying hard to act as if he felt fine, as if this were just another Christmas at the lodge. But he stopped frequently to rest, his breath came raspily, and when he poured us each a drink the bottle was shaking in his weak hand. He looked up at me, eyes watery, blinking, where once they could have frozen the water in the glass.

Hugh did it . . . it was Hugh . . .

When the tree was secured and it was fully dark outside my father took his drink to the kitchen to do some pasta for our dinner. I heard him shuffling around, banging pots and pans.

I went to my bedroom and took the envelope from among the shirts and underwear and gear I'd packed in the suitcase for the trip to the lodge. I sat on the edge of the bed and took the dog-eared photograph from the envelope, sat there slowly turning it in my hands, trying to make myself realize that my sister Val was truly dead, that she'd never come bursting into my room again, that I'd never hear her laugh, and most of all that I'd never sit down before the fire again and remember all the same stuff together, all the life only the two of us knew, all the things we'd ever said to each other. It wasn't easy, convincing myself that she was gone forever.

I looked at the photograph.

Who had taken the picture of Torricelli, Richter, D'Ambrizzi, and LeBecq?

Archduke. That's what gave everything a shape that made sense.

Summerhays. That had surprised my father. Well, of course it had. How could it not?

Summerhays, Indelicato, and Sandanato had conspired to save the Church, *their* Church, *their* way, and that had included killing my sister. . . .

She'd had a lot on her mind when she got back to Princeton. She had inevitably wanted to tell Father and me about what she'd discovered about the cancer eating at the Church. . . . But she'd also remembered what my mother had been saying. *Hugh did it . . .*

Now I was facing decisions of my own. What could I tell my father? Was there any point in bringing up what my mother had said? Was it true? And if my father had killed Father Governeau— which certainly explained why it was covered up—why had he done it?

Of course it mattered. But that didn't tell me what to do.

And someone was out in the cold and snow and dark watching us. Should I tell him? Would he have any idea who it might be? I wished to God I knew. . . .

* * *

Dinner was quiet, my father picking at his pasta as if his mind were far away. He managed to tell me a couple of funny stories about his nurses, Peaches, Margaret Korder's mother-hen concern, the stack of Artie Dunn's novels I'd left for him. He'd tried to read a few of them and said they weren't his cup of tea "but the covers weren't bad." That was my father's idea of a joke. Finally he looked at me and said, "You've got something on your mind, Ben—"

"You as well," I said.

"Well, we might as well talk about things. Watching you tie yourself in knots is giving me indigestion. Unless I'm having another heart attack. And if I am, promise me one thing—promise you'll let me die." He pushed his chair back. "I'm just about ready to make my exit. Now, let's go trim the tree."

I got the damned lights draped around the vast green girth. My father handed me the colored glass balls and tiny reindeer and snowmen and little frosted mirrors. While I tried to figure out how to say the things I needed to say, he began talking. As he rambled on I found myself thinking it would all have been so much simpler if my father hadn't had the heart attack. I was used to hating this man. He'd very nearly ruined my life. He'd once told me I should have succeeded in killing myself. Everything I'd ever done had offended him, irritated him, humiliated him, and enraged him. I had failed to become a priest and ever after I was unwelcome in his heart and mind. Maybe that was what D'Ambrizzi had meant: forgive yourself for failing your father. It was doubtless good advice, rather easier to take than to act upon. But now my father had done me the final unfairness: he'd gotten old, he'd gotten sick and almost died, and the hatred had gone out of him.

And I was left alone with my own sense of having failed my father, as well as with my own festering, guilt-ridden hatred of him. I knew it was wrong and as a result I felt my hatred turning back on myself. I looked at what was left of him and I was seeing the memory of his obsessive coldness and contempt and harsh, unforgiving judgments, all of it fading before my eyes. . . .

"I've been thinking, Ben," he said, handing me a tiny Santa Claus in a green sleigh full of presents, "about all this Nazi-Church business, all these connections, this mutual blackmail, the Pius Plot, all this Archduke stuff. It's all so insidious, Ben, but it's almost over, this generation of men is going to be gone soon. They're dying out, it's inevitable. Is it really so important now?"

"Aside from the murders—aside from that there's the art stockpiled in the subbasement of Indelicato's villa. And it's going to last a long time."

"Fine. The Church will benefit. Nazis don't endure. Art does. Chalk one up for the Church."

So far as I could tell, he was wandering up a blind alley, directly away from what mattered. "Look, Dad, don't you want to get through the reasons Val had to die? Isn't that really why I'm here?"

"I thought you came to have Christmas with your father—"

"She knew it all, everything—"

"No, no, I'm not so sure we should go over all this now, Ben."

"Wait a minute, just hold on." I finished dangling another little doodad on a limb and stood up straight. He was fumbling around with a small mountain of tinsel. "We're talking about Val. Don't you want to know why Horstmann followed her all the way to Princeton? Why he had to kill her? Who ordered it? Why he had to kill Lockhardt, Heffernan, and your daughter?"

"Ben—" He handed me a clump of tinsel.

"Because Indelicato and Archduke were afraid of her. Because they were afraid of what she knew, afraid she'd tell you and me and Lockhardt . . . that's why they tried to kill me, using Sandanato to set me up, because she might have told me the story already, before they killed her. They'd have killed you, but then you had your heart attack, so they must have decided to wait and see what happened to you. . . . But then after Ireland they stopped trying to kill me, maybe even before that, maybe they got the word to stop after the one attack on me. Why did they stop? I wish I knew. I wish I knew how deep Archduke runs in all this. They decided to kill other people who could hurt them *but not me*—why?"

My father poured out two glasses of Laphroaig with some ice and handed one to me. "Confusion to our enemies," he said, clinking his glass against mine.

I waited for him to say something, anything, but he walked, instead, over to the tree and draped some glittering strips of tinsel on several branches.

"Hasn't it occurred to you to wonder why Val started asking all the questions about Father Governeau?" I had to get him into it, get his attention, make him react. "Didn't that seem odd right from the beginning? The last day of her life and she was asking about the murder of Father Governeau—it *was* murder, there's no point in arguing about it. I just couldn't see the connection—it was what she'd found out about the Church in the past and present that brought her home . . . and what does she do when she gets here? Starts asking about Father Governeau. There *had* to be a connection. Val didn't do silly, pointless things. It took some time, but I figured it out, at least part of it anyway—"

"Did you? You must be very clever, Ben. I'm damned if I know what you're talking about. Why don't you drink some of that and get on with the tree." He was leaning against the face of the fireplace, swirling the scotch in his glass. The flames reflected in the prism of the cut crystal caught my eye, a violent rainbow. Ragged as his face appeared, he was really a picture of ease in his gray slacks and yellow button-down and pearl-gray cashmere sweater. There was some life back in his eyes. It was the change in my attitude. My frustration was suddenly reflected in those flat icy eyes. He loved the aggression he read in me. He fed on it. It gave him strength.

"Val came with her questions about Governeau because she'd remembered something our mother told both Val and me. I just got it straight after all these years—"

"Your mother? You're dragging her poor soul into this? Sober or under the influence of her demons?" The fire crackled and the winter wind whistled in the chimney. "Are you barking up a tree you can't climb, son?"

"You killed Father Governeau," I said. "That's what Val had on her mind."

"Well," my father said after a long pause, "he *was* murdered." His voice was smooth and calm, the way I'd heard it once or twice before in my life. Worlds were moving in his brain. "You're on the right track there. But not by your sainted father. If I'd killed the miserable bastard, I'd have admitted it and I'd have been a hero. A hero, Ben. But I didn't kill him—I just made a fool of myself and caused myself a lot of trouble, but there wasn't a whole helluva lot else I could do. I strung him up out in the orchard—look, I was half nuts and half in the bag and it all had begun to have something of the quality of a Halloween prank, like tipping over outhouses. . . . I pulled every damned string I could get my hands on to cover up the truth. You can believe me or not. There are risks a man has to take, Ben." He sipped the scotch and watched me.

"What are you saying? Why cover up something that could do you no harm and make you a hero?"

"Chivalry. Don't be a dull boy, Ben. It was your mother who killed Governeau. Made a damn good job of it, too, she did."

I felt my legs shaking. The tree seemed to sway. He was slipping away from me, the man I had hated for so long. "What are you talking about?"

"Your mother was a strange woman—God, how awful and pedestrian that sounds! She was very ill for a very long time. It wasn't just her drinking, and I'm damned if I'll go into that any further with you, her son. She deserves some dignity, and what I'm about to tell you doesn't leave her or anyone else with much of that valuable commodity. When it came to bashing in Father Governeau's head, well, I'll tell you what happened because I am an eyewitness." He sighed, frowning. "I wish you'd left all this alone, I truly do. You're my son, but you're a kind of monster, Ben—you don't know when you're well off, it's in your nature. What the hell gets into you? You can't just behave yourself. Neither could Val. It's some aberrant gene, I suppose. And it'll all turn out to be my fault." He freshened up his drink. "I wasn't supposed to be home that night. I had a meeting in New York. Damn near half a century ago, but I remember it in detail. Meeting got canceled at the last minute, I drove home. Got to Princeton about nine-thirty. Winter, snowing, cold. There was an old Chevy parked in the drive and the lights were on in the chapel. I didn't give it a thought. I put my car in the garage and did all my usual banging around, went inside. . . . Well, they'd heard me coming, things weren't going too well in the house. Father Governeau didn't have anything on but his undershirt and socks, like some old stag film, and your mother was naked— remember, son, you've accused me of murder and I'm explaining what actually happened, you brought all this on yourself and you're stuck with it. She was pushing him away—fighting him off supposedly, all for my benefit, you see, and he was standing there in the Long Room, sexually excited and very confused, seeing me standing in the doorway, he was looking right at me, frozen like a rabbit in the headlights, they'd obviously been on the floor before the fireplace . . . and while he was staring at me, wilting and doubtless trying to figure out what he was going to say to the bishop when word of this got back, your mother blindsided him with a very heavy Waterford sherry decanter . . . scratch one very surprised philandering priest. You look like you could use a refill, son."

I nodded, splashed more scotch into my glass, sipped. I could hear the wind and the sleety snow snapping at the skylight.

"She tried to convince me he'd raped her. He was lying there like a walleye, she was naked and babbling and, well, hell, it wasn't a scene from Burns and Allen. I told her to get dressed and forget she'd ever opened the door for Governeau—of course they'd been carrying on for a long time. I told her to shut up and have a drink. Then I called Drew Summerhays in New York and told him he had to get to Princeton ASAP. The kind of guy Drew is, he got up and got the Packard out and was on the scene a little after one o'clock. Your mother was in bed, out cold, and I told Drew what had happened. I didn't touch a thing until he got there. I had a couple of drinks, Governeau just reclined on the rug. Drew and I decided, most importantly, we couldn't implicate your mother in this in any way—she was fragile enough, something messy like having an affair with or being raped by a priest, regardless of whether she or I killed him, would have finished her for good. So we dressed the corpse—now, there's a nasty job for you. We wondered what the hell to do with the body. Drew was for dumping it somewhere, but that's harder than you think, and then we wouldn't have had any control over the investigation which might lead back to your mother. . . . We were both a little groggy. We argued and came up with various ideas and we both got loaded, I'm afraid, and then I said I wanted to make him a suicide and Drew said why the hell not and we carried him out to the orchard and it was snowing like all get out and we strung him up to find later. . . . There's no point in telling me I was acting like a nitwit, Ben, because the fact is, it worked! Drew drove the old Chevy off on some country road and left it. I followed him in his Packard, picked him up, he drove on home. Called to tell me the sun was up by the time he got to New York. And that's all you need to know about that. Your mother and I never—repeat, never—spoke of it again. That's the kind of people we were, goddammit! And that's the true story. . . . I don't know how you feel about it, but I look at it this way. Your mother was a lonely woman, I wasn't such a great husband, so she had an affair with a sweet-talking priest. And he paid for it. Governeau was the guilty party, not your mother—I didn't want that bastard buried in consecrated ground! Well, it was all a long time ago." He threw a handful of tinsel at the tree. "Relax, Ben. A skeleton in the closet. So what?" He came to me with a bemused smile on his flat, canny face, and turned to look at the tree. "We need more tinsel." Then I felt his hand on my back, patting me. I smelled, in the shameful recesses of my memory, the wet wool of the nun's habit, felt the relief again as she reached out to embrace me, the seduction which was so cruel and so fatal, and I was a little boy again. "Surprised you, didn't I, son?"

"Yes," I said, "I guess you did." My father's story was the first time in either of our lives that he'd shared a confidence with me. Idiotically I felt my eyes filling up and I turned away. I couldn't bear his seeing me in this state. We were pitching tinsel at the tree when a noise came from outside somewhere, a loud crack, a brittle sound blown on the wind. I flinched.

"Tree limb breaking in the wind," he said.

"Was I right about Val? Did she have it all backward, too?"

He nodded. "Funny, both my children thought I was a murderer. Both my children think too much and wind up not knowing what the hell they're talking about." His voice was shifting and I wondered if it was the tide of scotch or maybe something worse. The calm was retreating, anger seeping in. Maybe it really was the scotch. Maybe it was the memory of the awful night nearly half a century ago. Maybe it was me.

"When did Val tell you all this? Her suspicions?"

"Ben, I don't have to go back over all this with you. I've lost my daughter and as far as my son goes . . . there's been many a time when I'd have been better off without a son—Christ, you come here and accuse me of murder! I should have expected that of you, I guess." He muttered an oath, then dropped the surge of anger and said, "We need some music, Ben." He waved me toward the stereo cabinet. "Put on that Beethoven trio. Suits me tonight. You know, there's a story goes with that trio. I'd met D'Ambrizzi over in Rome back in the thirties, we seemed to hit it off, a couple of young comers, one night one of us had tickets for a concert . . . it was a damn fine evening, we went together, and it was brilliant, fine playing, and it was this piece. I've loved the music ever since. He bought me a recording of it, those big heavy seventy-eights in an album. Beethoven's Trio Number Seven in B-Flat Major." He lifted his glass to his lips.

I went to the stack of LPs and found it under the Kabalevsky cello concerto, the second record in the stack.

It was the single most heartbreaking and revelatory moment of a misspent life. It was not unlike the instant when I looked down at Val's lifeless body, smelled her blood and the singed hair. And now I was getting another whiff of burning, the hellfire, the Antichrist. That had been simple, this was different. That had been like a bullet in my own brain. This was new and subtler and so evil there was no name for it in my lexicon. New and worse and unspeakable because it reached into my belly and ripped me open and spilled my own hatred and my father's until I knew it was the night we would drown in it.

The recording had been made in 1966 by the Suk Trio, which included Josef Suk and Josef Chuchro and Jan Panenka.

While it was known formally as the Trio No. 7 in B-Flat Major, Opus 97, it had another name. The piece of music my father and D'Ambrizzi had heard and enjoyed so much that night in Rome before the war, before they had marched onward to their destinies—it had two names. And the other name was written clear across the dog-eared old album cover.

The "Archduke" Trio.

I finally slid the disc onto the spindle and set it playing. My hands were shaking.

I turned back to my father.

"Val had it all figured out, didn't she?"

"I've told you, Ben. Your sister was all fouled up—"

"Val knew it was you. Somehow she figured it out. She knew the whole damn thing . . ." I was having bad trouble catching my breath. "She knew you were Archduke."

"What the hell are you saying?"

"She knew you were Archduke. She knew you were in it with Indelicato to stop D'Ambrizzi's becoming pope—"

"You fool! You don't understand any of it!"

"She came home to warn you that she was going public—you *did* see her the day she was killed. I don't give a good goddamn about your alibi, your meeting in New York, nobody ever checked on that and you're Hugh Driskill, for chrissakes, you could fix an alibi with the President. . . . She wanted you to convince her that somehow she'd gotten it wrong, that it wasn't true . . . and you, you fucking monster, you made sure Horstmann killed her! You had to save the whole dirty plot. . . . So Val"—I was choking on my rage, a kind of red and purple flare searing and fusing everything balled up inside my head—"so Val had to die. . . ."

The music played and the glass fell from my father's hand and shattered on the stone hearth.

"I had to save the Church!" He staggered backward, white-faced, and fell heavily on the broken glass. He looked at his hand, smeared with blood, glass driven into the palm. "I had to sacrifice the thing I loved most in the world! It was the Church, Ben, it was the Church!"

3

DRISKILL

They say that confession is good for the soul, but as I listened to my father I began to wonder about his soul. It had been sold so long ago, I couldn't imagine the confession that might have reclaimed it. The soul was gone, whatever the soul was, and what I saw before me was nothing but wreckage, a man with no center but grief and sorrow and an endless capacity for treachery, all in the name of his God and his ever-abiding damned Church. It was as if he'd worshipped the tiger and served it and killed for it and brought it sustenance and then had become the tiger's feast.

He sat on the stone ledge beside the fire, leaned back against the stone facing, and talked to me, cradling his bloody hands in his lap, the great Hugh Driskill, who might have gone to the White House, who presided over the eternal and monumental fortune and exercised the power it conveyed and which he had enlarged—the great Hugh Driskill, who had seen to the murder of his daughter and the betrayal of his friend and had, by God, saved the life of a pope. Hugh Driskill had covered up a murder committed by his wife and seen to it that the victim was buried outside the boundaries of the Church. Hugh Driskill had looked at the Church of Rome and had decided he knew best, he knew what it was all about, and had spilled enough blood to keep it afloat the way he wanted. He had despised his son and now he was sitting in a puddle of his own blood, his palms impaled on glittering shards of glass, while he made his confession to the same son who returned his hatred in all its festering fullness, who wondered if he had the nerve to pick up the cast iron poker and beat him to death with it. . . .

"Indelicato said Val knew too much." My father's voice was low. As he spoke he looked from me to his hands and back, as if I might have some reasonable explanation for what had happened to him. His face was smeared with blood. He looked like an Indian on the warpath, but he wasn't, not anymore. Not by a hell of a long shot.

"Indelicato," I said. The dagger protruded from his chest, the elegant gold handle. I saw it all before me again as the fire popped and crackled before me. My father was sweating. He didn't seem to notice. He was having trouble with his confession. He was struggling to get it right.

"Indelicato and I, we were all that was left from the old days. And D'Ambrizzi, of course, but he was . . . unsound, he didn't understand the Church. He thought he could make it do tricks for him. . . . Manfredi and I knew about the Church, we knew it was . . . it *is*. Its nature is immutable, we serve it, it doesn't serve us. D'Ambrizzi never grasped that. And his spirit had infected Val—Indelicato told me she was going to bring down the Church as we knew it, she and D'Ambrizzi and Callistus, who was D'Ambrizzi's creature, but God stepped in to take care of Callistus. But we were up against time, we had to be ready when Callistus died. . . ."

He rambled on and I would find myself staring into his face, slick with blood and sweat, or watching the fire, or blocking it all out and hearing only the whine of the wind and the rattle of snow on the skylight. The Christmas tree shone like a child's dream, perfect and full of wonder.

"She'd found out about all of it, reconstructed it, it was an impossible accomplishment but Val, well, you know, she kept making shots that weren't on the table, she did it all her life—"

"You don't have to tell me about Val," I said.

"Murders. In the war, murders now, she had figured out all of it, D'Ambrizzi and Simon and Indelicato and the Collector and me, the man who saved the pope, only she saw me as something else, she would, oh, she would. The Church had survived so many attacks— Indelicato and I went over and over the ground, trying to figure out another way—but Val's story, the evidence she'd accumulated, it was too much . . . too much in this age of instant media, this age of television and investigative reporters who'd get hold of it and shake it and chew it and . . . you must understand, Ben, for the first time in all of history there was someone who could destroy the Church, turn it into a sideshow, someone who could drag it across every television screen in the world—a nun who was known in every corner of the world for her good works and intelligence and wit and writings, she could do it.

"Think of her, television loved your sister, she'd have made sure the story didn't end, it would have gone on and on, reporters would have dug all the way to China, there would have been fatal meltdown, don't you see that? The pope was dying and then all the stories about the murders of John XXIII and John Paul I would have surfaced and this time they wouldn't have gone away, they wouldn't have been covered up and written off as slightly kooky, and then the mess at the Vatican Bank, the suicides and murders and frauds, it would all have been brought out again, only this time Sister Val would have been there to fuel the flames and it would have been out of control. . . ." He wiped the sweat from his face and some of the glass in his palms scratched his forehead. He'd have liked the symbolism, the bleeding forehead, the crown of thorns, the martyr bleeding for his beliefs, his Church. "It *was* the triumph of the Antichrist, the end of the Church of Rome . . . and it was my daughter, Ben, it was the person in my life I've loved most . . . but I told her all this, I couldn't stop her, she had uncovered all of it, made all the connections. I don't know how she knew I was Archduke, but she had that miserable photograph she'd stolen from Richter, and she said, 'I know you're Archduke . . . I know you've been in it all along, the old OSS agent, the wartime hero, eternal servant of the Church. . . .'" I listened to him talk, but I could hear her voice. She could be tough, like a fighter boring in, all fists and short, quick punches that took your breath away. She had the killer instinct, it was embedded in her nature, and I could hear her, going for the kill. "She said, 'And you, dear Daddy, took the picture of the others, didn't you?

And you betrayed your friend D'Ambrizzi to that slimeball Indelicato.'
She called Manfredi Indelicato a slimeball—what the hell was going
on, Ben? A nun saying that, what did it mean?"

"It meant Indelicato was a slimeball. She was right." I wondered if I
was smiling at the memory of Val. I think I was. "She was going easy
on him," I said, "in deference to your finer sensibilities."

"She didn't understand that men like Indelicato and Pius—I knew
him, Ben, I knew the man—they have the good of the Church at heart,
not some passing whim, some cheap momentary morality . . . my God,
Ben, D'Ambrizzi wanted to kill the pope! He had to be stopped. But I
was a good friend . . . I could have killed him! But I loved him . . . so I
betrayed, as she put it, the plot—I was wrong for saving the pope! She
was mad, Ben, there was madness all around her! Nothing mattered to
her anymore, she'd forsaken her vows. She was Lockhardt's *whore*! She
was going to destroy it all—you don't see it, do you? You don't
understand anything I'm saying to you . . . I did what I could. When I
left the house that afternoon, Horstmann was waiting on the road to
Princeton. My leaving was the signal for him. . . ." He was crying. "It
was the worst moment of my life. *That* was the heart of darkness, Ben,
and you can't imagine what it was like. . . ."

"Damn, it has been tough for you, Dad. You've been through hell—"
The impulse to murder was bubbling over, flooding my brain.

"I'm in hell! My God, don't you see? I'm in hell and I'm never
coming out. . . ."

"And people say there's no justice," I said. "I just want to get
this straight. . . . You gave Indelicato or Horstmann the sign to kill
your daughter. I don't care when, I don't care how . . . but what
was her crime? Had Val murdered anyone? Whom had she left for
dead by the roadside? Or out in the chapel? She was a nun who
loved her Church, who believed in its essential goodness and its
power to do good. She wanted to rid it of the evil—and she wasn't
a fanatic, a nut, she had the proof that the inmates had been
running the asylum. That was the big difference between you and
Val. You don't believe in the essence of the Church, and she did.
She believed in the goodness and decency and kindness and
strength of the Church, she knew it would survive and prosper and
flower once it was clean again—"

"But I saved you, Ben! They wanted to kill you—I lay in that
hospital . . . wanting to die because of Val . . . and you'd been
attacked . . . and I told Indelicato that if you died, then I would go
public because there'd be nothing left for me . . . because the

Church would already have gone over the edge into the shrieking pit. . . . Do you hear me? I saved you and I saved the Church!"

"Congratulations, Dad."

"And then she started on Governeau. She said murder was my style . . . it was all going to come out . . . the darkness had taken her and she was pulling me down into it with her. . . ."

"I know all about the heart of darkness. I'm looking into it." I saw Val, the sunlight playing on her, the little girl in her red bathing suit, prancing in the arcs of the sprinkler, the sun beading up on her little body so she seemed to be dripping with diamonds, and I moved toward my father. It was time to end the misery. It was time to put him down like the rabid thing he was.

He shrank back. He knew what was coming. Patricide would have gone rather nicely in the family dossier.

He lifted his hand to defend himself. His sleeves and sweater were soaked with blood.

I heard a noise. A rapping noise, a muffled crying out over the wind. I looked behind me. The room was empty but for us. The tree mocked me with its bright lights, its tinsel. The lights were reflected in the eyes of the bear, as if he'd come to life. I heard the rapping turn to pounding and I heard something cracking and it was overhead.

A man lay on the skylight, arms outstretched, fists beating weakly on the glass, and the glass and the frame were beginning to go.

Then the sky was falling. The skylight seemed to explode into the room under the weight of the body. The aluminum frame began to twist and pop, pieces splitting apart, glass cracking, then shattering, and then a kind of glittering, shimmering rain of glass and metal rods caught in the light of the fire and the brightly colored bulbs on the tree, and there was a blast of wind and millions of snow crystals swirling down, and my father was screaming somewhere in the back of things and in the middle of the glass and metal and snow a man was hurtling down upon us like a meteorite from a cosmic light show.

The body hit the back of a couch, banged off onto a coffee table, and sprawled facedown on the floor at the foot of the Christmas tree. The man moved, jerking his legs, struggling to turn over. His gloved fingers were pulling at the black ski mask as if he were choking, suffocating beneath the wool.

I knelt beside him. I turned him over. The front of the white parka was soaked with blood. There was a neat entry hole on the lower left side of his trunk, just above the waist, and turning him, I saw the shredded exit hole. There was a lot of blood. It hadn't been a tree limb breaking. He kept pulling at the ski mask. The parka and the mask were embedded with bits of glass. He was coughing beneath the mask, trying to say something.

I helped him with the mask, pulling it up over his face. The face was scratched and leaking blood through the holes. It was Artie Dunn.

He looked up at me, licked blood from his lips.

"What a lousy day," he whispered. His chest was shaking with a chuckle. "Bastard shot me. *Me* . . . I've been watching over you . . . I'm no camper, pal . . . I knew he'd come after your father . . . He's here. . . ."

"You *knew*?"

"I knew Summerhays wasn't Archduke, for God's sake . . . I knew it was your father, it had to be, and I knew you'd never realize it . . . oh shit, this hurts. . . . Sorry about your roof . . . had to warn you . . ." His eyes were slightly glazed. He looked around, moving his head slowly, working hard at it. "Your father doesn't look so great. . . . You need a protector, Ben, honest to God." He coughed, licked his dry lips. His saliva was pink. Maybe it was from the cuts on his mouth. "I've felt better. . . . Listen to me—he's here. He's come back and he's out there . . . I knew he'd come, I waited, watched . . ." He was panting. I had my arm around his shoulders, was supporting him. His strength was going fast.

My father was holding his head in his hands, still sitting before the fire. He kept wiping his eyes and smearing blood from his hands across his face. Beneath the blood he was gray, like wet cement. "What's he saying? Tell me what he's saying? Who's here? Who's come?"

A voice came from behind me and I'd heard it once before. I'd heard it in the church in Avignon and it had been telling me to go home. Now I knew why he hadn't killed me when he had the chance. My father had sent the word from his hospital bed in Princeton. My father had spared me alone.

I turned and looked up into the bottomless eyes of August Horstmann. He was wearing a long black overcoat and a black fedora with the brim turned down all the way around. His eyes stared out from behind the circular lenses. He wore a scarlet muffler. There was snow clinging to his hat and coat. He was utterly calm.

"He's telling you that I've come for you, Archduke. You knew I'd have to come." He was standing just in front of the gigantic bear. It seemed to be threatening him from behind and he was unaware. It seemed to be reaching for him.

I started to speak and he put his hand up. The hand without the 9mm Walther. "I'm not here for you," he said in his accented voice. He briefly considered me down the long length of his bold nose. I could see the Christmas tree reflected in his glasses. Then he turned to my father. I felt Father Dunn's hand moving behind me, slowly, in the pocket of his parka. He coughed softly. Horstmann said, "It is time, Archduke. The time for a Judas is as inevitable as death. It *is* death." My father was staring at him with a look of disbelief that was slowly transforming itself into something closer to a trance. "You betrayed Simon, and many men died because of you. And now you have led me to slaughter the innocents. . . . I have come to avenge them, Archduke. There are so many. They are here now. They are all around us. Close your eyes and you will see their faces."

My father slowly rose, stood facing him. He closed his eyes.

"Can you see them, Archduke?"

He put a bullet in my father's head. My father fell over backward, his head and shoulders crashing into the fireplace, sparks showering, burning logs cracking through under the weight. Flames reached up, curled around his face, the waves of heat blurring his features as if he were melting. His feet kicked on the floor, a paroxysm, a dance of death.

Dunn sighed. I felt him sliding something into my hand, something cold and heavy. Then he slumped onto his back again, pink foam all around his mouth. He was breathing slowly, but the stain of the bullet wound was forming an ever-widening circle. I squeezed the butt of the army-issue Colt .45 and leveled it at Horstmann.

He turned from the mesmerizing sight of my late father catching fire and stared at me. Something in the fireplace was sizzling.

"I have no quarrel with you," he said to me. The Walther was pointing at me. He seemed barely to notice the huge automatic in my hand.

"I should think not," I said. "I've done nothing to you. But you shot my friend Father Dunn and you killed my sister. . . . Does it surprise you to learn that I couldn't care less about your excuse? You were led astray—I've heard all that. But I have a tough time feeling sorry for what you've been through."

"I have done what I could to even accounts."

I shook my head. "It's not enough. You're not avenging my sister. I'm the one avenging my sister. You killed my sister and I swore I'd find you. Now I'm going to kill you. I really have no choice."

He smiled at me. "Another toy gun, Mr. Driskill?"

"No," I said. "It's real."

The first slug blew his rib cage open and smashed him backward into the arms of the bear, where he hung, unable to deal with the shock, his eyes bulging against the restraints of the sockets. Maybe that first slug killed him, or would have, but it wouldn't have gotten the poison out of my system. I'd waited a hellish long time, and I wished there were an audience because I felt like making a statement. The gun was doing the talking for me. It was wiping away the frustration. Catharsis. Epiphany with a .45.

The second slug took off one side of his face and skull and a big hairy chunk of the bear's shoulder. Unendurable noise.

The third slug made his throat and chin explode and knocked both him and bear over into the hallway.

I heard Dunn's voice weakly behind me.

"I think you got him, Ben."

I called the police and the fire department in Menander and left it to them to get an ambulance out to the lodge, matter of life and death. Then I dragged my father's charred body from the fireplace. I could smell my father burning. There wasn't much I could do for Artie Dunn. He would either make it or he wouldn't. I held him in my arms, trying to talk him into staying alive. I kept telling him to look at the Christmas tree towering above us. I felt the icy wind and the wet snow drifting down through the night onto my face.

After a while I began to sing softly to myself, Christmas carols, and Father Dunn stirred in my arms and I heard him whispering.

God rest ye merry gentlemen
Let nothing you dismay . . .

That's how they found us.

Snow drifting down on us, the lights of the tree merry and bright, three men shot to pieces, a bear down, and one heathen whose mind had gone for a long walk, wandering aimlessly in the darkness which had engulfed us all.

REST
IN PEACE

My father's death had to compete for press coverage and the attention of great men with the passing of His Holiness, Pope Callistus. The papal ticker gave out, by my reckoning, about twelve hours after August Horstmann killed my father. When I viewed it from a fair psychological distance, the whole business took on the look of one of those nineteenth-century English tontines, in which the last member left alive collects the big prize. It looked as if Cardinal D'Ambrizzi was the last warrior standing. Would his prize be the Throne of Peter?

There was a considerable amount of skullduggery to be pulled off in the immediate aftermath of that last night at the lodge, if extraordinarily unanswerable questions were to be avoided. It never occurred to me to turn to anyone but Drew Summerhays, who was, I suspect, pushed to the limits of his influence to keep the lid from blowing all the way to Rome. He dragged Archbishop Cardinal

Klammer from his bed to start pulling strings, and the rest was just a blur so far as I was concerned. Whatever markers he called in, he pulled it off. He constructed an impenetrable cover-up. He hadn't turned out to be Archduke, but in his veins flowed the blood of both Hercules and Machiavelli.

When I asked him about why he'd been in Avignon he tried to shrug it away. Pressed, he said only that he'd feared something was "rotten in the heart of things but I wasn't sure who was behind it. I was trying to keep everything from coming down on you. Ben, I'm sorry for all the prices you had to pay." For God's sake, he'd been trying to *protect* me.

The story that went out had my father's ailing heart not unexpectedly failing. *Sic transit. We shall not see his like again. Hero of the war, diplomat of the peace, servant to the Church for all the days of his life.*

August Horstmann was quietly buried in a small cemetery serving a largely Catholic village in the coal-mining country of Pennsylvania, near a retirement home for elderly and penniless priests. Father Artie Dunn was taken to a private hospital which was well trained in the discreet care of the very rich, very famous, and very powerful. We knew within twenty-four hours that he would survive.

For its part in the elaborate charade, the village of Menander was given certain assurances that were bound to be met, without fail, by funds from Church coffers and the deep pockets of anonymous Catholic billionaires, the kind of men who were called upon for very special favors. It was obvious that as my father's heir I would be expected to make a large contribution toward these civic improvements involving the fire station, the local hospital, a new hockey rink, and the high school gymnasium. Ripples, ripples, ripples, and even in death, Drew Summerhays told me, my father was doing good.

The state funeral—I call it that because in a very real way that's what it was—for Hugh Driskill was held at St. Patrick's Cathedral on Fifth Avenue. The limousines jammed the street, the blue sawhorses were in place, New York's finest in brass-buttoned tunics and shiny leggings with steam snorting from their horses' nostrils were out in full force, the sun shone like the clear, perfect light of God, the television cameras watched every arrival and made Klammer happy by making him a talking head on the evening news, the

Christmas tree towered over the skaters in the Rockefeller Center skating rink, the shoppers put up with the inconvenience of having the avenue blocked off for a few hours on the morning of Christmas Eve. Once everybody had run out of wind and clichés they took my father and a few of the rest of us away together, and the mighty and the powerful went back to Wall Street and Albany and Washington and London and Rome. A great many of them would gather only a few days hence in Rome for the pomp and circumstance of Callistus's funeral. The rest of us went only as far as St. Mary's Church in New Prudence.

I missed Artie Dunn, who would have kept it all in such crystalline perspective. I missed my sister, but that was becoming a familiar ache that would never be cured. I'd be carrying it with me for the rest of my life. And of course I missed Sister Elizabeth. But she was in Rome, she belonged in Rome, and in the back of my mind I saw her there, imagined the bustle and excitement she must be feeling with the passing of Callistus and the final moves in the game that would crown the new winner, the successor to Callistus. I stood in the spare little graveyard, thinking, remembering. The icy wind, the clear, cold sky with the sun dipping toward a rim of silvery clouds that lay like frost on the horizon. The shadows lengthened quickly across the crusty snow. Peaches was getting to do his bit. Margaret Korder was there, some of his old pals, a former Secretary of State, a retired television anchorman, some of his longtime partners, Drew Summerhays, who had seen so many comrades fallen and buried.

While we waited for the casket to be unloaded from the hearse and brought to the graveside, Summerhays stood beside me. He looked somewhat self-conscious, as if we shared a disreputable secret which, I suppose, we did, though I had no idea just how much of it he knew. He smiled at me, the familiar wintry look that survived every season.

"I don't know what to say," I said softly. "You've taken care of everything, every detail. I have no way of thanking you. I wish I did."

"Oh, you do, Ben, you do." The casket passed before us. Peaches was speaking to Margaret Korder. Summerhays seemed to be fighting off the desire to salute the remains of my father. "One day soon it will be my turn. I've left a letter saying I want you to handle everything. It won't be complicated, but there will be some people who will insist on coming and will need special care. There are instructions for you. You'll make it all go smoothly. I'll be watching." He took my arm as we moved slowly toward the freshly dug grave. My father would lie next to my sister on one side, my mother on the other. "Forget all this, everything we've been through since your sister's death. . . . Do you hear me, Ben?"

"What are you saying? What are you afraid of now?"

"I'm much too far along the road to be afraid of anything. What am I saying? I'm saying this—when ignorance is bliss, 'tis folly to be wise."

"Ah. Well, when it comes to the Church, past or present, ignorance is the condition I aspire to. It's odd, Drew. Lately I've been remembering . . . faith."

"Ignorance and faith. Made for each other. We've been proving that for centuries. The Church is far from finished, you know."

"That's the thing that reminds me of faith. If the Church can survive all this . . ."

"Your father," he said at last. "This is all very involved, everything about him. It all stemmed from his commitment to the Church."

"It's only complicated if you think about it," I said. "I'm going to spend the rest of my life trying not to."

"Well, you are doomed to fail, Ben. Your father was a great man. And in all the ways that matter you are very much like him." The wind was so cold I felt brittle, as if I might crack. "He never forgave himself for the way he'd handled things with you. But he didn't know how to fix it."

"It doesn't matter, Drew. We are what we are, each one of us, the sum total of the past."

We stood at the graveside and I thought of my sister, all our family, all dead now. I was the only Driskill left. It was a peculiar sensation, seeing the row of graves, seeing the place next to my sister where someday I, too, would seek my rest.

I was trembling and then I heard the sound of a car drawing up behind us, out by the roadside, nearer Father Governeau's grave. I heard a car door slam, a muffled, heavy thud. Peaches was saying things about my father, about the Driskills.

I felt tears on my cheeks and I was too confused to know exactly why.

The service ended and my father was lowered into his grave

and everyone was moving past me, touching me, mumbling all the things people mumble at such times. Then I was alone beside the grave, the darkness gathering quickly.

"Ben . . ."

I recognized the voice, of course, and turned, feeling my heart leap against my ribs.

She was coming toward me, the wind swirling the long woolen cape, giving her the look of a swaggering freebooter. The toes of her boots kicked feathers of snow. Her long stride quickly covered the ground from the car parked at the side of the road. Her long thick hair was blown across her face and she raked it away with gloved fingers. She looked at me with that steady, level gaze.

"I'm sorry I'm late. I got lost. . . ." I was sinking into her eyes, her face, as she spoke. I knew it would happen and there was nothing I could do about it. "It seems we were just here . . . for Val." She reached out and took my hand. "How are you, Ben?"

"I'm all right, Elizabeth. You didn't have to come all this way."

"I know that."

"You must be going crazy in Rome . . . Callistus's funeral, the cardinals gathering, all of it. You should be setting the odds for the pools."

She smiled. "D'Ambrizzi's leading the field at three to five. Indelicato's troops are confused and in disarray. The way things are going lots of people think it's two to one D'Ambrizzi drops dead just before the election. . . ."

"Saint Jack's main chance."

She shrugged her broad shoulders, her smile lingering. "It doesn't really make any difference, does it? Not really?"

"Doesn't it? Funny thing for you to say. How long can you stay?" In my mind I saw her walking back to the car, heading back to Kennedy, her courtesy call behind her.

"That's pretty much up to you," she said.

"What's that supposed to mean?"

"I'm where I want to be, Ben. I'm here."

"You've thought it through?" It took me a long time to get it out. I was afraid to believe my ears.

"Ben, that's a slightly dumb question." She slid her arm through mine and squeezed me to her. "Now I'm afraid you're going to have to put up or shut up. As we say in the Church." There was another slow smile breaking like a perfect morning across her face.

"Well, I'll be damned," I said more to myself than to her.

She was pulling me along. Her cheeks were pink with the cold. I heard the wind whistling in my ears. In the midst of death I seemed to be coming to life. Had I heard my sister's ghostly, joyous laughter on the wind?

"I have a lot to tell you," I said.

It was dark by then. We were walking toward the lights and the warmth, toward the little church.

PACE